NEW YORK REVIEW BOOKS
CLASSICS

THE RETURN OF MUNCHAUSEN

SIGIZMUND KRZHIZHANOVSKY (1887–1950), the Ukrainian-born son of Polish emigrants, studied law and classical philology at Kiev University. After graduation and two summers spent exploring Europe, he was obliged to clerk for an attorney. A sinecure, the job allowed him to devote most of his time to literature and his own writing. In 1920, he began lecturing in Kiev on theater and music. The lectures continued in Moscow, where he moved in 1922, by then well known in literary circles. Lodged in a cell-like room on the Arbat, Krzhizhanovsky wrote steadily for close to two decades. His philosophical and phantasmagorical fictions ignored injunctions to portray the Soviet state in a positive light. Three separate efforts to print collections were quashed by the censors, a fourth by World War II. Not until 1989 could his work begin to be published. Like Poe, Krzhizhanovsky takes us to the edge of the abyss and forces us to look into it. "I am interested," he said, "not in the arithmetic but in the algebra of life."

JOANNE TURNBULL's translations from Russian in collaboration with Nikolai Formozov include Sigizmund Krzhizhanovsky's *The Letter Killers Club* (winner of the AATSEEL Award for Best Literary Translation into English) and *Autobiography of a Corpse* (winner of the PEN Translation Prize).

D0972384

OTHER BOOKS BY SIGIZMUND KRZHIZHANOVSKY
PUBLISHED BY NYRB CLASSICS

Autobiography of a Corpse
Translated by Joanne Turnbull with Nikolai Formozov
Introduction by Adam Thirlwell

The Letter Killers Club
Translated by Joanne Turnbull with Nikolai Formozov
Introduction by Caryl Emerson

Memories of the Future
Translated by Joanne Turnbull with Nikolai Formozov
Introduction by Joanne Turnbull

zhizhanovski., Sigizmu
e return of
nchausen /
016]
505237512870
04/03/17

THE RETURN OF
MUNCHAUSEN

SIGIZMUND KRZHIZHANOVSKY

Translated from the Russian by
JOANNE TURNBULL *with*
NIKOLAI FORMOZOV

NEW YORK REVIEW BOOKS

New York

THIS IS A NEW YORK REVIEW BOOK
PUBLISHED BY THE NEW YORK REVIEW OF BOOKS
435 Hudson Street, New York, NY 10014
www.nyrb.com

Copyright © 2002 by Éditions Verdier
Translation and introduction copyright © 2016 by Joanne Turnbull
All rights reserved.

Published with the support of the Institute for Literary Translation, Russia

ИНСТИТУТ ПЕРЕВОДА

AD VERBUM

Library of Congress Cataloging-in-Publication Data
Names: Krzhizhanovskiĭ, Sigizmund, 1887–1950, author. | Turnbull, Joanne,
    translator, writer of preface.
Title: The return of Munchausen / by Sigizmund Krzhizhanovsky ; translated
    and with an introduction by Joanne Turnbull.
Other titles: Vozvrashchenie Miunkhgauzena. English | New York Review
    Books classics.
Description: New York : New York Review Books, 2017. | Series: New York
    Review Books classics | Includes bibliographical references.
Identifiers: LCCN 2016026846 (print) | LCCN 2016028315 (ebook) | ISBN
    9781681370286 (alk. paper) | ISBN 9781681370293 (epub)
Classification: LCC PG3476.K782 V6913 2017 (print) | LCC PG3476.K782
    (ebook) | DDC 891.73/42—dc23
LC record available at https://lccn.loc.gov/2016026846

ISBN 978-1-68137-028-6
Available as an electronic book; ISBN 978-1-68137-029-3

Printed in the United States of America on acid-free paper.
10 9 8 7 6 5 4 3 2 1

CONTENTS

INTRODUCTION

BARON Munchausen's hold on the European imagination dates back to the late eighteenth century when that resourceful raconteur first pulled himself (and his horse) out of a swamp by his own up-turned pigtail. The year was 1786 and Gottfried August Bürger had turned his impecunious hand to a German translation of *Baron Munchausen's Narrative of his Marvellous Travels and Campaigns in Russia*. With embellishments of his own, however anonymous. The lyric poet did not want his name attached to this racy récit printed scant months before at Oxford and already in its third edition. French and Russian translations followed soon after.

The mythical Munchausen's monologue begins with him riding through deep snow in Russia. Overcome by night and sleep, he ties his horse to a tree stump poking up out of the snow. He wakes to find himself lying in a village graveyard, his horse dangling from the church steeple, the snow having melted. He is astonished, but then: "I took one of my pistols, shot off the halter, brought down the horse and proceeded on my journey."* Before we know it, the baron is fighting the Turks and telling us what Nabokov called "Munchausen's horse-decorpitation story." With the enemy put to flight, the baron races into a walled town and stops at a fountain to let his Lithuanian drink: "He drunk uncommonly—with an eagerness not

*Rudolf Raspe and others, *The Singular Adventures of Baron Munchausen*, a definitive text edited by John Carswell and illustrated by Fritz Kredel (New York: The Heritage Press, 1952), 4.

to be satisfied, but natural enough, for when I looked round for my men, what should I see, gentlemen? The hind part of the poor creature, croup and legs were missing, as if he had been cut in two, and the water run out as it came in."* The mystified baron goes back to the town gate and puts two and two together: the portcullis had been dropped on his horse ("unperceived by me") as he came rushing in. He finds the frisky back half larking about in a field full of mares.

These tall and infectious tales attributed to a garrulous flesh-and-blood baron, a former cavalry officer given to hunting and entertaining at his Bodenwerder estate, were in truth the anonymous work of a versatile but insolvent assay master at a tin mine in Cornwall, Rudolf Erich Raspe. A distinguished geologist and ambitious polyglot, Raspe had been elected a fellow of the Royal Society; a literary scholar and antiquarian, he had been appointed the curator of collections belonging to the Landgrave of Hesse-Cassel. Caught embezzling from those collections to pay off creditors, Raspe had fled his native Germany for London, his ruined reputation hard on his heels. Before long the Royal Society had taken the unprecedented step of expelling the Hanoverian, who was eventually reduced to living in a remote Cornish village and rifling his old notebooks for the odd bit of material that might garner a few guineas. Enter: the baron.

The real Baron Hieronymus von Münchhausen (1720–1797) had spent twenty-odd years in the Russian service and taken part in various campaigns against the Turks, including the siege of Oczakov, before retiring at the age of forty to his country seat. An ordinary career for a German nobleman of the time was made extraordinary in the baron's cavalier retellings at his hospitable dinner table. The guests upon one occasion, in the spring of 1773, may have included a red-haired curator named Raspe.

While Raspe's English-language narrative ridiculing the hyperbolic baron might have gone unnoticed by him, Bürger's more luxuriant German version could not. Overnight the real Münchhausen had become a legend in his own land, his estate deluged with

*Ibid., 16–17.

gawkers whom the lone gamekeeper was powerless to keep back. The baron abandoned his storytelling. The dinner parties ceased—and their once genial host crept through his last decade a dispirited recluse.

But his sprightly namesake lived on. The mythical Munchausen's boundless faith in his own imaginative powers, his invented worlds and impossible situations proved irresistible. Translators felt free to edit and embroider. Some of the best vignettes had been added by Bürger. In one episode Munchausen catches several dozen ducks with one very long dog leash to which he has attached a small piece of lard. The first duck swallows the slippery pork fat and passes it undigested; the second duck does the same, then the third, and so on, until they have all been strung like so many pearls. In another episode Munchausen, while at war with the Turks, leaps astride an outgoing cannonball, the better to infiltrate an unassailable fortress. Halfway there, he thinks better of this plan: "Once inside I'll be taken for a spy and hung from the first gibbet." Just then he sees an incoming cannonball whizzing by in the opposite direction. The baron quickly switches cannonballs—and returns to his regiment unscathed.

THE RETURN OF MUNCHAUSEN

Like Bürger, Sigizmund Krzhizhanovsky has taken certain liberties with the mythical baron. As the hero of this half phantasmagoria, half roman à clef set in 1920s Berlin, London, and Moscow, Munchausen remains a dreamer and fierce champion of his own unfettered imagination. At the same time, the two-hundred-year-old baron, a self-taught philosopher who long ago joined "the struggle for nonexistence," has emerged from his retreat on the Weser so as to take part in some real-world postwar diplomacy. In addition to the manor house at Bodenwerder, he now has a pied-à-terre in Berlin.

Krzhizhanovsky's novella opens in March 1921 to news of the Kronstadt rebellion. Thousands of sailors at a naval bastion near

Petrograd* have risen against the Bolsheviks in what could spell, so some Western observers thought at the time, the end of Lenin's fledgling regime. On the other hand, *The New York Times* reported, "there is a great deal of fog and smoke, and it is hard to find out who is fighting whom."[†]

Krzhizhanovsky's Munchausen has strong opinions about both: smoke and fog—associated as they are with his phantasms. "We Germans have not learned how to deal even with smoke," he tells the poor poet Unding. "We swallow it, like the foam from a mug, before it has done swirling and settled inside our pipe bowl. The imaginations of men with stubby cigars in their teeth are equally stunted." Before long the baron will leave Berlin for London—to visit the fogs: "Yes, the albescent veils rising from the Thames can unshape shapes, shroud landscapes and worldviews, shade facts, and . . ."

Unding takes umbrage. Why rush away to foreign fogs when you have at hand homegrown "fictionalism"? The poet is alluding to the philosophy of "as if" advanced by Hans Vaihinger. A popular Kant scholar, he held that the human mind, in order to think and to preserve itself, constructs conscious fictions, such as God, immortality, and freedom; while it knows these faiths to be false, it may benefit by acting "as if" they were not. "The 'As if' world, which is formed in this manner," wrote Vaihinger, "the world of the 'unreal' is just as important as the world of the so-called real or actual."[‡] If not more so, Munchausen might add.

The "exceedingly egocentric" baron cares only about his own imagination, Krzhizhanovsky remarked in an essay on countries that don't exist. "Traveling across Germany by diligence, he looks after the tunes that have frozen up in the postilion's horn, but is indifferent to the symphony of landscapes gliding past his eyes." Krzhizhanovsky's affection for his fantastical hero is palpable. As

---

*St. Petersburg (1914–1924).
†"The Fog of Petrograd," *The New York Times*, March 12, 1921.
‡Hans Vaihinger, *The Philosophy of "As If": A System of Theoretical, Practical and Religious Fictions of Mankind*, translated by C. K. Ogden (New York: Harcourt, Brace, 1925), xlvii.

soon as Munchausen is settled in London, he begins giving dinner parties, pressing the local fogs into service, and filling his guests' heads full of them "more deftly than an expert milkmaid decanting her ware into canisters."

When not receiving, the baron rambles through Kensington Gardens, past the statue of Peter Pan "who never existed," then up Piccadilly and along the Strand to "the most nonexistent of all": to God. Inside St. Paul's he often gazes at a particular pair of allegorical figures and engages a lay brother in this ritual exchange:

> "What is that?"
> "A true representation of Truth and Falsehood, sir."
> "And which one of them is Truth?" The baron squints.
> "If I may say so, sir, that one."
> "The last time, as I recall, you said that one was Falsehood."

Is it any wonder then that Munchausen should reverence not Saint Paul, not a conventional saint, but Saint Nobody? Or Nemo, as he was called in the eleventh century when he apparently sprang from the impudent head of an intractable French monk named Radulfus Glaber. Radulfus had the idea of treating the Latin word *nemo* (nobody, no man) in biblical and classical texts as a proper noun. His superhuman Nemo is not bound by the usual constraints. "All those endless stingy and gloomy negatives—'no one can,' 'no one knows,' 'no one must,' 'no one dares,'" writes Mikhail Bakhtin, "become giddy affirmatives: 'Nemo can,' 'Nemo knows,' 'Nemo must,' 'Nemo dares.'"[*]

The baron's London idyll comes abruptly to an end when he agrees to return to Russia. Undercover. Kronstadt and other uprisings have prompted Lenin to announce his New Economic Policy, a temporary return to private trade. At the same time, he is tackling what Maxim Gorky ruefully termed "the annihilation of the intelligentsia

---

[*]M. M. Bakhtin, *Tvorchestvo Fransua Rable* (Moscow: Khudozhestvennaya literatura, 1990, 2nd edition), 458.

in our illiterate and uncultured country."* The so-called dreamer in the Kremlin is especially exercised about the professors and writers: "counterrevolutionaries all."†

The religious philosopher Nikolai Berdyaev, for instance. From the very start Berdyaev perceived "the Bolsheviks' moral deformity"; he rejected their image "both aesthetically and ethically."‡ In February 1920 he was arrested and interrogated by Dzerzhinsky himself. The interrogation turned into a forty-five-minute lecture by Berdyaev on his religious, philosophical, and moral opposition to communism. His candor clearly disarmed the head of the Cheka. The philosopher was freed and delivered to his frigid apartment on Maly Vlasevsky where the small stove was sometimes fueled with sticks of ancestral furniture. All the same, it didn't so much heat the apartment as fill it with smoke.

It was there, in the spring of 1922, that Berdyaev received a tall, unknown writer from Kiev in search of work and a room: Sigizmund Krzhizhanovsky. Berdyaev could help with neither: his life in Moscow was by then too tenuous. In September the philosopher found himself forced to board a ship to the West along with two dozen other leading lights. Krzhizhanovsky found a room on the Arbat and began fighting for the printed existence of his unorthodox phantasms at odds with the times—to little or no avail. In 1927, as Soviet Russia prepared to celebrate the tenth anniversary of the Bolshevik coup, he was closeted with his much loved Munchausen. For the baron, Krzhizhanovsky fought hardest of all.

—JOANNE TURNBULL

*Letter to Alexei Rykov, July 1, 1922, in *Pisma i documenty: 1917–1922* (Moscow: Tsentrpoligraf, 2014).
†Letter to Felix Dzerzhinsky, May 19, 1922, in *Vysylka vmesto rasstrela: 1921–1923* (Moscow: Russky put, 2005).
‡N. A. Berdyaev, *Samopoznanie* (Moscow: Kniga, 1991), 229.

THE RETURN OF
MUNCHAUSEN

1. EVERY BARON HAS HIS FLIGHTS OF FANCY

A PASSERBY cut across Alexanderplatz and stretched out a hand toward the faceted panes of an entrance door. But just then from the star of in-streaming streets came the crying mouths of newspaper boys:

"Rebellion in Kronstadt!"

"End of the Bolsheviks!"

The passerby, shoulders hunched against the spring chill, thrust a hand into a pocket: his fingers fumbled from seam to seam—damn!—not a pfennig. He dashed open the door.

Now he sprang up the length of a long runner; leaping after him, taking the stairs two at a time, came muddy footprints.

On reaching the first landing: "Who shall I say is calling?"

"Tell the baron: the poet Unding."

The manservant eyed the caller—from his shabby boots to the crumpled crown of his ginger fedora—and asked again, "Who?"

"Ernst Unding."

"One minute."

His footsteps retreated—then returned; his voice betrayed genuine surprise.

"The baron will see you in his study. Pray come up."

"Ah, Unding."

"Munchausen."

Their palms met.

"Now then. Come and sit by the fire."

No matter how one looked at it, guest and host bore little resemblance to one another: side by side—soles to the fender—were a pair of impeccable patent-leather pumps and the muddy boots we have already met; side by side—leaning back in Gothic armchairs—were a long, clean-shaven face with hooded eyes and fine aristocratic nose versus a jowly face with red button nose and prickly-lashed pupils under tufts of draggled hair.

The two sat for a minute watching the dance of blue and scarlet sparks in the grate.

"The cigars are on that side table," the baron said at length.

His guest extended a hand: after it crept a striped and crumpled cuff. The lid of the cigar box clicked open—then came the chirring of the clipper against dried leaves, then wreathes of fragrant gray smoke.

The baron squinted slightly at the pulsating flame.

"We Germans have not learned how to deal even with smoke. We swallow it, like the foam from a mug, before it has done swirling and settled inside our pipe bowl. The imaginations of men with stubby cigars in their teeth are equally stunted. Permit me. . . ."

The baron got up and crossed over to an antique wardrobe. A little key clinked, the heavy carved doors creaked open—and Unding, following after with his eyes and the gleam of his cigar, saw poking out from behind the baron's long thin back on the wardrobe's wooden pegs: an old embroidered waistcoat of a kind not worn in over a century; a long sword in a battered sheath; a curved tobacco pipe in a beaded case; and a straggly pigtail minus its powder, but still with the bow.

The baron took the pipe from its peg and, having inspected it, resumed his seat. A minute later his Adam's apple jumped out of his collar as he sucked in his cheeks to meet the smoke streaming up from the chibouk into his nostrils.

"We understand still less about fogs," the baron went on between puffs, "metaphysical ones for a start. Incidentally, Unding, you did well to look in today: Tomorrow I intend to pay a visit to the London fogs. And to those who inhabit them. Yes, the albescent veils rising from the Thames can unshape shapes, shroud landscapes and worldviews, shade facts, and . . . in a word, I am off to London."

Unding's shoulders bristled.

"You do Berlin a disservice, baron. We too have mastered a few things: ersatzes, for instance, and the metaphysics of fictionalism—"

Munchausen broke in: "We shall not revive that old debate. Older, incidentally, than you think. Some hundred years ago Tieck and I sat up all night disputing about this—in other terms, true, but does that alter the gist? He was seated, as you are now, on my right. Knocking the ashes out of his pipe, he threatened to smite reality with dreams and blow it asunder. I reminded him that even shopkeepers have dreams, and that a rope, though in moonlight it resemble a snake, cannot bite. With Fichte, on the other hand, I argued far less. 'Doctor,' said I to the philosopher, 'now that "not-I" has jumped out of "I," it had better look back more often at its *whence*.' In reply, Herr Johann smiled politely."

"Allow me to smile not so politely, baron. That stands up to criticism no better than a dandelion clock to the wind. My 'I' is not waiting for 'not-I' to look back at it. Rather it turns away from all nots. As it was taught. My memory does not go back centuries,"—Unding nodded to his host—"but I do remember our first meeting, five weeks ago, as if it were today. A small marbled tabletop, the chance proximity of two pairs of eyes and two mugs of beer. I sat sipping mine, while you never brought the glass to your lips, only nodding now and then to the waiter, who replaced the undrunk mug with another, which also went undrunk. When tipsiness had slightly misted my mind, I asked you what it was you needed from glass and beer since you did not drink. 'I am interested in the bursting bubbles,' you said, 'and when they have all burst, I must order a fresh dollop of foam. Every man amuses himself after his fashion; what pleases me about this swill is its counterfeitness, its surrogateness.' And with a shrug of your shoulders you eyed me—I must remind you, Munchausen—as if I too had been a bubble stuck to the rim of your mug."

"You bear grudges."

"I bear many things in mind: still spinning in my brain is the colorful carousel that began turning right there, by two tangent mugs. We crossed continents and oceans together at a speed greater than the earth's rotation. And when I, batted about like a tennis ball, from country to country, from past to future and back to the past, happened to drop out of the game and ask, 'Who are you and how can a single lifetime have sufficed for so many wanderings?'—you, with a courteous bow, told me your name. Counterfeit beer makes for a counterfeit and confusing intoxication, realities burst like bubbles and phantasms slip in to take their place. Is that shake of your head ironic? You know, Munchausen—just between us—as a poet I am ready to believe that you are *you*, but as a sensible person—"

The jangle of a telephone bell bored into the conversation. Munchausen reached for the instrument with a long thin hand whose index finger wore an oval moonstone.

"Hello! Who is speaking? Ah, it's you, Mr. Ambassador. Yes, of course. I will be with you in an hour."

The receiver returned to its metal cradle.

"My dear Unding, that a poet should acknowledge my existence flatters me exceedingly. But even were you to cease to believe in me, Hieronymus von Munchausen, diplomats would not. You raise your eyebrows: you wonder why? Because to them I am indispensable. That is all there is to it. Existence de jure, from their point of view, is not a whit worse than existence de facto. As you can see, there is far more poetry in diplomatic pacts than in all your valueless verses."

"You're joking."

"Not at all: life, like any ware, is subject to supply and demand. Have newspapers and wars not taught you that? The state of the political stock exchange is such that I may count not only on life, but on flourishing good health. Do not hasten, my friend, to reckon me a ghost and place me on a library shelf. Do not."

"Well"—the poet grinned, eyeing his tall and angular interlocutor—"if shares in the Munchauseniad are going up, then I, perhaps, am ready to speculate on the rise in prices: up to and including existence. But what interests me is the specific *how*. I do of course recognize a certain diffusion between fact and fiction, the reality in 'I' and the reality in 'not-I'; but even so, how is it possible that we can sit here and converse without aid of an aural and visual hallucination? I need to know that. If the word 'friend,' given me by you, means anything at all, then...."

Munchausen seemed to hesitate.

"A confession? That would be more in the style of Saint Augustine than Baron Munchausen. But if you insist.... Only allow me to escape here and there—I cannot do otherwise—from the trammels of truth into free phantasms. So then, to begin: Picture a gigantic clockface of the centuries, the tip of its black hand moving from division to division, from date to date; straddling the tip of that hand, one may discern sailing by below: 1789, 1830, 1848, 1871, and on, and on. Indeed, my head still reels from the racing years. Now imagine, my good friend, your humble servant gripping with his knees that same clock hand suspended over the changing years (and everything in them) as he whirls around the clockface of time. Incidentally, the pegs in my wardrobe, which I forgot to lock, will help you to see my then self more clearly and particularly: my pigtail, my waistcoat, and my sword, suspended over the clockface, jouncing about with the jolts. The jolts of clock hand against numbers become more and more violent: at 1789 I squeeze my knees harder; at 1871 I have to grip the clock hand with both my arms and my legs; but by 1914 the numbers' shocks have become unbearable; banging into 1917 and 1918, I lose my balance and go tumbling head over heels, down.

"Coming toward me through the air I see the mottles—obscure at first, then more distinct—of oceans and continents. I stretch out a hand, seeking support: air, nothing but air. Suddenly I feel a blow to my palms, I clench my fingers, and in my hands I have a steeple— imagine that—an ordinary church steeple. A few feet above my head is a weathercock. I shinny up. A gentle breeze is batting the weathercock this way and that—and I may calmly behold the earth spread out beneath my soles some twenty or thirty yards below: radial patterns of paths, flights of marble steps, clipped columns of trees, translucent hyperboles of fountain jets—it all seems somehow familiar, seen not for the first time. I slide down the steeple and, coming to rest on a chimney pot, survey the scene: Versailles, but of course! Versailles, and I am on the roof of the Trianon. But how to get down? The springy billows of smoke bounding past my back suggest a simple and easy means. I remind you: if now I have solidified, so to speak, and amassed a certain weight, then on that first inaugural day I was not much heavier than smoke. I plunged into the smoky flows, like a diver into water and, gently sinking, found myself by and by at the bottom, that is, casting metaphors aside, in a fireplace—exactly like this one." A patent-leather pump poked the cast-iron fender inside which the flames had gone out. "I looked around: not a soul. I stepped out onto the hearth. I had landed, judging by the long shelves crowded with books and folders, in the palace library. I listened: through the wall I heard the scrape of chairs being drawn up, then silence marked off by only the tick-tock of a pendulum clock, then someone's even, wall-muffled voice slapping over words like slippers over floorboards. Having just fallen from the clock hand onto the clockface, I of course did not know that this was a session of the Versailles Conference. On the library table I found a card file, the latest editions of newspapers and folders full of official reports. These I set about reading, quickly apprising myself of the political moment. Suddenly I heard the scrape of chairs being pushed back, low voices, and someone's footsteps approaching the library door. Now I. . . . No, I see I must again visit my old wardrobe."

Ernst Unding, leaning far forward in anticipation of the story, watched with impatient eyes as the baron broke off, shuffled back to the pegs protruding from the depths of the wardrobe, and reached into the puckered pocket of his ancient waistcoat.

"Now then." Munchausen turned around to his guest. In his outstretched hand there glowed the morocco of a small gilt-edged octavo with leather corner pieces. "Here is a thing with which I am rarely parted. Feast your eyes: first London edition, 1785."

He opened the frail worn volume. Unding's pupils pounced on the title page and skimmed down the letters: BARON MUNCHAUSEN'S NARRATIVE OF HIS MARVELLOUS TRAVELS AND CAMPAIGNS IN RUSSIA. The book clapped shut and slipped in beside the storyteller on the broad flat arm of his chair.

"Afraid lest I be taken for a spy in search of diplomatic secrets," Munchausen continued, his soles resting once more on the fender, "I hastened to hide: opening my book—like this—I crouched down, knees touching my chin, head drawn into my shoulders, as compact as could be, and leapt into the pages, banging the book shut behind me, as you, say, might bang the door of a call box behind you. At that instant the footsteps strode into the library and approached the table on which, flattened between pages sixty-eight and sixty-nine, lay I."

"I must interrupt you." Unding started from his chair. "How could you have made yourself as small as that pocket book? That's in the first place, and—"

"And in the second place," the baron rapped the red morocco with the heel of his hand, "I will *not* be interrupted. . . . And in the third place, you are a bad poet, I swear by my pipe, if you do not know that books, if only they are books, may be commensurate with, but never proportionate to reality!"

"Very well," muttered Unding.

And the story went on.

"As luck would have it, the man who nearly took me by surprise (by the way, he was one of the honor cards in a tattered diplomatic deck) caused us both a fresh surprise: The fingers of that diplomatic ace, hunting for some reference, sliding over books and bindings, happened to catch in the morocco door of my refuge, the pages flew apart, and I, somewhat abashed I will admit, now three-dimensionalizing myself, now flattening myself anew, did not know what to do. The ace let fall the cigar from his mouth and, throwing up his hands, collapsed into an armchair, round eyes riveted on me. I had no choice: I stepped out of my book and tucked it under my arm, like this. Then I drew up a chair and sat down opposite the diplomat, knees to knees. 'Historians will claim'—I nodded encouragingly—'that it was you who discovered me.' When at last he found his tongue, he asked, 'To whom have I the honor?' I reached into my pocket and, without a word, offered him this."

A square visiting card flickered before the eyes of Unding, now slumped back in his chair; the Gothic script on the heavy stock read:

Baron
HIERONYMUS VON MUNCHAUSEN
Supplier of Phantasms and Sensations
In and Out of This World
Since 1720

The five lines hung in the air, then flipped about in the baron's long fingers and disappeared. The wall clock's pendulum had not ticked ten times when the story resumed.

"During that pause, which lasted no longer than this one, I noticed that the diplomatic expression on the diplomat's face was changing in my favor. While his mind moved from major to minor premise, I kindly supplied the conclusion: 'A more necessary man than I, Baron von Munchausen, you shall never find. I give you my word of honor. As for the rest. . . .' I opened my octavo, preparing to retire from this world to that, so to speak, but then the diplomat seized my elbow: 'For goodness' sake, I beg you.' Well, having thought a moment, I determined to stay. My old abode—right here, between pages sixty-eight and sixty-nine, if you care to look—has been left empty: for a long time, I suspect, if not forever."

Unding looked: on the bent-back page between parted paragraphs were the fine black rules of an oblong box: but inside the box was only the blank stare of white space—the illustration had disappeared.

"So there it is. My career, as I'm sure you know, began with a modest secretaryship in an embassy. After that . . . but now the minute hand means to separate us. My dear Unding, I must go."

The baron pressed a button. In the doorway darted a footman's side-whiskers.

"Bring me my dress coat."

The whiskers flashed out. The baron got up. His guest got up also.

"Ye-e-s," Munchausen drawled, "they have stripped me of my waistcoat and cut off my pigtail. So be it. Only remember, my friend, the day will come when this frippery"—a long finger, moonstone oval gleaming, pointed prophetically at the open wardrobe—"when these moldering castoffs will be taken from their pegs, placed on cushions of brocade, and carried in solemn procession, like holy relics, to Westminster Abbey."

But Ernst Unding was looking away.

"You have out-Munchausened Munchausen. I give you credit—as a poet."

The moonstone dropped down. To Unding's surprise, the baron's face now crinkled into countless laughing creases, aging him at least a hundred years; his eyes narrowed to sly slits, while his thin lips unpursed to reveal long yellow teeth.

"Indeed. Back in the days when I lived in Russia, they invented a saying about me: Every baron has his flights of fancy. The 'every' was added later—names, you see, like anything else, become forgotten. In any case, I flatter myself with the hope that I have made better and wider use than other barons of *my right to flights of fancy.* I thank you, and also as one poet to another."

A withered but tenacious palm grasped Unding's fingers.

"Do as you please, my friend: You may believe or not believe Munchausen and . . . in Munchausen. But if you should doubt my handshake, you will deeply offend an old man. Goodbye. And one more bit of advice: Do not bore into all and sundry with your eyes. If you bore through a barrel the wine will run out and inside the hoops will remain only a foolish and booming hollowness."

Unding smiled from the doorway and was gone. The baron was helped into his coat. Then an elegant secretary whisked into the room, clicked his heels, and handed the baron a heavy briefcase. Having straightened the lapels of his dress coat, Munchausen ran his left thumb and forefinger over the edges of the folders poking out of the briefcase. He riffled past: protocols from the League of Nations; original documents to do with the Brest peace; verbatim reports from sessions of the Amsterdam conference; numerous pacts and treaties, including Washington, Versailles, and Sèvres.

Eyeing these with fastidious distaste, Munchausen picked the briefcase up by its two bottom corners and shook the entire contents out on the floor. While secretary and manservant gathered up the paper piles, the baron went back to the morocco-bound tomelet patiently waiting on the arm of his chair; the tomelet dove inside the disencumbered briefcase, which shut over it with a loud click.

2. SMOKE THAT ROARS

STAIRS scurried under Unding's feet and then, damply through his worn-out soles, sidewalk asphalt. The baron's motorcar blared up from behind, spattering the pedestrian with mud as its yellow lamp-eyes rushed through the brumous spring gloaming.

Turning up his coat collar, Unding strode through a droning archway under four parallel rails suspended in air, then down the broad straight course of the king's quondam street. Looming up on his right were the stone cubes, arcs, and cornices of the palace. Down the asphalt's glassy tire-smoothed glair there stretched—like a string of violet beads—the reflections of streetlights; from the eaves of the dusk-enshrouded palace drooped rain-soaked flags of revolution. Farther on, right and left, the cast-iron benches of Unter den Linden went past Unding's eyes, which now descried—pounding the air with bronze hooves—the black quadriga atop the Brandenburg Gate.

He still had a way to go. Through the long Tiergarten and then down Bismarckstrasse, past ten crossroads to the far edge of Charlottenburg. The air, moist and smoky, seemed like a cheap and crude counterfeit air; the streetlamps' glass globes seemed like light bubbles of foam about to fly up into the sky, while down onto roofs and pavements in a soundless avalanche darkness tumbled. The bare Tiergarten trees flickering past his footsteps reminded the poet of thickets butchered by missiles, but then his associations came closer than his eyes, came inside his skull, a web of fantastical trench-like streets. Unding stopped, listened for a moment, and decided that the thrum of the city, over there, beyond the Tiergarten, sounded like the receding rumble of an artillery battle. Under the thumb and forefinger of his right hand, which still recalled the recent pressure of Munchausen's palm, he suddenly distinctly felt, almost burning his skin, the incandescent steel of a musket lock that had just fired.

"Phantasmagoria," Unding muttered, looking around at the stars, lamps, trees, and scatter of paths.

Someone's unsteady shadow, as if called by name, moved half-heartedly toward the poet. Under the soggy shell of a hat he saw cheekbones etched with hunger and rouge: a prostitute. Unding looked away and walked on. First he tried to think of a diminutive suffix for the name Phantasmagoria. But neither "-chen" nor "-lein" stuck. Then, listening to the rhythm of his footsteps, he began turning assonances and rhythms over in his mind, a familiar exercise that reduced his external world to the radius of his fedora—and a mute keyboard of words began fidgeting its keys.

The shock of someone's shoulder against his shoulder upset a line: Dropping rhymes, the poet raised his eyes and looked around. He had gone well past his entrance. Suddenly he felt—like heavy weights tied to his knees—his exhaustion. Unding mulled the irksome sum: two times two hundred made a dead loss of four hundred steps—his only reward.

Ernst Unding was hardly a regular reader of the morning papers. But after his parting conversation with Munchausen, he happened to see a three-line item about a member of the diplomatic corps, Baron von M., having left on the express—on some mysterious errand—for London. Then a week later the large type of a dispatch announced the successful agency in influential English circles of von M. The name's remaining letters seemed to have vanished in the London fog. Unding put the paper aside with a smile. Further reports went past him: he caught cold and took to his bed where he lay oblivious of events for five or six weeks. When he had recovered strength enough to creep to the casement and open it, he met a sunny blast of spring air. From below, ricocheting off walls, came the rivalrous voices of newspaper boys. Leaning over the sill, Unding caught first the end, then the beginning, then the whole cry:

"Extra! Extra! Baron Munchausen on Karl Marx!"

"Munchausen on . . ."

The wind began to blow. The convalescent closed the window and, breathing hard, let himself down into a chair. His lips articulated the soundless words: "Here we go."

Meanwhile, Baron Munchausen, safely arrived in London, was being received, as he put it, with extreme solicitude by the local fogs. The fogs served him humbly and faithfully. He could fill heads full of them more deftly than an expert milkmaid decanting her ware into canisters.

"Horses and voters," the baron liked to say among friends, "if you do not put blinkers on them, they will throw you into the nearest ditch. I have always admired Teniers's technique of allowing black to become white and white to grade into black: through gray. Neutral tones in painting, neutrality in politics, and let the Johns, Günthers, and Pierres go on goggling into the fog: 'What is that? The moon or a streetlamp?'"

However, these paradoxes rarely set foot outside the three-story cottage on Bayswater Road where the baron was now ensconced. He had deliberately chosen a house at some distance from rackety Charing Cross, with its waves upon waves of people. Behind the cottage were the wide and not too noisy streets of Paddington, while from the top-floor windows one could see, beyond the long wrought-iron railings, the silent walks of Kensington Gardens: in winter, the trees were festooned with cottony tufts of snow; in summer, under those same trees, the paths of saffron sand were dappled with shadows like inkblots.

Once settled, Baron Munchausen had the small front garden dug up; in place of the parterre of patterned flowers and greensward running up to the cottage's red bricks, he planted with his own hands the Turkey-bean seeds he had brought with him in a little antique box at the bottom of his portmanteau. After the first few waterings, the beans twined up the façade with supernatural speed, up and up. If at midday they were curling about the first floor, then by nightfall, when a hazy sickle moon cut through the gray-brown fog, the fine spirals of their green whorls had reached the windows of the third-floor study, where the baron was poring over the minute script in some old notebooks by the light of a green-shaded lamp. The beans went on twirling upward with their thread-like tendrils, obviously aiming for the sickle moon. But Munchausen gave the wanderers a stern look and, wagging an admonitory finger, said, "Again?"

The next morning dumbstruck passersby could only shake their heads as they contemplated the tremendous trellis that, having twirled right up to the roof, had suddenly sagged with its curly green pendants back down to the ground. From that day forth the house on Bayswater Road was known as Mad Bean Cottage.

Munchausen's daily round confirmed the words of a popular American author: "The world is managed by people who do about two hours work a day—that is, on the days when they work at all." On rising from his bed, the baron usually glanced through the morning papers, drank a cup of coffee *mehr weiss*,* and, having smoked his first pipe, exchanged his carpet slippers for a pair of pointed gaiters. Then he went out for an airing. To start, he went on foot: strolling through green-leaved Kensington from north gate to west. He liked to see the many-colored sunbeams gamboling along the paths, the sand castles, and the tiny tadpoles being read to by superannuated English misses from large-lettered picture books of fairy tales. Curving away to the left were the shimmering gray scales of the Serpentine. Off to the right, coming toward him through a filigree of branches, was the statue of Peter Pan who never existed, and, waiting at the west gate, a limousine. Johnny the chauffeur opens the door for the baron, who, as it clicks shut, invariably says, "To the most nonexistent of all."

Johnny: "Very good, sir." The limousine swings around the railings of Kensington and Hyde Park, and, bearing left, adds four more wheels to the thousands of wheels gliding up glass- and stone-clad Piccadilly. Then eases along the Strand toward the Temple—towers

*More white: coffee with milk. (German)

swathed in fog above the ribs of roofs—and finally to the round dome of St. Paul's. By the cathedral steps, Johnny again opens the door: "Here we are, sir."

The baron dispenses pennies to beggars on his way inside. Most often he visits the famous Whispering Gallery, where the faintest murmur of a word can be heard a hundred feet away; but sometimes he stands before the majestic marble of the Wellington Monument. Here there is always a gaggle of tourists gawping now at the capitals' acanthus curls, now at the canopy's tassels, now at the letters carved in stone. But this is not what interests Munchausen. Beckoning to a lay brother, he points to a pair of allegorical figures.

"What is that?"

"A true representation of Truth and Falsehood, sir."

"And which one of them is Truth?" The baron squints.

"If I may say so, sir, that one."

"The last time, as I recall, you said that one was Falsehood." The baron winks, arching his right eyebrow. The lay brother, long accustomed to this visitor's caprices, knows that now he must look not at Truth and not at Falsehood, but at the silver shilling glinting between the rich man's fingers, and then back gratefully away and disappear. Munchausen emerges from St. Paul's with a serene, almost joyful expression. Then, one foot on the running board of his motorcar, he invariably declares, "Whenever you go to God, he is never at home. We shall try others."

The baron gives an address, and Johnny turns the wheel either to the right, toward Paternoster Row, or to the left, toward the bustle of Fleet Street, shier of words all over the world; from here London's twenty-mile radiuses—now this one, now that—fan away beneath the whoosh of the limousine's wheels.

After paying two or three calls, the baron nods to Johnny: "Home." They usually drive back by way of the squalid East End. The grimy houses resemble compressed fog, and the man with his head thrown back on the limousine's leather cushions reflects that only one thing in this world will never be winnowed away by the winds: squalor.

At Mad Bean Cottage reporters are already waiting, pencils poised. Munchausen patiently and graciously answers all questions.

"My opinion of parliamentarism? Certainly. Only yesterday I finished calculating the amount of muscle power required to raise and lower the tongues of all the orators in England: using a rate of three opponents to one speaker, taking the Upper and Lower Houses, if we multiply the number of annual sessions by the number of years (from 1265 to 1920), adding all factions, committees, and subcommittees, then convert all of this into foot-poods and horse-powers, we obtain—just imagine!—an energy discharge sufficient to build two Cheops pyramids. What a majestic achievement. Just think! And yet the socialists will insist that we never do any physical labor.

"My battle plan? In the social sphere? Extremely simple. To the point of primitivism. Even African savages have put it into words. Yes indeed: they have a waterfall at Lake Victoria; its racket and roar can be heard for miles around; as you approach you see a gigantic cloud of watery dust—from sky to earth. The savages called this Mosi-oa-Tunya, which means 'smoke that roars.' So there you have it."

"Have you ever been there, sir?" inquires a reporter.

"I have been to what has never been, which is significantly farther. As a rule, I consider—are you taking this down?—I consider only two powers real: racket and reason. And if they were ever to join forces, why then.... But let us end on that note."

The baron rises to his feet; the reporters put away their notebooks and take their leave.

Then the manservant announces: Luncheon is served. Munchausen goes down to the dining room. Among the many dishes there are always his favorite roast ducklings. Having eaten his fill, the baron passes into the study and settles into a deep armchair; while the manservant fusses at his outstretched feet, replacing gaiters with down slippers, the baron, his kindly eyes half closed, gazes in sated reverie out the window at the London rain streaking the park's green landscape. Now comes the hour known at Mad Bean Cottage as the hour of postprandial aphorisms. In the doorway, stepping soundlessly, appears a prim miss. She pulls the little table with the typewriter out of its corner and applies her fingers to the keys. Munchausen does not immediately begin to dictate: first he sucks at length on his pipe, shifting it from one corner of his mouth to the other, as if considering out of which corner to smoke and which to speak. The baron smokes in an amazing way: first come swirling dove-colored spheroids, then curling around them, like Saturn's transparent rings—now to the right, now to the left—slow smoky coils.

"Now then. An old Limburger cheese pities no one, but still it cries.

"Before the oyster can form an opinion of the lemon's smell, it has been eaten."

The typist's ears are hidden under a straight red bob; she sits with her back to the aphorisms and her eyes on the slanting lines of rain, but her fingers tap at the keys, the rain taps at the panes, and the dictation continues until the baron, knocking the ashes out of his pipe, says, "Thank you. Tomorrow—as usual."

He tries to get up, but drowsiness has made his body heavy, his thoughts foggy—and reality, along with the soundlessly stepping red-haired miss, is slipping out the door.

Behind his closed eyelids visions stream: a dreamed automobile is ferrying him through dreamed streets, strangely peopleless and mute; without having once honked the horn, Johnny stops the whoosh of wheels by the colonnade of St. Paul's. Munchausen has already lowered a foot onto the running board when suddenly the cathedral comes to life: its head under its gigantic round hat swoops down, butting the air with its cross. Arching its ridged back, the monster, all of its bell clappers clacking, shouts, "Sir, how can I turn into Saul without turning around?" Quick-witted Johnny starts the engine and with a hard turn of the wheel sheers away; but the monstrosity, lugging its colossal stone trunk on twelve gigantic columns, comes crashing after. The gearbox, gnashing its teeth, flings the needle to full speed. But the fleet-columned monster is coming closer and closer. The car careers down a narrow street in the East End. The cathedral tries to wedge in after, thrusting an angular stone shoulder into the crack-like bystreet. Now Munchausen, bouncing up from his seat, shouts to the hundreds of square eyes stretching away to right and left, "Hey there! Look lively, don't let it in!" The houses instantly obey, moving their windows toward the windows opposite and cutting the cathedral off. With a sigh of relief the baron sinks back among the cushions only to see turned toward him Johnny's deathly pale face: "What've you done? We'll be killed!" And indeed, only now does the baron see that the houses in the squalid East End are row houses; soldered together, bricks inside bricks, they form a solid phalanx divided only by numbers: as soon as the brick boxes behind have come together, the ones ahead must do the same—the street's walls are slowly closing in, threatening to flatten the speeding automobile and the people in it; the car's axles keep grinding against the walls—faster!—ahead is the light of a public square; but too late—the gigantic flattener has caught the feebly whirring motor in a vise of many-storied boxes, its steel fenders and body crackle like the wing covers of an insect crunching underfoot. With a sharp kick Munchausen knocks out the window frame bearing down on his right and leaps inside the house. But luck has deserted poor Johnny, pinioned between two windows—wall collides with wall— his short shriek is lost in the crash of bricks against bricks, then all is quiet. And suddenly from behind: "You'll have to pay for that broken glass, mister." Munchausen turns around—he is in a shabby, but neatly kept room; in the middle is a plain deal table laid with piping bowls of soup before which sit a middle-aged man in shirtsleeves, a gaunt woman with flushed cheeks, and two little boys on a bench. Legs adangle, spoons stuck in their mouths, the boys stare wide-eyed at the visitant. "And I should warn you, the price of glass has gone up," the man goes on, stirring the contents of his bowl. "Tom, pull up a chair for the mister, he might as well sit down."

But Munchausen has no thought of sitting down. "How can you sit there when Saul has turned into Paul, when the street is gone and there is nothing left?"

The man, to the baron's surprise, is not surprised. "If you add nothing to nothing, it still makes nothing. Someone with nowhere to go doesn't need a street. Eat up, boys, before it gets cold."

The baron, as if another wall were bearing down on him, backs away to the door, knocking over the extra chair, and hurries down the stairs to find: a square yard inside four walls. "What if these are like those?" He ducks through a low gateway: another square inside four close walls; a lower and narrower gateway—and again a square inside even closer walls. "Confounded chessboard," a frightened Munchausen whispers, then sees in the middle of the square, on an enormous round leg, its black varnished mane bristling: a chess knight. Without wasting a moment, he jumps onto the horse's high neck; the horse twitches its wooden ears, and Munchausen, gripping the slippery varnish with his knees, feels the one-legged chessman crouch down, then jump forward, again forward and sideways, once more forward, forward and sideways; the ground now falls away, now strikes the horse's round heel with its swinging steeples and roofs; but the felt-shod heel—Munchausen remembers this well— gallops furiously on: squares flicker past, then patchwork fields and checkerboard cities—more and more—forward, forward, sideways and forward; the round heel pounds now grass, now stone, now black earth. The wind whistling in the baron's ears dies down, the horse's jumps grow shorter and slower—now over a flat snowy field whose drifts exude cold; the black horse, baring its teeth, makes one more jump and a jump and suddenly stops in the middle of the icy plain, felt-shod foot frozen to the snow. What to do? Munchausen tries to urge the horse on. "Kt. g8–f6; f6–d5, damn, d5–b6," he cries, recalling the zigzag of Alekhine's defense. In vain! The knight is played out: the wooden jade retires. Munchausen weeps with fury and frustration, but his tears freeze to his lashes; one cannot withstand this cold for even a second. Rubbing his ears with his palms, he trudges on—forward, forward and sideways, and again forward, forward and sideways—searching for the tiniest speck on the smooth snow-white cloth covering the vast, round, horizon-fringed table. And suddenly he sees, away in the distance, rippling like a faint shadow, a nimble string of pointed Gothic letters, a sort of prickly centipede. Next Munchausen catches sight of the individual letters and reads—his own name. He is stunned. Meanwhile, the eighteen-letter BARON VON MUNCHAUSEN is losing no time: bending its syllables, it slithers toward a frontier post that has popped up out of the ground: on the post is a board, on the board are symbols. Munchausen, barely tearing his soles away from the ground to which they have frozen, runs after his escaping name. But his name has already reached the post and barrier raising red and white stripes over the white plain; it turns around to glimpse its pursuer— is he far behind? At that same moment—Munchausen sees this clearly—the barrier swings swiftly down: the red and white stripes strike the eighth letter, and his name, like a snake cloven in two, is left writhing in pain: MUNCHAUSEN on that side of the post, BAR-ONVON on this. Standing up on its ink-bleeding N, poor BARON-VON rushes this way and that, not knowing what to do. Munchausen's eyes fly from the letters in the snow to the symbols on the frontier post: USSR. He stands there for a minute, mouth agape, then thinks: Leave your name and run. But the soles of his shoes have again frozen to the snow. He tries to wrest his right foot, then tugs his left—suddenly the four frontier letters bestir themselves. Terrified, Munchausen jumps out of his shoes and bounds over the snow's icy crust in just his socks; the cold nips at his heels, in despair he rushes this way and that and . . . wakes up.

His right slipper has come off, and his heel is resting on a cool square of waxed parquet. Rain is pattering on the study window, but its fine streaks are sheathed in darkness. The cuckoo on the chimneypiece cries seven times. Baron von Munchausen reaches for his little bell.

Mad Bean Cottage now lights its lamps and prepares to receive the evening guests. Downstairs the knocker knocks and knocks again at the oaken door: First to arrive is a stock-market king, followed a minute later by a diplomatic ace. Next is an elderly lady addicted to spiritualism. When the door is finally darkened by the drooping mustache of the Labor Party leader, Munchausen gets up to greet the knave, clucking like a lucky cardplayer:

"Royal flush! Come and join our game. You are just the man we need."

But besides the much-needed man, there now arrives a former minister without portfolio, whom the cozy cottage welcomes, for all that, with no less warmth and cordiality.

The guests exchange the latest news, forgetting neither bedchambers nor Parliament; they speculate about forthcoming appointments, about events in China; the baron talks to the minister without portfolio about a certain portfolio without minister, while the lady spiritualist recounts, "Yesterday, at the Pytchleys', we summoned the spirit of Li Hung Chang: 'Spirit, if you are here, knock once; if not, knock twice.' And just imagine, Li knocked twice."

Just then downstairs the door knocker knocks twice.

"Can that really be Li?" The baron leaps up, ready to greet the ghost.

But standing in the doorway is his manservant.

"His Holiness the Bishop of Northumberland."

A minute later a beringed hand is blessing all present.

The conversation resumes. The manservant hands around bread and butter, tea in porcelain cups, and liqueur in small glasses. For a while words whirl from mouth to mouth and then His Holiness, pushing teacup aside, asks the baron to tell them a story. With the lady's permission Munchausen lights his pipe and, over its wheezing bowl, launches into one of his adventures. His listeners are all ears, and right away he begins to bend them: first around the edges, then along the auricular cartilage, inward and inward, until they curl up like autumn leaves and, ear by ear, softly and unrustlingly, flutter to the floor. But now his disciplined manservant, who has appeared behind the guests' backs with dustpan and brush, quietly sweeps up the ears and carries them out.

"This happened during my last sojourn in Rome," the baron's voice wafts the whorls of smoke. "One fresh autumn morning I descended the steps of St. Peter's, crossed the piazza embraced by Bernini's colonnades, and turned left down the narrow Borgo Sant'Angelo. If you have ever been there, then you must recall the dusty windows

full of *antichità** and the dingy little commission shops whose owners, upon receiving something of yours and a few silver soldi, promise to return it the following week without the soldi, but with a
papal blessing. As the blessing's presence in the thing is invisible,
these commissions are carried out briskly and always on time. Here
one may also acquire for a small price an amulet, a snake's tooth to
ward off fever, a coral *jettatura* against the evil eye, and various
ashes—from Saint Francis to Saint Januarius, inclusive—poured
neatly into little paper packets. I turned into one of those shops and
asked for the ashes of Saint Nobody. The shop owner ran his fingers
over the paper packets: 'Perhaps signore would be satisfied with
Saint Ursula?' I shook my head. 'I could oblige signore with Saint
Pacheco: extremely rare ashes.' I repeated my request: '*Der heilige
Niemand*.'† The shop owner was, evidently, an honest man. He threw
up his hands and sadly confessed that he had no such ashes. I was
very nearly out the door when my eye fell upon an object in the corner, on a shelf: a tiny black box with yellow wisps of matted flax
poking out from under its half-open lid. 'What is that?' I asked,
turning around to the counter. The ashman's obliging fingers produced the ware at once. It turned out to be a partly burned piece of
flax from the coronation of Pius X. As we all know, during the inves-
titure of a new pope, a piece of flax is set alight over his tonsure to
the sacramental words *Sic transit gloria mundi*.‡ The shop owner,
whom I had no reason to disbelieve, swore to me that during the
performance of that ceremony, just as the sacramental words were
being said over Pius, a sudden gust of wind had carried off this piece
of flax, which he, a collector of rare objects, had managed to acquire
for a certain sum. 'You may see for yourself, signore,' he opened the
little box, 'the flax is singed and has a burnt smell.' Indeed it had. I
asked the price. He named a round number. I halved it. He came

---

*Antiquities. (Italian)
†Saint Nobody. (German)
‡Thus passes the glory of the world. (Latin)

down, I went up, and the little box of papal flax wound up in my pocket.

"Two hours later I was on the train to Genoa. I, you see, did not want to miss the next Christian Socialist congress, due to take place in that city's Palazzo Rosso: for lovers of impracticabilities—and I count myself one—gatherings of this sort can be instructive. The windows in my carriage were open to the damp sea air; closer to Genoa, we passed through a series of tunnels, stuffiness relieved by drafts, and I caught cold. During the very first Christian Socialist session I felt positively ill. Curative measures were in order. I happened to put my hand in my pocket and find the little box, at which point I recollected that cotton or—if you have none—flax inserted in the ears is a radical remedy for colds. I opened the black lid and stuffed a bit of the papal flax in either ear. And right away.... Oh, if you only knew what happened! The speakers went on speaking, as before the flax; their lips moved, articulating phrases, but not a single sound, except the ticking of my watch, reached my ears. I could not understand it: if I was deaf to words, then why not to the ticking of a timepiece? If the flax in my ears muffled sounds, if it weakened my hearing, why were loud voices softer than the barely audible mechanism of a watch? Discomfited, I walked out of the hall, past soundlessly speaking mouths, and was happily amazed when, outside once more and barely down the palace steps, I suddenly heard through my flax: 'Mancia.'* The word came from an old woman in rags. The flax's inhibitory effect had clearly ceased. She held out a grimy palm, but I, anxious to test my conclusion, rushed back into the assembly hall. I was quick, but my conclusion was quicker: again I saw moving lips, articulating nothing but silence. What the devil! (Forgive me, Your Holiness, I take that devil back.) What could this mean? I formed hypothesis after hypothesis, then suddenly remembered that the flax in my ears was special sacramental flax against smoke and all *gloria mundi*; nothing ephemeral, no worldly glory

---

*Alms. (Italian)

could pass through it. Undoubtedly, that was so. I had not overpaid the ashman from the Borgo Sant'Angelo: but then why was it that speeches by adepts of Christian socialism became mired in the flax and could not penetrate my hearing?

"Deep in onerous thought, I returned to my hotel room. For the next session, I decided to refine my filter separating Christians from pseudo-Christians and repelling all worldly vanity. My reasoning went as follows: If not a single sinful word could permeate the hallowed flax, if such words always got stuck in the dense fibers, what would happen if those dry and stiff fibers were made somewhat *slippery*? What would happen, quite naturally, is this: The words, given their slowness and crudeness (they consist of air, after all), would still get stuck in the slippery flax, whereas the thoughts they concealed, owing to their subtlety and etherealness, would most likely slip through the slippery strands and leap into my hearing. I took the bits of flax out of my ears and inspected them: both were coated with a rather dirty residue. Left, no doubt, by the speeches. I cleaned off that verbatim report, so to speak, and, before replacing the bits of flax in my ears, dipped each in a spoonful of fat, ordinary goose fat melted over a candle. My watch reminded me that the congress was about to resume. Passing through the lobby, I heard faint voices coming from the assembly hall: the session had already begun. I half opened the door and cocked my flax-caulked ears: a fine-looking man in a proper frock coat buttoned up to his chin stood at the lectern smiling unctuously and swearing lustily. In bewilderment, I surveyed the object of his abuse: the audience was listening reverently, hundreds of heads nodded approval in time to the insults raining down on them. Now and then the speaker was interrupted by applause and shouts of 'Cretin!,' 'Lickspittle!,' 'Hypocrite!,' 'Scoundrel!' In response he clasped his hands to his chest and bowed. Unable to bear it any longer, I stopped my ears. Or rather, I unstopped them: the speaker was discussing the congress's contributions to the struggle against class struggle. From all sides came cries of 'Bravo!,' 'Isn't that the truth!,' and 'How right you are!' Only now did I understand that the few grams of flax pressed inside my tiny box were worth a good philosophical method. I decided to filter the entire world through my deglorifying flax. I drew up a schedule of experiments and departed that night on an express bound for...."

The story continues. The cuckoo cries eleven times, then twelve, and only long after midnight does Munchausen's pipe knock out its ashes, while the baron, having finished his story, sees his guests to the front hall. His workday is done. And around Mad Bean Cottage, more and more spirals weave, casting their lines wider and wider with every evening: their fine tendrils have already curled past La Manche, the better to reach the earth's most distant meridians. The baron's aphorisms, he knows this, are on lecterns in both houses of Parliament, next to the agenda and the verbatim report. The stories and old anecdotes, begun by the slow bluish smoke of his pipe, swirl around Mad Bean Cottage like smoky mists, slithering up under all ceilings, from mouth to mouth, and into unhearing ears. Slapping upstairs in his slippers to his warm bed, the baron smiles vaguely and mumbles, "Munchausen sleeps, but not his cause."

3. KANT'S COEVAL

THOUGH Baron von Munchausen preferred slippers to gaiters and leisure to work, he soon had to give up his postprandial snooze and stay-at-home life. The smoke from his old pipe was easily dispersed with the palm of his hand, but the roar "made" by that smoke was swelling with the abandon of ocean breakers. The telephonic ear, which had hung peacefully from its metal hook in the baron's study, now fidgeted incessantly on its stand. The door knocker knocked without respite at the oaken door, telegrams and letters poured in from all parts, staring up at Munchausen with their round post-marks. Among them the baron's absently skimming eyes came across an elegant invitation printed on card stock in old-fashioned script: a group of admirers requested the honor of Baron Hieronymus von Munchausen's presence at a fete to celebrate the bicentennial of the esteemed baron's career. The Anniversary Committee. Splendid Hotel. Date and hour.

The formal rooms of the Splendid Hotel glittered with electric lights innumerable. The plate-glass entrance door, soundlessly re-volving, admitted more and more guests. The round central hall had been draped with the Munchausen coat of arms: along the shield's heraldic bend five ducks flew—bill, tail, bill, tail, bill—threaded on a string; from under the last tail, in roman letters, streamed the motto: MENDACE VERITAS.*

Seated at long tables forming an Old Slavonic *M* were women in décolleté and men in full dress—members of the diplomatic corps,

---

*Truth in lies. (Latin)

prominent columnists, philanthropists, and financiers. Champagne glasses had already clinked many times and rapturous cheers flown up to the ceiling after the corks when the baron rose to respond.

"Ladies and gentlemen," he began, surveying the now-silent tables, "it says in the Gospel: 'In the beginning was the Word.' That means: Any deed must be begun with words. I said as much at the last international peace conference, and I take the liberty of repeating myself on the present occasion. We Munchausens have always faithfully served fiction: my ancestor Heino embarked with Frederick II on a Crusade, and a descendant of mine joined the Liberal Party. What can one say against that? History, meanwhile, brought us—myself and Kant—into the world at the same time. As this distinguished gathering no doubt knows, Kant and I are almost the same age, and it would be wrong at this celebration in my honor not to mention his name. Of course, I do have my differences with the creator of the *Critique of Pure Reason*. Where Kant says: 'I know only what is introduced by me into my experience,' I, Munchausen, say, 'I introduce; let others try to know what I have introduced, if they have experience enough to do so.' But on the whole, our thoughts have often coincided. Thus when I saw a platoon of Versaillais take up rifles and level them at unarmed Communards (this was by the walls of Père-Lachaise), I could not help but recall an aphorism coined by the old man of Königsberg: 'Man is the ultimate purpose for man and should not be anything but the ultimate purpose.' In one of his witty plays, Mr. Bernard Shaw"—the baron turned toward an end of the flower-trimmed *M*—"maintains that we do not live forever only because we do not know how to wish for our immortality. But I—and Mr. Shaw will forgive me—have come much closer to the secret of immortality: I need not myself wish to prolong my life to infinity; it is enough that others wish me, Munchausen, a long life. Indeed, it is owing to your wishes," the baron's voice trembled, "that I have set out on the path of Methuselah. Yes, ladies and gentlemen, now you must not object. In your hands you hold not only glasses of champagne; you have opened a savings account for me in Being. Today from that account I have withdrawn two hundred. Henceforth it shall be as you please: maintain the account or close it. In essence, you have only to shake me out of your pupils and I shall be as poor as Nothing itself."

But these last words were washed away by a wave of applause, crystal tinkled against crystal as dozens of palms sought out that of the honoree; he barely managed to return all the smiles, to bow and express his thanks. Then tables were pushed against walls, violins and castanets struck up a fox-trot, and the baron, accompanied by several silvery pates, proceeded past the dancing pairs to the smoking room. They drew up chairs in a snug circle, and a diplomatic official, leaning toward the baron's ear, made him a confidential offer. This moment, as will be seen, was portentous. In response to this offer Munchausen's eyebrows rose, while the forefinger with the moonstone half tickled his ear, as if trying to test the words to the touch. Moving closer still, the official named a number. Munchausen hesitated. The official appended a zero to the number. Munchausen still hesitated. Finally, coming out of his quandary, he squinted at the moonstone's dimly glinting oval and said, "I sojourned in those latitudes some hundred and fifty years ago, and I do not know, truly.... You have jogged the pendulum—it is oscillating between yes and no. Of course, I am not a man one can frighten or knock out of the saddle, so to speak. The experience of my first journey to that nation of barbarians just named by you, sir, afforded ample material for judgments both about them and about me. Incidentally, not counting a few minor publications, this material has never seen the light of day. My acquaintance with Russia took place during the reign of my late friend the empress Catherine the Great. However, I stray from the matter at hand."

The diplomatic official, correctly calculating his chances, made a sign to the others, whose faces shone with rapt enthusiasm.

"Here, here!"

"It would be so interesting to hear."

"I am all ears."

"We are listening."

An underling, swallowtails flying, ran to the door and motioned to the dancers; the fox-trot betook itself to a more distant hall. The baron began:

"As our diligence approached the frontier of that astonishing country, the landscape changed abruptly. This side of the frontier post lush trees bloomed; that side, snowy wastes stretched as far as the eye could see. While the horses were being changed, we traded our light riding cloaks for fur coats. Then the barrier rose and.... But I shall not tell you about the tunes that froze up in our postilion's horn, or about my horse dangling from a church steeple, or many other adventures. Any cultivated person knows these stories no worse than his wallet or, shall we say, his prayers. Instead we shall stop the wheels of the diligence at the entrance to that barbarous nation's northern capital, Petersburg.

"Here I must tell you that an earlier diligence had delivered to the city of Saint Peter a philosopher not unknown in his day, one Denis Diderot: he was, to my mind, a most intolerable scribbler of philosophemes, a petit bourgeois parvenu, and of a clearly materialistic bent to boot. I, as you know, have never suffered and do not suffer materialists, persons fond of reminding one—apropos and not so—that sweet-smelling ambergris is in fact the excrement of a sperm whale, while the fresh-cut flowers in which a lovely girl has hidden her face are in fact a blooming bunch of genitalia. Who needs that silly *in fact*? I am at a loss to conjecture. But to return. We were both received at court: Diderot and I. I must admit that at first the empress appeared to favor—if you can imagine it—that ill-mannered upstart: in perpetual breach of etiquette, Diderot might strut back and forth in front of her nose, interrupt her, and even, in the heat of argument, slap her on the knee. Catherine, smiling graciously, listened to all his nonsensical plans: to eradicate drunkenness in Russia, to fight bribe-taking, to reform manufacturing and trade, to rationalize fisheries on the White Sea. I remained in the shadows, calmly awaiting my chance. No sooner had that driveler in ink-spattered dress clothes set about enlarging fisheries than I too turned from plans to action: from local hunters I acquired several trap-caught foxes and began, in the walled backyard of the country house where

I then dwelt, my own experiments—mentioned in my memoirs, if you recall—in the forcible eviction of foxes from their skins. Everything went on swimmingly, with no one the wiser. While Diderot was busy trying to catch fish from a frozen sea, I presented myself to the empress, by now somewhat disenchanted with her favorite, and requested the honor of her presence at a demonstration that might revolutionize the fur trade. On the appointed day and hour, the empress and her court arrived in my backyard. Four strapping footmen with whips and a fox tied by its tail to a post were at the ready. At a signal from me, the whips went to work till the fox, having jerked this way and that, jumped out of its skin—straight into the arms of a waiting fifth footman. Anyone who has read Darwin, gentlemen, knows the extraordinary adaptability of animals to their surroundings. Having jumped out into the bitter cold, the bald fox instantly began to grow a new coat which, though thin at first, thickened— right before our eyes—into a fine new pelt; the poor thing stopped shivering only to find itself, alas, tied to the post for a fresh flogging. And so on it went—just imagine—until there were seven pelts, and the fox finally jumped, so to speak, out of life. I had the carrion taken away, then laid the seven pelts out on the snow and, bowing down, said, 'Seven hundred percent pure profit!' The empress found this highly amusing and allowed me to kiss her hand. I was then asked to make a written report on methods and prospects for the fur trade, which I did on the spot. Having marked my report 'wary goot,' Her Majesty, in her own hand, crossed out every 'fox' and all 'foxes,' replacing these with a 'person' and 'people,' respectively. At the bottom she added: 'As amended. Catherine.' An original mind, don't you think?"

The baron ran his eyes around the circle of smiles and went on.

"After that Monsieur Diderot's nose was distinctly out of joint, as if it had got jammed in his snuffbox an instant before the delicious whiff. The Paris sage, accustomed to a hail-fellow hand from both the truth and the tsarina, was now left with just the truth. Society entirely fitting for such a parvenu, ha-ha! The poor man hadn't the means to take himself off home, so had to sell—for a few hundred livres—his library: it was acquired by the empress. She received me the very next day: I presented Her Majesty with a copybook full of my travels and adventures. Upon reading, she exclaimed, 'This is worth whole libraries!' I was granted an estate and one hundred thousand serfs. Wishing to escape from the adulation at court and certain circumstances of a more delicate nature, on which I shall not comment except to note that I am not overly fond of corpulent women, I set off to inspect my new possessions.

"The Russian landscape, I must tell you, is strange: in the midst of a field, like mushrooms under caps, a clutch of huts appears with roofs askew and chimneyless stoves; peasants pass into and out of these huts through the stovepipe, along with the smoke; towering over their wells, who knows why, are long sweep barriers, though often far from roads; their bathhouses, unlike the hovels they inhabit, are huge affairs of seven stories, or 'shelves.' But I digress.

"Wandering that foreign land I often recalled my native Bodenwerder: the pointed tile roofs like circumflex accents, the old graven mottos half effaced on whitewashed walls. Nostalgia compelled me to restlessly roam the hummocky bogs and reedy thickets with a rifle over my shoulder, if only to kill time. However, my game pouch was never empty, and soon my renown as a hunter—mentioned in my memoirs, but why repeat what any schoolboy knows by heart—had spread from the White Sea to the Black. Instead of snipes and partridges, I soon found myself hunting Turks. Russia, you see, had declared war on Turkey, and now I, having hung up my hunting rifle, had to take into these very hands, figuratively speaking, two hundred thousand guns, not counting the field marshal's baton which, given my former relations with the tsarina, I felt I could hardly refuse. After the very first engagement we saw nothing but our enemies' backs. At the battle on the Danube I captured one thousand, no, two thousand cannons, more cannons than we knew what to do with—whiling away our leisure in the field, we took potshots with them at passing sparrows. During one such lull in the fighting, I was called away from headquarters to the capital, where I was to be decorated with the Order of Basil the Blessed, a confection of fourteen golden crosses encrusted with diamonds. The verst posts flashed past my eyes faster than the spokes of my curricle's wheels, which, now and then, I craned out of my seat to see. Racing into the capital on smoking axles, I bid the driver slow the horses so that I might tip my tricorne to the welcoming crowds on our way to the palace. Bowing right and left, I noticed that these Russians were none of them wearing hats. At first this struck me as a natural expression of their feelings for my triumphant self, but even after the official ceremonies were over, there they still stood, despite the cold wind from the sea, with bare heads. This struck me as somewhat strange, but there was no time for questions. Again the versts flashed past—and soon I saw the even ranks of my armies formed up to greet their leader. On coming closer, I saw that they too were hatless. 'Cover your heads!' I commanded, but—a thousand devils!—my command went unheeded. 'What does this mean?' I turned, incensed, to my aide-decamp. 'It means,' he said, touching trembling fingers to his own uncovered head, 'that we trounced the enemy at the drop of a hat, of all our hats, Your Most High Excell—'

"That night a sudden idea woke me under the mantle of my field marshal's tent. I rose, dressed, and, without waking my orderlies, slipped away to the line of foreposts, whereupon two short words—password and watchword—opened the way for me to the Turkish camp. The Turks were still busy extricating themselves from the waist-deep heaps of hats, so I reached the gates of Constantinople unhindered, but there too everything was buried and behatted, right up to the rooftops! On arriving at the sultan's palace, I gave my name and received an immediate audience. My scheme was extremely simple: to buy up all the hats bedeviling soldiers, residents, roads, and paths. Sultan Mahmud did not know himself what to do with this embarrassment of hats and I was able to buy them for a song. By now autumn had turned to winter, and the still-hatless Russian populace was freezing, catching cold, grumbling, threatening to rebel and ring in a new Time of Troubles. The government could not rely even on the worthies: the senators' bald pates were the first to freeze and their fervent love for the throne was cooling by the day. So I loaded ships and caravans with my hats and sent them through neutral countries to myriad-headed Russia. Trade was extremely brisk: the lower the mercury fell in thermometers, the higher hat prices climbed.

"Soon millions of hats had returned to their rightful heads and I was the richest man in war- and indemnities-ravaged Turkey. By now the sultan and I were as thick as thieves and I had decided to invest my capital in rebuilding his country. However, palace intrigues obliged the sultan, his harem, and myself to change residence: we moved to Baghdad, a city rich if not in gold and silver, then in tales and legends. Again I began to long for my faraway Bodenwerder which, though wretched, was dear to my heart. When I asked my crowned friend to allow me to return home, he, tears trickling into his beard, said he would not survive the separation. Well then, wishing to shorten as far as possible those inevitable separations—for I too could not live without paying occasional visits to the ancestral aerie of my forefathers—I decided to connect Bodenwerder and Baghdad with parallel tracks of steel. Thus arose my project—implemented only much later, alas—for a Baghdad railway. We were just about to begin work, but—"

The baron suddenly interrupted his story and fell silent, eyes fixed on the shimmering moonstone on the index finger of his right hand.

"But why did you stop halfway?" burst from someone's lips.

"Because"—the baron turned to the voice—"at the time railways, you see, had not yet been invented. As simple as that."

Faint laughter ran around the circle. But the baron remained serious. Leaning toward the diplomatic official, he nudged the man's knee and said, "My memories have overwhelmed me. All right. I will go. As they say in Moscow: 'When a Russian is at death's door, a German feels fit as a fiddle.' Ha-ha!"

And raising his voice to meet the ears craning from all sides, the baron added: "Yes, our heraldic duck has never yet folded its wings."

Now there ensued a shaking of hands and shuffling of feet. A minute later the porter by the revolving glass panes at the entrance to the Splendid Hotel was shouting, "Baron von Munchausen's motorcar!"

A door clicked shut, a siren rent the air, and the leather cushions, gently swaying, sailed off into the glorious night brilliant with stars and streetlights.

4. *IN PARTES INFIDELIUM*

OFFER and acceptance had been duly concluded. The baron was leaving for the Land of the Soviets as a correspondent for two or three of the most influential newspapers delivering political credo in millions of copies to the outermost meridians of the British Empire. Munchausen had to preserve the strictest incognito, owing to which the quantity of top hats showing black under the windows of his private car was extremely limited, while the Kodaks and interviews had been dispensed with altogether. A moment before the departing whistle, the baron appeared on the car's open platform sporting a worn gray cap, a gleaming leather jacket under flared topcoat, and boots with accordion pleats. This costume elicited nods of approval from the top hats, and only the Bishop of Northumberland, come to catch perhaps his last glimpse ever of the baron, sighed and said, "*In partes infidelium, cum Deo.* Amen.*"

A diplomatic official hoisted himself up onto the step and made a sign to Munchausen, who bent down.

"My dear baron, do not joke with the perlustrators, sign your letters with an assumed name, something like—"

The baron nodded. "I understand: 'Zinoviev' or—"

The train, buffers clanking, jerked forward. The official was scooped up by his elbows; top hats were tipped; the curtain in the sailing-away window was drawn—and the not-finished sentence along with its not-finished speaker started off.

Dover. La Manche. Again the curtained window slid past droning

---

*To the land of the unbelievers, God be with you. (Latin)

railway platforms; again kilometers were subtracted from kilometers.

Only one man on the entire Continent knew the day and hour when Munchausen would pass through Berlin. That was Ernst Unding. But the letter sent to the poet from London did not immediately find him. The cycle of sonnets on which he was then at work might have been a crown of thorns fumbling his brain; it paid him not in pfennigs, but in sleepless nights. After much futile wrangling with hunger, Unding had had to accept the proposal of a cosmetics concern called Veritas to act as their agent, traveling to cities and towns around Germany. The London letter chased after its addressee for days on end, amassing postmarks, before finally catching him up in the city of Insterburg on the Königsberg–Eydtkuhnen line, some thirty kilometers from the border. It arrived just in time. Checking the numbers in his guidebook against the information in the letter, Unding easily deduced that Munchausen's train from Berlin would pass through Insterburg that evening at half past nine. His pocket watch showed eight fifty. Afraid of being late, Unding dressed for the station. At the time stated, the Berlin express rolled up to the platform. Unding quickly passed down the length of the train—from locomotive to caboose and back—glancing in all the windows: no Munchausen. A minute later the train had unsheathed the tracks. Puzzled, Unding went off to inquire: Was that the right train and when was the next? Yes, came the reply; the next train to the border would not arrive for two hours and some minutes. Unding hesitated: business required him to catch the ten o'clock to Königsberg; he already had his ticket. He fiddled with the cardboard rectangle and turned it in. Seated on a bench inside the station, he began following the hour hand on the wall with his eyes. He clearly pictured the approaching reunion. A car window would drop down and out would come Munchausen's hand—the long bony fingers with the moon glint on the index; their palms would meet and he, Unding, would say that even if there were no other reality in the world besides this handshake, he. . . . Through the wall he heard a rumbling: the express. Unding shook off his thoughts and rushed out onto the platform: the advancing lights of a locomotive, hissing brakes. Again he passed down the length of the train, to the head-light, and back to the red carbuncle at the tail end: not one window dropped down, no one's voice called, no one's hand reached out to meet his. Copper banged against copper—and again the rails were bare. The poet Unding stood a long while on the nighttime plat-form, pondering the situation. It was perfectly clear: Munchausen had taken a different route.

Next morning, sitting in a cheap hotel room in Königsberg, Un-ding jotted down some verses about a train, forty or fifty car-years long, loaded with life; the years, clanking against one another, race up steep hills and around sharp bends; lackadaisical signals switch them from track to track; the blood and emerald stars of horoscopes prophesy death and prosperity, until some senseless catastrophe smashes all the couplings of years with years and hurls them helter-skelter down an embankment.

After that, to use Unding's images, the days of an entire year churned past, buffers clanking, and now, as the next was advancing with "1923" scrawled above a still-sealed door, Munchausen's name, which had disappeared from the world press, suddenly reappeared on the front pages of papers in England and America. As a result, their enormous circulations became more gigantic still. And not only their circulations: the eyes of those who snapped up reports by Baron Munchausen invariably widened, as though his communica-tions contained atropine. Only one pair of eyes, inside red-rimmed lids fringed with prickly lashes, narrowed their pupils on seeing Munchausen's byline and twitched an eyebrow. To whom they be-longed, those two mistrustful eyes, one need hardly say.

5. THE DEVIL IN A DROSHKY

MEANWHILE the multiplying lines of Munchauseniads went on flinging his again-flickering name from candle to candle, as saltpeter threads will fling fire, and soon the entire world press, tangled in tinsel and wire-ribbon flashes, was clad like a Christmas tree in small yellow tongues. A week went by, another week, a month, and the baron's name began to feel cramped in newspaper columns: leaping out of newssheets, it slithered up playbill pillars and rippled down from illuminated signs—over the asphalt, the brick, and the flat bottoms of clouds. The playbills announced: Baron von Munchausen, who has just returned from the Land of the Soviets, will give an account of his journey in the grand hall of the Royal Society of London. The box office was mobbed, but only the chosen entered the old building in Piccadilly.

At the hour promised on the playbills, Munchausen materialized at the lectern: his lips were still calmly pursed, but the sharp Adam's apple between the wings of his starched collar was bobbing like a cork barely resisting the pressure of champagne. Thunderous and protracted applause from the packed hall forced the baron to bow his head and wait. Finally, the applause died away. He glanced around: by his elbow stood a tumbler and a carafe of water; to his left was the screen for the magic lantern; leaning against the screen was a varnished pointer resembling an over-long marshal's baton. And craning forward on all hands—from the right, the left, and in front—were hundreds upon hundreds of ears; even the marble busts of Newton and Cook, now leaning out of their niches, looked entirely alert. It was to them that Baron Hieronymus von Munchausen addressed his opening remarks.

I

If Captain Cook once set off in search of savages only to be eaten by them, then the winds that filled my sails were patently more merciful. As you can see, ladies and gentlemen, I am alive and well (slight flutter in the hall). The great British mathematician (Munchausen gestured toward Newton) watched the fall of an apple that had broken away from a branch and summed up the movement of a spheroid called Earth, that gigantic apple that had broken away from the Sun. Listening on nighttime street corners in Moscow to a revolutionary song sung by one and all about a little apple, I tried to understand where it had rolled off to, that little apple. Or rather, where it had wound up. But to the facts. Starting off for the land where everyone from commissars to cooks runs the state, I decided to avoid by hook or by crook the Russian customs; I had with me, not only in my head, but in my jacket pocket, words not meant for inspection. Before reaching Eydtkuhnen I took no steps. But once my train had passed through a tiny buffer state and its own buffers were nearing the frontier of the RSFSR,* I decided to effect a change: from rail to air. As you no doubt know, ladies and gentlemen, in my salad days I could break in not only wild horses, but flying cannonballs. Not counting the contents of my pockets, I had no baggage to speak of, so soon reached one of the guard towers with its muzzles trained on the Union of Soviet Socialist Republics. Upon learning who I was from my papers, the kindly commandant, whose name began with a "Pshtsh," agreed to put at my complete disposal an eighteen-inch steel suitcase. We proceeded to a concrete platform on which towered, its long straight trunk sticking up in air, a steel-gray

* Russian Soviet Federal Socialist Republic (Russia under Communist rule).

monstrosity. At a signal from the commandant, the gun crew began packing me on my way: the breechblock opened, a cart rolled up with my conical suitcase, steel clicked against steel, and the commandant saluted: "The baggage is loaded, the passenger will take his place." Now that enormous piece of ordnance, like an elephant after the peanut a child has poked through the bars, lowered its long trunk. I leapt up onto the edge and peered into the cavity: mustn't miss my chance. Then the metal-plated cavity climbed back up into the air and Pshtsh gave the command: "Ready fuse zero-zero-zero. Aim Herr Baron at the RSFSR. Fire!" I shut my eyes and jumped. Was I already there? But when I opened my eyes I saw that I was sitting under the steel elephant, surrounded by all those smiling Pshtshes. Yes, I had at once to admit that you cannot outrun technology. Even phantasms cannot outstrip it: a modern-day missile is not as easy to bestride as the old clumsy cast-iron bomb. Indeed, it was only after two failed attempts that I finally managed to straddle the humming steel. For some ten seconds the wind whistled in my ears, trying to blow me off the missile; but I am an excellent horseman and gripped its round overheated sides with my knees until a jolt against the ground arrested my flight. This jolt was so powerful that I bounced up like a ball, then down, then up again, until I found myself sitting on the ground. Looking about me, I saw that the spent missile had, fortunately, banged into a haystack standing in a bog. True, the stack had been flattened into mounds, but those mounds, like springs, had softened the blow and saved me not only from death, but from so much as a bruise.

So then, I was over the border. I sprang to my feet and ran my eyes around the horizon. A flat, unsown field. A low ceiling of dark clouds, supported only somewhere in the distance by a dozen columns of smoke. "A village," thought I, bending my steps toward the smoke. Soon houses too were poking up out of the ground. Upon coming within earshot of the village, I saw human figures moving from house to house, but did not call to them. The sun and I, having completed our trajectories, were both ready to drop. In that lonely little village lamps flickered to life, the smell of burnt meat singed my nostrils, and long black shadows crept toward me. Slowing my step involuntarily, I asked myself: Ought the main dish rush to dinner? My situation was tricky: there was no one to ask, no one with whom to consult. Another man in my place would have lost his head, but I had not come to the Land of the Soviets for advice and after a moment's reflection I knew just what to do.

As it happens, my boots had been made over from my old hunting boots, which possessed certain singularities. Many years ago when I lost my favorite hound—she appears in my memoirs—I decided not to burden my heart with new attachments, whose loss would lead to new sorrows, and took to hunting without a dog. A dog, you see, can easily be replaced with a well-trained pair of boots. Indeed. And since the futile memories of my late hound had been joined by an old rheumatic pain that prevented me wading through swamps, I, with a patience and tenacity typical of all Munchausens, set about training my hunting boots. In the end I achieved favorable results, and my solitary walks with a gun over my shoulder usually went like this: on reaching a boggy place full of game birds, I would take off my boots, stand them with toes pointing in the right direction, and say, "Seek! Seek!" My boots would stride from hummock to hummock, their leather rustling against the reeds, and rouse the game. As for me, seated on some dry patch, I had only to pull the trigger. The birds dropped straight into my boots. Then a brief "Fetch!" and my trained boots would trot back and meekly receive their master's heels.

And so it went now: I pulled off my boots, stood them with toes pointing toward the village, and—"Seek!" My boots, restive after several days shut up in a train, marched quickly off toward the lights. They advanced with their ear-loops pricked up, now straining ahead, now crouching down on their accordion pleats, with the look of cautious and experienced scouts. I watched them as far as the village. But then something unforeseen happened: a group of people noticed the boots coming toward them and, screaming with horror, scattered in confusion. It was then the idea struck me: here I was in a country of superstitious know-nothings, and if a pair of boots could terrify this village, the next, and the one beyond that, then off we would go, my boots and I, driving before us panic-stricken herds of ignorant peasantry which, wiping out cities in their path, infecting the masses and multitudes with their ancient Cimmerian horror, pillaging huts and palaces alike, would surge past the Urals. Then I would pull my boots back on by their ear-loops and send a radiogram from, say, Krasnokokshaisk: TOOK RUSSIA WITH MY BARE FEET. NO REINFORCEMENTS NECESSARY.

Expanding on my success, I got up, ready to deploy my stratagem to the end, even at the cost of calluses to my heels. But the situation had abruptly changed: the village in retreat from my boots had suddenly become a wild horde armed with pikestaffs and pitchforks, bucketing back for a counterattack. My boots made to turn tail, but too late. The bellowing horde, crossing itself with hundreds of hands and brandishing as many pitchforks, had surrounded them. Then the din died down. I could not see what was happening inside the ring of people. Creeping up as close as I could to my captured boots, I heard several voices arguing, but these soon yielded to the slow cadences of an old man. Having heard him out, everyone went away, everyone but the old man, who kicked off his bast shoes and began unhurriedly pulling on my boots. Hiding in the high grasses, I waited until he had finished. First I whistled softly (at the sound of my voice, the boots turned in my direction), then I shouted, "Fetch!" The old man wanted to go home, but no such luck: holding his decrepit legs fast, my boots began marching him in the opposite direction. Grabbing at bushes and grasses, the old man tried to stop his legs, but my faithful boots kept walking back to their master. The poor wretch saw he was no match for such a strong adversary and lay down flat on his back. But the boots, forcing his knees to bend, went on dragging his body over the ground until the abductor lay outstretched before me. I do firmly believe, ladies and gentlemen, that sooner or later everything nationalized will return to its rightful owners, as my boots returned to me. That is exactly what I said to the prostrate old man. I also told him he should be ashamed, at his hoary age, of trading God for socialism. Seized with holy horror, he yanked off my boots and ran, foot wrappings flying, all the way back to the village. Presently all the villagers came out to greet me in a religious procession with bread and salt, kneeling in prayer as church bells tolled. I accepted the invitation of these kind country folk and stopped for the night. While I slept, the rumor about me, ever wakeful, went around the neighboring hamlets. By morning an enormous crowd of complainants and petitioners had gathered under my window. I listened to all their entreaties and refused no one. The inhabitants of one small village, for example, asked me to resolve a longstanding dispute that had split them into two hostile camps. The rub was that one half of the village worked as carriers, the other half as farmers. But the civil war had reduced the number of horses. Harness the horses to the carts, and the farmers would have to drag their plows themselves; harness them to the plows, and the carriers would have to pull their carts themselves. My memoirs helped me to solve this difficult case: I ordered a saw to be brought and had the horses sawed, one by one, in two, owing to which their numbers doubled. The front legs were harnessed to carts, the hind legs to plows, and matters began to improve. Thus I fought horselessness. Had the Soviet government adopted my point of view in this and other spheres of the national economy, it might have avoided years of ruination and impoverishment. (A rustle of applause through the hall.) The peasants did not know how to thank me. They gave me one of the two-legged horses. I saddled it and continued on my way, tending toward the nearest railway station.

2

The peasants had warned me of the dangers near railroad tracks where, on a dark night, one could easily fall into the hands of bandits. Had I not lost my way on the impassable Russian roads, I would have reached the station before dusk. But the tangled cart tracks spun me around until nightfall. My weary half-horse was picking its way on its two hooves when I heard the fast-approaching clatter of many horses. A band! I applied my spurs, but you cannot gallop away from four-legged horses on a two-legged one. Soon I was surrounded: I reached for my sword only to remember that I had left it in Berlin, in my wardrobe, on Alexanderplatz. The bandits circled closer: now I reached for the back of my head, intending to pull myself out of this unsuitable society by my pigtail (as I once pulled myself out of a swamp), but—damn it!—my fingers found only a shorn nape. Alas, I would have to surrender. And I did. But these bandits did me not the slightest harm, treating me instead with cordiality, almost as one of their own. That night they elected me their ataman.* Inasmuch as this all took place in the pitch-dark, I do not know what governed these people, perhaps instinct.

Gritting my teeth, I had to comply: people are kind so long as you do not contradict them. For example, our relations, ladies and gentlemen, are based on my not contradicting you. You say that I exist. Very well, we will not argue. But if you were to say. . . . Then again, let us return to the events. I am not an ambitious man, and the title of ataman hardly flattered me: most every day I suggested that my men overthrow me, switch to a republican form of government, and banish me, at least to Moscow. In the end the band agreed to let me go if I paid a ransom: in banknotes or good advice, as I pleased. Well then, having thought a minute, I drew up a plan to rationalize brigandage. As everyone knows, in that ruined country the position of the hardworking highwayman is extremely troublesome and not to be envied. By day he must hide in the forests for fear of meeting Red Army rifles, and only on moonless nights may he engage in transferring valuables, so to speak, in pocketing stray coins as an entomologist nets butterflies. By the same token, all moonlit nights are without profit. Well, on just such a night flooded with the moon's silvery light, I took my bandits to the verge of a forest, lined them up, all thirty mouths to the moon, and ordered them to blow on that heavenly body. These men had enviable lungs (the Russian people develop their lungs by blowing on their samovars): at these con-

*Leader.

certed gusts of breath, the moon winked, stuck out its green tongues, and went out. Caught unawares by the moonlessness, wagons and wayfarers fell into our hands.

A few more exercises of this sort, and my gang no longer needed an instructor. This explains the spate of eclipses in recent years and other mysterious occurrences in the firmament: their cause lies, if I may say so here, in that sanctuary of science, in that forest near the Russian frontier. My friend Albert Einstein, whom I neglected to warn in advance, jumped to conclusions concerning these celestial anomalies. But what can be explained economically (and here Marx was right) requires no astronomical calculations; in searching for the cause, rather than ransack the stars, one should look right here, underfoot, on earth. And if in years to come, despite what I have said, anyone should wish to write about the "unextinguished moon," let him beware of meeting me, Munchausen, for I shall expose him as a liar.

The speaker now paused for a moment and inclined the crystal carafe at his elbow toward the tumbler; the hush in the hall was such that even in the last rows one could hear the water gurgling in the spout.

3

Thirty rifles saluted me at the hour of my farewell. Leaving the forest verge behind, I set off toward the locomotive whistles that now and then oriented me in that tangled clew of country roads. At length I reached a small station lost in the flatlands and began waiting for the train to Moscow. The platform was heaped with sacks and bundles, by which and on which people were sitting and lying, waiting, as I was, for the train. The wait was long and tedious. The clean-shaven face of the man next to me—his sack was empty (so I thought at first), but tied with three knots—had grown a red beard by the time the much looked for whorl of smoke appeared on the horizon. The train was inching along at the speed of an earthworm, and I feared it might, in the manner of an earthworm, disappear into the earth, leaving nothing behind but a trail of gray smoke.

Many of those present in this hall may find this notion of mine strange, but to me, a sanguine sort, everything slow, measured, and long-drawn-out has always seemed imaginary, unreal, and perhaps that is why Russia, unhurrying, ever in slow motion, switched from second hands to hour hands, afforded me a whole host of ghostlinesses and hallucinatory sensations. Seated in the train waiting for the signal to depart, I again found myself next to the red-bearded man with the empty sack over his shoulder. True, this emptiness now clinked against a wooden bunk.

"What do you have there?" I could not help but ask.

"An awl in a sack."*

"You think you can sell it?"

"Of course. There's a demand for it in Moscow."

This cheered me. My ware, you see, was of roughly the same sort. And then the train started, lifting my mood still higher. But not for long. That confounded earthworm stopped at every crosstie, as if each crosstie were a station. My fellow passengers, however, expressed no surprise, as if this were only natural. Toward evening we finally reached the next small station. Wishing to stretch my legs, I strolled down the length of the train to the smokestack. It was spewing fistfuls of red grains into the earth-black night: in their light I saw that the firebox was filled not with coal and not with wood, but with piles of books. Astonished at this strange state of bibliophilic affairs, I waited for the train's starting jolt to wake my neighbor, then put more questions to him. Other passengers broke into our conversation, and soon much had become clear to me—including the reason for our jolting progress from crosstie to crosstie.

"You see," they began explaining on all hands, "our engine-driver,

---

*Part of a Russian proverb meaning "the truth will out": You can't hide the truth (or an awl in a sack).

a professor of the greatest erudition, refuses to throw a single book into the firebox until he has read it from cover to cover, and thus we must advance log by log, or rather book by book, until we—"

"But how can this be?" I sputtered. "We must make a complaint! They must get rid of him and give us another engine-driver."

"Another one?" Alarmed necks craned from all bunks. "But there's no telling what kind we'd get: the engine-driver on the next line over reads nothing but *Anti-Dühring*. He hurls all books, heaps at a time, into the firebox until it's white-hot and the train at full speed. But should he, God forbid, come across *Anti-Dühring*, he's blind to all else … and has another wreck. Certainly not, we don't need another engine-driver; this one at least knows that haste makes waste. We may inch along, but we do advance. Ask for 'another,' and in no time we'll be hanging upside down from an embankment, station stop not Moscow, but Heavenly Kingdom."

I did not argue. Instead I added another nota bene to those already hidden in my notebook: On arriving in Moscow, I must find out how long the supplies of Russian literature would last.

4

We were nearing the Moscow Station and I had already taken hold of the door handle when the switchman unfurled a red Soviet flag, which in their country means: WAY CLOSED. Thus in full view of Moscow, with its thousands of belfries cast up to heaven, we had to cool our heels for a good hour until the switch allowed us to approach the platform.

The first thing that caught my eye was a notice on the station wall: Health Commissar Semashko was asking, for some reason, that he not be nibbled. At this I raised my eyebrows and indeed I did not lower them during my entire sojourn in Moscow. Prepared for extraordinary things, my heart pounding, I now entered that city built on blood and mystery.

Our European tales of the Soviet capital paint it as a topsy-turvy city where houses are built from the roof down, where people walk with their half soles in the clouds and cross themselves with their left hand, where the first are always last (in lines, for example), where the official paper *Pravda* (Truth) is somehow the reverse, and so on and so forth—one cannot remember them all—but they are all untrue. In Moscow, houses are not built from roof to foundation (nor are they built from foundation to roof), people cross themselves with neither their left hand nor their right, and as for whether they have the ground or the clouds under their half soles, I do not know: Muscovites walk about with no soles at all. Indeed, hunger and penury accost one on all sides in thousands of outstretched palms. Everything has been eaten, including the onion domes; for a while people tried eating their hats, but this disordered their digestion. Food shops—when I arrived—had been boarded up, but around their painted signboards festive with hams and garlands of sausages, framed with festoons of radishes, around the models of golden pretzels and boars' heads, crowds gathered to feast their eyes. More prosperous Muscovites, who could afford to hire an artist, honored the culinary traditions of old. At dinner, for the first course, they would serve a Dutch-school still life depicting all sorts of comestibles, and for dessert, Christmas-tree decorations (various fruits) made of papier-mâché. The shortages extended even to goods: shop shelves displayed almost nothing but dust. It is comical now to recall that when I needed a sword stick, an ordinary sword stick (the sidewalks there are full of pits and hollows), there was not a single double-edged sword stick to be found: I had to content myself with a single-edged one. Or another example: When a Muscovite driven to despair by the shortages of goods tried to hang himself, the rope turned out to be made of sand: instead of death, he had to limit himself to a few bruises. Outrageous!

Internal disagreements during my sojourn in the capital were further exacerbated by the general ruination and poverty. One day, walking past a succession of gray houses the color of cobwebs, I stopped to admire a mansion that stood out with its fresh gleaming paint and glazed windows. But when chance took me to that very same house the very next day, I saw that the paint had cracked and the walls sagged, while the street in front was buried under huge chunks of stucco that had fallen away from the façade as well as broken glass.

"What went on in that house?" I asked a passerby gingerly picking his way and trying not to cut his bare feet on the glass.

"A discussion."

"Well, and after that?"

"After that the leader of the opposition left, slamming the door behind him. That's all."

"Nonsense," said a second man coming toward us. "On his way out, he pinched his finger in the door. The point is—"

"The point is," the first man, now limping, broke in gloomily, "that because of your questions I have cut my foot."

The two men turned their backs and stalked off in opposite directions, leaving me utterly bewildered.

Munchausen pressed a button. Light was replaced by darkness, and on the screen's matte square there trembled the blurry, then clear duplicate contours of the twice-photographed house: before and after.

Through some heads in the hall there threaded an association: old, half-forgotten photographs of the Martinique earthquake. But before that memory could become conscious, the button had snapped the lights back on and Munchausen was again speaking, not allowing attentions to wander.

5

If you look at Moscow from a bird's-eye view, you will see: a stone spider in the center—the Kremlin, peering out of four wide-open archways at the web of streets it has woven, their gray threads, as in any web, stretching away radially, attaching themselves to distant gates; the radiuses are laced with short crossbars, the bystreets; in some places, these have knitted into long arcs forming boulevard rings and embankments; in other places, the ends of the spidery threads have been torn away by the wind—the cul-de-sacs; and winding through this web, its fractured body caught in the rigid embrace of bridges, is a dark blue caterpillar, the river. But now allow the bird to alight on a Moscow roof, and me to take a seat in a horse-drawn cab.

"Where to?" the cabby asks, roused by a tap on the shoulder.

"Tabachikhinsky Lane."

"Only a billion, your Lordship."

The driver lashes his half-dead nag, the cab plods from cobble to cobble, and we, having taken the hump of a bridge, trundle down into the tangle of Zamoskvorechye lanes. In one of these lanes we find a tiny house with squinting windows and creaky porch.

"Is Professor Korobkin at home?"

"Pray come in."

I enter. The venerable scientist comes blinking toward me over the lenses of his spectacles. I explain the object of my visit: As a foreigner I would like to acquaint myself with the material conditions now facing Russian science. The professor apologizes: He cannot shake hands. Indeed, his fingers are wrapped in gauze and bandages. I inquire as to why. It turns out that scientists, deprived of such basic materials as, for instance, slates, are obliged to wander about with chalk in hand, searching for slatelike surfaces on which to jot their calculations, diagrams, and formulas. Thus Professor Korobkin, only the previous day, had come upon the appealing black back of a carriage, stopped at a nearby entrance. The professor settled to work with his chalk, and the algebraic symbols began rasping across his improvised slate when suddenly that slate, wheels turning, made off with his as yet only half-discovered discovery. Needless to say, the poor man raced off after his bolting formula, but the formula, spokes flashing, swerved down a side street, while he collided with an oncoming cart. Crash! Here the professor's gauze-wrapped extremities told the rest without words.

Upon leaving the professor, I began studying the backs of carriages and motorcars. Presently, as I was passing an entrance surmounted with hammer and sickle, a motorcar pulled quickly up to the curb; its black canvas back was scored with the white lines of an unfinished diagram. Glancing in the direction whence the diagram had come, I soon saw the drawer: from far down the street, a piece of chalk showing white in his outstretched hand, an asthmatic man was rushing, butting the air with his bald pate. A purely sporting interest caused me to pull out my chronometer and set the second hand in motion. But just then a door slammed: a man with eyes hidden by the visor of his cap and a briefcase under one elbow strode away from the motorcar, interrupting my observations:

"Foreigner?"

"Yes."

"Curious?"

"Yes."

"Well then"—the man pointed to the bald pate now puffing up to us—"tell your countrymen: Red science is forging ahead."

Inviting me to follow him, he turned toward the entrance door. We walked upstairs to a private study with thirteen telephones. Running his lips over these instruments, like a reed-pipe player over the whistles of his woodwind, he motioned me to an armchair and sat down opposite. I did not like to ask, but it was immediately obvious that I was about to converse with a man of great importance. My interlocutor spoke tersely (without incidental or dependent clauses), preferring question marks to all others. He put his questions the way people put buckets and basins under cracks in the ceiling ahead of rain, and waited. I had no choice: I began speaking of the impression of penury, of the food shortages and goods shortages that a visitor from the West positively could not fail to see. At first I spoke with restraint, choosing my words with care, but then my recent impressions overwhelmed me: I gave the facts their freedom—and down they sluiced into his waiting basin. I had forgotten nothing—not even the single-edged sword sticks.

Having heard me out, the man removed his cap. Now I saw the

famous eyes and forehead, familiar to anyone who has ever glanced through an illustrated Russian yearbook.

"Yes, we are poor." He caught my pupils with his. "Our life is like an exhibition: one of everything, but not more. (Perhaps that is why we are so fond of exhibitions?) I guessed your thought, did I not? It is true: our sword sticks are single-edged, our government is single-party, our socialism single-country, but one mustn't forget the advantages of a sword stick with only one edge: at least one knows with which edge to strike. To strike without having to choose between this and that. We are poor and shall be poorer still. But all the same, sooner or later, our country of huts shall become a country of palaces."

For a minute I listened to the drumming of his fingers on the edge of the desk.

Then: "Why don't you ask about our literature?"

I confess I flinched: his squinting eyes had obviously stolen under the lapel of my jacket and were making free with the contents of my notebook.

"You guessed my thought."

"And your name." His laugh lengthened, then shortened the crack of his mouth, like an aperture during a short exposure. "A literary hero is naturally curious about literature. About 'how life smells.' It smells of printer's ink to the people who populate books or have emigrated to them. So then, all of our penmen are given a choice: feast or fast. Some work steadily; others starve."

"But then," I objected, gradually recovering my composure, "what was begun by the locomotive firebox you mean to end...."

He got up. I got up also.

"For specifics, apply to this address." An inky line torn from a notepad presented itself to me. "Our bald scientist has, I believe, finished his diagram. I must go. I could send you back the way you came, through a stovepipe, as was the custom in the Middle Ages: this telephone here plus three letters in place of an exorcism, and you would be driven away like chaff by the wind. But knowing your *nomen*, I foresee your omen. Fine. Go on feigning foreignness."

We exchanged smiles, but did not shake hands. I went out the door. Steps, like piano keys, slipped away from under my soles. Only the cool street air restored my calm.

6

The address on the notepad scrap led me to the columns of a manor house on a quiet Moscow street, away from the wagon clatter and tramcar bells. That same scrap of paper opened the door of a workroom in which, the servant told me, I would find the master of the house. Upon entering, I observed an enormous, high-ceilinged hall with no signs of furniture. The entire floor—from wall to wall—was blanketed with a gigantic, blindingly white sheet of paper held in place with tacks: running my eyes across the vast expanse of that page, I descried at its far end a man on hands and knees, moving from left to right along invisible ruled lines. On closer inspection I saw protruding from the man's fingers and toes fountain pens, swiftly fidgeting across the paper plains. Working with the speed of a true floor polisher, he was etching four inky furrows from wall to wall with four raspy pens, gradually coming nearer and nearer to me. Now, if I squinted, I could make out: a tragedy unfolding along the top line; lower down, a treatise on basso continuo and strict counterpoint forms; his left foot was knocking out essays on Russia's economic situation, his right foot a musical comedy in verse.

"What are you making?" I strode toward the floor polisher, no longer able to contain the question.

The toiler turned toward me and raised his head, peering myopically through the sweating lenses of his pince-nez: "Literature."

I tiptoed out, for fear of disturbing the birth.

My acquaintance with Moscow's scientific and literary world did not end there: I visited the compiler of *The Dictionary of Omissions, Complete & Unabridged*; looked up the famous geographer who discovered the Spur of the Moment; called on a modest man who collects cracks; and attended a ceremonial session of the Association for the Study of Last Year's Snow. In other words, I apprised myself of those burning questions to which Red science has devoted its efforts. Tempted as I am to expand on this subject, a lack of time prevents me.

7

Wandering from mind to mind, knocking on all scholarly brows, I failed to notice what was happening two or three feet lower down. The Russian saying about letting the cat out of the bag needs correcting: the cats were all eaten long ago, and when they tried not to let the hunger problem out of the bag, it fought back, furiously rumbling from all stomachs and threatening, if not given bread, to swallow the revolution. I am a philanthropist by nature, the names Howard and Haass bring tears to my eyes. So I determined to do what I could to help this country burnt by fires and the sun: I sent off a telegram in cipher—and soon several trains had arrived from Europe loaded with toothpicks. Can you imagine, ladies and gentlemen, the feelings with which residents of hungry districts met those trains? This first success redoubled my powers. The soup kitchens set up by the Soviet government could not combat the scourge of hunger: they gave out one poppy seed per person so that no one could say that no food had passed their lips; this prevented grumbling, but left stomachs empty. I suggested they enlist the help of rat charmers: they mobilized every last one. Every soup kitchen received a piper who, circling the houses, lured out the rats hiding in cellars and under floorboards: led by the melody the victuals marched themselves single-file—nose to tail, tail to nose—straight into the kitchen kettles and vats.

Medical hypnotists were also pressed into service. They seated the starving patient in a comfortable chair and, making passes over him, intoned, "This is not an ashtray full of cigar ends, you see, but a plate of soup with dumplings. Eat. That's right. Now you're full. Wipe your mouth with this napkin. Next!"

But most popular of all were the so-called munchkitchens opened at my suggestion (I had to cite my literary source without, of course, revealing my incognito). Each kitchen was equipped quite simply with a long piece of string and, by way of food, a tiny piece of pork fat, more than enough for any number of ... covers, shall we say, since the food was served somewhat under cover. At the lunch hour, people would line up facing the server: the server tied the slippery piece of pork fat to the string and gave it to the first mouth to swallow and then—well, you remember my ducks. So there it is: if the line grew longer, another piece of string would be tied to the free end of the first piece and, if need be, another piece of string to that, and so on. I refer those interested to my practical munchkitchen manual, printed in an edition of several hundred thousand copies under the title *Hungry as a Hunter*. Incidentally, people who lunched in this manner were not immediately able to part with one another; the second person trailed after the first, the third—willy-nilly—after the second, and so on. This led to those triumphal parades that have become so widespread, even without hunger, in Russia today. Even such common expressions as to "string along," "pull strings," and "string up" are, I dare say, echoes of the munchkitchen period.

While I was busy observing, wandering among meanings, decanting them into my notebooks, promoting public-mindedness, and fighting the cataclysm of hunger, time was pulling its string of days, tying days to days and months to months. Like a tear-off calendar slowly strewing its small square leaves, the trees on Moscow's boulevards began to lose their leaves. "Satisfying bodily hunger," I reflected, "is only half the battle. Awakening a spiritual hunger, that is the other half." I am an incorrigible old idealist. My long conversations with Hegel left their mark both on me and, I think, on him: Freedom, immortality, God—those are the three legs of my chair on which I calmly si— Beg pardon, I mean to say that materialists succeed only insofar as they are ... *idealists of their materialism*. Revolution's notorious broom, which raises more dust than it sweeps out, tried to sweep the idealists out of Russia's house, but of course, so I reflected, many of them got stuck in the doorway—so many bushels, so many leading lights. I would have to have a peek inside busheldom. At least once. Chance came to my help. Walking through a market one day where beggars and vendors hold out hands and wares pell-mell, my eye was caught by a dignified lady offering a pair of fire tongs for sale: both lady and tongs stood leaning against a wall, evidently weary of waiting for a buyer. I walked up and tipped my hat.

"To reach the coals in my hearth, madam, one would need tongs a thousand kilometers long. I am afraid yours will not do."

"But you can kill mice with them," she said anxiously.

Rather than argue, I paid the requisite sum and tucked the tongs under my arm: the wooden handle poking out from under my elbow was engraved with a count's crest. I turned to go, but the countess stopped me.

"It distresses me to think that my tongs fall somewhat short of those you require."

"Yes, by nine hundred ninety-nine whole kilometers and nine hundred ninety-nine thousandths."

"A great pity. But perhaps I might make up for this shortcoming by acquainting you with a man who sees a thousand versts and a thousand years ahead."

To this I assented—and soon one of those bushels had half opened. That is, the creaking door of a hovel had half opened to reveal, instead of wallpaper patterns, stains from dampness and bed-bugs and, poking out of a small stove, the charred ends of a family tree. The gloomy man to whom the gracious countess now introduced me, naming the rather famous author of books about Russia's impending fate, sat staring at the toes of his boots. The countess, seeing my impatience, tried to shift the seer's eyes from the ends of his boots to the end of the universe. The man bit his lip, but said not a word. Exchanging glances with me, the countess changed the subject.

"Have you noticed that the crows on Tverskoi Boulevard, instead of cawing, have started hurrahing? Now what could be the point?"

"There is no point," the prophet muttered, shifting his eyes from the ends of his boots to the ends in the stove.

The countess gave me a nod: now he will begin. And indeed: "In the chronicles it says: 'City of smoke.' And also: 'A blood-red sun rises over Muscovy beyond the smoke.' And in the *Domostroi*: 'As bees from smoke, so God's angels shall fly away.' And when we became angelless, the smoke rose up from space to time and so began our beclouded (as through a haze) Time of Troubles. Time itself became troubled and the centuries confused, the thirteenth with the twentieth, and then: revolution. One of our great writers titled it long ago: *Smoke*. Another, still longer ago, wrote about 'the smoke of the Fatherland' that is 'sweet and dear to us.' The numbers of gluttons who loved to gorge on smoke, to sup on cinders and decay, swelled and swelled until their native land, dwindling and dwindling, departing with the smoke, turned into the smoke that was so sweet and dear to them. Look at the street-clock disks: are their hands not trembling with disgust, flicking off the seconds' soot and cinders? Are your eyes not crying, stung by the smoke of the times? Are.... Incidentally, countess, your stove is smoking. Be so good as to hand me the tongs."

Again the countess and I exchanged glances: what if the prophet were to guess that his inklings about the smoke had been sold along with the tongs to me? Wishing to avoid any awkwardness, I ventured to speak in my turn, unpacking a whole collection of novelties brought from the West. The prophet sat with his head sunk in his palm, locks of unruly hair hiding the expression on his face. But the countess positively beamed with pleasure and begged me to tell her more. I spoke of European capitals thundering like waterfalls, of nights transformed into electric day, of rivers of automobiles, diplomatic routs, spiritualistic séances, fashionable ladies' dresses, sessions of the Amsterdam International and equipages of the English king, of a fashionable Boston religion and rising stars of the music-hall stage, of Churchill and Chaplin, of.... Through the blue haze (the stove was indeed playing pranks) I caught glimpses of the countess's face melting with delight, but, oblivious of the consequences, I went on and on. When I came to the description of an audience given me by the Russian emperor, I raised my eyes ... and saw no countess: her chair was empty. In my bewilderment I turned to the seer. He rose, sighed, and said, "Yes, no tongs, no countess: she melted. And *you* are the murderer."

Turning up his trouser cuffs, he waded through the pool of water that only a moment ago had been the countess. I could only do the same. Bound by our secret, we slipped out, closing the door tightly behind us.

Down a crooked street with dim lamps vainly gleaming, we walked in silence between blank walls: suddenly on one of them we saw four freshly painted symbols: USSR. My companion gestured toward the letters: "Read that."

I read it, decoding each letter. He shook his wrathful head.

"Lies! Listen and I shall reveal to you this cryptogram divined by the chosen: USSR—Una Sancta Sancta Russia—One Most Holy Russia. If you press your ear to the letters and listen to them breathe, you will notice only their exhalations, whereas I hear their inhalations as well: verily, verily they say, one most holy and godlike."

The crooked street led us onward. Upon reaching a crossroad, my companion suddenly stopped.

"I may go no farther."

"Why is that?"

"From here the street is cobbled," the prophet mumbled dully, "people of my profession had best stay away from stones."

Leaving my companion's motionless figure at the end of the asphalt ribbon, I strode on over the cobblestones: in the Munchausen line, thank God, there are no prophets.

Striding along beside me was the thought: Two million backs, bushels, lives fenced off by fear of denunciations and chekaneries; raise your eyes to theirs and you see pupils like point-blank muzzles, an endless *dos à dos*. Experience now confirmed my thought in all its bleakness: noticing a man walking quickly away from his dwelling, I stopped him with the question: "Where are you going?"

In reply I heard: "To relieve myself."

Those words filled with bitter lyricism are forever etched in my memory. That poor, lonely man, thought I as I watched him out of sight, he has neither friend nor beloved with whom to relieve his feelings—only the dark streets remain! Two million backs; bushels-bushels-bushels.

8

Munchausen paused: his Adam's apple dove down into the crack of his collar to rest. Meanwhile a bell jangled once or twice—and an image burst on the screen. A frightened "Ah!" blew through the hall like a wind, and suddenly dozens of people were knocking into one another in the darkness as they rushed for the doors.

"Lights!" cried the speaker and, when the chandeliers blazed up: "Take your seats, I shall continue."

The transparency that so frightened you, ladies and ... gentlemen, would seem to merit other emotions: what flashed and faded before you just now was the second-long life of a creature embodying the ideal of social justice. Each part of his body corresponds strictly in size to its value. In other words, you have just seen the "average man"; his portrait is well known to anyone who has ever dealt with workers' insurance. The constitution of this average man is such that every organ is directly proportionate in size to the sum paid by the insurer in case of that organ's loss. Thus in this average man the eyes—an organ that in us is significantly smaller than, say, our buttocks, which is unfair as their value for work is far greater—his eyes, as you surely noticed, are as big as balloons; his left arm barely reaches his hip, while the fingers of his right graze the ground, and so on, and so forth. I will admit that when I first encountered those balloon-size eyes, they gave me quite a turn. But in addition to Horace's maxim "Be surprised at nothing," I have a rule of my own invention: "Surprise with nothing." So then, one day I found myself sitting next to this average man on a Moscow boulevard bench. Boys licking toffees were scampering by. Shoeblacks were chasing after dirty bootlegs. The face of my accidental neighbor was hidden behind a newspaper.

Running my eyes down the paper screen, I said, "So, the reformists have gone to the right again."

"Zeroes, if they want to mean something, can only go to the right."

The newspaper folded up its pages, and now my inquiring gaze was met by two giganticized eyes exploding out of their sockets. I jerked away, but an overlong arm came after me: the outsize thumb and index finger, dwarfing the other three, made the hand look like a lobster claw. Catching me at the very end of the bench, the claw gripped my fingers.

"How do you do. My name is Visual Aid. And yours? It seems to me that you too"—his bulging nostrils quivered—"smell of printer's ink."

"Visual indeed," I replied, avoiding the question. "You certainly are a sight."

"Such a sight"—he grinned, exposing his mixed-caliber teeth—"that no woman will ever call me a sight for sore eyes."

"Who knows," I said, attempting a compliment, "in this world there is not much beauty, but a lot of bad taste."

"Yes, and the worse, the better. They used to call it the preestablished harmony, *harmonia predestinate*. But if you want me to be your aid, ask me anything: all numbers from zero to infinity at your service."

I produced my notebook.

"How many suicides were there during the civil war?"

"Zero."

"How is that?"

"Here's how: before you got around to it yourself, others had ... for you."

9

Meanwhile the October winds had torn the last leaves from the boulevard trees, the days like the mercury in thermometers had grown shorter, roofs and ground were covered with snow. I usually warmed myself with brisk walks. One day, as I was striding past a dilatory caravan of trams clanking along frozen rails, I noticed that at the front of every one, next to the driver, sat an old man stooped with age, snowy wisps of gray hair poking out from under his hat. I stopped and let pass the caravan of trams with their drivers and decrepit old men. Puzzled, I asked a passerby, "Who are they?"

"Braces," he growled and passed on.

I set off at once for the library in the History Museum. A dozen aristocratically hooked noses and as many protruding lower lips filed by in my mind's eye. I asked for the *Velvet Book* and began leafing through the genealogies: there were Berses, there were Bruces, but no Braces.

What could this mean? Pondering the fate of the ancient line of Braces lost in books, I left the museum—and soon learned the answer: walking down one of the seven hills over which Moscow is sprawled, I saw yet another tram which, steel grinding against steel, was struggling in vain to conquer the ascent. Finally, at a sign from the driver, the ancient brace got down and hobbled on ahead of the car: no longer worth his salt, he sprinkled it left and right, and the tram, also groaning old-mannishly, toiled up the salt-coated rails.

Given such a system, Moscow trams are convenient only for functionaries who, with their help, arrive late for work. I entrusted myself only once to one of those steel tortoises, and I must confess it very nearly took me . . . too far. I had confused the stops, you see, and so I bought, instead of an eleven-kopeck ticket, an eight-kopeck one. The inspector caught me. My misdeed was reported and an investigation conducted, after which the case and I were sent to trial. The case of the unpaid three kopecks was heard by the Supreme Court: they escorted me between two sabers to the dock. An enormous crowd of curiosity seekers had filled the courtroom. The words "capital crime" and "death penalty" went from mouth to mouth.

In my defense I argued as follows: Inasmuch as my deed, deemed a misdeed, had been the result of conditional reflexes, my punishment should also be conditional. After due deliberation, the court pronounced me guilty and sentenced me to be shot . . . by popguns.

The morning of my execution they stood me against a wall facing a dozen muzzles—before I could blink a volley crackled and they shot me. Taking off my hat, I apologized for the disturbance and passed out into the street. I was now in the position of a conditional corpse.

As executions usually take place at dawn, the streets were still empty, like the paths in a graveyard; moreover, it was a Sunday, when life wakes a bit later. I walked along in a state of some excitement: I could still feel the muzzles' stare. The city was beginning to stir. Taverns and beerhouses were opening their doors. My throat was parched. Turning in under a green and yellow sign, I was greeted by a beery smell and vehement voices. I sat down and glanced around at the mugs and faces. Much struck me as strange: none of the customers sitting and staring into their mugs were conversing with the others, yet they were all talking a blue streak. I listened more closely and began to make out the words. There were fewer words than speakers as these last were all repeating, with only slight variations, the same string of Russian obscenities. As the beer in their mugs grew less, their red faces and bloodshot eyes grew more and more furious, so that the air's every pore seemed to burst with their vile abuse. Faces and eyes all looked past one another, no one was angry at anyone else; only the leaves of an artificial palm trembled nervously beneath the hail of invective. Unable to make head or tail of what was going on, I beckoned to a waiter and asked him to explain. He gave me a lazy smile and said, "Vendors."

"What of it?"

"Here's what: for six days you put up with everything from buyers—not a moment's peace for you or your ware. They grab it, grab it again, ask, ask again, not that, no this, you take it out, put it away, measure it, measure it again, and hold your tongue. You suffer in silence for six days, but on the seventh...."

Brushing a peapod off a table with his dishcloth, the waiter went back to the counter.

I smiled: so then these people were giving back to the air—on their one day of rest—everything they had taken in through their eyes and ears during the long workweek.

Yes, I smiled, not at the crude curses sounding all around me, but at the dim memory they evoked: I recalled the postilion's horn—I dare say you have not forgotten it—that amazing horn in which, like a snail in its shell, the tunes had frozen up so as to come out of their own accord when the warmth and spring returned. But curses have better luck than tunes: in the poet's calendar, alas, there are no Sundays, and even if he manages not to freeze on the road, his heart is still frostbitten. Thus I, a conditional corpse in a beerhouse, sat musing on conditional reflexes.

10

From the back of the hall, from last row to first, diving down and darting up from behind shoulders, came a scrap of paper folded in four; on reaching the lectern, it put a momentary stop to the speech.

"I have received a note!" Munchausen beamed, brandishing the missive.

A female hand asks about the woman's position in Soviet society, about her rights in love and marriage. I had not intended to broach this matter, but as you insist, here it is in a nutshell: the attitude toward women in the former Russia has radically improved: those disharmonious creatures, "long of hair, but short of brain," have at last won the right to have their hair short too.

As for any practical study of love and marriage, my two hundred years absolve me somewhat of the duty to report on this point. However, wishing to be entirely conscientious and remembering that curiosity may pass for passion, I did attempt a mild flirtation with a pair of charming eyes. Walking down the street one day, I saw ahead of me a sylphlike girl leading a little boy by the hand. "His nurse, no doubt," thought I. Catching her up, I glanced under the brim of her hat. She turned away, embarrassed, but just then the child's red balloon on a string slipped out of her fingers, floating up past windows toward the rooftops. In a twinkling, I had shinnied up a drainpipe in pursuit. There I was, running over the rattling sheets of tin, when a gust of wind swept the errant balloon to a neighboring roof. I bent my knees and jumped from this house to that: the string was in hand. Pushing off from the roof ledge, I floated gently down with my red balloon to the feet of the astonished girl and open-mouthed little boy. After that, everything took its natural course: her eyes invited me to call on them. Inwardly I was already crowing, but then a silly mix-up spoiled everything. Wishing to hasten success, I stopped at a shop on the way. In Moscow, under one and the same signboard, they sell: fresh-cut flowers and horseflesh, bloodsucking leeches and tinned meat, and so on and so forth. The black letters on the blue rectangle above this particular shop read: CONFECTIONARY and COFFINS. I asked for one of the larger boxes of chocolates, but must have pointed inexactly. They handed me a large oblong box wrapped in elegant paper and tied up with pink ribbon. With pounding heart I knocked at the door of my temptress. On seeing my present, her eyes lit up—all was going marvelously well. When I sensed I was halfway from gazes to kisses, I pulled off the ribbon, then she, with the smile of one who loves sweets, undid the paper—and we both reeled back against the sofa: out of the crackling wrappings came— dark blue with a white border—a baby's coffin. The train to Happiness whistled—and raced past. Oh, how steep and narrow are those confounded Moscow stairwells!

Yes, I am not afraid to be frank, so I will tell you that men with imagination have nothing to do in love. A grandmaster, after all, can play a game of chess without looking at the board; and as for romance, better to love without looking at the woman. Just think! Who has success with the ladies? To this day I cannot forget the somewhat pimply visage of a certain archivist from Hanover, who, having fiddled his whole life with the ribbons of archival folders, learned to undo them so quickly that, by transposing this light-fingeredness, he became, so he claimed, irresistible. Before they could say "yes" or "no," this archivist liked to brag, their ribbons had all been undone. I tend to think that not all his words were mere boasting.

At any rate, I abandoned the practice of love and thereafter confined myself to a theoretical acquaintance with this problem. Piles of Soviet belles lettres led me to extremely pleasing conclusions and prognoses: while Soviet newspapers harp on the implacable hatred of one class for another, their novels extol only the love of the Chekist for the beautiful White Guard girl, of the Red female partisan for the White officer, the laborer for the lady aristocrat, the detitled prince or count for the simple black-earth peasant girl. That is why we, trusting in the old realistic traditions of Russian literature, may confidently expect all that has been driven in with a hammer to be cut down by a sickle...moon: sooner or later the nightingale will outwarble the factory whistle. So it always was, so it will always be: antitheses will always trail after theses, but let them marry—and their old friend synthesis will be there like a shot.

Opinions on this score are still up in the air; they have not had time to settle down and take hold. Some people champion the slogan EVERYONE INTO THE STREETS for love, while others will fight tooth and nail to keep the home fires burning. Titian's *Amor Sacro* and *Amor Profano*, shown sitting peaceably either side of a well, have suddenly grabbed each other by the hair, the better to push each other down that well.

Without entering the realm of speculation, one must nevertheless note that a great start has been made in the business of reorganizing love. "A great start is worth more than money," as one girl, deflowered five minutes before, said when the agreed-upon sum was not paid her. I do not believe that laws invented by jurists can fight the laws of nature. The great methodologist Francis Bacon defined the experiment thus: "We merely increase or decrease the distance between bodies—nature does the rest." If one considers that living conditions in the country from which I have just returned will not permit of any further decrease in distances, then.... But allow me to return to my paper.

11

Restoration of the Soviet economy has begun slowly, imperceptibly, exactly like their northern spring, which scarcely manages to push new leaf buds through the bare icy skin of branches. If I remember correctly, it all began with the beams that people began casting out of each other's eyes. In the past they had been loath to notice even the motes, but necessity makes us sharp-sighted: soon the supply of beams hauled out of people's pupils was such that one could set about building. On the city outskirts, now here, now there, log huts began to appear, residential cooperatives sprang up, and overall things began to improve.

Saplings were planted along the boulevards (of the old trees there remained only stumps) and made to grow quickly by a simple, but ingenious means: to each little tree they attached one end of a rope; the other end was attached to a pulley, and the tree was pulled up until it reached the prewar height. Within a few weeks, the bare boulevards were thick with shade trees and arrayed as of yore.

Quantities of posters placarded on all the walls and fences edified passersby with bits of practical advice, such as SINCE A FISH ROTS FROM THE HEAD DOWN, EAT IT FROM THE TAIL UP or SAVE YOUR SOLES, WALK ON YOUR HANDS. I cannot remember them all. Competing with the posters were playbills announcing extravagant productions and popular entertainments. Swept up in this wave, I could not remain a passive spectator and proposed various projects of my own design. Thus it was that I, while consultant to a Moscow theater director, advised him to stage Gogol's *Inspector General* on my grand scale, so to speak, in a Munchausenian manner that would turn everything upside down, beginning with the title.

The play, as we envisaged it, would be called *Thirty Thousand Messengers*: the main plot would shift from the individual to the masses; the main characters would be the poor souls who slaved as messengers for that cruel exploiter, the Petersburg minister Khlestakov. He drives them hard, causing packages to rain down on their heads until one day they organize, decide to strike, and stop delivering. Meanwhile, Khlestakov is making love to the beautiful wife of either a cabinet governor or kitchen gardener, I forget which. He sends her a letter by the first messenger fixing a rendezvous for that evening in the kitchen garden (as is the custom in Russia); but the striking messenger does not deliver the letter. Khlestakov waits all night in the garden, then returns, rather nettled, to his ministry and sends a second letter to the same effect to the same address by the second messenger. With the same result. The second, the third, the thousandth, the thousand and first all fail him. Khlestakov waits every night in the kitchen garden for three long years without result, but also without abandoning hope of winning the heart of his stand-offish lady love. He grows old and thin, but goes doggedly on sending her letters by messenger: the 1,450th, the 1,451st, the 2,000th. In scene after scene. A seasoned skirt-chaser abhors foot-dragging in love. He puts all work aside and every day he writes not one, but ten, twenty, a hundred letters, unaware that they are all being taken to the strike committee. Meanwhile, the gardener's wife, who is not at all standoffish, has waited these many years for even a line from her heart's desire; her kitchen garden is choked with weeds and overgrown with thistles. But now, from among the strikers, there emerges a lone strikebreaker: this is the last messenger, the thirty thousandth, who, unable to bear the strain of the strike any longer, delivers Khlestakov's letter to the addressee.

Following this event, Khlestakov runs as fast as his feet will carry him to meet the gardener's wife: at long last! But the strikers, too, are not napping: they track down the strikebreaker only to discover that letter No. 30,000 has slipped through their fingers. Now they tear open the twenty-nine thousand nine hundred and ninety-nine undelivered letters. Imagine the effect of this scene! Envelopes flying everywhere, thirty thousand white squares falling on spectators' heads! A chorus of furious voices—a collective recitation—reads thirty thousand nearly identical texts aloud, roaring so the walls and ceiling shake: "Come to the kitchen garden!" Then all thirty thousand descend in orderly ranks on the kitchen garden so as to do away with the minister-seducer. The couple is discovered whispering by the wattle fence. The two try to flee, but from all sides stride messengers—messengers—messengers. The night is now white as day with the thirty thousand envelopes being waved in Khlestakov's face. His life is hanging by a thread. The selfless gardener's wife cries that she is ready to give herself to all thirty thousand, if only to save her one and only. This embarrasses the messengers, who want to hide inside their envelopes. Then a repentant Khlestakov publicly confesses that he is not the minister they take him for, but a common titular counselor, working class like all the rest. Reconciliation. Every one of the thirty thousand holds a spade in his hand; to strains of the folk song "Don't Lead Me Up the Garden Path," their spades strike the earth, disenthistling the thistle-choked garden. Crimson streaks of sunrise. Wiping the sweat from his laborious brow, Khlestakov reaches toward the new day: "The scales have fallen from my eyes." After the scales, the curtain too falls. How about that? Eh?

Rehearsals had already begun when we ran up against an unexpected obstacle: to play the thirty thousand messengers we had engaged two military divisions from districts near Moscow. But the authorities, fearing a coup no doubt, balked at bringing so many troops into the capital. I left soon after, having asked the director, should my staging ever come to fruition, not to reveal my real name on the playbill. I think he will not break his promise.

During my stay in Moscow I tried not to miss a single scientific or scholarly lecture. The general economic revival has had a most beneficent effect on the pace of scientific research and experimentation. With your permission, ladies and gentlemen, I shall now summarize the last two lectures it was my good fortune to attend.

The first was devoted to proto-rhyme: the lecturer, an esteemed academician who had devoted his life to the study of Slavic etymologies, had gone in search of the first rhyme ever heard in Old Russian. Years and years of work had taken him back to the ninth century: it appeared that the inventor of rhyme was Saint Vladimir, who rhymed the words "think" and "drink." From this proto-rhyme, which grew gradually more complex, sprang all of Russian versification. But take away its "drink," said the silver-tongued lecturer, and it would have nothing with which to rhyme its "think," its now-trembling base would leave all its superstructures wobbling, and its house of books no more stable than one of cards. In conclusion, he suggested revising the terminology and classifying poetry not as "lyric" and "epic," as in the past, but as "home-distilled" and "purified."

The second lecture was part of a series organized by the Institution of Leveling Psyches (ILP). The title alone—"Either Side of the Part"—intrigued me. A respected physiologist would present ILP studies in the electrification of thought. A group of ILP scientists had proven that nervous currents, which arise in the brain like electrical currents, travel only over the surface of the brain's hemispheres, the two poles of electro-thought. From there it was technical child's play to raise a person's consciousness by two or three more centimeters so as to localize it on the surface of the cranium, at which point a part made from forehead to nape could comb thought processes to the left or to the right, depending. I need hardly explain to you that, in this bold experiment, strands of hair replaced the wires that radio thought into space.

After a brief theoretical summary, the physiologist proceeded to the demonstrations. A man in a brass helmet pulled down around his ears was led up onto the stage. The helmet was removed to reveal a neat straight part and hair so smooth it seemed to have been ironed into the man's skull—from right to left and from left to right. The physiologist picked up a glass wand and brought it to the man's left hemisphere.

"The idea of 'the State' is localized in this subject just here, at the end of this strand of hair to the left of the part. A red dot marks the spot. I invite those of you who are nearsighted to come forward and see for yourselves. Now watch: I shall press 'the State.'"

The tip of the glass wand poked the red dot: a spark flashed from the right side of the part to the left, the subject's jaws unclenched and out came "The State is organized violence...." The hand with the wand jerked back; the jaws, teeth grinding, snapped shut. The physiologist signaled to his assistant.

"Part his hair on the left. Good. Now, as you can see, the red dot is on the right side of the part. Contact!"

Again the glass wand poked the dot, a spark flashed from left to right, the jaws flew open and "The state is a necessary stage on the way to...."

"Better hold your tongue," the physiologist waved his wand.

The jaws clamped shut, and the subject was replaced with another. This one had a disheveled rebellious look. Four ILP guards barely managed to maneuver him up onto the stage. His hair stood on end, spitting sparks with a dry crackle, while his convulsively twisting mouth was gagged with a gag.

"Switch on the words," the physiologist gave the command.

The gag was removed, and out gushed words eliciting a soft murmur among the many-headed audience—"counterrevolution," "White ideology," "one hundred percent bourgeois," "the revolution is in danger"—until someone jumped up and shouted, "For that you should be shot!"

The physiologist held out both hands, calming the audience.

"Citizens, come to order! I ask that you not interrupt the experiment. Switch on the shaver!"

The assistant dashed to the instrument panel—and suddenly an ordinary electric hair shaver (but with long handles sheathed in glass) was gliding over the subject's skull, rapidly shearing off his thoughts. With every pass of the metal teeth over the top of the counterrevolutionary's head, his vocabulary became smaller, duller, more confused. When the shaver had completed its task, a guard began sweeping up the shorn-off worldview. The subject's arms hung limp as whips, but his doleful tongue, like the wooden rattle around a cow's neck, kept knocking out just two words: "freedom speech—speech freedom—freedom speech—freedo—"

With a look of concern, the physiologist set about inspecting the subject's shaved head. Suddenly his face brightened. He pointed a stubby finger at the patient's crown.

"Here are two last hairs." He grinned at the audience and, squeezing two square fingernails to an invisible something, yanked. "There! Clean as a whistle. And not a peep!"

The physiologist blew on his fingers and went back to the lectern. The guard, who had finished sweeping up, was about to dispose of the mental rubbish. But just then, from the back rows, came a soft sound: either a yawn, or a muffled sob. After a long pause, the bespectacled physiologist cast a stern look around the now hushed rows and said, "Remain calm. Let's remember the Russian saying: Having cut off the hair, one does not cry over the head."

12

If you have never been to a May Day parade in Moscow, you have never seen a public celebration. Come May, all windows are flung wide; red flags ripple in the spring puddles, mingling with the reflections of white clouds; from street to street drums beat, one hears the steady tread of columns as million-legged streams eddy across Red Square so as to cascade down to the vernally rushing Moscow River, free of ice and overflowing its banks. Trumpets hurl into the air "The Internationale," red standards fidget in the wind like gigantic cockscombs as the skyward beaks of bayonets sway past the reviewing stands. Squeezed in among the crowd, I observed at length this Celebration crying its battle cries, fluttering its red plumage of banners and ribbons, its gigantic trihedral beak ready to peck out all the stars in the sky like grains of millet so as to throw back fistfuls of ruby-red pentagonals, its wings spread from pole to pole ready to fly, a celebration full of fury that suddenly brought to mind a legend I had found not long before in a Moscow library, but instantly forgotten in the press of days and doings. Now I began to recall this legend about a Frenchman who traveled to Moscow in 1761 so as to.... But just then, for the thousandth time, brass trumpets screamed "The Internationale," the crowd reeled, someone trod on my toes, and I lost the thread.

Only toward evening did the celebration begin to fall off, like a cherry blossom in the wind. The walls still glowed with zigzags of lights, but the crowds had thinned away; then the windows closed their glass eyelids, the lights went out, and I alone strode down a deserted street trying to recollect the details of a half-forgotten legend. Little by little it all came back to me, down to the title page with its bold: THE DEVIL IN A DROSHKY.

In 1761, so the legend went, a Frenchman traveled all the way to Moscow for the purpose of finding a certain person of the greatest importance to him, but along the way he lost the address and only dimly remembered that this person lived by the Church of Little Nikola on Rooster Legs. On arriving in Moscow, the Frenchman hired a carriage and bid the driver take him to Nikola on Rooster Legs. The driver shook his head and said he knew no such church: there was Wet Nikola, Nikola Red Bells, Nikola on Three Hills, but as for Nikola on Rooster Legs. . . . Then the visitor bid him proceed from crossroad to crossroad that he might ask passersby. The driver flourished his whip and started off. The people they met in passing recalled different churches, some Nikola in the Pillars or Nikola in Pyzhi, others Nikola on Chicken Legs or Nikola in the Carpenters. But no one knew Nikola on Rooster Legs. The carriage wheels spun on, searching for the lost church. Night fell; horse, driver, and whip began to flag—but the insistent Frenchman said he would not get down until they had found Rooster Legs. The driver flicked the reins, and again the wheel rims rattled through the benighted streets of Moscow. In those days the city went early to bed, and only two or three passers, stopped by a voice bowling out of the darkness, hastened to say "Don't know" before ducking inside their doors. The sun blazed up, went out, again flared, and again sank into the gloom, and still the search went on. The weary nag, now stumbling, could barely pull the carriage, the driver swayed sleepily on his box, but the stubborn visitor, mangling the unfamiliar words, demanded they continue—on and on. Now they stopped at every church, and if it were night, the driver would go and knock on the windows next door. Sleepy people peered out at the question of Nikola on Rooster

Legs, but then the windows slammed shut with a curt "No." And again the spokes spun around their axles in search of the lost church. One night the keeper of Little Nikola on Chicken Legs, whose crosses tower over a tangle of side streets intersected by two Molcha-novkas, heard a bony knock at the window of his lodge. Getting up from the stove bench, he saw (the night was moonlit) a shaggy face pressed to the pane. "Who's there?" the keeper called out. "What is it?" Through the door he heard a mangled, yet intelligible, "P'tit Nikola on Rooster Leg." The keeper crossed himself in fright, mur-muring prayers, while the persevering Frenchman returned to his carriage and went on with his search. Soon a legend grew up around this strange visitor: people who had come across the mysterious car-riage spoke of a devil in a droshky who rode about the nighttime streets of Moscow searching for the underground church of Satan, whose left heel, as we all know, is a rooster's.

Now passersby, on hearing the rattle of the mysterious carriage, would dart away into side streets, dodging any encounter or ques-tion. And the devil in a droshky would whirl on in vain from cross-road to crossroad without ever meeting a single living soul.

Giving myself up to images from this old legend, I walked along the now noiseless streets, treading on shadows and moon blots, until chance led me into a long and narrow cul-de-sac. I turned around so as to make my way out of the stone sack, but just then, from around the bend, came the soft but distinct rattle of approaching wheels. I quickened my step in an effort to outpace them. But too late: the dilapidated carriage had barred my way. Yes, it was they: the flogged nag, through whose panting ribs the moon cast a skeletal weave of shadows; the driver holding the reins in his bony hands; and the dim silhouette of his passenger peering into the perspective of streets. I pressed my back to the wall, trying to hide behind the corner of a house. But they had already seen me. A low top hat of a kind long in disuse rose up over the passenger's head and his dead lips moved. But I, forestalling the question, shouted at his guttural mutterings:

"Listen, you, vision, where is your vision? Stop playing the legend. You are searching for the church on Rooster Legs. But there are thousands here: knock on any door, and see if it is not so. Don't you see the red cockscombs fluttering over the roofs of their houses, the gleaming steel beaks raised up to the sky? Every house (if you credit their tales), every idea (if you credit their books) is on rooster legs. Only touch it—and all this, feathers bristling, will come rushing after and peck us up, with all our millionaires, like so much millet. As for your driver, I would urgently advise him to join a union: let it exact from you what the man is owed for a hundred and sixty-two years. You are an exploiter, and a devil to boot!"

Incensed, I walked right through the apparition without further ado. The day's events had thoroughly exhausted me. Sleep had long awaited my return. Come morning I scarcely managed to untangle that clew of reality, dream, and legend.

13

What I have reported here to this distinguished gathering is but a few meager pennies, shaken out of my mouth as out of the slot of a tightly packed coin box. All of Russia is right here, under the crown of my head. I would need at least a dozen tomes to contain the entire experience of my journey to the Land of the Soviets.

At any rate, sensing that my coin box was full, I decided it was time to give some thought to my return. Few in the USSR manage to obtain a passport to travel abroad. The first official to whom I applied replied in the tone of the inscription over the gates of Dante's hell: "Not a living soul."

But I did not bat an eye.

"I beg your pardon! How can I be a living soul when I have been conditionally shot?"

I set about procuring the necessary documents and moved my case off dead center. After several weeks of bureaucratic hoops, I had in my pocket both ticket and pass.

My last day was at hand. My train would leave a few minutes after six. High in the midday sky a July sun was shining: I still had a few hours at my disposal—I decided to devote these to bidding Moscow farewell. Setting off at a leisurely pace, I soon reached one of the bridges spanning the river and, hanging over the railing, gazed for the last time at the waves and foam being swept away by a current quick as time. From the silt-covered banks came the long drawly croaks ("Kva! Kva!") of frogs, recalling for the last time the legend of how that astonishing city was built (the beginning of this legend you may read in the famous history by Zabelin) in a bygone age when in place of houses there were hummocks, in place of squares slimy bogs, in place of people frogs, and Tsarevich Mos came from heaven knows where and wooed heaven knows why Tsarevna Kva. They built a marital house amidst the bogs and marshes and celebrated their wedding. But as soon as Mos and Kva were left alone, Kva heard someone calling her. "Go," said she to her husband, who would sooner be with his wife than away from her. "See who is calling me." Vexed as he was, Mos went out and saw sitting on a hummock a toad: "Kva! Kva!" Mos shooed the toad away, but as soon as he returned to his wife, someone from another hummock began calling her by name. Again his wife said, "Go and find out." Mos grew angry and commanded a marital house to be built in another place. But there too, as soon as he was alone with his young wife, the calls came on all hands and all hummocks, distracting Tsarina Kva from her husband. Tsarina Kva began to cry and asked that a house be built in a third place. And then a fourth, and a fifth, and a thirty-third. The axes pounded and pounded, and house after house grew up; where there had been hummocks, now there were roofs; where there had been lakes, now there were squares; where there had been marshes and bogs full of croaking frogs, now there was a big city full of people who spoke a pure local dialect of the purest Russian. And now no one could prevent Mos and Kva from being joined, even in name: "Moskva."*

Tearing myself away from the railing, I set off again at the same leisurely pace down the familiar streets. A gust of wind overturned the tray of a little boy selling fruit jellies; he scrabbled about in the

*Moscow. (Russian)

dirt after the scattered sweets, rinsed them in the nearest puddle, and replaced them neatly on the tray. I walked on. A familiar wooden fence swam into view. Scrawled across the top board, warming their rust-colored letters in the sun, were the words HANGING BY A THREAD. For a second I slowed my step and tried to picture the meaning of that phrase. Then, with a feeling of resignation, I again walked past and on.

Slumped against a playbill pillar, an accordion slung between his jumping elbows, a drunk was singing: "Eh, little apple with leaves either side, I'd surely love you, but fear the great divide." Suddenly the pillar turned, dropping singer and song on the ground. Onward.

Floating toward me was an enormous square: in the center of the square, with five crosses raised up to the sky, stood a cathedral; next to the huge cathedral stood the high marble pedestal of a statue evidently knocked down by the revolution. I must confess I have never been able to let an empty pedestal pass. The incompleteness, the unfinishedness always irritates me. So it was now: I quickly scrambled up onto the marble base and assumed an attitude of serenity, full of dignity and grandeur. Passing by below was a street photographer. I had only to throw him a silver coin for his head to dive under his dark cloth. Standing with hand outstretched to the sinking sun, I could see a crowd gathering to watch with oohs and aahs this impressive tableau. But the screen will convey this more quickly and convincingly. There. (Thunderous applause greeted the tableau that leapt from the magic lantern up onto the flatness of the screen. Munchausen bowed, then motioned for silence.)

I would not like, ladies and gentlemen, for this to be taken as a hint. But in returning to my story, I must tell you that the Muscovites thronging the square around my statue responded to me exactly as you have, here in this hall: their clapping, their shouts of "Come back soon," "Don't go!" and "Why are you leaving us?" prevented me climbing down from my pedestal. What's more, the photographer made a very long exposure. So it should not strike you as strange that I was late for my train: it pulled out right in front of my nose, leaving me alone with ticket in hand, on the empty platform.

My situation turned out to be extremely serious. The problem was that trains left Moscow for the border (left, that is, during the time of which I speak) not more than once a month. This would ruin all my plans. Worse still, it would prevent me honoring promises I had given my contractors in the West, thus making me, Baron Munchausen (strange even to think, much more to say aloud), a liar and a cheat who goes back on his word.

But I had no choice. I returned to the city and spent the whole night sitting on a bench on Strastnoi Boulevard considering what to do. In the meantime, time was stretching seconds into minutes, and minutes into hours. The date stamped on my ticket was now yesterday's, and suddenly I had a thought: Why not try to find yesterday?

I set off directly for a newspaper office and poked through the little window where they accept such notices this text: "LOST: Yesterday. If found, please return for a substantial reward to..." and so on.

"Fine, in a couple of days."

"Excuse me," I sputtered, "in a couple of days yesterday will not be yesterday, but, how do you call it?"

"Three times yesterday," the little window replied. But then the man behind me in line advised, "Write 'four times yesterday.' To be on the safe side. They won't print it before then."

"But how can I do that?" Now I was completely confused. "I don't need three times yesterday or nine times yesterday, I need plain yesterday and I am telling you this in plain Russian—"

"Well, if you must have plain yesterday," the little window shot back, "you should have placed your notice on the third. That's the rule."

"But how—" I nearly burst out, but knew I would only be wasting my time. I decided to take a different tack. Turning over in my mind the names of institutions and persons to whom I might apply, I remembered the Association for the Study of Last Year's Snow. A telephone call, a brief conversation, and soon a horse-drawn cab was conveying me to the association's archives. The cab cut across Moscow on a diagonal and passed through a city gate. Beyond the city, some distance from the dusty summer road, the red roof of the archives loomed, half hidden behind a high stone wall. We drove up to the gate. I gave the rusty bellpull a tug. In reply there was a long dead hush. Another tug. Through the stone wall I heard slowly approaching steps. But how strange: the ground under those steps crunched and crackled. What could it be? Finally I heard the rusty whine of a key, and the hammered-copper gate cracked open. I was dumbstruck: July snow. Yes indeed. Inside the high stone wall, having lingered for several months, was winter. Long icicles depended from the bare branches, while the unkempt vegetable patches encircling the archives' dilapidated building were buried under drifts of snow and a brittle frozen crust. An old servant, gnarled and wizened, led me slowly down a path to the porch through air thick with soft white flakes fluttering soundlessly to the ground. I did not ask, for I knew: this was last year's snow.

The head of the Department of Yesterdays—a bald gentleman, eyes glazed with dark blue glass—had been alerted as to my visit, so greeted me most cordially.

"It happens, it happens." He smiled. "One man lets an instant slip by, another his entire life. But apply to us for your *diem perdidi** and you will find that we, like the biblical Ruth gleaning ears of corn dropped by the sickle, gather up all that is reaped and spent. We waste nothing: not a single second that has ticked by. Ruth gathers up Rus,† ha! Here you are—take your yesterday."

He handed me a neatly numbered little box the color of cobwebs. I opened the lid: inside, swaddled in cotton wool and bristling with fidgety second hands, my yesterday tossed sleepily. I did not know how to express my thanks.

The dark blue glasses suggested showing me the Ruth-Rus archives, but I, afraid of again losing what I had lost, made my excuses and hurried to the door. Flakes of last year's snow saw me to the gate. Completely white, I let myself out. The summer sun melted my

---

*Lost day. (Latin)
†Russia.

snowy mantle in a trice and dried my clothes. I sprang into the waiting cab.

"To the station!"

The cabman flicked the reins, and we started off. I somehow could not believe in the reality of what had just happened, and although time is invisible, my eyes kept searching for proof. Then suddenly, glancing at a street clock, I saw the hour hand jerk backward: from six to five, from five to four, and so on. A newsboy came bounding up.

"Extra! Extra! Read all about it!"

Touching the cabman's jacket, I stopped him so as to exchange a coin for a paper. With pounding heart I opened the sheet folded in four: thank God—printed in plain letters under the nameplate was yesterday's date. And on we raced.

Now I could calmly regard the street streaming away from under the wheel rims. There was yesterday's little boy: yesterday's wind had overturned his tray of fruit jellies, and he was again rinsing the sweets in a puddle and replacing them on the tray. And there was that drunk slumped against a playbill pillar, an accordion between his jumping elbows: "Eh, little apple with leaves either side, I'd surely love you, but fear the great divide..." I knew that now the pillar would turn, dropping singer and song in the dirt. I looked away. In essence, that "eternal return" about which Nietzsche theorized deserves if not criticism, then yawns.

Finally we reached the station. I was again standing on the platform. There was my train; it backed slowly in and wheezed to a halt. For me, a conditional corpse, there was a special boxcar made of rough red-painted boards: a storeroom on wheels; in chalk over the door: EXTREMELY PERISHABLE PERS.; above the words green pine branches. On the gloomy side, but it couldn't be helped: I presented myself for loading. The sliding door shuddered open. Sitting in complete darkness, I could hear them sealing my boxcar shut.

And then ... and then two days' journey in that dark cell—time enough to consider all that I had seen and heard, to winnow the husk from the grain and come to final conclusions. But with your permission, ladies and gentlemen, all of that for now shall remain sealed. I have finished.

Baron Munchausen made a bow and was about to walk off the stage when a standing ovation stopped him. The walls of London's Royal Society had never heard such a racket and roar: thousands of palms pounding palms and all mouths shouting one and the same name: Munchausen!

6. THE THEORY OF IMPROBABILITY

THE BARON was a man fairly inured to the ways of fame. Inasmuch as fame is made of words, he knew to only half listen to it while politely posing for the cameras' glass eyes, half smiling, half answering, extending now three fingers, now four, now two, lest his hand swell from all the handshakes. At Mad Bean Cottage his manservant knew to empty the wastepaper basket every two hours since letters, telegrams, and radiograms rained down with the persistence of the London rain.

But even his seasoned ability to deal with fame could not save Munchausen this time from a certain feeling of weariness and surfeit. Every day certificates poured in from every sort of academy and university making him a corresponding member or a doctor of philosophy; the American Journalists Association elected him their president; on the baron's longish torso there was no longer room for more medals, which had to be pinned to places less fitting. From the Spanish king he received an exquisite tongue of gold studded with diamonds, and from an heir to the Russian throne a bronze medal inscribed: FOR SAVING THE PERISHING.

A committee was formed to collect donations for a statue of Hieronymus Munchausen; coins rolled in from all parts—and soon a London square saw the ceremonial laying of the first stone.

The baron rarely found time to commune with his old pipe, the typewriter keys waited in vain to tap out postprandial aphorisms: Munchausen was engaged in work of a more serious and important nature. His lecture, which had been picked up by newspapers around the world, was fast growing into a book over which he labored day and night, often refusing food and sleep. True, the occasional reporter who slipped into the house through some keyhole did manage to stop Munchausen's pen. Invariably civil, he would turn an angry face on the truckling interloper:

"Ten seconds. My stopwatch has started. I am counting: one, two...."

The flummoxed reporter would throw out the first question that came to mind, such as: "Of what sections should an authoritative newspaper consist?"

In a sixth of a second came the reply: "Of two: the formal and the fawning. Eight, nine, ten. It has been a pleasure."

Standing on the sidewalk, the reporter would read and reread the scrawled line, not knowing what to do with it.

Indeed, as even habitués of Mad Bean Cottage had begun to notice, the baron was not his genial self. At the same time, his behavior betrayed certain oddnesses that no one had noticed before.

The first oddness made itself known on that memorable day when the baron's three-cornered hat, threadbare waistcoat, sword, and pigtail were borne triumphantly through the streets of London on cushions of gold brocade to the strains of thundering orchestras and singing clergy. The parade, which began at Guildhall, was supposed to pass by Munchausen's house then swing around toward Westminster Abbey under whose arches, beside the holiest relics of old England, the baron's sword, waistcoat, and tricorne would be laid to immortal rest.

Friends had conspired to keep all preparations for this festivity a secret from Munchausen. These same friends (including the Bishop of Northumberland) had been happily anticipating the effect of their magnificent surprise on the very kind and obliging baron. But a cruel disappointment was in store: upon hearing the clamor of the approaching procession and singing clergy, Munchausen padded to the window in his slippers and looked out, trying to understand what was the matter. Below, he saw floating slowly by, among the swaying crowd, cushions of brocade, and on those cushions—what the devil!—his own waistcoat, pigtail, sword, and tricorne. The crowd's joyful roar soared up to greet the baron, but he, taking a step back, turned around and saw the Bishop of Northumberland, who had just tiptoed into the room.

"Where are they going?" the baron asked hoarsely.

Beaming and rubbing his hands together, the bishop replied, "To the shrines of Westminster. Indeed, not every king—"

But now there occurred something unexpected, unbecoming, and unforeseen by ceremonial etiquette. Turning suddenly purple, Munchausen removed his right slipper and flung it at the exultant crowd: the slipper described a parabola then tumbled down among the gonfalons and glittering brocades, coming to earth like a missile in the middle of an expanding funnel of fast-retreating feet.

"Perhaps," the baron bellowed out the window at the now silent crowd, "you would also like my chamber pot!"

Thousands of frightened faces looked up at the open window only to see it slam shut. The discomfited bishop slipped out the door. The masters of ceremonies bent over backwards trying to restore order, but since the end of the parade, around a bend in the street, kept pressing on the head, the procession continued of its own momentum. Meanwhile, the choir sang out of tune and off-key, the fussing gonfalons pitched this way and that, and the celebration paled and soured.

The evening papers covered the event in cautious language, skirting or suppressing the regrettable fact of the unforeseen slipper missile. But this oddness in the baron's behavior was only the first in a series that caused Londoners' souls to run the gamut of emotion: the keynote was delight, the mediant bewilderment, the octave indignation.

The procession dispersed, Bayswater Road emptied, and the man who had banished delight from a thousand heads paced from corner to corner, furiously muttering to himself, then sat down at his desk and began crossing out whole paragraphs and pages of his manuscript. He had calmed down only a little when he set about his second oddness: two hours after the relics had been settled in Westminster, the abbey's chief custodian received a hand-delivered letter engraved with the von Munchausen coat of arms. In words sharp and terse, the letter demanded the immediate return of the expropriated waistcoat to its rightful owner. "I sincerely hope," the letter ended, "that the United Kingdom of Great Britain and both Indies does not wish to enrich itself by depriving a poor man of his everyday clothes."

The custodian, utterly perplexed, turned for advice to the vicar, the vicar told the father treasurer, the treasurer.... In a word, London had not yet lit its lamps before the odious words leapt over the abbey's crenellated wall, slid down telephone lines, and rustled in instruments, preparing to dive inside the coils of a transatlantic cable. The atmosphere was turning tense. Shortly before midnight the order came down from on high: "Pursuant to the written request of foreign subject Munchausen, revoke all rights and privileges assumed by relic No."—there followed a number—"and return said relic to the abovenamed foreigner."

Next morning not a single reporter dared go near the cottage on Bayswater Road, not counting Jim Chilchur, a staffer at a third-rate rag to which all doors were closed in perpetuity. Chilchur did not have money for the bus, so always began his morning route from Oxford Street to Moscow Road earlier than others and covered it on foot. Today, as usual, he was striding down the long camber of Bayswater Road, glancing at the gates of Kensington Gardens. His head, drawn into his shoulders by the morning chill, was solving a mathematical problem: if from the pence saved every day on bus fare one subtracted the pence required to amortize one's falling-apart shoes, then by what number of days must one multiply the difference so as to obtain the twelve shillings fifty pence needed to buy a new pair of gaiters? This was something like Newton's famous problem involving cows in a meadow—the cows graze the grass unceasingly, but meanwhile the grass continues to grow—and so engrossed was Chilchur in solving this difficult puzzle that he did not at first notice someone's furtive tug at his right sleeve, putting a stop to his steps and numbers. Actually, not someone's: looking over his shoulder, Jim Chilchur saw not a soul, yet someone's tenacious fingers would not let go of the button on his cuff. Chilchur jerked his hand away, and a long green spiral came trailing after, still clinging with its tendrils to his hand, caught as if in a spring trap. The reporter raised his eyes, saw a wall entirely covered with green curlicues, and realized that he was standing in front of Mad Bean Cottage. At that same instant the front door swung open; an old footman looked out and asked amiably, "Are you a reporter?"

"Ye-es. . . . Your beans—"

"The baron will see you." The footman bowed, opening the door wider.

Jim Chilchur was so stunned by this invitation he failed to notice that it had made the mad bean unhook its tendrils. Wobbly legs carried him up the stairs to a hall: the footman had already opened the door to the study where the baron was rising to greet the baffled reporter. An obliging armchair slid up from behind, knocking into Chilchur's knees and forcing him to sit down, while a question fired point-blank caused his fingers to jump from pocket to pocket in search of pencil and paper.

"Forgotten your pad?" The baron smiled. "Do not trouble yourself: this little notebook will do just as well. You mustn't thank me. A pencil? It has already done its work: asked the questions and answered them. You see, you wish to know—forgive me, your name . . . pleased to meet you—so then, you wish to know, Mr. Chilchur, why Munchausen needs his waistcoat. Isn't that so? Well, in your hands you hold documentary proof that this waistcoat is needed *not by me*. You, no doubt, are in a hurry. So am I."

Jim Chilchur dashed out into the street in a state of such joyful stupefaction he did not notice the mischievous stirrings in the morning wind of the long green tendrils entwining the cottage like gossamer snakes.

A special edition of the venal rag for which Chilchur worked cost five pence at ten that morning; by midday people were paying a shilling; and by two o'clock it could not be had even for half a pound. It contained news of the relics—more than enough to draw millions of eyes to a sensational "interview" that had turned the matter of the waistcoat inside out, so to speak. Munchausen's pen, it emerged, had been guided not by a desire to wound the British lion, not at all, but by a decision to give the prickly five-pointed star a lesson in generosity. A conditional corpse, he was expressing an access of rather lively gratitude by donating his two-hundred-year-old waistcoat to the Scientists Welfare Commission of the USSR. "The American Relief Administration," the baron ended the interview by saying, "will not, I think, refuse to dispatch my textile for presentation to the very poorest of young Russian scientists."

This gesture was so magnanimous and Christian (in the best sense of the word) that some newspapers refused to believe it. But Chilchur's rag had documentary proof, a photograph of which showed the baron's sloping script and dispelled the last doubts. Munchausen's fame, capital that he had seemed anxious to squander, suddenly increased, amassing countless round teardrops, which clung to eyelashes like tiny zeroes to the oblique stroke signifying %. The *Daily Mail* raved about this ever young heart donating all seventy-two beats a minute to the good of humanity. *The Times* said that the very kind Baron Munchausen had revived the image of the Dickensian eccentric, who even in his kindly deeds contrives to be a bit of a kook. A priest in the Chapel Royal at St. James's preached a sermon about the widow's mite, while grand Pall Mall, which as we know leads to Buckingham Palace, rolled out its asphalt carpet for Munchausen: in short, the baron was to be granted an audience with the king. But now we come to the third oddness, which.... Then again, let's begin at the beginning.

Baron Munchausen and Mr. Wilkie Dowly, their armchairs drawn together, were conversing in the study of the cottage on Bayswater Road. The sun in the windows was shining so uncommonly brightly for that city of fogs that even the trumpet emerging from the elderly professor's ear shimmered with giddy glints.

"In an hour you are to appear—" Dowly made to push back his armchair.

But the baron's fingers restrained him.

"One hour is three thousand six hundred tick-tocks on the part of a pendulum clock. Will you not allow me to share with you, Mr. Dowly, as an indisputable authority in the field of mathematics, a doubt of mine, a thought oscillating between two numbers?"

The ear trumpet drew nearer the baron, indicating a readiness to listen. After a minute's pause Munchausen went on:

"I am, of course, a dilettante in mathematics. But I have always been extremely interested in the so-called theory of probability, its development and practical conclusions, to which many of your profound and detailed treatises are devoted, my worthy Mr. Dowly. My first question is: Does the theory of probability not lead us to a theory of errors?"

The trumpet nodded: Yes.

"Then my question is: What if the theory of errors, applied to the theory of probability, should declare it an error? I mean to say that the symbolic snake biting its own tail may even choke on it—isn't that true?—in which case cause is devoured by effect, and the theory of probability turns out to be improbable, if only the theory of errors does not turn out to be erroneous."

Rippling over Mr. Dowly's forehead, as over the surface of water into which one has thrown a stone, came wrinkles.

"But permit me, Bernoulli's theorem—"

"My meaning precisely. Bernoulli's idea may be formulated thus: The greater the number of trials, the greater the exactness of the calculated probability. The difference $m/n-p$ becomes indeterminately small. That is, as the number of events becomes greater and greater than one, the oscillation of the numbers' pendulum diminishes, the thing supposed becomes the thing proven, the theory of probability assumes a firm mathematical shape and practical existence: in other words, the numbers and the facts coincide. Have I stated his law of large numbers correctly?"

Mr. Dowly bit his lip. "If we exclude your somewhat bizarre terminology, then I would not object."

"Excellent! Now then, the number of 'events' or trials has only to exceed one for Bernoulli to appear, for his theorem of large numbers and the theory of probability to be set in motion. But let the number of events become slightly stooped, become *less than one*, and just as surely you will see: Munchausen with his counter-theorem, a law of events that never happened, of expectations never fulfilled, wheels whirling in the opposite direction, and a *theory of improbability* going full tilt. You have dropped your trumpet, sir. Here you are."

But the aged mathematician was already knocking his long black aural appendage against the arm of his chair, his words against the nonsense.

"But have you taken into account, my dear Mr. Munchausen, the fact that the theory of probability uses whole numbers, assigning each event a value of one? Like all dilettantes fighting for mathematical symbols, you make them overly abstract; you wish to be more mathematical than the mathematician. Substantive *reality*, which consists of actions (mine, yours, whosesoever you like), knows no event with a value of less than one. We are real people, in a real world: we either act or do not act; events either happen or do not happen. I repeat: The theory of probability uses only whole numbers, one and numbers divisible by one."

"In that case," Munchausen enunciated into the appendage now returned to his guest's ear, "in that case, the facts and the numbers diverge: they must bow and part ways. You say, 'Events either happen or do not happen.' Whereas I maintain that events always only *half happen*. You offer me your *whole numbers*. But what have they, those whole numbers, to do with a *not-whole being*, a so-called person? People are fractions passing themselves off as ones, raising themselves up with words. But a fraction standing on tiptoes is still not a whole number, not a one; and the acts of a fraction are all fractional, all events in the world of the not-whole are not whole. Only the goals of the not-whole are whole, and those goals, please note, are never achieved because your theory of probability, mumbling something about the coincidence of an expected event with an event that has happened, is not fit for our world of improbabilities, where the expected never comes to pass, where vows say one thing and facts another, where life is forever promising to begin tomorrow. Mathematicians, who denote success with a p and failure with a q, understand less about their symbols than the silly cuckoo, which always predicts the same thing for everyone: q—q."*

By now the elderly mathematician, his trumpet fixed on the baron's words, was breathing hard through his nose and furiously clicking his false teeth.

"But if I may say so, sir, you are throwing the world out with our numbers. No more, no less. Your... eh-eh... metaphysics, were they to become widespread, would turn into an intellectual disaster. You cross out all numbers, save zero. But I say: Show greater loyalty to existence. A gentleman must recognize reality as real, otherwise he... well, I don't know how to put it.... These walls, you see, these streets, London, the ground, the world, are not the ash that I flick with the tap of a finger from the tip of my cigar. This is far more serious, and I am amazed, sir—"

"And I am amazed that you can accuse me of disrespect toward your houses and walls: after all, it is only my innate courtesy that compels me to walk not through them, but past them. Your streets are for me as field roads, your palaces and churches as grass over which I might easily stride did I not respect the rules that have Londonized the world: NO PICKING TRADITIONS—IDEAS NOT ALLOWED—KEEP OFF THE HOLIES. Do tell me, my dear Mr. Dowly, why legless people should bother bargaining for my seven-leagued boots? Far simpler and cheaper would be, before taking even one step, to consider those steps."

For a minute silence drove a wedge into the conversation, then the old professor said, "All this is not without its diverting aspects. But no more than that. The walls stand where they stood, the facts as well. And even the ash from my cigar has not disappeared; it is right here—in this ashtray. You deliberately speak in broad terms, my dear Mr. Munchausen, so as to avoid the narrow and cramped facts into which your theory of improbability will not possibly fit: for the feet of an ichthyosaur, Cinderella's glass slippers, ha-ha, would be, you must agree, a bit tight. Your theory of improbability,

*In Russian, the Latin letter q is pronounced "koo."

forgive me, rests on metaphors, whereas our theory of probability is the result of having worked with material of the most concrete kind. Give me even one living example, and I will gladly—"

"Certainly, from one of your monographs, Mr. Dowly. You write: 'If one takes a marble from a box containing only black and white ones, then one can predict with a certain percentage of probability that that marble will be, say, white, and with complete confidence that it will not be red.' But have you and I in our lives, Mr. Dowly, not run up against an extraordinary case when, from a box containing only blacks and whites, the hand of history—to the discomfiture of all—drew . . . a red?"

"More metaphors!" the professor fumed. "But we have gone on too long: the hour of your audience is approaching. I fear you will not have time to give me even one concrete example, even one improbability, having confined yourself to pure theory."

"You never know," said Munchausen, half rising as his guest unbent his own stiff knees. From below, through the thickness of the walls, came the rumble of a motorcar being brought around to the front. Also from below came the sound of footsteps climbing the stairs, the manservant on his way to say it was time to go.

"You never know," Munchausen repeated, merry eyes squinting at Dowly. "Tell me, what act on the part of a man due in twenty minutes to meet the king would you agree to call the most improbable?"

"If he were—" Wilkie Dowly was on the point of replying, but then the manservant appeared in the doorway.

"Very well. Tell Johnny I shall be right down. Now then, Mr. Dowly. I am all ears. You were saying, 'If he were. . . .'"

"Why yes. If he (you are speaking, of course, of yourself, sir), if he were, at the very hour, or rather minute of his audience, to turn his back on the king—"

"Mr. Dowly"—Munchausen leaned into the ear trumpet's bell—"will you give me your word as a gentleman not to tell a soul about the little thing I shall now produce from my vest pocket?"

"You may rest assured. Not a single soul."

The baron's moonstone dove into his vest pocket and flashed forth: between thumb and forefinger, now nearing Dowly's frightened eyes, was the yellow pasteboard of a railway ticket.

"Be so kind as to check the symbols: the train is at four nineteen, the audience is at four twenty. By the way, you know London better than I, tell me: Is it possible to walk out onto the platform at Charing Cross without turning one's back on Buckingham Palace?"

"But that would be most imp—"

"Improbable, you mean to say? My worthy Mr. Dowly, in order to carry out one more plan I shall require one more improbability, one on which I am firmly counting. Bring your trumpet a little closer—that's it. And that improbability is this: that the man who has given his word shall keep it. Is that not true, sir?"

Such was the third oddness: Munchausen had managed to dodge a swipe of the British lion's powerful paw. The journey from London to Dover is a mere two hours. Then again, how hard could it be for a man who had slipped through the five beams of a star to elude five claws?

7. THE HERMIT OF BODENWERDER

AT FOUR twenty-two the king knit his brows. At four twenty-three the palace master of ceremonies rushed to the telephone and rang Bayswater Road: the man at Mad Bean Cottage said the baron was on his way. The master of ceremonies ordered the clocks turned back five minutes and the doors from the private apartments to the throne room opened. At four twenty-five the palace walls began to shiver with murmurs of "Shocking!" At four thirty the king shrugged a furious shoulder and turned on his heel, while the master of ceremonies, catching the monarch's gaze, announced to the courtiers that the audience had been canceled.

But too late: the king had been made to wait! If punctuality is the politeness of kings, then punctuality with respect to kings is a sacred duty. Ten centuries of history had crashed down in ten minutes: the king had waited. Even the executioners who lopped off the heads of English kings did not dare to be a second late; their ax struck on the stroke of the old clock in the Tower. And suddenly... some foreign chatterbox. A German agent who fraternized with Moscow Bolsheviks.... Ten cumbrous centuries pitched and plunged, picking up gravestones the better to strike, while ten merry minutes, legs dangling from an hour hand, rapped out: Late—wait—wait.

The rumor that Munchausen had been abducted on the way from his cottage to the palace by a gang of communists was quashed within hours. Johnny, the chauffeur, testified that he had driven the baron to the station himself for the four nineteen train. The baron's house was searched, but nothing suspicious, save a left slipper missing its mate, was found. The venerable Wilkie Dowly, closeted with the baron not half an hour before the lèse majesté (maid's testimony), was also questioned, but he comported himself like an accomplice. Asked again and again whether he had or had not known, he invariably replied, "I gave my word, not a word more." The theory of improbability, as if to celebrate its triumph, put the blameless mathematician in prison where he soon died, of either old age or chagrin.

Work on the statue of Baron Hieronymus von Munchausen came, of course, to an immediate halt, and in the middle of a vast London square, surrounded by whirling wheels and hooting motorcar horns, an empty pedestal was left to loom, reminding certain people with good memories of Munchausen's story about his last day in Moscow.

The British press reacted briskly, if briefly, to the back that had shown its shoulder blades to the king; the whole herd of literary slop buckets sloshed with this latest scandal, only to slosh the next day with the next latest scandal. Jim Chilchur got his new pair of gaiters, but that was all: his career was hopelessly lost. Newton's cows had gobbled all the flowers of his hopes along with the algebraic grass.

Meantime Baron Munchausen, who had reached the Continent, was whirling along the weavings of railway filaments like a spider whose web has been torn asunder. The policeman on duty that night at the corner of Friedrichstrasse and Unter den Linden saw the baron's automobile race past in the direction of Alexanderplatz. But by noon the next day, when news of the baron's unexpected arrival had spread through the city, the porter at the house on Alexanderplatz was replying to all calls: "Come and gone."

That same morning a functionary on duty at the ministry had received a packet addressed in Munchausen's familiar hand. The functionary gave the packet to his chief. Though this functionary was not an indiscreet sort, he still could not resist telling two or three people about the strange return address on the envelope: "Someplace, Somewhere, Beyond the Seven Seas."

A day later a Berlin acquaintance of the baron, returning from Hanover to the capital, saw what he took to be Munchausen's face in the window of a westbound train stopped at an intermediate station.

The Berliner raised his bowler hat, but then the windows opposite floated past, and the bowler, unacknowledged, returned in a bewildered zigzag to its owner's temples.

Several months passed. The fields had been close shorn. The summer dust had been pinned to the earth by the rains. And the flocks of cranes that not long ago had cut across the sky from south to north like crooked boomerangs had now fallen back—closing the circle—to the south. The name of the mysteriously disappeared baron made a great stir at first, then less of one, before fading away altogether. Fame is like a sound thrown at the mountains: a succession of echoes, pauses more and more prolonged, a last dull distant reverberation—and again the stony silence pressing its gigantic crags of ears to some new sound. Munchausen's admirers and venerators were now venerating and worshiping someone else. His friends.... But didn't the great Stagirite say, "My friends, there is no friendship in this world!" One should note that he could complain of this state of affairs only to... his friends. This psychological antinomy is mentioned here only so that the reader will not be surprised on learning that one autumn morning the poet Ernst Unding received a letter signed: "Munchausen."

Unding's fingers trembled slightly as he reread the scant lines brought him by the narrow sealed envelope. The baron begged the poet not to refuse him "a last meeting with a last person." There followed an address that, the baron suggested, the poet should memorize and then destroy.

Unding might well have mistrusted the words from the narrow envelope: he still remembered the empty station platform and the trains going past. But as it happens, he counted his marks earned working for Veritas and left Berlin that same evening on a train bound for Hanover.

As instructed by the letter, Unding, who had thrashed about all night on the car's hard bunk, alighted two or three stations before Hanover. The little village was still asleep; only its roosters, in eager rivalry, were calling out the dawn. Upon reaching the last house— again he had to refer to the letter—he must stop, knock, and ask for

Michael Heinz. In response to his knock, a man's head poked out. On hearing the name, he asked no more questions and said, "All right. I'm coming."

Then from the fenced-in yard came the sound of hooves and wheels. A minute later the gates creaked open—a country conveyance trundled out onto the road and proffered its iron footboard to the visitor.

The first streak of daybreak was etched on the horizon. Michael jogged the horses; splashing through pools, the wheels proceeded at right angles to the dawn. Unding fumbled in his side pocket and felt—next to the envelope's prickly corners—a notebook folded in half. He smiled self-consciously, but proudly, as poets will when asked to read their verses. The road ran on through bare fields, then swept up over a hill. The rising sun dazzled Unding's eyes: looking away to the left, he saw a rank of four-armed windmills waving hospitably, but Michael tugged the right rein and the carriage, turning its rear wheels to the windmills, jounced down a side road toward the blue-gray shimmer of a pond. A bridge clattered under the wheel rims, a stagger of ducks started quacking and scattered before the hooves, and Michael, gesturing with his long whip toward two or three yellow-tile roofs visible above the double embrace of trees and stone coping, said: "Bodenwerder."

The gates stood wide to welcome Unding. Trudging toward him down the park's main avenue, gripping a walking stick and dragging one leg, came an old, hunched steward. Bowing low, he invited Unding to follow him:

"The baron is unwell. He is waiting for you in the library."

Barely containing his impatience, the poet restrained his muscles and adjusted his pace to the old man's dilatory hobble. They advanced beneath a fantastic weave of branches. The trees stood close together, carpeting the morning avenue with long black shadows. Finally, steward and guest reached the stone steps leading to the house. While the steward hunted for the keys, Unding glanced at the ancient façade, now cracked and sagging: either side of the door, in Gothic letters of gray-yellow stucco half effaced by the rains, were

mottos. On the right: BUY NEITHER RED NOR WHITE; SAY NEI-
THER YES NOR NO. On the left: THE MAN WHO BUILT ME IS
NOT ALIVE; THE MAN WHO LIVES IN ME IS AWAITED BY THE
NOT-LIVING.

The floorboards, creaking underfoot, led them past a whimsical
forest of deer antlers growing out of one wall in branching horizon-
tals. Over a tangled arabesque of carpets, guest and steward plodded
past a series of darkened portraits dimly lighted by narrow windows.
Finally, a spiral staircase quickly set the poet's steps spinning, up to
the musty smell of moldering books: Unding found himself in a
long and dusky chamber with a lancet window at the far end. The
walls were crowded with cabinets and shelves; one sensed that one
had only to take away the books stacked up to the ceiling, and it,
deprived of those supports, would sink down, flattening as it went:
worktable, armchairs and those in them.

But at the moment the armchairs were empty: sitting back on his
heels, Munchausen was arranging some little white squares on the
floor. Absorbed in his work, the skirts of his old dressing gown grazing the carpet, he did not hear Unding's footsteps. The poet came
closer:

"My dear baron, what are you doing?"

Munchausen got quickly to his feet, whisking the little squares
off his knees; their palms met in a firm and long handshake.

"Well, well. Here you are at last! You wonder what I am doing? I
am bidding the alphabet farewell. It is time."

Only now did Unding notice that the little squares scattered
about the carpet's design were the makings of an ordinary alphabet,
pieces of pasteboard each emblazoned in black with a Greek letter.
One of these remained in the baron's fingers.

"Do you not find, my good Unding, that omega—its strange
shape—recalls a bubble on duck feet? Look here a minute." Munchausen held the little square out to his guest. "Sadly enough, this is the
only letter that remains to me of the entire alphabet. I insulted these
letters, and they deserted me, as mice will desert an untenanted
house. Indeed. Any schoolchild, by putting these letters together,

may learn to join worlds with worlds. But for me these symbols have lost all meaning. I must grit my teeth and wait for that slimy bubble on duck feet, stepping soundlessly, to steal up from behind and...."

Munchausen tossed the omega on the table and fell silent. Unding, unprepared for such a speech, looked in alarm at his host: his unshaven cheeks were hollow; an Adam's apple like a sharp triangle gashed the line of his neck; from under the fitful pen stroke of his brows, sunk to the bottom of his eye sockets, centuries stared; the straw-colored hand curled about his prickly knee had the look of a desiccated leaf; even the moonstone on the forefinger had lost its lambency and luster.

For a minute there was silence. Then somewhere by the wall a spring wheezed. Guest and host turned toward the sound: a bronze cuckoo peeped out from behind the clockface and cried nine times. The triangular Adam's apple stirred.

"That silly bird pities me," the baron remarked. "Amusing, isn't it? To my omega it suggests joining its 'koo' (q), the letter by which mathematicians denote failure (when the actual result does not coincide with the one expected). But I do not need this bird's gift: I long ago left behind that little world where failure goes before success, where joy is in suffering and the resurrection in death itself. Cuckoo, keep your q—for it is your only worldly possession, not counting the spring that serves you for a soul. No, Unding my friend, the clockface wheel, turning its two spokes, must sooner or later run against a stone—and crack!"

"But that's just it!" The poet half rose. "Our images have converged, and if you will allow...."

Unding's hand slipped into his jacket pocket. But Munchausen's eyes were gazing absently past him, while around his mouth peevish creases twitched. The pages of the notebook crackling under the poet's fingers never left their hideaway. Only now did Unding see that, to a person bidding the alphabet farewell, all those letters forming stanzas and meanings were futile and belated. His palm returned to the arm of his chair. He understood that the only art required of him was the art of listening.

A wind ruffled the yellow leaves, tapping the window at times with a branch; from under the now silent cuckoo came the pendulum's measured clacket. The baron lifted his head:

"Perhaps you are tired from your journey?"

"Not at all."

"Well I am tired. Though there has been no journey, save tramping about a triangle: Berlin—London—Berlin—Bodenwerder—London—Berlin—Bodenwerder. That is all. Perhaps the absence of Moscow from my route surprises you?"

"No, it doesn't."

"Excellent: I knew you would catch my meaning at once. For though our views on poetics may differ, we both know this: One cannot turn to face one's 'I' without showing one's back to one's 'not-I.' And I, of course, would not be Munchausen were I to think of looking for Moscow... in Moscow. For people, meaning consists of certain realities that they may enter and exit, having left the key with the porter. Whereas I have always known only creations: before entering a house, I must build it. Thus in accepting my assignment to the USSR, I received a moral visa for every country in the world, except the USSR. And so I set off for my old, quiet Bodenwerder, for this place here—for the hush and bookshelves among which I might calmly conceive and build my MSSR.* Having slipped away from all eyes, I wove myself into a close and muffling cocoon so that then, when my hour came, I might break out of it and throw my gaudy dust into the air over the gray dust of the earth. But for purposes of refining this metaphor, the wings of a bat will better adhere to the imagination than those of a butterfly. You of course know the experiment: into a dark room strung with a string maze arrayed with little bells, you release a bat. No matter how the bat swoops about, slashing the gloom with its wings, not a single bell tinkles—the wings always elude the strings, wise instinct threads their spiral flight through the maze, shielding the bat from jolts against not-air.

"And so I released my imagination into that dark and empty (for

*Munchausenian (or Mythical) Soviet Socialist Republic.

me) fourletterdom: USSR. Swooping about from symbol to symbol, its wings seemed not to catch even once on reality; my phantasms glided past the facts until there began to appear an imaginary country, a world plucked from my own Munchausenian eye, which was, in my view, not a whit worse or more lackluster than the world that squeezes inside our eyes from without with its rays.

"I worked with a passion, happily anticipating the effect of my swaying tower of inventions, piled one on top of another, when it crashed down on the heads of my listeners and readers. Oh, how the jaws of London gapers would drop, how they would gawp at the green spirals of my beans as I wove their minds into the many-colored spirals of my phantasms.

"Only one circumstance muddled my images and weakened my composition: now as always, in preparing to impress my phantasmagorisms on other people's brains, I had to find the exact slant from sublime invention to vulgar lies, the one pitch accessible to eyes in blinkers, to turbid sixteen-candlepower thinking, to short-radius imaginations. As always, I had to muddy my colors, blunt my sharp edges, and prime my canvas with the daily ravings from popular newssheets, keeping only my ducks. At any rate, when I had finished composing my Russia that little spiral staircase returned me to people. The result of my lectures you know.

"Again I was surrounded by staring eyes, by ears cocked to catch my every word, by palms outstretched for a handshake, a handout or an autograph. The long-simmering resentment of an artist forced for two hundred years in succession to debase his art rose up in me this time with particular violence. When would these solicitous beings understand, I wondered, that my existence was no more than a courtesy? When would they see, and would they ever, that my pure inventions had come into the world for gasps and smiles, not blood and dirt? So it always is with you on earth, my dear Unding: minor mystifiers, all those Macphersons, Mérimées, and Chattertons who mix their wine with water, fantasy with fact, are declared geniuses, whereas I, a master of pure, unadulterated phantasms, am defamed as a frivolous liar and windbag. That's right. Now you must not contradict me. I know that only children in nurseries believe that old fool Munchausen. Then again only children understood Christ. Why are you silent? Or do you disdain to argue with a muddleheaded man muddled in his own muddles? There you have it, the earth's bitter payment: for myriads of words—silence."

Unding sought out the baron's eyes with his own and gently stroked the old man's withered knuckles: the moonstone on the hooked forefinger suddenly glinted dully and faintly. Munchausen recovered his rapid breath and went on:

"Forgive an old man. His bile. But now it will be easier for you to understand the resentment I felt then and the terrible nervous strain. The slightest shock would have been enough.... Indeed that shock was not long in coming. You recollect our conversation in Berlin when I, pointing to the pegs in my wardrobe—"

"Predicted," Unding joined in, "that sooner or later your waistcoat, pigtail, and sword would make their way on cushions of brocade to Westminster Abbey."

"Precisely. So you may imagine my amazement when, on opening the window one confounded morning, I saw all those castoffs, plucked from their pegs and placed on brocade, floating above the heads of a huge crowd toward Westminster. For the first time in two hundred years I had told the truth. My cheeks flushed with shame and my ears were suddenly ringing, as though the bat's wing had caught on a string with its tinkling bell. Ha! My phantasms had banged into facts. This shock so took me aback that it was some time before I could collect myself. Those fools clamoring in the street understood, of course, nothing. It is a wonder their priests did not canonize my slipper and entomb it in their reliquary.

"I spent the remainder of the day poring over draft pages of my book devoted to the USSR. Now, however, it struck me that here and there I had sinned against falsehood; I crossed out many lines. But having once suspected myself of truthfulness, I could not calm down; in every word there seemed to lurk some truth. Toward evening I pushed the butchered manuscript aside and sank into uneasy reflection: Did this mean that I had fallen ill with the truth? Did this mean that that dreadful and shameful *morbus veritatis*,* leading to either martyrdom or madness, had stolen into my brain too? Even if this attack were brief and not virulent, all those Pascals, Brunos, and Newtons had also begun with trifles, only to suffer thereafter from . . . ugh . . . acute chronic *hypotheses non fingo*.†

"After two or three days of hesitating, I made up my mind to throw off this muddle of conjecture and doubt: I would compare my portrait with the original, the country extracted from the split of my pen with the genuine article contained within real borders. I left London and returned here, to my seclusion. On the way I stopped for only a few hours in Berlin: to liquidate my diplomacy and ensure that I would be left in peace. I renounced all my special powers and enclosed a letter to my contractors saying that, should they even attempt to disclose my whereabouts, I would disclose their secrets. Now I had no worry: they would not allow me to be found. Indeed, the number of curiosity seekers seems to drop every day: my fame, like the Munchausen duck, has folded its wings, never to spread them again.

"I then had to auscultate my ailing manuscript and set about its treatment. With the help of several intermediaries I entered into a correspondence with Moscow; I managed to obtain their books and newspapers. Using these I made a comparative study of domestic Russia and émigré Russia, whose press and literature we all have at hand. Intending to systematically correct my manuscript, I decided to deal with those passages where my story and reality ran parallel as a musician deals with parallel fifths in a score.

"Little by little material from Moscow began to arrive and accrue; that faraway *there* flung hundreds of envelopes right here." Munchausen pointed to a shadowy corner of the library where stood an antique escritoire, its back to the book spines, its slender legs bowed, as if beneath some onerous burden. "Yes, hundreds of envelopes, every one of which, the moment its mouth was torn open, began saying

---

*Truth disease. (Latin)
†I frame no hypotheses. (Latin)

such extraordinary things that...but perhaps you think I am exaggerating? Alas, my illness has robbed me of even that joy. See for yourself. Now then."

With Unding trailing behind, Munchausen crossed over to the escritoire and opened its slanting lid. A heap of opened envelopes showed white; through their postage-stamp windows peered tiny men in Red Army helmets and workers' blouses. Munchausen's fingers rummaged the pile and abstracted a letter at random. Then a second and a third, another and another. Inky lines flickered before Unding's eyes. Munchausen's long fingernail, springing from sheet to sheet, entrained the poet's attention.

"Now then, this, for example: 'Genosse* Munchausen, In reply to your question about the famine on the Volga, I hasten to reassure you: the information contained in your lecture is not so much incorrect as incomplete. The reality, I would venture to say, somewhat surpa—' How do you like that? Or this: 'Dear Colleague, I did not realize that the extinguished *Tale of the Unextinguished Moon* echoed a fact that took place with you on your way from the border to Moscow. It is now clear to me that the author of that seasonably extinguished tale was misleading readers concerning the source of his story and that the whole truth—from beginning to end—belongs to you, and only you.... Allow me, as one writer to another—' What fantastic stupidity! I could never have concocted a tale like that. Or this: '...about that empty pedestal, it does exist. Only no Munchausen, allow me to report, ever stood on it, although a papier-mâché Tsar Alexander did sit on it for three or four days before they climbed him down with ropes, and where there was nothing, now there's nothing again, and nobody knows if there'll be anything else. There was an inscription about a "—berator," I saw it with my own eyes, only now, because of the construction, it's been painted over. But do you really doubt—' and so on. This one is even better." Munchausen's fingernail skimmed over the lines. "Finished? And

*Comrade. (German)

this. I would never have guessed! No. You must tell me what this means: either I have gone mad, or—"

Unding just managed to jerk his fingers away—the lid banged shut, and the baron's slippers slapped wrathfully back to his armchair. The poet turned around to see Munchausen sitting with his face hidden in his palms. There was a long pause before the two returned to words.

"The books by their émigrés were my undoing. When I sat down to concoct my story of Moscow's bushels and prophet, I did not know there were people who could so easily out-Munchausen Munchausen and mock that washed-up fibber. I do not envy them, but I am sad, as an old tree may be sad when it has lost its leaves and is dying, pressed on all sides by lush, young woods.

"But enough of lyricism. I might have gone on with my revisions, but I had had enough. I saw that facts by and large had become phantasms, and phantasms facts, and the darkness around that laboratory bat was tinkling with thousands of little bells; around every shock of wing against string, around every word, every pen stroke, was chiming chuckling air. I hear it still. Both in waking and dreaming hours. No, no. I have had my fill. Throw open the darkness and set the bird free: why go on torturing it now the experiment is ruined?

"You, no doubt, are annoyed with me. You wonder why you have come hundreds of kilometers to see an old curmudgeon of no use to you or to himself, why—"

"If only you knew, dear teacher, how essential you are to me, you would not speak that way!"

Munchausen righted his ring, about to slip around his withered finger, and seemed to smile at some memory.

"Then again, I did not summon you, my illness did. I would never have guessed that one day I would bare my soul like some old trollop through the grille of a confessional, that I would allow the truth into my speech. Did you know that my favorite book as a child was a German collection of marvels and legends ascribed in the Middle Ages to a certain Saint Nobody? Wise and good *der heilige Niemand* was the first saint to whom I addressed my childish prayers. In his colorful stories about the nonexistent, everything was different, otherwise. And when I, a boy of ten, recast his Otherwise and tried to acquaint my playfellows and school friends with his mysterious country of nonexistences, they called me a liar. In defending Saint Nobody, I met not only with jeers, but with fists. However, *der heilige Niemand* rewarded me a hundredfold; having taken away one world, he gave me a hundred hundred others. People, you see, are cheated of their share of the world: they are given only one for all of them. The poor souls live shut up always in their one and only world, whereas I, in my youth, was given a whole host of worlds—for me alone. In my worlds time went more quickly and space was more spacious. Lucretius Carus once asked: If a slinger stands at the edge of the world and shoots a stone, where will it fall: on the boundary or beyond the boundary? I answered that question a thousand times, for my sling always shot beyond the bounds of the existent. I lived in the boundless realm of imagination. To me the debates of philosophers, grabbing the truth out of each other's hands, resembled a fight among beggars over a single coin. Those unfortunate men could not do otherwise: if everything is equal to itself, if the past cannot be remade, if every object has one objective meaning, and thinking is harnessed to cognition, then there is no way out, except through the truth. Oh, how silly all those scholars seemed to me, those unifiers and fathomers. They were searching for 'one in many' and not finding it, whereas I could find *many in one*. They closed tight the doors of consciousnesses, whereas I flung them wide to nothingness, which is indeed everything. I withdrew from the struggle for existence (which makes sense only in a dark and meager world where there isn't enough existence to go around) so as to join *the struggle for nonexistence*: I created not yet created worlds, lighted and doused suns, ripped up old orbits, and traced new paths in the universe; I did not discover new countries, oh no, I *invented* them. In that complex game of phantasms against facts played on a chessboard divided into squares by lines of longitude and latitude, I particularly loved that moment (denoted by chess players with a colon) when, having waited my turn, I swept a fact away with a phantasm, replaced the existent with the nonexistent. Always and invariably my phantasms won—always and invariably, that is, until I chanced upon the country about which *one cannot lie.*

"Indeed, I found that flat square between black and white waters populated with such countless meanings, reconciling in themselves so many irreconcilabilities, extending over such impossible distances, and advancing such extraordinary facts, that my phantasms could only try to catch up. Yes, the Country About Which One Cannot Lie! I could never have guessed that that gigantic red queen would break through my line of pawns and upset the entire game. I remember the queen withstood attacks from almost all my pieces. Finally, my heart pounding in triumph, I pounced with a pawn, and out she went; but before my lips could break into a smile, I saw that my pawn, suddenly colossal and deeply blushing, had turned into that just discarded queen. Such things happen only in dreams: drawn into this nightmare, I grasped my knight's bristling mane, made a zigzag jump, and again knocked the queen off the board. I heard her gigantic crenellations crash to the ground, and then out of nowhere, there she was again, her bloody battlements towering over the lattice of meridians. I castled and captured her with my rook; again came the crash, again the transformation. Enraged, I struck that accursed queen an oblique blow with my bishop—in vain! And then I saw that my squares were empty and my king was in check, whereas the indestructible red queen was where she was, straddling the open lines of her star. The moment has come when I have nothing left with which to make a move: all my phantasms are played out. But I do not think of resigning. In this game, given the scale on which we conduct it, if one has nothing left to play, one has one's self. I tried this once before—when I took hold of my pigtail and pulled myself out of that hummocky swamp. So then—I will play myself: the played-out player cannot do otherwise, and my feet are none too firmly planted on the ground. But my chess clock is running out. It is time. Please leave me, my friend. If indeed you are my friend."

Unding lifted up first his leaden eyelids, then himself. He

searched for words of farewell and found none. But having heard the baron out, he could not walk away as if he hadn't heard. He ran his eyes around the room: serried ranks of book spines, the clockface disk in its bronze rim, the clicked-shut lid of the escritoire, in the corner a previously unnoticed rack for Turkish tobacco pipes with one old, smokeless exhibit, and next to it, hanging on the back of a chair, sleeves grazing the floor, the aged waistcoat that had fled Westminster. Gazing at its puckered shoulder blades, Unding exclaimed, "What! Do you mean to say you didn't send that waistcoat, as the papers claimed, to some young scientist in Moscow?"

"I may still find some use for it myself," came the equivocal reply. "And as for that poor scholar from the country about which one cannot lie, do not worry. I have sent him, by way of compensation, my rough drafts; if he possesses so much as a pair of scissors and a pot of glue, the resulting manuscript should help him on his literary way."

Host and guest said goodbye. On reaching the door, Unding turned around and saw, peeking out from under the baron's cap, which had slipped down onto his forehead, the long gray strands of a neatly braided pigtail.

The creaky spiral again set Unding's slow steps spinning.

8. THE TRUTH THAT DODGED THE MAN

MICHAEL Heinz pulled on the reins, and the wheels stopped. The footboard, then the worn steps of the little station house. Unding raised his eyes to the clockface set in the wall and thought: "A metaphor should be set in a clockface wheel—no matter how you spin the spokes, the rim remains motionless." With that there threaded through his brain a long sequence of images. Meetings with Munchausen always quickened and brightened the pulse of his ideas (Unding was not alone in experiencing this) and set his imagination madly ticking. To the rhythmic clacket and sway of the carriage, Unding's pencil reeled across blue ruled lines, refusing to release his fingers as it traced the shape of a new poem. The train was approaching Berlin by the time he had found a title: "A Speech to the Backs of Chairs." Such catastrophic moments occur even on a ship of words, when the soul whistles "All hands on deck!" and from every quarter, from the plunging bunks, from behind closed doors and even the dark pier glass, the summoned words rush to the surface of the paper pages, now rising, now falling like a sloop in a storm: immersed in his work, Unding missed the Friedrichstrasse stop, alighted at Moabit, and walked through the city hearing neither the clatter of wheels nor the hubbub of people for the resonance of his verses.

It was only when he reached the door of his room with the name Ernst Unding on the outside panel that the poet remembered who he was and where.

Then a deep sleep moved the hour hand nine hours ahead. Unding swung his feet down from the bed and shoved them into shoes, but he hadn't tied the laces before *yesterday* flooded back into his mind and took hold of his now rested consciousness. The peripeteias of his journey to Bodenwerder appeared to him in all their irreparableness. "If I went to help," the thought began to rankle, "then why was I silent? What sort of help is silence?" By his bed lay yesterday's jottings. Unding eyed the penciled scrawls and laughed bitterly. "There I was talking to the backs of chairs, why not to a person?" The written words, however, had hooked his pupils, and the poet did not notice that his verses, which had not done talking, were again pressing his fingers to the page while the poem's will had become his will: again he saw the imagined hall with its endless rows of wooden creatures receding into the perspective, and by each one—in front and behind—a motionless back on four bent legs; surveying the close ranks, the poet pelted the dead backs with words, giving himself up to the bombast of hopelessness; he spoke of the soundlessness of all thoughts that want to become words, and of the deaf Beethoven playing on clavichords whose strings had been unscrewed from the tangents; he rejoiced in the noble candor of his non-listeners and made them models for people afraid to admit that they too, no matter how you approached them, were only backs on legs bolted to the ground; from stanza to stanza, growing flushed with bitterness and rage, he wrote.... However, you shouldn't look over the shoulder of a lyric poet when he is addressing not you, but the back of his chair.

At any rate, it was not until dusk, when the air turned the color of graphite lines, that the poem was finished in rough and the pencil released his fingers. Unding had had nothing to eat all day; throwing on his coat, he went out into the evening street and pushed open the door of the first beerhouse. With the help of a knife, a fork, and a pair of jaws the famished poet quickly dispatched a serving of knackwurst; of the cabbage there remained only a faint cabbagy smell, while the fried eggs stared up with yellow eyes, begging in vain for mercy. Having assuaged his initial hunger, Unding reached for his mug of beer, pulled it toward him, then suddenly his fingers jerked back: on the surface of the ale, sticking to the thick glass rim, tiny bubbles of foam were swelling and bursting, exactly like the ones that, a few years ago, had introduced him to Munchausen. Now that his attack of egoism—what literary historians call "inspiration"—had passed, the image of his forsaken friend strode into the very center of his consciousness and refused to go away. That night Unding tossed about on hot pillows before finally falling asleep. But into that sleep came a dream: a low ceiling supported by stacks of books; behind him he hears quiet bird steps; Unding turns around to see, stealing cautiously across the writing table, a bubble on duck feet; he wants to flee, but his legs are of wood and bolted to the floor; he mustn't let the omega come up from behind—of this he is certain—but behind him is a back, in front of him is a back, and on all sides; the bubble, its shimmering glints distending, begins to balloon, bigger and bigger, until desk, books, ceiling, the entire room, and Unding himself are inside the bubble, still now expanding, until . . . it explodes—into death. Unding closes his eyes more tightly and sees . . . himself with eyes wide open in bed. And through the window sash, the dawn.

All through the day Unding's uneasiness increased. Whether picking up a newspaper, or making a note of his latest instructions from Veritas, through any distraction there appeared a man with his face hidden in palms of parchment, while his limp pigtail, slowly lengthening, seemed to threaten something irreparable. Once again, the passengers on the evening train from Berlin to Hanover included Ernst Unding.

Michael Heinz, woken by a knock and a voice, again, as a few days before, rumbled out of the yard in his country conveyance; Unding jumped onto the footboard, and the wheels trundled off toward Bodenwerder. This time it was a little colder and, as he gazed at the slow-blazing dawn, Unding kept hearing the panes of ice on pools burst and crackle under the hooves. Then, as the windmills with arms upraised loomed out of the morning fog to meet the clatter of wheels, his brain was struck by an unexpected thought: "What if everything that the baron had related the last time was mystification, the nimblest and most whimsical of all his Munchauseniads?" Unding pictured the laughing countenance of the Bodenwerder hermit, pleased at having pulled the wool over his eyes, at having made him believe the unbelievable. Unding no longer felt the cold, his heart was beating faster, but the wheels turned just as slowly. In his impatience, he leaned toward the driver:

"Would it be possible, Herr Heinz, to wake the horses?"

Michael flicked his whip, and the carriage swung down the side road. A frightened flock of ducks scrambled away with despairing quacks from the quickening hooves; under the wheels something snapped. Unding looked back—one duck, evidently, had gone too late: wings flattened to the ground, its immobilized neck still craned across the track. Picking up speed, Heinz's conveyance swept jauntily over the rise and was already rattling over the wooden bridge when Unding shouted, "Stop!"

The morning fog had lifted to reveal a group of people on the shore observing the slow progress of a boat: in the boat sat four men, all holding gaffs; now diving down, now rising up, the gaffs were probing the lake bottom. Among the onlookers Unding discerned the bent figure of the old steward who, turning around at the noise of the wheels, had also recognized the guest. He now hastened as quickly as his years would allow toward the bridge. Unable to wait, Unding leapt out of the carriage and ran to meet him.

"Has something bad happened? Tell me."

The old man hung his head. "My Lord Baron disappeared two days ago. I roused all the servants. We searched the house, the park, the forest, now we are searching the lake. Nowhere."

For a minute Ernst Unding was silent. Then: "Call off your search. It's pointless. Get in."

Unding's voice had the ring of certainty. The old man did as he was told. Having been masterless for two days, he felt the need for at least someone's orders. The boat returned to its mooring, the gaffs were left on the shore, while the carriage proceeded to the house. Along the way Unding learned the details.

"After you left," the steward began, "everything went as usual. Although no: the baron refused his lunch and asked not to be disturbed unnecessarily. At six, as always, I went up to his study. At that hour the baron generally takes a glass of kümmel. I set the tray down on the table; the baron was, as always, seated in an armchair with a book. I wanted to ask if I shouldn't warm up his lunch, but he motioned me to withdraw—"

"I must interrupt you: Do you happen to remember what book was in the baron's hands?"

"The binding was red; morocco, I believe; gilt-edged. It is lying on the baron's table still, just as he left it. The thing is—"

"Thank you. Now go on."

"I went back downstairs, but did not go off anywhere. It seemed to me the baron had taken ill and might call me at any minute. The house was so quiet that I distinctly heard his footsteps in the library. Then they ceased. I called Fritz (my grandson) and told him to stay put at the bottom of the stairs and listen in case the baron should call. I then went about my duties, one thing and another; by the time I returned it was night. 'Has the baron come out of his study?' I asked Fritz. 'No.' 'Has he called?' 'No.' What could the matter be? Fritz could barely keep his eyes open. I sent him off to bed then drew up a stool, sat down, and began to listen. There were no footsteps. Not a sound from above. An hour passed like that, and another. Then shortly before midnight I suddenly heard overhead what sounded like the tinkling of a little bell, then silence. Perhaps I imagined it, I thought, and perhaps not. I climbed the stairs to the library, knocked at the door, and waited. Not a sound. I opened the door a crack. 'Lord Baron, did you call me?' No answer. With that I made up my mind and walked in: I saw there was no one in the room. The armchairs were empty; on the edge of the table lay a closed book—the very same, bound in morocco; the empty kümmel glass had fallen to the floor and rolled under the table; and only the tablecloth fringe swayed slightly, as if someone had brushed against it with their knee. I went to the window: it was closed. Mother of God, what had happened? I looked at the shelves: books and more books. Perhaps the baron was hiding: but where? And besides, we are too old, he and I, for childish games of hide-and-seek. I woke Fritz: we searched high and low. Then I asked the watchman, 'Had the baron gone out?' 'No.' We took torches and went all around the garden. So it began—we have been at it for two days now. Tell me, sir, is it possible for a person to leave a room without having left it? Eh?"

Just then the carriage stopped at the manor gates, sparing Unding the need to reply. He jumped down and rushed toward the house without waiting for the steward's footsteps. Fritz, tousled and sleepy, opened the door to him, and the poet, passing down the row of old portrait squares framed in faded gold, hurried up the spiral stairs leading to the library. He thrust the door open and, hat in hand, strode into the room. Everything was just as before. But no: the clock, which someone had evidently forgotten to wind, was silent; and the back of the armchair, from which the baron's old waistcoat had hung its empty arms, was bare. And the morocco volume? Yes, it lay exactly as the steward had described: on the edge of the table, within reach of the armchair. Unding walked up and touched one of the leather corner pieces. Yes, the very same. His agitation might have momentarily stopped his fingers, but there was no time to lose—downstairs a door slammed and footsteps could be heard approaching. Taking hold of the corner piece, Unding flung the book open and began leafing through the pages: three—and on—thirty-nine—farther on—sixty-five, sixty-seven—now. His fingers trembled slightly as he turned the page: the empty square inside the black typographical rule was *not empty*: in the center, shoulders hunched, stood Baron Munchausen.

He was wearing his traditional waistcoat and straggly pigtail. True, by his right hip there was no sword, as in the edition of 1785, and his hair was noticeably whiter. But the casual observer, who had seen other copies of this edition, would have said, "The color has rubbed off with time and faded." In any case, in the whole world one could not have found another eccentric who thought what the poet Ernst Unding did: "So that was his last move—he played himself." And felt what he did: an acrid tear tingling in his lashes. That was really too much! Frowning angrily, he reached for a pencil, but an epitaph would not come. For a minute he sat with his elbows on the arms of the chair, peering at the dim and shrunken outline of his friend who had finally returned to his old book. The sweetly musty pages smelled to Unding of eternity itself.

Then suddenly the footsteps of the steward, who had seemed to linger in the mazelike passage, sounded close by. He would have to hurry. Taking the binding gently and reverently by its leather corner pieces, Unding lowered the morocco lid. Then, book in hand, he turned to the shelves crowded with spines and considered where to stand the morocco coffin. Right here: between leather and parchment, between decorous Adam Smith and the tales of *A Thousand and One Nights*. The door behind him creaked open. Turning around, he saw the steward.

"The baron will not return," said Unding, brushing past him, "for he never left."

The old man went hobbling after in hope of a plainer answer, but could overtake neither the answer nor the poet. Within five minutes, Unding was seated in the carriage gazing at the back of Michael Heinz, who now and then quickened the hooves' clip-clop with a whistle of his long and melodious whip. Crunching over the half-frozen ground, the wheels were already bowling toward the bridge when Unding suddenly leaned forward and touched Heinz's shoulder.

Heinz turned around on the box and saw, pressed to the passenger's knees, an open notebook. He expressed no surprise. Rather he adjusted the harness, then settled down to smoke and wait. Meanwhile the text, a weave of jumping gray letters, said:

> Here, beneath a morocco shroud,
> waiting for the judgment of the living,
> flattened into two dimensions, lies
> he who walked through the world's walls,
> Baron Hieronymus von Munchausen.
> As a true warrior, this man
> never once dodged the truth:
> All his life he fenced against her,
> parrying facts with phantasms.

And when, in response to her thrusts,
he made a decisive lunge, Truth itself,
as I am a witness, dodged the man.
Pray for his soul to Saint Nobody.

Ernst Unding put his notebook away and made a sign to the driver: onward. From under the wheel rims once more came the tinkling of fine icy panes on pools.

1927–1928

NOTES

INTRODUCTION

vii   *Gottfried August Bürger:* A German poet (1747–1794) best known for such ballads as "Lenore" and "The Wild Huntsman." His embellished translation of the baron's *Travels* became the model for Munchausens on the Continent.

     what Nabokov called "Munchausen's horse-decorpitation story": In *Bend Sinister* (1947), Vladimir Nabokov's novel involving a police state run by the Party of the Average Man. The characters include a "very *ancien régime*" baron who, to avoid arrest, decamps to a defunct elevator where he receives the philosopher Adam Krug with touching hospitality.

viii *Rudolf Erich Raspe:* For a scrupulous account of the life of Raspe (1737–1794) and the real Baron Münchhausen, see John Carswell, *The Prospector* (London: The Cresset Press, 1950).

x   *Hans Vaihinger:* A German philosopher (1852–1933) partly educated in Berlin and best known for his *Philosophy of "As If"* (1911); by 1924, when it first appeared in English, the book was in its sixth edition.

xi   *Radulfus Glaber:* Or Raoul Glaber (985–1047), the author of an idiosyncratic five-volume history of tenth-century France. For a sketch of his mischief-making character, see Helen Waddell, *The Wandering Scholars* (New York: Doubleday Anchor Books, 1955), 191. One suspects that Radulfus the historian did not want to be known for his comic creation, Nemo; a mock sermon on Saint Nobody, supposed to have been written by Radulfus, surfaced only in 1290.

xii *the so-called dreamer in the Kremlin:* So called by H. G. Wells, who spoke to Lenin in situ in October 1920. The interview appeared in *The*

New York Times on December 5, and later in Wells's controversial book *Russia in the Shadows* (London: Hodder and Stoughton, 1921).

xii *the small stove…didn't so much heat the apartment as fill it with smoke:* See Olga Volkogonova, *Berdyaev* (Moscow: Molodaya gvardiya, 2010), 210.

two dozen other leading lights: "There were around twenty-five exiles, with families this came to approximately seventy-five people. Therefore from Petersburg to Stettin we hired a whole steamship, which we completely filled. The steamship was called the *Oberbürgermeister Haken*." See N. A. Berdyaev, *Samopoznanie* (Moscow: Kniga, 1991), 246.

1. EVERY BARON HAS HIS FLIGHTS OF FANCY

3 *Alexanderplatz:* The heart of 1920s Berlin; renamed in honor of Alexander I after the Russian tsar's visit in 1805.

"Rebellion in Kronstadt!": An anti-Bolshevik revolt in March 1921 at a naval base near Petrograd by sailors whom Trotsky had called "the pride and glory of the Russian Revolution." Kronstadt and other risings around the country prompted Lenin to institute his tactical New Economic Policy.

Ernst Unding: Earnest Nonsense. (German)

5 *ersatzes:* An allusion to the substitute foods, substitute goods, and substitute substitutes that Berliners were reduced to consuming during World War I.

fictionalism: Or the philosophy of "As If" advanced by Vaihinger (see note above), who held that the human mind, in order to think and to preserve itself, constructs fictions, such as God, immortality, and freedom; while it knows these faiths to be false, it may benefit by acting "as if" they were not.

Tieck and I sat up all night disputing…I reminded him that…a rope, though in moonlight it resemble a snake, cannot bite: Ludwig Tieck (1773–1853), the Berlin-born son of a rope maker, was a leading exponent of German Romanticism, an inventor of folktales, and translator of *Don Quixote*.

5 *Fichte:* Johann Gottlieb Fichte (1762–1814), an idealist German philosopher who held that the non-ego ("not-I") is the unconscious product of the ego ("I"): the mind creates everything that we think of as the reality which we inhabit.

7 *Saint Augustine:* An early Christian church father and philosopher (354–430) who, in his *Confessions*, insisted on the truth: "He who knows the truth, knows the light."

1789, 1830, 1848, 1871: Years of revolutionary upheaval in Europe, from the French Revolution to the Paris Commune.

and in my hands I have a steeple ... an ordinary church steeple ... it all seems somehow familiar: The mythical Munchausen's adventures begin with him riding through deep snow in Russia. Overcome by night and sleep, he ties his horse to a tree stump poking up out of the snow. He wakes to find himself lying in a village graveyard, his horse dangling from the church steeple, the snow having melted.

8 *Versailles Conference:* Or the Paris Peace Conference, a meeting to establish the terms of the peace after World War I; it resulted in various agreements, including the Treaty of Trianon, signed on June 4, 1920, at the Grand Trianon.

10 *My career ... began with a modest secretaryship in an embassy:* The real Münchhausen began his professional life as a page in the Russian service, in the Brunswick Regiment under Prince Anton Ulrich, nephew-in-law of Tsarina Anna.

11 *League of Nations:* An intergovernmental organization that came out of the Paris Peace Conference with a mission to maintain world peace.

Brest peace: The Treaty of Brest-Litovsk (March 3, 1918) between Bolshevik Russia and the Central Powers (Austria-Hungary, Bulgaria, Germany, the Ottoman Empire); a separate peace that extricated Russia from World War I.

Amsterdam conference: Convened by labor and socialist groups (April 26–29, 1919), partly in an effort to influence the Paris Peace Conference.

treaties, including Washington, Versailles, and Sèvres: The Washington Naval Treaty (February 6, 1922), an agreement between the major powers that won World War I to limit naval armaments; the Treaty of Versailles (June 28, 1919), the Allies' peace agreement with Germany; and the Treaty of Sèvres (August 10, 1920), the Allies' peace agreement with the Ottoman Empire.

2. SMOKE THAT ROARS

13 *four parallel rails suspended in air:* The Berlin Stadtbahn, or elevated railway.

   the king's quondam street: Königstrasse, now Rathausstrasse.

   the stone cubes, arcs, and cornices of the palace: Berlin's city palace (Stadtschloss), the residence of the ruling dynasty of Brandenburg-Prussia until 1918.

   flags of revolution: The German Revolution of 1918–1919.

15 *Teniers:* David Teniers the Younger (1610–1690), the Flemish genre painter.

16 *The beans went on twirling upward with their thread-like tendrils, obviously aiming for the sickle moon…"Again?":* While enslaved to the Turkish sultan, the mythical Munchausen threw his silver hatchet at two bears; by mistake, it flew up to the moon. The baron managed to retrieve the precious hatchet by planting a fast-growing Turkey bean, which "actually fastened itself to one of the moon's horns."

   [in] the words of a popular American author: "The world is managed by people who do about two hours work a day—that is, on the days when they work at all": W. E. Woodward (1874–1950), whose best-selling novel *Bunk*, about a professional debunker, was soon followed by *Bread & Circuses* (New York: Harper & Brothers, 1925), the source of this quote (47).

17 *a pair of allegorical figures:* On the Wellington Monument (1858–1912) in St. Paul's; the female figure of Truth is shown bracing one foot against the chest of the unmasked male figure of Falsehood as she pulls his long forked tongue out of his mouth.

   Paternoster Row…Fleet Street: The third edition of Munchausen's *Travels* (1786) was sold in London by M. Smith at No. 46 Fleet Street and by the booksellers in Paternoster Row.

18 *Mosi-oa-Tunya:* The indigenous name for Victoria Falls, on the border between Zambia and Zimbabwe, which is nowhere near Lake Victoria.

19 *"Sir, how can I turn into Saul without turning around?":* An absurdist question suggesting that the cathedral would like to return to pre-Christian times when Paul was Saul.

21 *Alekhine's defense:* Introduced in 1921 by the Russian-French world chess champion Alexander Alekhine; a provocative opening in which Black runs his king's knight across the board, inviting White's pawns to chase it.

22 *the drooping mustache of the Labor Party leader…the knave:* Ramsay MacDonald (1866–1937), the illegitimate son of a Scottish servant girl; he had a shaggy, circumflex-shaped mustache.

23 *Li Hung Chang:* Li Hongzhang (1823–1901), a Chinese general and leading statesman; he attended the coronation of Tsar Nicholas II and was decorated by Queen Victoria.

24 *Saint Nobody:* Or Saint Nemo, a nonexistent saint evidently invented by the medieval French monk Radulfus Glaber (see note above). Radulfus had the idea of treating the Latin word *nemo* (nobody, no man) in biblical and classical texts as a proper noun. His superhuman Nemo *can* see and do what no man can.

Pius X: Pope Pius X (1835–1914); his coronation took place on August 9, 1903.

25 *Genoa:* In 1922 the city hosted the Genoa Conference, a failed postwar effort to negotiate a commercial relationship between capitalist Europe and Bolshevik Russia.

27 *"Munchausen sleeps, but not his cause":* A reworking of the Soviet-era slogan, "Lenin died, but his cause lives."

3. KANT'S COEVAL

28 *Kant's Coeval:* The real Baron Münchhausen was a contemporary of the German philosopher Immanuel Kant (1724–1804).

29 *the last international peace conference:* The Paris Peace Conference (1919).

29   *My ancestor Heino embarked on a crusade with Frederick II:* A fore-
father of the historical Münchhausens, Heino did in fact accompany
the Holy Roman Emperor to Palestine in 1228.

Kant says: 'I know only what is introduced by me into my experience':
In his introduction (1787) to the *Critique of Pure Reason*, Kant wrote:
"But, though all our knowledge begins with experience, it by no means
follows that all arises out of experience. For, on the contrary, it is quite
possible that our empirical knowledge is a compound of that which we
receive through impressions, and that which the faculty of cognition
supplies from itself.... Knowledge of this kind is called a priori, in con-
tradistinction to empirical knowledge, which has its sources a posteri-
ori, that is, in experience." (Translated by J. M. D. Meiklejohn)

*when I saw a platoon of Versaillais take up rifles and level them at
unarmed Communards (this was by the walls of Père-Lachaise):* A reference to the summary executions on May 28, 1871, that marked the end of
the Paris Commune, which Lenin saw as a pioneering attempt at a proletarian dictatorship.

*'Man is the ultimate purpose for man and should not be anything
but the ultimate purpose':* In his *Critique of Judgment*, Kant wrote:
"[Man] is the ultimate purpose of creation here on earth, because he is
the only being upon it who can form a concept of purposes." (Translated
by J. H. Bernard)

*Shaw ... maintains that we do not live forever only because we do not
know how to wish for our immortality:* In his preface (1911) to *The Doctor's Dilemma*, George Bernard Shaw wrote: "Do not try to live forever.
You will not succeed."

Methuselah: The longest-lived man in the Bible (Genesis 5:27); he
died at the age of 969.

30   *not counting a few minor publications, this material has never seen
the light of day:* By the 1920s, Munchausen's adventures (under various
titles) had been a bestseller in the major European languages for well
over a century at more than three times the original length.

*My acquaintance with Russia took place during the reign of my late
friend the empress Catherine the Great:* The real Münchhausen's first acquaintance with Russia took place during the reign of Tsarina Anna in

the late 1730s. By the time of Catherine's accession in 1762, he had re-tired to his patrimonial estate at Bodenwerder to hunt and entertain. But in 1744, when the German princess Sophia of Anhalt-Zerbst (the future Catherine II) passed through Riga on her way to St. Petersburg, she was met by an honor guard commanded by Hieronymus von Münchhausen. See A. N. Makarov, ed., *Priklyucheniya Barona Myunkh-gauzena* (Moscow: Nauka, 1985), 253.

31   *Denis Diderot:* The French encyclopedist and Enlightenment thinker (1713–1784) was, unlike Münchhausen, an intimate friend of Catherine the Great (1729–1796). At her invitation, Diderot spent five months in St. Petersburg in 1773–1774.

persons fond of reminding one—apropos and not so—that sweet-smelling ambergris is in fact the excrement of a sperm whale: Such as Mel-ville in *Moby-Dick*: "Who would think, then, that such fine ladies and gentlemen should regale themselves with an essence found in the inglo-rious bowels of a sick whale! Yet so it is."

in perpetual breach of court etiquette, Diderot might strut back and forth in front of her nose, interrupt her, and even, in the heat of argument, slap her on the knee: During their long tête-à-têtes in the Winter Palace, Catherine delighted in the brilliance and passion of this "quite extraor-dinary man" despite the violence to her person. "My thighs are bruised and all black," she wrote Mme Geoffrin, "I have been obliged to put a table between him and myself so as to shield myself and my limbs from his gesticulations." Quoted in Blake Hanna, review of Denis Diderot's *Mémoires pour Catherine II,* in *Études françaises,* vol. 2, no. 3 (1966): 367.

Catherine, smiling graciously, listened to all his nonsensical plans: Diderot had made a careful study of Russia and devised plans for its re-form. But by the time he arrived in Petersburg, a decade after first being asked, various challenges to Catherine's rule, including the then unfold-ing Pugachov Rebellion, had cooled her reformist zeal.

32   *my own experiments—mentioned in my memoirs, if you recall—in the forcible eviction of foxes from their skins:* The mythical Munchausen once flogged a fine black fox in a Russian forest "out of its fine skin."

The poor man . . . had to sell . . . his library: it was acquired by the em-press: Diderot sold his library in 1765, long before he went to Russia, to provide a dowry for his daughter; Catherine bought it on the condition that it remain at his disposal for his lifetime.

33 *certain circumstances of a more delicate nature, on which I shall not comment except to note that I am not overly fond of corpulent women:* Catherine's licentiousness was legend: "Lover after lover was admitted to the embraces of the Messalina of the North, until soldiers of the guards were employed in fatiguing an appetite which could not be satiated." See Henry Lord Brougham, *Historical Sketches of Statesmen Who Flourished in the Time of George III* (Philadelphia: Lea & Blanchard, 1839), 206.

I soon found myself hunting Turks. Russia, you see, had declared war on Turkey: "As a cornet in the Brunswick Regiment, [the real Münch-hausen] served against the Turks in the campaigns fought by Count Munich between 1738 and 1740, and was present at the capture of Ocza-kov which marked the turning point of the war." See John Carswell, introduction, in Rudolf Raspe et al., *The Singular Adventures of Baron Munchausen* (New York: The Heritage Press, 1952), xxvii.

Order of Basil the Blessed: The nonexistent order of a holy fool, Ba-sil the Blessed (d. 1552), who lived under Ivan the Terrible. Basil had the gift of prophecy and told the truth to everyone, including the Tsar.

34 *verst:* An old Russian measure of length, slightly more than a kilo-meter (3,500 feet).

curricle: A light two-wheeled chaise, usually drawn by two horses.

Time of Troubles: A fifteen-year period of political crisis and convul-sions in Russia in the absence of a hereditary tsar—from the end of the Rurik dynasty in 1598 to the beginning of the Romanov dynasty in 1613.

35 *'When a Russian is at death's door, a German feels fit as a fiddle':* An inversion of the Russian catchphrase, "What's good for a Russian is death to a German."

4. *IN PARTES INFIDELIUM*

37 *perlustrators:* Those who open and inspect correspondence.

'Zinoviev': The assumed name of G. E. Radomyslsky (1883–1936), a Bolshevik revolutionary and Soviet politician; then chairman of the Communist International.

5. THE DEVIL IN A DROSHKY

40   *the old building in Piccadilly:* The Royal Society was then located in Burlington House with other leading scientific societies.

Newton: Isaac Newton (1642–1727), an English mathematician, natural philosopher, and past president of the Royal Society, where his bust remains.

Cook: Captain James Cook (1728–1779), a British explorer, navigator, and cartographer; elected a Royal Society Fellow in 1776; stabbed to death by Pacific islanders on Hawaii.

41   *a revolutionary song…about a little apple:* A Russian folk song that amassed many new verses after the revolutions of 1917. Of these, the best known was: "Hey, little apple, / Where are you rolling? / You're mine to gobble, / So stop your bowling!"

the land where everyone from commissars to cooks runs the state: An allusion to a phrase ascribed to Lenin. In 1917 he wrote that cooks could not run the state yet, but the Bolsheviks would teach them. In 1925, the year after his death, a poster appeared with this "quote": EVERY COOK MUST LEARN TO RUN THE STATE—Lenin.

Eydtkuhnen: The easternmost terminus of the Prussian Eastern Railway, on the border with Lithuania. Now part of Russia (Chernyshevskoye).

a tiny buffer state: Lithuania.

in my salad days I could break in not only wild horses, but flying cannonballs: While taking tea with the ladies of a noble country house in Lithuania, the mythical Munchausen heard shouts of distress coming from the yard. A young horse had just arrived from the stud, "so unruly that nobody durst approach or mount him." The baron dashed downstairs, jumped on the horse's back, then forced it to leap in at an open window of the tea room to show the ladies. Later, while fighting the Turks, he leapt astride an outgoing cannonball so as to infiltrate an unassailable enemy fortress.

43   *my favorite hound—she appears in my memoirs:* A greyhound that ran so fast, so much, and for so long in the baron's service that she ran off her legs; he kept her on as a terrier.

44 *Cimmerian:* Of an ancient nomadic people thought to have inhabited southern Russia as early as 1300 BC.

45 *foot wrappings:* Pieces of cloth worn with shoes or boots in place of socks.

bread and salt: Traditional symbols of hospitality.

the civil war: Five years of armed struggle (1917–1922) between the Bolshevik Red Army and various adversaries.

My memoirs helped me to solve this difficult case: I ordered a saw to be brought and had the horses sawed, one by one, in two: The mythical Munchausen's "spirited Lithuanian" is cut in two by a dropped portcullis as he races into a walled Turkish town. He finds the back half larking about outside in a field full of mares.

The peasants had warned me of the dangers near railroad tracks where, on a dark night, one could easily fall into the hands of bandits: "The peasants reacted to food requisitioning by sowing less, so that food output by 1921 had fallen to less than half the 1913 level. Disbanded Red army men, with axes, bludgeons and pistols, roamed for food and plunder, setting up camps by railroad tracks." See Brian Moynahan, *The Russian Century* (New York: Random House, 1994), 117.

46 *I reached for the back of my head, intending to pull myself out of this unsuitable society by my pigtail (as I had once pulled myself out of a swamp):* Having miscalculated the width of a swamp, the mythical Munchausen once found himself about to drown in slime when he famously grabbed his own pigtail with his own strong arm, rescuing both himself and his horse.

47 *Albert Einstein…jumped to conclusions concerning these celestial anomalies:* An allusion to Einstein's general theory of relativity.

"unextinguished moon": An allusion to Boris Pilnyak's *Tale of the Unextinguished Moon* about an army commander who submits to a murderous medical operation ordered by "the Unbending Man." It ran in *Novy Mir* (1926). Party officials said the story was not a work of imagination, as Pilnyak claimed, but clearly based on "slanderous" talk about the recent death in hospital of Army Commander Mikhail Frunze. (The fatal ulcer operation to which Frunze submitted had been ordered by Stalin.)

48 *My ware, you see, was of roughly the same sort:* Truth in lies.

49 Anti-Dühring: Engels's 1878 attempt to summarize and popularize Marxist theory was, wrote Lenin, "a wonderfully rich and instructive book."

Health Commissar Semashko was asking, for some reason, that he not be nibbled: Munchausen has mistaken a public notice from the Health Commissariat asking citizens not to nibble sunflower seeds (*semechki*) for a private plea from Semashko not to nibble him. Health Commissar Nikolai Semashko (1874–1949) was also a professor of public hygiene at Moscow University.

51 *the Martinique earthquake:* A "convulsion of nature" in 1902 that wiped out St. Pierre, the cultural capital of the French Caribbean island.

52 *"Only a billion, your Lordship":* Inflation spiraled out of control after the Bolshevik coup. In 1924 a currency reform exchanged fifty billion "old" rubles for one "new" ruble.

Zamoskvorechye: A large loop of land on the south side of the Moscow River, opposite the Kremlin.

Professor Korobkin: Ivan Ivanovich Korobkin, the mathematician hero of Andrei Bely's 1926 novel *Moskovsky chudak* (The Moscow Eccentric).

53 *thirteen telephones:* Here Lenin is apparently associated with God, in communication with his twelve apostles and a thirteenth, Judas (Trotsky). Years before the revolutions of 1917, Lenin had referred to Trotsky as a "little Judas."

54 *our country of huts shall become a country of palaces:* A rewording of Lenin's revolutionary slogan "Peace to the huts, war to the palaces!," derived from the French revolutionary motto "War to the châteaux, peace to the cottages!"

'how life smells': The title poem of a popular collection (*Kak pakhnet zhizn*, 1924) by Alexander Bezymensky.

This telephone here plus three letters: Presumably a direct line to the Cheka (secret police) plus the letters VMN, *vysshaya mera nakazaniya* (supreme measure of punishment), a Soviet-era euphemism for the death penalty.

54   *you would be driven away like chaff by the wind:* Psalm 1:4.

55   *"What are you making?"....."Literature":* An allusion to Vladimir
Mayakovsky's *How Are Verses Made?* (1926) in which he contends that
poetry is an "industry" and "only an industrial attitude toward art can
put different types of literary labor on the same plane: both verses and
news items."

a modest man who collects cracks: Either Gottfried Lövenix, the
hero of Krzhizhanovsky's story "The Collector of Cracks," or Krzhizhanovsky himself, "collector of the most exquisite cracks in our fissured
cosmos," according to the poet Maximilian Voloshin.

Association for the Study of Last Year's Snow: In Russian, the expression "like last year's snow" refers to anyone or anything for which a person has absolutely no use (for example, a comb for the man who is bald).

56   *Howard and Haass:* The English philanthropist John Howard
(1726–1790), a reformer of prisons at home and abroad who died of an
infectious fever in Russia; and Friedrich Joseph Haass (1780–1853), a
German physician who spent his professional life in Moscow working
to alleviate the suffering of prisoners.

*the [rats] marched themselves single-file...straight into the kitchen
kettles and vats:* An inversion of the German legend in which a pied
piper charms all the rats out of the town of Hamelin and into the Weser
River.

Medical hypnotists were also pressed into service: In 1922, Vladimir
Bekhterev (1857–1927), a neurologist and Russian pioneer in the field of
hypnosis, organized (with Bolshevik support) a special Commission for
the Study of Mental Suggestion.

57   *you remember my ducks:* The mythical Munchausen caught several
dozen ducks with one very long dog leash to which he had attached a
small piece of lard. The first duck swallowed the slippery pork fat and
passed it undigested; the second duck followed suit, then the third, and
so on, until they had all been strung like so many pearls.

those triumphal parades that have become so widespread: "What
makes a Moscow demonstration more imposing and more ominous is its
complete organization: the tides are on leash and the leash is in the grip

of a small group on Red Square." See Eugene Lyons, *Assignment in Utopia* (London: George G. Harrap & Co., 1938), 103.

57 *My long conversations with Hegel left their mark both on me and, I think, on him: Freedom, immortality, God—those are the three legs of my chair:* Munchausen is mixing Hegel with Kant. Freedom of will, immortality of the soul, and the existence of God are Kant's three postulates of pure practical reason: unprovable things that must be assumed as true for man to lead a moral life. In his *Philosophy of Nature* (1817), Hegel says that man, inasmuch as he is dependent on others to satisfy his animal appetites, is not free: "This is the unpleasant feeling of need. The defect in a chair which has only three legs is in us." (Translated by A.V. Miller)

materialists succeed only insofar as they are . . . idealists of their materialism: Possibly a playful allusion to Schopenhauer's *The World as Will and Representation* (1818), in which the German philosopher discusses "the fundamental absurdity of materialism" and likens the materialist to Baron Munchausen pulling himself and his horse out of a swamp by his own upturned pigtail.

Revolution's notorious broom, which raises more dust than it sweeps out, tried to sweep the idealists out of Russia's house: A reference to the expulsion from Russia in 1922 of leading members of the anti-Soviet intelligentsia—professors, writers and philosophers, including Nikolai Berdyaev—in an operation initiated by Lenin. See *Vysylka vmesto rasstrela: Deportatsiya intelligentsii v dokumentakh VChK-GPU 1921–1923* (Moscow: Russky put, 2005).

so many bushels, so many leading lights: Dissenting intellectuals who remained in Russia after 1917 had to hide their light under the proverbial bushel.

58 *The gloomy man to whom the gracious countess now introduced me, naming the rather famous author of books about Russia's impending fate:* Nikolai Berdyaev (1874–1948), the outspoken religious philosopher, idealist turned pessimist, and author of *Sudba Rossii* (The Fate of Russia, 1918); his maternal grandmother was a French countess.

the crows on Tverskoi Boulevard, instead of cawing, have started hurrahing: An allusion to Soviet Moscow's command-performance parades.

The crows have evidently begun parroting the "hurrahs that rolled through Red Square like waves." See Lyons, *Assignment in Utopia*, 102.

59   Domostroi: Domestic Order, a sixteenth-century compendium of religious, social, and household rules.

Smoke: A novel (1867) by Turgenev in which the wind-driven smoke billowing from the train returning the hero to Russia serves as a metaphor for man's inconstancy and life's hopelessness.

'the smoke of the Fatherland' that is 'sweet and dear to us': A line from *Woe from Wit* (act 1, scene 7), which Griboyedov likely borrowed from Derzhavin ("The Harp"), who may have been paraphrasing Ovid in exile (*Ex Ponto: Book 1*): "Even Ulysses prayed that he might see the smoke of his ancestral hearth again."

Amsterdam International: The International Federation of Trade Unions, reconstituted at a congress in Amsterdam in July 1919.

a fashionable Boston religion: Christian Science, founded in 1879.

60   *no tongs, no countess: she melted*: Like all members of Russia's old nobility, the countess became under Soviet rule a disfranchised "former person."

Una Sancta Sancta Russia: An allusion perhaps to Berdyaev's 1927 article on Orthodoxy and ecumenism ("Una Sancta," in German); in it he argues that the Truth of Orthodoxy has long been "hidden under a bushel," but that now Orthodoxy represents the best way to an ecumenical Christian unity while the Russian Orthodox Church has the advantage of being a church of martyrs and sufferers (that is, godlike).

"From here the street is cobbled," the prophet mumbled dully, "people of my profession had best stay away from stones": In addition to the stoning of biblical prophets, this Russian prophet may be alluding to *Stone as a Weapon of the Proletariat* (1927), the Soviet sculptor I. D. Shadr's bronze of a worker wrenching a cobblestone loose from the pavement.

chekaneries: Searches and arrests or worse by the Cheka.

61   *Horace's maxim "Be surprised at nothing"*: "*Nil admirari*" (*Epistles* 1.6.1); critical detachment is the key to happiness.

62 *preestablished harmony:* A harmony said by the optimist Leibniz (our God-created world is "the best of all possible worlds") to be established eternally in advance between all monads, but especially between mind and matter.

63 Velvet Book: *Barkhatnaya kniga* (1787), an official register bound in velvet of Russia's most distinguished boyar and noble families.

64 *a conditional corpse:* "Conditional death by shooting" (*uslovny rasstrel*) was a form of suspended sentence instituted by the Bolsheviks in 1919 and applied in July 1921 to the structural engineer and inventor Vladimir Shukhov. Halfway through his construction of a 150-meter hyperboloid radio tower in Moscow, an accident destroyed most of the work. Shukhov was convicted of sabotage and would have been shot but for his indispensability to the project. He went on working, now as a conditional corpse. Only eight months later, when the radio tower went into operation, was his sentence repealed.

65 *the postilion's horn ... in which, like a snail in its shell, the tunes had frozen up so as to come out of their own accord when the warmth and spring returned:* The mythical Munchausen left Russia in the bitter cold, traveling day and night by post. On narrow roads the postilion tried to signal with his horn to warn oncoming travelers, but no sound came out. At the next stage, the postilion hung his horn up by the kitchen fire and suddenly: *Tereng! Tereng, teng, teng!* The tunes, which had frozen up in the horn, came out of their own accord by thawing.

66 *a certain archivist from Hanover:* Rudolf Erich Raspe, the author of *Baron Munchausen's Narrative of his Marvellous Travels and Campaigns in Russia* (1785).

67 *Some people champion the slogan EVERYONE INTO THE STREETS for love:* An allusion to "Down with Shame!," a pro-nudist movement promoted by Alexandra Kollontai, the Bolshevik feminist and champion of promiscuity. In September 1924, Mikhail Bulgakov noted in his diary that "absolutely naked people (men and women) appeared the other day on the streets of Moscow with 'Down with Shame!' banners over their shoulders. They boarded a tram. Passengers balked, and tried to stop the tram."

67 *others will fight tooth and nail to keep the home fires burning:* "One prominent university professor... advises Russian youth in almost St. Paul's own words that it is better to marry than to burn. 'Take a wife,' says this professor, 'a woman who shares your earnest ideals and will collaborate in your work for the communist state; be as continent as possible, because sex is a waste of vital energy which the state needs.'" See Dorothy Thompson, *The New Russia* (New York: Henry Holt, 1928), 275–76.

Titian's Amor Sacro *and* Amor Profano, *shown sitting peaceably either side of a well:* An allusion to Titian's *Sacred and Profane Love*, a symbolically mysterious painting (ca. 1514) of two women seated on an ancient Roman sarcophagus filled with water.

"A great start is worth more than money": An allusion to a famous pamphlet by Lenin (*A Great Start*, July 1919) in praise of communist subbotniks, unpaid days of voluntary labor for the good of society, "the actual beginning of communism."

"We merely increase or decrease the distance between bodies—nature does the rest": An allusion to an aphorism in Bacon's *Novum Organum* (1620): "Towards the effecting of works, all that man can do is to put together or put asunder natural bodies. The rest is done by nature working within." (Translated by James Spedding et al.)

living conditions in the country from which I have just returned will not permit of any further decrease in distances: An allusion to that signature Soviet invention, the communal apartment. "An apartment originally intended for a single family becomes home for half a dozen or more families, depending on the number of rooms, the largest of which may be subdivided.... This way of life, aside from being incredibly cramped, involves constant contact with total strangers." See Andrei Sinyavsky, *Soviet Civilization* (New York: Arcade, 1990), 165–66.

68 *Restoration of the Soviet economy... began with the beams that people began casting out of each other's eyes. In the past they had been loath to notice even the motes:* A mixture of two gospels, Christian (Matthew 7:5) and Soviet (a famous photograph of Lenin shows him pitching in at a subbotnik on the Kremlin grounds by helping to haul a log).

68   *A FISH ROTS FROM THE HEAD DOWN*: A Russian catchphrase meaning that corruption starts at the top (of the government, army, etc.); all bad things come from the powers that be.

SAVE YOUR SOLES: A number of Soviet posters of the period advertised the powers of rubber galoshes against rain and slush; some were produced by Mayakovsky.

Thus it was that I, while consultant to a Moscow theater director, advised him to stage Gogol's Inspector General *on my grand scale... [turning] everything upside down*: An allusion to the avant-garde Moscow stage director Vsevolod Meyerhold, whose dynamic montages rendered plays unrecognizable. In his hands, Martinet's *Night* became *The World Turned Upside Down*. His extravagant and exhausting production of *The Inspector General* (1926) had, according to some critics, no Gogol in it. Others derided Meyerhold for the inflated role he had given his ambitious actress wife, Zinaida Raikh. "A major point of contention is his use of velvet and silk, fourteen costumes for his wife," Walter Benjamin wrote in his *Moscow Diary*, "the performance, moreover, lasts five and a half hours."

Gogol's Inspector General: A social satire (1836) about a minor civil servant, Khlestakov, from St. Petersburg who, stuck in a small provincial town, is mistaken by the corrupt officials there for a government inspector. Khlestakov plays along while wooing the governor's daughter and wife. He is found out when a boastful letter to a friend in St. Petersburg is read by the local postmaster, though by then he has skipped town.

The play, as we envisaged it, would be called Thirty Thousand Messengers: *the main plot would shift from the individual to the masses:* Meyerhold, who publicly embraced the Bolshevik revolution, soon launched a movement (Theatrical October) to revolutionize the theater with politically relevant performances for a mass audience.

70   *to play the thirty thousand messengers we had engaged two military divisions from districts near Moscow:* An allusion to Yuri Annenkov's *Hymn to Liberated Labor* (1920), a one-off, open-air mass spectacle, whose cast of four thousand included (in the last act) units of Red Army infantry and cavalry. "The primitive plot consisted of three acts: the oppression of labor by capital, labor's fight for liberation, the triumph of

labor over capital. . . . In a formal sense the newest and most interesting achievement was precisely this participation of the Red Army, i.e. the introduction of concrete pieces of reality into a theatrical performance. Subsequently this device was often used in Meyerhold's theater." Yuri Annenkov, *Teatr! Teatr!* (Moscow: MIK, 2013), 216, 217.

70 *the general economic revival:* Lenin's New Economic Policy (NEP), a temporary return to private trade in the 1920s.

Saint Vladimir: Canonized Grand Prince Vladimir I of Kievan Rus; in 986, according to the *Primary Chronicle,* he chose Christian Orthodoxy over Islam because "Russians find merriment in drink, without which we cannot think."

From this proto-rhyme . . . sprang all of Russian versification: An allusion to the half-Scottish, Georgian-born, St. Petersburg–educated orientalist and linguist Nikolai Marr, an esteemed academician who in 1924 maintained that all the world's languages sprang from a proto-language consisting of "four elements": *sal, ber, yon,* and *rosh.*

71 *A respected physiologist presented ILP studies in the electrification of thought:* An allusion to Bernard Kazhinsky (1890–1962), a Soviet engineer and pioneer of the "brain radio" hypothesis. In 1922 he launched his scientific work in Moscow with a lecture called "Human Thought Is Electricity." His 1923 book *Peredacha myslei* (Thought Transference) contained the blueprint of an "electromagnetic microscope" for receiving and registering brain thought emissions.

"The State is organized violence . . .": Said by Gandhi: "The State represents violence in a concentrated and organized form."

72 *"The state is a necessary stage . . .":* Said by Marx: "Between capitalist and communist society lies . . . a political transition period in which the state can be nothing but the revolutionary dictatorship of the proletariat."

73 *Having cut off the hair, one does not cry over the head:* An inversion of the Russian saying, "Having cut off the head, one does not cry over the hair."

this legend about a Frenchman who traveled to Moscow in 1761: Munchausen is half remembering a half-forgotten Frenchman of flesh and blood. Jean Chappe d'Auteroche (1728–1769), an abbot and astronomer, was sent to Tobolsk (Siberia) in 1761 to observe the transit of Venus. He stopped in Moscow to replace his sledges, "broken to pieces with the continual shocks they had received" on the way from St. Petersburg. After that Chappe's pace was fairly relentless, to the despair of his clockmaker and interpreter. At Tobolsk, he set up an observatory. Unused to foreigners, the locals took this strange man with a nineteen-foot telescope for a magician. They blamed the catastrophic floods of that spring on him. He had frightened the stars. Undeterred, Chappe went on taking notes ("love of glory and one's country are unknown in Russia where despotism destroys the spirit, talent and all manner of feeling... no one dares think in Russia... fear is, so to speak, the only force that animates the entire nation") and talking to the odd prelate. His unflattering account (*Voyage en Sibérie fait par ordre du roi en 1761*) so enraged Catherine the Great that she published a refutation. Politics aside, Chappe had mangled many names, including those of churches.

74 *Wet Nikola:* A seventeenth-century church that stood near a pier on the Moscow River; Nikola (Nicholas the Miracleworker) was also a patron saint of seafarers, whom he often saved from drowning.

Nikola Red Bells: A seventeenth-century church known for the unusually beautiful ("red") sound of its bells.

Nikola on Three Hills: A seventeenth-century church built on high ground outside Moscow's Three-Hills Gate.

Nikola in the Pillars: A seventeenth-century church whose name may in part derive from its icon of the pillar saint Simeon Stylites.

Nikola in Pyzhi: A seventeenth-century church whose name derives from its locale, a place in Zamoskvorechye.

Nikola on Chicken Legs: The official name of a seventeenth-century church built near Tsar Aleksei Mikhailovich's chicken yard. By the 1920s it stood on Great Molchanovka Street, a stone's throw from Small Molchanovka Street.

Nikola in the Carpenters: A seventeenth-century church in a carpenters' settlement on the Arbat; Nikola was also a patron saint of the poor.

76 *Every house...is on rooster legs:* Munchausen is mangling an idiom. He means "on chicken legs." He is referring both to the hut on
chicken legs inhabited by the old folktale sorceress Baba Yaga and to all
rickety Russian houses, literal and figurative.

the inscription over the gates of Dante's hell: "Abandon hope, all ye
who enter here."

77 *Zabelin:* Ivan Zabelin (1820–1908), an historian-archaeologist; the
author of *History of the City of Moscow* (in Russian, 1905).

78 *Floating toward me was an enormous square: in the center of the
square, with five crosses raised up to the sky, stood a cathedral:* The Cathedral of Christ the Savior, commissioned by Nicholas I in 1837 and completed more than forty years later under Alexander II.

Standing with hand outstretched: Like Lenin, pointing the way to
communism.

80 *like the biblical Ruth gleaning ears of corn dropped by the sickle:*
Ruth 2:2–3.

81 *"eternal return":* Or eternal recurrence, an ancient doctrine which
holds that every actual state of affairs must recur an infinite number of
times; Nietzsche proposed something of the kind in *Thus Spake Zara-
thustra* (1883–1885).

I could hear them sealing my boxcar shut: Munchausen is being returned to Germany by the Russians in 1923 the same way Lenin was returned to Russia by the Germans in 1917.

6. THE THEORY OF IMPROBABILITY

88 *Scientists Welfare Commission: Komissiya po uluchsheniyu byta
uchenykh* (KUBU); created in 1920 in Petrograd by Maxim Gorky to
provide Soviet scientists and writers with food, shoes, clothes, and medicine. "This establishment to fight indigence was located on Million-
naya Street. The scientists who came there in rags, in torn shoes, with
bast sacks and children's sleds, were given a week's ration: so many
ounces of horsemeat, so much buckwheat, salt, tobacco, fat substitutes
and a bar of chocolate." Yuri Annenkov, *Dnevnik moikh vstrech* (Moscow: Khudozhestvennaya literatura, 1991), I, 33.

88 *American Relief Administration:* An American relief mission after World War I to Europe and later to Soviet Russia (1921–1923) in the wake of widespread famine.

the widow's mite: The small offering that represents a large sacrifice on the part of the giver (Mark 12:42).

89 *Bernoulli's theorem:* Or the law of large numbers, a fundamental theorem in probability theory first proven by Jacob Bernoulli (1654–1705), a Swiss mathematician. This law describes what happens when the same experiment is repeated a large number of times: The greater the number of trials, the closer the results will come to the expected value.

91 *seven-leagued boots:* Boots that allow the wearer to take strides of seven leagues. They appear in European folklore, including in Adelbert von Chamisso's *Peter Schlemihl* (1814). Peter, who has sold his shadow to the devil, bargains at a fair for some old boots that turn out to be seven-leagued. Shut out from human society by his shadowlessness, he strides all over the natural world "spread out like a rich garden before me."

7. THE HERMIT OF BODENWERDER

96 *But didn't the great Stagirite say: "My friends, there is no friendship in this world!":* In *The Nicomachean Ethics*, Aristotle (384–322 BC) distinguishes between passing friendship, based on utility or pleasure, and perfect friendship, based on a mutual desire for each other's good.

antinomy: A contradiction between two philosophical principles, each taken to be true.

99 *(q), the letter by which mathematicians denote failure:* In a Bernoulli trial, a random experiment such as the tossing of a coin, with only two possible outcomes, "success" and "failure"; then p equals probability of success (e.g., heads), and q equals probability of failure (e.g., tails).

101 *blood and dirt:* Capital, as described by Marx in *Das Kapital*: "If money, according to Augier, 'comes into the world with a congenital blood-stain on one cheek,' capital comes dripping from head to foot, from every pore, with blood and dirt." (Translated by Samuel Moore et al.)

minor mystifiers, all those Macphersons, Mérimées, and Chattertons: The Scottish poet James Macpherson (1736–1796), the French novelist and dramatist Prosper Mérimée (1803–1870), and the English poet Thomas Chatterton (1752–1770), authors of successful literary hoaxes. Macpherson produced ostensible translations of epic poems by the ancient Gaelic bard Ossian. Mérimée passed off six of his own plays as translations from the work of a Spanish actress, the imaginary Clara Gazul. Chatterton presented his archaic poems as the work of a fifteenth-century monk, the nonexistent Thomas Rowley.

103 *all those Pascals, Brunos, and Newtons had also begun with trifles, only to suffer thereafter from—ugh ... acute chronic hypotheses non fingo:* Blaise Pascal (1623–1662), a French mathematician, physicist, and moralist; Giordano Bruno (1548–1600), an Italian philosopher, Dominican, and unorthodox thinker denounced to the Inquisition; and Newton (see note above) whose phrase *hypotheses non fingo* ("I frame no hypotheses") appears in his *General Scholium* (1713): "Hitherto we have explained the phenomena of the heavens and of our sea by the power of gravity, but have not yet assigned the cause of this power ... and I frame no hypotheses." (Translated by Andrew Motte)

parallel fifths: Or consecutive fifths, a recurrence of the same interval between two parts or voices; long an object of academic condemnation.

104 *the famine on the Volga:* "Famine swept the Volga in 1921; in that year and the one following, it and the diseases that rode with it—typhus, typhoid, dysentery and cholera—would kill perhaps five million." See Brian Moynahan, *The Russian Century,* 118.

I did not realize that the extinguished Tale of the Unextinguished Moon *echoed a fact that took place with you on your way from the border to Moscow:* Pilnyak's tale (see note above) was "extinguished" by the Politburo, which ordered the entire print run of the issue of *Novy Mir* in which it appeared withdrawn from circulation. In the tale's epilogue, a little girl gazes at the moon from her window and tries to blow it out.

about that empty pedestal, it does exist: In 1918, the Bolsheviks knocked down the statue of Alexander III by the Cathedral of Christ the Savior. They left the pedestal intact for an anticipated statue of Liberated Labor. The statue was never executed; the huge pedestal stood empty until 1931 when it was razed along with the cathedral.

104 *a papier-mâché Tsar Alexander:* Alexander II, the "Tsar Libera-
tor"; he had planned to consecrate the Cathedral of Christ the Savior in
1881, but was assassinated shortly beforehand.

105 *Moscow's bushels and prophet:* Soviet Moscow's dissenting intellectuals and foremost philosopher Nikolai Berdyaev.

106 *Lucretius Carus:* Roman poet and philosopher (ca. 98–55 BC); the
author of *On the Nature of Things*, a complete science of the universe. By
way of proving the infinity of the universe, Lucretius places a man on its
"extremest part" and has him try to throw a dart. Either way, says Lucretius, if "the dart would fly forward, or, hindered, stay...that's not the
end." (Translated by Thomas Creech)

107 *my phantasms won—always and invariably, that is, until I chanced
upon the country about which one cannot lie:* Soviet Russia. The world's
greatest liar, Munchausen, has been beaten at his own fantastical game
by still more fantastical Soviet reality. His tales of the USSR are, as it
turns out, not tales at all. Some of the facts they contain are mentioned
in these notes.

   that flat square between black and white waters: The USSR, bounded
   to the north by the White Sea and to the south by the Black Sea.

   *I heard her gigantic crenellations crash to the ground, and then out
   of nowhere, there she was again, her bloody battlements towering over the
   lattice of meridians:* Here the red queen is a symbol of Soviet rule, which
   by 1927, when Krzhizhanovsky sat down to write his *Munchausen*, appeared indomitable and aspired to world supremacy.

8. THE TRUTH THAT DODGED THE MAN

114 *the empty square inside the black typographical rule:* The title page
of the first printed mock-sermon on the mock-saint Nemo (ca. 1510) was
illustrated with an empty frame and the caption: *Figura neminis quia
nemo in ea depictus* (A picture of nobody because nobody is depicted in
it). See Gerta Calmann, "The Picture of Nobody: An Iconographical
Study," *Journal of the Warburg and Courtauld Institutes*, vol. 23, no. 1/2
(1960): 64.

ACKNOWLEDGMENTS

FOR THEIR contributions to our work on Krzhizhanovsky, beginning with *Seven Stories* (GLAS, 2006), we thank Natasha Perova, Robert Chandler, Caryl Emerson, Maxim Amelin, Sergei Kazachkov, Solomon Apt, Anatoly Teriokhin, Vassili Belov, Katerina Grigoruk, Daniel McBain, Alisa Ballard, Stephen Twilley, and Vadim Perelmuter.

—J.T. *and* N.F.

TITLES IN SERIES

For a complete list of titles, visit www.nyrb.com or write to:
Catalog Requests, NYRB, 435 Hudson Street, New York, NY 10014

J.R. ACKERLEY Hindoo Holiday*
J.R. ACKERLEY My Dog Tulip*
J.R. ACKERLEY My Father and Myself*
J.R. ACKERLEY We Think the World of You*
HENRY ADAMS The Jeffersonian Transformation
RENATA ADLER Pitch Dark*
RENATA ADLER Speedboat*
AESCHYLUS Prometheus Bound; translated by Joel Agee*
LEOPOLDO ALAS His Only Son *with* Doña Berta*
CÉLESTE ALBARET Monsieur Proust
DANTE ALIGHIERI The Inferno
KINGSLEY AMIS The Alteration*
KINGSLEY AMIS Dear Illusion: Collected Stories*
KINGSLEY AMIS Ending Up*
KINGSLEY AMIS Girl, 20*
KINGSLEY AMIS The Green Man*
KINGSLEY AMIS Lucky Jim*
KINGSLEY AMIS The Old Devils*
KINGSLEY AMIS One Fat Englishman*
KINGSLEY AMIS Take a Girl Like You*
ROBERTO ARLT The Seven Madmen*
WILLIAM ATTAWAY Blood on the Forge
W.H. AUDEN (EDITOR) The Living Thoughts of Kierkegaard
W.H. AUDEN W.H. Auden's Book of Light Verse
ERICH AUERBACH Dante: Poet of the Secular World
DOROTHY BAKER Cassandra at the Wedding*
DOROTHY BAKER Young Man with a Horn*
J.A. BAKER The Peregrine
S. JOSEPHINE BAKER Fighting for Life*
HONORÉ DE BALZAC The Human Comedy: Selected Stories*
HONORÉ DE BALZAC The Unknown Masterpiece *and* Gambara*
VICKI BAUM Grand Hotel*
SYBILLE BEDFORD A Legacy*
SYBILLE BEDFORD A Visit to Don Otavio: A Mexican Journey*
MAX BEERBOHM The Prince of Minor Writers: The Selected Essays of Max Beerbohm*
MAX BEERBOHM Seven Men
STEPHEN BENATAR Wish Her Safe at Home*
FRANS G. BENGTSSON The Long Ships*
ALEXANDER BERKMAN Prison Memoirs of an Anarchist
GEORGES BERNANOS Mouchette
MIRON BIAŁOSZEWSKI A Memoir of the Warsaw Uprising*
ADOLFO BIOY CASARES Asleep in the Sun
ADOLFO BIOY CASARES The Invention of Morel
EVE BABITZ Eve's Hollywood*
EVE BABITZ Slow Days, Fast Company: The World, the Flesh, and L.A.*
CAROLINE BLACKWOOD Corrigan*
CAROLINE BLACKWOOD Great Granny Webster*

* *Also available as an electronic book.*

DANIEL PAUL SCHREBER Memoirs of My Nervous Illness
JAMES SCHUYLER Alfred and Guinevere
JAMES SCHUYLER What's for Dinner?*
SIMONE SCHWARZ-BART The Bridge of Beyond*
LEONARDO SCIASCIA The Day of the Owl
LEONARDO SCIASCIA Equal Danger
LEONARDO SCIASCIA The Moro Affair
LEONARDO SCIASCIA To Each His Own
LEONARDO SCIASCIA The Wine-Dark Sea
VICTOR SEGALEN René Leys*
ANNA SEGHERS Transit*
PHILIPE-PAUL DE SÉGUR Defeat: Napoleon's Russian Campaign
GILBERT SELDES The Stammering Century*
VICTOR SERGE The Case of Comrade Tulayev*
VICTOR SERGE Conquered City*
VICTOR SERGE Memoirs of a Revolutionary
VICTOR SERGE Midnight in the Century*
VICTOR SERGE Unforgiving Years
SHCHEDRIN The Golovlyov Family
ROBERT SHECKLEY The Store of the Worlds: The Stories of Robert Sheckley*
GEORGES SIMENON Act of Passion*
GEORGES SIMENON Dirty Snow*
GEORGES SIMENON Monsieur Monde Vanishes*
GEORGES SIMENON Pedigree*
GEORGES SIMENON Three Bedrooms in Manhattan*
GEORGES SIMENON Tropic Moon*
GEORGES SIMENON The Widow*
CHARLES SIMIC Dime-Store Alchemy: The Art of Joseph Cornell
MAY SINCLAIR Mary Olivier: A Life*
WILLIAM SLOANE The Rim of Morning: Two Tales of Cosmic Horror*
SASHA SOKOLOV A School for Fools*
VLADIMIR SOROKIN Ice Trilogy*
VLADIMIR SOROKIN The Queue
NATSUME SŌSEKI The Gate*
DAVID STACTON The Judges of the Secret Court*
JEAN STAFFORD The Mountain Lion
CHRISTINA STEAD Letty Fox: Her Luck
GEORGE R. STEWART Names on the Land
STENDHAL The Life of Henry Brulard
ADALBERT STIFTER Rock Crystal*
THEODOR STORM The Rider on the White Horse
JEAN STROUSE Alice James: A Biography*
HOWARD STURGIS Belchamber
ITALO SVEVO As a Man Grows Older
HARVEY SWADOS Nights in the Gardens of Brooklyn
A.J.A. SYMONS The Quest for Corvo
MAGDA SZABÓ The Door*
MAGDA SZABÓ Iza's Ballad*
ANTAL SZERB Journey by Moonlight*
ELIZABETH TAYLOR Angel*
ELIZABETH TAYLOR A Game of Hide and Seek*
ELIZABETH TAYLOR A View of the Harbour*
ELIZABETH TAYLOR You'll Enjoy It When You Get There: The Stories of Elizabeth Taylor*
TEFFI Memories: From Moscow to the Black Sea*

Ⓑ 8117

$ 3⁵⁰

Happy
Birthday
Fran

Fran Nancy &
Jeff

Christmas 1980

D0972278

The Best
of
Sholom
Aleichem

*Edited by Irving Howe
and Ruth R. Wisse*

A TOUCHSTONE BOOK

*Published by Simon and Schuster
New York*

Copyright © 1979 by New Republic Books
All rights reserved
including the right of reproduction
in whole or in part in any form
First Touchstone Edition, 1980
Published by Simon and Schuster
A Division of Gulf & Western Corporation
Simon & Schuster Building
Rockefeller Center
1230 Avenue of the Americas
New York, New York 10020
TOUCHSTONE and colophon are trademarks of Simon & Schuster
Published by arrangement with New Republic Books
Designed by Susan Marsh
Manufactured in the United States of America

The publishers wish to acknowledge the following copyright holders:

"Yom Kippur Scandal," "The Clock That Struck Thirteen," "Home for Passover," and "Dreyfus in Kasrilevke," are taken from THE OLD COUNTRY by Sholom Aleichem, translated by Julius and Frances Butwin. © Copyright 1946, 1974 by Crown Publishers, Inc. Used by permission of Crown Publishers, Inc.

"The Bubble Bursts," "Chava," "Get Thee Out," and "If I Were Rothschild" are taken from TEVYE'S DAUGHTERS by Sholom Aleichem, translated by Frances Butwin. © Copyright 1949, 1977 by The Children of Sholom Aleichem and Crown Publishers, Inc. Used by permission of Crown Publishers, Inc.

"On Account of a Hat," and "Eternal Life," are from TREASURY OF YIDDISH STORIES, edited by Irving Howe and Eliezer Greenberg. © Copyright 1953, 1954 by The Viking Press, Inc. Reprinted by permission of Viking Penguin, Inc.

All the stories in this book are translated and reprinted with the permission of the Family of Sholom Aleichem, and their cooperation is gratefully acknowledged.

1 2 3 4 5 6 7 8 9 10

Library of Congress Cataloging in Publication Data

Rabinowitz, Sholom, 1859-1916.
    The best of Sholom Aleichem.
    "A Touchstone book."
    1. Jews in Eastern Europe—Fiction. I. Howe,
Irving. II. Wisse, Ruth R. III. Title.
[PZ3.R113Bc 1980] [PJ5129.R2] 839'.0933   80-12492
ISBN 0-671-41092-X Pbk.

Contents

Introduction

HOW DO TWO editors write an essay together when one lives in New York City and the other in Montreal? They follow the epistolary tradition of Yiddish literature and send one another letters. That is what we did, sent real letters that we soon began to look forward to receiving. It could have gone on almost forever, but we stopped because Sholom Aleichem said, "Enough, children, enough."

IH to RW

Reading through the Sholom Aleichem stories we have brought together, I have an uneasy feeling that this is a Sholom Aleichem seldom before encountered. Or at least, seldom before recognized. Yet the stories, apart from the few translated here for the first time, are familiar enough, part of the Sholom Aleichem canon.

The writer universally adored as a humorist, the writer who could make both Jews and Gentiles laugh, and most remarkable of all, the writer who could please *every kind of Jew*, something probably never done before or since—this writer turns out to be imagining, beneath the scrim of his playfulness and at the center of his humor, a world of uncertainty, shifting perception, anxiety, even terror.

Let no innocent reader be alarmed: the stories are just as funny as everyone has said. But they now seem to me funny in a way that almost no one has said. Certainly if you look at the essay on Sholom Aleichem

The Best of Sholom Aleichem

by the preeminent Yiddish critic S. Niger, which Eliezer Greenberg and I anthologized in our *Voices from the Yiddish*, you will find described there a writer of tenderness and cleverness, with a profound grasp of Jewish life (all true, of course)—but not the Sholom Aleichem I now see.

Is my view a distortion, the kind induced by modernist bias and training? I'm aware of that danger and try to check myself, but still. . . . As I read story after story, I find that as the Yiddish proverb has it, "a Jew's joy is not without fright," even that great Jew who has in his stories brought us more joy than anyone else. True, there are moments of playfulness, of innocent humor, as in the portions of the adventures of Mottel the orphan that we've excerpted here—he, so to say, is Sholom Aleichem's Tom Sawyer. But the rest: a clock strikes thirteen, a hapless young man drags a corpse from place to place, a tailor is driven mad by the treachery of his perceptions, the order of *shtetl* life is undone even on Yom Kippur, Jewish children torment their teacher unto sickness. And on and on.

Perhaps the ferocious undercurrent in Sholom Aleichem's humor has never been fully seen, or perhaps Jewish readers have been intent on domesticating him in order to distract attention from the fact that, like all great writers, he can be very disturbing.

No, he isn't Kafka, and I don't at all want him to be. (The world doesn't need more than one Kafka.) Still, aren't there some strands of connecting sensibility? When Kafka read his stories aloud, he roared with laughter. And now, in reading Sholom Aleichem, I find myself growing nervous, anxious, even as I keep laughing. Like all great humorists, he attaches himself to the disorder which lies beneath the apparent order of the universe, to the madness beneath the apparent sanity. In many of the stories one hears the timbre of the problematic.

Of course, I'm exaggerating a little—but not much. And what I'm not trying to say is merely that we now see Sholom Aleichem as a self-conscious, disciplined artist rather than merely a folk-voice (or worse yet, the "folksy" tickler of Jewish vanities). For while it is true that Sholom Aleichem is tremendously close to the oral tradition of Yiddish folklore (you once remarked that a number of his stories are elaborations, or complications, of folk anecdotes), still, that folk material is itself not nearly so comforting or soft as later generations of Jews have liked to suppose.

Given the nature of Jewish life in Europe these past several centuries, how could the folk tradition have been as comforting or soft as it has

viii

come down to us through both the popularizers and the sentimentality of people who have broken from the Jewish tradition even as they have felt drawn to it? The Chelm stories, the Hershel Ostropolier stories, the Hasidic tales, even sometimes the folk songs: all have their undercurrents of darkness. Life may have been with people, but the people often lived in fright. Sholom Aleichem, then, seems to me a great writer who, like all the Yiddish writers of his moment, was close to folk sources yet employed them for a complicated and individual vision of human existence. That means terror and joy, dark and bright, fear and play. Or terror in joy, dark in bright, fear in play.

Am I wrong?

RW to IH

Your concluding words remind me of the description by Ba'al Makhshoves (the Yiddish critic and one of Sholom Aleichem's earliest admirers), of the feeling we have when we think we've committed a terrible sin, or experienced catastrophe, and wish it were all just a dream. This, according to him, is Sholom Aleichem's incomparable achievement: he conjures up the collective anxiety and then dispels it magically, laughing the danger away.

I guess Sholom Aleichem's contemporaries took the nightmarish uncertainties for granted and enjoyed the relief he alone provided. But you're right. Nowadays his name has become such a byword for folksy good humor, innocent "laughter through tears," that we're surprised to rediscover the undertone of threat in his work. It may be, as you say, our "modernist bias" that attracts us to the darker side, but there it *is*, menacing and grotesque. There is fear, not just confusion, and guilt, a nastier emotion than sorrow. That recurring image of the sick father, once powerful but now coughing fitfully between sentences, or the humiliated teacher, never able to recover his authority, suggests the fatal weakness in the culture and—more to the point—the narrator's sense of his own shared culpability in having brought it low.

And actually, how could it be otherwise? For the author of these works is a sophisticated literary man, living at some remove from the insular and cohesive society he delights in depicting. Remember I told you how startled I was to find that all the correspondence between the author and his family, his wife and children, was in Russian, obviously the language of the home. Unlike Tevye, Sholom Aleichem encouraged his children's Russification, realizing that the centrifugal force of change would leave little of the old way of life intact. Oh, to be sure, he was still the product of "tradition," and confined to a Jewish fate. Raised in a Ukrainian *shtetl*, he later suffered the indignities of living in Kiev without a residence permit, scrambled like a thousand other Menachem-Mendels to provide for his family, fled the pogroms, joined the great migration to America. In some ways it's the very typical Jewish story. But he was also the consummate artist, working the full range of modern literary genres; the shrewd journalist, attuned to every nuance of socialist, Zionist, or assimilationist politics and polemics; the exacting editor, forging a new cultural idiom and enjoying a cosmopolitan milieu. Small wonder that there is so much masking and unmasking in his stories, so many instances of dislocation and social ambiguity. Everyone was remaking himself, with varying degrees of success. And among them was Sholom Rabinowitz, experiencing all the personal and social upheavals that as "Sholom Aleichem" he would reorder with amusing grace.

Far from distorting, your comments begin to set the record straight. And if you're particularly struck by the generally overlooked "ferocity" of the work, I'm amazed by the ingenious and *self-conscious* artist behind the widely accepted notion of the folk-voice. Take "Station Baranovich," one of the train stories we decided to include. Early Yiddish readers were likely to know that their author, the man you once called "the only modern writer who may truly be said to be a culture-hero," had suffered a complete collapse at that fateful stop during a grueling speaking tour, an attack of "acute pulmonary tuberculosis" that was followed by years of convalescence. At Baranovich the great entertainer, the spellbinding story teller, had almost left the train for good.

So much for fact. What about the fiction? The story is narrated by a traveling salesman. The passengers' conversation runs appropriately grim—to pogroms, murders, anti-Jewish decrees. The interior story of a certain Kivke, alternately a victim of the czarist regime and a blackmailer of his own community, might have been used by many another Jewish writer (God save us!) to demonstrate the demoralizing effects of persecution. But Sholom Aleichem, who at Baranovich was warned of his own mortality, makes this a writer's story: the fate of Kivke and of the Jewish community are ultimately in the hands of the gifted *story teller* whose untimely departure at Baranovich constitutes the story's only really fatal event. The artist can transform reality at will—a potent charm in desperate times—but his magic is subject to temporal claims. Hilarious the story is. But doesn't it also comment bitingly on the relation of the artist to his audience and to his material, of the audience to its artists and environment, of reality to art? It even manages a stroke of revenge in its parting shot: "May Station Baranovich burn to the ground!" Our colleagues analyzing "self-reflexiveness in art" should have a field day here!

It must be some fifty years since Van Wyck Brooks drew attention to Samuel Clemens lurking behind the sprightlier Mark Twain. If anything, we're a little late in exposing the negative, the harsher "World of Sholom Aleichem" and the canny Mr. Sholom Rabinowitz behind the man with the avuncular smile. Or should we stick to the compulsively naive and cheerful? As in his, "What's new with the cholera epidemic in Odessa?"

IH to RW

We've been stressing, so far, the "modern" Sholom Aleichem, a comic writer whose view of Jewish, and perhaps any other, life tends to be problematic, rather nervous, and streaked with those elements of guilt and anxiety that we usually associate with writers of the twentieth century. To see Sholom Aleichem in this way seems a necessary corrective to the view, now prevalent in Jewish life, that softens him into a toothless entertainer, a jolly gleeman of the *shtetl*, a fiddler cozy on his roof. And insofar as we reject or at least complicate this prevailing view, it's especially important to remark that Sholom Aleichem is not a "folk writer," whatever that might mean. No, he is a self-conscious artist, canny in his use of literary techniques, especially clever in his use of the monologue, which in his stories may seem to be meandering as pointlessly as an unemployed Jew on market day in the *shtetl* but which actually keeps moving toward a stringent and disciplined conclusion.

Still we should not go too far in trying to revise the common view of Sholom Aleichem. He came out of a culture in which the ferment of folk creation was still very lively, and in which the relationship between writer and audience was bracingly intimate, certainly different from what we have come to accept in Western cultures. A good many of Sholom Aleichem's stories are drawn from familiar or once-familiar folktales and anecdotes. One of his best stories, "The Haunted Tailor," is based on such materials, though as Sholom Aleichem retells it, the story emerges intellectually sharpened and complicated. It moves in its tone toward both the grotesque and the satiric, and in characterization it progresses from folk figure to individual. Tevye the dairyman, probably Sholom Aleichem's greatest character, emerges from the depths of Jewish folk experience in Eastern Europe, yet he is far more than a representative type. Tevye is a particularized Jew with his own nuances and idiosyncrasies, even as we also recognize in him a *shtetl* Everyman.

In Sholom Aleichem, then, the balance between collectivity and individual, between Jewish tradition and personal sensibility, is very fine. Coming at the point in the history of the Eastern European Jews where the coherence of traditional life has been shattered, only to let loose an enormous, fresh cultural energy, Sholom Aleichem stands as both firm guardian of the Jewish past and a quizzical, skeptical Jew prepared (as the unfolding of the Tevye stories makes clear) to encounter and maybe accept the novelty and surprise of modern Jewish life. It's just this balance, so delicate and precarious, that I find enchanting in his work. And this may be one reason that I think of him as a "culture hero," in the sense that Dickens and Mark Twain were culture heroes in their time and place. For Sholom Aleichem embodies the culture of the Eastern European Jews at a high point of consciousness, at the tremor of awareness that comes a minute before dissolution starts.

He embodies the essential values of Eastern European Jewish culture in the very accents and rhythms of his language, in the pauses and suggestions, the inside jokes and sly references. This relationship between the writer as culture hero and the culture itself is something so intimate and elusive we hardly have a way to describe it—except to say that every Jew who could read Yiddish, whether he was orthodox or secular, conservative or radical, loved Sholom Aleichem, for he heard in his stories the charm and melody of a common *shprakh,* the language that bound all together. The deepest assumptions of a people, those tacit gestures of bias which undercut opinion and rest on such intangibles as the inflection of a phrase, the movement of shoulders, the keening of despair, the melody of a laugh—all these form the inner substance of Sholom Aleichem's work.

Take as an example the brilliant little story, "A Yom Kippur Scandal." Wit and cleverness turn upon one another; the bare anecdote on which the story is based becomes an occasion for revealing the deepest feelings of a culture. Yet Sholom Aleichem's own quizzical voice is also heard at the end. There are at least two scandals: one that a stranger, a guest of the synagogue on the holiest of days, Yom Kippur, is robbed of a substantial sum of money (or pretends that he has been robbed); the other that a youth is a violator of the fast, discovered at the service with chicken bones hidden away. Both scandals are serious, but in the eyes of the rabbi, one of Sholom Aleichem's innocents, the first seems a sin against man, the second a sin against God, and thereby the second is the greater. Sholom Aleichem doesn't stop there, for he leaves the story up in the air—it is a characteristic narrative strategy of his—so that we don't know whether the stranger really was robbed, who did it, or how the problem was solved. As if that matters in the light of the greater scandal of the chicken bones, wildly funny as it struck many of the congregants! The story follows the Jewish habit of answering a question with another question: all life is a question, and if you ask me why, I can only answer, how should I know?

The dominant quality of Sholom Aleichem's work, then, seems to me not his wit or verbal brilliance or playfulness, remarkable as all these are; it is his sense of moral poise, his assurance as both Jew and human being, his ease in a world of excess. The image of the human, drawing upon traditional Jewish past and touching upon the problematic Jewish future, has seldom received so profound a realization as in these stories. His controlling voice tells us of madness, to be sure; but so long as we can hear *that* voice, we know the world is not yet entirely mad.

So I'd like to keep in balance the two Sholom Aleichems, the traditional and the modern, who, as we read him, are of course really one.

RW to IH

I've been thinking about your emphasis on the cultural balance and "moral poise" of Sholom Aleichem, wondering how much of what you describe derives from the historical moment, and just what is specific to him. The end of the nineteenth century, that very critical period for East European Jews, when they were still thickly rooted in their traditions but freshly vulnerable to social and political changes, provided great artists with a unique literary opportunity. Yiddish, the common language, was ripe for the kind of harvest yielded during the Renaissance, when Western European writers in an analogous period of secularization and rising national awareness, plowed their vernaculars with heady expectations of gain. There are periods when the culture and its language seem to be at just the right point of tension between maturity and untried possibilities. No accident that all three of the Yiddish classical masters—Mendele Mocher Sforim (Abramovitch), I. L. Peretz, and Sholom Aleichem (Rabinowitz)—flourished almost together.

But of the three, Sholom Aleichem alone really struck the note of balance. Mendele and Peretz were both embattled writers, fiercely critical of their society, and only gradually softened by pity, doubt, and age. As underpaid employees of the Jewish community—Mendele was a school principal and Peretz a bureaucratic official—they spent most of their adult years torn between the daily routine of duty and the personal drive for literary self-expression. The strain of this divided existence, and the resentment, shows in their work. Their writing has a strong dialectic tendency, pitting the old and new, the impulses and ideas against one another in sharp confrontations. Peretz's favorite literary arena is the law court. As for Abramovitch-Mendele, his fictional autobiography literally splits his personality in two and has the critical, crotchety intellectual facing the kindly philosophic book peddler with no middle ground between them.

Sholom Aleichem is different. Though he too felt the impending break in the "golden chain" of Jewish tradition, and felt the cracks in his own life, he makes it his artistic business to *close* the gap. In fact, wherever the danger of dissolution is greatest, the stories work their magic in simulating or creating a *terra firma*. Maybe this, in part, is what the

Yiddish critic, Borukh Rivkin, had in mind when he wrote that Sholom Aleichem provided the East European Jews with a fictional territory to compensate for their lack of a national soil.

The Tevye stories, of which we include a few, provide the most striking instance of stability where one would least expect it. If you follow the line of the plot, it traces nothing less than the breakup of an entire culture. At the beginning Tevye "makes a fortune," becomes a dairyman, and begins to provide for his large family. By the end he is a widower, supporting a destitute widowed daughter. A second daughter is in Siberia, a third is a convert, a fourth has committed suicide, the fifth—who married for money—has fled with her bankrupt husband to America. Tevye is attacked (albeit mildly) by his peasant neighbors and forced to flee from the land to which he feels he has as good a claim as anyone. He says, "What portion of the Bible are they reading this week? *Vayikro?* The first portion of Leviticus? Well, I'm on quite another chapter. *Leykh lekho:* get thee out. Get going, Tevye, they said to me, *get out of thy country and from thy father's house,* leave the village where you were born and spent all the years of your life and go—*unto the land that I will show thee*—wherever your two eyes lead you!" Pretty bitter stuff! God's mighty prophecy to Abraham of a promised land is applied by Tevye to himself with the caustic inversion of all the terms. This is Lear on the heath, but as his own jester. Tevye, who is actually defenseless against the barrage of challenges and attacks that lay him low, should have been a tragic victim. Instead, balancing his losses on the sharp edge of his tongue, he maintains the precarious posture of a comic hero.

All Tevye's misquotations, puns, and freewheeling interpretations that cause such hardship to even our best translators have been offered as proof of his simplicity and ignorance. Ridiculous! Tevye may not be the Vilna Gaon, but he is the original stand-up comic, playing to an appreciative audience of one: his impresario, Sholom Aleichem, who then passes on this discovered talent to us readers. Tevye has been endowed with such substantiality, so much adaptive vigor of speech and vision, that the dire events he recounts almost cease to matter. He gives proof of his creative survival even as he describes the destruction of its source. (I thought it was very fine when the Broadway production of *Fiddler on the Roof* placed Tevye, in the finale, on a revolving stage, as though he were taking his world along with him wherever he went.)

This character worked so well for Sholom Aleichem it's not surprising that he created other versions of Tevye, including the narrator of "A Thousand and One Nights" whom we're introducing here. Yankel Yonever of Krushnik is another sturdy father, telling Sholom Aleichem the sorry tales of his children—only here the events are uglier and deadlier. The Jews are trapped between the anti-Semitic Cossacks and the invading Germans in the murderous chaos of World War I. The survivors, Yankel the narrator and Sholom Aleichem his listener, are in flight from Russia, suspended aboard ship in midocean with no ground at all underfoot. Yet even here the effect is one of moral and psychological balance, though the author has gone as far as he can go in achieving it. Yankel describes how the venerable rabbi was murdered by the Cossacks and left hanging for three days in the public square. This is the kind of brutal reality Sholom Aleichem had always avoided, and, in fact, Yankel says that at first he refused to pass the square, unwilling to witness the shame with his own eyes. When he finally goes, though, what does he see? Not the terrifying symbol of Cossack might, but the rabbi *"hanging shimenesre,"* the eighteen benedictions. Whereas ordinary Jews stand in their daily recitation of these blessings, the rabbi sways back and forth in an ultimate act of devotion. The image is so comfortingly homey; it domesticates the violence and shows us the rabbi as we can bear to look at him. Without inflated rhetoric, it also transforms a vile humiliation into triumphant martyrdom. It's just the turn of the phrase that does it, the simple substitution of "hanging" for "standing" *shimenesre* in one of the commonest Yiddish terms for praying. The English, because of the need for explanation, has to work almost too hard for the required effect, pressing on consciousness as a deliberate interpretive act. In Yiddish the redemption seems effortless.

Reading the last chapters of Tevye and this ironic version of Sheherezade, the tales of "A Thousand and One Nights," all written during Sholom Aleichem's final years, I wonder whether he could have kept the "comedy" going much longer. It is almost impossible to avoid sentimentalizing on the one hand or falling into cynicism on the other when attempting a balanced humanism in the face of this kind of barbarity.

Introduction

IH to RW

I know we have to be moving along to the literary aspects of Sholom Aleichem's work: his inventiveness with language, his fondness for the monologue as a narrative form, his curious habit of seeming to end a story before it comes to climax. But I can't resist a few more words on the matter of "moral poise"—by which, of course, we mean not some abstract doctrine but a vibrant quality of the stories themselves, communicated through details of language. It's when you come to Sholom Aleichem's stories about children that you see how balanced, at once stringent and tender, severe and loving, is his sense of life.

Some of the children's stories, like "Bandits" and "The Guest," are not at all carefree. Their dominant tone is nervousness and fright, their dominant theme, the enforced discovery, at too early an age, of the bitterness of the world. Sholom Aleichem does not hesitate to register the psychic costs of traditional Jewish life, costs in denial, repression, narrowness. But there are other stories, happier in voice, where the life-force, the child's sheer pleasure in breathing and running, breaks through. In the group translated as "Mottel the Cantor's Son," from which we've taken a few self-contained portions, the tone is lighthearted and playful. If Tom Sawyer could speak Yiddish, he'd be at home here. It's as if Sholom Aleichem were intent upon reminding his Jewish readers that we too deserve a little of the world's innocence.

Mottel represents the sadly abbreviated childhood of the traditional *shtetl,* where life does not flow evenly from one phase of experience to another, but all of them, childhood, adolescence, and manhood, are compressed into one. But Mottel does not yet know this, or pretends not to know it—who can be sure which? He is a wonderful little boy, celebrating his friendship with a neighbor's calf and stealing apples from the gardens of the rich. He is full of that spontaneous nature which Jewish upbringing has not yet suppressed ("Upon one leg I hop outside and—naturally straight to our neighbor's calf"). But he has an eye for the life about him; he is beginning to seep up that quiet Jewish sorrow which is part of his life's heritage ("That's an old story: a mother's got to cry. What I'd like to know is whether all mothers cry all the time, like mine"). Perhaps in a kind of tacit rebellion against the heaviness, the weighted ethicism, of Jewish life, Sholom Aleichem makes Mottel into something of a scamp, especially in the breezy chapters we've excerpted here, where Mottel, after the death of his father the cantor, becomes a little businessman, selling the cider and ink that his overimaginative brother manufactures ("Jews, here's a drink:/Cider from heaven/If you order just one/You'll ask for eleven").

The Mottel stories are notable because the note they strike is heard infrequently in Yiddish literature. The hijinks of an adventurous boy, so favored in American and English writing, is something (I would guess) that Sholom Aleichem chose to write about only after conscious deliberation, as if to show his fellow Jews in Eastern Europe and in the American slums what life might be, or in their long-lost youth might once have been. In his autobiography Sholom Aleichem writes about childhood pleasures: ". . . this is not meant for you, Jewish children! Yellow sunflowers, sweet-smelling grass, fresh air, fragrant earth, the clear sun—forgive me, these are not meant for you. . . ." Mottel shows us what has been lost.

Still, even in the saddest and most burdened Yiddish writing, there is something else shown about the life of Jewish children, and now, in retrospect, this seems to form an overwhelming positive contrast to the literatures of our century. In Yiddish literature the family is still a cohesive unit; fathers may be strict, mothers tearful, brothers annoying, but love breaks through and under the barriers of ritual. If there are few carefree children in Yiddish literature, there are few unloved or brutalized children.

Perhaps all that I'm saying is that in the world of Sholom Aleichem there are still some remnants of community. And this gives him strength and security as a writer; simply because he is so much at home with his materials, he can move from one tone to another. The Mottel stories can be casual, offhand, charming, even mischievous, but then suddenly Sholom Aleichem will drop to a fierce irony, a harrowing sadness. At the end Mottel and his family are aboard ship for America. All is fun, pranks, jokes, and then comes a brief lyrical description of a Yom Kippur service in the hold of the ship, "a Yom Kippur," says this Jewish little boy, "that neither God nor man would ever forget." And it is a token of Sholom Aleichem's genius, his "moral poise," that we are entirely prepared to accept the claim that these words come from the same boy who sells cider and ink and hops on one leg toward the neighbor's calf.

RW to IH

The other day I came across a 1941 essay by Max Weinreich that runs oddly parallel to some of our main concerns. I say "oddly" because as a linguist Weinreich was dealing strictly with Sholom Aleichem's language and linguistic influence: yet he too concludes that the folksiness of Sholom Aleichem received undue attention and had a deleterious effect on its imitators, while the hard precision and richness of his language have gone almost unnoticed. Weinreich argues that the compulsive association of Yiddish with joking—an unfortunate tendency among modern Jews—has prevented a deeper appreciation of the master's verbal craftsmanship and artistic range.

It does seem that in its literary imitations of the voices and mannerisms of ordinary Jews, Sholom Aleichem's oral styles were almost *too* effective. Even sophisticated readers were so amused and dazzled by the natural flow of the language that they considered the writer to be a ventriloquist, his art a superior form of realism. As if Sholom Aleichem had anticipated the tape recorder!

This may be a compliment in its way, but in fact, the "artless garrulousness" of the characters is under surprisingly tight control, and in ways that translation may sometimes have to sacrifice. What, for example, can we do with the opening sentence of *"Dos tepl"* ("The Pot")—that famous Sholom Aleichem monologue: *"Rebbe! Ikh vil aykh fregn a shayle vil ikh aykh!"* Natural English can't attempt much more than "Rabbi, I've come to ask you a question." But the original circles back on itself, rather like this: "Rabbi, I want to ask you a question is what I want to do." The woman's circular style is the most accurate literary expression of the closed circle of her thoughts and her life. She labors within the same rounds of work and obligation set out for her by her mother; her son is dying of the very illness that claimed her husband; her poverty traps her in such narrow constraints of time and space that she cannot grasp those very possibilities that might mitigate her poverty. Above all, her mind is imprisoned in its own obsessive circularity, unable to come to the point even long enough to pose her question. Though her speech may be generally "true to life," it is actually used to give truth to her particular embattled consciousness, self-protecting and self-defeating in equal measure, and preoccupied with impending death.

At some point we would also have to admit that Sholom Aleichem's success as a stylist has frustrated our editorial choices, at least in part. The sly mockery of American Jewish assimilation, rendered through the crude, overeager borrowings of Yiddish immigrants fresh off the boat, falls flat in English, the host language. It's also difficult to distinguish in translation, as Sholom Aleichem does in the original, the many degrees of social climbers who oil their Yiddish with Russian phrases to ease the way up, and then slip comically on their malapropisms and mistakes. Sholom Aleichem's speakers are characterized as much by the quality of their language as by its apprehended meaning. I doubt that any translation can get this across.

In addition to being a marvelous tool, Yiddish is also Sholom Aleichem's metaphor for the culture. While many of his contemporaries and even some of his successors were hampered by the novelty of Yiddish as a modern literary language, Sholom Aleichem turned the fluidity and newness of Yiddish prose style to penetrating advantage. What better medium for conveying the critical changes of East European Jewish life than a "language of fusion"—to use Max Weinreich's term—in which the sources of fusion are still identifiable and in active flux? Sholom Aleichem uses the nuances of Yiddish to communicate the degree to which a speaker is integrated into the traditional culture or deviates from it in any direction—toward the "German" enlightenment, the Slavic identification with the folk, or the higher pretensions of St. Petersburg society. From the speaker's tendency to use certain aspects of the German or Slavic components of the language, one can determine his origins and aspirations, his relation to the values of his home, and the lure of the environment.

Yet too extreme an emphasis on the Hebraic element, the most indigenous component of Yiddish, is not a good sign either. Characters who affect too traditional a language are either sanctimonious hypocrites, like the members of the Burial Society in the story "Eternal Life," or con-artists of whom Sholom Aleichem provides a peerless variety. The positive characters are those who tend neither inward nor outward but speak a perfectly balanced tongue.

For Tevye, the most trustworthy of Sholom Aleichem's speakers, the fused elements of Yiddish are an eternal delight. Like a true musician, he enjoys showing the speed and grace with which he can skip from one

Introduction

note or one tone to another. His best jokes and quotations are polyglot, drawing attention to their mixture of high and low, old and new, indigenous and imported. He can use these combinations to achieve both comic and sentimental effects.

Even this technique of linguistic crosscutting, however, does not automatically guarantee a reliable character. Shimon-Eli, the haunted tailor, is like Tevye, a man who loves to speak in quotations which he translates, or mistranslates, or occasionally invents. His level of speech, like Tevye's, reveals his limited *cheder* education, his easy familiarity with the tradition, and an intellectual reach that exceeds its grasp. But Shimon-Eli uses quotations and linguistic jokes as clichés, the same stock phrases reappearing whoever the listener and whatever the situation. He moves instinctively back and forth through his repertoire, just as he passes through the same phases of his journey over and over again without reflection or insight. At the end, his failure to adapt, his application of tried explanations instead of fresh, deductive questions, dooms him to madness. Tevye's movement through levels of speech is the manifestation of his adaptive intelligence. Shimon-Eli's automatic movement through a similar set of paces is the surest sign of his stultification.

By the end of the nineteenth century, I. L. Peretz, who was quickly becoming the dominant influence in Yiddish literature, tried to stabilize a literary language for the purposes of normal narration. He drew attention away from the specificities of Yiddish, away from its folk expressions, the interplay of its source languages, the different dialects and levels of its various speakers. In Peretz's stories a Lithuanian rabbi and a Polish Hasid speak the same Yiddish.

But for Sholom Aleichem the unfixed nature of Yiddish was its greatest attraction, and its infinite range of dialects and oral styles the best literary means of capturing the dynamic changes—or the resistance to change—in the culture. There are times, reading Sholom Aleichem in the pulsating original, when I think we ought to have put out a Yiddish reader for the fortunate few who can use it, leaving translation to the gods.*

---

*The difficulties of translating Sholom Aleichem are almost beyond recounting. They go far deeper than the problem of rendering Yiddish idiom into English, a problem sometimes solved by finding enough English equivalents, and more often acknowledged as beyond solution because the Yiddish idiom is

IH to RW

In talking about Sholom Aleichem's stories, we both remarked on the seeming oddity that many of them do not really end. Especially in those told by an internal narrator (a character who is seen and heard telling a story either to other characters or to "Mr. Sholom Aleichem"), there is roughly the following sequence: the stories move toward climax, they arouse suspense, they bring together the elements of conflict, and then, just when you expect the writer to drive toward resolution, they seem deliberately to remain hanging in the air. They stop rather than end. And this happens often enough to make us suspect that it cannot be a mere accident or idiosyncrasy. Sholom Aleichem is a self-conscious artist and he must have had something in mind. Thus, in "A Yom Kippur Scandal" we never really find out who stole the money; in "The Haunted Tailor" we are spared following the central figure to his fate; and in "Station Baranovich" the story teller provocatively refuses to complete his story. What is this all about? I have a few speculations:

1. Sholom Aleichem is persisting in the old tradition of oral story telling (though, in fact, he is a literary artist and not an oral story teller)

so deeply planted in Jewish tradition it is virtually untranslatable. A more serious problem is that of rendering the Hebraic component, which in some stories like "The Haunted Tailor" and "Tevye Strikes It Rich," is crucial to the development of both narrative and meaning.

Previous translators have simply evaded this problem by omitting the Hebrew, either in translation or transliteration, and the result has been a serious impoverishment of the work. In the present volume such gifted translators as Leonard Wolf and Hillel Halkin struggle heroically with this difficulty, each employing a different approach. What compounds the difficulty here is that the relationship between the two languages, Hebrew and Yiddish, is so complex: at some points they are two separate languages, though historically linked, but at other points they form a linguistic continuum. Yet we may also be certain that for some of Sholom Aleichem's Yiddish readers these Hebrew passages, many of them taken from the Bible and some cleverly distorted for comic effect, were almost as inaccessible as they are for most English readers. The jokes, then, are not only on one or another character, but also on us, readers who have lost or abandoned the tradition.

which takes pleasure in leading the listener on, teasing him further and
further. Then, as if to demonstrate the emotional power of the narrator
or the moral perplexities of existence, there is a sudden, abrupt
blockage—as if to say, figure out the rest for yourself, make up whatever
denouement you can, it's all equally puzzling. . . .

2. Sholom Aleichem is suggesting rather slyly that, really, there are
far more important things in the world than the resolution of an external
action, suspenseful and exciting though it may be; indeed, what one
learns along a narrative journey matters more than the final destination.
Thus in "A Yom Kippur Scandal" the question of the visitor's money—
was it ever really there? did someone steal it? is he a confidence man?—
counts for very little in comparison with the scandal, the shocked
laughter, when it is discovered that one of the *shtetl's* pious young
favorites has been secretly nibbling on chicken bones during the fast day
of Yom Kippur. And the reasoning is obvious once you ponder it: the
money is merely a worldly matter, while the behavior of the youth raises
an issue of faith.

3. Sholom Aleichem often uses in these stories a narrating figure that
might be called "the clever Jew," one who is rather worldly though still
tied to some of the old ways of piety. This narrator has "been around," as
merchant or traveler. In his ambiguous person he seems to straddle old
world and new. Almost always there is a duel between the narrator and
his audience of gullible and/or skeptical listeners within the story; or
between the narrator and the readers of the story, who are in effect
challenged to figure out what to make of him; or sometimes, one
ventures to say, between the narrator and Sholom Aleichem himself,
who stands somewhat bemused by his own creation. The puzzlement
this narrator spins out in a story like "A Yom Kippur Scandal" becomes
a trail toward evident laughter and possible wisdom. In "Eternal Life"
the narrator is now an experienced man, one of those solid but still
reasonably pious merchants that Yiddish writers liked to use as the
center of their fictions. He recalls the foolishness but also the charming
innocence of his youth; and if he now flees from the prospect of seeking
"eternal life," is that, within the bounds of the world view by which he
purports to live, so entirely a gain in maturity and rightness? In "Dreyfus
in Kasrilevke" the narrator is placed within the action; he tells his
"stories" (the reports he reads in the paper about the Dreyfus case) to
other Jews in the little *shtetl* of Kasrilevke. At the end they refuse to
believe him; they cannot credit so gross an injustice. In their "rejection"

of this narrator figure, Sholom Aleichem has created an overpowering moment, a deeply poignant image of the Jewish refusal to believe in the full evil of the world. The "clever Jew" is thus shown in many aspects—complicated, quizzical, problematic.

4. Sholom Aleichem uses, as I've said, traditional devices of oral story telling, but he is also a sophisticated writer very much aware of his departures from that tradition. He can no longer regard a story as something that is always fixed, secure, knowable (e.g., the rebellious clock in "The Clock That Struck Thirteen," a wonderfully appropriate and homey image for the sense of collapsing order). Sholom Aleichem lived at a time when stories could be begun but not always brought to an end. Before him stories could be brought to an end; after him they could hardly be begun. What, then, one wonders, would he have made of Cocteau's remark that "Literature is a force of memory that we have not yet understood"? Perhaps he would have amended the last clause to "that we can no longer understand."

5. Sholom Aleichem knew intuitively that the boundary between comedy and tragedy is always a thin and wavering line—and for Jews, often nonexistent. Almost all of his best comic stories hover on the edge of disaster. All exemplify the truth of Saul Bellow's remark that in Jewish writing "laughter and trembling are so curiously intermingled that it is not easy to determine the relations of the two." Reading Sholom Aleichem is like wandering through a lovely meadow of laughter and suddenly coming to a precipice of doom. At the end of "The Haunted Tailor" we have a vista of madness, at the end of "A Passover Expropriation" a prospect of social violence, at the end of "A Yom Kippur Scandal" the shame of Jewish disintegration. Sholom Aleichem takes us by the hand, we are both shaking with laughter, and he leads us. . . . "And would you like to hear the rest of the story?" asks one of his narrators. "The rest isn't so nice." Assuredly not.

RW to IH

I appreciated your speculations on Sholom Aleichem's endings and narrative art. As a mundane footnote, one could also note the influence in this—as in every conceivable linguistic, stylistic, and

Introduction

narrative aspect of Sholom Aleichem's work—of Mendele Mocher Sforim, the man he dubbed the grandfather of modern Yiddish literature, the man who was really his own artistic progenitor. Indeed some of Mendele's finest work, also in the oral tradition, does not seem to end; but Sholom Aleichem draws attention to the inconclusiveness of his conclusions in a way his forerunner did not. It's as you say: he actively challenges our notion of the denouement or solution and avoids the verdict, the finality, of what would usually be an unhappy fate.

In general, Sholom Aleichem did not do very well with a direct approach to the great, climactic, and decisive moments of plot. When he did attempt a big love scene, or a tough social confrontation, he could be surprisingly inept. You have only to look at one of his earliest efforts, the thinly disguised autobiographical novella where the wealthy young heroine, who has been playing fantasias by moonlight, rushes through the garden and into the arms of her indigent tutor to the following momentous dialogue:

He: Polinka!
She: Rabovsky!

Impossible to read the scene without laughing—at the author's expense.

Lest this seem just the failure of a novice, one could turn to a ripe novel, like *The Storm* (1905), where Sholom Aleichem depicts the ideological clashes among the Jews in pre-Revolutionary Russia. At the moment of intended climax, when the Zionist hero is to win over the uncommitted heroine to both his politics and himself, he can do no better than to stop in the middle of the street, whip from his pocket a famous poem by Chaim Nachman Bialik, and *read* her its text for the better part of the chapter! It is not that Sholom Aleichem avoided the romantic subject, the heroic possibility, the grand style of the novel: he was simply unconvincing and demonstrably *uncomfortable* in this mode, especially at the high points of resolution, and of course, conclusion.

No, his mastery is of quite the opposite order. Beginning with no more than an anecdote, sometimes an item that his adoring readers sent him, sometimes a joke that already had whiskers on it, he would invent a speaker, give him a story to tell and the merest pretext for a tale—the amusement of a fellow passenger, the enlightenment of a stranger to town, etc. The story would be either about himself, or more often, about

xxv

a third party, someone from his *shtetl* perhaps, more of a character type than a differentiated personality. And if that were not layered and indirect enough, the speaker would tell the story not to the readers, but to an intermediary who was often the author's invented self, this all-embracing soul called "Sholom Aleichem." Veiled, then, like Salome, the anecdote begins its tantalizing, captivating play, a dance of words that is meant to leave you, as the author boasts, laughing your head off!

The kernel "story" of "On Account of a Hat," one of your favorites, I know, was once told to me as a regional Jewish joke, in about ten seconds. Out of this insubstantial matter, Sholom Aleichem has woven a masterpiece with a dozen interpretations: it is the plight of the Diaspora Jew, an exposure of rootlessness, a mockery of tyranny, the comic quest for identity, a Marxist critique of capitalism, and, of course, an ironic self-referential study of literary sleight of hand. . . . It's easy to mock the highfalutin readings this story has received, but those who catch its serious import are not wrong either. Magically witty and unpretentious as it is, the story leaves you with an eerie, troubling sense of reality that begs attention. (Isaac Bashevis Singer, whose anecdotal style owes much to Sholom Aleichem, occasionally forces the serious mien of his stories with sermonettes on good, evil, and the meaning of existence. In Sholom Aleichem, you get no such prompting.)

What we have is an author who works best by indirection, in the smaller modes of fiction, from the worm's angle of vision, and with apparently flimsy materials. Even the main, archetypal figures of Sholom Aleichem are not full-blown heroes of novels, but characters or speakers in short story sequences, written over a period of years and later assembled in book form. The stature and personalities of Tevye, Menachem-Mendel, Mottel the Cantor's Son, as well as the town of Kasrilevke (Sholom Aleichem's fourth, collective "hero"), emerge from a run of episodes, each only slightly different from the one before it, that cumulatively establish their dimensions. As distinct from the normal novel, which develops a single architectonic structure, growing from introduction to a central point of resolution, Sholom Aleichem's major works beat like waves against a shore, one chapter resembling and reinforcing the last in variations of a theme. The normal novel lays human destiny out as a one-way trip, with important encounters, intersections, and moments of decision that determine one's rise or fall, success or failure, happiness or misery. The major works of Sholom Aleichem have no such suspenseful vision. A man is what he is to begin with—even Mottel, the child. He confronts all the things that happen to him and forces himself upon life again and again, and the sum of these trials shape the rhythm, constitute the meaning, of his existence.

It's the old literary knot of form and content. Sholom Aleichem's admiration for the stubborn ruggedness of Jewish faith and the surprising vitality of the people comes to expression not just thematically, in story after story, but in the resilient, recuperative *shape* of all his major works.

Before ending, I should tell you that this serious correspondence of ours about Sholom Aleichem appeared to me the other day in a comical light. I was lecturing about Sholom Aleichem to a nice synagogue audience, and every time I illustrated a point with a quotation or the plot of a story, the audience broke into happy, appreciative laughter. After a while I must admit I found myself adding quotations and dramatizing more stories to elicit that laughter, and when the lecture was over, people came over to tell me what a good story teller I was!

You see the point. Expostulate on Kafka or Dostoevsky and people are fairly begging for your explanations and interpretations. Lecture on any other Yiddish writer—Mendele, Peretz, Asch, Grade, the brothers Singer—and your words will illumine, clarify, edify. But set out to discuss the "narrative structure" or "comic techniques" of Sholom Aleichem, and he undercuts your very best attempt. I have the uncomfortable feeling that readers may look through these letters not for any insights, but for their illustrative examples. And Sholom Aleichem would be right behind, egging them on. Consider the deliberate irreverence of his literary memoir, *Once There Were Four*, and contrast this mountaineering saga of Jewish writers with all the high, serious climbs of other European literati. He gives us no disquisitions on literature, no pen portraits of his contemporaries, no contemplative philosophy from the heights. Just four "anecdotes" on the subject of forgetting, in which three of the greatest Jewish writers of the age, and one choleric literary companion, are revealed as ordinary, anxious Jews, faltering and trembling in ordinary, if not humiliating circumstances. He deflates intellectual and artistic pretentiousness, and even undercuts the grandeur of the Alps!

We set out—I think justifiably—to take a serious new look at a well-known but not well-appreciated author. What confronts us, finally, is the quizzical smile of the author, compulsively skeptical about everything but the story.

Part
One

The Haunted Tailor

ISH HOYO BE-ZOLODIEVKA, there was a man in Zolodievka, a village near Mazapevke, not far from Haplapovitch and Kozodoievka, between Yampoli and Stristch, just on the way from Pistchi-Yavadeh to Petschi-Khvost to Tetreve and from there to Yehupetz. *U'shmo Shimon-Eliyohu,* and his name was Shimon-Eli, but he was called "Shimon-Eli *Shma-Koleynu*" because when he said his prayers in the synagogue he had a way of working himself up, putting a trill into his prayers and singing them at the top of his voice. *Vehoyo ho-ish khayet,* and the man was a tailor—not, God forbid, one of those "ascended" tailors who sew according to the latest fashions. Rather, he was a genius patch tailor who could make a hole or a patch invisible. He could, for example, take an old caftan and turn it into a cloak; then the cloak into a pair of trousers; of the trousers he could make a shirt; and of

"Untranslatable" is the translator's constant complaint, after which he goes back to work. What I have not been able to retain in this English version of "The Haunted Tailor" is the especially corrosive quality which Shimon-Eli's frequent—and frequently mistaken—quotations in Hebrew give to the story. It pleases me to believe that Sholom Aleichem's genius has overleaped my limitations.

—*Translator's Note.*

the shirt something else again. Don't think that's such easy work—and it was on this account that Shimon-Eli *Shma-Koleynu* was a somebody in his world, since Zolodievka was a very poor village where the making of a new suit was not so frequent a matter. In Zolodievka, therefore, they thought the world of him.

However, he had one fault—he could not get along with the well-to-do and the authorities. He liked to meddle in communal business, taking always the side of the village poor. He spoke openly against the philanthropists who busied themselves with the public welfare; and he publicly maligned the tax gatherer, calling him a money-leech, a bloodsucker, a cannibal. As for the rabbis and the ritual slaughterers, the tax gatherer's accomplices, he called them a gang of thieves and liars, deceivers, killers, gangsters, highwaymen—may the devil take them and their fathers' fathers to the generation of grandfather Terah and Uncle Ishmael into the bargain.

Among the laborers and guildsmen, Shimon-Eli *Shma-Koleynu* was thought of as a scholar. For them this meant that he was someone who understood the small print of Torah explication, because Shimon-Eli liked to sprinkle his speech with passages—sometimes whole chapters— of *Gemara*, of *Midrash* made out of whole cloth: "The people . . ." . . . "I am small . . ." . . . "Today the world was created . . ." . . . "Here you are, creator of all light . . ." . . . and other such words which he always had ready at hand. On top of all this he had a tolerably good, if somewhat loud, voice, tending toward a treble. He understood all the styles of prayer and knew all the melodies and variations by heart.

He was madly eager to get at the podium.

He was also the president of the tailor's synagogue, which cost him blows from time to time, particularly on Simkhas-Torah during the *Ato Horeyso* prayer when those who did not get to carry a Torah vented their anger at him.

All his life Shimon-Eli had been poor, but the fact had never disheartened him. On the contrary, he liked to say, "Where there is poverty, there is life;" "Where there is hunger, there is song." As the *Gemara* says: "Poverty fits a Jew like a red handkerchief on a pretty girl." In short, Shimon-Eli was one of those of whom it is said that he was poor but happy.

He was short and ugly and his clothes were always stuck around with needles and pins. There were bits of cotton clinging to his curly black hair. He had a little goatee, a flattened nose, and there was a groove down his lower lip. His eyes were large, black, and constantly smiling. He moved with a little dance step and with a melody under his breath: *"Ha'yom haras oylem,* the world was created today—nothing to worry about."

Vayhi lo bonim u'vonoys, and he had sons and daughters. He was burdened with children of all sizes, most of them female, some of them already grown.

Sheym ishto, his wife's name was Tsippa-Beila-Reiza. She was altogether his opposite, a Cossack of a woman. From the day of their wedding she took Shimon-Eli in hand and never let go. She wore the pants, not he. He had tremendous respect for her. When, as she could do, she opened her mouth at him, he simply shivered. But more. When there was no one to see, she did not hesitate to give him a slap or two. Shimon-Eli tucked the slap into his pocket, saying *"Ha'yom haras oylem,* the world was created today—nothing to worry about." "It is written in the holy Torah, 'And he, that is to say, the husband . . . he will reign over you . . . .' Well . . . well . . . never mind. If all the kings from West to East came, it wouldn't help matters."

It happened one day that Tsippa-Beila-Reiza came home from the market. She threw her basket with her few purchases—a bit of garlic, some parsley, a few potatoes—to one side and cried angrily, "To hell with it. Racking one's brain every day thinking what to cook. You need to be smart as a prime minister. Beans and dumplings, dumplings and beans, and again beans and dumplings. May God not punish me for these words. And all the while Nekhama Brukha—a poverty-stricken, penniless, indigent, needy pauper of a woman—*she* has a goat. Why does *she* have a goat? Because she has a husband, Lazer Shloimo—also a tailor—but he's a man!

"No small matter, a goat. Nothing trivial about it. When there's a goat in the house, the children can have a glass of milk. One can cook up some groats and milk, and a meal becomes an easy matter. You can manage the evening meal. And you can have a pitcher of sour cream, some cheese now and then, some butter. One can live."

"You're right, no doubt," Shimon-Eli said gently. "There is a saying, 'Every Jew should have a goat.' As it is written."

Tsippa-Beila-Reiza shrieked, "I say a goat and he gives me a quotation. I'll give you quotations . . . I'll quotation your eyes! He feeds me quotations. My fine breadwinner, my *schlimazel*. I'll give you the entire Torah for a cream borscht."

And the like. And so on. She gave him such lectures several times a day until Shimon-Eli gave her his word that, with God's help, she should have a goat. She could sleep soundly on it.

From that time Shimon-Eli saved groschen upon groschen. He denied himself necessary things. He pawned his sabbath caftan, on which he paid weekly interest. Finally he had only to take the money he had saved and go to Kozodoievka to buy a goat.

Why especially to Kozodoievka? There were two reasons: first, the name of the town itself translated into Yiddish means "milkgoats"; the second, Tsippa-Beila-Reiza had overheard a neighbor to whom she had not spoken in several years. She, the neighbor, had heard from her Kozodoievka sister, who had come for a visit, that there, in Kozodoievka, there was a primary school teacher who was sardonically called "Chaim-Chono the Wise" because he was so stupid. This man had a wife, Thema Gittel, who was called "Thema Gittel the Silent," because, as it is said about women, she had nine measures of speech. And this quiet Thema Gittel had two goats, both of them milk-givers. It is natural to ask, "Why does she deserve two goats, milk-givers to boot? What would be the catastrophe should she not have so much as one? There are people who do not have so much as half a goat. Well . . . do they die of it?"

"You're very right," Shimon-Eli said to his wife. "You know . . . it's an old complaint. As it is written, 'To own is to bemoan.'"

"Just listen to him. Here he is again with his quotations," his wife interrupted. "One talks of a goat, and he quotes. You'd better go to the Kozodoievka teacher and say to him: 'We've heard that you own two goats, and both of them give milk. Why do you need two milk-giving goats? For scapegoats? No doubt, then, you must want to sell one of them. Sell it to me.' That's how to talk with him, do you understand?"

"Of course I understand. What do you mean?" said Shimon-Eli. "With money, will I have to beg? With money one can buy anything. Silver and gold will clean bastards and pigs. What's bad is when there is no money, as Rashi says, 'Daddy's not there, go to sleep.' Or as it is said, 'Without fingers you can't thumb your nose.'"

"Again a quotation, and once more a quotation. My head's quotationing. May you sink . . . ," said his wife, Tsippa-Beila-Reiza, burying him under nine ells of earth as she rehearsed him over and over in how to talk with Chaim-Chono the teacher in case he was willing to sell. Well, and what if he was unwilling? Why should he be unwilling? Why should he be entitled to two goats, and milkers to boot? There are Jews in the world, God be praised, who do not have so much as half a goat. If so, do they die of it?

And so on and so on, always the same theme.

Two

Ha'boyker or, it was dawn. Our tailor rose eagerly, said his prayers, took his stick and a leading rope, and peacefully started off on foot. It was Sunday, a bright, lovely summer's day. It had been a long time since Shimon-Eli could remember such a delightful day, and long since Shimon-Eli had been out in the countryside in the open air—since his eyes had seen such green traceries of branches in the wood, such a lovely blanket of green fields strewn with every kind of color. It had been long since his ears had heard such a piping of birds and the flutter of tiny wings, long since his nose had smelled such fine odors of grass and freshly turned earth.

Shimon-Eli *Shma-Koleynu* spent his days in quite another world. He looked at quite different pictures: a dark cellar . . . an oven near the door . . next to the door, shovels and spades and a slop pail filled to the brim. Next to the slop pail, a bed made of three boards on which there were many children, God be praised, each child smaller than the next, half-naked, entirely barefoot, unkempt, and always hungry. He usually heard quite other sounds: "Mama, bread. . . . Mama, a roll. . . . Mama, something to eat." And above the clamor the voice of Tsippa-Beila-Reiza, "Eat? May the worms not eat you, dear God, together with your father, that *schlimazel.* You and him together."

And other such cries. His nose was used to other smells: the dank walls which in winter were humid and in summer bred mold . . . the smells of yeast and bran, onions and cabbage, scraped fish and tripe . . . the smell of old clothes making themselves known under the steam iron—thick steam and strange odors.

Having torn himself away for a little while from that poverty-stricken, bare, dark world to this new, bright, fragrant light, our Shimon-Eli felt

6

like someone who, on a hot day, has plunged naked into the sea. And the sea takes him. . . . The waves move him. . . . He bobs and he dips and he drifts. . . . He takes deep breaths glorious to the soul. For all practical purposes he is in Eden.

He thinks, "Let us consider, for example . . . how would it have hurt . . . how would it have done God any harm if every working man, for instance, came out every day . . . or let's say, just once a week . . . into something like this, into the open . . . to enjoy God's little world. *Oy*, what a little world!"

And Shimon-Eli sang a little song in the Talmudic fashion: *Ato yotsarto*, Thou has created; *Oylamkho*, your world; *mikedem*, long ago; *bokharto bonu*, and Thou hast chosen us, that we might live there in Zolodievka, jammed together head to head, hardly able to breathe. *Vatiten lonu*, and Thou hast given us . . . ah, hast Thou given us, sorrows and pain, and griefs . . . and fevers and chills . . . in your great mercy . . . cy . . . cy."

Thus sang Shimon-Eli under his breath, and he was tempted to throw himself down where he stood in a field of grass to enjoy for a while God's little world. Then he remembered his mission and said, "Enough singing, Shimon-Eli, get a move on, brother. You'll have time to rest at Dodi the Rendar's Oak Tavern. There, with God's help, one can get a little whiskey—as it is written: 'The study of Torah is the culmination of all things.'" And Shimon-Eli *Shma-Koleynu* walked on.

Three

Halfway between the two towns, Zolodievka and Kozodoievka, stood the Oak Tavern. The tavern had something like magnetic power and drew to it wagon drivers and passengers. Whether they were traveling from Zolodievka to Kozodoievka or from Kozodoievka to Zolodievka, they all had to stop at the Oak for at least a few moments. No one knew the secret, not to this day. Some say it was because the host of the inn, Dodi Rendar, was a genial fellow—which is to say that one could buy a good little glass of whiskey and something good to snack on along with it. Others said that it was because Dodi was one of those people called "finders" or "prophets" who, though they are not themselves thieves, are, just the same, pals of well-known crooks such as the famous Reb Schmelke. But since no one knew this for certain, it's better not to mention it. . . .

Dodi was one of those hairy, thickset Jews with a big belly and a potato nose and the voice of a wild ox. A prosperous fellow who owned cattle, he had no troubles to plague him. In his later years he had become a widower and was now without ties. He was a coarse fellow who could not tell the difference between a prayer book and a Passover manual. For this reason Shimon-Eli was ashamed of him. He didn't like the notion that he, Shimon-Eli, a learned man and chairman of his synagogue, was related to a toll keeper, a common fellow. And Dodi, for his part, was just as ashamed that he was related to a real tailor. Each was ashamed of the other. Just the same, when Dodi saw Shimon-Eli *Shma Koleynu*, he welcomed him warmly because he was afraid, not so much of Shimon-Eli himself, but of his big mouth.

"Oh, a guest, a guest. What are you up to, Shimon-Eli? And how is your Tsippa-Beila-Reiza? And how are the children?"

"'Now what are we, and what is our life? How should we be?'" the tailor replied with a citation, as was his wont. "'Sometimes up, sometimes down.' As long as we're healthy, as it is written: 'Wisdom is smoke; smoke is wisdom.' How are you, dear kinsman? What's going on in your village? I still remember your dumplings and the bit of liquor from last year. That's the main thing for you, isn't it? Your kind are not fond of looking into books. What do you care about a Yiddish word? Ah, Reb Dodi, Reb Dodi, if your father, my Uncle Gedaliah-Wolf, were to rise from his grave and see what has become of his little Dodi, lost among village Gentiles, he would die a second death. Ah, your father, your father, Reb Dodi. A devout Jew. May he forgive me, but he used to drink from a bitter cask. In short, 'There is no man without his burden.' Give us some whiskey. As the Reb Bimbon says, 'Pawn your caftan and take a little whiskey.'"

"There you go again with your hash of quotations," Dodi said, and brought him some whiskey. "You'd do better just to tell me where you're traveling."

"I'm not traveling," Shimon-Eli said, lifting his glass, "I'm walking. As we say in the Hallel prayers, 'If you have feet, are you too sick to walk?'"

"In that case, dear cousin, where are you walking?"

"I'm walking. . ." Shimon-Eli said, drinking another glass, "to

Kozodoievka to buy a goat. As it is written, 'Thou shalt buy goats.'"

"Goats?" the astonished Dodi said. "How does a tailor happen to be buying goats?"

"'Goats' is a way of speaking," Shimon-Eli said. "What I mean is 'a goat.' May God send me the proper goat—cheap, that is. I myself would not be buying a goat. But my wife, may she live long, Tsippa-Beila-Reiza, that is . . . you know her . . . when she makes up her mind she's set for all time. She wants a goat. And a wife, you will agree, must be obeyed. It is specified in the *Talmud,* of course. You remember, eh?"

"You know that as regards *Midrash,* you and I are . . . distant cousins. But there's something I don't understand. How is it that you're an expert on goats?"

"How does a Rendar come to be an authority on prayer passages?" said Shimon-Eli, irritably. "Just the same, at Passover, with God's help, you keep time to a true Yom Kippur's 'Who shall live and who shall die?' Isn't that so?"

Dodi the Rendar well understood the insult, but he bit his lip, thinking, "Wait, wait, my tailornik, you. You're a bit too greedy today, showing off just a little too much with your Torah. Wait, I'll give you a goat . . . that will give you the itch."

And Shimon-Eli ordered another glass of that bitter drop which is the remedy for all sorrows. There's no way to avoid the truth: Shimon-Eli liked his little drop now and then—though he was no drunkard, God forbid. When could he afford a glass of whiskey? His problem was that no sooner did he have one little drop, than he immediately had to have another. Two such drops made him tipsy, and his cheeks flamed and his eyes glittered and his tongue was set to tolling without end.

"Speaking of guilds," Shimon-Eli said, "To my guild—Shears and Press-iron: the people. There's a quality to our people that makes us all want 'honor,' no matter how little. A nothing of a shoemaker yearns to be a chairman, never mind of what—even of only his garbage can. So I say to them: 'Brothers, I need it like a hole in the head. Choose some shoemaker for your chairman. Spare me the honor. I'd rather avoid the blows.' They say, 'To hell with it. If the guild decides, that's it. Take the chairmanship and take the blows.' Shhh . . . I'm wandering a bit . . . I forgot that I have a goat to buy. *'Od hayom godol,'* time does not stand still. Good-bye, Reb Dodi. 'Mighty, mighty! We will be strong!' Good-bye, be well. And remember, make dumplings."

"Don't forget," Dodi said to him, "If the Blessed Name permit' on your way back—if the Lord spares us—don't forget, blessed be his name, and stop in on your way back."

"If God wills, if God wills," Shimon-Eli said. *'Bosser v'dom,'* that is, 'One is no more than flesh and blood: *Odem,* a person; *Tsipor,* a bird'— it's simple. Just you have something proper to drink and a little bite to go with it. As our motto is: 'Steam-iron and shears: the people.'"

Four

And Shimon-Eli left the Oak Tavern in high spirits. *Vayovoy,* and he arrived in peace and health in Kozodoievka. Once in Kozodoievka, he asked around for the home of Reb Chaim-Chono the Wise, who had a wife Thema Gittel the Silent, who owned two milk-goats. He did not need to ask for long, because the village of Kozodoievka was not one of those "towns of the seacoast towns," in which one could, God forbid, get lost. The whole town was spread out before one's eyes as on a plate: there were the butcher shops, the butchers with their cleavers and the inevitable dogs; there was the marketplace where stockinged women moved from one peasant woman to another, squeezing various fowl:

> *Tshuish, tshuish. A scho tobi za kurkuh?*
> *Yaka kurkuh? Tseh piven, a ne kurkuh.*
> *Nekhai budeh piven.* *

Two paces beyond was the synagogue courtyard where old women with basins sat selling pears, sunflower seeds, and beans; teachers conducted their classes while children yelled; and goats, goats without end, leaped about pulling wisps of hay from thatched roofs, while other silk-bearded goats warmed themselves in the sun and chewed their cud.

Not far away was the bathhouse with its sooty walls. After that, the lake, covered with a green scum that crawled with leeches and frogs that croaked away. The lake gleamed in the sun, glistening like diamonds

---

Listen, what do you want for this hen? What hen? It's not a hen, it's a rooster. All right, a rooster. How much do you want for this hen?

and stinking to high heaven. Farther on, on the other side of the lake, there was nothing but earth and sky—no more Kozodoievka.

When the tailor entered the house of Reb Chaim-Chono the Wise, he found him at work, wearing his large fringed prayer undergarment and a pointed *yarmulke*. He was bent over the *Gemara,* leading his pupils at the tops of their voices through the *Talmud* passage "On Damages": "Now that goat, when it saw that there was food on the top of the barrel, that same goat leaped toward that same food . . . "

"*Tsifra teva l'mariah dakhita dakufa d'mata*," Shimon-Eli called out in Aramaic, translating at once into ordinary Yiddish: "Good morning to you, Rebbe, to you and to your students. You are studying, I see, just such a case as has brought me here. To wit, a goat. Enough. . . . I myself would not have thought of buying a goat, but my wife, Tsippa-Beila-Reiza, that is to say, has gotten it into her head once and for all that she wants a goat. And a wife, you will agree, needs to be obeyed. It is specified in the *Gemara.*

"Why do you stare at me? Because I know *Gemara*? Though I am a working man? 'You can't tell a book by its cover.' It may be you've heard of me. I am Shimon-Eli of the blessed town of Zolodievka, member of the guild and president of the tailor's synagogue, though I need the honor like a hole in the head. 'Thanks a lot,' I told them. 'You keep the honor and spare me the blows.' They answer, 'Too bad.' If the guild says so, it's done. 'Take the honor along with the blows.' I've wandered a little from my subject and almost forgot to say, "*Sholem.*" *Sholem aleichem* to you, teacher. *Sholem aleichem* to you, pupils—holy sheep, snot-nosed troublemakers, unruly mice—may you yearn to dance the way you yearn to study. Ah, ha, did I hit it right?"

Hearing these words, the pupils pinched each other under the table and made snorting noises. Actually, they were well pleased with their guest and would have been delighted had the good Lord often sent them such visitors. But Chaim-Chono the Wise was not as happy as they were. He did not like to be interrupted in the midst of things. Calling in his wife Thema Gittel, he turned his attention to his pupils and to the goat that had been nibbling at the fodder. Once more they sang at the tops of their voices: "Rabah said, 'Guilty,' and set it down that she must pay for the fodder and the barrel that was damaged."

Shimon-Eli *Shma-Koleynu*, seeing that there was no more to be had from the teacher, turned his attention to the teacher's wife, and while the goat of the *Gemara* was being interpreted on the one hand, Shimon-Eli kept up a conversation with the teacher's wife about her goats.

"I am, as you see me, a Jew—a working man," Shimon-Eli said. "It may be you've heard of me, I am Shimon-Eli, tailor of Zolodievka, member of the guild, and president of the tailor's synagogue—an honor I need like a hole in the head. 'Thanks a lot,' I told them. 'You keep the honor and spare me the blows.'

"I've come, let me say, about one of your goats. That is, I would not myself buy a goat, but since my wife, Tsippa-Beila-Reiza, that is, is set on having a goat once and for all, and since a wife, you would agree, needs to be obeyed—it is specified in the *Talmud*."

Thema Gittel, a small woman with a nose like a bean—a nose which she continually wipes with her fingers—listened to him a while. Then, interrupting, "So you've come, I take it, to bargain with me for one of my goats. In which case, let me tell you this, my dear man: in the first place, I'm not about to sell one of my goats. Why not? Let's not deceive ourselves. For money? What is money? Money is round and disappears, while a goat . . . is a goat. Especially a goat like this. A goat? Who says it's a goat? She's a mother, I tell you, not a goat. May the Lord avert the evil eye from her. What an easy milker, and gives so much, not to speak of how little she eats. Eats! Does she eat anything? A measure of bran and some wisps of straw from the House of Study roof.

"But never mind . . . if I were to get the right price, I might consider it. Money is . . . how would you say? . . . a temptation. For money I could buy another goat, though a goat such as my goat is hard to find. A goat? She's a mother, not a goat. Never mind. No use talking. I'll bring her in and you can see for yourself."

Thema Gittel went off and brought the goat in along with a full pitcher of milk which she said the goat had given that very morning.

Seeing the milk, the tailor's mouth watered. He said, "Tell me, dear woman. *Ma yokor*, what is the price? Because if the price isn't right, I won't buy. Do you know why? Because, in the first place, I need a goat like a hole in the head. But since my wife, may she live long, Tsippa-Beila-Reiza, that is, has got it into her head once and for all. . . . "

"What difference does it make, how much?" Thema Gittel said, interrupting. Taking a wipe at her nose, she said, "Let's hear *your* price. I'll tell you something: no matter what you pay, it will still be a bargain. Do you know why? Because if you buy this goat, you'll really have a goat."

"Listen to you," the tailor interrupted. "That's just why I want to buy her, because she's a goat—not a dragon. What I mean . . . actually, I myself don't want to buy a goat. I need a goat like a hole in the head. But since my wife, may she live long, Tsippa-Beila-Reiza, that is, has taken it into her head once and for all. . . ."

"Listen to you, that's just what I've been saying," interrupted Thema Gittel, and began once more to add up the virtues of her goat. But the tailor interrupted in his turn. They went on in this fashion until their interrupting litanies merged into a hash and a mishmash: "A goat . . . a mother, not a goat . . . I myself wouldn't buy a goat . . . a measure of bran . . . she's got it in her head, once and for all . . . money is round . . . may the Lord keep her . . . what an easy milker . . . Tsippa-Beila-Reiza, that is . . . does she eat anything? . . . once and for all . . . as for the rest . . . a wisp of straw from the House of Study roof . . . a wife needs to be obeyed . . . a goat . . . a mother . . . not a goat."

"That's enough goating between you," interrupted Chaim-Chono the Wise, turning to face his wife. "Have you ever heard the like? We are right in the midst of 'On Damages,' while they 'Goat, goat, goat, goat.' One or the other of you make up your mind. Sell the goat or don't sell the goat. My head is aching with goats."

"He's right," agreed Shimon-Eli, 'Where there is Torah, there is wisdom.' Make up your mind. Who needs more speech? '*V'li hakessef, v'li hazohov*.' My money, your wares. Just say three words: one word plus two, without garbling them . . . as it is written in the prayer book for the High Holy Days."

"Who needs your explanation? Just say what you'll give for the goat," Thema Gittel said quietly, crouched like a kitten as she licked her lips.

"What I'll give . . . " said Shimon-Eli, also quietly. "What do you mean, 'Say what you'll give'? Am I some kind of a 'sayer'? I see that it is all wasted effort. I see that there's going to be no goat bought from you today. I'm very sorry to have disturbed you." And Shimon-Eli turned and made his way to the door, as if he were leaving.

"Just look at him," said Thema Gittel, taking him by the sleeve. "What's your hurry? Is the lake burning? Make up your mind. After all, it was you who started to say something about a goat. . . . "

To be brief, the woman named her price, and the tailor named his. She came down a bit; he went up a bit. One coin up, another down, until they agreed. Shimon-Eli counted out the money and tied the goat to his rope.

Thema Gittel spat on the money and wished the tailor the best of luck, her eyes moving from the money to the goat and back again. Meanwhile, keeping up a constant patter, she led the tailor out of the house, where she wished him many blessings.

"Go well and be well, and use her in good health. May she be to you as she has been to me and no worse. Better there is no equal. May she last long, may she give milk and never cease to give milk."

"Amen, and the same to you," the tailor said and started toward the door. But the goat wouldn't budge. She twisted her horns about, planted her hind feet, and made a resounding bleat like a young cantor going to the podium for the first time. She sang, "Mehhh . . . what is my crime?" and "Mehhh . . . what is my sin?" as one might say, "Where are you dragging me?"

Reb Chaim-Chono the Wise, in all his dignity, using his switch, helped drive the goat from the house. The gang of students urged her on: "*Hai Kozeh! Kozeh! Pashol Kozeh*, move it."

And the tailor went on his way.

Five

Vatima'en, and she would not. The goat, that is to say, would by no means go with the tailor toward Zolodievka, but tore herself in the direction of home with all her force. It did her no good. Shimon-Eli yanked at her rope and gave her to understand that she was wasting her time with her turnings and bleatings. He talked to her as follows: "It is written—you have been driven into exile by necessity. Whether you like it or not, no one wants your opinion. I, too—not now, God forbid—was once a free bird, a proper bachelor, wearing a vest and boots that creaked splendidly. What did I lack? Headaches! So God said unto me: 'Shimon-Eli, crawl into your sack. Marry Tsippa-Beila-Reiza. Beget children. Darken the days of your life.'"

In this fashion Shimon-Eli discoursed to the goat as he moved along quickly, all but running. A warm breeze tugged at the lappets of his patched caftan and stole under his earlocks and caressed his beard, bringing to him the sweet fragrance of mint and rosemary, of wildflowers and herbs that had the odor of the heavens in them and to which he was anything but accustomed. In sheer ecstasy, he began his early evening prayers, reciting the *Pitum haktoyres*, in which are enumerated all good things, rattling them off nicely in a fine cantorial melody but in a different mode. All at once . . . out of no place, Satan, the tempter, whispered into his ear: "Listen to me, Shimon-Eli, you fool. Why are you standing here, singing away on an empty stomach? It's nearly night and you've had nothing in your mouth but a couple of glasses of whiskey. Also you gave your cousin your holy word that, God willing, on your way back with the goat, you'd stop in to have a bite with him. A word given is a word given. A mouth is not a boot top." And Shimon-Eli cut short "the eighteen prayers," whizzed through the *takhnun* prayer, and made his joyful way to Dodi Rendar's.

"Good evening to you, my dear cousin, Reb Dodi. I have news for you. Congratulate me—I have bought a goat. But a goat from goatland, a goat which not even our fathers goated. Look at her and judge for yourself—you are in some fashion a learned man. Well then, guess. How much do you think I paid?"

Dodi put his hand to the visor of his cap, shielding his eyes from the setting sun that was making a golden line in the sky. He studied the goat in the manner of an expert, then guessed her value at just twice what Shimon-Eli had paid for her. This made Shimon-Eli so cheerful that he slapped the Rendar across the shoulders. "Dear Reb Dodi. This time may we both live long and well—you've guessed wrong."

Dodi Rendar pursed his lips, nodded, then spat as if to say, "A bargain, a steal."

Shimon-Eli cocked his head and crooked a finger into his vest as if he were plucking a needle from it to thread. "Well, Reb Dodi. What do you say to that? Do we know our business, eh? And if you saw how much milk she gave, God keep her, you'd die on the spot."

"Rather you than me," Reb Dodi replied.

"Amen, and the same to you," said Shimon-Eli. "Now, since my welcome is so warm, kindly put the goat into your barn so no one will steal her while I finish up the evening prayer. Then we'll have a little drink and a snack. Is it not written in the *Megillah:* 'No dancing before meals'?"

"Who knows?" said Dodi. "If you say it's written, no doubt it's written. After all, you're the Torah Jew."

Having rattled off his prayers, the tailor said, "Pour a bit of liquor from that green bottle for our health's sake. 'Health is the first wisdom,' as we say in our prayers."

With a bite to eat and little whiskey inside him, our tailor's tongue was soon unleashed. He ticked off Zolodievka, the congregation, the affairs of the synagogue, guilds, tailoring—"Shears and steam-irons: the people." He denounced the civic leaders and the rich and the way they gave orders, saying they deserved to be sent to Siberia, "or his name wasn't Shimon-Eli."

"Do you hear," he said, tangling his speech with snatches of Torah, as was his habit: "May the devil take their parents . . . our philanthropists, I mean. All they know is how to suck blood, how to flay the poor. They get a quarter of a ruble a week out of my measly three rubles. Never mind. Their time will come. They haven't paid God's reckoning. Tsippa-Beila-Reiza, my wife, tells me I'm a *schlimazel* because, if I wanted to, I could put the squeeze on them. I've had such notions myself. But who listens to a wife? In our holy Torah it is written, 'And he shall rule over you.' You know where the passage is. The words are sweet to the tongue. Listen closely: 'He, the husband that is, shall rule. . . . ' Well, never mind. As it is written, 'If you are pouring, pour some more.'"

More and more, Shimon-Eli's speech wandered. His eyelids grew heavy until, to make a long story short, he leaned against the wall and dozed off with his head tipped to one side, his hands folded over his chest—though three fingers still clung to his goatee, like a man engrossed in thought. Except that he was wheezing and snorting and whistling through his teeth—"ts . . . ts . . . ts . . . ts . . . "—nobody in the world would have said that he was sleeping.

And though he slept his mind worked on delightedly. And he dreamed that he was at home beside his workbench, that soon there would be a touch of prosperity in his home, and the idea pleased him. Never in his life had he seen so many little pitchers of milk, so many sacks of cheese. And butter! Whole mixing bowls of butter! One day, buttermilk; one day sour cream or sour milk with whole lumps of clabber. And buttercakes without end. Milk pancakes baked in butter and sprinkled with granulated sugar and cinnamon. And the smell, the smell. . . .

Some kind of familiar smell—ugh. He felt something crawling along his neck between his collar and his ear, across his face. The something that stank tickling his nose. . . . He felt about and touched—a bedbug. He opened an eye, then another eye, and looked toward the window. Oh, oh. Trouble, damn it. It was dawn.

"That was a good nap," Shimon-Eli said, stretching. He woke the Rendar, then hurried to the courtyard, opened the barn, took the goat's rope and shot off like an arrow toward home, racing like a man pursued. Pursued by what? The devil only knows.

Six

V'hoisho, and the woman, Tsippa-Beila-Reiza, when she saw that her husband was long in coming home, could not understand it. She began to imagine, God forbid, some disaster. Highwaymen had captured her husband, taken away his few rubles, killed him and thrown his body into a ditch, while she, Heaven help her, was left an eternal *aguna*. With so many children, God bless them, one might as well—may it happen to the enemies of Zion—drown them and oneself along with them. Such were poor Tsippa-Beila-Reiza's thoughts that night, during which she never closed an eye. When the first rooster crowed in the morning, she dressed quickly and went out. Seating herself on the porch sill, she scanned the horizon to see whether a pitying God would let her catch a glimpse of her husband. "A *schlimazel* doesn't get lost," she thought and set herself to give him the dreadful scolding he deserved. But when she saw him and saw that he was trailing a goat behind him by a rope, her anger evaporated and she called to him, "What took you so long, my little canary? My little almond cake? I was sure that by now you were six feet under, my jewel, or that some similar misfortune had overtaken you, God forbid."

Shimon-Eli led the goat into the house, untied its rope, and started on the tale of his adventures, talking a blue streak.

"Do you hear, my wife? Have I bought a goat? From goatland. Is this a goat? A goat such as our ancestors have not goated. Let them do their best, our rich folk. Still in their wildest dreams they will not see a goat like this one. As for its food, it eats nothing except once a day a measure of bran; as for the rest, a little straw from the roof of the House of Study. And does it give milk, God save her? Like a cow—and twice a day. I saw for myself a full milk basin, as I hope to live and breathe. Is it a goat? 'It's a mother, not a goat,' that's what Thema Gittel said. I tell you, the goat is a steal, but what a deal of haggling. It took all night to get her to come down, and it was like pulling teeth. Not to mention that at the beginning she simply did not want to sell a goat. I got her down to six and a half rubles."

17

As he spoke, Tsippa-Beila-Reiza was thinking, "*Nekhama Brukha* . . . damn the woman. Thinks she's the only one who knows how to run a proper household. Only Eli's wife also has a goat. And wait till Blumeh-Zalteh and Khayah-Maiteh and the rest of the sisterhood . . . Oh, Lord, Lord, may they get only half the evil they wish me. Wait till they hear." Meanwhile, she fired up the stove and got buckwheat noodles cooking for breakfast. Shimon-Eli put on his *tefillin* and said heartfelt prayers with great fervor. It had been a long time since he prayed this way. He sang the hallelujahs, made cantorial trills, snapped his fingers, and woke all the children with his singing. The children, hearing from their mother that their father had bought a goat and that noodles and milk were cooking (instant "joy and happiness"), jumped from their beds, held hands, and danced about in their shirts, accompanying themselves with a little song which, that minute, they invented:

> "A goat, a goat, a little goat—
> Daddy brought a little goat;
> The little goat will give mi . . . lk,
> And mama will cook noo . . . dles . . . "

Watching the children's joy, Shimon-Eli expanded. He thought, "Poor children, to yearn so for milk. Never mind. From now on they will have God's plenty. Each day a little glass of milk, and boiled groats with milk, and milk with tea. A goat is truly a comfort to one's bones. What do I care about Fishel? I can just hear the tomcat, 'No meat for you. Just bones.' Let him choke on his bones. I don't need his meat now that, God be thanked, I have milk. And what about the Sabbath? For the Sabbath one buys fish. Where is it written that a Jew has to eat meat? I've never seen such a law. If all Jews were of my mind, they'd buy goats. Then what would our little potbellied Fishel look like? The devil take his grandfather."

Thus Shimon-Eli *Shma-Koleynu* folded his *tefillin,* washed his hands, blessed the bread, and prepared himself for a feast. Suddenly the door opened and in came Tsippa-Beila-Reiza with an empty basin, her face as red as fire, angry to the bursting point, and cursing a blue streak, all of it directed at Shimon-Eli. They weren't just curses, but more like stones falling from the sky. Pitch and sulphur spewed from Tsippa-Beila-Reiza's mouth, "May the devil take your father, the drunkard, and you, too. May you turn to stone, to bone. May you land in purgatory. May a musket shoot you. May you be hanged, drowned, and burned and roasted, and be flayed and quartered! Go, you bandit, you highwayman. Go see . . . you, you . . . apostate. What kind of goat did you bring me? A black nightmare on your head, your hands, and your feet. Good God in Heaven, dear compassionate father . . . "

The rest Shimon-Eli did not hear. He pulled down his hat and left the house to discover what the catastrophe was. Outside he looked at the goat, his beautiful jewel, and the goat stood tied to the doorpost of the house, chewing his cud. Shimon-Eli stood, stupefied, thinking what to do, where to go. He thought and thought, then said, "May he be damned to his grandfather's generation, that teacher and his wife. They've found someone to make a fool of, have they? I'll give them a fool. They'll see. Oh, that teacher. One would think from looking at him that butter wouldn't melt in his mouth. A helpless fellow—so innocent. And just see what's come of it. What a story. No wonder his pupils giggled when I was sent off with the goat while the teacher's wife was wishing me milk into eternity. I'll give them a milking. I'll milk the blood of those holy worthies."

Brooding thus, Shimon-Eli *Shma-Koleynu* started back toward Kozodoievka, with the idea of giving them the comeuppance they deserved.

Passing by the Oak Tavern, he saw the Rendar at the door with his pipe between his teeth. The tailor, though he was still some distance away, burst into laughter.

"What are you celebrating?" Dodi asked him. "What's so funny?"

"Take a look if you please. Maybe you'll laugh, too," the tailor said, laughing eerily, like a man tickled by ghosts. 'Wherever there's trouble, it comes my way.' If you know what I mean. Have I had a scolding from my wife, Tsippa-Beila-Reiza, may she live long. She gave me a belly full, and on an empty stomach, too. May the teacher and his wife get some of it. You can be sure I'm not going to hold still. There will be 'an eye for an eye.' I don't like to be played for a fool. In the meanwhile, Reb Dodi, give me a glass of whiskey to ease my heart, to rinse my throat so I may have the strength to speak, and to give my soul some consolation.

"To your health, Reb Dodi, let's be Jews, that's the main thing. As it is written: '*Ha'yom haras oylem*,' today the world was created, nothing to worry about.' I'll show them how to play tricks. Shears and steam-irons: the people."

Dodi, innocently sucking at his pipe, asked, "Who told you it was a trick? Maybe you misunderstood each other."

Shimon-Eli fairly leaped for anger. "What are you talking about? Do you know what you're talking about? I went to them specifically to buy a goat and made it as clear as when Jacob asked for the naked Rachel: a goat, just a goat."

Dodi pulled on his pipe, shrugged his shoulders, threw up his hands as if to say, "What have I done, in God's name? Is it my fault?"

And Shimon-Eli grabbed up the rope and started off toward Kozodoievka, seething with anger.

Seven

V'hamlamed, and the teacher was at his work. That is, he sat teaching his pupils, leading them through every case in the Talmud section "On Damages." The boys' chanting could be heard all over the courtyard: "She flicked her tail—the cow, that is—and she broke the pitcher."

"Good morning, Rebbe, to you and to your pupils," Shimon-Eli said. "Stop for a minute. It doesn't matter. The cow won't go anywhere and the pitcher won't mend itself. . . .

"Why am I standing on ceremony? You've played me a dirty trick. Never mind. I don't like such tricks. Of course, you know the story of the two Jews in the bathhouse on Friday afternoon. They were on the highest bench. One says to the other, 'Here, take my bunch of twigs and switch me.' The other took him at his word and laid on till the blood came. The injured man said, 'What are you trying to prove? If you wanted to get even with me for something while I lay naked here on the highest bench, and you had the twigs in your hand, that I can understand; but if you meant it as a practical joke, let me tell you—I don't like such jokes.'"

"What point are you making?" the teacher asked, taking his glasses off and scratching his ear with them.

"The point has to do with you and the beautiful goat you passed off on me so innocently by way of a joke. A joke like that can end by making you laugh out of the other side of your mouth. Don't think you're

ing with some kind of a simpleton. My name is Shimon-Eli, tailor of
the holy community of Zolodievka, member of the guild, and president

By this time Shimon-Eli was in a frenzy. The teacher put his glasses
back on and studied the tailor as if Shimon-Eli were in a fever of
hallucination. The pupils, for their part, nearly choked with suppressed
laughter.

"Why are you looking at me like that, as if I were a clown?" the tailor
asked. "I come to buy a goat and you palm off the devil only knows what
on me."

"You don't like the goat?" the teacher asked, innocently.

"The *goat!*" he said. "If it's a goat, then you're the governor."

"The class exploded with laughter and Thema Gittel the Silent came
in. Now the party really began. Shimon-Eli spoke; Thema Gittel
interrupted. The teacher watched; the pupils roared. Shimon-Eli and
Thema Gittel kept interrupting each other until Thema Gittel, in a burst
of anger, grabbed the tailor by the arm. "Come," she cried. "Come to the
rabbi," she said, dragging him. "Let all Jews know how a Zolodievka
tailor can make trouble. How he frames innocent people."

"Yes," Shimon-Eli said. "Very well. We'll let the world know what so-
called devout, *honest* people there are here, who take a stranger for all
he's worth. Come along then, come on."

The teacher put on his plush hat over his *yarmulke* and all four of
them went off—the tailor, the teacher, his wife, and the goat.

When the group arrived at the rabbi's house, they found him in his
robe, washing his hands, just finishing the prayer one makes after using
the bathroom, the *Asher yotsar* as thou wishest . . . ." He spoke slowly,
with deliberation, squeezing his words out, "*Ne'kuvim,* holes . . .
khalulim. . . kha . . . lu . . . lim, orifices." The prayer finished, he
gathered up the skirts of his robe and seated himself on a chair without a
seat—an old chair, with nothing left but legs and armrests and rails that
were as shiny and shaky as teeth still miraculously in place long after
they ought to have fallen out.

Having heard the two contenders who would not let each other talk,
the rabbi sent for the deputy rabbi and the ritual slaughterer, as well as
various other worthies of the town. To the tailor he said, "Be good
enough to tell *your* story from beginning to end. Then we can get *her*
story."

Shimon-Eli was not at all reluctant to tell his story, and to tell it again and once more. To wit: that he, Shimon-Eli the tailor, of the blessed community of Zolodievka, member of the guild and chairman of the synagogue— though much against his will: "I need it like a hole in the head. But they say, 'Take the blows and be the chairman. . . .' In brief, I came to Kozodoievka to find a goat. That is, myself I didn't want a goat. I needed a goat like a hole in the head, but since I have a wife, may she live long, Tsippa-Beila-Reiza, clamoring at me, what was there to do? She wanted a goat, and a wife, don't you agree, needs to be obeyed. So I came to Reb Chaim-Chono, the Talmud teacher, and bargained with him for a goat. 'The naked Rachel was specified.' A goat, that is to say. Well, they took my rubles and passed off the devil only knows what. For fun! Fun! He, Shimon-Eli that is, hates such tricks. Perhaps you've heard the story of the two Jews who were in the bathhouse on Friday. . . "

Here Shimon-Eli the tailor repeated the tale of the two Jews in the bathhouse, while the rabbi, the assistant rabbis, and other dignitaries laughed.

The rabbi said, "We've heard one side of the argument. Now let's hear the other."

Chaim-Chono the Wise got up, pulled his hat down over his *yarmulke* and said, "Hear me, oh assembly. The story is as follows: I was sitting teaching my pupils the tractate 'On Damages' . . . Then this Jew from Zolodievka . . . yes, this one . . . says he's from Zolodievka . . . from Zolodievka, he says . . . bids me *sholem* . . . *sholem* he bids me . . . and tells a story . . . a story he tells me . . . that he's from Zolodievka . . . from Zolodievka, that is . . . and that he has a wife . . . he has a wife, that is. Tsippa-Beila-Reiza. Yes, I think so. Tsippa-Beila-Reiza." The teacher nodded toward the tailor who, all this while, stood clasping his beard, his eyes closed and his head tilted a little to one side. He rocked back and forth, murmuring a response in his fashion, "True, certain and sure. She has all three names: Tsippa and Beila and Reiza. That's how she was named, and it's the name I've known her by for thirty long years. But . . . what else were you going to say, old friend? But you'd do better to get things straight: 'What I said and what you said.' As King Solomon puts it: 'There is nothing new under the sun.' No tricks please."

"I don't know anything," the teacher said, frightened, pointing to his wife. *"She* talked to him. She dealt with him. She. Me, I don't know anything."

"Very well then," the rabbi said. "Let's hear what she says." Here the rabbi pointed a finger at Thema Gittel the Silent. Thema Gittel, her face suffused with red, leaned on an elbow and, gesticulating with her other hand, began an endless rapid-fire monologue.

"Listen to me, my fellow Jews. The story is as follows: This Jew, this tailor from Zolodievka, that is either—you'll pardon the expression—crazy or drunk, I don't know which. Did you ever hear such a story? A man comes to me from Zolodievka, that fellow over there. He grabs on to me like a leech and begs me to sell him a goat—God be praised, I had two. He gives me a song and dance about how he, personally, would not buy a goat; he needs it like a hole in the head. But he has a wife, Tsippa-Beila-Reiza, that is, who has taken it into her head once and for all that she wants a goat. And a wife, he says—do you see what I mean?—needs to be obeyed. So I said, 'What's that to me? If you want to buy one of my goats, I'm willing to sell it. That is, I personally would not sell a goat because what is money after all? Money is round and rolls away; but a goat is always a goat. And especially this goat. Is it a goat? It's a mother, not a goat. God bless her, how easily she milks. And talk about eating? Does she eat anything at all? Once a day a measure of bran, and after that a wisp of straw from the roof of the House of Study.' But thinking it over, it occurred to me that, after all, I had two goats, and money *is* a temptation. . . . To make a long story short, my husband, may he live long, mixed in at this point and we agreed with the tailor on a price. How much? You will want to know. May my enemies be paid as little, so help me God. And I gave him the goat. May those I love best have such a goat. She's a mother, not a goat.

"Then he comes back, the tailor, with his libel. 'It's not a goat,' he says. Enough talk. You know what? Here stands the goat. If you'll kindly lend me a milking bucket, I'll milk her right before your eyes." And Thema Gittel borrowed a bucket from the rabbi's wife and milked the goat before them all, then passed the bucket around, first of course, to the rabbi, then to the assistant rabbis, dignitaries, and other folk.

What a tumult and shouting followed—as if the heavens had split open. Some said that the Zolodievka tailor should be required to buy drinks all around; others said that wasn't a sufficient fine—the goat should be taken from him. "No," said someone else, "the goat is a goat. May they live in prosperity and honor together." "Honor," said still another. "Let's beat some honor into him, him and his cursed goat."

Shimon-Eli, seeing how matters were going, slowly edged his way out of the rabbi's house and made off.

Eight

Va-iso hakhayat es raglaim, and the tailor took to his heels and ran off with the goat, like a man pursued by wildfire, looking back from time to time to see if he was being chased. And he thanked God that he got away, free and clear.

Approaching the Oak Tavern, Shimon-Eli thought, "I'll be damned if I'll tell him what happened." And he hid the matter from Dodi.

"Well, how did it go?" Dodi asked eagerly.

"How should it have gone?" Shimon-Eli said. "They treated me with respect. Because I'm not just anybody. I really let them have it. As for the teacher, we talked a little Torah together, and it's clear that I know a little more about the fine print than he does. In short, everyone begged my pardon, and they gave me the first goat I had bought. 'Here she is. Take her for a while,' as it is written, 'Take thou this creature and give me a drink.'"

"Not only is he a boaster, he's a liar, too,' thought Dodi the Rendar. "One has to play the trick again and see what he'll say then." To the tailor, Dodi said, "I've got a little really fine old cherry wine, if you're interested."

"Ah, the Messiah wine," Shimon-Eli said, licking his lips. "Let's have a bit, and I'll test its quality. Not everyone is a connoisseur of such things."

After the first glass our tailor's tongue was unleashed, and he said to the Rendar, "Tell me, my dear cousin. After all, you are a man of some experience and certainly no fool. Tell me, do you believe in magic? In delusions?"

"For instance?" Dodi said, astonished.

"For instance," replied Shimon-Eli, "in possession, in goblins, wraiths, in reincarnated creatures."

"Why do you ask?" Dodi said, affecting a simpleton's look.

"Just because," Shimon-Eli *Shma-Koleynu* said, and started off on an endless monologue about *gilguls*, warlocks, witches, devils, gnomes, wraiths, ghosts, and spirits.

Dodi appeared to be amazed. He puffed on his pipe, then spat to avert the evil eye. "I'll tell you what, Shimon-Eli, I'm going to be afraid to sleep tonight. It's true. I've always been afraid of the dead, and now you've got me believing in *gilguls* and gnomes as well."

"How can you help it?" the tailor said. "Just try not believing. Just let one of those goblins come, overturning your kneading trough, drinking your water, sucking your pitchers dry, breaking your pots, tying the fringes of your prayer garment into knots, throwing your cat into your bed so it sits on your chest like a ten-ton weight and you can't move, and when you do get up you find the cat staring into your eyes like a soul in hell."

"Enough, enough," said the Rendar, spitting and waving his hands. "I don't want to hear any more of that. Night's coming on."

"Good-bye, then. I'm sorry if I've upset you. It's not really my fault. Goodnight."

Nine

Khshebo hakhayat, arrived at home. The tailor went into his house, intending to give Tsippa-Beila-Reiza the sound scolding she deserved, but he resisted the impulse, thinking, "A woman, after all, is only a woman. Let it pass." And for the sake of peace he told his wife a handsome lie: "I'll tell you, Tsippa-Beila-Reiza, my dear, those people have tremendous respect for me. Let me not talk about the scolding I gave the teacher and his wife. I'll spare you that, though I gave them plenty. But then I dragged them off to the rabbi and his judgment was that they should pay a fine, because when a Jew like Shimon-Eli comes to buy their goat, he should be given the greatest respect. "Because Shimon-Eli," said the rabbi, "is a Jew who is a somebody.""

Tsippa-Beila-Reiza, however, had no interest in hearing how her husband had been praised. Eagerly, she went into the house to milk the *real* goat, but it was not long before she came running out, speechless. Grabbing Shimon-Eli by the collar, she gave three great thrusts that landed him outside the house, damning him and his lovely goat together.

Immediately a crowd of men, women, and children gathered around the tailor and his fine goat and learned that this goat, whose leading rope he now held, was in Kozodoievka a goat that gave milk, but no sooner did she come to Zolodievka than she stopped being a goat. Shimon-Eli swore up and down, with oaths even an apostate would have believed, that with his own eyes he had seen the goat milked in the rabbi's house and that she had given a full bucket of milk.

People in the crowd studied the goat earnestly, asked for more details, and were told the story over and over again to their amazement. Some laughed, others cracked jokes or poked fun at the tailor. Still others shook their heads, spat against the evil eye, and said, "Some goat. If it's a goat, I'm the rabbi's wife."

"Then what is it?"

"A *gilgul*, that's what it is."

The word *gilgul* was taken up by the crowd and *gilgul* tales were soon bandied about: some that had happened here in Zolodievka, in Kozodoievka, in Yampoli, in Pistchi-Yavadeh, in Khaplapovitsch, in Petschi-Khvost—all over. Who, for example, didn't know the story of Lazer Wolf's horse and how it had to be taken out of the town, killed, and buried in shrouds? And who had not heard the story of the quarter of a chicken which, when it was being served at a Sabbath meal, moved its single wing—and other such true tales?

Finally Shimon-Eli started off toward Kozodoievka, followed by an honor guard of pupils shouting, "Hurrah *Shma-Koleynu!* Hurrah the Milking Tailor!" and holding their sides for laughter.

This wounded Shimon-Eli to the quick. Bad enough the ill luck that had come his way—now, to be ridiculed as well. He led his goat through the town and complained to his guild, demanding to know why its members were silent on the matter. He told them the story of his adventures in Kozodoievka and showed them the goat.

Whiskey was immediately sent for, a meeting was held, and it was concluded to send a delegation to the rabbi, to the assistant rabbis, and to the other town dignitaries, to stir things up. "Who ever heard of such scoundrels? To take a poor Jew and cheat him out of his last few rubles; to sell him a so-called goat, then to pass off on him the devil only knows what. Not only that, but to play the same trick twice. Such a thing was unheard of, not even in Sodom."

And so it was. The delegation went to the rabbi, to the assistant rabbis, and to the town dignitaries and lodged their complaint as follows: "Who ever heard of such scoundrels? To take a poor Jew and cheat him out of his last few rubles; to sell him a so-called goat, then to pass off on him the devil only knows what, and to play the same trick on him twice. Such a thing was unheard of, even in Sodom."

The rabbi, the assistant rabbis, and the town dignitaries listened to the complaint and called a meeting for that evening at the rabbi's house. There it was decided, on the spot, to send a letter to the rabbi, the

assistant rabbis, and the town dignitaries of Kozodoievka. And so it
was. They sat themselves down and wrote a letter in Hebrew, all very
fine and florid. This is the letter they sent—every jot and tittle:

> To the rabbis, assistant rabbis, town dignitaries, and
> renowned learned men, pillars of the world against which
> the entire house of Israel leans: peace and honor. First
> unto you, and peace unto the entire and sanctified
> community of Zolodievka, and may all excellence
> descend upon it, amen.
>
> Whereas it has come to our ears that a great wrong has
> been done to a man of our town, Shimon-Eli, son of the
> Reb Bendit Leib of blessed memory—who is known as
> Shimon-Eli *Shma-Koleynu*—to wit: that two of your
> people, the teacher Chaim-Chono and his wife, now and
> in the world to come, with cunning extracted from the
> tailor six and a half rubles of silver which they conveyed
> into their own vessels, then wiped their lips as if to say,
> "We have done no injustice."
>
> We, the undersigned, therefore, since such a thing is not
> done among Jews, bear witness that the above-mentioned
> tailor is an honest and poor workingman who is burdened
> with children, that he supports himself by the sweat of his
> brow—and did not King David say long ago in his
> Psalms, "When thou eatest of the weariness of thy hands
> it shall be well with thee." As our sages say, the meaning
> of it is: Well in this world and well in the world to
> come. . .
>
> Therefore, we implore you to scrutinize the matter
> closely and set down a judgment sentence that shall shine
> like the sun on one of the parties. Either let the tailor have
> his money repaid to him or the goat that he bought shall
> be returned to him, since the goat with which he arrived in
> Zolodievka is not a goat—on that the whole town is
> willing to take a solemn oath.
>
> And let there be peace among Jews, as our sages have
> said: "For Jews, there is no vessel holier than peace."
>
> Peace, then, unto you. Peace, near and far. Peace unto

all. Amen. From us, your servants, to you, whose littlest finger has more girth than our thighs.

These are the words of the Rabbi————, son of the Rabbi————of blessed memory . . . and the words of the Rabbi————, son of the Rabbi———— —— of blessed memory . . . and the words of Baruch Caftan, Zerah Bellybutton, Fishel Tavern-bouncer, Chaim Squeak, Nissel Wallow, Mottel Peeling, Yehoshuah Heshel Kiss-kiss.

Ten

Balayla ha-hu, that night, the moon gazed down at Zolodievka's gloomy half-ruined houses that stood squeezed together without courtyards or fences or trees, looking for all the world like a cemetery—an old cemetery whose gravestones looked like penitents; they were bowed so perilously that they would long ago have toppled over if they had not been propped up.

Despite the foul evening air and the unsavory smells that came from the market and the synagogue courtyard—despite the dust, dense as a wall, people, like cockroaches, were out of their holes for the evening. Men and women, old folks and children, were taking the air after a broiling day. Some sat on their stoops, chatting, exchanging nonsense, or just sitting around, or looking at the sky, at the face of the moon, or at the billions of stars which if you had eighteen heads you could not count them.

That night Shimon-Eli, the tailor, roamed the town's back streets, trailing the precious goat he had bought in Kozodoievka, trying to avoid as best he could the urchins of the town. His plan was to wait for daylight when he would make his way back to Kozodoievka.

To pass the time, he dropped in at the tavern run by Hodel, "the excise tax man's wife," to have a little drink to ease his heart, to talk with Hodel and get her advice about his trouble.

Hodel, the excise tax man's wife, was a widow with "a man's brains," who was familiar with all the leading citizens of the town and was friendly with laborers as well. How does it happen that she was called the excise tax man's wife?

The story goes that when she was young, she was a *Yefas toyar,* a very great beauty. One day the excise tax collector, a very rich man, was passing through Zolodievka and came upon her carrying a couple of geese to the *shochet*. He stopped her and asked, "Whose daugher are you?"

This man made Hodel so shy that she laughed and ran off.

Since that time, she was known as the excise tax man's wife. There were those who said that the excise tax man later went to her home and talked with her father, Nekhamiah Vinokur, offering to marry Hodel just as she was, without a dowry. More than that, the tax man promised to put some money into Nekhemiah's pocket as well. It almost came to an engagement contract, but the town gossips made so much fuss that nothing came of it. Later she was quietly married off to some poor fellow, an epileptic. She wept bitterly and refused to go to the wedding ceremony. It was a scandal that rocked the whole town.

It was said that she was still madly in love with the excise tax man, and there was a song made up about her that women and girls in Zolodievka sing to this day. The songs begins:

> The moon shone—
> It was midnight
> And Hodel sat by the door.

The song ends:

> I love you, oh my soul,
> Love without end,
> I can't live without you.

This then was the story of Hodel the excise tax man's wife, and it was to her that our tailor poured out his anguished heart. He told her everything and asked for her advice.

"What's to be done?" he said. "You are, after all—as King David says in the Song of Songs—'Black and comely.' Wise is not comely, but you are both . . . so give me some advice. What's to be done?"

"What's to be done?" Hodel said, spitting against the evil eye. "Can't you see that the thing is a *gilgul?* It's like a bomb that's going to explode. Get rid of the damn thing. Or, God forbid, the same thing will happen to you as happened to my Aunt Pearl, may she rest in peace. She's in a better world now."

"What happened to her?" a frightened Shimon-Eli asked.

"What happened?" Hodel sighed. "My Aunt Pearl, may she rest in peace, was a devout, honorable woman—my family are all honorable folk—though in this Godforsaken Zolodievka, may it burn in hell, you might not know that for the catty gossip that goes on—behind one's back, of course. To one's face it's all flattery and sweet talk. Anyway, my Aunt Pearl, may she rest in peace, went to do her shopping one day and saw a spool of thread on the ground. 'A spool of thread,' she thought. 'One can always use a spool of thread.' So she bent down and picked it up and went on her way, but the spool leaped up into her face, then fell to the ground. So she bent down and picked it up again; and again, it leaped up into her face. So she spat on it to keep away the evil eye and threw the damn thing away and started on home, but looking back, she saw it following her. She tried running, but the spool of thread followed after. In short, by the time she got home, the poor thing was half-dead. She fell into a faint. After that, she pined away for more than a year. Well, what do you make of that? Just take a guess."

"Ah," said Shimon-Eli. "All women are alike. It's all old wives' tales. Stuff and nonsense. If you pay attention to the prattling of women, you end by jumping at your own shadow. As it is written, 'Women are geese.' But never mind. 'Today the world was created—nothing to worry about.'"

And Shimon-Eli the tailor went on his way.

It was a star-filled night. The moon strolled through drifting clouds that looked like high dark mountains touched with silver. The half-moon looked down on Zolodievka that was now deep in sleep. A few householders, dreading bedbugs, had dragged their yellow bedclothes outside and were snoring away, dreaming sweet dreams: dreams of good profits at the fair, of large incomes, of profitable little shops, dreams of a bit of bed, of honorable income, or of honor itself. All sorts of dreams.

The streets were empty; not a sound to be heard anywhere. Even the butchers' dogs, now tired of their daytime strife and weary with barking, squeezed themselves under the butchers' blocks, put their muzzles between their paws, and—hush! From time to time, half a bark escaped a dog dreaming of a bone for which other dogs were already baring their teeth; or when it dreamed of a fly hovering above its nose, hummmming like the string of a bass fiddle, until the fly landed somewhere and was still. Even the nightwatchman, whose job it was to tap at shop doors—tap,

tap, tap—was in keeping with the evening, drunk tonight, and stood leaning against a wall, fast asleep.

It was on this hushed night that Shimon-Eli the tailor roamed alone through the town, not knowing whether to go or stand or sit. He moved about muttering lines from the Passover song about the cat that ate the kid. "*Khad gadyah*—an only kid. A . . . a . . . a . . . an . . . on . . . on . . . only kid. 'May destruction take the damned goat.'"

He burst into laughter that immediately frightened him. Just then he passed the "Cold Synagogue"—a synagogue in which, it was said, the dead came to say their prayers on Saturday nights, wearing white garments under their prayer shawls. Shimon-Eli thought he heard singing, "*U . . . U . . . U . . . ,*" like a wind blowing down the chimney on a winter night. He hurried by the "Cold Synagogue" and into one of the Gentile streets where suddenly he heard "*Psssssss.*" It was a bird that had flown to the tip of the church steeple. And Shimon-Eli was overwhelmed by a mixture of fear and despair, against which he struggled to give himself courage as best he could, trying to find a *Talmud* passage that could be said at night to keep fear away. But he was assailed by the image of throngs of people he had known who had died long ago, and through his mind rushed all the terror tales he had ever heard: tales of ghosts and devils, of demons in the form of calves, and tales of elves that scurried about on wheels, of werewolves that crawled on all fours, of all sorts of one-eyed creatures, of tales of the living dead, inhabitants of chaos who moved about dressed in shrouds.

Finally Shimon-Eli persuaded himself that the goat trailing after him was not a goat at all, but a *gilgul* or a demon that would, any minute now, stick out a tongue ten yards long, or flap its wing, or cry *ku . . . ku . . . ri . . . ku . . .* for the whole town to hear. Shimon-Eli's brain began to whirl. He paused and untied the rope—at least he could get rid of the "bomb" trailing him. But . . . nothing doing. The creature would not go. Not for a minute. It kept right on following him. Shimon-Eli tried moving away a few paces; the creature followed. He turned to the right; so did the beast. He turned to the left; so did the goat.

"'*Shma Yisroel*,' Hear O Israel," cried Shimon-Eli, his voice no longer his own, and dashed off every which way. As he ran it seemed to him that something pursued him, and though it bleated like a goat it spoke with a human voice, with the intonation of a cantor.

"*Mehhh . . . lehkh*, King over life and of death, and the resurrection."

Eleven

Baboyker—in the morning, when Jews rose to say their prayers and women to go to market and girls to tend their flocks, Shimon-Eli the tailor was discovered sitting on the ground, with the goat, its feet tucked under, sitting beside him, chewing his cud, his beard bobbing up and down. When people spoke to the tailor he replied not a word, but stared ahead like a *golem* made of clay.

Immediately a crowd gathered, making a racket as if the sky were falling down: "Eli . . . goat . . . *Shma-Koleynu* . . . *gilgul* . . . ghost . . . werewolf . . . demon . . . *gilgul* . . . made to ride all night . . . tormented . . . exhausted." Meanwhile, rumors circulated. Everyone claimed to have seen somebody riding something.

"Who rode on what?" asked a Jew, sticking his head among the crowd. "Shimon-Eli the goat; or the goat, Shimon-Eli?"

The crowd roared with laughter.

"Damn you and your laughter," said one of the Jews, a laborer. "You should be ashamed of yourselves. Jews. Grown men. Husbands, fathers of children. What are you laughing at? Can't you see the poor tailor is in a stupor? Sick. You'd do better to get him home and send for the doctor, the devil take your grandfather." The man spoke with authority, his words as if fired from a gun, and the crowd stopped laughing. Somebody ran to get water. Somebody else to get Yudel, the healer.

They took Shimon-Eli under the arms, if you'll pardon the expression, and led him home where he was put to bed. Yudel the healer, with all his instruments, arrived shortly and gave him his "serious" treatment. He cupped him, set leeches on him, and bled him endlessly.

"The more blood we take, the better," Yudel said, "because all illness comes from bad blood." Thus Yudel explained his medical theory and promised to come back that night.

When Tsippa-Beila-Reiza saw her poor husband, the *schlimazel*, lying on the collapsed cot, covered with rags, his eyes turned up to the ceiling, speaking deliriously through parched lips, she wrung her hands, beat her head against the wall, and mourned as if she were mourning for the dead. "Oh, woe is me! What a disaster! What will become of me and of our little children?" And the children, naked and barefoot, ran in and gathered about their poor mother, helping her to mourn. The older ones wept silently, swallowed their tears, and hid their faces. The little ones, who did not understand what was going on, cried as loudly as they could. Even the smallest one, a worn, sallow-faced boy with a swollen belly, crept up to his mother's side to wail, "Mama, I'm hungry." All of them together made such a terrible music that no one seeing them could stand it for long. Those who came to the tailor's house left at once, overwhelmed and sick at heart. Asked how Shimon-Eli was, he was likely to gesture with his hand as if to say, "Bad. Too bad."

Several housewives, near neighbors, stood around, their faces tear-stained, their noses red. Before Tsippa-Beila-Reiza's very eyes, they pointed to their temples and shook their heads or nodded, as if to say, "Too bad, Tsippa-Beila-Reiza. Too bad."

Then the wonder began. Shimon-Eli *Shma-Koleynu* had lived in poverty for fifty years in Zolodievka, as unobserved as a worm in the dark. No one had talked of him; nobody knew what sort of man he was. Now that he was sick, suddenly all of his good deeds were visible, and it turned out that Shimon-Eli was a unique, pure, good soul. A saintly fellow. It was said of him that he would take from the rich to give to the poor; that, though it cost him blows, he would take the part of the poor against the whole town. Or that he would share his last bite with a hungry man. And more such virtues and praises were told about him— the way at a funeral, one speaks only good of the departed.

Suddenly nearly the entire town came to visit the sick man, and every possible effort was made to save him from dying, God forbid, an untimely death.

Twelve

V'hapoalim, and the working people of Zolodievka met together in Hodel, the excise tax man's wife's, tavern. Whiskey was put on the table. There was a tremendous shouting and racket. Tales were told, the rich were splattered with curses—behind their back, as usual.

"Zolodievka—may it burn in hell. What keeps them quiet, our big shots? All of them ready to bathe in our blood, and no one to take our part. Who is it that pays the community's expenses? We do. When troubles come, who helps? We do. Who pays the *shochet*? We do. Who supports the ritual bath? We do. Whom do they flay? Us. Jews, why are you silent? Let's go to the rabbi, to the assistant rabbis, and to the dignitaries and beat their guts out. What kind of anarchy is this—to let them kill a whole family?

And the workers went off to the rabbi, where they made an outcry, to which the rabbi replied by letting them see the letter that had just been handed to him by a wagon driver. The letter came from the rabbis, the assistant rabbis, and the dignitaries of Kozodoievka.

Here is that letter:

> All honor to the rabbis, the assistant rabbis, the famous scholars (may they shine in heaven as they shine on earth), of the blessed city of Zolodievka, amen.
>
> As soon as we received your words, which were as honey to our mouths, we all met together to inquire accurately into the matter; and we have concluded that our people have been innocently maligned. Not only is your tailor a wicked fellow, he has invented a frame-up and created enmity between two communities. He is worthy to be fined. We, the undersigned, take oath and swear that with our own eyes we saw that the goat gave milk, may God grant that all Jewish goats should give so much! Pay no attention to him, that tailor, who tells lies, whatever tales he tells. Do not believe the inventions of scoundrels, may their mouths be stopped. Peace be unto you, and to all Jews from now and into eternity.
>
> These are the words of your younger brothers who are not worthy to kiss the dust of your feet:
> The words of the Rabbi, son of the Rabbi ———— of blessed memory; and the words of the Rabbi, son of the Rabbi ———— of blessed memory; and the words of Henikh Gullet, Yekutiel Lumpenclod, Shepsel Potato, Fishel Wallower, Berel Whiskey, Leib Growler.

When the rabbi had read this letter to the workers, they were more furious still. "Ah, Kozodoievka scoundrels! They're making fun of us. We'll teach them respect. 'Shears and steam-irons: the people.'"

And a new meeting was called at once, whiskey was sent for, and it was concluded to take that fine goat and march to Kozodoievka and tear the place apart—the school and the whole town together.

Oymer v'oyseh, no sooner said than done. Some sixty of the workers quickly formed a mob. Tailors, shoemakers, carpenters, butchers, blacksmiths—rough, tough-looking fellows all, and all of them armed: some with tailors' yardsticks, others with steam-irons, still others with bootlasts, some with cleavers or hammers or whatever other household implements they could grab—a rolling pin or a cheese grater.

And the cry was "On to Kozodoievka—war! To destroy and to kill without quarter, once and for all. Death to the Philistines, and an end to the matter!"

"Hold on, fellows," one of the guild members called out. "You're ready for anything, but where's the goat?"

"Just look at us. Where the damn hell is the *gilgul?*"

"That *gilgul* is no dummy. Where the hell could it be?"

"Probably ran home to the teacher."

"You're crazy. You're talking like a cow."

"Then you're a horse. Where else could he be?"

But what good were these guesses? If one searched for a month of Sundays, they would not have found the goat.

Thirteen

Ka'eys, now, let us leave the haunted tailor in his wrestling with the angel of death, and the guild members readying themselves for war, and let us follow the *gilgul*—that is, the goat.

The *gilgul*, seeing the commotion in the town, considered the matter and concluded that it was none of his business. What good did it do him, dying of hunger, to be dragged about here and there after the *schlimazel* of a tailor? How much better to follow his nose into the wide world.

And the goat took off crazily, his hooves not touching the earth—taking no care for anything at all, leaping over men and women, creating destruction in the marketplace—a real terror, knocking over tables of pancakes and bread, bowls of cherries and berries, springing over pots and glassware, leaping, breaking, jumping, clatterty-bang-bang. The market women panicked, screeching, "What is it . . . what kind of *schlimazel? . . . a goat . . . a creature . . . a gilgul . . .* woe is me . . . a disaster . . . where is it? . . . what is it? . . . catch him . . . catch him. Catch." And the mob of men with their sleeves rolled up and women with their skirts tucked up, if you'll forgive the expression, milled about, searching. It was useless. Our goat had discovered the meaning of freedom and took off wherever his feet would take him.

And the tailor, poor fellow! "What is the moral of this tale?" the reader will ask. Don't press me, friends. It was not a good ending. The tale began cheerfully enough, and it ended as most such happy stories do—badly. And since you know the author of the story—that he is not naturally a gloomy fellow and hates to complain and prefers cheerful stories—and you know that he hates insisting on a story's "moral," and that moralizing is not his manner. . . . Then let the maker of the tale take his leave of you smiling, and let him wish you, Jews—and all mankind— more laughter than tears. Laughter is good for you. Doctors prescribe laughter.

Translated by Leonard Wolf

A
Yom
Kippur
Scandal

"THAT'S NOTHING!" called out the man with round eyes, like an ox, who had been sitting all this time in a corner by the window, smoking and listening to our stories of thefts, robberies, and expropriations. "I'll tell you a story of a theft that took place in our town, in the synagogue itself, and on Yom Kippur at that! It is worth listening to.

"Our town, Kasrilevke—that's where I'm from, you know—is a small town, and a poor one. There is no thievery there. No one steals anything for the simple reason that there is nobody to steal from and nothing worth stealing. And besides, a Jew is not a thief by nature. That is, he may be a thief, but not the sort who will climb through a window or attack you with a knife. He will divert, pervert, subvert, and contravert as a matter of course; but he won't pull anything out of your pocket. He won't be caught like a common thief and led through the streets with a yellow placard on his back. Imagine, then, a theft taking place in Kasrilevke, and such a theft at that. Eighteen hundred rubles at one crack.

"Here is how it happened. One Yom Kippur eve, just before the evening services, a stranger arrived in our town, a salesman of some sort from Lithuania. He left his bag at an inn and went forth immediately to look for a place of worship, and he came upon the old synagogue. Coming in just before the service began, he found the trustees around the collection plates. 'Sholem aleichem,' said he. 'Aleichem sholem,' they answered. 'Where does our guest hail from?' 'From Lithuania.' 'And your name?' 'Even your grandmother wouldn't know if I told her.'

'But you have come to our synagogue!' 'Where else should I go?' 'Then you want to pray here?' 'Can I help myself? What else can I do?' 'Then put something into the plate.' 'What did you think? That I was not going to pay?'

"To make a long story short, our guest took out three silver rubles and put them in the plate. Then he put a ruble into the cantor's plate, one into the rabbi's, gave one for the *cheder,* threw a half into the charity box, and then began to divide money among the poor who flocked to the door. And in our town we have so many poor people that if you really wanted to start giving, you could divide Rothschild's fortune among them.

"Impressed by his generosity, the men quickly found a place for him along the east wall. Where did they find room for him when all the places along the wall are occupied? Don't ask. Have you ever been at a celebration—a wedding or circumcision—when all the guests are already seated at the table, and suddenly there is a commotion outside— the rich uncle has arrived? What do you do? You push and shove and squeeze until a place is made for the rich relative. Squeezing is a Jewish custom. If no one squeezes us, we squeeze each other."

The man with the eyes that bulged like an ox's paused, looked at the crowd to see what effect his wit had on us, and went on.

"So our guest went up to his place of honor and called to the *shammes* to bring him a praying stand. He put on his *tallis* and started to pray. He prayed and he prayed, standing on his feet all the time. He never sat down or left his place all evening long or all the next day. To fast all day standing on one's feet, without ever sitting down—that only a Litvak can do!

"But when it was all over, when the final blast of the *shofar* had died down, the Day of Atonement had ended, and Chaim the *melamed,* who had led the evening prayers after Yom Kippur from time immemorial, had cleared his throat, and in his tremulous voice had already begun— '*Ma-a-riv a-ro-vim . . .*' suddenly screams were heard. 'Help! Help! Help!' We looked around: the stranger was stretched out on the floor in a dead faint. We poured water on him, revived him, but he fainted again. What was the trouble? Plenty! This Litvak tells us that he had brought with him to Kasrilevke eighteen hundred rubles. To leave that much at the inn—think of it, eighteen hundred rubles—he had been afraid. Whom could he trust with such a sum of money in a strange town? And yet, to keep it in his pocket on Yom Kippur was not exactly proper either. So at last this plan had occurred to him: he had taken the money to the synagogue and slipped it into the praying stand. Only a Litvak could do a thing like that! . . . Now do you see why he had not stepped away from the praying stand for a single minute? And yet during one of the many prayers when we all turn our face to the wall, someone must have stolen the money . . .

"Well, the poor man wept, tore his hair, wrung his hands. What would he do with the money gone? It was not his own money, he said. He was only a clerk. The money was his employer's. He himself was a poor man, with a houseful of children. There was nothing for him to do now but go out and drown himself, or hang himself right here in front of everybody.

Hearing these words, the crowd stood petrified, forgetting that they had all been fasting since the night before and it was time to go home and eat. It was a disgrace before a stranger, a shame and a scandal in our own eyes. A theft like that—eighteen hundred rubles! And where? In the Holy of Holies, in the old synagogue of Kasrilevke. And on what day? On the holiest day of the year, on Yom Kippur! Such a thing had never been heard of before.

"'*Shammes,* lock the door!' ordered our rabbi. We have our own rabbi in Kasrilevke, Reb Yozifel, a true man of God, a holy man. Not too sharpwitted, perhaps, but a good man, a man with no bitterness in him. Sometimes he gets ideas that you would not hit upon if you had eighteen heads on your shoulders. . . . When the door was locked, Reb Yozifel turned to the congregation, his face pale as death and his hands trembling, his eyes burning with a strange fire.

"He said, 'Listen to me, my friends. This is an ugly thing, a thing unheard of since the world was created—that here in Kasrilevke there should be a sinner, a renegade to his people, who would have the audacity to take from a stranger, a poor man with a family, a fortune like this. And on what day? On the holiest day of the year, on Yom Kippur, and perhaps at the last, most solemn moment—just before the *shofar* was blown! Such a thing has never happened anywhere. I cannot believe it is possible. It simply cannot be. But perhaps—who knows? Man is greedy, and the temptation—especially with a sum like this, eighteen hundred rubles, God forbid—is great enough. So if one of us was tempted, if he were fated to commit this evil on a day like this, we must probe the matter thoroughly, strike at the root of this whole affair. Heaven and earth have sworn that the truth must always rise as oil upon the waters. Therefore, my friends, let us search each other now, go through each other's garments, shake out our pockets—all of us from the oldest householder to the *shammes,* not leaving anyone out. Start with me. Search my pockets first.'

"Thus spoke Reb Yozifel, and he was the first to unbind his gabardine and turn his pockets inside out. And following his example all the men loosened their girdles and showed the linings of their pockets, too. They searched each other, they felt and shook one another, until they came to Lazer Yossel, who turned all colors and began to argue that, in the first place, the stranger was a swindler, that his story was the pure fabrication of a Litvak. No one had stolen any money from him. Couldn't they see that it was all a falsehood and a lie?

"The congregation began to clamor and shout. What did he mean by this? All the important men had allowed themselves to be searched, so why should Lazar Yossel escape? There are no privileged characters here. 'Search him! Search him!' the crowd roared.

"Lazer Yossel saw that it was hopeless, and began to plead for mercy with tears in his eyes. He begged them not to search him. He swore by all that was holy that he was as innocent in this as he would want to be of any wrongdoing as long as he lived. Then why didn't he want to be searched? It was a disgrace to him, he said. He begged them to have pity on his youth, not to bring this disgrace down on him. 'Do anything you wish with me,' he said, 'but don't touch my pockets.' How do you like that? Do you suppose we listened to him?

"But wait . . . I forgot to tell you who this Lazer Yossel was. He was not a Kasrilevkite himself. He came from the devil knows where, at the time of his marriage, to live with his wife's parents. The rich man of our town had dug him up somewhere for his daughter, boasted that he had found a rare nugget, a fitting match for a daughter like his. He knew a thousand pages of *Talmud* by heart, and all of the Bible. He was a master of Hebrew, arithmetic, bookkeeping, algebra, penmanship—in short, everything you could think of. When he arrived in Kasrilevke— this jewel of a young man—everyone came out to gaze at him. What sort of bargain had the rich man picked out? Well, to look at him you could tell nothing. He was a young man, something in trousers. Not bad looking, but with a nose a trifle too long, eyes that burned like two coals, and a sharp tongue. Our leading citizens began to work on him: tried him out on a page of *Gemara,* a chapter from the Scriptures, a bit of Rambam, this, that, and the other. He was perfect in everything, the dog! Whenever you went after him, he was at home. Reb Yozifel himself said that he could have been a rabbi in any Jewish congregation. As for world affairs, there is nothing to talk about. We have an authority on such things in our town, Zaidel Reb Shaye's, but he could not hold a candle to Lazer Yossel. And when it came to chess—there was no one like him in all the world! Talk about versatile people . . . Naturally the whole town envied the rich man his find, but some of them felt he was a little too good to be true. He was too clever (and too much of anything is bad!) For a man of his station he was too free and easy, a hail-fellow-well-met, too familiar with all the young folk—boys, girls, and maybe even loose women. There were rumors . . . At the same time he went around alone too much, deep in thought. At the synagogue he came in last, put on his *tallis,* and with his skullcap on askew, thumbed aimlessly through his prayerbook without ever following the services. No one ever saw him doing anything exactly wrong, and yet people murmured that he was not a God-fearing man. Apparently a man cannot be perfect . . .

"And so, when his turn came to be searched and he refused to let them do it, that was all the proof most of the men needed that he was the one who had taken the money. He begged them to let him swear any oath they wished, begged them to chop him, roast him, cut him up—do anything but shake his pockets out. At this point even our rabbi, Reb Yozifel, although he was a man we had never seen angry, lost his temper and started to shout.

"'You!' he cried. 'You thus and thus! Do you know what you deserve? You see what all these men have endured. They were able to forget the disgrace and allowed themselves to be searched; but you want to be the only exception! God in heaven! Either confess and hand over the money, or let us see for ourselves what is in your pockets. You are trifling now with the entire Jewish community. Do you know what they can do to you?'

"To make a long story short, the men took hold of this young upstart, threw him down on the floor with force, and began to search him all over, shake out every one of his pockets. And finally they shook out . . . Well, guess what! A couple of well-gnawed chicken bones and a few dozen plum pits still moist from chewing. You can imagine what an impression this made—to discover food in the pockets of our prodigy on this holiest of fast days. Can you imagine the look on the young man's face, and on his father-in-law's? And on that of our poor rabbi?

"Poor Reb Yozifel! He turned away in shame. He could look no one in the face. On Yom Kippur, and in his synagogue . . . As for the rest of us, hungry as we were, we could not stop talking about it all the way home. We rolled with laughter in the streets. Only Reb Yozifel walked home alone, his head bowed, full of grief, unable to look anyone in the eyes, as though the bones had been shaken out of his own pockets."

The story was apparently over. Unconcerned, the man with the round eyes of an ox turned back to the window and resumed smoking.

"Well," we all asked in one voice, "and what about the money?"

"What money?" asked the man innocently, watching the smoke he had exhaled.

"What do you mean—what money? The eighteen hundred rubles!"

"Oh," he drawled. "The eighteen hundred. They were gone."

"Gone?"

"Gone forever."

Translated by Julius and Frances Butwin

Eternal Life

IF YOU LIKE, I'll tell you a story of how I once took a burden upon myself and came close, perilously close, to misfortune. And why, you may wonder, did it happen? Because I was very young, neither experienced nor shrewd. It's possible, of course, that I'm still far from wisdom, for if I were clever, wouldn't I be rich? If you have money you're clever and handsome, and you can sing, too.

In short, I was a young man, living, as the custom was, off my in-laws, sitting at my studies, dipping into forbidden books on the sly when my father-in-law and mother-in-law weren't looking. My father-in-law wasn't so bad. It was she, the mother-in-law, who made the trouble; she wore the pants; she was boss! All by herself she ran the business, made matches for her daughters—everything singlehanded. She picked me, too; it was she who examined me in the Law; it was she who brought me to Zwihil from Radomishli. I'm from Radomishli myself—surely you've heard of Radomishli! It was written up in the papers not so long ago.

Well, so there I was in Zwihil, living off my in-laws, sweating over Maimonides' *Guide for the Perplexed*, hardly stepping across the threshold of the house, you might say, until the time came to register for military service and I had to bestir myself, arrange my papers, figure out a way of getting an exemption, obtain a passport, and all the rest of it. This, you might say, was my first journey into the world. To show that I was now a man, I went to the market all by myself and hired a conveyance. God sent me a bargain, a lucky find—a peasant from Radomishli with a sleigh, a broad red sleigh with two wings on the sides, like an eagle. I never even noticed that he had a white horse, and a white

43

horse, said my mother-in-law, means bad luck. "May I be lying," she said, "but I'm afraid this journey will end in trouble." "Bite off your tongue," exclaimed my father-in-law and regretted it immediately, for he soon got what was coming to him. But to me he said on the sly, "Women's superstitions."

I began to prepare for the trip—prayer shawl and phylacteries, cakes made with butter, a few rubles in my pocket, and three pillows: one to sit on, one to lean on, and one for my feet. But when the time came to say good-bye, the words stuck in my throat. It's always like that with me: I lose my tongue. What does one say? I don't know! To me it's always seemed rather coarse to turn your back on people and leave them, just like that. I don't know how you feel about it, but farewells for me are, to this day, a torment. But I seem to be losing the thread of my story. . . . I was on my way to Radomishli.

It was the beginning of winter; the snow was thick and made excellent going for the sleigh. White though it was, the horse ran like a song, and the peasant I had drawn was a silent one, the kind that answers "Eh-heh," meaning Yes, or "Ba-nee," meaning No. If you threatened him with the cholera you couldn't get another word out of him. Having eaten well, I departed happily, settled cozily in the sleigh, a pillow under me, a pillow at my shoulders, a pillow at my feet.

The nag leaps ahead; the peasant clucks; the sleigh glides; the wind blows. Snow whirls in the air and floats down upon the great wide highway. My heart is full of a strange, outlandish joy. For the first time I am going into God's little world, all by myself, my own master. And I lean back and stretch my legs in the sleigh, as proud and easy as a squire.

But in winter, no matter how warm your clothes may be, you want to stop, to catch your breath and warm your sides before you go on. I began to imagine a warm inn, a blazing samovar, a roast with hot gravy. These dreams pressed upon my heart—that is, they made me hungry. So I took up the matter of an inn with my peasant. "Ba-nee," he said, meaning No. "Is the inn far?" I asked. "Eh-heh," he drawled, meaning Yes. "How far?" But that I couldn't pry out of him. And then I began to think: imagine if the driver had been a Jew instead of a peasant! He'd have told me not only where the inn was, but who was the owner, what he was called, how many children he had, how much he had paid for the inn, how much he earned by it, how long he's been there, and whom he had bought it from—he'd have recited me an epic. A strange people. Our Jews, I mean. God bless them.

So I dreamed on about my inn and the hot samovar and the little delicacies to eat. Until God took pity on me. The peasant clucked to his nag, turned the sleigh off to a side, and there stood a small gray hut covered with snow, a country tavern. Standing alone on the white snowy plain, it seemed strangely solitary, like a remote and forgotten gravestone. We drove up to it as grand as you please, and my peasant took the horse and sleigh to the stable while I went right into the tavern, opened the door, and remained standing on the threshold, perplexed. Why, you wonder? It's a pretty story, and a short one. In the middle of the floor, on the ground, lay a corpse covered with black. At its head stood two brass candlesticks with tiny candles. Tattered children sat beside it, beating themselves on their heads with their tiny hands, weeping, yammering, crying, "Ma-ma! Mama!" And a tall, long-legged man in a torn, summer-thin, loose coat paced back and forth, wringing his hands and muttering to himself, "What's to be done? What can I do?"

Seeing this, my first thought was to escape. "Noah," I said to myself, "clear out!" I began to back away. But the door closed behind me and something soldered my feet to the threshold. I couldn't move from the spot. Catching sight of me, the long-legged man rushed over to me with arms outstretched, like someone begging to be rescued. "What do you say to this misfortune!" he cried, showing me the weeping children. "Their mother has left them. What shall I do? What's to be done?"

"Blessed be God's righteousness," I said to him and wanted to console him with kind words, as the custom is among us. But he interrupted me and said, "It's an old story, you understand. She's been all but dead this past year. It was the true blessing, consumption. Poor thing, how she begged and prayed for death! But what shall we do, here in the middle of this barren field? What's to be done? If I go to a farm and hire a wagon to take her to town, how can I leave the children? And night is coming on. What's to be done!"

With these words my long-legged Jew burst into a strange tearless weeping, almost like laughter, and sounds resembling coughs came from his throat. "Oohoohoo! Oohoo!"

I forgot my hunger, my cold, I forgot everything and said to him, "I'm traveling from Zwihil to Radomishli and have a fine sleigh. If the village you speak of is not far, I can lend you the sleigh and wait here. If it won't take too long."

He threw his arms around me and almost kissed me. "Oh, long life to you for this good deed! You'll gain Eternal Life! As I am a Jew, Eternal

Life! The village isn't far from here. Four or five miles, no more. It will hardly take an hour, and I'll send your sleigh right back. It'll bring you Eternal Life, I swear it, Eternal Life! Children, get up from the ground and give thanks. Kiss this young man's hands and feet. He's given us his sleigh, and I will take your mother to the consecrated ground. Eternal Life! As I am a Jew, Eternal Life!"

You could scarcely say there was rejoicing. The children, when they heard their mother was to be taken away, fell upon her with still more tears. All the same, these were good tidings. Someone—a man, myself— had turned up to do them a mercy; God alone had sent him there. They looked at me as though I were a redeemer, a sort of Elijah the Prophet, and to tell the honest truth I began to see myself as no ordinary person. Suddenly I grew in stature before my own eyes, becoming what some people call a hero. At that moment I was ready to lift mountains, to overwhelm worlds. Nothing seemed impossible. So I blurted out, "You know what? I'll take her myself, with the help of my peasant, so you won't have to leave the children alone at such a time."

The more I talked this way, the more they all wept. They wept and they looked at me as if they were seeing an angel that had come down from heaven. In my own eyes I kept getting bigger by the minute, unbelievably great, so much so that I forgot I had always lived in terror of corpses, being afraid even to touch them. With my own hands I helped carry out the body and put it in the sleigh. I promised my peasant an extra half-ruble and a shot of brandy. He scratched his head doubtfully and mumbled under his breath, but after his third drink he grew more reasonable, and the three of us—the peasant, the corpse, and I—were off. Her name was Chava Nechama, daughter of Raphael Michael. I remember this name as if I had heard it today, because I kept repeating it to myself, Chava Nechama, daughter of Raphael Michael. Her husband had taken great pains to make sure I got it correctly, since the burial service could not be performed properly unless her full name was invoked. So I kept repeating, "Chava Nechama, daughter of Raphael Michael."

As I was doing this I forgot her husband's name! If you threatened to cut my head off, I couldn't remember what he called himself. He had told me his name and assured me that as soon as I came to the village I had only to mention it and the body would be taken from me, so I could continue my journey. He was well known in the village, he went there on the High Holidays, he was a liberal contributor to the synagogue and to such good causes as the ritual bath; to hear him tell it, he was virtually a legendary benefactor. He stuffed my head with instructions and directions, where to go and what to say. But I forgot every word of it. Nothing remained with me. Nothing! All my thoughts were centered on one thing only: I had a corpse on my hands. And this caused me so much tumult and panic that I nearly forgot *my* name. From early childhood I have dreaded the sight of the dead. It seemed to me, as we drove along, that the half-closed frosty eyes were looking at me and that the locked dead lips might soon open and some strange subterranean voice issue from them. Just to imagine such a sound would be enough to make you lose your senses. Not for nothing are stories told among us of people swooning or even losing their minds from fear of the dead!

We drove on with the corpse. I gave the dead woman one of my pillows; she lay there at my feet. To avoid weird and oppressive thoughts I looked toward the heavens and began to repeat silently, "Chava Nechama, daughter of Raphael Michael, Chava Nechama, daughter of Raphael Michael," until the names grew confused in my mind and I found myself saying, "Chava Raphael, daughter of Nechama Michael" and "Raphael Michael, daughter of Chava Nechama." I failed to notice that it had been growing darker, the wind was blowing fiercely, and the snow fell and fell until it covered the road marks. The sleigh now seemed to be gliding forward at random into a white waste. The peasant grumbled more and more loudly; I could have sworn he was heaping threefold blessings upon me. "What's the matter?" I asked. He spat with rage—may God defend me! He opened his mouth and pelted me with words. I was leading him to ruin, he said, him and his horse, too. Because of the corpse in the sleigh the horse had lost its way, we had lost the road, night was coming on, and soon we would be utterly forsaken.

When I heard this I was ready to turn back with the corpse and undo my good deed. But the peasant said there was no going back; there were no longer any recognizable signs; we were circling about, lost in the fields. The road was snowed under, the sky was dark, it was night, the little nag was tired to death. "May a filthy end overtake the innkeeper and all the innkeepers of the world!" cursed the peasant. "If only he had broken his leg," he continued—and by "he" he meant himself—"before he decided to stop at that inn! If only the first drink had choked him before he let himself be talked into this folly of taking a calamity into his sled, for a few dirty coins, and being lost to the devils, nag and all, in these fields." About himself, he said, he didn't complain; maybe it was fated so. But the little nag, this innocent creature that knew nothing, what had it done to deserve such a fate?

I could have sworn that there were tears in his voice. I promised him another half-ruble and two more glasses of brandy to make him feel better, but this only made him furious, and he said that if I didn't keep quiet he'd throw the corpse out of the sleigh altogether. And I thought to myself, what will I do if he does throw out the corpse, and me with it, leaving the two of us there together in the snow, the corpse and me? Can anyone tell what a peasant will do when he becomes angry?

I grew dumb. I huddled into the pillows and tried to stay awake. After all, how can you fall asleep with a corpse in front of you? And besides, I had often heard that one must not sleep in the winter frost; from such sleep one may never waken. But my eyes began to droop. At that moment I would have given anything to be able to drop off, but I fought against it and held my eyes open with my fingers. Nevertheless they kept closing, again and again, while the sleigh flew across the soft white deep drifts, and a curious sweetness poured through my limbs. I experienced a strange, close pleasure, and I wished this sweetness to last forever, but some power kept waking me, cruelly rousing me, poking me in the sides and saying, "No, Noah, don't sleep. Stay awake!" And I forced my eyes and found this imagined sweetness to be a terrible chill that crept through my bones, and I began to know a deep fear—terror! May God have mercy on me! I imagined that the corpse stirred, uncovered itself, and looked at me with those frosty half-open eyes as though to say, "What are you doing to me, young man? Destroying a daughter of Israel who has died, the mother of tiny children, not bringing her to rest in consecrated ground?" The wind howled in my ears as if it were a human voice, and hideous thoughts ran through my mind. I saw us all under the snow, buried there, the horse, the peasant, the dead woman, and myself, the living frozen to death and only the corpse, the innkeeper's wife, come to life.

Suddenly I heard the peasant urge his horse on more cheerfully, thank God. He crossed himself in the dark with a sigh. It was as if he planted a new soul in me. Far off a tiny fire could be seen; it appeared, disappeared, and then we saw it again. A settlement, I thought, and I gave thanks to God with a full heart. To my peasant I said, "Apparently we've found the way. That's a town we're approaching, isn't it?"

"Eh-heh," said the peasant, without anger and in his usual laconic style. Right then and there I wanted to embrace him, to kiss him on the back for his good tidings and for his laconic "Eh-heh," which was dearer to me than the cleverest sermon.

"What's your name?" I asked, wondering why I hadn't thought to ask before.

"Mikita."

"Mikita!" I repeated, and found a rare charm in the sound.

"Eh-heh!" he said, and I wanted him to say more, at least a few words, for Mikita had become so dear to me, and his horse too, lovely little nag. I spoke to Mikita about him. "That's a fine little horse," I said.

"Eh-heh," answered Mikita.

"Fine sled, too."

"Eh-heh."

And more than that, though you broke him into a dozen pieces, Mikita wouldn't say.

"Don't like to talk, do you, Mikita my heart?"

"Eh-heh."

I laughed. I felt gay, happy. If I had found a treasure or a juicy piece of news the world had never heard of I couldn't have been happier. In short, I felt lucky—oh, so lucky! Do you know what I wanted? I wanted to raise my voice in song. That's my nature, I sing when I'm happy. My wife, who knows me inside out, will ask, "Well, what's happened now, Noah? How much money have you made that you're singing so loud?" Women, with their women's brains, seem to think that a man is happy only when he's making money. I wonder why it is that our women are so much more concerned with money than we, the men. Who works for it? We or they? But there, I've fallen off the track again.

So, with God's help, we arrived in the village, and it was still quite early. The place was still deep in slumber, there were many hours before day would come, and nowhere was a fire to be seen. I caught sight of a wide-gated house with a little broom hung on it to signify a hotel. We stopped, crawled down, and began to beat our fists upon the gate. We knocked and we knocked, and finally we saw a little light in the window; then we heard someone scuffing his feet and a voice came from within: "Who is it?"

"Open up, uncle," I shouted, "and you'll win Eternal Life."

"Eternal Life?" came the voice from behind the gate. "Who are you?" The lock began to turn.

"Open up," I said. "I've brought a corpse."

"A corpse? What do you mean, a corpse?"

"A corpse means someone who has died. The body of a Jewish woman from the country. From an inn."

Silence on the other side of the gate. I heard a lock turn and feet scuffle away into the distance. The light went out. What was I to do!

The whole thing angered me so that I called my peasant to help me, and we beat so hard that at last the lamp reappeared and we heard the voice again.

"What do you want from my life? What kind of plague are you?"

"In the name of God," I pleaded as with a bandit. "Take pity. I have a corpse here."

"What kind of a corpse?"

"The innkeeper's wife."

"What innkeeper?"

"I've forgotten how he calls himself, but her name is Chava Michael, daughter of Chana Raphael—Chana Raphael, daughter of Michael Chava—I mean, Chana Chava Chana—"

"Get away from here you *schlimazel*, or I'll pour a bucket of water over you."

That's what the innkeeper said. He clumped away from the window and put out the light. There was nothing we could do.

About an hour later, when the dawn began to show, the gate opened a bit. A black head streaked with pillow feathers looked out and said, "Was it you, pounding on the windows?"

"Of course. Who else?"

"What did you want?"

"I've brought a corpse."

"A corpse. Take it to the *shammes* of the Burial Society."

"Who is this sexton of yours? What's his name?"

"His name is Yechiel. You'll find him down the hill, not far from the bath."

"And where is your bath?"

"You mean to say you don't know where the bath is? I guess you don't live here. Where do you come from?"

"From Radomishli. I'm a Radomishler myself, but now I'm coming from Zwihil, and I've brought along the corpse from an inn not far from here. It's the innkeeper's wife—she died of consumption."

"A pity. But what's that to do with you?"

"Nothing, nothing at all. I was just passing through and he asked me—the innkeeper, that is. He's all alone out there in the fields, with little children, and no one to leave them with. So he asked me. And since it was a chance to win Eternal Life, I thought, why not?"

"There's something fishy about your story," he said to me. "You'll have to see the Burial Society. I mean the officers."

"Who are these officers? Where can they be found?"

"You mean to say you don't know? Reb Shepsel, one of them, lives on this side of the marketplace, and Reb Eliezer Moishe, another one, lives right in the middle of the marketplace, while Reb Yosi is near the old synagogue. The most important one is Reb Shepsel. He's the boss. He's a hard man, I may as well warn you. He won't be easy to get around."

"Thanks," I said. "May you live to give better tidings. When can I meet them?"

"When? What sort of a question is that? Why, in the morning of course, after prayers."

"Great," I said. "And in the meantime, let me come in to warm myself. What kind of a town is this anyway, a Sodom?"

Hearing these words, my host quickly locked his gate again, and the silence of a cemetery descended on the street. What could we do now? We remained standing by the sleigh, in the middle of the road, as Mikita murmured angrily, scratching his head, spitting and cursing. "May this innkeeper and all the innkeepers of the world meet a foul end." For himself, he said, meaning himself, personally, he won't complain. But this little nag of his—what do they have against such a sweet little nag that they try to kill it with hunger and cold? An innocent creature, a beast of the field that has never sinned.

I felt ashamed. "What," I asked myself, "must he be thinking in that head of his about us Jews? How must we look—we the merciful and sons of the merciful—to peasants like this, coarse and boorish, when one Jew shuts the door against another and won't even let him in to warm himself on a freezing night?" It seemed to me then that our fate, the fate of the Jews, made sense after all. I began to blame every one of us, as usually happens when one Jew is wronged by another. No outsider can find more withering things to say of us than we ourselves. You can hear bitter epithets among us a thousand times a day. "You want to change the character of a Jew?" "Only a Jew can play such a trick." "You can't trifle with a Jew." And other such expressions. I wonder how it is among the Gentiles. When they have a falling out, do they curse the whole tribe?

In any case, we sat in the sleigh in the middle of the marketplace and waited for daylight to bring a sign of life. By and by we heard doors creaking, the occasional groan of a windlass as a bucket was hauled from the well; smoke rose from chimneys, and the crowing of cocks grew stronger and livelier. Presently all doors opened and God's creatures appeared in a plenitude of forms: cows, calves, goats, and also Jews, women and girls wrapped in warm shawls and bundled up like dolls, bent triple and as frozen as winter apples in the cellar. In short, the town had revived from its cold sleep. The inhabitants awakened and poured the ritual water over their fingers before saying the prayers. The men were off to their labor of worship, prayers, study, and chanting of psalms; the women to their ovens, kneading troughs, and the tending of cows and goats.

I began to inquire after the officers of the Burial Society. "Where does one find Reb Shepsel? Where does Reb Eliezer Moishe live? Reb Yosi?" Those whom I asked, asked me in turn, "Which Reb Shepsel? Which Eliezer Moishe? What Yosi?" There were several Shepsels and several Eliezer Moishes and even several Yosis in the town, they told me. And when I said that I was looking for the officers of the Burial Society, they grew frightened and wanted to know, "Why does a young man like you need the Burial Society so early in the morning?"

Well, I didn't give them time to feel me out and come at the facts gradually. I told them my story at once, straight from the heart, and revealed what a burden I had taken upon myself. You should have seen what happened. Do you think they set about helping me in my misfortune? Nothing of the sort! They all ran to the sleigh to peer into it and see for themselves whether I really had a corpse. A crowd formed around us, a changing crowd; because of the cold some spectators left, others came over, looked into the sleigh, shook their heads, shrugged their shoulders, inquired of one another whose corpse that could be and from where it had come, and who I might be and how I happened to have brought it. But of help they gave me none whatever. It was only with the greatest difficulty that I persuaded someone to show me the house of Reb Shepsel.

I found him facing the wall, standing, wrapped in his prayer shawl and phylacteries, and praying so sweetly, so melodiously, so raptly, that the very room seemed to sing with him. He snapped his fingers, bumbled harmoniously, twisted his trunk back and forth, made many queer and pious gestures. I had the double satisfaction of watching this extraordinary prayer—I love to listen to spirited praying—and of warming my frozen bones at the same time. And when at last he twisted his head around to me, his eyes were still full of tears and he had, for me, every appearance of a godly man, a man whose soul was as far from earth as his round fat body from heaven. And because he had not yet finished his prayers and didn't want to break off in the middle, he communicated with me in the holy tongue—that is, by means of winks and twirling of his fingers, shrugs, movements of the head, and twitching of the nose, with a few words of Hebrew thrown in for good measure. If you like, I can report our conversation word for word.

"*Sholem aleichem,* Reb Shepsel."

"*Aleichem sholem. Iyo*, sit. Sit down."

"Thanks. I've had enough sitting."

"*Nu? Ma?* What, what?"

"I've come to you on a great errand, Reb Shepsel. You'll win Eternal Life."

"Eternal Life? Good! But what? What?"

"I've brought you a corpse."

"A corpse? What corpse?"

"Not far from here there's an inn, and there lives a poor man, pitifully poor, and this poor man has lost his wife—she died of consumption—and he is left with small children. A great pity. If I hadn't taken pity on them I don't know what he would have done, this poor man, out there in the fields with an unburied corpse."

"Blessed be God's righteousness! But *nu?* Money? The Burial Society?"

"What money? He's poor as a mouse. Down to nothing. Burdened with children. Rep Shepsel, you'll gain Eternal Life."

"Eternal Life? But what? What? Poor folk, poor Jews here, too. *Iyo nu? Feh!*"

And because I hadn't quite grasped his meaning he turned angrily to the wall once again and resumed his prayer, much less ardently this time, squeaking somewhat and rocking himself swiftly in a sort of galloping courier's tempo. He then threw off his prayer shawl and phylacteries and turned to me with great heat, as though I had spoiled a sale for him at the fair.

"Look here," he said to me, "this is a poor town and has enough of its own paupers who have no shrouds when they die. We have to hold collections for them. And still people come here from everywhere, from the very ends of the earth. Everyone has to die here!"

I defended myself as well as I could. I said I was innocent of any design against his town, that I was merely performing a good deed. "As though," said I, "one had found a corpse in the street! It's entitled to decent burial and last rites. You're an honest Jew, and a pious one. You can win Eternal Life by this deed."

He became even more furious. You might almost say he nearly drove me out—that is, he didn't literally drive me, but pummeled me with words. "Is that so! You are a young man representing Eternal Life? Go and make a little inspection of our town. See to it that people are prevented from dying of hunger and cold and *you* will win Eternal Life. Eternal Life indeed! A young man who trades in Eternal Life! Go, take your goods to the shiftless and the unbelievers, and peddle your Eternal Life to them. We have our own charities, and if we develop a craving for Eternal Life we'll know where to find it. What do we need you for?"

So spoke Reb Shepsel and angrily escorted me to the door, which he loudly slammed after me.

I swear to you that from that morning I took a rooted dislike to those people who are always worshiping and conversing with God. You will tell me that modern unbelievers are even worse than the orthodox old-fashioned communers-with-God, but I disagree. Now at least the hypocrisy is less glaring.

Well, Rep Shepsel had shouted at me and shown me the door. What should I do now? I turned to the others, his colleagues. But at this point a miracle occurred, a miracle straight from heaven. There was no need for me to seek them; they had come looking for me. We met nose to nose, at Reb Shepsel's door.

"Do you happen to be the young man with the goat?" they asked.

"What goat?"

"The young man, that is, who brought the corpse to our town? Is it you?"

"Yes, it's me. I'm the one."

"Come in with us to Reb Shepsel's and we'll talk it over."

"What's there to talk about? Take the corpse off my hands and you'll gain Eternal Life."

"No one's keeping you here," they said to me. "You can go any time you wish. You can even drive your corpse to Radomishli and gain our thanks for it."

"Many thanks for the advice," I said to them.

"You're welcome," they said to me.

So we made our way into Reb Shepsel's house, the three of us, and they began to dispute among themselves, quarreling, disagreeing, all but cursing one another. The two newcomers declared that Reb Shepsel had always been a hard man to deal with, a stickler for the letter of the law, a literalist. For his part, Reb Shepsel twisted to and fro, hitting back with quotations from Scripture. *The poor of your city have prior need.* But the others attacked him with strong arguments. "So? Does that mean that this young man should be turned away with his corpse?"

"God forbid!" said I. "Go off again with this dead woman? Why, I barely made it here alive. We were nearly lost in the storm. The blessed peasant wanted to throw me into the snow. I beg you, take pity. Free me from this burden. You will purchase Eternal Life."

"Eternal Life, that's quite a mouthful," answered one of the two, a tall, lean, long-fingered Jew, the one they called Eliezer Moishe. "We'll take the corpse from you and see that it's properly buried. But it'll cost you a little something."

"What do you mean?" I said. "Isn't it enough that I took this good deed upon myself, nearly perished in the field, was almost thrown from the sleigh by the peasant? And you still speak of money?"

"But you'll be winning Eternal Life, won't you?" said Reb Shepsel with such an ugly face that I loathed his soul. Only by a great effort did I hide my feelings—after all, I was at the mercy of these people.

"Listen to us," said the one called Reb Yosi, a little Jew with a meager beard, half plucked out. "You'd better realize young fellow, that there's another obstacle. You have no burial papers."

"What papers?"

"We don't know who this corpse is. She may not be the person you say she is," said the lean one with the long fingers, Eliezer Moishe.

I stared from one to the other, and the long-fingered Eliezer Moishe pointed at me and said, "Yes. Who knows? Maybe you killed a woman somewhere. Maybe she's your own wife, whom you brought here with a story about a poor innkeeper, the innkeeper's wife, little children, consumption, and Eternal Life."

Apparently I myself looked like a corpse when he said these things, for the little one they called Reb Yosi began to console me, explaining that they had nothing against me. Why should they have? They didn't suspect me of a crime. They knew I wasn't a murderer or a thief. Nevertheless, he said, I was a stranger, and a corpse is no mere sack of potatoes. A human being is involved, a corpse. They had a rabbi, they gave me to understand, and a police official. One had to think of protocol.

"Yes," said Eliezer Moishe, pointing to me and looking me up and down as if I had already been convicted of a crime, "there's protocol."

I was struck dumb. Sweat started forth, my forehead grew cold, and I felt ill, as if I were going to faint. I understood my situation only too well. I saw how I had been snared. Shame, sorrow, and heartbreak overcame me. But I thought, why enter into long negotiations with these three? I took out my small purse and said to them, "Listen to me. This is how matters stand. I see that I have gotten myself badly tangled. It was just my luck to have gone to that inn to warm myself right after the death of this innkeeper's wife, and to have listened to the pleas of the poor widower with children who promised me Eternal Life if I would give him a helping hand—and the upshot is that it's going to cost a pretty penny. All right, here's my purse. I have some seventy rubles in it. Take what you want. Just leave me enough to get me to Radomishli. But relieve me of the corpse and let me go."

I must have spoken with great emotion, for the three of them exchanged looks, refused to touch my money, and said that after all this town was not Sodom. True, it was poor, with more paupers than rich men, but to fall upon a stranger like robbers, no, that wasn't their way. They had no intention of abusing me. They would take whatever I felt I could offer in a spirit of good will, but not a penny more. Still, I would have to contribute something, it was such a poor town. The beadles, the pallbearers, the shrouds, the plot, brandy for the services—all cost money. Naturally they didn't expect any extravagance. You start to spend carelessly on an occasion like this and there's no telling how much money may spill between your fingers.

Well, what else can I tell you? Even if the innkeeper had been a man of great wealth his wife's funeral couldn't have been more impressive. The townspeople came out in droves for a sight of the young man who had brought a corpse. The rumor spread, increasingly detailed and complicated, that I was a wealthy young man who had brought the body of his mother-in-law, a woman of vast fortune, to be interred—where did they get the idea she was my mother-in-law? Crowds came into the streets to welcome me, the wealthy mourner with the rich mother-in-law. I was said to be flinging money to the poor by the fistful. People pointed at me from all sides. And the poor—an endless multitude! Never, never have I seen such a quantity of paupers. Not even on the eve of Yom Kippur was there ever so great a throng before the doors of the synagogue. They snatched at my coat, they nearly tore me to pieces. After all, an immensely rich young man pouring money! It was no ordinary thing. Luckily the officials of the Burial Society were there to protect me. They prevented me from giving away all of my money, especially the tall sexton who kept by my side all the while and kept admonishing me with his long finger. "Young man, don't throw your money away. There's no end to this." And the more he admonished, the more the beggars crowded me and tore at my flesh. "It's all right," they cried. "When you bury a rich mother-in-law you can afford to spend a few more pennies. She's left him plenty—plenty! Wishing him no bad luck, *we* should have as much as he's inherited."

"Young man," shrieked one of the beggars as he tugged at my coat, "give up half a ruble for two of us here! Or forty kopecks at least. We're two born cripples, one blind and the other lame. Give us fifteen kopecks at least for the two. Two cripples are always worth that much!"

"Cripples," shouted another beggar as he kicked the first one out of the way. "You call these cripples? My wife, there's a cripple for you! No hands, no feet, nearly lifeless, and with sick little ones. Give me five kopecks, will you, and I'll say *Kaddish* for your mother-in-law and brighten her Paradise."

Now it's easy to laugh, but it was no laughing matter at the time, for the poor multiplied all around me. They covered the marketplace within half an hour, like a plague of locusts. The pallbearers couldn't move forward. The officials had to beat the beggars off with sticks, and a free-for-all broke out. Peasants too began to collect around us, and at last the police took action. The inspector himself appeared, mounted and sporting a whip, and with a single glare and several lashes he scattered them all as if they were sparrows. Then he dismounted and approached the casket. He began to make inquiries. Who was it that had died? Of what illness? And why such disorder in the marketplace? It pleased him to begin with me. Who was I? What was my business here? Where was I bound to? I was terrified. I lost all power of speech. Why it is I don't know, but whenever I see a policeman I fall into a cold terror. I've never harmed a fly, and I know that a policeman is, after all, merely a mortal. I'm even acquainted with a man who is on friendly terms with a policeman; they visit each other; the policeman eats fish with him on High Holidays, and he is received as a guest in the policeman's house, where he feasts on eggs. This Jew is forever telling everyone what a gem his policeman is. But all the same, when I see a policeman my impulse is always to run. Perhaps it's hereditary, for I myself, you must remember, am a descendant of pogrom survivors from the days of Vailchikov. About those days I have heard stories and stories to tell you, but enough—I've fallen off the track again.

The inspector gave me a thorough grilling. I had to tell him who I was and what I was doing and where I was going, details about details. How could I explain that I lived with my in-laws at Zwihil and had to journey to Radomishli to obtain some papers? I was deeply thankful to the officers of the Burial Society for disentangling me. One of them, the fellow with the half-plucked beard, called the inspector aside and the two of them conferred in whispers of secrecy, while the tall one with the thin fingers coached me meantime, half in Hebrew and half in Yiddish, telling me what explanations to make. "You will say you live a short way from town. And that is your mother-in-law who just died. And you've come here to bury her. And while you slip him a few rubles, invent a name straight from the *Haggadah*. Meanwhile we'll get your driver away and give him a glass of spirits and keep him out of sight. Everything will be fine."

The inspector took me into a house and began to examine me. I'll never be able to repeat what I told him. I don't remember what I said; whatever came to my head, that's what I babbled. He took everything down.

"Your name?"

"Moishe."

"Your father's name?"

"Itzko."

"Age?"

"Nineteen."

"Single."

"Married."

"Children?"

"Children."

"Occupation?"

"Merchant."

"Who is the corpse?"

"My mother-in-law."

"Her name?"

"Yente."

"Her father?"

"Gershon."

"Her age?"

"Forty."

"Cause of death?"

"Fright."

"A fright?"

"Yes, a fright."

"What sort of fright?" he said, putting down his pen, smoking his cigarette and glaring at me from head to foot.

My tongue seemed to stick to my palate. I decided that, since I had begun with lies, I might as well continue with lies, and I made up a long tale about my mother-in-law sitting alone, knitting a sock, forgetting that her son Ephraim was there, a boy of thirteen, overgrown and a complete fool. He was playing with his shadow. He stole up to her, waved his hands over her head, and uttered a goat cry, *Mehh!* He was making a shadow goat on the wall. And at this sound my mother-in-law fell from her stool and died.

As I wove this tale he kept looking at me, never once dropping his gaze. I mumbled, repeated myself, lost the sense of what I was saying. He heard me out, spat, wiped his red mustachios, accompanied me to the casket, raised the black lid, looked at the face of the dead woman, and shook his head with suspicion. He said to the three officials, "Well, you can bury the woman. But I'll have to detain this fellow while I investigate his story and find out whether she really is his mother-in-law and really died of fright."

You can imagine how I felt. I turned aside and burst into tears, the tears of a very small child.

"What are you crying for, young man?" said the one called Reb Yosi. He consoled me: I had nothing to fear. If was I innocent.

"If you've eaten no garlic your breath will be clean." Reb Shepshel smiled with such a grin that I wanted to slap both his cheeks.

Why had I let myself be so misled as to tell such a tale and involve my mother-in-law? To make things worse, it would now reach her ears that I had killed her with fright and buried her alive.

"Don't be afraid. God is with you. The inspector isn't a bad sort. Just slip him something and tell him to drop the whole thing. He's a clever man. He knows you've told him a yarn." So spoke Eliezer Moishe as he pointed his long fingers at me. If I could, I would have torn him to pieces, the way one tears a herring.

I can relate no more. What happened afterward I hardly remember.

The rest of my money was taken away, I was put in prison, and there was a trial. But all this was nothing compared with what happened when my in-laws discovered that I was in prison because I had somehow acquired a corpse. They came at once and declared that they were my father-in-law and mother-in-law—and things really began to boil. On one side the police kept asking, "Now that we know your mother-in-law is alive, this one who says she is Yente, tell us who the dead woman was." And on the other side my mother-in-law kept demanding, "There's only one thing I want to know. What did you have against me that you wanted to bury me while I was still alive?"

At the trial I was, naturally, found to be innocent. But it cost a lot of money. Witnesses were brought. The innkeeper and his children appeared, and I was freed. But what I had to endure from my mother-in-law—I wouldn't wish on my worst enemy.

From then on, when anyone mentions Eternal Life, I run.

Translated by Saul Bellow

Station Baranovich

IN THIRD-CLASS our handful of Jews sat closely packed—you might say grafted together. Actually not all sat, only those who had pounced on the few seats. The others stood, jammed against the compartment walls, freely butting into the deliberations of the sitters. And a lively forum it was. Everyone had something to say. At the same time.

As usual, having slept well, prayed, eaten breakfast (more or less) and topped it off with a smoke—we were on the morning train, fresh and chirpy as April. Jabbering about what? Mention anything. Each in turn tossed out something lively or shocking to hold his audience. None succeeded. We flitted from subject to subject. The drift to war was resolved (talk of mixing Scripture!) by the price of wheat, which somehow led to the Revolution. After the Revolution we bore into the Constitution until we struck the pogroms—the outrages, the martyrs, the new anti-Jewish decrees, the expulsions from the villages, the stampede to America—with detours into other afflictions and evils of this gracious age: bankruptcy, expropriation, war, hangings, hunger, cholera, the anti-Semite Purishkevich . . .

"A-z-e-v!"

Like a terrorist, someone lobbed the name and blew out the compartment. Voices exploded from all sides: "Azev's a czarist spy! . . . Azev's on our side! . . . Azev's for Azev! . . . A double agent on both sides!"

"I beg your pardon, but all of you (don't be offended) are fools. Why start a riot? Over Azev? Eh . . . who's Azev? A freak, a sneak, a squealer, a flea, a Mr. Nobody descended from Nobodies. I can tell you a story about someone from my village of Komink, who makes Azev (don't be offended) look like a saint."

This was said by one of the passengers leaning against the compartment wall. I turned and looked up at a large head squeezed into a silk hat, a face the color of glue setting, a grin shy two front teeth. Through this gap his z's whistled, and "Azev" came out "Azhev."

He appealed to me. I envy breeziness in a Jew, and I was attracted to his openness, to his calling us "fools." For a moment the passengers were dumbfounded by this unexpected appraisal, but they rallied quickly, traded shrugs, and took turns urging him:

"You want us to beg? . . . We're begging, with pleasure."

"Tell us what happened in Komink."

"But why are you standing? Sit."

"Where? We'll snug up a bit. Here! Please . . ."

Packed tightly, they squirmed and jockeyed, and somehow pried open a patch of chair. The Kominker Jew sat with a flourish, as if he were the godfather at a circumcision, waiting for the infant to be handed over and cradled in his arms. Raking his silk hat over one eye and cuffing his sleeves, he took the floor.

"This is not a parable and not a fantasy from the *Thousand and One Nights*. I'm reporting to you an incident that took place (don't be offended) in my own Komink, told to me by my father, who heard it from his father. I understand that the story was recorded in one of our village chronicles, since destroyed in a fire. I tell you, the loss deprives us all. The chronicles, they say, were delightful, much more engaging than the stories printed today in books and magazines.

"To begin, it was in the time of Nicholas the First, when striping was common. Don't smile—ask. You never heard of striping? Striping means—you could be striped. What's a stripe? Again you're in the dark? Then I'll start even before the beginning. Picture this: two rows of cavalry wielding horsewhips, and you strut along between, obliged to complete (don't be offended) twenty-odd laps, as naked (forgive the expression) as you were born. The cavalry inflict on you what your *rebbe* inflicted when you got lost in the text. Have I made striping clear? Good. Then I can go on.

"So on this day there arrived from the commissioner—Vasilchikov was then commissioner—an order to stripe a Jew named Kivke. Who exactly this Kivke was, I cannot tell you. He owned a tavern and by reputation was not a rock of reliability, which may explain why at his age he was still a bachelor. Among his other qualities he counted a loose tongue, and in his bar he started to bandy words with the peasants—he had to go and pick a Sunday!—about theology. A little gabble-gibble here, a bit of my God-your God there, and the peasants called in the constable and filed (don't be offended) a complaint. Bartender, set up a round of drinks, and the whiskey will wash away the heresy! Instead he trumpets, 'No! Kivke never eats his words!' as if being headstrong is balm for burned fingers. After that, what could he expect? A light fine and a good day? On the other hand, who would suspect that for a few foolish words he would be flogged? To make a long story short, the constable collared Kivke and led him to the local bastille, to wait for absolution under twenty-five lashes.

"Well, you can imagine the commotion in Komink. And when was the sentence handed down? Naturally, at night—and just as naturally, Friday night. On Saturday morning the synagogue seethed.

"'Flogging?'

"'Kivke? Why? For what?'

"'For nonsense, for a loose tongue.'

"'A frame-up.'

"'Who framed him? Kivke has a mouth like a gate.'

"'A mouth like two gates, but flogging?'

"'Who flogs Jews? . . .'

"The Jews of Komink sizzled all day. In the evening after blessing the *havdoleh* candle, they descended on my grandfather: 'Reb Nisel, why haven't you raised your voice? You can't let them get away with this, flogging a Jew, one of our own, a Kominker . . .'

"You're wondering, why did they besiege my grandfather? I have to explain. My grandfather (may he enjoy sunny days in Paradise) was—not that I want to brag—the most sympathetic, substantial, prominent, influential citizen of our community, respected by the authorities and somewhat of a thinker, too.

"When the uproar wore itself out, my grandfather measured the room, pacing off the length, then the width—a habit of his, according to my father (may he rest in peace)—for my grandfather to think, he had to measure. Eventually my grandfather beat his way to a stop and announced: 'Children! Go home. Stop working yourselves up.

Everything, with God's help, will be straightened out. No one in Komink has ever, thank God, been whipped, and with God's help we'll see to it no one ever is . . .'

"They left with my grandfather's assurance, and in the village they understood for Reb Nisel Shapiro (may he rest in peace) a word is a deed. Cross-examination—how and what and when—would only upset him. A Jew of substance, who carries weight with the authorities—a thinker, too—such a citizen is entitled to good manners. And why not? My grandfather did what he said he would do. But what is it that he did? If you're interested, pay attention."

Seeing that everyone in the compartment was spellbound, straining to hear, the Jew from Komink put a bridle on his tongue. He brought out a sack of tobacco and rolled a cigarette, choosing among several eagerly struck matches. He inhaled contentedly, drawing the ash slowly to his lips, then snuffed out the stub. Refreshed, he continued.

"Now pay attention to how a manager manages. My grandfather (bless his saintly memory) arrived, after careful deliberation, at a simple solution. He persuaded the constable that his prisoner, Kivke that is, should (don't be offended) give up the ghost. Why the looks of alarm? Are you in pain because my grandfather, God forbid, poisoned Kivke? Rest easy. We're not assassins. What then? He worked it out—with finesse. The prisoner would retire for the night, fit and fine, and in the morning would wake up dead. . . . Now, is it going down, or can't you swallow without a finger in your mouth?

."Well . . . the day came. One morning a notice arrived from the prison, addressed to my grandfather: since a Jew named Kivke passed away in his cell during the night, and since Reb Nisel Shapiro is head of the community and administrator of the Burial Society, he is directed to assume responsibility for the corpse and arrange for its removal to the Jewish cemetery. . . . A clever blind, will you agree? But wait. Don't cheer yet. Words have it easier than deeds. Remember, this wasn't just another Jew who'd died. This Jew had been up to his elbows in heresy . . . flogging . . .

"To begin with, my grandfather had to avoid an autopsy. Then an affidavit was required, signed and sealed, certifying that a doctor had examined the cadaver immediately after death, and that death had been caused by a heart attack—it should never happen to us—a kind of apoplexy. Kivke's end. Kivke, dead.

"On top of that, there was the cost to the community—I wish

everyone in this compartment earned as much in a month. And who stood the expense? My grandfather, may he rest in peace. The village knew that on him they could rely. He worked everything out, you understand, with finesse and ingenuity, square and round, tucked and stitched. The very same day, at nightfall, the beadles of the Burial Society washed and prepared the body. Led by an honor guard of soldiers, followed by the entire community, the corpse was escorted from the prison to the cemetery. Do I have to tell you, Kivke had never looked forward to such a funeral? At the gate to holy ground, the soldiers were dismissed with a few tumblers (don't be offended) of fine brandy. The bier was carried into the court for burial, and there, with his *droshky* and span of fired-up stallions, waited Simon the leather-puller (so my father, may he rest in peace, called him when he told me the story). Before the cock crowed, our cadaver (don't be offended) was on the far side of Rogatke. With luck and our blessings, Kivke was slipped into Rodevil, and from there—good-bye forever—over the border into Brod.

"You understand, of course, that Komink waited impatiently for Simon to return from Rodevil. No one slept much. Least of all, my grandfather, may he rest in peace. Anything could happen. If the corpse—our Kivke—fell into their hands at the border and was brought back alive and beaming, the village would be exiled to the far side of Siberia.

"But God lent a hand, and Simon the leather-puller rolled in from Rodevil behind his fired-up stallions, bringing a handwritten note from Kivke: '*I wish to report . . . I'm in Brod!*'

"Our village went wild. Immediately, a feast was patched together—in my grandfather's house, of course—and runners were sent for the prison guard, the constable, the doctor, and other notables. The music was loud, the drinking heavy, and soon the prison guard (don't be offended) was kissing my grandfather and his family. And the constable was discovered at dawn, waltzing on my grandfather's roof without (forgive the expression) his pants.

"A trifle? A life redeemed! A Jew delivered from striping! Splendid, no? Well, dear Jews, don't rush to conclusions. This is all preamble. The story itself hasn't even begun. If you're interested, please bear with me. I must get off at this station to ask the dispatcher how far is Baranovich. There I change trains."

Tipping back his silk hat, he left. The passengers waited, exchanging appraisals of the Kominker and his Kominker chronicle.

"How do you fancy our friend?"

"He's pleasant enough."

"Colorful."

"He'll never have to beg for words."

"Uses them well."

"But the story?"

"Entertaining."

"Too short."

Someone recalled a similar episode in his village. Not exactly similar, but a similar circumstance. Which stirred another passenger's memory. The two began to talk at once, and others took sides about who interrupted whom. The growing brawl was cut short by the entrance of the Jew from Komink. Unresolved, the dispute collapsed. Like a wall, the passengers, open-eyed and open-eared, closed around the Kominker.

"Where were we? Finished, thank God, with a Jew named Kivke? Yes . . . you would agree? Then, my dear friends, you would be mistaken. Six months passed, or a year, the time isn't important, and a letter from Kivke arrived addressed to my grandfather: *'First, I wish to report that I am well, thank God, and look forward to hearing the same from you. Secondly, I don't understand the Germans, and they don't understand me. Thirdly, I'm without a groschen and without a job, and without help. I can only lift up my heels, stretch out, and wait for the angel of death. . .*

"Are you following this prodigy? To help means to help with money. The village had its laugh, tore the letter (don't be offended) into little pieces, and forgot Kivke. In less than three weeks a new letter was delivered, again from our corpse, again addressed to my grandfather, again *I wish to report*, and again *without help . . .* Only this *without help* was bitter: *'What do you want from me? I should have accepted my punishment. By now the wounds would have healed. I'd be keeping body and soul together, not roaming around idle, surrounded by Germans, swollen with hunger. . .*

"This time, my grandfather (may he rest in peace) called the community together: 'We have to send him something . . .' And when Reb Nisel Shapiro opened his hand, you couldn't have a cramp in yours. Funds were collected (my grandfather, I don't have to spell out, gave most), and the village (don't be offended) forgot there ever existed a Jew named Kivke.

"Kivke, however, did not forget Komink. Six months went by, maybe a year—the months aren't important. Again an envelope arrived, again addressed to my grandfather, again *I wish to report*, and once again *without help*. . . . But this time, thank God, with a *mazel-tov: 'Since I am soon to be married, with a jewel for a bride—the daughter of a fine family—and since, without help, I will be forced to break my word, please send the two hundred in gold I pledged toward the dowry.'*

"Our problem! Kivke's wedding plans! What can I tell you, the letter went from hand to hand, and the village held its sides laughing. Komink took turns snickering: 'That's a *mazel-tov*? . . . Did you hear, two hundred in gold for a dowry? . . . A jewel of a family . . . Cheh-cheh-cheh . . .'

"The 'cheh-cheh-cheh' was good for two weeks, until a new envelope was delivered, again from Kivke, again addressed to my grandfather. This letter left out the *I wish to report* but not the *without help*: '*I am puzzled by your failure to forward the two hundred in gold that I pledged. Unless the funds are received promptly, the wedding will be called off, and out of shame I will face two choices: either to drown myself in the river or to return to Komink to face the whip . . .'*

"These last words flew up the community's nose (don't be offended) like pepper, and the cackling stopped. That night my grandfather assembled the pillars of the village, who concluded that a delegation, led by my grandfather, would pass among the Jews of Komink to raise Kivke's dowry.

"They had no choice, but don't run out of sympathy yet for Komink.

"With the two hundred in gold they sent their best wishes and their hope that Kivke and his bride would grow old together, in health and prosperity, honored by their children and grandchildren. The village was convinced the normal complications and disappointments of marriage would overwhelm Kivke and he would forget that Komink ever existed. As it turned out—when? who? Not Kivke. In less than six months, certainly in less than a year—I don't remember exactly—my grandfather heard from him again! *My bride was sent to me by the Almighty, may all Jewish husbands know such contentment. But . . . no one is perfect. She has a father—before you deal with him, pray for redemption. He lies, cheats, swindles—a fox with two legs. He drove us into the street, but not before he bled us of the two hundred in gold. Therefore please send another two hundred immediately. Otherwise I must either throw myself into the river or return to Komink to face the whip . . .'*

"The village was not amused. Two dowries? That seemed greedy. Komink ignored the letter. Kivke brooded two or three weeks, and then my grandfather (don't be offended) heard from him again, here and there . . . Why hadn't they sent the two hundred? What was there to think about? He would wait another ten days, and if the money hadn't come, Komink would soon, God willing, have a guest. And he closed the letter with a *together let us say amen.* The devil—you understand—asking for their prayers!

"Komink belched fire and fury. But again the leaders of the community met in my grandfather's house, and again a delegation, led by my grandfather, went through the village. Few (don't be offended) found charity in their hearts. No one wanted to send another groschen to the rascal, but it isn't easy to turn you back on Reb Nisel Shapiro. Still my grandfather had to agree to one condition: this was the last collection.

"My grandfather wrote to him—Kivke, that is—letting him know whatever the circumstances, without exception, not to dream of appealing to them again. Naturally, as you'd expect, Kivke was terrorized . . . Before the next holiday, the righteous one wrote from Brod again. Now what? *Since I have come across a German, respected and honest, and have become his partner in crockery, a business without risk, and since from this business I expect to support my new bride . . . therefore, please send four-hundred-fifty in gold. And for God's sake, don't dillydally. My partner has many offers, ten for one. Without crockery, God forbid, I have nothing to turn to, and with nothing to turn to, I can only throw myself into the river or go home to face the whip. . .* The old story!

"In closing, Kivke served notice that if they didn't send four-hundred-fifty in gold, it would end up costing them more, since they would have to reimburse his expense from Brod to Komink and from Komink back to Brod. The devil—they should understand—could call down not only prayers, but curses, too.

"Do I have to tell you how this soured the holiday? Most of all, my grandfather's, may he rest in peace, who was left (don't be offended) with the hot coal in his hand. At the meeting in his house, he heard only grumbling.

"'Enough! He thinks he's tapping a mine.'

"'There's an end to everything.'

"'If I can get tired of eating *kreplach,* I can get tired of Kivke.'

"'Your Kivke will make beggars of us all.'

"My grandfather asked, 'Why is he my Kivke?'

"'When he was in prison, whose idea was it? Who sent him apoplexy?'

"My grandfather saw— he was no fool—that he was wasting words. The community had closed its purse. So he turned to the authorities, to the constable, to the prison guard . . . But who? Where? For Kivke, they wouldn't give up even a glass of kvass. A peasant isn't a Jew; he doesn't take someone else's suffering to heart. So my grandfather sent the cutthroat (may his name be erased) a number of *zhlotys* and some plain words. (My grandfather, bless his memory, knew how when he wanted to!) He called Kivke a fraud, a boor, a sinner, a leech, Satan, spiteful, degenerate, and a few other things; warned him, for the last time, not to write again; and reminded him that the Almighty saw everything and punished severely. My grandfather (his was still a Jewish heart!) closed by begging Kivke to spare the village further pain and to have pity on him as he approached his midnight years. Kivke's reward would be happiness in marriage and prosperity in business.

"So my grandfather (may he rest in peace) wrote to Kivke—and in a clear, strong hand he signed, *Nisel Shapiro.* A folly you'll agree, if you listen carefully (don't be offended) to what happened next."

Here the Kominker paused, drew out his sack of tobacco, and painstakingly rolled a cigarette. He inhaled deeply, once . . . twice . . . exhaling pleasurably, ignoring his audience who waited expectantly for the story's end. After he puffed the cigarette into smoke and ash, he coughed, blew his nose, rolled up his sleeves, and continued.

"Don't think my grandfather's letter made the scoundrel lose his courage. Not even a lick. A half-year went by, or a year, and a letter arrived (don't be offended) from the swindler, with this news: *First, I wish to report that my partner, the German—may he be driven mad by nightmares—is a thief; he picked me clean and threw me out. I considered filing charges, but I'd lay eyes on more holding a candle to the sun than suing a German. Instead I rented a shop, right next to his, and opened my own business—also crockery. With the Almighty's help*

I'll bury him, and with both hands feed him dirt! However, there's one loose end—I need a thousand in gold. Therefore, please send. . .'

"There and here . . . and he—Kivke, that is—closed his letter: '. . .*if I don't receive my thousand in gold in eight days, I'll mail your last letter, which you signed in your own hand, 'Reb Nisel Shapiro,' to Valchikov to the Commissioner, and tell him everything from A to Z: how I suffered my stroke, how I rose from the dead, how Simon the leather-puller smuggled me into Brod, and how you've been sending me money to keep me quiet.'*

"Well how do you like that for regards? As soon as my grandfather, may he rest in peace, finished reading Kivke's sweet message, he felt (don't be offended) dizzy and fainted. The paralysis, may it never happen to us . . . Say, have we stopped? Where are we?"

The conductor called out, "Baranovich! Station Baranovich! and rushed past the window of our car.

As soon as he heard "Baranovich" the Jew from Komink jumped up and wrestled loose his bag, a packsack crammed with odd bulges. Straining, he dragged it behind him toward the door, toppled the bag to the platform, and plunged after it. Jostled and driven by the crush of passengers, he held tight to his bag, sweating, nosing into one face after another and asking, "Baranovich?"

"Baranovich."

The passengers of our compartment, I among them, swarmed after the Kominker, clinging to his sleeve.

"That's not fair!"

"You can't leave us like this!"

"What happened next?"

"Finish the story! We won't let you go until you tell us the end!"

The Kominker struggled to free his sleeve. "What end? It was just the beginning! Take your hands off. You want me to miss my train? Baranovich! This is Station Baranovich! Didn't you hear? Can't you see?"

See? Before we could blink, he was gone.

May Station Baranovich burn to the ground!

Translated by Reuben Bercovitch

The Pot

RABBI! A QUESTION'S what I want to ask you. I don't know if you know me or if you don't know me. Yente's who I am, Yente the dairy-vender. I deal in eggs, see, and also geese, hens, and ducks. I have my steady customers, two-three households—may God give them health and long life, because if they didn't support me, I couldn't buy the bread to make a prayer over. I manage, see—grab a groschen here, grab a groschen there, sometimes here, sometimes there, give a little, take a little—manage, if you can call it that. Of course, if my husband (may he rest in peace) was with me now, in the flesh—*well!* . . . Though to tell the truth, life with him was not what you'd call milk and honey. A wage earner (you should pardon the expression) he wasn't. He'd just sit and study, sit and study, while I slaved away. That's what I'm used to, slaving away—ever since I was a child in my mother's house (may she rest in peace). Batya was her name, see—Batya the candle-fitter. She'd buy up tallow from the butchers and braid the candles. Who'd heard then about gas? Or about lamps with glass tops, that drip all the time? Just last week a glass top of mine burst, and two weeks before that . . .

Now, what were we saying? Yes, you said, *died young* . . . . When my Moishe Ben Zion died (may he rest in peace), he was all of twenty-six years old. Huh? Twenty-six? Let's try that again. Nineteen he was at our wedding; eight years it's been since he died; that makes it, altogether, nineteen and eight . . . Seems it's as much as twenty-three! So how did I get twenty-six? Because I forgot about those seven years he was sick. Though as for being sick, he was sick much longer than that. He was always sickly. I mean, he was really *healthy,* except for that cough. It

71

was the cough, see, that did him in. He was always coughing (may it never happen to you, Rabbi). Not *always,* of course, but at times when the cough got into him he'd start coughing, and once he'd start, he'd cough and cough and cough. The doctors said he had some kind of "spasm"—that is, the kind that if you want to cough, you cough, and if you don't want, you don't. One-two skidoo! Fiddlesticks! Goats should know as much about getting into strange gardens as they know (the doctors, I mean) about what's going on. Take Reb Aaron, the *shochet's* boy, Yockel they call him. He had a toothache, see, and they tried everything, from soup to nuts, but nothing helped. So he went and put garlic in his ear (Yockel, that is). He'd heard that garlic's a cure for toothaches. Well, there he was climbing the walls, and he kept the garlic a secret. So the doctor came and took his pulse. Why his pulse, you idiot? Anyway, if they hadn't carried him off (Yockel, that is) to Yehupetz, do you know where he'd be by now? *There,* with his sister Pearl. Poor thing, her luck left her (God forbid it should happen to you, Rabbi) in childbirth . . .

But what we were saying? Yes, you said, *a widow* . . . I became a widow (may it never happen in this house) when I was still young, a girl you might say, with a small child, and half a house on Pauper's Street, the other half of Lazer the carpenter's place. Do you know it? It's not far from the bathhouse. But you're wondering, aren't you, why only half a house? Actually it's not mine. It belongs to my brother-in-law; Ezriel's his name. You must know him—he's from Vesselikut, some sort of town somewhere, and as for a living, he makes a living from fish, quite a good living, depending on what the river's like. If it's calm outside, fish get caught, and if fish get caught, then the price is cheap. When the wind's out, fish don't get caught, and then the price is high. But things go better if fish get caught. That's what he says, Ezriel I mean. So I asked him, "Where's the logic?" So he said, "The logic is simple logic. If it's calm outside, fish get caught, and if fish get caught, then the price is cheap. When the wind's out, fish don't get caught, and then the price is high. But things go better if fish get caught." So I said to him, "Yes, but where's the *logic?*" So he said, "Simple. If it's calm outside, fish get caught, and if fish get caught, then the price is cheap." "Phooey on you!" I said to him. Go and reason with a clod! . . .

What were we saying, now? Yes, you said, *your own house* . . . . Naturally it's better to have a little corner of your own. "What's mine is mine," as they say, "and not anyone else's." So I have my bit of what's mine, my half a house. I can't complain. But I ask you, why does a poor widow with a one-and-only child need all of half a house? A place to lay my head, that's plenty! Especially when the place needs a roof—it's been years since the house had a decent roof on it. He kept pestering me, my sweet brother-in-law (Ezriel, I mean), that the house needs to be covered by a roof! "It's time," he said, "for it to be covered!" "So cover it," I said. So he said, "Let's cover it!" "Right," I said. "Let's cover it." Cover-cover, cover-shmover—that's how things remained. Because for a roof you need straw, not to mention shingles. Where could I get the money? Well, I rented out two rooms, see. One little room to Chaim Chono, an old man, deaf and already senile. His children pay me five gulden a week for rent, and he eats at their place every second day. That is, one day he eats and one day he fasts. And on the day that he eats, he eats boils and scabs. That's what he says (Chaim Chono, I mean), and maybe it's a lie— maybe old people grumble, you know. No matter how much you give them, it's not enough; wherever you sit them down, the chair's too hard; whatever you do for them, it's the wrong thing. . .

Now, what were we saying? Yes, you said, *boarders* . . . No decent Jew should have to trouble with them! Still, Chaim Chono's deaf, a quiet boarder. As they say, "never seen, never heard." But it was my luck to rent out the other room to Gnessi. She's a flour dealer, see—has a stall for flour. Some piece of goods! But you should have seen her at the start: soft as honey-pie, all sweetness and light, couldn't do enough for me. Butter wouldn't melt in her mouth. What did *she* need, after all? A corner of the oven to heat her pot, that's all; the edge of the board once a week, maybe, to salt her scrap of meat; an inch or two of the table, once in a blue moon, for rolling her strip of noodle dough. "And the children?" I asked her. "Where will you put your children, where? Gnessi, I know you have children, they should be well." So she said, "What are you talking about, Yente darling? Do you know what kind of children they are? *Children!* They're diamonds, not children! Summer, they roam outside all day long. Winter, they climb up on a shelf over the oven, like sweet lambs. You won't hear a peep from them."

A pretty kettle of fish I got myself into—may it happen to all my enemies! Some children! God forgive me for my words, but one brat's worse than the other! A piece of bread isn't enough for them! Day and night they're at it. They scream, they tear and claw, they murder each other. It's hell! What am I saying, *hell*? Hell's paradise, I tell you, compared to them! And that's not all. In fact, that's not even the problem. Children you can deal with. A whack, a pinch, a smack—after all, they're children! But God sent her a husband. Oyzer's his name. I'm sure you know him, he's the assistant *shammes* in the lower prayer-house. A kosher Jew, poor thing, and no fool either, it seems; but you should hear how she lets him have it, Gnessi I mean. Oyzer, here! Oyzer, there! Oyzer, this! Oyzer, that! Oyzer-Oyzer! And him, either he makes some wisecrack (he's a smart aleck too, on top of everything else), or else he grabs his hat and goes off. I tell you, it's a great success, that marriage—a real winner and that's all! . . .

What were we saying? Yes, you said, *bad neighbors* . . . Bad isn't the word! I hope God Almighty won't think I have an evil tongue. Anyway, *I* don't have to be the one to spread rumors. What do I have against her? She's a woman who likes to give bread to the poor. But who can figure her out? When she gets into one of her moods, God help and defend us all! It's a shame to talk of it—I wouldn't say it to anyone else, but with you, I know, it'll stay a secret. . . . *Shh* . . . . She beats him up—her husband, I mean, when no one's looking! "Oy!" I said to her, "Gnessi, Gnessi! Aren't you afraid of God? Of God, Gnessi, you're not afraid?" So she said, "Go bother your grandmother." So I said, "The devil take it!" So she said, "Whoever keeps an eye on someone else's pot, let that person be the scapegoat!" So I said, "Whoever has nothing better to watch than *that* pot, should have his eyes taken out." So she said, "May every eavesdropper drop dead!" What do you say, Rabbi, to such a big mouth? . . .

But what were we saying? Yes, you said, *I like things clean.* . . . Why should I deny it? I really do like it to be clean in every nook and corner. How does that make me guilty? Maybe it's just that she can't stand it (Gnessi, I mean) that my place is clean, my place is nice and tidy, my place is bright. And by her? You should see—chaos and darkness, everything topsy-turvy, like a hurricane hit it. The chamber pot's always full—up to your neck, Rabbi. Up to your eyes! Phooh! Comes morning, it's thunder and lightning! Call those children? Demons, not children! Just like my Dovidel—as black to white! Because my Dovidel, he should be well, he's in *cheder* all day, see, and as soon as he comes home at night he gets to work: either he prays, see, or else he studies, or else he looks through some book or other. And *her* children—God shouldn't punish me for these words, but if it's not eating, it's crying, or it's banging their heads against the wall. You understand me, Rabbi? Is it my fault that God blessed her with such brats, terrors of the earth, and that me He gave such a gift, a piece of gold, a jewel, he shouldn't be taken from me (my Dovidel, I mean), because he costs me enough tears, see! Don't think it's that I'm just a woman! A man in my place couldn't bear it! Don't be insulted, Rabbi, but some men, see, are a thousand times worse than women. If they feel the pinch, they don't know if they're coming or going. Do you need examples? Here, take Yosi, Moishe-Avram's boy. As long as Frumme-Neche was alive, he managed; and when she died (may it never happen in this house), he just let go and gave up, body and soul. "Reb Yosi," I said to him, "God help you! All right, your wife died. What's there to do? That's God's business. The Lord gives and the Lord takes away—how's it written there in our Holy Scriptures? You don't have to be told, do you, Rabbi? You probably know it all. . . ."

Now, what were we saying? Yes, you said, *an only son* . . . He's my one and only, as they say—the apple of my eye, Dovidel I mean. You don't know him? He's named after my father-in-law, see, Dovid Hirsch. You should see him, my Dovidel (may he live a long life)—the image of his father, exactly Moishe Ben Zion, even the same height. And that face! Just like *his* (may he rest in peace)—yellowish, exhausted, skin-and-bones, and *weak,* weak and worn out, poor thing, from studying, from the *Gemara.* "Enough is enough," I said to him; "my sweet son, rest a little. Just look at your face, will you! Here, take something to eat, drink something. Have this glass of chicory. Here, take it!" "The chicory," he said, "*you'd* better drink, mother. You work beyond your strength," he said. "I'd do better to help you carry the parcels from market." What an idea! "Do you know what you're talking about?" I said. "What do you mean, you'll carry parcels? My enemies won't live to see the day, and I have plenty of enemies! You have to study," I said, "so study already! Sit and study."

And meanwhile I can't keep my eyes off him, Dovidel I mean. Just like *him* (may he rest in peace). Even the cough's the same, woe is me. Woe and desolation! Every time he coughs it tears my heart out. Because, you know, it almost did me in just to get him to grow up. To begin with, no one believed the child would live (may he live a long life). Whatever the sickness, the plague, the disease, him it hit. If it's measles you want, *he's* got it. You'd like chicken pox? He's got chicken pox. Diphtheria or the measles? He has it. Scarlet fever, the mumps, whooping cough? Why not? *What* not? How many nights I spent at his bedside only God can count. It seems, though, that my tears did the trick (and maybe also his father's spirit, a bit), because I did live to see his *bar mitzvah,* after all.

You think that's that, don't you? Well, listen to this gem. One night, wouldn't you know, he was coming home from *cheder,* it was winter, and he met something, someone, dressed all in white and beating the air with both hands. Naturally the child was scared to death. Poor thing, he fell in a faint on the snow, and they brought him to me half-dead, see, just barely alive. And when he came to, then he really collapsed. Lay there burning with fever for no more or less than six weeks! How I survived is a miracle from heaven. What didn't I do? I made deals with all the angels! I bargained for him a hundred times over, and pulled him back out of the jaws of death! I even tagged another name on him: Chaim, for *life*—Chaim Dovid Hirsch. And tears . . . *tears!* What's the point of talking about tears? "Dear God," I said, arguing my case with the Almighty. "You want to punish me? Punish! Any way you like, but my child, see, you mustn't take from me!"

After God granted me the gift, made my son well again, Dovidel said to me, "Know what, mother? I've got regards for you from Father. Father came to visit me." Well, I felt the life go out of me and my heart pounding, *bam, bam, bam!* "Let him intercede for us," I said; "it's a sure sign you'll live long, God willing, and be well." That's what I said, with my heart going *bam, bam, bam!* It was only much later, quite a while afterwards, that I found out about the one dressed in white. He was, do you know who? . . . Well, guess, Rabbi. After all, you're a wise man! . . . Reb Lippa, that's who it was, Lippa the water-carrier! Just that day, see, he had to go and buy himself a new fur pelt, a white one yet. And since there was a burning frost outside, he decided he'd like to warm himself, so he stood there clapping one hand against the other. May my troubles come to rest on his head! Did you ever hear of such nerve? That a Jew should suddenly put on a white fur pelt, without rhyme or reason!

Now, what were we saying? Yes, you said, *health.* . . . Health, that's the main thing. That's what our doctor says. He told me I should give him pills (my Dovidel, that is), and cook broths, see, every day a broth, made from at least a quarter chicken. And if I can manage it, he said, I should also feed him with milk and butter, and with chocolate, too, he said, if I can manage *that.* A fine story—*if* I can manage it! Think, is there anything in the world I couldn't manage for my Dovidel? Just suppose, for some reason, they'd tell me, "Go Yente, dig the earth, chop wood, carry water, knead clay, rob a church, just for Dovidel." Would I find some excuse not to? I'd do it in a split second, even in the middle of the night, in the biggest frost! Look, he took a notion this summer (my

Dovidel I mean) that he wanted certain books, prayer books probably. And since I go into the best houses, see, he asked me could I get him these books, or prayer books, and he wrote me down the books on paper. So I came and showed them the paper and asked for the books, or prayer books . . . once, twice, three times. They laughed at me. "Yente," they said, "why do you need such books? Do you feed the hens with them, or maybe the geese and ducks?" "Laugh, laugh," I thought to myself, "as long as my Dovidel has what to read." All night long, night after night, he looked through those books, or prayer books, and asked me to bring him more and more. Should I begrudge him? I brought those back and took others. And here that doctor came, the wise-guy— "Can you manage, for Dovidel's sake, to make a broth every day, from at least a quarter chicken?" Rabbi, if he'd said three quarters of a chicken, would I have tried to find a way out? Where in the world, I ask you, do such doctors come from? Where do they grow? What sort of yeast do they use to cook them up? What kind of ovens? . . .

What were we saying? Yes, you said *broth* . . . Every day I've made a broth for him (my Dovidel, I mean) from a quarter chicken, and in the evening, when he comes home from his studies, he eats and I sit opposite him with some work in my hands, and I feel just ready to burst with joy. And I pray to God, God should help me so that tomorrow, God willing, I'll be able to prepare another broth from a quarter chicken. Sometimes he'll say to me, "Mother, why don't you eat with me?" So I say, "Eat and be healthy. I ate already." So he says, "What did you eat?" "What I ate, I ate," I say, "so long as I ate. Eat well." And when he's done with studying the books, or prayer books, it's only then, see, that I'll take a couple of baked potatoes from the oven, or else I'll rub a piece of bread with onion, and make myself a feast. And I swear to you by all that's holy—I should only live so long and see my Dovidel happy—that I get more pleasure from that piece of onion than I'd get from the most delicious meal, because I remember that Dovidel (God preserve him) just ate a broth made from a quarter chicken, and tomorrow, God willing, there'll be another broth made from a quarter chicken.

Still, there's one little problem—that cough he coughs all the time, poor thing. I begged the doctor, see, to get him something for the cough. So he said (the doctor I mean), "How old was your husband when he died, and what did he die of?" So I said, "He died of death. His years ran out, see, and he died. What kind of comparison is that to this?" So he said, "I need to know it. I've examined your son," he said. "You have a fine son, a fine upstanding boy." "Thank you very much," I said, "that much I know myself. What you'd better give me, see, is a remedy for his cough so he'll stop coughing and coughing." So he said, "That can't be done. You just have to watch that he doesn't study so much." "What else should he do?" I said. So he said, "He should eat a lot, and go for a walk every day. And the main thing," he said, "he mustn't sit at night studying his books. If it's his fate to be a doctor someday, it won't do him any harm to wait a few years longer."

"What I dreamed last night," I thought to myself, "and tonight and every night of the year—may all my worst dreams! . . . But there's something fishy here. He's not talking straight. How come my Dovidel's to be a doctor, of all things? Why shouldn't he become something better, a governor, why not?"

So I went home, see, and told it all to my Dovidel. His face got red as a flame. "Do you know what, mother?" he said to me. "Don't go to the doctor any more, and don't talk to him." So I said, "I can't stand him already. Can't I tell he's a lunatic?" Imagine, a doctor with such habits— prying into a patient's life! "How do you live? From what do you live? Where do you get your living?" What's *his* business? Doesn't he get his half a ruble? Why can't he just take it and write the prescription? . . .

What were we saying? Yes, you said, *a chicken without a head . . .* Of course I run around like a chicken without a head! What else would you expect, with all I've got to worry about—eggs and hens and geese and ducks, and those rich ladies always on my back, each of them wanting to have first pick, each one trembling that maybe the others got the best eggs and fattest hens. I sleep in my street clothes! So when do I have time, tell me yourself, Rabbi, to cook a broth? I'm never at home! But as they say, if you set your mind on it you find a way. Very early, see, before I get off to market, I heat the oven. Then I rush back from the market for a minute to salt the quarter chicken, and then I'm off again to work. And rush back again, to rinse the meat and put on the cooking pot. Then I ask her, that lodger of mine (Gnessi, I mean), to watch my pot. That is, when the pot boils, she should cover it and rake over the ashes. Some big job! How often does it happen that I'll cook a whole supper for her? After all, we're Jews, God help us. We're among people, aren't we, not wandering in the desert! Then in the evening, when I come home from work, I blow up the fire, and warm up the pot, see, and a fresh broth is what he gets to eat (my Dovidel, I mean). So it seems everything's fine, right? But there's the lodger of mine, that big . . . No, I won't say it. Let not the word be spoken! This morning, of all mornings, she had to go and cook a dairy meal for her children—*halushkas,* or *balabeshkas* with milk. What got into her that she had to make *balabeshkas* with milk? Why all of a sudden this morning out of the clear blue? I should know so much about hard times! She's a strange bird, that flour dealer. With her it's all or nothing. Three days go by and she won't light a fire in the oven. Then suddenly, she'll get in the mood—start up a casserole pot with buckwheat *kasha.* That's what *she* says, but you've got to put on your glasses to see a speck of buckwheat. Or else she'll put on a soup of beans and barley, or a pot of fish-potatoes, and you can smell the onion a mile off, not to mention the pepper she peppered it with. After that, her children can go open-mouthed and empty-bellied for the next half a week, yowling "Hoo-ah! Hoo-ah!" . . .

What were we saying? Yes, you said, *schlimazel.* . . . She started in, that lodger of mine, and rolled out a dough of *balabeshkas* from buckwheat flour, and put a pot of milk to boil on the oven. And her children set up such a celebration, such cries of joy—my God! You'd think they'd never seen a drop of milk. Though mind you, all our enemies should earn as much, as there was milk in that pot! Maybe two spoonfuls, the rest water. But for such poor people, I guess, that's something, too. Meanwhile, guess who the wind blew in? The *shammes!* Oyzer must have sniffed all the way out there at his prayer-house that back here a royal feast was cooking. So he came flying home, with a wisecrack as usual: "Happy holidays!" "A miserable, a dark and bitter day to you!" she said. "Why so early?" So he said, "I was afraid. God forbid I should come late for the blessing! Tell me Gnessi, what's cooking there on the oven?" "The plague," she said, "in a little pot, especially for you." So he said, "Why not a big pot? It could be for both of us!" So she said, boiling mad, "Damn you with your wisecracks!" And she reached for the potholder to get the pot. Well, the pot turned over, and the milk—splash! all over the oven! What shrieks and screams! Gnessi was cursing her husband with deadly curses—lucky for him he managed to slip out fast—and the children were yowling as if someone has just killed their father and mother. "A curse on *balabeshkas* with milk," I said. "What if the broth's spoiled? The milk, God forbid, might have made my pot *treyf!"* So she said, "The devil take you, together with your broth and your pot! Maybe my *balabeshkas* with milk," she said, "are just as precious to me as all your pots and all the broths you cook for that precious son of yours!" "I'll tell you what," I said. "May you all be sacrificed for the smallest fingernail from the smallest finger of my Dovidel!" So she said, "I'll tell *you* what. Your Dovidel should be sacrificed for all of us—he's only one!" What do you say to a slut like that? Shouldn't she have her mouth slapped shut with a wet towel? . . .

What were we saying? Yes, you said, *from dairy and meat on the same oven, no good can come.* . . . So there was the pot, see, upside-down, and the milk spilled all over the oven. Rabbi, I'm afraid that (God forbid) it may *just* have touched my pot, and then I'm a lost soul! Come to think of it, though, how could the milk have reached it? My pot was standing there in a far corner, shoved away somewhere at the opposite end of the oven. But it's the old story—the chicken or the egg? Anything's possible; how can I be sure? Just my rotten luck! What if. . . ? Rabbi, I'll tell you the honest truth, see. Never mind the broth. A broth is a broth. Of course, it breaks my heart—what will Dovidel eat, poor thing? But I'll probably think up something, probably. Yesterday, I bought some geese at the market, made some roasts to sell, so there are a few giblets left for Saturday—heads, innards, this, that. You can make *something* from it! But woe is me, Rabbi, how *can* I, if I don't have a pot? I'm afraid if you say the pot is *treyf,* I'm left without a pot, see; and without a pot, it's like I'm without a hand, because I've only got one pot. That is, as for pots, I used to have three meat pots. But then Gnessi (may she sink into the earth) once borrowed a pot from me, a brand new pot, and then she goes and gives me back a crippled pot. So I said to her, "What kind of pot is this?" So she said, "It's your pot." So I said, "How come I get back a crippled pot when I gave you a brand new pot?" So she said, "Shut it. Don't yell like that, who needs your things? First of all, I gave you back a brand new pot. Second, the pot I took from you was a crippled pot. And third, I never even took a pot from you. I have my own pot, so get off my back!" There's a slut for you! . . .

Now, what were we saying? Yes, you said, *no such thing as having too many pots.* . . . There I was, see, left with two pots, two good pots I mean, and one crippled pot. Two pots. But how can a poor person dare to have two pots? It must have been decreed in heaven that when I came home today from the market with two hens, one hen should get loose and be scared by the cat. I bet you're wondering how a cat got into this. It's *her,* Gnessi and her brats! They got their grimy hands on a cat somewhere, so day and night they torture it to death. "It's a pity," my Dovidel keeps telling them, "a shame and a pity! That's a living thing!"

But try and argue with such rotten, no-good do-nothings. To make a long story short, they tied something to the cat's tail, and she started jumping (the cat I mean), doing cartwheels, standing on her head. So the hen got scared and flew right to the top shelf, and crash, a pot gone to hell! Do you think it was the crippled pot? Of course, what else! If something's got to break, count on it, it'll be the good pot! That's the way it's been since the world began. What I'd like to know, see, is why that is. For example, two people go along, this one goes along and that one goes along. One is an only son, a one-and-only, his mother trembles over him. And the other . . . Rabbi, God be with you! What's the matter with you? . . . *Rebbetsen!* What are you hiding for? Quick, get over here! Hurry up! The Rabbi looks sick! Looks like he's going to faint! . . . Water! *Water!*. . .

Translated by Sacvan Bercovitch

The Clock
That Struck
Thirteen

THE CLOCK STRUCK THIRTEEN.

That's the truth. I wasn't joking. I am telling you a true story of what happened in Kasrilevke, in our own house. I was there.

We had a hanging clock. It was an ancient clock that my grandfather had inherited from his father and his father's father straight back to the days of Count Chmielnitzki.

What a pity that a clock is a lifeless thing, mute and without speech. Otherwise what stories it could have told and told. It had a name throughout the town—Reb Nochem's clock—so unfaltering and true in its course that men came from all directions to set their own clocks and watches by it. Only Reb Leibesh Akoron, a man of learning and philosophy, who could tell time by the sun and knew the almanac by heart, said that our clock was—next to his little watch—just so much tin and hardware, not worth a pinch of snuff. But even he had to admit that it was still a clock. And you must remember that Reb Leibesh was the man who, every Wednesday night, climbed to the roof of the synagogue or to the hilltop nearby, before the evening prayers, to catch the exact moment when the sun went down—in one hand his watch, and in the other—his almanac. And just as the sun sank below the housetops he muttered to himself: "On the dot!"

He was always comparing the two timepieces. Walking in without so much as a "good evening," he would glance up at our hanging clock, then down at his little watch, then over to his almanac, again at our clock, down to his watch, over to the almanac, several times, and away he went.

Only one day when he came in to compare the two timepieces with his almanac, he let out a yell, "Nochem! Quick! Where are you?"

My father, more dead than alive, came running. "What—what's happened, Reb Leibesh?"

"You are asking me?" shouted Reb Leibesh, raising his little watch right up to my father's face, and pointing with his other hand up to our clock: "Nochem, why don't you say something? Can't you see? It's a minute and a half fast! A minute and a half! Cast out the thing!" He hurled the words like an angered prophet with a base image before him.

My father did not like this at all. What did he mean, telling him to cast the clock out? "Where is it written, Reb Leibesh, that my clock is a minute and a half *fast?* Maybe we can read the same sentence backward—that your watch is a minute and a half *slow*. How do you like that?"

Reb Leibesh looked at my father as at a man who has just said that Sabbath comes twice a week or that the Day of Atonement falls on Passover. Reb Leibesh didn't say a word. He sighed deeply, turned around, slammed the door, and away he went.

But we didn't care. The whole town knew that Reb Leibesh was a man whom nothing could please. The best cantor you ever heard sounded like a crow; the wisest man was—an ass; the best marriage—a failure; the cleverest epigram—a dull commonplace.

But let us return to our clock. What a clock that was! Its chimes could be heard three doors away. Boom . . boom . . . boom . . . Almost half of the town ordered its life according to it. And what is Jewish life without a clock? How many things there are that must be timed to the minute—the lighting of the Sabbath candles, the end of the Sabbath, the daily prayers, the salting and the soaking of the meat, the intervals between meals . . .

In short, our clock was the town clock. It was always faithful to us and to itself. In all its existence it never knew a repairman. My father, himself, was its only master. He had "an intuitive understanding of how it worked." Every year before Passover he carefully removed it from the wall, cleaned the insides with a feather duster, took out from within a mass of spiderwebs, mutilated flies which the spiders had lured inside, along with dead cockroaches that had lost their way and had met their sad fate there. Then, cleaned and sparkling, he hung the clock on the wall again and it glowed. That is, they both glowed, the clock because it had been polished and cleaned, and my father—because the clock did.

But there came a day when a strange thing happened. It was on a beautiful cloudless day when we were sitting at the noonday meal. Whenever the clock struck I liked to count the strokes, and I did it out loud.

"One, two, three . . . seven . . . eleven, twelve, thirteen . . . "

What . . . thirteen!

"Thirteen!" cried my father, and burst out laughing. "A fine mathematician you are—may the evil eye spare you. Whoever heard of a clock striking thirteen?"

"Thirteen," I said. "On my word of honor. Thirteen."

"I'll give you thirteen smacks," cried my father, aroused. "Don't ever repeat such nonsense. Fool! A clock can't strike thirteen."

"Do you know what," my mother broke in, "I'm afraid that the child is right. It seems to me that I counted thirteen, too."

"Wonderful," said my father. "Another village heard from."

But at the same time he too began to suspect something. After dinner he went to the clock, climbed on a stool, and prodded around inside until the clock began to strike. All three of us counted, nodding our heads at each stroke: "One, two, three . . . seven . . . nine . . . eleven, twelve, thirteen."

"Thirteen," repeated my father, with a look in his eye of a man who had just beheld the wall itself come to life and start talking. He prodded once more at the wheels. Once more the clock struck thirteen. My father climbed down from the stool pale as a sheet and remained standing in the middle of the room, looking down at the floor, chewing his beard and muttering to himself, "It struck thirteen . . . How is that? What does it mean? If it was out of order it would have stopped. What then?"

"What then?" said my mother. "Take down the clock and fix it. After all, you're the expert."

"Well," agreed my father, "maybe you're right." And taking down the clock he busied himself with it. He sweated over it, he worked all day over it, and at last hung it back in its place. Thank the Lord, the clock ran as it should, and when midnight came we stood around it and counted each stroke till twelve. My father beamed at us.

"Well," he said, "no more thirteen."

"I've always said you were an expert," my mother said. "But there is one thing I don't understand. Why does it wheeze? It never used to wheeze like this before."

"You're imagining it," my father said. But listening carefully, we heard the clock wheeze when it got ready to ring, like an old man catching his breath before he coughs—"wh-wh-wh"—and then the boom . . . boom . . . boom. But even the boom itself was not the boom of olden days. The old boom had been a happy one, a joyous one, and now something sad had crept in, a sadness like that in the song of an old, worn-out cantor toward the end of the Day of Atonement . . .

As time went on the wheezing became louder and the ringing more subdued and mournful, and my father became melancholy. We could see him suffering as though he watched a live thing in agony and could do nothing to help it. It seemed as though at any moment the clock would stop altogether. The pendulum began to act strangely. Something shivered inside, something got caught and dragged, like an old man dragging a bad leg. We could see the clock getting ready to stop forever. But just in time, my father came to the decision that there was nothing wrong with the clock itself. What was wrong was the weight. Not enough weight. And so he fastened to the weight the pestle of my mother's mortar—a matter of several pounds. The clock began to run like a charm, and my father was happy again, a new man.

But it didn't last long. Again the clock began to fail. Again the pendulum began to act strangely, swinging sometimes fast and sometimes slow. It was heartrending, it tore you apart, to see the clock languish before your eyes. And my father, watching it, drooped also, lost interest in life, suffered anguish.

Like a good doctor devoted to his patient, considering every known treatment or possible remedy, my father tried every way imaginable to save the clock.

"Not enough weight, not enough life," said my father, and attached to the weight more and more objects. First an iron frying pan, and then a copper pitcher, then a flatiron, a bag of sand, a couple of bricks . . . Each time the clock drew fresh life and began to run. Painfully, with convulsions, but it worked. Till one night when a catastrophe took place.

It was a Friday night in winter. We had just eaten the Sabbath meal of delicious spicy fish with horseradish, fat chicken soup with noodles, pot roast with prunes and potatoes, and had said the grace that such a meal deserved. The candles were still flickering. The servant girl had just brought in the freshly roasted sunflower seeds, when in came Muma Yente, a toothless, dark-skinned little woman whose husband had abandoned her years ago and gone off to America.

"Good Sabbath," said Muma Yente, breathless as usual. "I just knew you'd have sunflower seeds. The only trouble is—what can I crack them with? May my old man have as few years to live as I have teeth in my mouth . . .

"M-m-m," she went on, faster and faster, "I can still smell your fish, Malka . . . What a time *I* had getting fish this morning, with that Sarah-Pearl—the millionairess—standing next to me at the market. I was just saying to Menasha the fishman, 'Why is everything so high today?' when Sarah-Pearl jumps up with, 'Quick, I'm in a hurry. How much does this pickerel weigh?' 'What's your rush?' I say to her. 'The town isn't on fire. Menasha won't throw the fish back into the river. Among the rich,' I let them know, 'there is plenty of money but not much sense.' Then she goes and opens her mouth at me. 'Paupers,' says she, 'shouldn't come around here. If you have no money you shouldn't hanker after things.' What do you think of her nerve? What was she before she married—a peddler herself—standing in her mother's stall at the market?"

She caught her breath and went on: "These people and their marriages! Just like Abraham's Pessel-Peiseh who is so delighted with her daughter just because she married a rich man from Stristch, who took her just as she stood, without dowry. Wonderful luck she has. They say she is getting to look a sight. The life those children lead her . . . What do you think—it's so easy to be a stepmother? God forbid! Look at that Chava for instance. A good, well-meaning soul like that. But you should see the trouble she has with her stepchildren. The screaming you hear day and night, the way they talk back to her. And what's worse—pitch-patch—three smacks for a penny . . . "

The candles begin to gutter. The shadows tremble on the walls, they mount higher and higher. The sunflower seeds crackle. All of us are talking, telling stories to the company at large, with no one really listening. But Muma Yente talks more than anybody.

"Listen to this," she lets out, "there is something even worse than all the rest. Not far from Yampola, a couple of miles, some robbers attacked a Jewish tavern the other night, killed everyone in the family, even an infant in a cradle. The only one left was a servant girl asleep on top of the oven in the kitchen. She heard the shrieks, jumped down from the oven, and looking through a crack in the door, saw the master and mistress lying murdered on the floor in a pool of blood. She took a chance—this servant girl—and jumped out the window, running all the way to town yelling, 'Children of Israel, save us! Help! Help! Help!'"

Suddenly, in the midst of Muma Yente's yelling, "Help! Help!"—we hear a crash—bang—smash—boom—bam! Immersed in the story, all we could think was that robbers were attacking our own home and were shooting at us from all sides—or that the room had fallen in—or a hurricane had hit us. We couldn't move from our seats. We stared at each other speechless—waiting. Then all of us began to yell, "Help! Help! Help!"

In a frenzy my mother caught me in her arms, pressed me to her heart, and cried, "My child, if it's going to happen, let it happen to me! Oh . . ."

"What is it?" cries my father. "What happened to him?"

"It's nothing. Nothing," yells Muma Yente, waving her arms. "Be quiet."

And the girl runs in from the kitchen, wild-eyed. "What's the matter? What's happened? Is there a fire? Where is it?"

"Fire? What fire?" shouts Muma Yente at the girl. "Go burn, if you want to. Get scorched, if you like." She keeps scolding the girl as if it's all her fault, then turns to us.

"What are you making this racket for? What are you frightened of? What do you think it is? Can't you see? It's just the clock. The clock fell down. Now do you know? Everything you could imagine was hung on it—a half a ton at least. So it fell down. What's strange about that? You wouldn't have been any better yourself . . ."

At last we come to our senses. We get up from the table one by one, go up to the clock and inspect it from all sides. There it lies, face down, broken, shattered, smashed, ruined forever.

"It is all over," says my father in a dull voice, his head bent as if standing before the dead. He wrings his hands and tears appear in his eyes. I look at him and I want to cry, too.

"Hush, be quiet," says my mother, "why do you grieve? Perhaps it was destined. Maybe it was written in heaven that today, at this minute, the end should come. Let it be an atonement for our sins—though I should not mention it on the Sabbath—for you, for me, for our children, for our loved ones, for all of Israel. Amen. *Selah*."

All that night I dreamed of clocks. I imagined that I saw our old clock lying on the ground, clothed in a white shroud. I imagined that I saw the clock still alive, but instead of a pendulum there swung back and forth a long tongue, a human tongue, and the clock did not ring, but groaned.

And each groan tore something out of me. And on its face, where I used to see the twelve, I saw suddenly number thirteen. Yes, thirteen. You may believe me—on my word of honor.

Translated by Julius and Frances Butwin

Home for Passover

TWO TIMES A YEAR, as punctually as a clock, in April and again in September, Fishel the *melamed* goes home from Balta to Hashtchavata to his wife and children, for Passover and for the New Year. Almost all his life it has been his destiny to be a guest in his own home, a most welcome guest, it is true, but for a very short time, only over the holidays. And as soon as the holidays are over he packs his things and goes back to Balta, back to his teaching, back to the rod, to the *Gemara* that he studies with the unwilling small boys of Balta, back to his exile among strangers and to his secret yearning for home.

However, when Fishel does come home, he is a king! Bath-Sheba, his wife, comes out to meet him, adjusts her kerchief, becomes red as fire, asks him quickly without looking him in the eye, "How are you, Fishel?" And he answers, "How are *you?*" And Froike, his boy, now almost thirteen, holds out his hand, and the father asks him, "Where are you now, Ephraim, in your studies?" And Reizel, his daughter, a bright-faced little girl with her hair in braids, runs up and kisses him.

"Papa, what did you bring me for the holidays?"

"Material for a dress, and for your mother a silk shawl. Here, give Mother the shawl."

And Fishel takes a new silk (or maybe half-silk) shawl out of his *tallis*-sack, and Beth-Sheba becomes redder than ever, pulls her kerchief low over her eyes, pretends to get busy around the house, bustles here and there, and gets nothing done.

"Come, Ephraim, show me how far you've got in the *Gemara*. I want to see how you're getting along."

And Froike shows his father what a good boy he has been, how well he has applied himself, the understanding he has of his work, and how good his memory is. And Fishel listens to him, corrects him once or twice, and his soul expands with pride. He glows with happiness. What a fine boy Froike is! What a jewel!

"If you want to go to the baths, here is a shirt ready for you," says Bath-Sheba, without looking him in the eye, and Fishel feels strangely happy, like a man who has escaped from prison into the bright, free world among his own people, his loved and faithful ones. And he pictures himself in the room thick with steam, lying on the top ledge together with a few of his cronies, all of them sweating, rubbing each other and beating each other with birch rods and calling for more, more . . .

"Harder! Rub harder! Can't you make it harder!"

And coming home from the bath, refreshed, invigorated, almost a new man, he dresses for the holiday. He puts on his best gabardine with the new cord, steals a glance at Bath-Sheba in her new dress with the new silk shawl, and finds her still a presentable woman, a good, generous, pious woman . . . And then with Froike he goes to the synagogue. There greetings fly at him from all sides. "Well, well! Reb Fishel! How are you? How's the *melamed?*" "The *melamed* is still teaching." "What's happening in the world?" "What should happen? It's still the same old world." "What's doing in Balta?" "Balta is still Balta." Always, every six months, the same formula, exactly the same, word for word. And Nissel the cantor steps up to the lectern to start the evening services. He lets go with his good, strong voice that grows louder and stronger as he goes along. Fishel is pleased with the performance. He is also pleased with Froike's. The lad stands near him and prays, prays with feeling, and Fishel's soul expands with pride. He glows with happiness. A fine boy, Froike! A good Jewish boy!

"Good *yontif!* Good *yontif!*"

"Good *yontif* to you!"

They are home already and the *seder* is waiting. The wine in the glasses, the horseradish, the eggs, the *haroses,* and all the other ritual foods. His "throne" is ready—two stools with a large pillow spread over them. Any minute now Fishel will become the king, any minute he will seat himself on his royal throne in a white robe, and Bath-Sheba, his queen with her new silk shawl, will sit at his side. Ephraim, the prince, in his new cap and Princess Reizel with her braids will sit facing them.

Make way, fellow Israelites! Show your respect! Fishel the *melamed* has mounted his throne! Long live Fishel!

      The wits of Hashtchavata, who are always up to some prank and love to make fun of the whole world (and especially of a humble teacher) once made up a story about Fishel. They said that one year, just before Passover, Fishel sent a telegram to Bath-Sheba reading like this: *Rabiata sobrani. Dengi vezu. Prigotov puli. Yedu tzarstvovat.* In ordinary language this is what it meant: "Classes dismissed. Purse full. Prepare *kneydlach.* I come to rule." This telegram, the story goes on, was immediately turned over to the authorities in Balta, Bath-Sheba was searched but nothing was found, and Fishel himself was brought home under police escort. But I can tell you on my word of honor that this is a falsehood and a lie. Fishel had never in his life sent a telegram to anyone. Bath-Sheba was never searched. And Fishel was never arrested. That is, he was arrested once, but not for sending a telegram. He was arrested because of a passport. And that not in Balta but in Yehupetz, and it was not before Passover but in the middle of summer. This is what happened.

Fishel had suddenly decided that he would like to teach in Yehupetz that year and had gone there without a passport to look for work. He thought it was the same as Balta where he needed no passport, but he was sadly mistaken. And before he was through with that experience he swore that not only he but even his children and grandchildren would never go to Yehupetz again to look for work ...

And ever since that time he goes directly to Balta every season and in the spring he ends his classes a week or two before Passover and dashes off for home. What do you mean—dashes off? He goes as fast as he can—that is, assuming that the roads are clear and he can find a wagon to take him and he can cross the Bug either over the ice or by ferry. But what happens if the snows have melted and the mud is deep, there is no wagon to be gotten, the Bug has just opened and the ferry hasn't started yet because of the ice, and if you try to cross by boat you risk your very life—and Passover is right in front of your nose? What can you do? Take it the way a man does if he's on his way from Machnivka to Berdichev for the Sabbath, or from Sohatchov to Warsaw—it's late Friday afternoon, the wagon is going up a hill, it's getting dark fast, suddenly they're caught in a cloudburst, he's dead hungry—and just then the axle snaps! It's a real problem, I can assure you ...

Well, Fishel the *melamed* knows what that problem is. As long as he has been a teacher and has taken the trip from Hashtchavata to Balta and from Balta to Hashtchavata, he has experienced every inconvenience that a journey can offer. He has known what it is to go more than halfway on foot, and to help push the wagon, too. He has known what it is to lie together with a priest in a muddy ditch, with himself on bottom and the priest on top. He has known how it feels to run away from a pack of wolves that followed his wagon from Hashtchavata as far as Petschani—although later, it is true, he found out that it was not wolves but dogs. . . . But all these calamities were nothing compared with what he had to go through this year when he was on his way to spend the Passover with his family.

It was all the fault of the Bug. This one year it opened up a little later than usual, and became a torrent just at the time when Fishel was hurrying home—and he had reason to hurry! Because this year Passover started on Friday night—the beginning of Sabbath—and it was doubly important for him to be home on time.

Two

Fishel reached the Bug—traveling in a rickety wagon with a peasant—Thursday night. According to his reckoning he should have come there Tuesday morning, because he had left Balta Sunday noon. If he had only gone with Yankel-Sheigetz, the Balta coachman, on his regular weekly trip—even if he had to sit at the rear with his back to the other passengers and his feet dangling—he would have been home a long time ago and would have forgotten all about the whole journey. But the devil possessed him to go into the marketplace to see if he could find a cheaper conveyance; and it is an old story that the less you pay for something, the more it costs. Jonah the Drunkard had warned him, "Take my advice, Uncle, let it cost you two rubles but you'll sit like a lord in Yankel's coach—right in the very back row! Remember, you're playing with fire. There is not much time to lose!" But it was just his luck that the devil had to drag an old peasant from Hashtchávata across his path.

"Hello, Rabbi! Going to Hashtchavata?"

"Good! Can you take me? How much will it cost?"

How much it would cost—that he found it necessary to ask; but whether or not he would get home in time for Passover—that didn't even occur to Fishel. After all, even if he went on foot and took only tiny steps like a shackled person, he should have been able to reach Hashtchavata in less than a week . . .

But they had hardly started out before Fishel was sorry that he had hired this wagon, even though he had all the room in the world to stretch out in. It became apparent very soon that at the rate at which they were creeping they would never be able to get anywhere in time. All day long they rode and they rode, and at the end of the day they had barely got started. And no matter how much he kept bothering the old peasant, no matter how many times he asked how far they still had to go, the man did not answer. He only shrugged his shoulders and said, "Who can tell?"

It was much later, toward evening, that Yankel-Sheigetz overtook them, with a shout and whistle and a crack of the whip—overtook them and passed them with his four prancing horses bedecked with tiny bells, and with his coach packed with passengers inside, on the driver's seat, and some hanging onto the rear. Seeing the teacher sitting alone in the wagon with the peasant, Yankel-Sheigetz cracked his whip in the air again and cursed them both, the driver and the passenger, as only he could curse, laughed at them and at the horse, and after he had passed them he turned back and pointed at one of the wheels: "Hey, *schlimazel!* Look! One of your wheels is turning!"

"Whoa!" the peasant yelled, and together the driver and passenger climbed down, looked at every wheel, at every spoke, crawled under the wagon, searched everywhere, and found nothing wrong.

Realizing that Yankel had played a trick on them, the peasant began to scratch the back of his neck, and at the same time he cursed Yankel and every other Jew on earth with fresh new curses that Fishel had never heard in all his life. He shouted louder and louder and with every word grew angrier and angrier.

"Ah, shob tubi dobra ne bulo!" he cried. "Bad luck to you, Jew! I hope you die! I hope you never arrive! Every one of you die! You and your horse and your wife and your daughter and your aunts and your uncles and your cousins and your second-cousins and—and—and all the rest of your cursed Jews!"

It was a long time before the peasant climbed into his wagon again and was ready to start. But even then he was still angry; he couldn't stop yelling. He continued to heap curses at the head of Yankel-Sheigetz and all the Jews until, with God's help, they came to a village where they could spend the night.

The next morning Fishel got up very early, before dawn, said his morning prayers, read through the greater part of the *Book of Psalms,* had a bagel for breakfast, and was ready to go on. But Feodor was not ready. Feodor had found an old crony of his in the village and had spent the night with him, drinking and carousing. Then he slept the greater part of the day and was not ready to start till evening.

"Now, look here, Feodor," Fishel complained to him when they were in the wagon again, "the devil take you and your mother! After all, Feodor, I hired you to get me home for the holidays! I depended on you. I trusted you." And that wasn't all he said. He went on in the same vein, half pleading, half cursing, in a mixture of Russian and Hebrew, and when words failed him he used his hands. Feodor understood well enough what Fishel meant, but he did not answer a word, not a sound, as though he knew that Fishel was right. He was as quiet and coy as a little kitten until, on the fourth day, near Petschani, they met Yankel-Sheigetz on his way back from Hashtchavata with a shout and a crack of the whip and this good piece of news: "You might just as well turn back to Balta! The Bug has opened up!"

When Fishel heard this his heart sank, but Feodor thought that Yankel was making fun of him again and began to curse once more with even greater vigor and originality than before. He cursed Yankel from head to foot, he cursed every limb and every bone of his body. And his mouth did not shut until Thursday evening when they came to the Bug. They drove right up to Prokop Baraniuk, the ferryman, to find out when he would start running the ferry again.

And while Feodor and Prokop took a drink and talked things over, Fishel went off into a corner to say his evening prayers.

Three

The sun was beginning to set. It cast its fiery rays over the steep hills on both sides of the river, in spots still covered with snow and in spots already green, cut through with rivulets and torrents that bounded downhill and poured into the river itself with a roar where they met with the running waters from the melting ice. On the other side of the river, as if on a table, lay Hashtchavata, its church steeple gleaming in the sun like a lighted candle.

Standing there and saying his prayers with his face toward Hashtchavata, Fishel covered his eyes with his hand and tried to drive from his mind the tempting thoughts that tormented him: Bath-Sheba with her new silk shawl, Froike with his *Gemara,* Reizel with her braids, and the steaming bath. And fresh *matzo* with strongly seasoned fish and fresh horseradish that tore your nostrils apart, and Passover borscht that tasted like something in Paradise, and other good things that man's evil spirit can summon . . . And no matter how much Fishel drove these thoughts from his mind, they kept coming back like summer flies, like mosquitoes, and they did not let him pray as a man should.

And when he had finished his prayers Fishel went back to Prokop and got into a discussion with him about the ferry and the approaching holiday, explaining to him half in Russian, half in Hebrew, and the rest with his hands, how important a holiday Passover was to the Jews, and what it meant when Passover started on Friday evening! And he made it clear to him that if he did not cross the Bug by that time tomorrow—all was lost: in addition to the fact that at home everybody was waiting for him—his wife and children (and here Fishel gave a heartrending sigh)—if he did not cross the river before sunset, then for eight whole days he would not be able to eat or drink a thing. He might as well throw himself into the river right now! (At this point Fishel turned his face aside so that no one could see that there were tears in his eyes.)

Prokop Baraniuk understood the plight that poor Fishel was in, and he answered that he knew that the next day was a holiday; he even knew what the holiday was called, and he knew that it was a holiday when people drank wine and brandy. He knew of another Jewish holiday when people drank brandy too, and there was a third when they drank still more—in fact they were supposed to become drunk, but what they called that day he had forgotten . . .

"Good, that's very good!" Fishel interrupted with tears in his voice, "But what are we going to do now? What if tomorrow—God spare the thought. . ." Beyond that, poor Fishel could not say another word.

For this Prokop had no answer. All he did was to point to the river with his hand, as though to say, "Well—see for yourself . . ."

And Fishel lifted his eyes and beheld what his eyes had never before seen in all his life, and he heard what his ears had never heard. For it can truthfully be said that never before had Fishel actually seen what the out-of-doors was like. Whatever he had seen before had been seen at a glance while he was on his way somewhere, a glimpse snatched while hurrying from *cheder* to the synagogue or from synagogue to *cheder*. And now the sight of the majestic blue Bug between its two steep banks, the rush of the spring freshets tumbling down the hills, the roar of the river itself, the dazzling splendor of the setting sun, the flaming church steeple, the fresh, exhilarating odor of the spring earth and the air, and above all the simple fact of being so close to home and not being able to get there—all these things together worked on Fishel strangely. They picked him up and lifted him as though on wings and carried him off into a new world, a world of fantasy, and he imagined that to cross the Bug was the simplest thing in the world—like taking a pinch of snuff—if only the Eternal One cared to perform a tiny miracle and rescue him from his plight.

These thoughts and others like them sped through Fishel's head and carried him aloft and bore him so far from the riverbank that before he was aware of it, night had fallen, the stars were out, a cool wind had sprung up and had stolen in under his gabardine and ruffled his undershirt. And Fishel went on thinking of things he had never thought of before—of time and eternity, of the unlimited expanse of space, of the vastness of the universe, of the creation of heaven and earth itself . . .

Four

It was a troubled night that Fishel the *melamed* spent in the hut of Prokop the ferryman. But even that night finally came to an end and the new day dawned with a smile of warmth and friendliness. It was a rare and balmy morning. The last patches of snow became soft, like *kasha,* and the *kasha* turned to water, and the water poured into the Bug from all directions . . . Only here and there could be seen huge blocks of ice that looked like strange animals, like polar bears that hurried and chased each other, as if they were afraid that they would be too late in arriving where they were going . . .

And once again Fishel the *melamed* finished his prayers, ate the last crust of bread that was left in his sack, and went out to look at the river and to see what could be done about getting across it. But when he heard from Prokop that they would be lucky if the ferry could start Sunday afternoon, he became terrified. He clutched his head with both hands and shook all over. He fumed at Prokop, and scolded him in his own mixture of Russian and Hebrew. Why had Prokop given him hope the night before; why had he said that they might be able to get across today? To this Prokop answered coldly that he had not said a word about crossing by ferry, he had only said that they might be able to get across, and this they could still do. He could take him over any way he wanted to—in a rowboat or on a raft, and it would cost him another half ruble— not a kopek more.

"Have it your own way!" sobbed Fishel. "Let it be a rowboat. Let it be a raft. Only don't make me spend the holiday here on the bank!"

That was Fishel's answer. And at the moment he would have been willing to pay two rubles, or even dive in and swim across—if he could only swim. He was willing to risk his life for the holy Passover. And he went after Prokop heatedly, urged him to get out the boat at once and take him across the Bug to Hashtchavata, where Bath-Sheba, Froike, and Reizel were waiting for him. They might even be standing on the other side now, there on the hilltop, calling to him, beckoning, waving to him . . . But he could not see them or hear their voices, for the river was wide, so fearfully wide, wider than it had ever been before.

The sun was more than halfway across the clear, deep-blue sky before Prokop called Fishel and told him to jump into the boat. And when Fishel heard these words his arms and legs went limp. He did not know what to do. In all his life he had never been in a boat like that. Since he was born he had never been in a boat of any kind. And looking at the boat he thought that any minute it would tip to one side—and Fishel would be a martyr!

"Jump in and let's go!" Prokop called to him again, and reaching up he snatched the pack from Fishel's hand.

Fishel the *melamed* carefully pulled the skirt of his gabardine high up around him and began to turn this way and that. Should he jump—or shouldn't he? On the one hand—Sabbath and Passover in one, Bath-Sheba, Froike, Reizel, the scalding bath, the *seder* and all its ceremonial, the royal throne. On the other hand—the terrible risk, almost certain death. You might call it suicide. Because after all, if the boat tipped only once, Fishel was no more. His children were orphans. And he stood with his coat pulled up so long that Prokop lost his patience and began to shout at him. He warned him that if Fishel did not jump in at once he would spit at him and go across by himself to Hashtchavata. Hearing the beloved word Hash-tcha-va-ta, Fishel remembered his dear and true ones again, summoned up all his courage—and fell into the boat. I say "fell into" because with his first step the boat tipped ever so slightly, and Fishel, thinking he would fall, drew suddenly back, and this time he really did fall, right on his face . . . Several minutes passed before he came to. His face felt clammy, his arms and legs trembled, and his heart pounded like an alarm clock: tick-tock, tick-tock, tick-tock!

As though he were sitting on a stool in his own home, Prokop sat perched in the prow of the boat and coolly pulled at his oars. The boat slid through the sparkling waters, and Fishel's head whirled. He could barely sit upright. No, he didn't even try to sit. He was hanging on, clutching the boat with both hands. Any second, he felt, he would make the wrong move, any second now he would lose his grip, fall back or tumble forward into the deep—and that would be the end of Fishel! And at this thought the words of Moses' song in *Exodus* came back to him: "They sank as lead in the mighty waters." His hair stood straight up. He would not even be buried in consecrated ground! And he made a vow . . .

But what could Fishel promise? Charity? He had nothing to give. He was such a poor, poor man. So he vowed that if the Lord brought him back home in safety he would spend the rest of his nights studying the Holy Writ. By the end of the year he would go, page by page, through the entire Six Orders of the *Talmud*. If only he came through alive . . .

Fishel would have liked to know if it was still far to the other shore, but it was just his luck to have sat down with his face to Prokop and his back to Hashtchavata. And to ask Prokop he was afraid. He was afraid even to open his mouth. He was so sure that if he so much as moved his jaws the boat would tip again, and if it did, where would Fishel be then? And to make it worse, Prokop became suddenly talkative. He said that the worst time to cross the river was during the spring floods. You couldn't even go in a straight direction. You had to use your head, turn this way and that. Sometimes you even had to go back a little and then go forward again.

"There goes one as big as an iceberg!" Prokop warned. "It's coming straight at us!" And he swung the boat back just in time to let a huge mass of ice go past with a strange roar. And then Fishel began to understand what kind of trip this was going to be!

"Ho! Look at that!" Prokop shouted again, and pointed upstream.

Fishel lifted his eyes slowly, afraid to move too fast, and looked—looked and saw nothing. All he could see anywhere was water—water and more water.

"There comes another! We'll have to get past—it's too late to back up!"

And this time Prokop worked like mad. He hurled the boat forward through the foaming waves, and Fishel became cold with fear. He wanted to say something but was afraid. And once more Prokop spoke up: "If we don't make it in time, it's just too bad."

"What do you mean—too bad?"

"What do you think it means? We're lost—that's what."

"Lost?"

"Sure! Lost."

"What do you mean—lost?"

"You know what I mean. Rubbed out."

"Rubbed out?"

"Rubbed out."

Fishel did not understand exactly what these words meant. He did not even like the sound—lost—rubbed out. He had a feeling that it had to do with eternity, with that endless existence on a distant shore. And a cold sweat broke out all over his body, and once again the verse came to him, "They sank as lead in the mighty waters."

To calm him down Prokop started to tell a story that had happened a year before at this same time. The ice of the Bug had torn loose and the ferry could not be used. And just his luck one day an important-looking man drove up and wanted to go across. He turned out to be a tax officer from Ouman, and he was ready to pay no less than a ruble for the trip. Halfway across, two huge chunks of ice bore down upon them. There was only one thing for Prokop to do and he did it: he slid in between the two chunks, cut right through between them. Only in the excitement he must have rocked the boat a trifle too much, because they both went overboard into the icy water. It was lucky that he could swim. The tax collector apparently couldn't, and they never found him again. Too bad . . . A ruble lost like that . . . he should have collected in advance. . .

Prokop finished the story and sighed deeply, and Fishel felt an icy chill go through him and his mouth went dry. He could not say a word. He could not make a sound, not even a squeak.

Five

When they were halfway over, right in the middle of the current, Prokop paused and looked upstream. Satisfied with what he saw, he put the oars down, dug a hand deep into his pocket and pulled out a bottle from which he proceeded to take a long, long pull. Then he took out a few black cloves and while he was chewing them he apologized to Fishel for his drinking. He did not care for the whiskey itself, he said, but he had to take it, at least a few drops, or he got sick every time he tried to cross the river. He wiped his mouth, picked up his oars, glanced upstream, and exclaimed, "Now we're in for it!"

In for what? Where? Fishel did not know and he was afraid to ask, but instinctively he felt that if Prokop had been more specific he would have added something about death or drowning. That it was serious was apparent from the way Prokop was acting. He was bent double and was thrashing like mad. Without even looking at Fishel he ordered, "Quick, uncle! Lie down!"

Fishel did not have to be told twice. He saw close by a towering block of ice bearing down upon them. Shutting his eyes, he threw himself face down on the bottom of the boat, and trembling all over began, in a hoarse whisper, to recite *Shma Yisroel*. He saw himself already sinking through the waters. He saw the wide-open mouth of a gigantic fish; he pictured himself being swallowed like the prophet Jonah when he was escaping to Tarshish. And he remembered Jonah's prayer, and quietly, in tears, he repeated the words: "The waters compassed me about, even to the soul; the deep was round about me. The weeds were wrapped about my head."

Thus sang Fishel the *melamed* and he wept, wept bitterly, at the thought of Bath-Sheba, who was as good as a widow already, and the children, who were as good as orphans. And all this time Prokop was working with all his might, and as he worked he sang this song:

Oh, you waterfowl!
You black-winged waterfowl—
You black-winged bird!

And Prokop was as cool and cheerful as if he were on dry land, sitting in his own cottage. And Fishel's "encompassed me about" and Prokop's "waterfowl," and Fishel's "the weeds were wrapped" and Prokop's "black-winged bird" merged into one, and on the surface of the Bug was heard a strange singing, a duet such as had never been heard on its broad surface before, not ever since the river had been known as the Bug . . .

"Why is he so afraid of death, that little man?" Prokop Baraniuk sat wondering, after he had got away from the ice floe and pulled his bottle out of his pocket again for another drink. "Look at him, a little fellow like that—poor, in tatters . . . I wouldn't trade this old boat for him. And he's afraid to die!"

And Prokop dug his boot into Fishel's side, and Fishel trembled. Prokop began to laugh, but Fishel did not hear. He was still praying, he was saying *Kaddish* for his own soul, as if he were dead . . .

But if he were dead would he be hearing what Prokop was saying now?

"Get up, Uncle. We're there already. In Hashtchavata."

Fishel lifted his head up slowly, cautiously, looked around on all sides with his red, swollen eyes.

"Hash-tcha-va-ta?"

"Hashtchavata! And now you can give me that half-ruble!"

And Fishel crawled out of the boat and saw that he was really home at last. He didn't know what to do first. Run home to his wife and children? Dance and sing on the bank? Or should he praise and thank the Lord who had preserved him from such a tragic end? He paid the boatman his half-ruble, picked up his pack, and started to run as fast as he could. But after a few steps he stopped, turned back to the ferryman: "Listen, Prokop, my good friend! Come over tomorrow for a glass of Passover brandy and some holiday fish. Remember the name—Fishel the *melamed!* You hear? Don't forget now!"

"Why should I forget? Do you think I'm a fool?"

And he licked his lips at the thought of the Passover brandy and the strongly seasoned Jewish fish.

"That's wonderful, Uncle! That's wonderful!"

Six

When Fishel the *melamed* came into the house, Bath-Sheba, red as fire, with her kerchief low over her eyes, asked shyly,

"How are you?" And he answered, "How are *you?*" And she asked, "Why are you so late?" And he answered, "We can thank God. It was a miracle." And not another word, because it was so late.

He did not even have time to ask Froike how he was getting along in the *Talmud,* or give Reizel the gift he had brought her, or Bath-Sheba the new silk shawl. Those things would have to wait. All he could think of now was the bath. And he just barely made it.

And when he came home from the bath he did not say anything either. Again he put it off till later. All he said was, "A miracle from heaven. We can thank the Lord. He takes care of us . . ."

And taking Froike by the hand, he hurried off to the synagogue.

Translated by Julius and Frances Butwin

On
Account of a
Hat

"DID I HEAR you say absentminded? Now, in our town, that is, in Kasrilevke, we've really got someone for you—do you hear what I say? His name is Sholem Shachnah, but we call him Sholem Shachnah Rattlebrain, and is he absentminded, is this a distracted creature, Lord have mercy on us! The stories they tell about him, about this Sholem Shachnah—bushels and baskets of stories—I tell you, whole crates full of stories and anecdotes! It's too bad you're in such a hurry on account of the Passover, because what I could tell you, Mr. Sholom Aleichem—do you hear what I say?—you could go on writing it down forever. But if you can spare a moment I'll tell you a story about what happened to Sholem Shachnah on a Passover eve—a story about a hat, a true story, I should live so, even if it does sound like someone made it up."

These were the words of a Kasrilevke merchant, a dealer in stationery, that is to say, snips of paper. He smoothed out his beard, folded it down over his neck, and went on smoking his thin little cigarettes, one after the other.

I must confess that this true story, which he related to me, does indeed sound like a concocted one, and for a long time I couldn't make up my mind whether or not I should pass it on to you. But I thought it over and decided that if a respectable merchant and dignitary of Kasrilevke, who deals in stationery and is surely no *litterateur*—if he vouches for a story, it must be true. What would he be doing with fiction? Here it is in his own words. I had nothing to do with it.

This Sholem Shachnah I'm telling you about, whom we call Sholem Shachnah Rattlebrain, is a real-estate broker—you hear what I say? He's always with landowners, negotiating transactions. Transactions? Well, at least he hangs around the landowners. So what's the point? I'll tell you. Since he hangs around the landed gentry, naturally some of their manner has rubbed off on him, and he always has a mouth full of farms, homesteads, plots, acreage, soil, threshing machines, renovations, woods, timber, and other such terms having to do with estates.

One day God took pity on Sholem Shachnah, and for the first time in his career as a real-estate broker—are you listening?—he actually worked out a deal. That is to say, the work itself, as you can imagine, was done by others, and when the time came to collect the fee, the big rattler turned out to be not Sholem Shachnah Rattlebrain, but Drobkin, a Jew from Minsk province, a great big fearsome rattler, a real-estate broker from way back—he and his two brothers, also brokers and also big rattlers. So you can take my word for it, there was quite a to-do. A Jew has contrived and connived and has finally, with God's help, managed to cut himself in—so what do they do but come along and cut him out! Where's justice? Sholem Shachnah wouldn't stand for it—are you listening to me? He set up such a holler and an outcry—"Look what they've done to me!"—that at last they gave in to shut him up, and good riddance it was, too.

When he got his few cents Sholem Shachnah sent the greater part of it home to his wife, so she could pay off some debts, shoo the wolf from the door, fix up new outfits for the children, and make ready for the Passover holidays. And as for himself, he also needed a few things, and besides he had to buy presents for his family, as was the custom.

Meanwhile the time flew by, and before he knew it, it was almost Passover. So Sholem Shachnah—now listen to this—ran to the telegraph office and sent home a wire: *Arriving home Passover without fail.* It's easy to say "arriving" and "without fail" at that. But you just try it! Just try riding out our way on the new train and see how fast you'll arrive. Ah, what a pleasure! Did they do us a favor! I tell you, Mr. Sholom Aleichem, for a taste of Paradise such as this you'd gladly forsake your own grandchildren! You see how it is: until you get to Zolodievka there isn't much you can do about it, so you just lean back and ride. But at Zolodievka the fun begins, because that's where you have to change, to get onto the new train, which they did us such a favor by running out to Kasrilevke. But not so fast. First there's the little matter of several hours' wait, exactly as announced in the schedule— provided, of course, you don't pull in after the Kasrilevke train has left. And at what time of night may you look forward to this treat? The very middle, thank you, when you're dead tired and disgusted, without a friend in the world except sleep—and there's not one single place in the whole station where you can lay your head, not one. When the wise men of Kasrilevke quote the passage from the Holy Book, *"Tov shem meshemen tov,"* they know what they're doing. I'll translate it for you: We were better off without the train.

To make a long story short, when our Sholem Shachnah arrived in Zolodievka with his carpetbag he was half dead; he had already spent two nights without sleep. But that was nothing at all to what was facing him—he still had to spend a whole night waiting in the station. What shall he do? Naturally he looked around for a place to sit down. Whoever heard of such a thing? Nowhere. Nothing. No place to sit. The walls of the station were covered with soot, the floor was covered with spit. It was dark, it was terrible. He finally discovered one miserable spot on a bench where he had just room enough to squeeze in, and no more than that, because the bench was occupied by an official of some sort in a uniform full of buttons, who was lying there all stretched out and snoring away to beat the band. Who this Buttons was, whether he was coming or going, he hadn't the vaguest idea—Sholem Shachnah, that is. But he could tell that Buttons was no dime-a-dozen official. This was plain by his cap, a military cap with a red band and a visor. He could have been an officer or a police official. Who knows? But surely he had drawn up to the station with a ringing of bells, had staggered in, full to the ears with meat and drink, laid himself out on the bench as in his father's vineyard, and worked up a glorious snoring.

It's not such a bad life to be a Gentile, and an official one at that, with buttons, thinks he—Sholem Shachnah, that is—and he wonders, dare he sit next to this Buttons, or hadn't he better keep his distance? Nowadays you never can tell whom you're sitting next to. If he's no more than a plain inspector, that's still all right. But what if he turns out to be a district inspector? Or a provincial commander? Or even higher than that? And supposing this is even Purishkevitch himself, the famous anti-Semite (may his name perish)? Let someone else deal with him, and Sholem Shachnah turns cold at the mere thought of falling into such a fellow's hands. But then he says to himself—now listen to this—Buttons, he says, who the hell is Buttons? And who gives a hang for Purishkevitch? Don't I pay my fare the same as Purishkevitch? So why should he have all the comforts of life and I none? If Buttons is entitled to a delicious night's sleep, then doesn't he—Sholem Shachnah, that is—at least have a nap coming? After all, he's human too, and besides, he's already gone two nights without a wink. And so he sits down on a corner of the bench and leans his head back, not, God forbid, to sleep, but just like that, to snooze. But all of a sudden he remembers he's supposed to be home for Passover, and tomorrow is Passover eve! What if, God have mercy, he should fall asleep and miss the train? But that's why he's got a Jewish head on his shoulders—are you listening to me or not? So he figures out the answer to that one, too—Sholem Shachnah, that is—and goes looking for a porter, a certain Yeremei (he knows him well), to make a deal with him. Whereas he, Sholem Shachnah, is already on his third sleepless night and is afraid, God forbid, that he may miss his train, therefore let him—Yeremei, that is—in God's name, be sure to wake him, Sholem Shachnah, because tomorrow night is a holiday, Passover. "Easter," he says to him in Russian and lays a coin in Yeremei's mitt. "Easter, Yeremei, do you understand, *goyisher kop?* Our Easter." The peasant pockets the coin, no doubt about that, and promises to wake him at the first sign of the train—he can sleep soundly and put his mind at rest. So Sholem Shachnah sits down in his corner of the bench, gingerly, pressed up against the wall, with his carpetbag curled around him so that no one should steal it. Little by little he sinks back, makes himself comfortable, and half shuts his eyes—no more than forty winks, you understand. But before long he's got one foot propped up on the bench and then the other; he stretches out and drifts off to sleep. Sleep? I'll say sleep, like God commanded us: with his head thrown back and his hat rolling away on the floor. Sholem Shachnah is snoring like an eight-day wonder. After all, a human being, up two nights in a row—what would you have him do?

He had a strange dream. He tells this himself—that is, Sholem Shachnah does. He dreamed that he was riding home for Passover—are you listening to me?—but not on the train, in a wagon, driven by a thievish peasant, Ivan Zlodi we call him. The horses were terribly slow, they barely dragged along. Sholem Shachnah was impatient, and he poked the peasant between the shoulders and cried, "May you only drop dead, Ivan darling! Hurry up, you lout! Passover is coming, our Jewish Easter!" Once he called out to him, twice, three times. The thief paid him no mind. But all of a sudden he whipped his horses to a gallop and they went whirling away, up hill and down, like demons. Sholem Shachnah lost his hat. Another minute of this and he would have lost God knows what. "Whoa, there, Ivan old boy! Where's the fire? Not so fast!" cried Sholem Shachnah. He covered his head with his hands—he was worried, you see, over his lost hat. How can he drive into town bareheaded? But for all the good it did him, he could have been hollering at a post. Ivan the Thief was racing the horses as if forty devils were after him. All of a sudden—tppprrru!—they came to a dead stop. What's the matter? Nothing. "Get up," said Ivan, "time to get up."

Time? What time? Sholem Shachnah is all confused. He wakes up, rubs his eyes, and is all set to step out of the wagon when he realizes he has lost his hat. Is he dreaming or not? And what's he doing here? Sholem Shachnah finally comes to his senses and recognizes the peasant. This isn't Ivan Zlodi at all, but Yeremei the porter. So he concludes that he isn't on a high road after all, but in the station at Zolodievka, on the way home for Passover, and that if he means to get there he'd better run to the window for a ticket, but fast. Now what? No hat. The carpetbag is right where he left it, but his hat? He pokes around under the bench, reaching all over, until he comes up with a hat—not his own, to be sure, but the official's, with the red band and the visor. But Sholem Shachnah has no time for details and he rushes off to buy a ticket. The ticket window is jammed; everybody and his cousins are crowding in. Sholem Shachnah thinks he won't get to the window in time, perish the thought, and he starts pushing forward, carpetbag and all. The people see the red band and the visor and they make way for him. "Where to, Your Excellency?" asks the ticket agent. What's this Excellency, all of a sudden? wonders Sholem Shachnah, and he rather resents it. Some joke, a Gentile poking fun at a Jew. All the same he says—Sholem Shachnah, that is—"Kasrilevke." "Which class, Your Excellency?" The ticket agent is looking straight at the red band and the visor. Sholem Shachnah is angrier than ever. I'll give him an Excellency so he'll know how to make fun of a poor Jew! But then he thinks: Oh well, we Jews are in Diaspora—do you hear what I say?—let it pass. And he asks for a ticket third class. "Which class?" the agent blinks at him, very surprised. This time Sholem Shachnah gets good and sore and he really tells him off. "Third!" he says. All right, thinks the agent, third is third.

In short, Sholem Shachnah buys his ticket, takes up his carpetbag, runs out onto the platform, plunges into the crowd of Jews and Gentiles, no comparison intended, and goes looking for the third-class carriage. Again the red band and visor work like a charm; everyone makes way for the official. Sholem Shachnah is wondering, what goes on here? But he runs along the platform till he meets a conductor carrying a lantern. "Is this third class?" asks Sholem Shachnah, putting one foot on the stairs and shoving his bag into the door of the compartment. "Yes, Your Excellency," says the conductor, but he holds him back. "If you please, sir, it's packed full, as tight as your fist. You couldn't squeeze a needle into that crowd." And he takes Sholem Shachnah's carpetbag—you hear what I'm saying?—and sings out, "Right this way, Your Excellency, I'll find you a seat." "What the devil!" cries Sholem Shachnah. "Your Excellency and Your Excellency!" But he hasn't much time for the fine points; he's worried about his carpetbag. He's afraid, you see, that with all these Excellencies he'll be swindled out of his belongings. So he runs after the conductor with the lantern, who leads him into a second-class carriage. This is also packed to the rafters, no room even to yawn in there. "This way please, Your Excellency!" And again the conductor grabs the bag and Sholem Shachnah lights out after him. "Where in blazes is he taking me?" Sholem Shachnah is racking his brains over this Excellency business, but meanwhile he keeps his eye on the main thing—the carpetbag. They enter the first-class carriage, the conductor sets down the bag, salutes, and backs away, bowing. Sholem Shachnah bows right back. And there he is, alone at last.

Left alone in the carriage, Sholem Shachnah looks around to get his bearings—you hear what I say? He has no idea why all these honors have suddenly been heaped on him—first class, salutes, Your Excellency. Can it be on account of the real-estate deal he just closed? That's it! But wait a minute. If his own people, Jews, that is, honored him for this, it would be understandable. But Gentiles! The conductor! The ticket agent! What's it to them? Maybe he's dreaming. Sholem Shachnah rubs his forehead and while passing down the corridor glances in the mirror on the wall. It nearly knocks him over! He sees not himself but the official with the red band. That's who it is! "All my bad dreams on Yeremei's head and on his hands and feet, that lug! Twenty times I tell him to wake me and I even give him a tip, and what does he do, that dumb ox, may he catch cholera in his face, but wake the official instead! And me he leaves asleep on the bench! Tough luck, Sholem Shachnah old boy, but this year you'll spend Passover in Zolodievka, not at home."

Now get a load of this. Sholem Shachnah scoops up his carpetbag and rushes off once more, right back to the station where he is sleeping on the bench. He's going to wake himself up before the locomotive, God forbid, lets out a blast and blasts his Passover to pieces. And so it was. No sooner had Sholem Shachnah leaped out of the carriage with his carpetbag than the locomotive did let go with a blast—do you hear me?—one followed by another, and then, good night!

The paper dealer smiled as he lit a fresh cigarette, thin as a straw. "And would you like to hear the rest of the story? The rest isn't so nice. On account of being such a rattlebrain, our dizzy Sholem Shachnah had a miserable Passover, spending both *seders* among strangers in the house of a Jew in Zolodievka. But this was nothing— listen to what happened afterward. First of all, he has a wife—Sholem Shachnah, that is—and his wife—how shall I describe her to you? *I* have a wife, *you* have a wife, we all have wives, we've had a taste of Paradise, we know what it means to be married. All I can say about Sholem Shachnah's wife is that she's A Number One. And did she give him a royal welcome! Did she lay into him! Mind you, she didn't complain about his spending the holiday away from home, and she said nothing about the red band and the visor. She let that stand for the time being; she'd take it up with him later. The only thing she complained about was the telegram! And not so much the telegram—you hear what I say?—as the one short phrase, *without fail.* What possessed him to put that into the wire: *Arriving home Passover without fail.* Was he trying to make the telegraph company rich? And besides, how dare a human being say "without fail" in the first place? It did him no good to answer and explain. She buried him alive. Oh, well, that's what wives are for. And not that she was altogether wrong—after all, she had been waiting so anxiously. But this was nothing compared with what he caught from the town—Kasrilevke, that is. Even before he returned, the whole town— you hear what I say?—knew all about Yeremei and the official and the red band and the visor and the conductor's Your Excellency—the whole show. He himself—Sholem Shachnah, that is—denied everything and swore up and down that the Kasrilevke smart alecks had invented the entire story for lack of anything better to do. It was all very simple: the reason he came home late, after the holidays, was that he had made a special trip to inspect a wooded estate. Woods? Estate? Not a chance— no one bought *that!* They pointed him out in the streets and held their sides, laughing. And everybody asked him, 'How does it feel, Reb Sholem Shachnah, to wear a cap with a red band and a visor?' 'And tell us,' said others, 'what's it like to travel first class?' As for the children, this was made to order for them—you hear what I say? Wherever he went they trooped after him, shouting, 'Your Excellency! Your excellent Excellency! Your most excellent Excellency!'"

"You think it's so easy to put one over on Kasrilevke?"

Translated by Isaac Rosenfeld

Dreyfus in Kasrilevke

I DOUBT IF the Dreyfus case made such a stir anywhere as it did in Kasrilevke.

Paris, they say, seethed like a boiling vat. The papers carried streamers, generals shot themselves, and small boys ran like mad in the streets, threw their caps in the air, and shouted wildly, "Long live Dreyfus!" or "Long live Esterhazy!" Meanwhile the Jews were insulted and beaten, as always. But the anguish and pain that Kasrilevke underwent, Paris will not experience till Judgment Day.

How did Kasrilevke get wind of the Dreyfus case? Well, how did it find out about the war between the English and the Boers or what went on in China? What do they have to do with China? Tea they got from Wisotzky in Moscow. In Kasrilevke they do not wear the light summer material that comes from China and is called pongee. That is not for their purses. They are lucky if they have a pair of trousers and an undershirt, and they sweat just as well, especially if the summer is a hot one.

So how did Kasrilevke learn about the Dreyfus case? From Zeidel.

Zeidel, Reb Shaye's son, was the only person in town who subscribed to a newspaper, and all the news of the world they learned from him, or rather through him. He read and they interpreted. He spoke and they supplied the commentary. He told what he read in the paper, but they turned it around to suit themselves, because they understood better than he did.

One day Zeidel came to the synagogue and told how in Paris a certain Jewish captain named Dreyfus had been imprisoned for turning over certain government papers to the enemy. This went into one ear and out of the other. Someone remarked in passing, "What won't a Jew do to make a living?"

And another added spitefully, "A Jew has no business climbing so high, interfering with kings and their affairs."

Later when Zeidel came to them and told them a fresh tale, that the whole thing was a plot, that the Jewish Captain Dreyfus was innocent and that it was an intrigue of certain officers who were themselves involved, then the town became interested in the case. At once Dreyfus became a Kasrilevkite. When two people came together, he was the third.

"Have you heard?"

"I've heard."

"Sent away for good."

"A life sentence."

"For nothing at all."

"A false accusation."

Later when Zeidel came to them and told them that there was a possibility that the case might be tried again, that there were some good people who undertook to show the world that the whole thing had been a plot, Kasrilevke began to rock indeed. First of all, Dreyfus was one of *ours*. Secondly, how could such an ugly thing happen in Paris? It didn't do any credit to the French. Arguments broke out everywhere; bets were made. Some said the case would be tried again, others said it would not. Once the decision had been made, it was final. All was lost.

As the case went on, they got tired of waiting for Zeidel to appear in the synagogue with the news; they began to go to his house. Then they could not wait that long, and they began to go along with him to the post office for his paper. There they read, digested the news, discussed, shouted, gesticulated, all together and in their loudest voices. More than once the postmaster had to let them know in gentle terms that the post office was not the synagogue. "This is not your synagogue, you Jews. This is not your community hall."

They heard him the way Haman hears the *grager* on Purim. He shouted, and they continued to read the paper and discuss Dreyfus.

They talked not only of Dreyfus. New people were always coming into the case. First Esterhazy, then Picquart, then General Mercies, Pellieux Gonse. . . .

There were two people whom Kasrilevke came to love and revere.

These were Emile Zola and Labori. For Zola each one would gladly have died. If Zola had come to Kasrilevke the whole town would have come out to greet him; they would have borne him aloft on their shoulders.

"What do you think of his letters?"

"Pearls. Diamonds. Rubies."

They also thought highly of Labori. The crowd delighted in him, praised him to the skies, and, as we say, licked their fingers over his speeches. Although no one in Kasrilevke had ever heard him, they were sure he must know how to make a fine speech.

I doubt if Dreyfus's relatives in Paris awaited his return from the Island as anxiously as the Jews of Kasrilevke. They traveled with him over the sea, felt themselves rocking on the waves. A gale arose and tossed the ship up and down, up and down, like a stick of wood. "Lord of Eternity," they prayed in their hearts, "be merciful and bring him safely to the place of the trial. Open the eyes of the judges, clear their brains, so they may find the guilty one and the whole world may know of our innocence. Amen. *Selah*."

The day when the good news came that Dreyfus had arrived was celebrated like a holiday in Kasrilevke. If they had not been ashamed to do so, they would have closed their shops.

"Have you heard?"

"Thank the Lord."

"Ah, I would have liked to have been there when he met his wife."

"And I would have liked to see the children when they were told, 'Your father has arrived.'"

And the women, when they heard the news, hid their faces in their aprons and pretended to blow their noses so no one could see they were crying. Poor as Kasrilevke was, there was not a person there who would not have given his very last penny to take one look at the arrival.

As the trial began, a great excitement took hold of the town. They tore not only the paper to pieces, but Zeidel himself. They choked on their food, they did not sleep nights. They waited for the next day, the next and the next.

Suddenly there arose a hubbub, a tumult. That was when the lawyer, Labori, was shot. All Kasrilevke was beside itself.

"Why? For what? Such an outrage! Without cause! Worse than in Sodom!"

That shot was fired at their heads. The bullet was lodged in their breasts, just as if the assassin had shot at Kasrilevke itself.

"God in heaven," they prayed, "reveal thy wonders. Thou knowest how if thou wishest. Perform a miracle, that Labori might live."

And God performed the miracle. Labori lived.

When the last day of the trial came, the Kasrilevkites shook as with a fever. They wished they could fall asleep for twenty-four hours and not wake up till Dreyfus was declared a free man.

But as if in spite, not a single one of them slept a wink that night. They rolled all night from side to side, waged war with the bedbugs, and waited for day to come.

At the first sign of dawn they rushed to the post office. The outer gates were still closed. Little by little a crowd gathered outside and the street was filled with people. Men walked up and down, yawning, stretching, pulling their earlocks and praying under their breath.

When Yadama the janitor opened the gates they poured in after him. Yadama grew furious. He would show them who was master here, and pushed and shoved till they were all out in the street again. There they waited for Zeidel to come. And at last he came.

When Zeidel opened the paper and read the news aloud, there arose such an outcry, such a clamor, such a roar that the heavens could have split open. Their outcry was not against the judges who gave the wrong verdict, not at the generals who swore falsely, not at the French who showed themselves up so badly. The outcry was against Zeidel.

"It cannot be!" Kasrilevke shouted with one voice. "Such a verdict is impossible! Heaven and earth swore that the truth must prevail. What kind of lies are you telling us!"

"Fools!" shouted Zeidel, and thrust the paper into their faces. "Look! See what the paper says!"

"Paper! Paper!" shouted Kasrilevke. "And if you stood with one foot in heaven and the other on earth, would we believe you?"

"Such a thing must not be. It must never be! Never! Never!"

And—who was right?

Translated by Julius and Frances Butwin

Two Anti-Semites

MAX BERLLIANT IS a lost cause. He travels from Lodz to Moscow and from Moscow to Lodz several times a year. He knows all the buffets, all the stations along the way, is hand in glove with all the conductors, and has visited all the remote provinces—even the ones where Jews are only allowed to stay twenty-four hours. He has sweated at all the border crossings, put up with all kinds of humiliations, and more than once has been aggravated—has eaten his heart out, in fact—and all because of the Jews. Not because the Jews as a people exist, but because he himself—don't shout, whisper it—is also a Jew. And not even so much because he's a Jew, as because—if you'll forgive me for saying so—he looks so Jewish. That's what comes of creating man in God's image! And what an image! Max's eyes are dark and shining, his hair the same. It's real Semitic hair. He speaks Russian like a cripple, and, God help us, with a Yiddish singsong. And on top of everything he's got a nose! A nose to end all noses.

As if that weren't enough, our hero is unlucky in his occupation. He's a traveling salesman and it's part of his job to be friendly. He has to talk a lot, and in his business it's important that he should not just talk, but that he should be heard, and not just be heard, but above all be seen. In short, he's a sorry creature.

True, our hero did avenge himself on his beard. Beardless now, and decked out like a bride, he curls his whiskers, files his nails, wears a tie as glorious as what the Lord God himself might have worn had he ever worn a tie. Max has accustomed himself to the food in railway restaurants, but he continually vents his bitterness on the pigs of the world. If even half the curses he heaps on the species were to come true, I would be happy. But what's the use of being fussy? Might as well be hung for a sheep as for a lamb, so Max took his life in his hands and began to eat lobster.

Why do I say he took his life in his hands? May our worst enemies know as much about their noses as Max Berlliant knows about eating lobsters. Should he cut them with a knife or stab them with a fork? Or should he eat them whole, just as they come?

Despite all these glorious achievements Max Berlliant can't hide his Jewishness; not from us, the Jews, nor from them, the Gentiles. You can pick him out like a counterfeit coin in a handful of change, and in a crowd of Abels he stands out like a Cain. At every twist and turn he is reminded who he is and what he is. In short, he's a sorry creature.

If Max Berlliant was unhappy up to the time of Kishinev, after Kishinev no one could touch him for misery. To harbor deep in your heart a great sorrow, and what's worse to be ashamed of it, is a special kind of hell. Max was as ashamed of what had happened in Kishinev as if he was personally responsible for it, almost as if Kishinev was part of himself. And as luck would have it, right after the incidents in Kishinev, his firm sent him into the very districts where it had all happened: Bessarabia.

That's when a new hell opened up under his feet. He had heard a thousand horror stories about Kishinev in his home town. Wasn't it enough that his heart had flooded with grief and filled with blood when he was told about the atrocities in Kishinev, atrocities such as never had been known or heard before? Will he ever forget the day they offered up special prayers in the synagogues for the slaughtered of Kishinev? Or how, on that day, the old men wept and the women fainted?

It must surely have happened to you while sitting on a train that you passed the place where some great catastrophe has occurred. You know in your heart that you are safe because lightning doesn't strike twice in the same spot. Yet you can't help remembering that not so long ago trains were derailed at this very point, and carloads of people spilled over the embankment. You can't help knowing that here people were thrown out head first, over there bones were crushed, blood flowed, brains were splattered. You can't help feeling glad that you're alive; it's only human to take secret pleasure in it.

Max knew he was bound to meet people in these parts eager to talk about the pogroms. He would have to listen to the wails and groans of those who had lost their near and dear, and he would also be forced to endure the righteous exhortations and malicious remarks of the Gentiles. So the closer they came to Bessarabia, the more he tried to find some way of escape, some way to hide from his own soul.

As they approached the region Max thought of staying behind when the other passengers got off. Then he changed his mind and jumped down onto the platform with the others when the train stopped. He made his way to the buffet as if he hadn't a care in the world. He ordered a drink, followed it up with some tasty tidbits forbidden to Jews, washed it all down with a beer, lit a cigar, and went up to the counter where they sell books and newspapers. There his glance fell on a certain ugly anti-Semitic newspaper called *The Bessarabian*, published by a certain ugly anti-Semite called Krushevan. And here in the very region where this fine newspaper was conceived, hatched, and born, it lay innocently— almost anonymously—all by itself on the counter. Not a soul was buying it, nobody even gave it a second look.

The local Jews don't buy it because it's so scurrilous, and the Gentiles don't buy it because they are sick and tired of it. So there it lies, nice and neat on the counter, put there to remind the world that somewhere on the face of this earth lives a certain Krushevan, a man who neither rests nor sleeps in his tireless search for new ways to warn the world against that dread disease: Judaism.

Max Berlliant is the only one to buy a copy of *The Bessarabian*. And why is that? Maybe because of the same urge that drives him to eat lobster. Or maybe he wants to see for himself what that dog of dogs has to say about Jews? It's a proven fact that the readers of anti-Semitic newspapers are mostly Jews. That means us, little brothers, with all due respect. . . And though the publishers of such newspapers know it, they act on the principle that even if the Jew is *treyf*, his money is *kosher*. . . .

Accordingly our Max buys himself a copy of *The Bessarabian*, brings it back to the train, stretches out on the seat, and covers himself with the newspaper the way you cover yourself with a blanket. And while he is thus busying himself, a thought flies through his head: "What, for instance, would a Jew think if he came across a man stretched out on the seat covered with a copy of *The Bessarabian?* Surely it would never occur to him that the man under the newspaper might be a Jew . . . What an idea, what a great way to get rid of Jews and at the same time keep a seat all to myself."

So reasoned our hero. And in order to make sure that no mother's son should find out who was lying there, he covered his face with the newspaper; he hid his nose, also his eyes and hair, and indeed the whole physiognomy—the one made in God's own image. He pictured to himself how in the middle of the night an old Jew, weighed down with packs and bundles, creeps onto the train, looks around for a seat, sees someone lying there covered with *The Bessarabian*, figures that he must be a squire at least, but a bad lot in any case, and probably an anti-Semite—possibly even Krushevan himself. So the old Jew with his packs and bundles spits three times and goes away, while he, Max, remains lying there in lonely splendor, lording it over the whole seat. "Oh, oh, as I live and breathe, what a great joke!"

So much did this plan please our Max as he lay under his *Bessarabian*, that he burst into laughter. After all, when you have eaten, washed it down with beer, smoked a cigar, and toward evening stretch out on a seat all to yourself—you have something to crow about. . . .

Hush now, let's have quiet. Our hero, Max Berlliant, the traveling salesman whose route stretches from Lodz to Moscow and from Moscow to Lodz, is lying on a seat covered with the latest issue of *The Bessarabian*. He has just dozed off, so let's not disturb him.

Let's admit it, Berlliant is smart. But this time fate outsmarted him. Everything happened almost as he imagined. Someone did come onto the train—a burly fellow with two suitcases, and someone did notice him as he lay there covered with his *Bessarabian*. But instead of spitting three times and going away, the newcomer stood there studying him, this queer anti-Semite with the Semitic nose (for, during his sleep the newspaper had slipped off Max's face to reveal his nose, his stigma).

Our new arrival stands there, smiling. After placing his suitcase on the seat opposite Max, he steps out on the platform and returns with a fresh issue of *The Bessarabian*. Out of his suitcase he takes a pillow, a blanket, a pair of slippers, a bottle of eau de cologne, and makes himself comfortable. Then, stretching out on the seat opposite, he covers himself with the newspaper in exactly the same way as our Max Berlliant. He lies there smoking, looking at Max and smiling. He closes first one eye, then the other, and finally dozes off.

So let's leave our two *Bessarabians* sound asleep, seat to seat. In the meantime we'll introduce the reader to our new character: who he is and what he is.

He is a general. Not a general in the army and not a governor-general, but a general inspector, an agent for a company. His real name is Chaim

Nyemchick, but he signs himself Albert, and everybody calls him Patti.

I admit it sounds a bit crazy. How from a Chaim you get an Albert is understandable. After all, among us Jews doesn't a Velvel become a Vladimir, an Israel an Isadore, and an Avrom an Avukem? But how does a Chaim get to be a Patti? To answer this we'll have to employ logic, study linguistics, and use common sense.

Our first move is to get rid of the "ch" in Chaim. Then we say good-bye to the "i" and the "m," leaving only the "a" by itself. So all we have to do now is to add on an "l" and a "b" and an "e" and an "r" and a "t." Now doesn't that add up to Albert? And from Albert it's just a step to Alberti, and from Alberti we get first Berti, then Betti, and finally—how could we miss?—Patti! *Sic transit gloria mundi.* In other words, this is how to make a turkey out of a duck.

Our character is called Patti Nyemchick and he's a general inspector who travels the world the same as Max Berlliant. But his nature is entirely different. He's lively, active, and expressive. And in spite of the fact that his name is Patti and he's a general inspector, he's a Jew like other Jews, and he loves Jews. He also enjoys entertaining people with stories and telling Jewish jokes.

Patti Nyemchick is known far and wide as a raconteur, but he has one fault: whatever the anecdote, he'll swear by all that's holy that his story is true and that it actually happened. The trouble is he keeps changing the locale of his stories and forgetting what he said last time. It's also rumored that Patti, this inspector general, skims over prayers, bluffs his way through difficult Hebrew passages, exaggerates—or as they say in our parts, he's a liar.

So, having come into the train and having noted how our Max Berlliant is stretched out on the seat under an issue of the notorious *Bessarabian*, and having recognized from his nose that Max could in no way be a relation, either close or distant, to Krushevan and his fancy anti-Semitic rag, Patti's first thought is: "This'll make a great story; this'll have them rolling in the aisles."

That's the reason why Patti slipped out, provided himself with a copy of *The Bessarabian*, and lay down opposite our Max. Wondering what would come of it, he dozed off.

Now let's leave Patti the general inspector under *The Bessarabian* copy two, and return to Max the traveling salesman under *The Bessarabian* copy one.

Two

Max Berlliant had a bad night. It must have been the things he ate at the station, because his sleep was troubled. He dreamed that he wasn't Max Berlliant at all, but Krushevan, the editor of *The Bessarabian*—and that he was riding, not on a train, but bareback on a wild boar, while a lobster, boiled and red, kept waving its claws at him, and all the while cries and echoes of "*Ki-shi-nev*" sounded from afar.

Now a little breeze seems to whistle in Max's ears. He hears the sound of rustling leaves and women's dresses and wants to open his eyes and can't. When he tries to touch his nose he finds he hasn't got one; his nose is gone—disappeared without a trace. And in the place where his nose used to be is a copy of *The Bessarabian*, and he can't remember where he is. He tries to move and can't. He knows he's dreaming but he can't wake up, he can't get hold of himself. He simply cannot.

He lies there stunned and suffering, in utter confusion. He feels his strength leaving and summons up his last bit of willpower. Finally he manages to squeeze out a groan, so low that he's the only one who hears it. He opens one eye a little, just a tiny little bit, and sees a ray of light. In the light he sees the figure of a man lying stretched out on the seat opposite him, also alone, and like him, taking up the whole seat. And that man is also covered with a copy of the same issue of *The Bessarabian*.

Our Max is amazed and bewildered. It seems to him that it's himself who is stretched out on the seat opposite, and he can't understand the logic of how he, Max, can possibly be lying there. How can a man see his own reflection without a mirror? Every single hair on his head stands on end, one at a time.

Gradually our Max begins to collect his thoughts and understand that the man on the seat opposite is not himself, Max, but someone else altogether. He wonders: "Where did the fellow come from and why is he lying on the seat opposite? And why is he covered with a copy of *The Bessarabian*?"

Max doesn't have the patience to wait for morning. He's in a hurry to answer the riddle, and right away. So he starts stirring, rattling his newspaper until he hears that the person on the seat opposite is also stirring and rattling his newspaper. He keeps still for a minute, then takes a quick look and sees the other fellow regarding him with a half-smile. Our two *Bessarabian* customers are lying there across from each other, staring but not talking. Although each anti-Semite is dying to know who the other one is, they hide their curiosity and keep mum.

Then Patti has an idea and starts to whistle the tune of that well-known Yiddish folk song:

> A little fire
> burns cosily
> in the old wood stove . . .

Our Max takes up the tune and whistles out the next line:

> And the room is hot . . .

Then slowly, slowly both anti-Semites sit up, throw off the *Bessarabians*, and together they burst into the familiar refrain. This time they don't whistle it, but sing the words with loud abandon:

> The rebbe sits
> with little children
> and recites with them
> the Hebrew alphabet . . .

Translated by Miriam Waddington

A Passover Expropriation

KASRILEVKE HAS ALWAYS danced to the tune of Odessa. Since the disturbances began, the two towns do not differ by a hair. A strike in Odessa—a strike in Kasrilevke. In Odessa, agitation for a constitution—in Kasrilevke, agitation for a constitution. Odessa, a pogrom—Kasrilevke, a pogrom. A joker started a rumor that people in Odessa are cutting off their noses, and people in Kasrilevke began to sharpen their knives. It's a good thing that in Kasrilevke each likes to look at what the other is doing; everyone waited for someone else to cut off his nose. They're still waiting.

After such a preface, it's no wonder that scarcely a day passes that you don't read in the papers of a new misfortune in Kasrilevke: a "gang" invaded a baker's and expropriated all he had baked; a cobbler had almost finished a pair of boots—all that remained was to add the soles and heels—when they attacked him in broad daylight, intoning the well-known verse, "Lift your hands in the sanctuary and bless you the Lord," and took away the boots. Or a poor man went begging house to house—it happened on a Thursday—when he was trapped somewhere in an alley; they pushed a pistol in his face and shook out everything he had. Or listen to a story that a woman tells . . . But what a woman tells is something not to be repeated. A female is nervous, the times are disturbing; she may mistake a milk cow for a pear tree . . . I don't want to be held responsible.

In short, the town has experienced a series of expropriations, each more frightful than the next. It is dangerous to be alive! One began to long for the good old days when a police inspector (you only had to slip him a ruble) knew how to keep a whole city in his hand. We began to turn to God and pray: "Lord of the universe! Help us—bring 'em back. 'Renew our days of old!'"

This is still no more than an introduction. Now the story really begins.

Benjamin Lastetchke is the richest man in Kasrilevke. There is no end to his greatness! For one thing, he has rich in-laws in all parts of the world. True, they're not as rich as they used to be. What with today's conditions and business failures, this is not surprising. It's only a wonder that Jews manage as well as they do. But Kasrilevke Jews—they're stronger than iron! They are packed together like herring in a barrel, and there they feed on one another. It's a bit of luck that each year America draws almost twice as many as die here from hunger, pogroms, or other calamities. But since God has willed it, there is still a rich man in Kasrilevke, one called Benjamin Lastetchke, the envy of all because he doesn't have to depend on anyone—except his rich in-laws. You may think that having to depend on a rich in-law is not exactly such a tasty piece of bread, since most rich in-laws (not to be repeated) are stingy by nature. Still, Benjamin Lastetchke is the rich man of Kasrilevke. If you need a favor, where do you go? To Benjamin Lastetchke. He listens. Sometimes he helps with a bit of advice or a wise saying, sometimes with a sigh. These don't hurt. Without them, would it be better? It's all down the drain anyway.

What is the difference between a rich man in Kasrilevke and one in Yehupetz? Rich men in Yehupetz have a soft heart. They cannot bear the misery of poor people. So they close the door, stand a butler at the threshold, and admit no son of Adam who is not well-dressed. Comes the dear summer, they rise like swallows and off to foreign parts—just try to find them! But let a rich man in Kasrilevke try to do it—they will tear him apart! Benjamin Lastetchke (he has no choice) is head and front of the community. In all matters pertaining to charity, he is the first among us not only to make a donation but to take his walking stick in hand and go house to house asking for contributions from paupers—for other paupers.

Especially before Passover, when it comes to collecting money for wheat—ah!—that is when you can take delight in watching Benjamin Lastetchke, even if only from afar. I doubt that the most zealous civic leader in the entire world, while engaged in the hottest campaign, has ever sweated as much as our Benjamin Lastetchke in the four weeks before the holidays! He swears that between Purim and Passover he sleeps in his clothing! Might as well believe him, because how does he stand to gain? He does not ask to be paid for his work. Ah, you may say he does it for the honor? Maybe. . . . But why should this disturb you? A man wants honor. Even princes don't disdain it. We won't change human nature it is too late.

Two

The custom of wheat for the poor is an old one. It's a very old-fashioned method of philanthropy. Nonetheless, I do not think it is as distasteful as our modern thinkers would like to persuade us. They say, "philanthropy is an offense against society." I don't want to join them in debate. I merely want to answer that, in my opinion, there is a custom which is even more offensive: that the wealthy do not give and you have to pluck it out of their teeth. What is even a thousand times worse is that the nice people who don't want to give will try, so to speak, to talk a child into your belly: they don't give because of a principle. These are the sort of people you ought to run away from. They are dry like a dried fish and gloomy like a cat. Thank God, in Kasrilevke this "principle" is not yet in fashion. Those who do not give do not because they have nothing to give. However, when it comes to contributions for wheat, even this will not serve as an excuse. There is a saying in Kasrilevke: everyone must either give money or take it.

Strange are the people of Kasrilevke! Thousands of years have passed since their great-grandfathers broke the chains of Egyptian exile—and they still can't lose the habit of eating unleavened bread eight days each year. I'm afraid this dry morsel won't be out of style for a long time. Other days of the year, a Jew in Kasrilevke may swell up with hunger; but as soon as Passover arrives, let the world stand on its head, he must be supplied with *matzos*. It has never happened yet that at this time a Jew should die of hunger. If such a thing occurs, it should be charged to the account of the whole year; that is, he died not because (God forbid) he had no *matzos* during the eight days, but because he had no leavened bread in 357 other days. As you understand, there is a big difference.

Three

There is no rule without an exception. This year, the one we are describing, was one whose like we had never heard of. It seemed there were more takers than givers. If they hadn't been ashamed, very few of the inhabitants would have refused money for wheat. Oh, a pity to look at our rich Benjamin Lastetchke, how he sits in "committee" this last day and keeps turning the applicants away: "There is no money . . . it has run out . . . do not take offense."

"Maybe next year," answered the people who had been refused, adding under their nose, "May *you* come to us for charity."

One after another, the poor people came out of the committee office, hands empty and faces red as if from a steam bath, cursing from one end of the world to the other—may it fall into the sea!

Among the last of those who were rejected was a pack of young fellows, workers who'd been idle, without a stitch of work, the entire winter. They'd already sold all of their belongings. One had pawned a silver watch and for what he got he bought cigarettes which they all smoked to quiet their hunger—it was a sort of communal affair.

When they came to the committee office, they put forward as their spokesman a ladies' tailor called Shmuel-Abba Fingerhut. Although he was the speaker-in-command, he was helped out by the entire group, all arguing and complaining they are dying of hunger, that they are falling face forward to the ground. The chairman of the committee, Benjamin Lastetchke, let them speak, and when they stopped he began in this fashion: "Do not take offense, but your words are wasted. In the first place, you are not married and we give only to those who are. In the second (no evil eye attend you), you are young fellows who can get a job and earn what is needed. In the third place, this year has brought a good crop of poor people—more takers than givers. Fourthly, I'm ashamed to say it, but since early morning we haven't even got a broken penny in the cash box. If you don't believe me—look!"

And the chairman of the committee turned his pockets inside out so they might see, with their own eyes, that he had no money. He was pure as gold. They were left speechless—except for their leader Shmuel-Abba Fingerhut. No one has to prime his tongue. He turned to the chairman with a full-length sermon, half Yiddish, half Russian, to the following effect: "A pity you didn't start at the very end—you would not have had to waste so much of your powder. But I'll give you an answer to each of your arguments. One, if we are bachelors, that is good for you: fewer poor in town. Two, you spoke of work. Do us a favor: give us work and we'll turn the wide world upside down. Three, when you use the phrase 'poor people'—capitalism is to blame for exploitation of the proletariat. And four, if you turn your pockets inside out, that proves nothing at all. We're sure that in your home your own cupboards are full of *matzos*, eggs, onions and potatoes, and goose fat and other such items, as well as wine for the 'four cups.' . . . You're all bourgeois, exploiters without conscience—*Bolsheh nitchevo*: You are nothing else. *Tovarishtchi*—comrades, let's go!"

We must admit that Kasrilevke, which dances to the tune of Odessa and other big cities, is not—as yet—so far advanced that an exploiter such as Benjamin Lastetchke should open his cupboards and give the poor his *matzos*, his eggs, onions and potatoes, and goose fat, as well as wine for his 'four cups,' while he himself, his wife and children are left just so. . . . But I am convinced, sure as twice two is four, that my Kasrilevke exploiters certainly will get to do it. Just let Odessa or Yehupetz or other big cities set an example. Kasrilevke, my friends, has no obligation to be the first one at the fair.

Four

With a clear conscience, bathed and festive, Benjamin Lastetchke sat with his wife and children at the first *seder*, calm and well-disposed, like a true king at ease in his kingdom. To his right, the queen, his wife Sarah-Leah, dressed in best regalia, with a new silken shawl near which hung two long earrings of genuine 84-karat silver. Around the board his children, princes and princesses—a bouquet of washed hair, red cheeks, gleaming tiny eyes. Even Zlotke the maid—who on other days is in yoke and harness, toiling like a donkey—has shampooed her hair with a scented soap and got herself into a new calico dress and new half-boots and put a wide red ribbon on her shiny, swarthy forehead. All feel so good, delighted, and free, as if they themselves just got out of Egypt.

Starting with a boom, the youngest of the princes rattled off the Four Questions. The king—his father Benjamin Lastetchke—began slowly, in a loud voice with a lovely tune, to give him the explanation, the old explanation, "*Avodim hayinu*—we were slaves, *lefaro bemitzrayim*—of Pharaoh in Egypt. And God delivered us with a mighty hand. He paid off Pharaoh with ten nice afflictions. . . ." In a loud voice, to a special tune, they began to count the nice afflictions. When suddenly . . .

Five

Suddenly a knock on the door; then another knock. Then two more. . . . Who could this be? Should they open or not? It was decided that yes, they would, because the knocking, as it went on, grew louder. King, queen, and princes were silent. Zlotke, the maid, opened the door. Into the house there rushed the whole pack of young fellows, the leader Shmuel-Abba Fingerhut, in front with a broad "Good *yontif!*" . . .

Our rich Benjamin Lastetchke, though his heart was in his boots, summoned up his courage to face them: "A good *yontif!* Look who's here. What is the good word?"

Shmuel-Abba Fingerhut, the official spokesman, came forward with a sermon in his own manner, Yiddish mixed with Russian, which might be translated: "You are in a well-lit room, sitting with a glass of wine, celebrating the holy feast. And we—poor proletarians—are perishing from hunger. I find this "*n'yesprovedle*": it is unjust. I "*prikozeve*," command, that you surrender your holiday dinner to us, and don't dare utter a peep. Don't open any window, don't call any police, or it will be too bad. We will smash you. . . . Comrade Moishe, where's the bomb?"

Six

The last few words were enough to paralyze the whole household; they sat riveted to their places. When this "Comrade Moishe," a young cobbler with a dark complexion, a black forelock, and grimy fingers, went to the table and with a flourish set down some sort of a long cylindrical object covered by a rag, the household became like Lot's wife when she turned around wanting to see what had happened to Sodom and Gomorrah.

Zlotke the servant, her teeth chattering, brought them first of all the hot peppered fish, then the broth with fat dumplings, pancakes, puddings, and other good things which the fellows put away with such appetite as if it really had been a long time since they had eaten. And they drank each morsel down with wine, as if they had promised themselves not to leave a drop. Even the symbolic shank bone, egg, greens, bitters, and sweet paste received the proper treatment. They didn't leave a trace or memory of the *seder*—only the *Haggadah*. While this was going on, the speaker-in-chief, Shmuel-Abba Fingerhut, continued to jeer at our rich man, the exploiter Benjamin Lastetchke, using these words: "As a rule, we read the *Haggadah* while you eat the dumplings. But this time *you* read the *Haggadah* while we eat the dumplings. . . . Your health, bourgeois. God grant—you'll become a proletarian like us. Next year, may we celebrate a constitution!"

The Epilogue of the Tragedy

It was midnight. The poor rich man, Benjamin Lastetchke, and his household still sat around the table, still in a fright. On the table still stood the "calamity"—the tall, cylindrical object covered with a rag. Before they left, members of the pack had warned them they'd better sit in place for the next two hours; otherwise it would be bad. . . . That night, no one fell asleep. They thanked God they had come out of it alive.

But what happened to the tall, cylindrical "calamity" that stood on the table? If you wonder, we will reassure you: a tin of shoe polish—filled with matzo meal—isn't dangerous at all. It may stand a thousand years and it won't blow up anything, unless, God forbid. . . . "a good *yontif!*"

Translated by Nathan Halper

If I Were Rothschild

IF I WERE Rothschild, ah, if I were only Rothschild—a Kasrilevke *melamed* let himself go once upon a Thursday while his wife was demanding money for the Sabbath and he had none to give her. If I were only Rothschild, guess what I would do. First of all I would pass a law that a wife must always have a three-ruble piece on her so that she wouldn't have to start nagging me when the good Thursday comes and there is nothing in the house for the Sabbath. In the second place I would take my Sabbath gabardine out of pawn—or better still, my wife's squirrel-skin coat. Let her stop whining that she's cold. Then I would buy the whole house outright, from foundation to chimney, all three rooms, with the alcove and the pantry, the cellar and the attic. Let her stop grumbling that she hasn't enough room. "Here," I would say to her, "take two whole rooms for yourself—cook, bake, wash, chop, make, and leave me in peace so that I can teach my pupils with a free mind."

This is the life! No more worries about making a living. No more headaches about where the money for the Sabbath is coming from. My daughters are all married off—a load gone from my shoulders. What more do I need for myself? Now I can begin to look around the town a little. First of all I am going to provide a new roof for the old synagogue so the rain won't drip on the heads of the men who come to pray. After that I shall build a new bathhouse, for if not today, then tomorrow—but surely soon—there is bound to be a catastrophe—the roof is going to cave in while the women are inside bathing. And while we are putting up a new bathhouse we might as well throw down the old poorhouse, too, and put up a hospital in its place, a real hospital such as they have in big towns, with beds and bedding, with a doctor and attendants, with hot broths for the sick every day. . . . And I shall build a home for the aged so that old men, scholars who have fallen upon hard times, shouldn't have to spend their last days on the hearth in the synagogue. And I shall establish a Society for Clothing the Poor so that poor children won't have to run around in rags with—I beg your pardon for mentioning it—their navels showing. Then I shall institute a Loan Society so that anyone at all—whether teacher or workman, or even merchant—could get money without having to pay interest and without pawning the shirt off his back. And a Society for Outfitting Brides so that any girl old enough to marry and without means should be outfitted properly and married off as befits a Jewish girl. I would organize all these and many other such societies in Kasrilevke.

But why only here in Kasrilevke? I would organize such societies everywhere, all over the world, wherever our brethren the Sons of Israel are to be found. And in order that they should all be run properly, with a system, guess what I would do. I would appoint a Society to head them all, a Board of Charity that would watch over all the societies under it. This Board of Charity would keep watch over all of Israel and see to it that Jews everywhere had enough to live on and that they lived together in unity. It would see to it that all Jews sit in *yeshivas* and study the Bible, the *Talmud*, the *Gemara*, and the various commentaries and learn all the seven wisdoms and the seventy-seven languages. And over all these *yeshivas* there would be one great *yeshiva* or Jewish Academy which would naturally be located in Vilno. And from there would come the greatest scholars and wise men in the world. And all of this education would be free to everyone, all paid for out of my pocket. And I would see to it that it was all run in orderly fashion, according to plan, so that there should be none of this grab-and-run, hit-and-miss, catch-as-catch-can business. Instead, everything would be run with a view to the common welfare.

But in order to have everyone think only of the common welfare, you have to provide one thing. And what is that? Naturally, security. For, take it from me, security from want is the most important thing in the world. Without it there can be no harmony anywhere. For alas, one man will impoverish another over a piece of bread; he will kill, poison, hang his fellow man. Even the enemies of Israel, the Hamans of the world—what do you think they have against us? Nothing at all. They don't persecute us out of plain meanness but because of their lack of security. It's lack of money, I tell you, that brings envy, and envy brings hatred, and out of hatred come all the troubles in the world, all the sorrows, persecutions, killings, all the horrors and all the wars. . . .

Ah, the wars, the wars. The terrible slaughters. If I were Rothschild I would do away with war altogether. I would wipe it off completely from the face of the earth.

You will ask how? With money, of course. Let me explain it to you. For instance, two countries are having a disagreement over some foolishness, a piece of land that's worth a pinch of snuff. "Territory" they call it. One country says this "territory" is hers and the other one says, "No, this territory is mine." You might think that on the First Day, God created this piece of land in her honor. . . . Then a third country enters and says, "You are both asses. This is everybody's 'territory'; in other words, it's a public domain." Meanwhile the argument goes on. "Territory" here, "territory" there. They "territory" each other so long that they begin shooting with guns and cannons and people start dying like sheep and blood runs everywhere like water. . . .

But if I come to them at the very beginning and say, "Listen to me, little brothers. Actually, what is your whole argument about? Do you think that I don't understand? I understand perfectly. At this feast you are concerned less with the ceremonial than with the dumplings. 'Territory' is only a pretext. What you are after is something else— something you can get your hands on—money, levies. And while we are on the subject of money, to whom does one come for a loan if not to me, that is, to Rothschild? I'll tell you what. Here, you Englishmen with the long legs and checkered trousers, take a billion. Here, you stupid Turks with the scarlet caps, take a billion also. And you, Aunt Reisel—Russia, that is—take another billion. With God's help you will pay me back with interest, not a large rate of interest, God forbid, four or five percent at the most—I don't want to get rich off you."

Do you understand what I've done? I have not only put over a business deal, but people have stopped killing each other in vain, like oxen. And since there will be no more war, what do we need weapons for? For what do we need armies and cannons and military bands, and all the other trappings of war? The answer is that we don't. And if there are no more weapons and armies and bands and other trappings of war, there will be no more envy, no more hatred, no Turks, no Englishmen, no Frenchmen, no Gypsies, and no Jews. The face of the earth will be changed. As it is written: "Deliverance will come—" The Messiah will have arrived.

And perhaps, even—if I were Rothschild—I might do away with money altogether. For let us not deceive ourselves, what is money anyway? It is nothing but a delusion, a made-up thing. Men have taken a piece of paper, decorated it with a pretty picture and written on it, *Three Silver Rubles*. Money, I tell you, is nothing but a temptation, a piece of lust, one of the greatest lusts. It is something that everyone wants and nobody has. But if there were no more money in the world there would be no more temptation, no more lust. Do you understand me or not? But then the problem is, without money how would we Jews be able to provide for the Sabbath? The answer to that is—How will I provide for the Sabbath now?

Translated by Frances Butwin

Part
Two

Tevye Strikes It Rich

IF YOU'RE MEANT to strike it rich, Pani Sholom Aleichem, you may as well stay home with your slippers on, because good luck will find you there, too. The more it blows the better it goes, as King David says in his Psalms—and believe me, neither brains nor brawn has anything to do with it. And vice versa: if it's not in the cards you can run back and forth till you're blue in the face, it will do as much good as last winter's snow. How does the saying go? Flogging a dead horse won't make it run any faster. A man slaves, works himself to the bone, is ready to lie down and die—it shouldn't happen to the worst enemy of the Jews. Suddenly, don't ask me how or why, it rains gold on him from all sides. In a word, *revakh ve'hatsoleh ya'amoyd la'yehudim*, just like it says in the Bible! That's too many words to translate, but the general sense of it is that as long as a Jew lives and breathes in this world and hasn't more than one leg in the grave, he mustn't lose faith. Take it from my own experience—that is, from how the good Lord helped set me up in my present line of business. After all, if I sell butter and cheese and such stuff, do you think that's because my grandmother's grandmother was a milkman? But if I'm going to tell you the whole story, it's worth hearing from beginning to end. If you don't mind, then, I'll sit myself down here beside you and let my horse chew on some grass. He's only human too, don't you think, or why else would God have made him a horse?

Well, to make a long story short, it happened early one summer, around Shavuos time. But why should I lie to you? It might have been a week or two before Shavuos too, unless it was several weeks after. What

I'm trying to tell you is that it took place exactly a dog's age ago, nine or ten years to the day, if not a bit more or less. I was the same man then that I am now, only not at all like me; that is, I was Tevye then too, but not the Tevye you're looking at now. How does the saying go? It's still the same lady, she's just not so shady. Meaning that in those days (it should never happen to you) I was such a miserable beggar that rags were too good for me. Believe me, I'm no millionaire today either. If from now until autumn the two of us earned what it would take to make me one, we wouldn't be doing half-bad. Still, compared to what I was then I've become a real tycoon. I've got my own horse and wagon. I've got two cows that give milk, bless them, and a third cow waiting to calf. Forgive me for boasting, but we're swimming in cheese, cream, and butter. Not that we don't work for it, mind you: you won't find any idlers at my place. My wife milks the cows. The kids carry the cans and churn butter. And I, as you see, go to market every morning and from there to all the rich summer *dachas* in Boiberik. I stop to chat with this one, with that one; there isn't a rich Jew I don't know there. When you talk with such people, you know, you begin to feel that you're someone yourself and not such a one-armed tailor any more. And I'm not even talking about the Sabbath. On the Sabbath, I tell you, I'm king. I have all the time in the world; I can even pick up a Jewish book if I want: the Bible, psalms, Rashi, Targum, Perek, you-name-it. . . . I tell you, if you could only see me then, you would say: "He's really some fine fellow, that Tevye!"

To get to the point, though . . . where were we? Oh, yes . . . in those days, with God's help, I was poor as a devil. No Jew should starve as I did. Not counting suppers, my wife and kids went hungry three times a day. I worked like a dog dragging logs by the wagonful from the forest to the train station for—I'm embarrassed even to tell you—half a ruble a day . . . and not even every day either. You try feeding a house full of little mouths on that, to say nothing of a horse who's moved in with you and can't be put off with some verse from the Bible, because he expects to eat every day and no buts! So what does the good Lord do? I tell you, it's not for nothing that they say He's a *zon u'mefarnes lakol*, that He runs this world of his with more brains than you or I could. He sees me eating my heart out for a slice of bread and says: "Now, Tevye, are you really trying to tell me that the world has come to an end? Eh, what a damn fool you are! In no time I'm going to show you what God can do when He wants. About face, march!" As we say on Yom Kippur, *mi yorum u'mi yishpoyl*—leave it to Him to decide who goes on foot and who gets to ride. The main thing is confidence. A Jew must never, never give up hope. How does he go on hoping, you ask, when he's already black in the face? But that's the whole point of being a Jew in this world! What does it say in the prayer book? *Ato b'khartonu!* We're God's chosen people; it's no wonder the whole world envies us. . . . You don't know what I'm talking about? Why, I'm talking about myself, about the miracle God helped me to. Be patient and you'll hear all about it.

Vayehi hayom, as the Bible says: one fine summer day in the middle of the night, I'm driving home through the forest after having dumped my load of logs. I feel like my head is in the ground, a black desert could grow in my heart; it's all my poor horse can do to drag his feet along behind him. "It serves you right, you *schlimazel*," I say to him, "for belonging to someone like me! If you're going to insist on being Tevye's horse, it's time you knew what it tastes like to fast the whole length of a summer's day." It was so quiet that you could hear every crack of the whip whistle through the woods. The sun began to set; the day was done for. The shadows of the trees were as long as the exile of the Jews. And with the darkness a terrible feeling crept into my heart. All sorts of thoughts ran in and out of my head. The faces of long-dead people passed before me. And when I thought of coming home—God help me! The little house would be pitch dark. My naked, barefoot kids would peek out to see if their *schlemiel* of a father hadn't brought them some bread, maybe even a freshly baked roll. And my old lady would grumble like a good Jewish mother: "A lot he needed children—and seven of them at that! God punish me for saying so, but my mistake was not to have taken them all and thrown them into the river." How do you think it made me feel to hear her say such things? A man is only flesh and blood, after all; you can't fill a stomach with words. No, a stomach needs herring to fill it; herring won't go down without tea; tea can't be drunk without sugar; and sugar, my friend, costs a fortune. And my wife! "My guts," says my wife, "can do without bread in the morning, but without a glass of tea I'm a stretcher case. That baby's sucked the glue from my bones all night long."

Well, one can't stop being a Jew in this world: it was time for the evening prayer. (Not that the evening was about to run away, mind you, but a Jew prays when he must, not when he wants to.) Some fine prayer it turned out to be! Right smack in the middle of the *shimenesre*, the eighteen benedictions, a devil gets into my crazy horse and he decides to go for a jaunt, I had to run after the wagon and grab the reins while shouting "God of Abraham, Issac, and Jacob" at the top of my voice— and to make matters worse, I'd really felt like praying for a change, for once in my life I was sure it would make me feel better. . .

In a word, there I was running behind the wagon and singing the *shimenesre* like a cantor in a synagogue. *M'khalkel khayim b'khesed,* who provideth life with His bounty. . . it better be all of life, do you hear me? *U'm'kayem emunoso lisheyney ofor,* Who keepeth faith with they who slumber in earth. . . who slumber in earth? With my troubles I was six feet underground already. And to think of those rich Yehupetz Jews sitting all summer long in their *dachas* in Boiberik, eating and drinking and swimming in luxury! Master of the Universe, what have I done to deserve all this? Am I or am I not a Jew like any other? *Gevalt! Re'eh-no b'onyenu,* See us in our affliction. . . take a good look at us poor folk slaving away and do something about it, because if you don't, who do you think will? *Refo'enu ve'nerofey,* Heal our wounds that we be whole. . . please concentrate on the healing because the wounds we already have. *Borekh oleynu,* Bless the fruits of this year. . . kindly arrange a good harvest of corn, wheat, and barley—although what good it will do me is more than I can say: does it make any difference to my horse, I ask you, if the oats I can't afford to buy it are expensive or cheap?

But God doesn't tell a man what He thinks, and a Jew had better believe that He knows what He's up to. *V'lamalshinim al tehi tikvo,* May the slanderers have no hope. . . those are the big shots who say there is no God. What wouldn't I give to see the look on their faces when they line up for Judgment Day! They'll pay with back interest for everything they've done, because God has a long memory, one doesn't play around with Him. No, what he wants is for us to be good, to beseech and cry out to Him. *Ov harakhamom,* merciful, loving Father! *Shma koleynu,* You better listen to what we tell you! *Hus v'rakhem oleynu,* pay a little attention to my wife and children, the poor things are hungry! *R'tseh,* take decent care of your people again, as once you did long ago in the days of the Temple, when the Priests and the Levites sacrificed before you. . .

All of a sudden—whoaaa! My horse stopped short in its tracks. I rushed through what was left of the prayer, opened my eyes, and looked around me. Two weird figures, dressed for a masquerade, were approaching from the forest. "Robbers!" I thought at first, then caught myself. "Tevye," I said, "what an idiot you are! Do you mean to tell me that after traveling through this forest by day and by night for so many years, today is the day for robbers?" And bravely smacking my horse on the rear as though what I saw were no affair of mine, I said, "Giddap!"

"Hey, a fellow Jew!" One of the two holy terrors called out to me in a woman's voice and waved a scarf at me. "Don't run away, mister. Wait a second; we won't do you any harm."

"It's a ghost for sure!" I thought to myself. But a second later I thought, "What kind of monkey business is this, Tevye? Since when are you so afraid of ghouls and goblins?" So I pulled up my horse and took a good look at the two. They really did look like women. One was quite old and had a silk kerchief on her head, while the other was young and wore a wig. Both were beet-red and sweating buckets.

"Well, well, well, good evening!" I said to them as loudly as I could to show that I wasn't a bit put out. "How can I be of service to you? If you're looking to buy something, I'm afraid I'm out of stock, unless you're interested in some fine hunger pangs, a week's supply of heartache, or a head full of scrambled brains. Anyone for some chilblains, assorted aches and pains, worries to turn your hair gray?"

"Calm down, calm down," they said to me. "Just listen to him run on! Say a good word to a Jew, and you'll get a mouthful of bad ones in return. We don't want to buy anthing. We simply wanted to ask whether you happened to know the way to Boiberik."

"The way to Boiberik?" I did my best to laugh. "You might as well ask me whether I know that my own name is Tevye."

"You say your name is Tevye? We're very pleased to meet you, Reb Tevye. We wish you'd explain to us, though, what the joke is all about. We're strangers around here; we come from Yehupetz and have a summer place in Boiberik. The two of us went out this morning for a little walk and have been going around in circles ever since without finding our way out of these woods. A little while ago we heard someone singing in the forest. At first we thought, who knows, maybe it's a highwayman. But as soon as we came closer and saw that you were, thank goodness, a Jew, you can imagine how much better we felt. Do you follow us?"

"A highwayman?" I laughed. "That's a good one! Did you ever hear the story of the Jewish highwayman who fell on somebody in the forest and begged him for a pinch of snuff? If you'd like, I'd be only too glad to tell it to you."

138

"The story," they said, "can wait. We'd rather you showed us the way to Boiberik first."

"The way to Boiberik? You're standing on it right now. This path will take you to Boiberik whether or not you want to go to Boiberik."

"But if this is the way to Boiberik, why didn't you say before that this is the way to Boiberik?"

"I didn't say that this is the way to Boiberik, because you didn't ask me whether this is the way to Boiberik."

"Well, if this is the way to Boiberik," they said, "would you possibly happen to know by any chance how far away to Boiberik it is?"

"To Boiberik," I said, "it's not a long way at all. Only a few miles. About two or three. Maybe four. Unless it's five."

"Five miles?" screamed both women at once, wringing their hands and all but breaking out in tears. "Do you realize what you're saying? Do you have any idea? *Only* five miles!"

"Well," I said, "what would you like me to do about it? If it were up to me, I'd make it a little shorter. But there are worse fates than yours, let me tell you. How would you like to be stuck in a wagon creeping up a muddy hill with the Sabbath only an hour away? The rain whips straight in your face, your hands are numb, your heart is too weak to beat, and suddenly. . . bang! Your front axle's gone and snapped."

"You're talking like a halfwit," said one of the two women. "I swear, there's a screw loose in your head. Why are you telling us fairytales from *The Arabian Nights*? We haven't the strength left to take another step. Except for a cup of coffee with a butter roll for breakfast, we haven't had a bite of food all day—and you expect us to stand here listening to your stories. . . "

"That," I said, "is a different story. How does the saying go? It's no fun dancing on an empty stomach. And you don't have to tell me what hunger tastes like; that's something I happen to know. It's not at all unlikely, in fact, that I haven't even seen a cup of coffee and a butter roll for over a year. . . " The words weren't out of my mouth when I saw a cup of hot coffee with cream and a fresh butter roll before my eyes, not to mention what else was on the table. "Idiot," I thought to myself, "a person might think you were raised on coffee and rolls; I suppose plain bread and herring would make you sick?" But just to spite me my imagination kept insisting on coffee and rolls. I could smell the coffee, I could taste the roll on my tongue—my God, how fresh, how delicious it was. . .

"Do you know what, Reb Tevye?" the two women said to me. "We've got a brilliant idea. As long as we're standing here chatting, why don't we hop into your wagon and give you the chance to take us back to Boiberik yourself. How about it?"

"I'm sorry," I said, "but you're spitting into the wind. You're going to Boiberik and I'm coming from Boiberik. How do you suppose I can go both ways at once?"

"That's easy," they said. "We're surprised you haven't thought of it already. If you were a scholar, you'd have realized right away: you simply turn your wagon around and head back in the other direction. . . . Don't get so nervous, Reb Tevye. We should only have to suffer the rest of our lives as much as getting us home safely, God willing, will cost you."

"My God," I thought, "they're talking Chinese. I can't make head or tail of any of it." And for the second time that evening I thought of ghosts, witches, and things that go bump in the night. "You block of wood," I said to myself, "what are you standing there for like a tree stump? Jump back into your wagon, give the horse a crack of your whip, and get away while the getting is good!" Well, don't ask me what devil got into me, but when I opened my mouth again I said, "Hop aboard!"

They didn't have to be invited twice. I climbed in after them, gave my cap a tug, let the horse have the whip, and one, two, three—we're off! Did I say off? Off to no place fast. My horse is stuck to the ground, a cannonshot wouldn't budge him. "Well," I told myself, "that's just what you get for stopping in the middle of nowhere to chat with a pair of females. It's just your luck that you couldn't think of anything better to do. . . "

Just picture it if you can: the woods all around, the eerie stillness, night coming on—and here I am with these two apparitions pretending to be women. . . . My blood began to whistle like a teakettle. I remembered a story I once had heard about a coachman who was driving by himself through the woods when he spied a sack of oats lying on the path. Well a sack of oats is a sack of oats, so down from the wagon he jumps, shoulders the sack, barely manages to heave it into his wagon without breaking his back, and drives off as happy as you please. A mile or two later he turns around to look at his sack. . . did someone say sack? What sack? Instead there's a billygoat with a beard. He reaches out to touch it and it sticks out a tongue a yard long at him, laughs like a hyena, and vanishes into thin air. . .

"Well, what are you waiting for?" the two women asked me.

"What am I waiting for? You can see for yourselves what I'm waiting for. My horse is happy where he is. He's not in a frisky mood."

"Then use your whip," they say to me. "What do you think it's for?"

"Thank you for your advice," I said to them. "It's very kind of you to remind me. The problem is that my four-legged friend is not afraid of such things. He's as used to getting whipped as I'm used to getting gypped." I tried to sound casual but I was burning with a ninety-nine year fever.

Well, why bore you? I let that poor horse have it. I whipped him as long as I whipped him hard, until he finally picked up his heels and we began to move through the woods. As we did, a new thought occurred to me. "Ah, Tevye, are you ever a numbskull! Once a beggar, always a beggar; that's the story of your life. Just imagine: here God hands you an opportunity that comes a man's way once in a hundred years—and you forget to clinch the deal in advance, so that you don't even know what's in it for you! Any way you look at it—as a favor or a duty, as a service or an obligation, as an act of human kindness or something even worse than that—it's certainly no crime to make a little profit on the side. When a soup bone is stuck in somebody's face, who doesn't give it a lick? Stop your horse right now, you imbecile, and spell it out for them in capital letters: "Look, ladies, if it's worth such-and-such to you to get home, it's worth such-and-such to me to take you; if it isn't, I'm afraid we'll have to part ways." On second thought, though, I thought again: "Tevye, you're an imbecile to call yourself an imbecile! Supposing they promised you the moon, what good would it do you? Don't you know that you can skin a bear in the forest but you still can't sell its hide there?"

"Why don't you go a little faster?" the two women asked, poking me from behind.

"What's the matter," I asked, "are you in some sort of a hurry? You should know that haste makes waste." From the corner of my eye I stole a look at my passengers. They were women, all right, no doubt of it: one wearing a silk kerchief and the other a wig. They sat there looking at each other and whispering back and forth.

"Is it still a long way off?" one of them asked me.

"No longer off than we are from there," I answered. "Up ahead there's an uphill and a downhill. After that there's another uphill and a downhill. After that there's a real uphill and a downhill, and after that it's straight as the crow flies to Boiberik. . ."

"The man's a numbskull for sure!" whispered one of the women to the other.

"I told you he was bad news," said the second.

"He's all we needed," said the first.

"He's crazy as a loon," said the second.

I certainly must be crazy, I told myself, to let these two characters treat me like this.

"Excuse me," I said to them, "but where would you two ladies like to be dumped?"

"Dumped? What kind of language is that? You can go dump yourself if you like!"

"Oh, that's just coachman's talk," I said. "In ordinary parlance we would say: 'When we get to Boiberik safe and sound, with God's help, where do I drop off *mesdames?*'"

If that's what it means," they said, "you can drop us off at the green *dacha* by the pond at the far end of the woods. Do you know where it is?"

"Do I know where it is?" I said. "I know my way around Boiberik the way you do around your own home. I wish I had a thousand rubles for every log I've carried there. Just last summer, in fact, I brought a couple of loads of wood to the very *dacha* you're talking about. There was a rich Jew from Yehupetz living there, a real millionaire. He must have been worth a hundred grand, if not twice that."

"He's still living there," said both women at once, regarding each other with a whisper and a laugh.

"Well," I said, "seeing as the ride you've taken was no short haul, and as you may have some connection with him, would it be too much of me to request of you, if you don't mind my asking, to put in a good word for me with him? Maybe he's got an opening, a position of some sort. Really anything would do. . . You never know how things will turn out. I know a young man named Yisroel, for instance, who comes from a town not far from here. He's a real nothing, believe me, a zero with a hole in it. So what happens to him? Somehow, don't ask me how or where, he lands this swell job, and today he's a bigshot clearing twenty rubles a week, or maybe it's forty, who knows. . . Some people have all the luck! Do you by any chance happen to know what happened to our slaughterer's son-in-law, all because he picked himself up one fine day and went to Yehupetz? The first few years there, I admit, he really suffered; he damn near starved to death. Today, though, I only wish I were in his shoes and could send home the money that he does. Of course, he'd like his wife and kids to join him but he can't get them a residence permit. I ask you, what kind of life is it for a man to live all alone like that? I swear, I wouldn't wish it on a dog. . .

"Well, bless my soul, will you look at what we have here: here's your pond and there's your green *dacha!*" And with that I swung my wagon right through the gate and drove like nobody's business clear up to the porch of the house. Don't ask me to describe the excitement when the people sitting there saw us drive up. What a racket! Happy days!

"*Oy,* grandma!"

"*Oy, oy, oy,* mama!"

"*Oy,* auntie, auntie!"

"Thank God they're back!"

"*Mazel tov!*"

"*Gevalt,* where have you been?"

"We've been out of our minds with worry all day long!"

"We had scouts out looking for you on all the roads!"

"The things we thought happened to you, it's too horrible for words: highwaymen or maybe a wolf! So tell us, what happened?"

"What happened? What happened shouldn't have happened to a soul. We lost our way in the woods and blundered about for miles. Suddenly along comes a Jew. What, what kind of a Jew? A Jew, a *schlimazel,* with a wagon and horse. Don't think we had an easy time with him either, but here we are!"

"Incredible! It sounds like a bad dream. How could you have gone out in the woods without a guide? What an adventure, what an adventure. Thank God you're home safe!"

In no time lamps were brought out, the table was set, and there began to appear on it hot samovars flowing with tea, bowls of sugar, jars of preserves, plates full of pastry and all kinds of baked goods, followed by the fanciest dishes, soup brimming with fat, roast meats, a whole goose, the best wines and salad greens.

I stood a ways off and thought, "So this, God bless them, is how these Yehupetz tycoons eat and drink. It's enough to make the devil jealous! I'd pawn my last pair of socks if it would help to make me a rich Jew like them." You can imagine what went through my mind. The crumbs that fell from that table alone would have been enough to feed my kids for a week, with enough left over for the Sabbath. "*Gevalt, Gottenyu,*" I thought. "They say you're a long-suffering God, a good God, a great God; they say that you're merciful and fair. Perhaps you could explain to me then why it is that some folk have everything and others have nothing twice over? Why does one Jew get to eat butter rolls while another gets to eat dirt?". . . A minute later, though, I said to myself: "Ach, what a fool you are, Tevye, I swear! Do you really think He needs your advice on how to run the world? If this is how things are, it's how they were meant to be; the proof is that if they were meant to be different, they would be. It may seem to you that they ought to have been meant to be different. . . but it's for that you're a Jew in this world! A Jew must have confidence and faith. He must believe, first, that there is a God, and second that if there is, and that if it's all the same to Him, and that if it isn't putting Him to too much trouble, He can make things a little better for the likes of you. . ."

"Wait a minute," I heard someone say. "What happened to the coachman? Has the *schlimazel* left already?"

"God forbid!" I called out from where I was. "Do you mean to suggest that I'd just walk off without so much as saying good-bye? Good evening, it's a pleasure to meet you all. Enjoy your meal; I can't imagine why you shouldn't."

"Come on in out of the dark," said one of them to me, "and let's have a look at your face. Perhaps you'd like a little brandy?"

"A little brandy?" I said. "Who can refuse a little brandy? God may be God but brandy is brandy." *"L'chayim!"* I emptied the glass in one gulp. "God should only help you to stay rich and happy," I said, "because since Jews can't help being Jews, somebody else had better help them."

"What name do you go by?" asked the man of the house, a fine-looking Jew with a *yarmulke*. "Where do you come from? Where do you live now? What's your work? Do you have a wife? Children? How many?"

"How many children?" I said. "Forgive me for boasting, but if each child of mine were worth a million rubles, as my Golde tries to convince me, I'd be the richest man in Yehupetz. The only trouble is that poor isn't rich and a mountain's no ditch. How does it say in the prayer book? *Hamavdil beyn koydesh l'khoyl*, some make hay while others toil. There are people who have money, and I have daughters. And you know what they say about that: better a house full of boarders than a house full of daughters. But why complain when we have God for our father? He looks after everyone; that is, He sits up there and looks at us slaving away down here. What's my work? For lack of any better suggestions, I break my back dragging logs. As it says in the *Talmud: b'makom she'eyn ish,* a herring too is a fish. Really, there'd be no problem if it weren't for having to eat. Do you know what my grandmother used to say? What a shame we have mouths, because if we didn't we'd never be hungry. . . But you'll have to excuse me for carrying on like this. You can't expect straight words from a crooked brain—and especially not when I've gone and drunk brandy on an empty stomach."

"Bring the Jew something to eat!" ordered the man of the house, and right away the table was laid again with food I never dreamed existed: fish, cold cuts, roasts, fowl, more gizzards and chicken livers than you could possibly count.

"What would you like to eat?" I was asked. "Come on, wash your hands and sit down."

"A sick man is asked," I answered, "a healthy one is served. Still, thank you anyway. . . a little brandy, with pleasure. . . but to sit down and make a meal of it when back home my wife and children, they should only be healthy and well. . . So you see, if you don't mind, I'll. . ."

What can I tell you? They seem to have gotten the point, because before I knew it my wagon was being loaded with goodies: here rolls, there a fish, a pot roast, a quarter of a chicken, tea, sugar, a cup of chicken fat, a jar of jam.

"Here's a gift to take home to your wife and children," they said. "And now please tell us how much we owe you for your trouble."

"To tell you the truth," I said, "who am I to tell you what you owe me? You pay me what you think it was worth. What's a few pennies more or less between us? I'll still be the same Tevye when we're done."

"No," they said, "we want you to tell us, Reb Tevye. You needn't be afraid. We won't chop your head off."

"Now what?" I thought to myself. I was really in a pretty pickle. It would be a crime to ask for one ruble when they might agree to two. On the other hand, if I asked for two they might think I was mad. Two rubles for one little wagon ride?

"Three rubles!" The words were out of my mouth before I could stop them. Everyone began to laugh so hard that I could have crawled into a hole in the ground.

"Please forgive me," I said, "if I've said the wrong thing. Even a horse, who has four feet, stumbles now and then, so why not a man with one tongue. . ."

The laughter grew even louder. I thought they would all split their sides.

"Stop laughing now, all of you!" ordered the man of the house. He pulled a large wallet from his pocket, and out of the wallet he fished—how much do you think? I swear you'll never guess—a ten ruble note, all red as fire, as I hope to die! And do you know what else he says to me? "This," he says, "is from me. Now children, let's see what each of you can dig up out of his pockets."

What can I possibly tell you? Five- and three- and one-ruble notes flew onto the table. I started shaking all over until I was sure I was going to faint.

"Well, what are you waiting for?" says the man of the house to me. "Take your money from the table and have a good trip home."

"God reward you," I said, "a hundred times over; may He bring you good luck and happiness for the rest of your lives." I couldn't scrape up that money (who could even count it?) and stuff it into my pockets fast enough. "Good night," I said. "You should all be happy and well—you, and your children, and their children after them, and all their friends and relations."

I had already turned to go when the old woman with the silk kerchief stopped me and said, "One minute, Reb Tevye. There's a special present that I'd like to make you. You can come pick it up in the morning. I have the strangest cow—it was once a wonderful beast, it gave twenty-four glasses of milk every day. Someone must have put a hex on it, though, because now you can't milk it at all—that is, you can milk it all you want, you just won't get any milk. . . ."

"I wish you a long life," I said, "and one you won't wish was any shorter. We'll not only milk your milk cow, we'll milk it for milk. My wife, God bless her, is such a wizard around the house that she can bake a noodle pudding from air, cook soup from a fingernail, whip up a Sabbath meal from an empty cupboard, and put hungry children to sleep with a box on the ear. . . .Well, please don't hold it against me if I've run on a little too long. And now good night to you all and be well," I said, turning to go to the yard where my wagon was. . . .Good Lord! With my luck one always has to expect a disaster, but this was an out-and-out misfortune. I looked this way, I looked that way—*ve'hayeled eynenu:* there wasn't a horse in sight.

This time, Tevye, I thought, you're really in a fix! And I remembered a charming story I had read in a book about a gang of goblins who once

played a prank on a Jew, a pious *Hasid*, by luring him to a castle outside
of town where they wined and dined him and suddenly disappeared,
leaving a naked woman behind them. The woman turned into a tigress,
the tigress turned into a cat, and the cat turned into a poisonous
snake. . . "Between you and me, Tevye," I said just to myself, "how do
you know that they're not pulling a fast one on you?"

"What are you mumbling and grumbling about there?" someone
asked me.

"What am I mumbling about?" I replied. "Believe me, it's not for my
health. In fact, I have a slight problem. My horse—"

"Your horse," someone said, "is in the stable. You only have to go
there and look for it."

I went to the stable and looked for it. I swear I'm not a Jew if the old
fellow wasn't standing there as proud as punch among the tycoon's
horses, chewing away at his oats for all he was worth.

"I'm sorry to break up the party," I said, "but it's time to go home, old
boy. Why make a hog of yourself? Before you know it you'll have taken
one bite too many. . . "

In the end it was all I could do to wheedle him out of there and back
into his harness. Away home we flew, on top of the world, singing Yom
Kippur songs as tipsily as you please. You wouldn't have recognized my
horse; he ran like the wind without my so much as mentioning the whip
and looked like he'd been reupholstered. When we finally got home late
at night, I joyously woke up my wife.

"Mazel tov, Golde," I said to her. "I've got good news!"

"A black *mazel tov* yourself," she says to me. "Tell me, my fine
breadwinner, what's the happy occasion? Has my goldfingers been to a
wedding or a *bris?"*

"To something better than a wedding and a *bris* combined," I said. "In
a minute, my wife, I'm going to show you a treasure. But first go wake up
the kids. Why shouldn't they also enjoy some Yehupetz cuisine. . . "

"Either you're delirious, or else you're temporarily deranged, or else
you've taken leave of your senses, or else you're totally insane. All I can
say is, you're talking just like a madman, God help us!" says my wife.
When it comes to her tongue she's a pretty average Jewish housewife.

"And you're talking just like a woman!" I answered. "King Solomon
wasn't joking when he said that out of a thousand females you won't find
one with a head on her shoulders. It's a lucky thing that polygamy's gone
out of fashion." And with that I went out to the wagon and began

unpacking all the dishes I'd been given and set them out on the table. When that gang of mine saw all the rolls and smelled all the meat, they fell on it like a pack of wolves. Their hands trembled so they could hardly snatch anything up. I stood there with tears in my eyes, listening to their jaws work away like a plague of starving locusts.

"So tell me," says my woman when she's done, "who's been sharing their frugal repast with you, and since when do you have such good friends?"

"Don't worry, Golde," I said, "you'll hear it all in good time. First put the samovar on, so that we can sit down and drink a glass of tea in style. Generally speaking, one only lives once, am I right? So it's a good thing that we now have a cow of our own that gives twenty-four glasses of milk every day; in fact, I'm planning to go fetch her in the morning. And now, Golde," I said to her, pulling out my wad of bills, "be a sport and guess how much I have here!"

You should have seen my wife turn pale as a ghost. She was so flabbergasted that she couldn't say a word.

"God be with you, Golde my darling," I said to her. "You needn't look so frightened. Are you worried that I've stolen it somewhere? *Feh*, you should be ashamed of yourself! How long haven't you been married to me that you should think such thoughts of your Tevye? This is kosher money, you sillyhead, earned fairly and squarely by my own wits and hard work. The fact is that I've just saved two people from great danger. If it weren't for me, God only knows what would have become of them. . ."

In a word, I told her the whole story from beginning to end, the entire rigamarole. When I was through we counted all the money, then counted it again, then counted it once more to be sure. Whichever way we counted, it came to exactly thirty-seven rubles and no cents.

My wife began to cry.

"Why are you crying like an idiot?" I ask her.

"How can I help crying," she says, "when the tears won't stop coming? When the heart is full, it runs out at the eyes. God help me if something didn't tell me that you were about to come with good news. You know, I can't remember when I last saw my Grandma Tzeitl (may she rest in peace) in a dream—and just before you came I dreamed that I saw a big milkcan filled to the brim, and my Grandma Tzeitl was carrying it under her apron to keep the evil eye away, and all the children were shouting, 'Look, mama, look. . .'"

"Don't go smacking your lips before you've tasted the pudding, Golde, my darling," I said to her. "I'm sure that Grandma Tzeitl is enjoying her stay in Paradise, but that doesn't make her an expert on what's happening down here. Still, if God went through all the trouble of getting us a milk cow, it stands to reason that He'll see to it that the milk cow will give milk. . . . What I wanted to ask you, though, Golde, my dear, is what should we do with all the money?"

"It's funny you asked me that, Tevye," she says, "because that's just what I was going to ask you."

"Well, if you were going to ask me anyway," I say, "suppose I ask you. What do you think we should do with so much capital?"

We thought. And the harder we thought, the dizzier we became planning one business scheme after another. What didn't we deal in that night? We bought a pair of horses and quickly sold them for a windfall; with the profits we opened a grocery store in Boiberik, sold out all the stock, and opened a drygoods store; after that we invested in some woodland, found a buyer for it, and came out a few more rubles ahead; next we bought up the tax concession at Anatevka, farmed it out again, and with the income started a bank. . .

"You're completely out of your mind!" my wife suddenly shouted at me. "Do you want to throw away our hard-earned savings lending money to good-for-nothings and be left with no more than your whip again?"

"So what do you suggest," I said, "that it's better to go bankrupt trading in grain? Do you have any idea of the fortunes that are being lost right this minute on the wheat market? If you don't believe me, go to Odessa and see for yourself."

"What do I care about Odessa?" she says. "My greatgrandparents didn't live there and neither will my greatgrandchildren, and neither will I as long as I have legs not to take me there."

"So what do you want?" I ask her.

"What do I want?" she says. "I want you to talk sense and stop acting like a moron."

"Well, well," I said, "look who's the wise one now. Apparently there's nothing that money can't buy, even brains. I might have known this would happen."

To make a long story short, after quarreling and making up a few more times we decided to buy, in addition to the beast I was to pick up in the morning, a milk cow that gave milk. . . .

It might occur to you to ask why we decided to buy a cow when we could just as well have bought a horse. But why buy a horse, I ask you, when we could just as well have bought a cow? We live close to Boiberik, which is where all the rich Yehupetz Jews come to spend the summer in their *dachas*. And you know those Yehupetz Jews—nothing is too good for them. They expect to have everything served on a silver platter: wood, meat, eggs, poultry, onions, pepper, parsley. . . . So why shouldn't I be the man to walk into their parlor with cheese, cream, and butter? They like to eat well, they have money to burn, you can make a fat living from them as long as they think that they're getting the best— and believe me, fresh produce like mine they can't even get in Yehupetz. The two of us, my friend, should only have good luck in our lives for every time I've been stopped by the best type of people, Gentiles even, who beg to be my customers. "We've heard, Tevye," they say to me, "that you're an honest fellow, even if you are a rat-Jew. . . ." I ask you, do you ever get such a compliment from Jews? My worst enemy should have to lie sick in bed for as long as it would take me to wait for one! No, our Jews like to keep their praises to themselves, which is more than I can say about their noses. The minute they see that I've bought another cow, or that I have a new cart, they begin to rack their brains: "Where is it all coming from? Can our Tevye be passing out phony banknotes? Or perhaps he's making moonshine in some still?" Ha, ha, ha. All I can say is: keep wondering until your heads break, my friends, and enjoy it. . . .

Believe it or not, you're practically the first person to have heard my story—the whole where, what, and when of it. And now, you'll have to excuse me, because I've run on a little too long. We all have our (what is the word?) *vocations* in life. How does it say in the Bible? *Kol oyrev l'mineyhu*, it's a wise bird that feathers its own nest. So you'd better be off to your books, and I to my milk cans and jugs. . . .

There's just one request I have of you, Pani: please don't stick me in any of your books. And if that's too much to ask, at least do me a favor and leave my name out of it.

And oh, yes, by the way: don't forget to take care and be well!

Translated by Hillel Halkin

The Bubble Bursts

"THERE ARE MANY thoughts in a man's heart." So I believe it is written in the Torah. I don't have to translate the passage for you, Mr. Sholom Aleichem. But, speaking in plain Yiddish, there is a saying: "The most obedient horse needs a whip; the cleverest man can use advice." In regard to whom do I say this? I say it in regard to myself, for if I had once had the good sense to go to a friend and tell him such and such, thus and so, this calamity would never have taken place. But how is it said? *"Life and death issue from thine own lips.*—When God sees fit to punish a man he first takes away his good sense."

How many times have I thought to myself: Look, Tevye, you dolt, you are not supposed to be a complete fool. How could you have allowed yourself to be taken in so completely and in such a foolish way? Wouldn't it have been better for you if you had been content with your little dairy business whose fame has spread far and wide, everywhere from Boiberik to Yehupetz? How sweet and pleasant it would have been if your little hoard still lay in its box, buried deep where not a soul could see or know. For whose business is it whether Tevye has money or not? Was anyone concerned with Tevye when he lay buried nine feet deep, wrapped in his poverty like a dead man in his shroud? Did the world care when he starved three times a day together with his wife and children?

But lo and behold! When God turned his countenance on Tevye and caused him to prosper all at once, so that at last he was beginning to arrive somewhere, beginning to save up a ruble now and then, the world suddenly became aware of his presence, and overnight, mind you, plain Tevye became Reb Tevye, nothing less. Suddenly out of nowhere a multitude of friends sprang up. As it is written: *"He is beloved by everyone."* Or, as we put it: "When God gives a dot, the world adds a lot."

Everyone came to me with a different suggestion. This one tells me to open a drygoods store, that one a grocery. Another one says to buy a building—property is a sound investment, it lasts forever. One tells me to invest in wheat, another in timber. Still another suggests auctioneering. "Friends!" I cry. "Brothers! Leave me alone. You've got the wrong man. You must think I'm Brodsky, but I am still very far from being a Brodsky. It is easy to estimate another's wealth. You see something that glitters like gold at a distance. You come close and it's only a brass button."

May no good come to them—I mean those friends of mine, those well-wishers—they cast an evil eye on me. God sent me a relative from somewhere, a distant kinsman of some kind whom I had never before seen. Menachem-Mendel is his name—a gadabout, a wastrel, a faker, a worthless vagabond, may he never stand still in one place. He got hold of me and filled my head with dreams and fantasies, things that had never been on land or sea. You will ask me: *"Wherefore did it come to pass?"* How did I ever get together with Menachem-Mendel? And I will answer in the words of the *Haggadah: "For we were slaves."* It was fated, that's all. Listen to my story.

I arrived in Yehupetz in early winter, with my choicest merchandise— over twenty pounds of butter fresh from butterland and several pails of cheese. I had salted away everything I had, you understand, didn't leave a smidgen for myself, not as much as a medicine spoon would hold. I didn't even have the time to visit all of my regular customers, the summer people of Boiberik, who await my coming as a good Jew waits for the coming of the Messiah. For say what you will, there isn't a merchant in Yehupetz who can produce a piece of goods that comes up to mine. I don't have to tell you this. As the prophet says: *"Let another praise thee.*—Good merchandise speaks for itself."

Well, I sold out everything to the last crumb, threw a bundle of hay to my horse and went for a walk around the town. *"Man is born of dust and to dust he returneth."* After all, I am only human. I want to see something of the world, breathe some fresh air, take a look at the wonders Yehupetz displays behind glass windows, as though to say: "Use your eyes all you want, but with your hands—away!"

Standing in front of a large window filled with seven and a half ruble gold pieces, with piles of silver rubles, and stacks of paper money of all kinds, I think to myself: God in Heaven! If I had only a tenth of what all of this is worth! What more could I ask of God and who would be my equal? First of all, I would marry off my oldest daughter, give her a suitable dowry and still have enough left over for wedding expenses, gifts, and clothing for the bride. Then I would sell my horse and wagon and my cows and move into town. I would buy myself a synagogue seat by the Eastern Wall, hang strips of pearls around my wife's neck, and hand out charity like the richest householders. I would see to it that the synagogue got a new roof instead of standing as it does now, practically roofless, ready to cave in any minute. I would open a school for the children and build a hospital such as they have in other towns so that the town's poor and sick wouldn't have to lie underfoot in the synagogue. And I would get rid of Yankel Sheigetz as president of the Burial Society. There's been enough guzzling of brandy and chicken livers at public expense!

"*Sholem aleichem*, Reb Tevye," I hear a voice right in back of me. I turn around and take a look. I could swear I have seen this man somewhere before.

"*Aleichem sholem*," I answer. "And where do you hail from?"

"Where do I hail from? From Kasrilevke," he says. "I am a relative of yours. That is, your wife Golde is my second cousin once-removed."

"Hold on!" I say. "Aren't you Boruch-Hersh Leah-Dvoshe's son-in-law?"

"You've hit the nail right on the head," he says. "I am Boruch-Hersh Leah-Dvoshe's son-in-law and my wife is Sheina Sheindel, Boruch-Hersh Leah-Dvoshe's daughter. Now do you know who I am?"

"Wait," I say. "Your mother-in-law's grandmother, Sarah-Yenta, and my wife's aunt, Fruma-Zlata, were, I believe, first cousins, and if I am not mistaken you are the middle son-in-law of Boruch-Hersh Leah-Dvoshe. But I forget what they call you. Your name has flown right out of my head. Tell me, what is your name?"

"My name," he says, "is Menachem-Mendel Boruch-Hersh Leah-Dvoshe's. That's what they call me at home, in Kasrilevke."

"If that's the case," I say, "my dear Menachem-Mendel, I really owe you a *sholem aleichem* and a hearty one! Now, tell me, my friend, what are you doing here, and how is your mother-in-law and your father-in-law? How is your health, and how is business with you?"

"As far as my health," he says, "God be thanked. I am still alive. But business is not so gay."

"It will get better, with God's help," I tell him, stealing a look meanwhile at his shabby coat and the holes in his shoes. "Don't despair, God will come to your aid. Business will get better, no doubt. As the proverb says: '*All is vanity.*—Money is round, it is here today, gone tomorrow.' The main thing is to stay alive and keep hoping. A Jew must never stop hoping. Do we wear ourselves down to a shadow in the meanwhile? That's why we are Jews. How is it said? If you're a soldier you have to smell gunpowder. '*Man is likened to a broken pot.*—The world is nothing but a dream.' Tell me, Menachem-Mendel, how do you happen to be in Yehupetz all of a sudden?"

"What do you mean how do I happen to be in Yehupetz all of a sudden? I've been here no less than a year and a half."

"Oh," said I, "then you belong here. You are living in Yehupetz."

"Shh!" he whispers, looking all about him. "Don't talk so loud, Reb Tevye. I *am* living in Yehupetz, but that's just between you and me."

I stare at him as though he were out of his mind. "You are a fugitive," I ask, "and you hide in the middle of the public square?"

"Don't ask, Reb Tevye. You are apparently not acquainted with the laws and customs of Yehupetz. Listen and I'll explain to you how a man can live here and still not live here." And he began telling me a long tale of woe, of all the trials and tribulations of life in the city of Yehupetz.

When he finished I said to him, "Take my advice, Menachem-Mendel. Come along with me to the country for a day and rest your tired bones. You will be a guest at our house, a very welcome guest. My wife will be overjoyed to have you."

Well, I talked him into it. He went with me. We arrive at home. What rejoicing! A guest! And such a guest! A second cousin once-removed. After all, blood is thicker than water. My wife starts right in, "What is new in Kasrilevke? How is Uncle Boruch-Hersh? And Aunt Leah-Dvoshe? And Uncle Yossel-Menashe? And Aunt Dobrish? And how are their children! Who has died recently? Who has been married? Who is divorced? Who has given birth? And who is expecting?"

"What do you care about strange weddings and strange circumcisions?" I tell my wife. "Better see to it that we get something to eat. As it is written, '*All who are hungry enter and be fed.*—Nobody likes to dance on an empty stomach.' If you give us a *borscht*, fine. If not, I'll take *knishes* or *kreplach*, pudding or dumplings. *Blintzes* with cheese will suit me, too. Make anything you like and the more the better, but do it quickly."

Well, we washed, said grace, and had our meal. "*They ate*," as Rashi says. "Eat, Menachem-Mendel, eat," I urged him. "'*Forget the world*,' as King David once said. It's a stupid world, and a deceitful one, and health and happiness, as my grandmother Nechama of blessed memory used to say—she was a clever woman and a wise one—health and happiness are only to be found at the table."

Our guest—his hands trembled as he reached for the food, poor fellow—couldn't find enough words in praise of my wife's cooking. He swore by everything holy that he couldn't remember when he had eaten such a dairy supper, such perfect *knishes*.

"Stuff and nonsense," I tell him. "You should taste her noodle pudding. Then you would know what heaven on earth can be."

After we had eaten and said our benedictions, we began talking, each one naturally talking of what concerned him most. I talk about my business, he of his. I babble of this, that, and the other, important and unimportant. He tells me stories of Yehupetz and Odessa, of how he had been ten times over, as they say, "on horseback and thrown off the horse." A rich man today, a beggar tomorrow, again a rich man, and once more a pauper. He dealt in something I have never heard of in my life—crazy-sounding things—stocks, bonds, shares-shmares. The devil alone knew what it was. The sums that he reeled off his tongue were fantastic—ten thousand, twenty thousand, thirty thousand—he threw money around like matches.

"I'll tell you the truth, Menachem-Mendel," I say to him. "Your business sounds very involved; you need brains to understand all of that. But what puzzles me most is this: from what I know of your better half it's a wonder to me that she lets you go traipsing around the world and doesn't come riding after you on a broomstick."

"Don't remind me of that," he says with a deep sigh. "I get enough from her as it is, both hot and cold. If you could see the letters she writes me you would admit that I am a saint to put up with it. But that's a small matter. That's what a wife is for—to bury her husband alive. There are worse things than that. I have also, as you know, a mother-in-law. I don't have to go into detail. You have met her."

"It is with you as it is written: '*The flocks were speckled and streaked and spotted.*—You have a boil on top of a boil and a blister on top of that.'"

"Yes," he says. "You put it very well, Reb Tevye. The boil is bad enough in itself, but the blister—ah, that blister is worse than the boil."

Well, we kept up this palaver until late into the night. My head whirled with his tales of fantastic transactions, of thousands that rose and fell, fabulous fortunes that were won and lost and won again. I tossed all night long dreaming in snatches of Yehupetz and Brodsky, of millions of rubles, of Menachem-Mendel and his mother-in-law.

Early the next morning he begins hemming and hawing and finally comes out with it. Here is what he says. "Since the stock market has for a long time been in such a state that money is held in high esteem and goods are held very low, you Tevye have a chance to make yourself a pretty penny. And while you are getting rich you will at the same time be saving my life, you will actually raise me from the dead."

"You talk like a child," I say to him. "You must think I have a big sum of money to invest. Fool, may we both earn before next Passover what I lack to make me a Brodsky."

"I know," he says, "without your telling me. But what makes you think we need big money? If you give me a hundred rubles now, I can turn it in three or four days into two hundred or three hundred or six hundred or maybe even into a thousand rubles."

"It may be as it is written: '*The profit is great, but it's far from my pocket.*' Who says I have anything to invest at all? And if there is no hundred rubles, it's as Rashi says: '*You came in alone and you go out by yourself.*' Or, as I put it, 'If you plant a stone, up comes a boulder.'"

"Come now," he says to me, "you know you can dig up a hundred rubles. With all the money you are earning and with your name . . . "

"A good name is an excellent thing," I tell him. "But what comes of it? I have my name and Brodsky has the money. If you want to know the truth, my savings come all in all close to a hundred rubles. And I have two dozen uses for it. First of all, to marry off my daughter . . . "

"Just what I've been trying to tell you," he breaks in. "When will you have the opportunity to put in a hundred rubles and to take out, with God's help, enough to marry off your daughter and to do all the other things besides?"

And he went on with this chant for the next three hours, explaining how he could make three rubles out of one and ten out of three. First you bring in one hundred rubles somewhere, and you tell them to buy ten pieces of I-forget-what-you-call-it, then you wait a few days until they go up. You send a telegram somewhere else to sell the ten pieces and buy twice as many for the money. Then you wait and they rise again. You shoot off another telegram. You keep doing this until the hundred rubles become two hundred, then four hundred, then eight hundred, then sixteen hundred. It's no less than a miracle from God. There are people in Yehupetz, he tells me, who until recently went barefoot—they didn't have a pair of shoes to their names. They worked as errand boys and messengers. Now they own palatial homes, their wives have expensive stomach ailments, they go abroad for cures. They themselves fly all over Yehupetz on rubber wheels; they don't recognize old friends any more.

Well, why should I drag out the story? I caught the fever from him. Who knows, I think to myself, maybe he was sent by my good angel? He tells me that people win fortunes in Yehupetz, ordinary people with not more than five fingers to each hand. Am I any worse than they? I don't believe he is a liar; he couldn't make all these things up out of his own head. Who knows, suppose the wheel turns, and Tevye becomes a somebody in his old age? How much longer can I keep on toiling and moiling from dawn until dark? Day in and day out—the same horse and wagon, night and day the same butter and cheese? It's time, Tevye, that you took a little rest, became a man among men, went into the synagogue once in a while, turned the pages of a holy book. Why not? And on the other hand, if I lose out, if it should fall buttered side down? But better not think of that.

"What do you say?" I ask my wife. "What do you think of his proposition?"

"What do you want me to say?" she asks. "I know that Menachem-Mendel isn't a nobody who would want to swindle you. He doesn't come from a family of nobodies. He has a very respectable father, and as for his grandfather, he was a real jewel. All of his life, even after he became blind, he studied the Torah. And Grandmother Tzeitl, may she rest in peace, was no ordinary woman either."

"A fitting parable," I said. "It's like bringing Chanukah candles to a Purim feast. We talk about investments and she drags in her Grandmother Tzeitl who used to bake honeycake, and her grandfather who died of drink. That's a woman for you. No wonder King Solomon traveled the world over and didn't find a female with an ounce of brains in her head."

To make a long story short, we decided to form a partnership. I put in my money and Menachem-Mendel, his wits. Whatever God gives, we will divide in half. "Believe me, Reb Tevye," he says, "you won't regret doing business with me. With God's help the money will come pouring in."

"Amen and the same to you," I say. "From your lips into God's ears. There is just one thing I want to know. How does the mountain come to the prophet? You are over there in Yehupetz and I am here in the country; and money, as you know, is a delicate substance. It isn't that I don't trust you, but as Father Abraham says, '*If you sow with tears you shall reap with joy.*—It's better to be safe than sorry.'"

"Oh," he says, "would you rather we drew up a paper? Most willingly."

"Listen," I say to him, "if you want to ruin me, what good will a piece of paper do me? '*The mouse is not the thief.*—It isn't the note that pays, but the man.' If I am hung by one foot I might as well be hung by both."

"Believe me, Reb Tevye," he says to me, "I swear to you on my word of honor, may God be my witness, that I have no tricks up my sleeve. I won't swindle you, but I will deal with you honestly. I will divide our earnings equally with you, share and share alike—a hundred to you, a hundred to me, two hundred to you, two hundred to me, four hundred to you, four hundred to me, a thousand to you, a thousand to me."

So I dug out my little hoard, counted the money over three times, my hands shaking the whole time, called over my wife as a witness, and explained to him again that this was blood-money I was giving him, and sewed it carefully inside his shirt so that no one would rob him of it on the way. He promised that he would write me not later than a week from Saturday and tell me everything in detail. Then we said good-bye with much feeling, embraced like close friends, and he went on his way.

When I was left alone there began to pass in front of my eyes all sorts of visions—visions so sweet that I wished they would never end. I saw a large house with a tin roof right in the middle of town, and inside the house were big rooms and little rooms and pantries full of good things, and around it a yard full of chickens and ducks and geese. I saw the mistress of the house walking around jingling her keys. That was my wife Golde, but what a different Golde from the one I knew. This one had the face and manner of a rich man's wife, with a double chin and a neck hung with pearls. She strutted around like a peacock giving herself airs, and yelling at the servant girls. And here were my daughters dressed in their Sabbath best, lolling around, not lifting a finger for themselves. The house was full of brightness and cheer. Supper was cooking in the oven. The samovar boiled merrily on the table. And at the head of the table sat the master of the house, Tevye himself, in a robe and skullcap, and around him sat the foremost householders of the town, fawning on him. "If you please, Reb Tevye. Pardon me, Reb Tevye."—And so on.

"What fiendish power money has!" I exclaimed.

"Whom are you cursing?" asked Golde.

"Nobody. I was just thinking," I told her. "Daydreams and moonshine . . . Tell me Golde, my love, do you know what sort of merchandise he deals in, that cousin of yours, Menachem-Mendel?"

"What's that?" she said. "Bad luck to my enemies! Here he has spent a day and a night talking with the man, and in the end he comes and asks me, 'What does he deal in?' For God's sake, you made up a contract with him. You are partners."

"Yes," I said. "We made up something, but I don't know what we made up. If my life depended on it, I wouldn't know. There is nothing, you see, that I can get hold of. But one thing has nothing to do with the other. Don't worry, my dear wife. My heart tells me that it is all for the best. We are going to make a lot of money. Say amen to that and go cook supper."

Well, a week goes by and two and three. There is no news from my partner. I am beside myself with worry. It can't be that he has just forgotten to write. He knows quite well how anxiously we are waiting to hear from him. A thought flits through my head. What shall I do if he skims off the cream for himself and tells me that there is no profit? But that, I tell myself, can't be. It just isn't possible. I treat the man like one of my own, so how can he turn around and play a trick like that on me? Then something worse occurs to me. Profit be hanged. Who cares about profit? "*Deliverance and protection will come from the Lord.*" May God only keep the capital from harm. I feel a chill go up and down my back. "You old fool," I tell myself. "You idiot. You made your bed, now lie on it. For the hundred rubles you could have bought yourself a pair of horses such as your forefathers never had, or exchanged your old wagon for a carriage with springs."

"Tevye, why don't you think of something?" my wife pleads with me.

"What do you mean why don't I think of something? My head is splitting into little pieces from thinking and she asks why don't I think."

"Something must have happened to him on the road," says my wife. "He was attacked by robbers, or else he got sick on the way. Or he may even be dead."

"What will you dream up next, my love?" I ask. "All of a sudden she has to start pulling robbers out of thin air." But to myself I think: "No telling what can happen to a man alone on the road."

"You always imagine the worst," I tell my wife.

"He comes of such a good family," she says. "His mother, may she intercede for us in Heaven, died not long ago, she was still a young woman. He had three sisters. One died as a girl; the other one lived to get married but caught cold coming from the bath and died; and the third one lost her mind after her first child was born, ailed for a long time, and died too."

"To live until we die is our lot," I tell her. "We must all die sometime. A man is compared to a carpenter. A carpenter lives and lives until he dies, and a man lives and lives until he dies."

Well, we decided that I should go to Yehupetz. Quite a bit of merchandise had accumulated in the meanwhile—cheese and butter and cream, all of the best. My wife harnessed the horse and wagon, and *"they journeyed from Sukos"*—as Rashi says. On to Yehupetz!

Naturally my heart was heavy and my thoughts gloomy as I rode through the woods. I began to imagine the worst. Suppose, I think to myself, I arrive and begin to inquire about my man and they tell me, "Menachem-Mendel? Oh, that one? He has done well by himself. He has feathered his own nest. He owns a mansion, rides in his own carriage, you wouldn't recognize him." But just the same I gather up courage and go to his house. "Get out!" they tell me at the door, and shove me aside with their elbows. "Don't push your way, Uncle. We don't allow that."

"I am his relative," I tell them. "He is my wife's second cousin once-removed."

"*Mazel-tov*," they tell me. "We are overjoyed to hear it. But just the same it won't hurt you to wait a little at the door."

It occurs to me that I should slip the doorman a bribe. As it is said: "*What goes up must come down*" or "If you don't grease the axle the wheels won't turn." And so I get in.

"Good morning to you, Reb Menachem-Mendel," I say.

Who? What? "*There is no speech. There are no words.*" He looks at me as though he has never seen me before. "What do you want?" he says.

I am ready to faint. "What do you mean?" I say. "Don't you recognize your own cousin? My name is Tevye."

"Tevye . . ." he says slowly. "The name sounds familiar."

"So the name sounds familiar to you. Maybe my wife's *blintzes* sound familiar, too? You may even remember the taste of her *knishes* and *kreplach?*"

Then I imagine exactly the opposite. I come in to see Menachem-

Mendel and he meets me at the door with outstretched arms. "Welcome, Reb Tevye. Welcome. Be seated. How are you? And how is your wife? I've been waiting for you. I want to settle my account with you." And he takes my cap and pours it full of gold pieces. "This," he tells me, "is what we earned on our investment. The capital we shall leave where it is. Whatever we make we shall divide equally, share and share alike, half to me, half to you, a hundred to me, a hundred to you, two hundred to you, two hundred to me, five hundred to you, five hundred to me. . . . "

While I am lost in this dream, my horse strays from the path, the wagon gets caught against a tree, and I am jolted from behind so suddenly that sparks fly in front of my eyes. "This is all for the best," I comfort myself. "Thank God the axle didn't break."

I arrive in Yehupetz, dispose of my wares quickly and, as usual, without any trouble, and set out to look for my partner. I wander around for an hour; I wander around for two hours. It's no use. It's as Jacob said about Benjamin: "*The lad is gone*." I can't find him anywhere. I stop people in the street and ask them, "Have you seen or have you heard of a man who goes by the elegant name of Menachem-Mendel?"

"Well, well," they tell me, "if his name is Menachem-Mendel, you can look for him with a candle. But that isn't enough. There is more than one Menachem-Mendel in the world."

"I see, you want to know his family name. At home in Kasrilevke he is known by his mother-in-law's name—Menachem-Mendel Leah-Dvoshe's. What more do you want? Even his father-in-law, who is a very old man, is known by his wife's name, Boruch-Hersh Leah-Dvoshe's. Now do you understand?"

"We understand very well," they say. "But that isn't enough. What does this Menachem-Mendel do? What is his business?"

"His business? He deals in seven and a half ruble gold pieces, in Putilov shares, in stocks and bonds. He shoots telegrams here, there, and everywhere—to St. Petersburg, Odessa, Warsaw."

They roll with laughter. "Oh, you mean Menachem-Mendel-who-deals-in-all-and-sundry? Turn left and follow this street and you will see many hares running around. Yours will be among them."

"Live and learn," I say to myself. "Now I am told to look for hares." I follow the street they pointed out to me. It's as crowded as our town square on market day. I can barely push my way through. People are running around like crazy—shouting, waving their hands, quarreling.

It's a regular bedlam. I hear shouts of "Putilov," "shares," "stocks . . . " "he gave me his word . . . " "here is a down payment . . . " "buy on margin . . . " "he owes me a fee . . . " "you are a sucker . . . " "spit in his face . . . " "look at that speculator." Any minute they will start fighting in earnest, dealing out blows. "*Jacob fled*," I mutter to myself. "Get out, Tevye, before you get knocked down. God is our Father, Tevye the Dairyman is a sinner. Yehupetz is a city, and Menachem-Mendel is a breadwinner. So this is where people make fortunes? This is how they do their business? May God have mercy on you, Tevye, and on such business."

I stopped in front of a large window with a display of clothing in it and whom should I see reflected in it but my partner Menachem-Mendel. My heart was squeezed with pity at the sight. . . . I became faint. . . . May our worst enemies look the way Menachem-Mendel looked. You should have seen his coat. And his shoes. Or what was left of them. And his face! A corpse laid out for burial looks cheerful by comparison. "Well, Tevye," I said to myself as Esther had once said to Mordecai, '*if I perish, I perish.*—I am done for.' You may as well kiss your savings good-bye. '*There is no bear and no woods.*—No merchandise and no money.' Nothing but a pack of troubles."

He looked pretty crestfallen on his part. We both stood there, rooted to the ground, unable to speak. There seemed to be nothing left to say, nothing left to do. We might as well pick up our sacks and go over the city begging.

"Reb Tevye," he says to me softly, barely able to utter the words, the tears are choking him so, "Reb Tevye, without luck, it's better never to have been born at all. Rather than live like this, it is better to hang from a tree or rot in the ground."

"For such a deed," I burst out, "for what you've done to me, you deserve to be stretched out right here in the middle of Yehupetz and flogged so hard that you lose consciousness. Consider for yourself what you've done. You've taken a houseful of innocent people who never did you a speck of harm, and without a knife you slit their throats clear through. How can I face my wife and children now? Tell me, you robber, you murderer, you—"

"It is all true, Reb Tevye," he says, leaning against the wall. "All true. May God have mercy on me."

"The fires of hell," I tell him, "the tortures of Gehenna are too good for you."

"All true," he says. "May God have pity on me. All true. Rather than to live like this, Reb Tevye, rather than to live—" And he hangs his head.

I look at him standing there, the poor *schlimazel*, leaning against the wall, his head bent, his cap awry. He sighs and he groans and my heart turns over with pity.

"And yet," I say, "if you want to look at it another way, you may not be to blame either. When I think it over, I realize that you couldn't have done it out of plain knavery. After all, you were my partner, you had a share in the business. I put in my money and you put in your brains. Woe unto us both. I am sure you meant it for the best. It must have been fate. How is it said? '*Don't rejoice today, because tomorrow—*' Or, 'Man proposes and God disposes.'

"If you want proof, just look at my business. It seems to be completely foolproof, a guaranteed thing. And yet when it came to pass last fall that one of my cows lay down and died and right after her a young calf—was there anything I could do about it? When luck turns against you, you are lost.

"I don't even want to ask you where my money is. I understand only too well. My blood money went up in smoke, it sank into the grave. . . . And whose fault is it if not mine? I let myself be talked into it. I went chasing after rainbows. If you want money, my friend, you have to work and slave for it, you have to wear your fingers to the bone. I deserve a good thrashing for it. But crying about it won't help. How is it written? '*If the maiden screamed—*You can shout until you burst a blood vessel.' Hindsight, as they say . . . It wasn't fated that Tevye should be a rich man. As Ivan says, 'Mikita never had anything and never will.' God willed it so. '*The Lord giveth and the Lord taketh away.*' Come, brother, let's go get a drink."

And that, Mr. Sholom Aleichem, is how my beautiful dream burst like a bubble and vanished into thin air. Do you think I took it to heart? Do you think I grieved over the loss of my money? Not at all. We know what the proverb says: "*The silver and the gold are mine.*—Money is worthless." Only man is important, that is, if he is really a man, a human being. For what did I grieve then? I grieved for the dream I had lost, the dream of wealth that was gone forever. For I had longed, how I had longed, to be a rich man, if only for a short while. But what did it avail me? The proverb says, "*Perforce you live and perforce you die.*—You live in spite of yourself and you wear out your shoes in spite of yourself."

"You, Tevye," says God, "stick to your cheese and butter and forget your dreams." But what about hope? Naturally, the harder life is the more you must hope. The poorer you are the more cheerful you must be.

Do you want proof? But I think I have talked too long already. I have to be on my way; I have to tend to business. As it is said: *"Every man is a liar.*—Everyone has his affliction." Farewell, be healthy and happy always. . . .

Translated by Frances Butwin

Chava

"GIVE THANKS UNTO the Lord, for He is good.— Whatever He ordains, His way is the best." It has to be the best, for if you had the wisdom of a Solomon could you improve on it? Look at me—I wanted to be clever, I turned and twisted this way and that, and tried everything I knew, and then when I saw it was no use, I took my hand off my chest, as the saying is, and said to myself, "Tevye, you're a fool, you won't change the world. The Lord has given us the *'pain of bringing up children,'* which means that in raising children you have to accept the bad with the good and count them as one."

Take, for instance, my oldest daughter, Tzeitl, who went and fell in love with the tailor Mottel Kamzoil. Have I got anything against him? True, he is a simple, unlettered fellow who can't read the learned footnotes at the bottom of the page, but is that anything against him? Everybody in the world can't be a scholar. At least he is an honest man and a hard-working one. She's already borne him a whole brood of young ones; they have a houseful of hungry mouths to feed, and both of them, he and she, are struggling along *"in honor and in riches,"* as the saying is. And yet if you ask her, she will tell you that she is the happiest woman in the world, no one could be happier. There is only one tiny flaw—they don't have enough to eat. *"That's the end of the first round with the Torah.*—There's Number One for you."

About my second daughter, about Hodel, I don't have to tell you. You know about her already. With her I played and I lost. I lost her forever. God knows if my eyes will ever behold her again, unless it should be in the next world. To this day I can't bring myself to talk about her calmly. I mention her name and the old pain returns. Forget her, you say? How can you forget a living human being? And especially a child like Hodel! If you could only see the letters she writes me. . . . They are doing very well, she tells me. He sits in prison and she works for a living. She washes clothes all day, reads books in between, and goes to see him once a week. She lives in the hope that very soon the pot will boil over, as they say, the sun will rise and everything will become bright. He will be set free along with many others like him, and then, she says, they will all roll up their sleeves and get to work to turn the world upside down. Well, what do you think of that? Sounds promising, doesn't it?

But what does the Lord do next? He is, after all, *"a gracious and merciful Lord,"* and He says to me, "Wait, Tevye, I will bring something to pass that will make you forget all your former troubles."

And so it was. It's a story worth hearing. I would not repeat it to anyone else, for while the pain is great, the disgrace is even greater. But how is it written? *"Shall I conceal it from Abraham?*—Can I keep any secrets from you?" Whatever is on my mind I shall tell you. But one thing I want to ask of you. Let it remain between you and me. For I repeat: the pain is great, but the disgrace—the disgrace is even greater.

How is it written in Perek? *"The Holy One, blessed be He, wished to grant merit to Israel—"* The Lord wanted to be good to Tevye, so He blessed him with seven female children, that is, seven daughters, each one of them a beauty, all of them good-looking and charming, clever and healthy and sweet-tempered—like young pine trees! Alas, if only they had been ill-tempered and ugly as scarecrows, it might have been better for them, and certainly healthier for me. For what use is a fine horse, I ask you, if you have to keep it locked up in a stable? What good are beautiful daughters if you are stuck away with them in a forsaken corner of the world, where you never see a live person except for Anton Poperilo, the village mayor, or the clerk Fyedka Galagan, a young fellow with a long mane of hair and tall peasant boots, or the Russian priest, may his name be blotted out?

I can't bear to hear that priest's name mentioned, not because I am a Jew and he is a priest. On the contrary, we've been on friendly terms for a number of years. By that I don't mean that we visit at each other's homes or dance at the same weddings. I only mean that when we happen to meet we greet each other civilly: "Good morning." "Good day. What's new in the world?"

I've never liked to enter into a discussion with him, for right away the talk would turn to this business of *your God* and *my God.* Before he could get started I would recite a proverb or quote him a passage from the Bible. To which he replied that he could quote me a passage from the Bible also, and perhaps better than I, and he began to recite the Scriptures to me, mimicking the sacred language like a Gentile: "*Berezhit bara alokim*—In the beginning the Lord created the Heavens. . . ." Then I told him that we had a folktale, or a *medresh* to the effect that. . . . "A *medresh*" he interrupted me, "is the same as *Talmud*," and he didn't like *Talmud*, "for *Tal-mud* is nothing but sheer trickery." Then I would get good and angry and give him what he had coming. Do you think that bothered him? Not in the least. He would only look at me and laugh and comb his long beard with his fingers. There is nothing in the world, I tell you, so maddening as a person who doesn't answer when you abuse him. You shout and you scold, you are ready to burst a gut, and he stands there and smiles. . . . At that time I didn't understand what that smile of his meant, but now I know what was behind it. . . .

Well, to return to my story. I arrived at home one day—it was toward evening—and whom should I see but the clerk Fyedka standing outside with my Chava, that's my third daughter, the one next to Hodel. When he caught sight of me, the young fellow spun around quickly, tipped his hat to me, and was off. I asked Chava, "What was Fyedka doing here?"

"Nothing," she said.

"What do you mean nothing?"

"We were just talking."

"What business have you got talking with Fyedka?" I asked.

"We've known each other for a long time," she said.

"Congratulations!" I said. "A fine friend you've picked for yourself."

"Do you know him at all?" she asked. "Do you know who he is?"

"No," I said, "I don't know who he is. I've never seen his family tree. But I am sure he must be descended from a long and honorable line. His father," I said, "must have been either a shepherd or a janitor or else just a plain drunkard."

To this Chava answered, "Who his father was I don't know and I don't care to know. All people are the same to me. But Fyedka himself is not an ordinary person, of that I am sure."

"Tell me," I said, "what kind of person is he? I'd like to hear."

"I would tell you," she said, "but you wouldn't understand. Fyedka is a second Gorky."

"A second Gorky? And who, may I ask, was the first Gorky?"

"Gorky," she said, "is one of the greatest men living in the world today."

"Where does he live," I asked, "this sage of yours, what is his occupation and what words of wisdom has he spoken?"

"Gorky," she said, "is a famous author. He is a writer, that is, a man who writes books. He is fine and honest and true, a person to be honored. He also comes from plain people, he was not educated anywhere, he is self-taught . . . here is his portrait." Saying this, she took a small photograph from her pocket and handed it to me.

"So this is he," I said, "this sage of yours, Reb Gorky? I can swear I have seen him somewhere before, either at the baggage depot, carrying sacks, or in the woods hauling logs."

"Is it a crime then if a man works with his hands? Don't you yourself work with your hands? Don't all of us work?"

"Yes, yes," I said, "you are right. We have a certain proverb which says, *'When thou eatest the labor of thine own hands*—If you do not work, you shall not eat.' But I still don't understand what Fyedka is doing here. I would be much happier if you were friends at a distance. You mustn't forget *'Whence thou camest and whither thou goest*—Who you are and who he is.'"

"God created all men equal," she said.

"Yes, yes," I said, "God created Adam in his own image. But we mustn't forget that each man must seek his own kind, as it is written: *'From each according to his means. . . .'*"

"Marvelous!" she cried. "Unbelievable! You have a quotation for everything. Maybe you also have a quotation that explains why men have divided themselves up into Jews and Gentiles, into lords and slaves, noblemen and beggars?"

"Now, now, my daughter, it seems to me you've strayed to the *'sixth millennium.'*" And I explained to her that this had been the way of the world since the first day of Creation.

"And why," she wanted to know, "should this be the way of the world?"

"Because that's the way God created the world."

"And why did God create the world this way?"

"If we started to ask why this, and wherefore that, *'there would be no end to it*—a tale without end.'"

"But that is why God gave us intellects," she said, "that we should ask questions."

"We have an old custom," I told her, "that when a hen begins to crow like a rooster, we take her away to be slaughtered. As we say in the morning blessing, *'Who gave the rooster the ability to discern between day and night. . . .'*"

"Maybe you've done enough jabbering out there," my wife Golde called out from inside the house. "The *borscht* has been standing on the table for an hour and he is still out there singing Sabbath hymns."

"Another province heard from! No wonder our sages have said, *'The fool hath seven qualities.—*A woman talks nine times as much as a man.' We are discussing important matters and she comes barging in with her cabbage *borscht*."

"My cabbage *borscht*," said Golde, "may be just as important as those 'important matters' of yours."

"Mazel-tov! We have a new philosopher here, straight from behind the oven. It isn't enough that Tevye's daughters have become enlightened, now his wife has to start flying through the chimney right up into the sky."

"Since you mention the sky," said Golde, "I might as well tell you that I hope you rot in the earth."

Tell me, Mr. Sholom Aleichem, what do you think of such crazy goings-on on an empty stomach?

Now let us, as they say in books, leave the prince and follow the fortunes of the princess. I am speaking of the priest, may his name and memory be blotted out. Once toward nightfall I was driving home with my empty milk cans—I was nearing the village—when whom should I see but the priest in his cast-iron *britzka* or carriage, approaching from the other direction. His honor was driving the horses himself, and his long, flowing beard was whipped about by the wind.

"What a happy encounter!" I thought to myself. "May the bad luck fall on his head."

"Good evening," he said to me. "Didn't you recognize me, or what?"

"It's a sign that you will get rich soon," I said, lifted my cap and was about to drive on. But he wouldn't let me pass. "Wait a minute, Tevel, what's your hurry? I have a few words to say to you."

"Very well. If it's good news, then go ahead," I said. "But if not, leave it for some other time."

"What do you mean by some other time?" he asked.

"By some other time, I mean when the Messiah comes."

"The Messiah," said he, "has already come."

"That I have heard from you more than once," I said. "Tell me something new, little father."

"That's just what I want to tell you. I want to talk to you about yourself, that is, about your daughter."

At this my heart almost turned over. What concern could he have with my daughter? And I said to him, "My daughters are not the kind, God forbid, that need someone to do the talking for them. They can manage their own affairs."

"But this is the sort of thing she can't speak of herself. Someone else has to speak for her. It's a matter of utmost importance. Her fate is at stake."

"And who, may I ask, concerns himself with the fate of my child? It seems to me that I am still her father, am I not?"

"True," he said, "you are her father, but you are blind to her needs. Your child is reaching out for a different world, and you don't understand her, or else you don't wish to understand her."

"Whether I don't understand her, or don't wish to understand her, is beside the point. We can argue about that sometime if you like. But what has it got to do with you, little father?"

"It has quite a lot to do with me," he said, "for she is now under my protection."

"What do you mean she is under your 'protection'?"

"It means she is now in my care."

He looked me straight in the eye as he said this and stroked his long, flowing beard with his fingers.

"What!" I exclaimed. "My child is in your care? By what right?" I felt myself losing my temper.

He answered me very calmly, with a little smile. "Now don't start getting excited, Tevel. We can discuss this matter peaceably. You know that I am not, God forbid, your enemy, even though you are a Jew. As you know, I am very fond of the Jewish people, even though they are a stiff-necked race. And my heart aches for them because in their pride they refuse to admit that we mean everything for their own good."

"Don't speak to me of our own good, little father," I said, "for every word that comes from your lips is like a drop of poison to me—it's like a bullet fired straight at my heart. If you are really the friend you say you are, I ask only one thing of you—leave my daughter alone."

"You are a foolish person," he said to me. "No harm will come to your daughter. She is about to meet with a piece of great good luck. She is about to take a bridegroom—and such a bridegroom! I couldn't wish a better fate to one of my own."

"Amen," I said, forcing a laugh, though inside me burned all the fires of hell. "And who, may I ask, is this bridegroom, if I may have the honor of knowing?"

"You must be acquainted with him," he said. "He is a gallant young man, an honest fellow and quite well-educated, though he is self-taught. He is very much in love with your daughter and wants to marry her, but cannot because he is not a Jew."

"Fyedka!" I thought to myself, and the blood rushed to my head, and a cold sweat broke out all over my body, so that I could barely sit upright in my cart. But show him how I felt? Never. Without replying I picked up the reins, whipped my horse, and *"departed like Moses."* I went off without as much as a fare-thee-well.

I arrived at home. What a scene greeted me! The children all lying with their faces buried in pillows, weeping; my Golde weaving around the house like a ghost. I looked for Chava. Where is Chava? She is nowhere to be found. I didn't ask where she was. I knew only too well. Then it was that I began to feel the tortures of a soul that is damned. I was full of rage and I didn't know against whom. I could have turned on myself with a whip. I began yelling at the children, I let out all my bitterness toward my wife. I couldn't rest in the house, so I went outside to the barn to feed my horse. I found him with one leg twisted around the block of wood. I took a stick and began laying it into him, as though I were going to strip off his skin and break his bones in half. "May you burn alive, you *schlimazel*. You can starve to death before I will give you as much as an oat. Tortures I will give you and anguish and all the ten plagues of Egypt. . . ."

But even as I shouted at him I knew that my horse did not deserve it; poor innocent creature, what did I have against him? I poured out some chopped straw for him, went back to the house and lay down. . . . My head was ready to split in two as I lay there thinking, figuring, arguing with myself back and forth. What could it all mean? What was the significance of all this? *"What was my sin and what my transgression?"* How did Tevye sin more than all the others that he should be punished thus above all the others? *"'Oh, Lord Almighty, what are we, and what is our life?'* What sort of cursed creature am I that you should constantly bear me in mind, never let any plague that comes along, any blight or affliction, pass me by?"

As I lay there torturing myself with such thoughts, I heard my wife groaning and moaning beside me. "Golde," I said, "are you sleeping?"

"No," she said. "What is it?"

"Nothing," I said. "Things are bad with us, very bad. Maybe you can think of what's to be done."

"You ask me what's to be done. Woe is me, how should I know? A child gets up in the morning, sound and fresh, gets dressed, and falls on my neck, kissing and hugging me, and weeping all the time, and she won't tell me why. I thought that, God forbid, she had lost her mind. I asked her, 'What's the matter with you, daughter?' She didn't say a word, but ran out for a while to see to the cows, and disappeared. I waited an hour, two hours, three hours. Where is Chava? There is no Chava. Then I said to the children, 'Run over and take a look at the priest's house. . . .'"

"How did you know, Golde, that she was at the priest's house?"

"How did I know? Woe is me. Don't I have eyes in my head? Am I not her mother?"

"If you do have eyes in your head, and if you are her mother, why did you keep it all to yourself? Why didn't you tell me?"

"Tell you? When are you at home that I can tell you anything? And if I do tell you something, do you listen to me? If a person says anything to you, you answer him with a quotation. You drum my head full of quotations and you've done your duty by your children."

After she finished I could hear her weeping in the dark. "She is partly right," I thought to myself, "for what can a woman understand of such matters?" My heart ached for her; I could not bear to listen to her moaning and groaning. "Look here, Golde," I said, "you are angry because I have a quotation for everything. I have to answer you even that with a quotation. It is written: *'As a father has mercy on his children.'* This means that a father loves his child. Why isn't it written: *'As a mother has mercy on her children'?* For a mother is not the same as a father. A father can speak differently with his child. You will see— tomorrow I will go and speak to her."

"I hope you will get to see her, and him also. He is not a bad man, even if he is a priest. He has compassion in his heart. You will plead with him, get down on your knees to him, maybe he will have pity on us."

"Whom are you talking about?" I said. "That priest? You want me to bow down to the priest? Are you crazy or out of your head? *'Do not give*

Satan an opening,' it is said. My enemies will never live to see that day."

"What did I tell you?" she said. "There you go again."

"Did you think," I said, "that I would let a woman tell me what to do? You want me to live by your womanish brains?"

In such talk the whole night passed. At last I heard the first cock crow. I got up, said my morning prayers, took my whip with me, and went straight to the priest's house. A woman is nothing but a woman. But where else could I have gone? Into the grave?

Well, I arrived in the priest's yard and his dogs gave me a royal welcome. They leaped at me and tried to tear off my coat and sink their teeth into my calves to see if they liked the taste of a Jew's flesh. It was lucky that I had taken my whip along. I gave them this quotation to chew on—*"Not a dog shall bark."* Or, as they say in Russian: *"Nehai sobaka daram nie breshe."* Which means, "Don't let a dog bark for nothing."

Aroused by the barking and the commotion in the yard, the priest came running out of his house and his wife after him. With some effort they drove off the happy throng that surrounded me and invited me to come in. They received me like an honored guest and got ready to put on the samovar for me. I told the priest it wasn't necessary to put on the samovar; I had something I wanted to say to him in private. He caught on to what I meant and motioned to his spouse to please be so kind as to shut the door on the outside.

When we were alone I came straight to the point without any preambles, and asked him first of all to tell me if he believed in God. Then I asked him to tell me if he knew what it felt like to be parted from a child he loved. And then I asked him to tell me what, according to his interpretation, was right and what was wrong. And one more thing I wanted him to make clear for me. What did he think of a man who sneaked into another man's house, and began tearing it apart, turning beds, tables, and chairs—everything, upside down.

Naturally he was dumbfounded by all this, and he said to me, "Tevel, you are a clever man, it seems to me, and yet you put so many questions to me and you expect me to answer them all at one blow. Be patient and I shall answer them one at a time, the first question first and the last question last."

"No, dear little father," I said. "You will never answer my questions. Do you know why? Because I know all your answers beforehand. Just tell me this: is there any hope of my getting my child back, or not?"

He leaped up at this. "What do you mean getting her back? No harm will come to your daughter—just the opposite."

"I know," I said. "I know. You want to bring her a piece of great good luck. I am not speaking of that. I only want to know where my child is and if I can see her."

"Everything, yes," he said, "but that, no."

"That's the way to talk," I said. "Come to the point. No mincing of words. And now good-bye. May God repay you in equal measure for everything you have done."

I came home and found Golde lying in bed all knotted up like a ball of black yarn. She had no more tears left to weep. I said to her, "Get up, my wife, take off your shoes, and let us sit down and mourn our child as God has commanded. *'The Lord hath given and the Lord hath taken away.'* We are neither the first nor the last. Let us imagine that we never had a daughter named Chava, or that like Hodel she went off to the ends of the earth. God is All-Merciful and All-Good. He knows what He is doing."

As I said this I felt the tears choking me, standing like a bone in my throat. But Tevye is not a woman. Tevye can restrain himself. Of course, you understand, that's only a way of speaking. First of all, think of the disgrace! And second, how can I restrain myself when I've lost my child, and especially a child like Chava. A child so precious to us, so deeply embedded in our hearts, both in her mother's and mine. I don't know why she had always seemed dearer to us than any of the other children. Maybe because as a baby she had been so sickly, and we had gone through so much with her. We used to stay up whole nights nursing her, and many a time we snatched her, literally snatched her, from the jaws of death, breathed life into her as you would into a tiny crushed chick. For if God wills it, He makes the dead come to life again, as we say in Hallel: *"I shall not die, but I will live.*—If you are not fated to die, you will not die." And maybe we loved her so because she had always been such a good child, so thoughtful and devoted, both to her mother and me. Now I ask you, how could she have done this thing to us?

Here is the answer: first of all, it is fate. I don't know about you, but as for me, I believe in Providence. Second, it was witchcraft. You may laugh at me, and I want to tell you that I am not so misguided as to believe in spirits, elves, and such nonsense. But I do believe in witchcraft, in the evil eye. For what else could it have been? Wait, listen to the rest of the story, and you will agree with me.

Well, when the Holy Books say, *"Perforce you must live.—*Man does not take his own life—" they know what they are talking about. There is no wound so deep that it does not heal in time; there is no sorrow so great that you do not forget it eventually. That is, you do not forget, but what can you do about it? *"Man is likened to a beast.—*Man must work, man must till the earth in the sweat of his brow." And so we all went to work. My wife and children got busy with the pitchers of milk, and I took to my horse and wagon and *"the world continued in its course—*the world does not stand still." I told everyone at home to consider Chava as dead. There was no more Chava. Her name had been blotted out. Then I gathered up some dairy stuff—cheese and butter and such, all fresh merchandise—and set off for Boiberik to visit my customers in their *dachas.*

I arrived in Boiberik and I was met with great rejoicing. "How are you, Reb Tevye?" "Why don't we see you anymore?" "How should I be?" I told them. *"'We renew our days as of old.—*I am the same *schlimazel* as always.' One of my cows just dropped dead." They appeared surprised. "Why do so many miracles happen to you, Reb Tevye?" And they began questioning me, wanting to know what kind of cow it was that had dropped dead, how much she had cost, and if I had many cows left. They laughed and joked and made merry over me as rich people will make merry over a poor man and his troubles, when they have just eaten their fill and are in a good mood, and the weather is perfect, sunny and warm and balmy, just the weather to drowse in. But Tevye is the sort of person who can take a joke even at his own expense. I would sooner die on the spot than let them know how I felt.

When I got through with my customers, I set out for home with my empty milk cans. As I rode through the woods I slackened the horse's reins, let him nibble at will, and crop a blade of grass now and then. I let my thoughts roam at will also. I thought about life and death, this world and the next, what the world is altogether about, what man has been created for, and other such things. Anything to drive my gloom away, to keep from thinking about Chava. But just as if to spite me she kept creeping in among my thoughts.

First she appeared before me in her own image, tall, lovely, blooming, like a young tree. Then I saw her as a little baby, sick and ailing, a frail little nestling, snuggled in my arms, her head drooping over my shoulder. "What do you want, Chaveleh? Something to suck on? A piece of candy?" And for the moment I forgot what she had done to me and my heart went out to her in longing. Then I remembered and a great anger seized me. I burned with anger against her and against him and against the whole world, but mostly against myself because I wasn't able to forget her, even for a minute. Why couldn't I forget her, why couldn't I tear her out of my heart completely? Didn't she deserve to be forgotten?

For this, I thought, Tevye had to be a Jew among Jews, to suffer all his life long, to keep his nose to the grindstone, bring children into the world—in order to have them torn from him by force, to have them fall like acorns from a tree and be carried away by the wind and by smoke. I thought to myself, "It's like this: a tree grows in the forest, a mighty oak with outspread branches, and an ignorant lout comes along with an axe and chops off a branch, then another and another. What is a tree without branches, alas? Go ahead, lout, chop down the whole tree and let there be an end. . . . What good is a naked oak in the forest?"

In the midst of these thoughts I suddenly became aware that my horse had stopped. What's the matter? I lift up my eyes and look. It is she, Chava. The same as before, not changed at all; she is even wearing the same dress. My first impulse was to jump off the wagon and take her in my arms. But something held me back. "What are you, Tevye? A woman? A weakling?" I pulled in my horse's reins. "Giddap, *schlimazel*." I tried to go to the right. I look—she is also going to the right. She beckons to me with her hand as though to say, "Stop a while, I have something to tell you."

Something tears at my insides, something tugs at my heart. I feel myself going weak all over. Any moment I will jump off the wagon. But I restrain myself, pull the horse's reins in, and turn left. She also turns left. She is looking at me wildly, her face is deathly pale. What shall I do? Should I stop or go on? And before I know what's happened, she's got the horse by the bridle and is saying to me, "Father, I will sooner die on the spot before I let you move another step. I beg you, father, listen to me."

"So," I think to myself, "you want to take me by force. No, my dear, if that's what you are trying to do, I see that you don't know your father very well." And I began whipping my horse with all my might. The horse obeys me, he leaps forward. But he keeps moving his ears and turning his back. "Giddap," I tell him. "*'Judge not the vessel but its contents.—* Don't look where you aren't supposed to.'" But do you think that I myself wouldn't like to turn my head and look back at the place where I left her standing? But Tevye is not a woman. Tevye knows how to deal with the Tempter.

Well, I don't want to drag my story out any longer. Your time is valuable. If I have been fated to suffer the punishments of the damned after death, I surely have expiated all my sins already. If you want to know about the tortures of hell that are described in our Holy Books, ask me. I can describe them all to you. All the rest of the way, as I drove, I thought I could hear her running after me, calling, "Listen, father, listen to me." A thought crossed my mind, "Tevye, you are taking too much upon yourself. Will it hurt you if you stop and listen to her? Maybe she has something to say that is worth hearing. Maybe—who can tell—she is regretting what she has done and wants to come back to you. Maybe she is being badly treated and wants you to save her from a living hell." Maybe and maybe and maybe . . . And I saw her as a little child once more and I was reminded of the passage: *"As a father has mercy on his children . . . "* To a father there is no such thing as a bad child. I blamed myself and I told myself, *'I do not deserve to be pitied*—I am not worthy of the earth I walk upon.'

"What are you fuming and fretting for?" I asked myself. "Stubborn mule, turn your wagon around and go back and talk to her. She is your own child." And peculiar thoughts came into my mind. What is the meaning of Jew and non-Jew? Why did God create Jews and non-Jews? And since God did create Jews and non-Jews, why should they be kept apart from each other and hate each other, as though one were created by God and the other were not? I regretted that I wasn't as learned as some men so that I could arrive at an answer to this riddle. . . .

And in order to chase away these painful thoughts I began to chant the words of the evening prayer: *"Blessed are they who dwell in Thy house, and they shall continue to praise Thee. . . ."* But what good was this chanting when inside of me a different tune was playing? *Chava*, it went. *Cha-va.* The louder I recited the prayer, the plainer the word *Chava* sounded in my own ears. The harder I tried to forget her, the more vividly she appeared before me, and it seemed to me that I heard her voice calling, "Listen, father, listen to me." I covered my ears to keep from hearing her voice and I shut my eyes to keep from seeing her face, and I started saying *Shimenesre* and didn't know what I was saying. I beat my breast and cried aloud, *"For we have sinned,"* and I didn't know for what I was beating my breast.

I didn't know what I was saying or doing. My whole life was in a turmoil, and I myself was confused and unhappy. I didn't tell anyone of my meeting with Chava. I didn't speak about her to anyone and didn't ask anyone about her, though I knew quite well where they lived and what they were doing. But no one could tell from my actions. My enemies will never live to see the day when I complain to anyone. That's the kind of man Tevye is.

I wonder if all men are like me, or if I am the only crazy one. For instance, let us imagine—just suppose it should happen—if I tell you this, you won't laugh at me? I am afraid that you will laugh. But just let us suppose that one fine day I should put on my Sabbath gabardine and stroll over to the railway station as though I were going away on the train, going to see them. I walk up to the ticket window and ask for a ticket. The ticket seller asks me where I want to go. "To Yehupetz," I tell him. And he says, "There is no such place." And I say, "Well, it's not my fault then." And I turn myself around and go home again, take off my Sabbath clothes and go back to work, back to my cows and my horse and wagon. As it is written: *"Each man to his labor*—The tailor must stick to his shears and the shoemaker to his last."

I see that you are laughing at me. What did I tell you? I know what you're thinking. You're thinking that Tevye is a big imbecile. . . . That's why I say: *"Read to this part on the great Sabbath before Passover,"* meaning, it's enough for one day. Be well and happy and write me often. And don't forget what I asked you. Be silent as the grave concerning this. Don't put what I told you into a book. And if you should write, write about someone else, not about me. Forget about me. As it is written: *"And he was forgotten*—" No more Tevye the Dairyman!

Translated by Frances Butwin

Get Thee Out

GREETINGS TO YOU, Mr. Sholom Aleichem, heartiest greetings. I've been expecting you for a long time and wondering why I didn't see you anymore. I kept asking, *"Where are you?"* as God once asked of Adam, and I was told that you have been traveling all over the world, visiting faraway countries—*"the one hundred and twenty-seven provinces of Ahasheurus,"* as we say in the *Megillah.*

But you are looking at me strangely. You seem to be hesitating and wondering, "Is it he, or isn't it he?" It is he, Mr. Sholom Aleichem, it is he, your old friend Tevye in person. Tevye the Dairyman, the very same as before, but not a dairyman any longer. Just an ordinary, everyday Jew, and greatly aged, as you can see. And yet I am not so old in years. As we say in the *Haggadah:"I look like a man of seventy.*—I am still far from seventy." Then why should my hair be so white? Believe me, dear friend, it's not from joy. My own sorrows are partly to blame and partly the sorrows of all Israel. For these are difficult times for us Jews—hard, bitter times to live in.

But that isn't what's troubling you, I can see. The shoe pinches on the other foot. You must have remembered that I told you good-bye once, as I was about to leave for Palestine. Now you are thinking, "Here is Tevye, just back from the Holy Land," and you are eager to know what's going on in Palestine—you want to hear about my visit to Mother Rachel's Tomb, to the Cave of Machpelah, and the other holy places. Wait, I will set your mind at rest; I will tell you everything, if you have the time and would like to hear a strange and curious tale. Then listen carefully, as it is written: *"Hear ye!"* And when you have heard me out,

179

you yourself will admit that man is nothing but a fool and that we have a mighty God who rules the Universe.

Well, what portion of the Bible are *you* studying this week in the synagogue? *Vaikro?* The first portion of Leviticus? I am on a different portion entirely—on *Lech-lecho* or *Get thee out.* I have been told, *"Get thee out*—get a move on you, Tevye—*out of thy country*—leave your own land—*and from thy father's house*—the village where you were born and spent all the years of your life—*to the land which I will show thee*—wherever your two eyes lead you." That's the lesson I am on now. And when was I given this lesson to study? Now that I am old and feeble and all alone in the world, as we say on Rosh Hashanah: *"Do not cast me off in my old age."*

But I am getting ahead of my story. I haven't told you about the Holy Land yet. What should I tell you, dear friend? It is indeed a *"land flowing with milk and honey,"* as the Bible tells us. The only trouble is that the Holy Land is over there and I am still here—*outside of the Promised Land.* He who wrote the *Megillah* or Book of Esther must have had Tevye in mind when he had Esther say, *"If I perish, I perish."* I have always been a *schlimazel*, and a *schlimazel* I will die. There I stood, as you remember, with one foot practically in the Holy Land. All I had to do was to buy a ticket, get on a ship, and I'm off. But that isn't the way God deals with Tevye. He had something different in store for me. Wait and you will hear.

You may remember my oldest son-in-law, Mottel Kamzoil the tailor from Anatevka. Well, our Mottel goes to sleep one night in the best of health, and never gets up. Though I shouldn't have said he was in the *best* of health. How could he be, a poor workingman, alas, sitting day and night *"absorbed in study and worship of God,"* meaning that he sat in a dark cellar day and night bent over a needle and thread, patching trousers. He did this so long that he got the coughing sickness, and he coughed and coughed until he coughed out his last piece of lung. Doctors couldn't help him, medicines didn't do any good, nor goats' milk, nor honey and chocolate. . . . He was a fine boy, the salt of the earth; it's true, he had no learning, but he was an honest fellow, unassuming, and without any false pretensions. He loved my daughter with all his heart, sacrificed himself for the children—and he thought the world of me!

And so we conclude the text with: *"Moses passed away."* In other words, Mottel died, and he left me with a millstone around my neck.

Who could begin to think about the Holy Land now? I had a Holy Land right here at home. How could I leave my daughter, a widow with small children and without any means of support? Though if you stop to think, what could I do for her, an old man like me, a sack full of holes? I couldn't bring her husband back to life or return the children's father to them. And besides, I am only human myself. I would like to rest my bones in my old age, take life easy, find out what it feels like to be a human being. I've done enough hustling and bustling in my lifetime. Enough striving after the things of this world. It's time to begin thinking about the next world. I had gotten rid of most of my goods and chattels, sold my cows and let my horse go quite some time ago. And all of a sudden in my old age I have to become a protector of orphans and provide for a family of small children. But that isn't all. Wait. More is coming. For when troubles descend on Tevye, they never come singly. The first one always brings others trailing after it. For instance, once when a cow of mine died, didn't another one lie down and die the very next day? That's how God created the world and that's how it will remain. There is no help for it.

Do you remember the story of my youngest daughter Beilke and her great good fortune? How she caught the biggest fish in the pond, the contractor Padhatzur who had made a fortune in the war and was looking for a beautiful young bride—how he sent Ephraim the Matchmaker to me, how he met my daughter and fell in love with her, how he begged for her on his knees, threatened to kill himself if he couldn't have her, how he was ready to take her just as she was, without any dowry, and showered her with gifts from head to foot, with gold and diamonds and jewels? It sounds like a fairy tale, doesn't it? The wealthy prince, the poor maiden, the great palace. But what was the end of this beautiful tale? The end was a sorry one. May God have pity on us all! For if God wills it, the wheel of fortune can turn backwards and then everything begins to fall buttered side down as we say in Hallel: *"Who raiseth up the poor out of the dust."* And before you can turn around— Crash! *"That looketh down low upon heaven and upon the earth—* everything is shattered into little pieces."

Thus God likes to play with us human beings. That's how he played with Tevye many times, raising him up, and casting him down, like Jacob ascending and descending the ladder. And that is what happened to Padhatzur. You remember his great riches, his airs and pretensions, the splendor of his mansion in Yehupetz with its dozen servants and thousand clocks and mirrors. What do you think was the outcome of all this? The outcome was that he not only lost everything and had to sell all his clocks and mirrors and his wife's jewels, but went bankrupt in the bargain, and made such a sorry mess of everything that he had to flee the country and become a fugitive. . . . He went to where the holy Sabbath goes. In other words, he ran off to America. That's where all the unhappy souls go, and that's where they went.

They had a hard time of it in America at first. They used up what little cash they had brought with them, and when there was nothing more to chew on, they had to go to work, both he and she, doing all kinds of back-breaking labor, like our ancestors in Egypt. Now, she writes me, they are doing quite well, God be thanked. Both of them are working in a stocking factory, and they manage to "scrape up a living," as they say in America. Here we call it being one jump ahead of the poorhouse. It's lucky for them, she tells me, that there are just the two of them—they have neither chick nor child. "*That too is for the best.*"

And now, I ask you, doesn't he deserve to be cursed with the deadliest curses, I mean Ephraim the Matchmaker, for arranging this happy match? Would she have been any worse off if she had married an honest workingman the way Tzeitl did, or a teacher, like Hodel? You might argue that their luck didn't hold out either, that one was left a young widow, and the other had to go into exile with her husband. But these things are in God's hands. Man cannot provide against everything. If you want to know the truth, the only wise one among us was my wife Golde. She looked about her in good time and decided to leave this miserable world forever. For tell me yourself, rather than to suffer the "*pain of bringing up children,*" the way I have suffered, isn't it better to lie in the earth and be eaten by worms? But how is it said: "*Perforce thou must live.*—Man doesn't take his own life, and if he does, he gets rapped on the knuckles for it." But in the meanwhile we have strayed off the path. "*Let us return to our original subject.*"

Where were we? At section *Lech-lecho* or *Get thee out*. But before we go on with section *Lech-lecho* I shall ask you to stop with me for a moment at section *Balak*. It has always been a custom since the world began to study *Lech-lecho* or *Get thee out* first, and *Balak* or the lesson of revenge later, but with me the custom was reversed and I was taught the lesson of *Balak* first and *Lech-lecho* afterward. And I was drilled in *Balak* so thoroughly that I want you to hear about it. The lesson may come in handy some day.

This happened some time ago, right after the war, during the troubles over the Constitution when we were undergoing *"salvations and consolations"*—that is, when reprisals were being carried out against Jews. The pogroms began in the big cities, then spread to the small towns and villages. But they didn't reach me, and I was sure that they never would reach me. Why? Simply for this reason: that I have lived in the village for so many years and had always been on such friendly terms with the peasants. I had become a *"Friend of the Soul and Father of Mercy"* to them—"Brother Tevel" was their best friend. Did they want advice? It was, "do as brother Tevel says." Did one of them need a remedy for fever? It was, "Go to Tevel." A special favor? Also to Tevel. Tell me, why should I worry about pogroms and such nonsense when the peasants themselves had assured me many times that I had nothing to be afraid of? They would never permit such a thing, they told me. *"But it came to pass."*—Listen to my story.

I arrived home from Boiberik one evening. I was still in my prime then—how do you say it?—in high feather. I was still Tevye the Dairyman who sold milk and cheese and butter. I unhitched my horse, threw him some oats and hay, and before I had time to wash my hands and say a prayer before eating, I take a look outside and see the yard is full of peasants. The whole village has turned out to see me, from the Mayor, Ivan Poperilo, down to Trochin the Shepherd, and all of them looking stiff and strange in their holiday clothes. My heart turned over at the sight. What holiday was this? Or had they come like Balaam to curse me? But at once I thought, "Shame on you, Tevye, to be so suspicious of these people after all these years you have lived among them as a friend." And I went outside and greeted them warmly, "Welcome, friends, what have you come for? And what good news do you bring?" Then Ivan Poperilo the Mayor stepped forward and said, right out, without any apologies, "We came here, Tevel, because we want to beat you up."

"What do you think of such talk? Tactful, wasn't it? It's the same as speaking of a blind man as *sagi nohor* or having too much light. You can imagine how I felt when I heard it. But to show my feelings? Never. That isn't Tevye's way. *"Mazel-tov,"* I said, "why did you get around to it at this late date? In other places they've almost forgotten all about it." Then Ivan said very earnestly, "It's like this, Tevel, all this time we've been trying to decide whether to beat you up or not. Everywhere else your people are being massacred, then why should we let you go? So the

Village Council decided to punish you, too. But we haven't decided what to do to you. We don't know whether to break a few of your windowpanes and rip your featherbeds, or to set fire to your house and barn and entire homestead."

When I heard this, my spirits really sank low. I looked at my guests standing there, leaning on their sticks and whispering among themselves. They looked as though they really meant business. "If so," I said to myself, "it's as David said in the psalm, '*For the waters are come in even into the soul.*' You are in bad trouble, Tevye. '*Do not give Satan an opening.*—You cannot trifle with the Angel of Death.' Something has to be done."

Well, why should I spin out the story any longer? A miracle took place. God sent me courage and I spoke up boldly. "Listen to me, gentlemen. Hear me out, dear friends. Since the Village Council has decreed that I must be punished, so be it. You know best what you do, and perhaps Tevye has merited such treatment at your hands. But do you know, my friends, that there is a Power even higher than your Village Council? Do you know that there is a God in Heaven? I am not speaking now of *your* God or *my* God, I am speaking of the God who rules over all of us, who looks down from Heaven and sees all the vileness that goes on below. It may be that He has singled me out to be punished through you, my best friends. And it may be just the opposite, that He doesn't want Tevye to be hurt under any circumstances. Who is there among us who knows what God has decreed? Is there one among you who will undertake to find out?"

They must have seen by then that they couldn't get the best of Tevye in an argument. And so the Mayor, Ivan Poperilo, spoke up. "It's like this, Tevel, we have nothing against you yourself. It's true that you are a Jew, but you are not a bad person. But one thing has nothing to do with the other. You have to be punished. The Village Council has decided. We at least have to smash a few of your windowpanes. We don't dare not to. Suppose an official passed through the village and saw that your house hadn't been touched. We would surely have to suffer for it."

That is just what he said, as God is my witness. Now I ask you, Mr. Sholom Aleichem, you are a man who has traveled all over the world. Is Tevye right when he says that we have a great and merciful God?

Well, that's the end of section *Balak*. They came to curse and remained to bless. Now let us turn to section *Lech-lecho* or *Get thee out*. This lesson was taught to me not so long ago and in real earnest. This time fine speeches didn't help me; orations didn't avail me. This is exactly the way it happened. Let me tell it to you in detail, the way you like to have a story told. . . .

It was in the days of Mendel Beiliss, when Mendel Beiliss became our scapegoat and was made to suffer the punishments of the damned. I was sitting on my doorstep one day sunk in thought. It was the middle of summer. The sun was blazing and my head was splitting. "Lord, Lord," I thought, "what times these are! What is the world coming to? And where is God, the ancient God of Israel? Why is He silent? Wherefore does He permit such things to happen?" Wherefore and why and wherefore once more? And when you ask questions of God you begin to ponder about the universe and go on asking: What is this world? And the next world? And why doesn't the Messiah come? Wouldn't it be clever of him to appear at this very moment riding on his white horse? That would be a master stroke! It seems to me that he has never been so badly needed by our people as now. I don't know about the rich Jews, the Brodskys in Yehupetz for instance, or the Rothschilds in Paris. It may be that they never even give him a thought. But we poor Jews of Kasrilevke and Mazapevka and Zolodievka, and even of Yehupetz and Odessa, watch and wait and pray for him daily. Our eyes are strained from watching. He is our only hope. All we can do is hope and pray for this miracle—that the Messiah will come.

And while I am sitting there deep in such thoughts, I look up and see someone approaching, riding on a white horse. He comes riding up to my door, gets off, ties the horse to the post, and comes straight up to me. "*Zdrastoi*, Tevel," he says—"Greetings, Tevye." "Greetings to you, your honor," I answer him with a smile, though in my heart I am thinking, "*Haman approacheth.*—When you're waiting for the Messiah, the village constable comes riding." I stand up and say to him, "Welcome, your honor, what goes on in the world? And what good news do you bring?" And all this time I am quaking inside, waiting to hear what he has to say. But he takes his time. First he lights a cigarette, then he blows out the smoke, spits on the ground, and at last he speaks up. "How much time do you need, Tevel," he says, "to sell your house and all your household goods?"

I look at him in astonishment. "Why should I sell my house? In whose way is it?"

"It isn't in anybody's way," he says, "but I came to tell you that you will have to leave the village."

"Is that all?" I asked. "And how did I come to deserve such an honor?"

"I can't tell you," he says, "I am not the one who's sending you away. It's the provincial government."

"And what has the government against me?"

"Against you? Nothing. You aren't the only one. Your people are being driven out of all the villages, out of Zolodievka and Rabilevka, and Kostolomevka, and all the others. Even Anatevka, which up to now has been a town, has become a village and your people are being driven from there too."

"Even Lazer-Wolf the Butcher?" I asked. "And Naphtali-Gershon the Lame, and the *shochet* of Anatevka? And the rabbi?"

"Everybody, everybody." And he made a motion with his hand as though he were cutting with a scythe. I felt a little easier at this. How do we say it? "*The troubles of the many are a half-consolation.*" But anger at this injustice still burned inside of me. I said to him, "Is your honor aware of the fact that I have lived in this village much longer than you have? Do you know that in this corner of the world lived my father before me, and my grandfather and grandmother before him?" And I began naming all the different members of my family, telling him where each one had lived and where each one died. The constable heard me out, and when I had finished he said, "You are a clever Jew and you certainly know how to talk, but what good are these tales of your grandfather and grandmother to me? Let them enjoy their rest in Paradise. And you, Tevel, pack up your things and go, go to Berdichev."

That made me good and angry. It wasn't enough that you brought me this glad tidings, you Esau, you have to poke fun at me besides? "Pack up and go, go to Berdichev," he tells me. I couldn't let that pass. I had to tell him a thing or two. "Your honor," I said, "in all the years you have been constable here, have you ever heard the villagers complaining of Tevye? Has anyone ever accused Tevye of stealing from him, or robbing him, or cheating him in any way? Ask any of the peasants if I didn't live alongside them like the best of neighbors? How many times did I come to you yourself, your excellency, to plead in their behalf, to ask you not to ill-treat them?"

I could see that this was not to his taste. He got up, crushed his cigarette between his fingers, threw it away, and said to me, "I have no time to waste on idle chatter. I received a paper and that's all I know. Here, sign right here. They give you three days to sell your household goods and get out of the village."

When I heard this, I said, "You give me three days to get out, do you? For this may you live three years longer '*in honor and in riches*.' May the Almighty repay you many times over for the good news you brought me today." And I went on, laying it on thick, as only Tevye can do. After all, I thought to myself, what did I have to lose? If I had been twenty years younger and if my Golde had still been alive, if I were the same Tevye the Dairyman as in ancient days, I would have fought to the last drop for my rights. But "*what are we and what is our life*?" What am I today? Only half of my former self, a broken reed, a shattered vessel. "Ah, dear God, our Father," I thought, "why do you always have to pick on Tevye to do Thy will? Why don't you make sport of someone else for a change? A Brodsky, for instance, or a Rothschild? Why don't you expound to them the lesson *Lech-lecho*—Get thee out? It seems to me that it would do them more good than me. In the first place they would find out what it means to be a Jew. In the second place they would learn that we have a great and mighty God."

But this is all empty talk. You don't argue with God; you don't give Him advice on how to run the world. When He says, "*Mine is the heaven and mine is the earth*," it means that He is the master and we have to obey Him.

I went into the house and said to my daughter, "Tzeitl," I said, "we are going away. We are moving to town. We've lived in the country long enough. '*He who changes his place changes his luck*.' Start packing right away, get together the pillows and featherbeds, the samovar and the rest. . . . I am going out to see about selling the house. An order came for us to get out of here in three days and not leave a trace behind us."

When she heard this, my daughter burst into tears. The children took one look at her and burst out crying, too. What shall I tell you? There was weeping and wailing and lamentation, just like on Tisha-Bov, the day on which we mourn the destruction of the Temple. I lost my temper and began scolding. I let out all the bitterness that was in my heart to my daughter. "What have you got against me?" I said. "Why did you have to start blubbering all of a sudden like an old cantor at the first *Sliches?* What do you think I am—God's favorite son? Am I the only one chosen for this honor? Aren't other Jews being driven out of the villages, too? You should have heard what the constable had to say. Even your Anatevka which has been a town since the world began has, with God's help, become a village too, all for the sake of the few Jews who live there. Are we any worse off than all the others?"

That is how I tried to comfort her. But after all she is only a woman. She says to me, "Where will we turn, father? Where will we go looking for towns?" "You talk like a fool," I said to her. "When God appeared to our great-great-grandfather Abraham and said to him, 'Get thee out of this country,' did Abraham question Him? Did he ask, 'Where shall I turn?'" God told him, 'Go unto the land which I will show thee.' Which means, ' . . . into the four corners of the earth.' And we too will go wherever our eyes lead us, where all the other Jews are going. Whatever happens to all the children of Israel, that will happen to this son of Israel. And why should you consider yourself luckier than your sister Beilke who was once a millionairess? If 'scraping up a living' in America with her Padhatzur is good enough for her, this is good enough for you. Thank God that we at least have the means with which to go. We have a little saved up from before, a little from the sale of the cows, and I will get something from the house. A dot and a dot make a full pot. *'That too is for the best.'* And even if we had nothing at all, we would still be better off than Mendel Beiliss."

And so I persuaded her that we had to go. I gave her to understand that when the constable brings you a notice to leave, you can't be hoggish and refuse to go. Then I went off to the village to dispose of my house. I went straight to Ivan Poperilo the Mayor because I knew that he'd had his eye on my house for a long time. I didn't give him any reasons or explanations, I am too smart for that. All I said was, "I want you to know, Ivan, my friend, that I am leaving the village." He asked me why. I told him that I was moving to town because I wanted to live among Jews. "I am not so young anymore," I said. "Who knows—I might die suddenly." Says Ivan to me, "Why can't you die right here? Who is preventing you?" I thanked him kindly and said, "You'd better do the dying here, instead of me. I will go and die among my own people. I want you to buy my house and land. I wouldn't sell it to anyone else, but to you I will."

"How much do you want for your house?" he asked me. "How much will you give me?" I said. Again he asked, "How much do you want?" And I countered with, "How much will you give?" We bargained and dickered thus until at last we agreed on a price, and I took a substantial down payment from him then and there, so that he wouldn't change his mind. I am too smart for that. And that was how in one day I sold out all my belongings, turning everything into good money, and went off to hire a wagon to move the few odds and ends that were left.

And now something else happened to me, something that can happen only to Tevye. Be patient a little longer and I will tell you in a few words.

Well, I arrived at home, and found not a house, but a ruin—the walls bare, stripped of everything, almost weeping in their nakedness. The floor was piled with bundles and bundles and bundles. On the empty hearth sat the cat, looking as lonely and forsaken as an orphan. My heart was squeezed tight and tears stood in my eyes. If I weren't ashamed before my daughter, I would have wept. After all, this was my homestead. This village was the nearest thing to a fatherland that I could ever have. Here I had grown up, here I had struggled all my days, and now all of a sudden in my old age, I am told, "Get thee out." Say what you will, it's a heartache. But Tevye is not a weakling. I restrained myself and called out in a cheerful voice, "Tzeitl, where are you? Come here." And Tzeitl came out of the other room, her eyes red and her nose swollen with weeping. "Aha," I thought, "my daughter has started wailing again like an old woman on the Day of Atonement. That's women for you— crying at the least excuse. Tears must come cheap to them. Fool," I told her, "why are you crying again? Aren't you being silly? Just stop and consider the differences between you and Mendel Beiliss." But she wouldn't listen to me. "Father," she said, "you don't know why I'm crying."

"I know very well why you're crying," I told her. "Why shouldn't I know? You are crying because you will miss your home. You were born in this house, this is where you grew up, and your heart aches at having to leave it. Believe me, if I were someone else and not Tevye, I'd be kissing these bare walls myself and embracing these empty shelves. . . . I would be down on my knees on this earth. For I shall miss every particle of it as much as you. Foolish child! Look, do you see the cat sitting there like an orphan on the hearth? She is nothing but an animal, a dumb creature, and yet she too is to be pitied, left alone and forsaken without a master."

"I want to tell you that there is someone who is more to be pitied," said Tzeitl.

"For instance?" I asked.

"For instance, we are going away and leaving a human being behind us, alone and forsaken."

"What are you talking about?" I said to her. "What's all this gibberish? Which human being? Whom are we forsaking?"

"Father," she said, "I am not talking gibberish. I am speaking of Chava."

When she uttered that name it was just as if she had thrown a red-hot poker at me, or hit me over the head with a club. I began yelling at her, "Why bring Chava up all of a sudden? How many times have I told you that she is dead?"

Do you think she was taken aback by this outburst? Not in the least. Tevye's daughters are made of sterner stuff. "Father," she said, "don't be angry with me. Remember what you yourself told me many times, that it is written that one human being must have pity on another the way a father has pity on his child."

Did you ever hear anything like this before? I grew even more furious with her. "Don't speak to me of pity," I shouted. "Where was her pity when I lay like a dog in front of the priest while she was probably in the next room and no doubt heard every word? Where was her pity when her mother lay covered with black in this very room? Where was she then? And all the sleepless nights I spent? And the heartache I suffered and that I suffer to this day when I remember what she did to me and for whom she forsook me? Where is her pity for me?" My throat went dry, my heart began to hammer, and I couldn't speak anymore.

Do you think that Tevye's daughter didn't find an answer to this too? "You yourself have said, father, that God forgives him who repents."

"You speak of repentance, do you? It's too late for that. The limb which has been torn from the tree must wither. The leaf which has fallen to the ground must rot. Don't say another word to me about it. '*Here ends the lesson for the great Sabbath before Passover.*'"

When she saw that she was getting nowhere with talk, and that Tevye was not the person to be won over with words, she fell on my neck and began kissing my hands and pleading with me, "May I suffer some evil, may I die here on the spot, if I let you cast her off as you cast her off that time in the forest when she came to plead with you and you turned your horse around and fled."

"What are you hanging around my neck for? What do you want from me? What have you got against me?" I cried.

But she wouldn't let me go. She clasped my hands in hers and went on, "May I meet with some misfortune, may I drop dead, if you don't forgive her, for she is your daughter the same as I am."

"Let me go. She is not my daughter. My daughter died long ago."

"No, father, she didn't die, and she is your daughter still. The moment she found out that we were being sent away she swore to herself that if we were driven out, she would go too. That's what she told me herself. Our fate is her fate, our exile is her exile. You have the proof right here. This bundle on the floor is hers," said Tzeitl, all in one breath the way we recite the names of the ten sons of Haman in the *Megillah*, and pointed to a bundle tied in a red kerchief. Then she opened the door to the next room and called out, "Chava."

And what shall I tell you, dear friend? There she stood in the doorway, Chava herself in the flesh, tall and beautiful, just as I remembered her, except that her face looked a little drawn and her eyes were somewhat clouded. . . . But she held her head up proudly and looked straight at me. I looked back at her, and then she stretched out both arms to me and said one word—"Father."

Forgive me if tears come to my eyes when I recall these things. But don't think that Tevye weakened and wept in front of his daughters. I have my pride to consider. But you understand that in my heart I felt differently. You are a father yourself and you know how you feel, when a child of yours, no matter how it has erred, looks into your eyes and says, "Father." But then again I remembered the trick she had played on me, running off with that peasant Fyedka Galagan. I remembered the priest, may his name and memory be blotted out, and poor Golde lying dead on the ground. . . . How can you forget such things? How can you forget?

And yet she was still my child. The same old saying came to me: "*A father has mercy on his children*." How could I be so heartless and drive her away when God Himself has said, "*I am a long-suffering God and slow to anger*"? And especially since she had repented and wanted to return to her father and to her God? Tell me yourself, Mr. Sholom Aleichem, you are a wise man who writes books and gives advice to the whole world. What should Tevye have done? Should he have embraced her and kissed her and said as we do on Yom Kippur at *Kol Nidre:* "*I have forgiven thee in accordance with thy prayers.*—Come to me, my child?" Or should I have turned my back on her as I did once before and said, "Get thee out. Go back where you came from"? Try to put yourself in my place and tell me truthfully what would you have done? And if you don't want to tell me right away, I will give you time to think it over. Meanwhile I must go—my grandchildren are waiting for me. And grandchildren, you must know, are a thousand times dearer and more precious than one's own children. *Children and grandchildren*—that's something to reckon with!

Farewell, my friend, and forgive me if I have talked too much. You will have something to write about now. And if God wills it, we shall meet again. For since they taught me the lesson—*Lech-lecho*, Get thee out—I have been wandering about constantly. I have never been able to say to myself, "Here, Tevye, you shall remain." Tevye asks no questions. When he is told to go, he goes. Today you and I meet here on this train; tomorrow we might see each other in Yehupetz; next year I might be swept along to Odessa or to Warsaw or maybe even to America. Unless the Almighty, the Ancient God of Israel, should look about him suddenly and say to us, "Do you know what, my children? I shall send the Messiah down to you." Wouldn't that be a clever trick? In the meanwhile, good-bye, go in good health, and give my greetings to all our friends and tell them not to worry. Our ancient God still lives!

Translated by Frances Butwin

Part
Three

From Mottel
the Cantor's Son

My Brother Elye's Drink

For One Ruble A Hundred!
Earn one hundred rubles a month or more
Just by knowing what's in this book.
The cost is one ruble plus postage.
Hurry! Offer Limited!

This my brother Elye read in a newspaper somewhere just after he'd left his father-in-law's table. He left the table not because his time was up—he'd been promised three whole years' board and got not even three-quarters of one year—but because of tragedy. Yoine the baker went bankrupt and instead of a rich man was now a poor one. How bad luck fell upon him I've already told you, and I don't tell a story twice unless asked. This time even asking won't help because I'm so busy. I'm earning money. I carry about a drink my brother Elye makes with his own hands. He found out how to do this from a book that costs only a ruble. With this book you can earn a hundred rubles a month and more. My brother Elye, soon as he read that such a book existed, sent off the ruble—our last—and told our mother she had nothing more to worry about: "Mama, thank God, we're saved. We'll have," he said, pointing to his throat, "money up till here."

"What's this?" she asked. "You got a job?"

"Better than that," my brother answered as his eyes lit up, apparently from joy. He told her to wait a few days until a book came.

"What book?"

"Wait, you'll see," he answered and asked if she could use a hundred rubles a month. She answered that she could live on one hundred a year so long as she could count on that amount. My brother Elye told her that her reach was too small and went off to the post office. He goes there every day now to inquire about the book. Over a week has passed and still no book. In the meantime, says my mother, we still have to live. "You can't just spit out your soul," she says. How you spit out a soul I have no idea.

Two

All right, calm down—the book's here. No sooner did we unpack it than my brother Elye sat down to read it. And he found there any number of different ways to make money. You can earn a hundred rubles by making the best inks or the best black shoe polish; or by driving off mice, roaches, and other pests; or by manufacturing liqueurs, sweet brandies, lemonade, soda water, kvass, and still cheaper drinks.

My brother Elye settled for the last idea. First of all because he'd earn over one hundred rubles a month. It says so, right there in the book. Second, that way you can keep away from ink, shoe polish, mice, roaches, and other pests. The only problem is which drink to choose. For liqueurs and brandies you need Rothschild's fortune. For lemonade and soda water you need a kind of machine, some kind of stone that costs who knows how much. What's left is kvass. Kvass is the kind of drink that costs little and sells fast, especially in a summer as hot as this. From kvass, you should know, our kvass-maker, Boruch, has grown rich. He makes bottled kvass. It's known all over the world. It shoots out of the bottle like a cannon. How it shoots nobody knows. That's Boruch's secret. They say he puts something in there that makes it shoot. Some say it's a raisin, others say hops. When summer comes along he doesn't have enough hands. He makes a bundle.

The kvass that my brother Elye makes from the formula isn't bottled and doesn't shoot. Ours is a completely different kind. How it's made I can't tell you. My brother Elye doesn't let anyone near him when he makes it. He pours in water—everyone sees that; but when he mixes in the other ingredients he shuts himself off in my mother's alcove. Neither

I, nor my mother, nor my sister-in-law Brokhe has the right to be near. Nevertheless, if you promise to keep a secret I'll tell you what's in the drink. I know the ingredients. There's lemon peel, loose honey, something called cream of tartar that's more sour than vinegar; the rest is water. There's more water than anything. The more water, the more kvass. This is stirred well with a plain stick—that's what the book says— and the drink is ready. After that it's poured into a big pitcher and you throw in a piece of ice. Ice is the main ingredient. Without ice the drink is nothing. This I know without the book. I once tried kvass without ice and thought I'd drop dead.

When the first barrel of kvass was ready it was decided I'd be the one to go out peddling it in the street. Who else? My brother Elye—it's beneath his dignity; he's a married man. My mother—definitely not. We'd never allow her to go around with a pitcher, yelling, "Kvass! Kvass! Everybody, kvass!" So it was decided this should be my work. I felt the same way. I was thrilled at the news. My brother Elye began showing me what to do. I'm to hold the pitcher in one hand by a rope, the glass in the other hand. In order to get people to stop I'm supposed to sing loudly:

> *Ice cold kvass*
> *a kopek a glass;*
> *cool and sweet*
> *can't be beat.*

I told you long ago that I have a nice voice, a soprano inherited from my father, he should rest in peace. I sang out heartily and turned the call upside down.

> *Cool as a beet*
> *can't be sweet;*
> *ice in a glass*
> *try some kvass.*

I don't know what was so great—my singing or the kvass, or maybe the day was so hot, but I sold the first pitcher in half an hour and came home with almost a ruble. My brother Elye handed the money over to my mother and immediately filled up another pitcher. He said if I could make five or six trips a day we'd take in exactly a hundred rubles for the month. Figure it out for yourself. Take off the four Saturdays plus expenses and you'll know the profits. The drink itself costs very little, almost nothing. The big expense is ice. This means we have to sell a pitcher very fast in order to use the ice for a second pitcher, a third, and so on. In fact, I have to run. Boys chase me, a whole gang of ruffians. They make fun of the way I sing. Who cares? I try to sell out the pitcher fast and run home for another. I don't even know how much I made the first day. I only know that my brother Elye, my sister-in-law Brokhe, and my mother all praised me to the skies. For supper I got a piece of watermelon, a slice of cantaloupe, two prunes, and, of course, kvass— we drink it like water. At bedtime, my mother prepared my mattress on the floor and asked if, Heaven forbid, my feet hurt. My brother Elye laughed at her and he said I'm the kind of boy that nothing ever hurts. "Of course," I said. "Proof is, if you want, I'll go right out in the middle of the night with the pitcher."

The three of them laughed at my ingenuity, but in my mother's eyes I saw tears. That's an old story: a mother has to cry. What I'd like to know is if all mothers cry all the time or only mine.

Three

Business keeps pouring in. One day's hotter than the next. It's roasting. People pass out from the heat; children fall like flies. If not for kvass we'd burn up. Without exaggeration, I make ten rounds a day with the pitcher. My brother Elye looked into the barrel and saw it was just about empty. He got the idea of adding a pail of water. He isn't the first to come up with the plan; I did it before him. I've played the trick several times. Almost every day I go over to our neighbor Peshe and give her a glass of our drink. Her husband, Moishe the bookbinder, I give two glasses. He's a good person. The children also get glasses; let them also know how good a drink we make. I give the blind uncle a glass to taste; poor man, he's a cripple. All my friends I give kvass, free. In order not to lose anything I add water to the pitcher. For each glass I give away free I add two of water. We do the same at home. If, for example, my brother Elye takes a glass of kvass, he immediately pours in some water. He's right: it's a sin to waste a kopek. My sister-in-law Brokhe drinks a few glasses of kvass—she's crazy about my brother Elye's kvass—she pours in water. My mother occasionally tastes some kvass—she has to be asked; by herself she won't take it—she pours in water. In other words, we never lose a drop of merchandise, and we make good money, knock on wood. My mother's paid off a lot of debts, redeemed a few big pledges, like the bedding. A table's come into the house; a chair. Friday night and Saturday we have meat, fish, and white *khale*. I've been promised for the holidays, God willing, a new pair of boots. Seems no one's as well off as we.

Four

Go be a prophet and guess that a tragedy would hit us—that our drink would spoil, good only for the slop pail. As if that wasn't enough, I was almost arrested. Listen to this. One day I wandered over to our neighbor Peshe with the pitcher of kvass. Her whole bunch took kvass and so did I. I was now short some twelve-thirteen glasses, so I went to the room where the water was. Apparently, instead of the drinking pail I found the washtub. I poured fifteen-twenty glasses into the pitcher and went to the street with a new tune I made up:

> *Drink, one and all*
> *only the best—*
> *the taste of Heaven*
> *for me and the rest.*

A man stops me, pays his kopek, and orders a glass of kvass. He drinks the whole glass and wrinkles up his face. "Hey! What kind of drink is this?" he wants to know. Let him talk to himself; I have two customers waiting for kvass. One sips half a glass, and the other a third. They pay, spit out, and walk away. Another brings the glass to his lips, tries it, and says it tastes of soap and is salty. The next one looks at the glass and gives it back with the comment, "What is this stuff?"

"A drink," I say.

"A drink? It's a stink, not a drink."

Somebody else comes over, tastes, and throws the glassful in my face. Soon I'm surrounded by a circle of men, women, and children. They talk, they gesticulate, they get excited. A Russian policeman sees the gathering and comes over to ask what's going on. They tell him. He looks into my pitcher and demands a taste. He drinks, spits, and gets ready to murder me: "Where'd you get the soapsuds?"

"From a book," I answer. "It's my brother's work; he makes the stuff himself."

"Who's your brother?" he asks.

"My brother Elye," I answer.

"Which Elye?" he asks.

"Idiot! Don't mention your brother," several men call to me half in Hebrew. Suddenly there's yelling, buzzing, and shouting. People keep coming over. The policeman holds me by the hand and wants to take us—me and the drink—to the police station. The noise grows. "An orphan! A poor orphan!" I hear from all sides. My heart tells me I'm in a tight squeeze. I look pleadingly about me: "Jews, have mercy." They want to slip the policeman a coin. He refuses. An old man with mischievous eyes calls out to me in Hebrew, "Mottel, tear your hand away from the *goy*. Lift your feet and beat it." I tear my hand away, pick up my feet, and run home. I fall into the house half-dead.

"Where's the pitcher?" my brother asks.

"In the police station," I answer and fall upon my mother in tears.

We Flood the World with Ink

What a fool I was. Just because I sold bad kvass I thought they'd chop off my head. Nothing happened. I got scared for nothing. Is is all right for Yente to sell lard as goose fat? For Gedalye the butcher to sell the town unkosher meat? That's how our neighbor Peshe comforted my mother. My mother's strange that way: she takes everything to heart.

That's what I like about my brother Elye. He didn't get flustered when we got burned with the kvass. So long as he has the book, everything's all right. He bought a book for a ruble. It's called, *For One Ruble A Hundred*. He's learning it by heart. There are endless formulas there for making money. He knows almost all of them. He knows how to make ink, how to make shoe polish, how to drive off mice, roaches, and other pests. He figures he'll try ink; it's a good item. These days everybody's learning how to write. He's gone to Yudel the scribe to check how much ink he uses. "A fortune in ink," he answers. Yudel the scribe has some sixty girls he's teaching to write. Boys don't study with him; they're afraid. He hits—with a ruler over the hand. Girls, he's not supposed to hit; spanking, certainly not. It upsets me I wasn't born a girl. First of all, I wouldn't have to pray every day. I'm sick of it; every day the same thing. Then I could be rid of *cheder*. I'm in school half a day. I study very little but I make it up in slaps. From the teacher? No, from his wife. What does she care if I take care of the cat? You should see that poor cat. She's always hungry. She whines quietly (pardon the comparison) like a human being. It tears my heart out. They have no pity. What do they want from the cat? If she sniffs at someone they scream "Scat!" and she runs off where no one can find her. They don't let her keep her head up. Once she disappeared for a few days, and I was sure, God forbid, she'd dropped dead. Finally, she came with a litter . . . All right, I'm coming back to my brother Elye's ink.

Two

My brother Elye says the world isn't what it used to be. There was a time, he says, when if you wanted to make ink you'd buy ink balls, crumble them, cook them over the flame—who knows how long— and throw them in copper-water. To make the ink shiny you added a bit of sugar—a complex procedure. Today, he says, it's a pleasure. You buy a powder at the druggist's and a bottle of glycerine. Mix it with water, a second over the fire—and it's ready. That's what my brother says. He went to the druggist and came home with a bunch of powders and a whole bottle of glycerine. Then he shut himself up in the alcove and did something. What, I don't know; it's a secret. To him everything's a secret. If he wants my mother to get him a bowl he calls her over quietly and says, "Mama, the bowl." He mixed the powders and the glycerine in a big pot bought for the occasion. The pot he then shoved into the oven and asked my mother quietly to bolt the house door. We couldn't imagine what was going on. Every minute my mother glanced at the oven. She was probably afraid the stove would explode. Next we rolled the kvass barrel into the room. Then we slowly took the pot out of the oven and gently poured the mixture into the barrel. After that we began adding water. When the barrel was over half full my brother Elye cried "Enough!" and sat down with the book, *For One Ruble a Hundred*. He read and then asked quietly for a new pen and a fresh sheet of white paper—"the kind you write appeals on," he whispered into my mother's ear. Then he dipped the pen into the barrel and scribbled on the white paper in curlicues and zigzags. He showed the scribble first to my mother, then to my sister-in-law Brokhe. Both stared, then called out, "It writes."

Soon he returned to the business of adding water. After a few pails he raised his hands: "Enough." He dipped the pen into the barrel, again scribbled on the white paper, and carried it to my mother, then to my sister-in-law Brokhe. Both looked at the paper: "It writes."

We did all this several times until the barrel was full; there was no more room for water. My brother Elye raised his hands: "Enough," and the four of us sat down to eat.

Three

After dinner we began pouring the ink into bottles, bottles my brother Elye had dragged together from the whole world. All kinds of bottles and flasks, large and small. Beer bottles, wine bottles, kvass bottles, whiskey bottles, plain bottles. He bought used corks to save money, a new funnel, and a tin dipper to pour ink from the barrel into the bottles. Once more he whispered to my mother to bolt the door, and the four of us threw ourselves into the work. The work was well divided. My sister-in-law Brokhe rinsed the bottles and handed them to my mother. My mother checked inside each bottle and handed it on to me. I had to put the funnel into the bottle with one hand and steady the bottle with the other. My brother Elye had only to fill the dipper from the barrel and empty it into the funnel. The work went well and was lots of fun. There was one problem—ink spots on the fingers, the hand, the nose, and whole face. Both of us, my brother Elye and I, grew black as demons. This was the first time I ever saw my mother laugh. My sister-in-law Brokhe, naturally, almost split her sides. My brother Elye hates to be laughed at. He yelled at my sister-in-law Brokhe and asked what she was laughing at. She only laughed harder. He gets angrier; she laughs harder. She falls into spasms which could kill her. This goes on until my mother pleads for a halt and tells the two of us to go wash. My brother has no time for washing; he thinks of nothing but bottles. We've used up the bottles. There aren't any more bottles. Where do you get more bottles? He calls over my sister-in-law Brokhe, gives her money, and whispers in her ear that she should go for bottles. She listens, stares at him, and bursts out laughing. He gets angry and whispers the same secret in my mother's ear. My mother goes for bottles and the rest of us pour water into the barrel. Not all at once, of course, but gradually. After each pail my brother lifts his hands and says to himself, "Enough." Then he dips the pen in the barrel, writes on the white paper, and says to himself, "It writes."

This went on until my mother returned with a load of bottles. Then we started all over, pouring ink from barrel to bottle, until we were once more without bottles.

"How long will this go on?" my sister-in-law Brokhe called out.

"Don't give us the evil eye," my mother shot back as my brother Elye gave Brokhe an angry look as if to say, "Maybe you're my wife, but God pity us, you're still a fool."

Four

How much ink we have I can't tell you. I'm afraid there may be a thousand bottles. What's the result of all this? There's nowhere to put the bottles. My brother Elye's been everywhere; selling them retail, one by one, is hopeless. That's what my brother Elye told our neighbor's husband, Moishe the bookbinder. When Moishe came over and saw, knock on wood, all our bottles, he grew frightened and stopped short. He turned to my brother and a strange conversation took place between them.

"What are you frightened of?"

"What do you have in the bottles?"

"What do you expect? Wine?"

"What wine? It's ink."

"If you know, why do you ask?"

"What are you going to do with so much ink?"

"Drink it."

"No, seriously. You're going to sell retail, too?"

"You think I'm crazy? When I sell, it'll be ten bottles, twenty bottles, fifty bottles. That's called wholesale. Do you know what wholesale is?"

"I know what wholesale is. Who'll you sell it to?"

"To the rabbi."

My brother went around to the storekeepers. He went to one large dealer who told him to bring a sample bottle—he wants to look it over. To another he brought a sample, but the man wouldn't touch it; it had no label. A bottle has to have a pretty label with a design. My brother told him "I don't make designs; I make ink."

"All right, go on making ink."

He tried Yudel the scribe. Yudel the scribe answers with something nasty. He's already bought enough ink for the whole summer. "How many bottles?" my brother Elye asked.

"Bottles?" Yudel the scribe answered. "I bought one bottle of ink and I'll use it up till it's done. Then I'll buy another one." This is what you get from a teacher. First he says he uses a fortune in ink. Now he says he uses a bottle that doesn't run out. My brother Elye was beside himself. What is he going to do with so much ink? First he said he wouldn't sell ink retail, only in volume. Now he's changed his mind. I'd like to know what retail means.

Here's what it means. It won't hurt you to listen.

Five

My brother Elye got hold of a big sheet of paper. He sat down and wrote in large, prayer book letters:

> *Ink Sold Here*
> *Wholesale and Retail*
> *Low Cost and Good Quality*

The words "Low Cost" and "Good Quality" were written so large they occupied almost the whole sheet. When the writing dried he hung the paper outside the door. Lots of people passed by and stopped to stare. I saw them through the window. My brother Elye also looked through the window and cracked his knuckles, a sure sign he was upset. He said to me, "You know what? Stand by the door and listen to what they're saying."

He didn't have to coax me. I stood by the door and watched to see who stopped by and hear what they said. After half an hour I went back inside. My brother Elye came over and asked quietly, "Well?"

"Well, what?"

"What did they say?"

"Who?"

"The people passing by."

"They said it's written nicely."

"That's all?"

"That's all."

My brother Elye sighed. What's he sighing about? My mother asked the same question: "What are you sighing about, you silly child. Wait a bit. In one day you expect to sell the whole thing?"

"At least a beginning," he said with tears in his throat.

"Listen to me; don't be a fool. Wait, my child, with the help of God you'll have your start." That's what my mother said as she set the table. We washed and sat down to eat, the four of us squeezed among the bottles. The bottles make it horribly crowded in the house. As soon as we made the blessing over the bread a strange young man came running into the house. I know him; he's already engaged. His name's Kopel. His father is a tailor, a ladies tailor.

"You sell ink here?"

"Yes, what do you want?"

"I want a little ink."

"How much do you need?"

"Just a kopek's worth."

My brother Elye almost went crazy. If he hadn't been ashamed in front of my mother he'd have smacked Kopel the bridegroom and thrown him out of the house. Instead, he controlled himself and poured out a kopek's worth of ink. A quarter of an hour goes by and a girl comes in. I don't know her. She picks her nose and says to my mother, "You make ink here?"

"Yes, what do you want?"

"My sister wants to know if you'd lend her some ink. She has to send a letter to her fiancé in America."

"Who's your sister?"

"Bashe the seamstress."

"Ah, see how she's grown. Knock on wood. I didn't recognize you. Do you have an inkwell?"

"How would we have an inkwell? My sister asks maybe you have a pen. She'll write the letter to America and give you back the pen and ink."

My brother Elye is no longer at the table. He's in the alcove quietly pacing back and forth, looking down and biting his nails.

Six

"Why did you make so much ink? You want to supply the world with ink in case of a shortage?" That's what our neighbor's husband, Moishe the bookbinder, said to my brother. He has a way of throwing salt on wounds; otherwise, he's not such a bad person, just somewhat annoying. He likes to bore into your insides.

But my brother Elye gave it to him. He told him to take care of himself instead of mixing things up, like a Passover *Haggadah* together with penitential prayers. Moishe the bookbinder knows well what this dig means. Once he took on a job from a coachman. The coachman gave him a *Haggadah* to bind. A tragedy occurred: by mistake he bound a few pages of penitential prayers into the *Haggadah*. The coachman himself may not have caught his mistake, but the neighbors heard him singing, "The soul is yours; the body, your handiwork" instead of "Pour out your wrath." He confused Passover deliverance with High Holiday mournfulness.

This became a big joke. The next day the coachman came to our neighbor the binder and wanted to tear him in two. "Thief!" he cried. "What do you have against me? Why did you mix yeast with *matzo*— "The soul is yours" with the Passover *Haggadah*? I'm going to tear your insides out."

That year we really had a lively holiday.

Don't be upset that I've thrown in this story. I'm coming right back to our marvelous business ventures.

Aftermath of the Ink Flood

My brother Elye goes around completely confused. What do we do with the ink?

"Ink, again?" my mother asks.

"I'm not talking about ink!" my brother Elye says. "The devil with it. I'm talking about the bottles. There's money in the bottles. We've got to empty them and make money."

From everything he has to make money. Now we're stuck with having to throw out all that ink. Where do you do this? It's ridiculous.

"The only thing we can do," says my brother Elye, "is to wait till nightfall. At night it's dark; no one will see."

We hardly get through till nightfall. Out of spite, the moon shines like a lantern. When you really need the moon it shuts itself up. Now it's here; who sent for it? That's what my brother Elye says as we carry bottle after bottle to dump outside. Dumping it in one spot makes a river, so you're not supposed to spill the whole thing in one place. That's what my brother Elye says, and I listen to him. I keep looking for new spots. Every bottle, a different place. The neighbor's wall—splash. The neighbor's fence—splash. Two goats grazing in the moonlight—splash.

"Enough for now," my brother Elye says, and we go to bed. It's quiet and dark. Crickets chirp. The cat purrs behind the stove. A very lethargic cat; day and night she'd snuggle and nap. From outside the door comes the sound of quiet footsteps. Maybe it's a demon? My mother isn't asleep yet; she seems never to sleep. I always hear her cracking her fingers; moaning, groaning, and talking to herself. That's her nature. Every night she unburdens her heart a little, pouring out her troubles. Whom does she speak to? To God? She keeps groaning, "God, oh God."

Two

I'm still lying on my mattress on the floor and in my sleep I hear a lot of yelling. Familiar voices. Slowly I open my eyes and it's bright daylight. The sun's rays force their way in through the window. Somebody's calling me outside. I try to recall what happened yesterday.

Aha! Ink. I jump out of bed and dress quickly. My mother's in tears—when isn't she? My sister-in-law Brokhe is enraged, as usual. My brother Elye is in the middle of the room with his head down; maybe I can milk something out of him.

What's the story? There's not one story, but many. Our neighbors got up in the morning and the hoopla started—they were being murdered. One had a whole wall sprayed with ink; another a new fence. The third had two white goats now unrecognizably black. All this would have been tolerable if not for the slaughterer's stockings. His wife had hung his new pair of white stockings on our neighbor s fence and now they were ruined. Who asked her to hang the stockings on a strange fence? My mother offered to buy her a new pair if she'll only keep still. What about the wall? The fence? It's been agreed that my mother and sister-in-law Brokhe will respectfully stand with two brushes and a pail of whitewash to clean off the spots.

"It's lucky you have nice neighbors," our neighbor Peshe said to my mother. "If you'd thrown your ink into Menashe the doctor's garden, you'd find out there's a God on earth."

"Well," my mother answered, "even in bad luck you still need some good luck."

What does that mean?

Three

"This time I'll be smarter," my brother Elye says to me. "We'll take the bottles to the river when night comes."

Of course, sure as I'm alive. What can be smarter than that? All kinds of junk is dumped into the river. They do laundry there and they water horses; pigs wallow. I'm a good friend of the river. I've already described how I catch fish there. You can now understand how I couldn't wait to get to the river.

With nightfall we packed baskets full of bottles and began carrying them to the river. We emptied the ink, carried the bottles back home, and filled them up again. We did this all night. I haven't had such an enjoyable night in a long time. Imagine: the town's asleep, the heavens are covered with stars, the moon shines down into the river. Gloriously still, the river comes alive. After Passover, when the ice melts, it really goes wild. It puffs up, spreads out, overflows. Later on it gets smaller, narrower, and shallower. By summer's end it's quiet altogether; it naps. Something on the riverbed makes noises like "*Bul, bul, bul.*" A few frogs croak back from the other bank, "*Khwul, khwul.*" This is a joke, not a river. I can get from one side to the other without taking off my pants.

The river rose somewhat from our ink—a thousand bottles can't be sneezed at. To empty a thousand bottles we had to work like oxen. We dropped off to sleep half-dead and were awakened by my mother's cry, "You've darkened my days! What did you do to the river?"

It turns out we've damaged the whole town. The washerwomen have nowhere to do laundry; the coachmen, no place to water their horses; the water carriers—they're all after us. That's what my mother says. We're not going to wait for them. We don't want to see how water carriers collect their debts. My brother Elye and I pick ourselves up and hurry over to his friend Pinye. "They'll look for us there if they need us," says my brother Elye as he takes my hand and we hurry downhill to Pinye's. When we see each other again I'll tell you about my brother's friend Pinye. It's worth knowing him; he has very interesting ideas.

A Street Sneezes

You want to hear the latest? Mice. A whole week my brother Elye has been studying the book that teaches how to make money, *For One Ruble A Hundred.* He's learned, he says, how to drive out mice, roaches, and other pests. Rats, also. Let him in with his powder and that's the end of the mice. They run away; lots of them die; no more mice. How he does this, I don't know. It's a secret, a secret only he and the book know—no one else. He keeps the book in his breast pocket and the powder in a paper. The powder is reddish and finely ground. It's called hellebore.

"What's hellebore?"

"Turkish pepper."

"What is Turkish pepper?"

"I'll give you a 'what is.' Soon I'll break open the door with your head."

That's what my brother Elye says to me. He hates to be asked questions in the middle of work. I look on and keep quiet. I notice that besides the red powder there's another ingredient, but you have to be very careful with that one. "Poison," says my brother maybe a hundred times, to my mother, Brokhe, and me. Mainly, me, so I won't go near it—it's poison.

The first test we made on our neighbor Peshe's mice. You couldn't count the mice over there. You know that Peshe's husband is a bookbinder. His name is Moishe. He always has a room full of books. Mice love books—not books so much, but the glue that holds them together. Because of the glue they eat the whole book. This causes a lot of damage. They've eaten holes through a holiday prayer book, a brand new one, just at the word "King" which is written in especially large letters. They've cut off the leg of the "K." "Let me in here for just one night," my brother Elye pleaded with the bookbinder.

The bookbinder didn't want him. "I'm afraid you'll ruin my books."

"How'll I ruin the books?"

"How do I know? I'm just afraid; the books aren't mine."

So. Try to talk to a bookbinder. We finally persuaded him to let us in there for the night.

Two

The first night was not a success. We didn't catch a single mouse. My brother Elye said that's a good sign; the mice smelled the powder and ran away. The binder shook his head and smiled with one lip; he didn't seem to believe. Nevertheless, the word has spread through town that we chase mice. The rumor started with our neighbor Peshe. She went very early to the market and proclaimed all over town that we "get rid of mice like no one else." She's made us a name. With the kvass she did the same thing. And again with the ink—ink that can't be beat. But what good did her talking do if nobody needs ink? Mice are not the same as ink. Mice are everywhere; almost everyone has them. Every house has a cat, but what's the good of one cat against so many mice? Especially rats. Rats are about as afraid of a cat as Haman is of a *grager*.

Some say the cat is afraid of the rat. Like Bere the shoemaker. He tells such horrible tales about rats. He tells tall tales but even if half of what he says is true, that's enough. He claims rats ate his new pair of boots. He swears oaths that would convince even an apostate. He says he saw two huge rats come out of their lair and eat up a pair of boots before his eyes. It happened at night. He was afraid to get near them, they were so huge—as big as calves. He tried to drive them off from a distance. He whistled, stamped his feet, and screamed, "Kish, kish, kish, kish, kish." Nothing helped. He threw a boot heel at them; they just looked at him and went about their business. He sent a cat after them and they ate it. Nobody wanted to believe him, but if a person swears . . .

"Let me in for a night," my brother Elye says, "and I'll get rid of all your rats."

"With pleasure," answers Bere the shoemaker. "I'll even say, 'thank you.'"

Three

We sat all night at Bere's. Bere sat up, too. The stories he told! He talked about the Russian-Turkish War in which he'd served. He was in a place called Plevne. They used cannon. Have you any idea how much a cannon holds? One cannonball is bigger than a house, and a cannon shoots a thousand balls a minute. Satisfied? The ball as it flies makes a noise so loud it makes you deaf. Once Bere was standing guard—that's what he says; suddenly he heard an explosion—and he was lifted into the air, up very high, over the clouds, and the ball split into a thousand pieces. He was lucky he fell on a soft spot; otherwise, he'd have broken his head. My brother Elye listened and his eyebrows smiled; not he—his eyebrows. A weird smile. Bere the shoemaker didn't notice; he went on with his stories, one stranger than the next. We sat that way until dawn. Rats? Not a one.

"You're a magician," said Bere the shoemaker to my brother Elye, and goes around town telling everyone how we drove out all the rats with a magic word in one evening. He swears he himself saw how my brother Elye whispered something and all the rats came out of their lairs and ran down to the river. They swam to the other side and never came back.

Four

"You get rid of mice here?" People keep coming to ask us if we'd please come to drive off their mice with our magic formula. My brother Elye, however, is an honest man; he hates lies. He says he chases mice not with magic but with powder. He has a powder that makes the mice run away when they smell it.

"A powder; a curse. Who cares just so long as you get rid of the mice. How much does it cost?"

My brother Elye hates to bargain. He says he wants so much for the powder, so much for labor. Usually he says more each time; every day he raises the price. Actually, it's not he who raises the price but my sister-in-law. "Make up your mind," she said, "if you're going to eat pig, let the juice run down your beard. If you drive away mice, at least make money."

"And what about justice? Where's God?" my mother interrupted.

"Justice? Here's justice," Brokhe answered, pointing to the stove. "God?" she said, slapping her pocket. "Here's God."

"Brokhe! What are you saying? God forgive you," my mother shouted as she wrung her hands.

"Why are you wasting your time with a fool?" my brother Elye said. He was walking around the room pulling at his beard. He already has quite a beard; it grows like the devil. He pulls at it and it grows. It looks funny: there's growth on the neck but the face is smooth. Have you ever seen such a beard?

Another time my sister-in-law Brokhe would have made him pay dearly for calling her a fool. Now she's quiet because he's bringing in money. When he earns money he becomes somebody special to her. I've also become dearer because I help my brother. Usually she calls me a pest, a wretch, a misfit. Now she has a new name for me, "Mottele."

"Mottele, pass me my shoes."

"Mottele, get me a quart of water."

"Mottele, take out the garbage."

When you make money, people talk differently.

Five

The trouble with my brother Elye is he does everything in bulk. Kvass—by the barrel. Ink—a thousand bottles. Mouse poison—a sackful. Our neighbor's husband asked him why he needs so much and my brother blasted him.

If only they'd locked up the sack on a shelf somewhere. They all went away and left me with the sack. So what if I sat down on it to ride? It was a good rocking horse. Should I know the sack would split and something yellow would shoot out of it? It was the powder my brother Elye used for catching mice. It has a smell so sharp you could faint. I bent over to pick up the spillage and fell into a sneezing fit. A whole box of snuff would not have made me sneeze so much. I sneezed so long I had to run outside; maybe I'd stop. Not a chance. I ran into my mother. She saw me sneezing and asked why. I could answer only, "Achoo! Achoo!" and more "Achoo!"

"What's wrong with you?" she asked, wringing her hands. "Where did you get such a cold?" I couldn't stop sneezing and pointed to the house. She went inside and came back sneezing worse than I. My brother Elye came by and saw us sneezing. He asked what's wrong. My mother pointed to the house. He went inside and ran back out excited.

"Who opened the—achoo! Achoo! Achoo!"

It was a long time since I'd seen my brother Elye so angry. He lunged at me. It's lucky he was sneezing, otherwise I'd have left his hands a cripple.

My sister-in-law Brokhe came by and saw us holding our sides, sneezing. "What's the matter with you people? Why the sneezing all of a sudden?"

What could we tell her? Could we talk? We pointed to the house. She went inside, ran back out red as a flame, and fell upon my brother Elye. "What did I tell—achoo! Achoo! Achoo!"

Fat Peshe our neighbor arrived. She spoke but no one could answer. We pointed to the house. She went inside, ran back out. "What have you—achoo! Achoo! Achoo!" She threw her hands about.

Her husband the binder came out. He looked at us and laughed. "Where did this sneezing fit come from?"

"Please go—achoo! Achoo! Achoo!" we said to him and pointed to the house.

The binder went inside and immediately reappeared, laughing. "I know what's going on. I took a sniff. It's hell—achoo! Achoo! Clutching his sides he sneezed heartily. After each sneeze he'd spring and land on his toes, where he remained until the next sneeze; a sneeze and a jump, sneeze and a jump, and so on. Within half an hour all our neighbors, their uncles, aunts, cousins, and friends—the whole street from beginning to end—was sneezing.

Why did my brother Elye become so frightened? He was afraid, I guess, they'd all let out their anger on him for their sneezing. He took me by the hand and still sneezing, we took off downhill to his friend Pinye. It was an hour and a half before we could talk like human beings. My brother Elye told his friend Pinye the whole story. His friend Pinye listened carefully the way a doctor listens to a patient. When my brother finished, Pinye said, "So, show me the book."

My brother Elye took the book out of his breast pocket and handed it to his friend Pinye. His friend Pinye read the title page, "For One Ruble A Hundred. How to make from scratch with your own hands one hundred rubles a month and more. . . ." He took hold of the book and threw it into the burning stove. My brother Elye thrust his hand toward the fire. Pinye held him back. "Slowly; take it easy," he said.

Within a few minutes my brother Elye's book was nothing but a pile of ash. One piece of page remained unburned. Barely legible, it read, "Hellebore."

Translated by Gershon Freidlin

Bandits

"IS HE STILL SLEEPING?"

"Dead to the world!"

"Wake him up! Wake him up!"

"Leyb-gizzard-fricasee!"

"Beautiful dreamer wake unto me—"

"Open your eyes and who do you see?"

The minute I open my eyes, lift my head, and look around, I see the whole gang of wise guys, my friends from *cheder*. The window is open. I can see the light in their eyes and the bright morning sunlight pouring into the room along with their joy and laughter. I look around.

"Look at him staring."

"Caught in the act."

"Don't you know who we are?"

"Don't you remember? It's Lag Baomer!"

Oh, my! Lag Baomer? The words go through me like a bolt of lightning. I shoot out of bed. In half a second I am on my feet, and a minute later dressed, washed, and ready to go. I look for my mother. She is distracted with breakfast and the little kids.

"Mama, today is Lag Baomer."

"Have a good holiday. What do you want?"

"Give me something to contribute for the meal."

"What should I contribute? My aggravation? Or my headaches?"

So Mama says, but she is ready to give me something anyhow. We bargain: I ask for more, she gives less. I want two eggs. She says, bellyaches is what you'll get. I get mad; she slaps me. I cry; she makes peace with an apple. I want an orange. She says, "Are you crazy? What are you going to dream up next?"

My friends outside are ready to explode.

"Are you coming or not?"

"Leyb-gizzard-fricassee!"

"Let's get going. We're wasting time!"

"Quick as a bunny—"

"Sonny!"

I finally manage to work it out with Mama, grab my breakfast and my contribution to the meal, and race out, fresh, frisky, happy, to my friends. In the bright warm sunlight, we rush downhill all together to *cheder*.

Two

Cheder is sheer noise. It's like a market day, a hollering unto the heavens. Twenty mouths all talking at once. The table is covered with treats. We've never yet had a Lag Baomer meal like this one. We even have brandy and wine, thanks to our friend Berl Yossel, the vintner's son. He brought a bottle of brandy, good brandy too, and two bottles of wine, the best, Yossel the vintner's own product. His father gave him the brandy. The bottles of wine he took on his own.

"What do you mean, on his own?"

"Don't you get it, dummy? He took it off the shelf when no one was looking."

"Well, that means he stole it, doesn't it?"

"Genius! So what?"

"What do you mean, so what? What about Thou shalt not steal?"

"For the holiday meal, turkey!"

"It's okay to steal?"

"Naturally. Look at this mastermind over here!"

"Where does it say so?"

"He wants us to tell him where it says so."

"Tell him in The Book of Pralnik."

"In the chapter on Taking."

"On page Lamed Bim-Bom."

"On the New Moon of Kremenitz."

"Ha, ha, ha!"

"Quiet everyone! Mazepa's coming."

Suddenly everyone gets as still as the silent standing prayer. We sit around the table like model pupils, innocents, quiet, well-behaved children, treasures, can't count to two, owe our souls to God.

Three

Mazepa is our *rebbe*. His name is really Boruch Moshe, but since he's come down recently from Mazepevka, the town calls him the Mazepevker, and we *cheder* boys have shortened it and turned it into Mazepa—"dark and ugly." Generally, when students crown their *rebbe* with a lovely name like that, he has earned it. Let me present him to you.

Short, shrivelled, and skinny—a creep. Without a trace of a beard, mustache, or eyebrows. Not, God forbid, because he shaves, but just because they don't care to grow. They talked themselves out of it. But to compensate, he has a pair of lips on him, and oh my! a nose! A braided loaf, a horn, a *shofar!* And a voice like a bell, a lion's roar. How did a creature like him get such a terrifying voice? And where did he get his strength? When he grabs your arm with his skinny, cold fingers, you can see the world to come. And when he slaps you, you feel it for the next three days. He hates lengthy discussions. For the least thing, guilty or not guilty, he has one law: Lie down!

"*Rebbe!* Yossel Yankev Yossel's hit me."

"Lie down!"

"*Rebbe*, it's a lie! He kicked me in the side first."

"Lie down!"

"*Rebbe!* Chaim Berl Lappes stuck his tongue out at me."

"Lie down!"

"*Rebbe*, lies and falsehood! It was just the opposite. He gave me the high sign."

"Lie down!"

And you have to lie down. Nothing helps. Even redheaded Eli, who is already *Bar Mitzvah* and betrothed and wears a silver pocketwatch— you think he isn't beaten? Oh my, isn't he! Eli says that he'll regret those beatings. He says he'll pay Mazepa back with interest; he says he'll give him something to remember him by until he has grandchildren. That's what Eli always says after a whipping, and we answer:

"Amen. Hope so. From your mouth to God's ears."

Four

When we've finished saying morning prayers—with the *rebbe*, as usual (he never lets us pray by ourselves; he knows that without him we would skip more than half of it), Mazepa announces to us in his lion's voice: "Well, children, wash up and sit down to the feast, and when we finish the grace after eating, I'll let you go out walking."

Actually we're used to having our Lag Baomer feast on the other side of town, in the fresh air, on the bare grass under God's heaven, throwing crumbs to the birds to let them know too that it's Lag Baomer in the world. But with Mazepa you don't start negotiating. When Mazepa says, "Sit down," you sit. Or he might order you to lie down.

"Blessed be all who are sitting at the table," the *rebbe* says after we've made the blessing over bread.

"Join us," we say, for form's sake.

"Eat in good health," he says. "I don't want to eat yet, but I think I wouldn't mind making a blessing over something to drink. What's in that bottle over there? Brandy?" he says, and puts out a dry hand with thin fingers for the bottle of brandy. He pours himself a little, tastes it, and makes such a face that we have to be strong as iron not to burst out laughing.

"This is strong stuff! Whose is it?" he asks and takes a little more. "It's not bad liquor, to tell you the truth." And he takes a little more and toasts us.

"*L'chayim,* children, may God grant we live to celebrate again next year, and . . . and . . . and isn't there something to eat with this? Well, I'll wash, and in honor of Lag Baomer, I'll have a bite to eat with you."

What's happening to our *rebbe?* This isn't our Mazepa at all. He's in a good mood, talkative, his cheeks red as beets, his nose red, his eyes shiny, chewing, talking, and pointing to the bottles of wine.

"What kind of wine do you have there? It looks like Passover wine."

(He tastes and smacks his lips.) "One of a kind!" (Drinks.) "I'll tell you the truth, it's been a long time since I drank wine like this." (To Yossel the vintner's son, with a laugh.' "Devil take your father's cellar, heh, heh! I've seen the barrels at his place, countless barrels for wine and fruit of the vine, and made from pure raisins, too, heh, heh! *L'chayim*, children! May God make you honest, good Jews, and may you . . . may you . . . open the second bottle . . . Take a drop, why don't you take some? And drink *l'chayim*. May God grant . . . (he licks his lips and his eyes shut) . . . all . . . all good to all of Israel . . . "

Five

When he has finished eating and said grace, Mazepa's tongue gets tangled in his teeth. "So, we've observed the *mitzvah*, ha? The commandment of the Lag Baomer feast. Well, what next? Ha?"

"Now we're going for our walk."

"Ha? For your walk? Excellent. Where to?"

"To the Black Forest."

"Ha? To the Black Forest? That's excellent! I'm going with you. It's very good, very healthy, to go for a walk in the forest, because the forest . . . Ah, now I'm going to explain the nature of a forest to you."

And we set out all together, with the *rebbe* in our midst, for the other side of town. At the outset, we feel a bit uncomfortable having the *rebbe* with us. But M—, -um, Mum! And the *rebbe* walks along gesticulating and explaining the nature of the forest to us.

"The nature of a forest, you see, is that the One Above created it to be full of trees, and on them—the trees, that is—there would be branches, and the branches would be covered with leaves, green ones, and they would give off an aroma, a delightful smell, a wonderful mustardy scent . . ."

And meanwhile, the *rebbe* sniffs the wonderful mustardy scent, even though we are still far off from the forest and the odors aren't yet especially wonderful or mustardy.

"Ha? Why don't you say something?" the *rebbe* asks us. "Say something good, sing a song. Ha? I was once a boy, a wise guy like you, heh, heh. I also had a *rebbe*, like you, heh, heh."

That Mazepa was ever a wise guy like us, and had a *rebbe* like us, seems strange and weird to us, practically beyond belief. Mazepa—a wise guy? We look at each other and heh-heh silently, imagining Mazepa as a wise guy, and his *rebbe*, and how his *rebbe* used to . . . But we are afraid to think such things. . . . Only Eli dares to say it out loud, "*Rebbe,* did your *rebbe* beat you the way you beat us?"

"Ha? And how! Heh, heh . . . "

We look at the *rebbe* and at one another and understand each other. We help him laugh heh-heh until we are well on the other side of the town, in the wide open fields not far from the Black Forest.

Six

Out in the fields it is marvelous, a paradise. Sweet-smelling grass. White blossoms. Yellow motes. Wings light as air. The blue skullcap above, spreading without end. The forest before us dressed for a holiday. And in the trees the little birds hop from one branch to another and twitter. That's their way of welcoming us on our beloved holiday of Lag Baomer. We look for the shadow of a leafy tree, protection from the burning sun, and all sit down on the ground with our *rebbe* in the midst of us.

The *rebbe* is tired from the walk. He flings himself down on the ground and stretches out with his face up. His eyes close. His tongue gets tangled in his teeth, and he just about manages to say: "You are dear, golden chi-children . . . Jewish children . . . saints . . . I love you, and you love me . . . isn't that so? You l-love me?"

"Like a pain in the eye," Eli answers.

"Ha? I know that you l-love me . . . " the *rebbe* says to him.

"May God love you as much," Eli says.

We get frightened and say, "For God's sake . . . "

"Dopes," Eli answers with a laugh. "What are you afraid of? Can't you see that he's drunk out of his mind?"

"Ha?" the *rebbe* says with one eye open (the other is already asleep). "What were you saying? Saints? All saints . . . on the other hand . . . it's all right . . . the Guardian of Israel chl- chl- chrrrrsss—"

And our *rebbe* falls fast asleep and his snoring resounds from his nose like the sound of a *shofar* far into the forest. And we sit around him feeling sad.

"This is our *rebbe* who makes us tremble at his look? This is Mazepa?"

Seven

"You guys!" Eli says to us. "Why are we sitting here like bumps on a log? Let's think up a punishment for Mazepa."

We suddenly feel afraid.

"What are you afraid of, fools?" Eli says again. "He's like a corpse now."

We grow even more frightened. Eli exhorts us, "We can do what we want with him now. He beat us all winter like sheep. Let's take revenge at least once."

"What do you want to do to him?"

"Nothing. Only to scare him."

"How are you going to scare him?"

"You'll see in a minute," Eli says. He gets up and goes over to the *rebbe* and takes off his sash and says: "You see this? We'll tie him to the tree with his own sash, so he can't get loose. And then one of us will go up close and yell in his ear, '*Rebbe,* bandits!'"

"What will that do?"

"Nothing. We'll run away and he'll yell *Shma Yisroel.*"

"How long will he yell?"

"Until he gets used to it."

And without further ado, Eli takes the sash and ties our *rebbe's* hands together and fastens both hands to the tree. We stand and watch. A shudder runs through us: "Is this our *rebbe,* whose looks made us tremble? This is Mazepa?"

"What are you standing there for? You're made of clay?" Eli says. "If God has made a miracle and delivered Mazepa into our hands, let's dance!"

And we take each other's hands and begin to circle around our *rebbe* like wild men, and dance and jump and sing like lunatics.

"So far so good!" says Eli. And we stop, and Eli goes over to the *rebbe,* leans down quite close to him, and yells into his ear loudly in a voice that could waken the dead: "Help, *Rebbe!* Bandits! Bandits! Bandits!!!"

Eight

Like a shot we all run off, afraid to stop even for a moment, afraid even to look back. We are all frightened, and so is Eli, even though he never stops yelling at us. "Fools, dopes, cattle! What are you running for?"

"Why are you running?"

"You're running, so I'm running, too."

We rush into town with all our might and with one cry: "Bandits! Bandits!"

People see us running and run after us. Other people see people running and run after them.

"What's the running about?"

"How should we know? Everyone's running so we're running, too."

Finally they stop one of us, and seeing this we all stop but keep on yelling, "Bandits! Bandits!"

"Where? Where? where?"

"Over there in the Black Forest, we were attacked by bandits . . . tied the *rebbe* to a tree . . . God knows if he's still alive . . . "

Nine

If you are jealous of us because we're free now and aren't attending *cheder* (the *rebbe* is sick), don't bother. You can never feel the shoe pinch the other person's foot. No one, but no one, knows who the real bandits are. We hardly go to see one another. And when we meet, the first thing is, "How's the *rebbe?*" (It's no longer Mazepa.) And when we say prayers, we pray to God for the *rebbe* and cry quietly: "Master of the Universe! Master of the Universe!"

And Eli—don't ask about Eli. May his name be wiped out. That Eli!

Epilogue

When the *rebbe* recovered (for six weeks he lay in a fever and talked to bandits) and we returned to *cheder*, we could scarcely recognize Mazepa; he had changed so much. Where was his lion's voice? He had tossed his whip away somewhere. No more "Lie down!" No more Mazepa. And a quiet, tender melancholy has transformed his features. A feeling of regret steals into us and Mazepa suddenly becomes dear to us, sealed in our hearts. Ah! If only he would blame us, get angry at us! It's just as if nothing had happened . . . But suddenly he breaks off in the midst of study and asks us to tell him again the story of the Lag Baomer bandits. We don't hold back; we tell him again and again the story that we have by heart: how bandits suddenly came out of the woods, flung themselves on him, tied him up, and would have killed him with a knife if we hadn't rushed into town with all our might and saved him with our cries for help . . .

The *rebbe* hears us out with eyes closed. Afterward he heaves a sigh and asks suddenly, "Are you sure they were bandits?"

"What else could they be?"

"Maybe a band of imps?"

And the *rebbe's* eyes look off somewhere, and it seems to us that a sly smile hovers on his incredibly thick lips.

Translated by Seymour Levitan

The Guest

"I HAVE A guest for you, Reb Yonah, for the Passover—a guest such as you've never had since you became a householder."

"You mean?"

"I mean, something special."

"What's 'something special'?"

"I mean, a really refined person, handsome and well-bred. He has only one failing, though. He doesn't understand our language."

"What language *does* he understand?"

"The holy tongue, Hebrew."

"From Jerusalem?"

"I don't know where he's from. All I know is that his speech is full of 'ahs'."

Such was the conversation that took place between my father and our *shammes* Ezriel several days before Passover. I was bursting with curiosity to get a good look at this rare person who does not understand Yiddish and speaks Hebrew with "ahs" exclusively. In the synagogue I had already observed an odd-looking man in a traditional fur-edged hat and a Turkish robe of yellow, blue, and red stripes. We youngsters surrounded him and proceeded to inspect him from all angles. For this we were sternly reprimanded by Ezriel: "What a bad habit children have of sticking their noses into a stranger's face!"

After services the congregation shook hands warmly with the goodlooking stranger, said "Sholem," and wished him a happy holiday, to which he responded with a charming smile, his red-cheeked face framed by a gray beard. His "Sha-lom, sha-lom!" in reply to each greeting elicited loud laughter in us boys. Infuriated, the *shammes* rushed toward us with an upraised hand, ready to deal out slaps, but we slipped out of his grasp and again edged up to the stranger, listening for his "Sha-lom, sha-lom" in order to explode once more into laughter and escape again from Ezriel's threatening hand.

Exultantly I walk behind my father and this personage to our home for the holiday, aware that my pals are envying me our extraordinary guest. Knowing that they are following us with their eyes from a distance, I turn around and stick my tongue out at them. The three of us walk silently all the way. When we enter the house, my father calls out to my mother, "Happy holiday!" Our guest nods, which makes his fur hat tremble, and says, "Sha-lom, sha-lom!" This makes me think of my pals and I turn my face aside so as not to burst into laughter.

I steal frequent glances at our guest and am pleased by what I see. I like his Turkish robe with the yellow, blue, and red stripes. I like his rosy cheeks inside the half-circle of gray beard. I like the shining black eyes which look out smilingly from under luxuriant eyebrows. I can see that my father, too, delights in him. My mother gazes at our guest as though at a divine creature. But no one speaks a word to him! With a respectful gesture my father requests that he be seated on the ceremonial chair bedecked with pillows. My mother goes into a frenzy of busyness, assisted by Rickel our maid. Only when the time comes to make the blessing does my father converse with his guest in the holy tongue. I am puffed up with pride because I understand practically everything that is being said. Here is their conversation in Hebrew, word for word:

Father: *"Nu?"* (Meaning in Yiddish, "Be so good as to say the *Kiddush* prayer.")

Guest: *"Nu, nu!"* (Meaning, "Go right ahead, *you* say it.")

Father: *"Nu, aw?"* ("How about you?")

Guest: *"Aw, nu?"* ("Why not you?")

Father: *"Ee-aw!"* ("Please, you first!")

Guest: *"Aw, ee!"* ("You first, please!")

Father: *"Eh, aw, ee!"* ("I beg of you, you say it first!")

Guest: *"Ee, aw, eh!"* ("You say it, I beg of you!")

Father: *"Ee, eh, aw, nu?"* ("Will it harm you to say it first?")

Guest: *"Ee, aw, eh, nu, nu!"* ("Well, since you insist, I'll say it!")

Our guest takes the cup from father's hand and recites the *Kiddush*. It is a benediction such as we have never heard before and do not expect to hear again. First, on account of the Hebrew with all the "ahs" in it; and second, on account of his voice which does not issue from his throat but from his Turkish robe with the gaily colored stripes. I think of my pals, of the laughter that would have pealed forth, of the slaps that would have flown about, had they been present at this *Kiddush.* But since I am alone, I restrain myself and ask my father the Four Questions in my usual tone of voice. All together we read the *Haggadah* and I am in a state of exaltation because this particular guest is *ours* and no one else's!

Two

Surely, the sage who advised that one should not speak during meals would pardon me for saying that he was ignorant of the exigencies of Jewish life. When, I ask you, does a Jew have time to converse if not at the dinner table? Especially at the Passover *seder* when there is such a great deal to narrate, during the meal and after it?

Rickel hands us the bowls of water for the washing of hands before saying the prayer at the breaking of the *matzo,* and my mother serves portions of the fish. It is only then that my father, rolling up his sleeves, begins a prolonged conversation with his guest in Hebrew. He starts with the first question that one Jew usually asks another: "What is your name?"

The reply is a mass of "ahs" in one breath, much as one reels off the names of Haman's sons when reading the Book of Esther: "Ack-Becker-Galush-Damat-Henoch-Yasam-Zen-Hafiff-Tatsik . . ."

My father remains sitting with an open mouth of food and gazes at him in astonishment, apparently because of the multitude of names, while I get an attack of coughing and stare down at my lap. My mother is alarmed and says, "Watch out when you eat fish. One can choke, God forbid, on a tiny bone."

She looks respectfully at our guest. Although she can make nothing of that string of names, she is awed by them. However, since my father does understand, he feels that an explanation is due her. "You see, 'Ack-Becker . . .'—it's the *aleph-beis,* and evidently, there, in that land, they have a custom of giving names in alphabetical order."

"*Aleph-beis, aleph-beis.*" Our guest catches it up with the sweetest of smiles and looks at us with the utmost friendliness beaming from his enchanting black eyes—even at Rickel, our maid.

Having learned the guest's name to his satisfaction, my father is now interested to learn from which country he has come. I comprehend this from the names of towns and cities which ring out and which my father immediately translates for my mother. Each word, almost, is accompanied by an explanation, and my mother is impressed by each name separately. This is no small thing, after all! A man has journeyed ten thousand miles or so from a land which can be reached only by swimming seven seas and crossing a desert which takes forty days and forty nights to cross. But in order to reach the desert, one must first climb a mountain so high that its peak, covered by ice and swept by biting winds, reaches to the very clouds. An awesome spot! In the end, however, when one has scaled this mountain safely, there lies on the other side spread out before one an earthly paradise teeming with all sorts of good things: with spices, cloves, and rare herbs, and all kinds of fruit in abundance—apples, pears and oranges, grapes, dates and olives, nuts and figs. The houses there are built of pinewood only and covered with pure silver. The dishes are made of solid gold. (While saying this, our guest glances briefly at our silver goblets and silver spoons, knives, and forks.) Precious stones and pearls and diamonds lie strewn about on the streets but no one bothers to bend down and pick them up because there they are valueless. (Here he peers at my mother's earrings and the yellowed pearl necklace about her milky-white throat.)

"Do you hear that?" My father motions to my mother with a radiant face.

"I hear," my mother replies, and wants to know, "Why don't they bring those treasures here? They'd make a fortune. Please, Yonah, ask him that."

My father relays the question and translates the reply to her in Yiddish. "You see, when you enter that land, you may gather as much as you wish, full pockets of the treasure, but when you leave, you must return everything. If they shake anything out of you, you're done for."

"What does that mean?" my mother asks fearfully.

"It means that they either hang you from a tree or stone you to death."

Three

The more our guest speaks, the more interesting become the stories he relates. We have finished the soup with *kneydlach* and are still taking small sips of wine when my father queries, "To whom does it all belong? Do they have a king ruling over them?"

To this he receives an immediate clear response which he transmits joyously to my mother: "He says that the entire wealth belongs to the inhabitants of the kingdom who are called *Sephardim;* and they have a king, he says, who is terribly pious and wears a fur-edged hat; and this king's name is Joseph ben Joseph. He serves as their high priest, he says, and rides in a golden carriage drawn by six fiery horses, and when he crosses the threshold of the synagogue, Levites come to greet him with song . . ."

"Levites sing in your *shul?*" my father asks in wonderment. Again he gets a swift reply which he promptly conveys to my mother, his face radiant as the sun.

"Wonder of wonders! He says they have a holy temple with priests and Levites and an organ . . ."

"An altar, too?" my father asks, and then tells my mother, "He says they have an altar with sacrifices and golden vessels, everything as it was in ancient times in Jerusalem, he says."

Concluding these words, my father sighs deeply, and watching him, my mother sighs too. I can't understand them. What is there to sigh about? Just the reverse: shouldn't they be proud and rejoice in the existence of such a land—a land ruled by a Jewish king who is also a high priest, a land where there is a holy temple and Levites and an organ and an altar and sacrifices . . .

Splendid, gleaming fantasies lift me up and transport me to that fortunate Jewish land where the houses are built of fragrant pinewood and covered with silver, where the dishes are made of gold and precious stones lie scattered about on the streets. Suddenly the thought comes to me that if I were there, *I'd* know what to do, *I'd* know how to conceal the treasure well. They would shake nothing out of me! I would bring back fine presents for my mother: sparkling earrings and more than one pearl necklace.

As I think this, I look at my mother's earrings and the pearls about her

lovely throat, and I am seized by an overwhelming desire to visit that
fabulous land. My mind is made up. After Passover I will go there with
our guest. Secretly of course, so that not a soul will know of it. I will
disclose my resolve to him only; I will pour out my heart to him and beg
him to take me with him, even for the briefest time. Surely he will not
have it in his heart to refuse me; surely he will do me this favor. He is
such a goodhearted, amiable person. He looks at each one of us with
such friendliness, even at Rickel the maid.

As I sit daydreaming and contemplate our guest, it seems to me that
he has guessed my thoughts and is winking to me with his beautiful dark
eyes, saying in his own language: "Be silent, little rogue. Not a word out
of you. Be patient and wait until Passover is ended. You'll see, *then* the
time will be ripe!"

Four

All night long I struggle with a tangle of dreams. I see a
desert, a holy temple, a high priest. I scale a deep mountain on top of
which grows precious stones, pearls, and diamonds. My playmates
climb into trees and shake down jewels from the branches. Standing
below, I pick them up and stuff them into my pockets. No matter how
much I put into my pockets, there's room for more. Endlessly. I put my
hand into my pocket and, instead of jewels, I pull out all sorts of fruit:
apples, pears, oranges, olives, dates, nuts, and figs. I am terror-stricken
and toss from side to side. The holy temple appears before me and I hear
priests chanting and Levites singing. An organ plays. I want to enter the
temple but can't because Rickel is holding me tight and will not let me
go. I scream at her, I yell, I plead. In anguish I toss from side to side, and
awake, and . . .

My parents are standing before me, disheveled and half-dressed, both
pale as death. My father's head is bowed, my mother wrings her hands,
tears welling in her dear eyes. I sense that something wicked has
happened, something so terribly wicked that my childish mind cannot
conceive of it.

Our guest, the kindhearted stranger from that magical faroff land where houses are made of pinewood and covered with silver and so forth, has disappeared. And with him much else has vanished, including our maid Rickel.

My heart is shattered. But not on account of the loss of our goblets and silverware or of my mother's scanty jewelry and the money. Not on account of Rickel the maid—the devil take her! But because now I will never see that happy, happy land where precious stones lie carelessly about in the streets, where there is a holy temple with priests, Levites, an organ, and an ancient altar with sacrifices. All these marvelous things cruelly, wantonly stolen from me . . .

I turn my face to the wall and weep silently.

Translated by Etta Blum

Part
Four

The Krushniker Delegation

SO WE'RE AT the point, aren't we, where my son Yekhiel was made mayor of Krushnik, and was running things, as they say, with an iron hand, and the Poles were scraping and digging, looking everywhere for lies to tell, spreading Haman's slanders against him and against all of us. Well, they kept at it, those Poles, may their names be blotted from memory, until finally the Germans began making "forays" into town. That is, they began searching and scavenging and shaking up people. And God helped them—they actually found something at Aba the *shochet*'s, some hidden circumcision knives, along with a packet of circumcision powder, which looks a bit like gunpowder. And then the fun began—God Almighty!

First off, they took the *schlimazel* (the *shochet*, I mean) and threw him into jail, solitary confinement, so that God forbid no evil should come near him, and no one disturb his rest. And the whole town became, what should I say, a very pit of desolation and bitter lament. And all at once they came running to me. "What's going on?" they said. "Yankel, why don't you speak up? Your son," they said, "is the mayor, isn't he? And

---

Translated here for the first time into English, the following sketch is taken from a longer narrative which Sholom Aleichem wrote toward the end of his life. It deals with the experiences of the East European Jews caught in the First World War between Germans and Poles. Some elements of the traditional Sholom Aleichem are still here, but the reader will quickly notice that the tone and substance have changed, as if the great humorist is giving way before the blows of modern history.—Editors' Note

you," they said, "you're such a big shot, if you said the word, that *schlimazel* (the *shochet*, that is) would be a free man."

Well, I tried to reason with them. "Get off my back," I said. "You're making a bad mistake, my dear friends. In the first place," I said, "I'm not the big shot you think me, and even if I am, let's say, that's no special advantage. On the contrary. Just because," I said, "my Yekhiel is mayor, and because I'm pretty important around here—a big shot, as you say—just because of this," I said, "I'd do more harm than good. Because if you knew the Germans," I said, "like I know them, you wouldn't talk that way. I'll tell you exactly what a German is," I said. "A German hates flattery as much as a kosher Jew hates pork. A German won't stand for empty words, and as for bribery," I said, "forget it. A German's not a Russian who'll watch your hand to see if you've got a bribe there for him. A German," I said, "needs delicate handling, if you see what I mean."

You'd think that that would do it, right? But you're dealing with Jews. You say salt, they say pepper. So you say pepper, they say garlic. And all the while the *shochet*'s wife and her children were standing off to one side, weeping and wailing, tearing their hair out. I don't know about you, Mr. Sholom Aleichem, but I have an odd habit—when I see tears, I'm struck dumb. I can't stand to see someone crying. I can't, that's all. I'm not bragging that I'm goodhearted; it's the power of tears, if you see what I mean. But in the long run all that made no difference anyway. As it turned out, I didn't have to be begged. The authorities ordered me to come. And not only me, but our rabbi too, and the *rabbiner* (the rabbi appointed by the government), along with all the other first citizens of Krushnik. Our hearts sank, I can tell you, but we gathered up our courage and got ready to go. That is, we dressed in our Sabbath best, with top hats—very elegant, very fitting and proper. It was as if we weren't being sent for, but had decided on our own to go as a delegation.

Meanwhile, my wife saw me all decked out on a Wednesday afternoon. "Yankel," she said, "where are you off to?"

Naturally I didn't tell her they'd sent for us. Does a woman have to know everything? So I made up a story that we were going as a delegation to the Germans, to the commandant I mean, in order to save a poor Jew from the gallows.

Well, she wrung her hands and started wailing. "Yankel, you musn't do it!" There was a terrible pain in her heart, she said. Lightning, she said, had struck her. Evil days were coming upon the children of Israel. . . .

As you'd expect, a wife. What does a woman know anyway? Though to tell the truth, my wife (may she rest in peace) was not as foolish as other women. In fact, she wasn't foolish at all. You might even say the opposite. She was clever, quite clever; and sometimes she could talk like a wise woman, a wonderfully wise woman! I don't say it because she was my wife or because she's now in heaven. After death, as they say, you become a saint on earth, but that's not why I praise her. I'm not like other men. Here's an example—if you'd go to Krushnik and ask around about Yankel Yunever's wife, Miriam Mirel, you'd hear only praise and praise and more praise! First, she was pious, and not just "respectable," God forbid, like other women who won't move an inch from the letter of the law. Besides that, she was religious, very religious! But who's discussing religion? We're talking about kindness, about the meaning of character. This was a woman! A vessel of goodness! A person without gall! Well, maybe not *without* gall. Everyone has a gall, naturally, and if you step on it, it's got to burst, because a human being can't be more than a human being, if you see what I mean.

But I don't want to mix things up, and as you know I hate to brag. So I'll get right to the point. We were going, I and the rabbi and the *rabbiner,* and the other good men of Krushnik, to the head authority, the commandant, to hear him out. And we went confidently. After all, we made quite a show, as they say, with the father himself of Krushnik's mayor there—you can't just dismiss something like that with a wave of your hand! And on our way we discussed what we'd say to the commandant. We decided that I would begin and address him in the words of Moses: "O Lord, you have begun to show your servants your greatness—that is to say, you have been gracious toward us, Herr German, from the day you set foot upon our land." And more of that kind of high talk. Why should we wait until he'd start? It would be best to get in a few words first, and then by the way, if you see what I mean, we could throw in something about the *shochet*—explain who the *schlimazel* was, why he'd hidden the ritual knives, just what that packet of circumcision powder meant—a regular lecture.

But as they say, if it's fated to be a disaster, you lose your tongue. That's where my real story begins. When I think of it even now, it makes my hair stand on end. . . .

In short then, we arrived at the commandant's headquarters, and there we found the *schlimazel,* Aba the *shochet* himself, tied up in the courtyard, and two soldiers with loaded rifles, one at each side of him.

The *shochet* was trembling like a leaf and muttering something, probably his last confession. We were going to cheer him with a word or two, something like "Aba, God is with you!" But the soldiers gave us a nudge with their rifles—meaning one word to him, the *shochet,* and we'd be shot dead. And if a German says he'll shoot, trust him, especially when the whole world has gone crazy. At the slightest whim they'd shoot. Do you see what I mean or not? For example, someone comes by and says, "Got some tobacco, pal? If you do, all right. If not, I'll shoot." He doesn't give you time to think it over, let alone to defend yourself, to explain that you never use tobacco. Your life wasn't safe, that's the kind of world it was—try and do something about it.

To make a long story short, I don't have to tell you how we Krushniker Jews felt when we saw the *shochet* tied up and making his last confession. You can imagine it for yourself. I could only think, great God Almighty, what's going to happen to this Jew? And what will happen to his wife, the poor widow, and to his children, the orphans, if God forbid we can't get them to listen?

As we were standing around like that, thinking, out came not the commandant, but some other devil—a redhead, fat, well-fed, a cigar in his teeth. He'd just had a good supper and apparently more than a few drinks to wash it down. Along with him came two other officers. They looked at us; we looked at them. We examined each other, that is, without words for a while. No one knew what would happen. Now if it had been the commandant himself, and if he'd received us like human beings in his house, not outside there in the courtyard, then it would have been a different matter altogether, and quite a different sort of conversation. But this way, nothing. We stood and were silent—I and the rabbi and the *rabbiner* standing right up front, in the firing line, if you see what I mean. The other Krushniker dignitaries were standing behind us and pushing us from behind to say something. But how can you say something if you can't talk? Besides I was waiting for the rabbi to start—he was older. And the rabbi was waiting for the *rabbiner* — *he'd* been appointed by the government.

When they saw what they had there—a speechless delegation, a feast without food—the fat one yelled out to us, "Who are you?" So I stepped forward, let happen what may, and introduced him to the old man. "This is our rabbi," I said. "And the younger one, he's the *rabbiner,* the rabbi appointed by the government, and as for me," I said, "I'm Yankel Yunever, the father," I said, "of the lord mayor of Krushnik."

You'd think, wouldn't you, that he'd be impressed? Not at all. He didn't move a muscle. So seeing that reputation didn't work, I began to plead, putting first things first, as they say. "We, the foremost citizens of Krushnik," I said, "come before you as a delegation," I said, "with a request, to beg mercy for this Jew"—and I pointed to the *schlimazel,* to Aba the *shochet,* that is.

The fat German heard me out, then motioned to the soldiers to take us away. So they took us, if you see what I mean, and put us into prison like real criminals, each in a separate cell. It all happened in a minute, much less time than it's taken me to tell you about it. Did they let us send word at least to our wives and children? No, they shoved us in, locked the doors, and that's that. Should we have asked them why? Useless! First, a German won't answer. That's one reason. Another is it could make things worse, God forbid. Wartime's a powderkeg. You have to watch what you say, if you see what I mean, because who knows which side will win and what the result will be? It could be that the top dogs will be turned out into the cold, and the winners wind up six feet below.

In short, we were in a tight spot. Although if you look at it another way, what could they have against us? After all, we were dealing with Germans, with gentlemen. But then again, this was a time when Germans weren't really German, or Frenchmen French, or Englishmen English. They were wolves, not men—human beings acting like animals, like wild beasts, a plague on them! It was worse now than at the time of the flood; it was the end of the world. You probably think they fined us or beat us with whips. Well, think again. But you'd never guess, not if you'd live nine lives, so don't trouble yourself. Give me a minute or two to catch my breath, and I'll tell you a pretty story. Then be so good as to tell *me* what it was—a joke? the real thing? or a dream? . . .

Let's call it a story about the new moon—I mean, a story about how we Krushniker Jews prayed to the new moon. You remember, don't you, where we left off? They had kindly seated us in prison, me and the rabbi and the *rabbiner* and the other good men of Krushnik, the town's pride and joy, because of the crime we'd committed—we'd taken the part of Aba the *shochet,* pleaded on his behalf, if you see what I mean, and tried to save a Jew from the gallows. So there we sat, each one of us in his own cell, not studying Torah and not sitting at work for ten rubles a week, but just sitting, like common thieves and drunkards, in prison. What could we do? We'd been seated, as they say, so we sat . . . sat one hour, sat two hours, sat three hours. . . . Soon it would be night—what were we sitting there for, I ask you? At home they didn't even know where we were, that's where it hurt! And besides, everything has to end sometime, as they say, so let it come, I thought, one way or another!

I tell you, my head was ready to burst. I kept thinking and thinking, and only of evil things, and of worse to come. I imagined, first, that they'd condemn us as criminals and sentence us according to the laws of war. Next they'd politely line us up—the finest Krushniker citizens, including the rabbi and the *rabbiner*, all in a row, and twelve soliders would stand ready, rifles loaded, waiting for the good word. And then the commandant enters in person, so I imagine, and asks us to say our last prayers—he's a German, after all, a gentleman! At this I get a bit hot under the collar and I think, "Yankel, the end's approaching. It's only a minute to death anyway; why not ease your conscience, as they say, and give him a piece of your mind?" And I begin in the language of our fathers, speaking as Abraham spoke before the gates of Sodom: "My Lord, harken to me, and hear me out. Do not take offense, O German, but let your servant's words find favor in the ears of his lord and master"—and so on, without putting the least emphasis on the fact that he's a German and a commandant and the conqueror of Krushnik.

And as I'm arguing with him (in my imagination, that is), the door opened and who do you think came in but a soldier with a loaded rifle. Once inside, he winked at me as if to say, "Be so kind as to follow me." Well, I could see there wasn't much choice, so I went. Outside it was pitch black. I looked around and saw the others were there, too—all of Krushnik's finest, the rabbi and the *rabbiner* included. Behind each of them stood a soldier, armed to the teeth.

Then the captain shouted "Forward!" and we went, the whole delegation, quietly, no words spoken, because talking wasn't allowed—strictly forbidden, as they say. Only sighs and groans that would break your heart, just like at Rosh Hashanah, during prayers before the *shofar* is sounded. Did you ever hear the groaning then? My heart ached, especially for our rabbi, an old man seventy years old. What am I saying, seventy? He must have been then, according to my calculations, at least seventy-five, and if you really want to know, maybe even eighty, because I can still remember him at my wedding in Yunev. I was married in Yunev, you know. They brought him down from Krushnik, and by that time he was already an old man—I mean, not an *old* man, but grey-haired. And since then it's been . . . let's see, to be exact . . . no doubt as much as—actually, I don't remember; and anyway, I don't want to get off the track. That weakens the point of the story, if you see what I mean. I might forget where I'm at. Though as for my memory—God keep it always as clear as it is now. And to prove it, I'll tell you where I left off.

I was telling you about the old man, our rabbi, how he was walking out in front, and we Krushniker dignitaries were walking behind him, sighing and moaning and not allowed to speak a word. If only our families knew where we were—if only we ourselves knew where they were taking us! But nothing doing; like sheep to the slaughter, as they say. No sign they might be taking us to something good, because if so why wouldn't the Germans tell us where we were going? And certainly no one was waiting there to heap honors upon us, because then they wouldn't be pushing and shoving us—"Forward, march! Forward, march!" Before we could look around we found ourselves on Death Street, which leads to the new cemetery. I say the new one because in Krushnik we had two cemeteries, thank God, an old one and a new one. Of course, the new one was already old enough, and well populated, one grave set snugly beside the other. Pretty soon we'd have to find space for a third cemetery, if only God would let us live, and put an end to the war, and let Krushnik remain Krushnik and Jews, Jews.

Well, I won't drag this out. As we were going along the moon came out, and we could see that we were at the cemetery. What was I to think? Had someone in town died, some important person, or were they bringing some dead person here from another town, to be buried in a Jewish grave? But then why should *we* be here, and why, for that matter, a funeral with soldiers? But then again what other reason could there be for marching us suddenly, in the middle of the night, to the burial grounds?

As we were thinking this over, we looked up and saw—there he was, too, the *schlimazel*, Aba the *shochet*, I mean. He, and two soldiers with him! What was *he* doing here? Nothing much—just standing there with a shovel in his hands, digging a grave, and weeping, tears streaming down his face. Well, we didn't like the looks of it. In the first place, who was he digging a grave for? Second, what sort of a gravedigger was Aba the *shochet*? And besides that, what was he weeping about? Any way you looked at it, it was a puzzle, if you see what I mean, a mystery of mysteries, incomprehensible.

But it didn't take long—maybe as long as it's taking to tell you this, maybe even less—and all questions were answered. The captain gave an order and there emerged from out of nowhere a group of soldiers carrying shovels, and they took us, if you see what I mean, and stood us several steps apart from each other. Then they handed each of us a shovel and asked us to be so good as to dig graves, every one on his own private plot, since in two hours at most, so they gave us to understand, we'd be shot.

You want to know how we felt when they told us the good news? I can't speak for the others; that's their business. But for myself I can say absolutely, and give you my oath, that I felt—nothing. Simply and truly nothing. What do I mean *nothing?* Take a healthy person, strong and able, with wife and children and suddenly put a shovel in his hand and order him to dig his own grave since he's about to be shot! I ask you, Mr. Sholom Aleichem, think it over carefully—do you have any idea of what that means? No, you have to go through it yourself. It's a waste of time to explain. Though actually it wasn't so complicated. If a person had brains and was levelheaded and could think around and about, he could see it all plainly for himself and stop worrying himself so much. "After all," I said to myself, "what's so special here? It's the old story. As they say, if God wants you to die, don't be a smart aleck; you've got to die. You're not the only one. People are dying in the thousands, tens of thousands, falling like flies, like straws in the wind. So just imagine, Yankel Yunever, that you're a soldier and in the heat of battle. Fool! Who thinks of death in the heat of battle? Or rather who thinks of anything *but* death? Because if you get right down to it, what's war if not the angel of death? And what's the point of telling the angel of death, if you see what I mean, to fear death?" Think it over, Mr. Sholom Aleichem. You'll soon see how deep that is!

Still, what's the good of philosophy? You want to get to the point, right? Well, I can tell you this much—I know as much about what happened next as you do. Suddenly confusion broke out, a clamor from heaven, a drumming of drums, a chaos of soldiers running and horses galloping. Great God Almighty, I thought, what's going on? A revolution? The earth opening under Sodom and Gomorrah? The end of the world? In an instant the soldiers vanished, and we Krushniker Jews remained all alone on the new burial grounds, shovels in hand, and—silence.

It was then we understood—not that we *understood* anything (why should I lie to you?), but we felt with all our five senses, if you see what I mean, that something extraordinary had happened, a true and genuine miracle from heaven, and we'd been saved from disaster. But for all that, we just couldn't say a word to each other, not a word! We'd lost our tongues, and that was that. And like one man, as if we'd decided on it beforehand, we threw down the shovels, pulled ourselves together, and hit the road, as they say—slowly at first, then a little faster, and then we ran, but really *ran,* if you see what I mean, like you run from a blazing fire.

Where did we get the courage? And especially the old rabbi, where did he get the strength to run like that? But he didn't last long, poor thing, and when he couldn't go any further he stopped short, with his hand on his chest, barely breathing. So we stopped too—it's not decent to leave a rabbi by himself in the middle of nowhere. We still couldn't say a word, and we still didn't know what was happening. But we could hear the drumming and the galloping and the shooting. Something was going on, God only knows what, but as it's written, "God will provide, so keep quiet." Quiet we were—we couldn't speak.

The first to say something was the old rabbi. "Children," he called to us, looking up toward the bright moon. "I can tell you that it's the Almighty," he said, "the Creator of heaven and earth who has done these things. God Himself," he said, "has taken pity on our wives and children and saved us from disaster. And so we owe it to God," he said, "to give thanks to His moon; it's the right time of the month." And without another word, he turned his face to the new moon—the rabbi, I mean— right there in the middle of town, and we stood around him. And the rabbi started chanting "Hallelujah," cheerfully, and we all followed him, growing livelier as we went along, chanting, clapping, and leaping. By the time he got to "Let us dance in praise of His name," we were really dancing! Such a prayer to the new moon, believe me, Krushnik had never heard of since Krushnik was Krushnik. Never had and never will again. It was, as they say, a once-in-a-lifetime prayer to the new moon.

You can imagine we didn't know where we were, whether in this world or the next, when it came to the "*Sholem aleichem's.*" I heard someone blubbering, right into my ear, "*Sholem aleichem.*" I answered "*Aleichem sholem!*" and looked around. It was him, the *schlimazel,* Aba the *shochet,* I mean. How did *he* get here? Had he also been with us there at the burial grounds? A curse on it all! I'd completely forgotten— he'd been the first one! We must have been out of our minds, if you see what I mean. I only wanted to hug and kiss that *schlimazel,* and at the same time I wanted to hug the rabbi (may his memory stay with us always—he's now in another world, a better one). And the way he died! God Almighty! May it happen to all our enemies! You'll hear about it, don't worry; I won't leave out the details. That was a Jew! Where can you find Jews like him today?

But just think what a rabbi can do. Once we'd finished our prayer to the new moon, he wanted to say a few more words. He'd decided, if you see what I mean, to explain a passage from the Song of Songs. "The voice of my beloved," he began. . . . I hope he'll forgive me for saying this, but he had one fault, our rabbi: he loved to hold forth, to give lectures. So we took counsel and decided nothing doing. A prayer to the new moon was one thing, but a commentary on the Song of Songs, with interpretations and illustrations and exhortations, in the middle of town, late at night, after such horrors and such miracles and wonders— *that*, brother, we could leave for another occasion. So we tucked in our coattails, as they say, and ran for home, each one of us. And there we met with another happy scene, I mean a real celebration. By comparison, everything we'd been through was mere child's play. You'll say that yourself when you hear the story. . . .

You know, Mr. Sholom Aleichem, Jews brag about the town of Kishinev. Kishinev, they say, was world-famous for its pogroms and its hooligans. Ha! I'd laugh at them if there were any Jews left there to laugh at. Kishinev! You call *that* a town? Kishinev was a dog compared to Krushnik. Do you hear me? Kishinev wasn't worthy of washing Krushnik's feet. Concerning the treatment of Jews, the Kishinever hooligans could have learned a lesson or two (if they don't mind me saying so) from our Russian Cossacks. To begin with, they didn't even have the right weapons. In Kishinev, if they felt like smashing a house, they'd have to gather up a hundred people, along with sticks and rocks and pebbles. But what good are such weapons?—if you can call them weapons. By the time you get something going, smash up a house or two, all the excitement's gone out of it and the party's over. Now in our town in Krushnik, there were dozens of good guns, or if you preferred there was a fine cannon. A few blasts of that cannon, and you've shot up the whole area, wiped out the marketplace with all its stores and stalls and the houses all around to boot. Do you see what I mean, or don't you? With one blow they wiped out all of Krushnik, didn't leave a shred behind, not a trace! They rooted us out from the bottom up, demolished everything Jewish, just as if it wasn't their own country they were in but the enemy's. As if Krushnik was some kind of fortress, another Paris, or a Warsaw! Though I must tell you that Krushnik was always, what should I say, a helter-skelter town, a town thrown open to the wind and the rain, without courtyards, without orchards, without gardens, without fences or walls—only houses and shacks, naked, bare Jewish homes; and these they smashed up, cut down, hacked apart, split in pieces, ground up, wiped out. Finished, no more Krushnik!

And was it only Krushnik, you think? The way it was with Krushnik, that's how it was with Rakhev, too, and with Mazel-Bozhetz, and with Bilgoray, and with every other Jewish town all around as far as Lublin. But not Lublin, of course—that was the provincial capital, and Poles lived there as well as Jews; and it was they, the Poles, who unleashed the furies. If not for them, if they hadn't poured oil on the fire with their lies, then maybe nothing would have happened.

The first to show up was the Honorable Mr. Pshepetsky, head of the administrative council. The morning after our prayer to the new moon, he ran to tell the Russian officials, personally, that we Krushniker Jews were hand in glove with the Germans. Proof was, he said, that no one wanted the job of mayor; only my Yekhiel, he said, would take it on.

Well, the Russians didn't have to hear more. They were furious, beside themselves with rage against all Jews, and especially against the mayor himself, against my Yekhiel. A summons was issued from headquarters that he should be taken—my Yekhiel, that is—dead or alive! And not only him. They were to take all of us, if you see what I mean, all the first citizens of Krushnik, along with the rabbi and the *rabbiner*, and bring us to Ivan, dead or alive—he desired to see us.

Don't you think I knew beforehand it would turn out that way? I knew! My word as a Jew I knew, and the proof is that I warned everyone. "Jews," I said, "as you love God, let's get out of here!" I told them in good time, too, that night, just as soon as we heard the Germans running and Ivan coming on with his Cossacks. Because I knew that where Ivan set foot no grass would grow. So I told them, "Let's get out of here, wherever our feet will carry us. Anywhere in the world," I said, "but not here."

Well, I almost convinced them—all but one. That was the old man, the rabbi. He just dug in his heels and refused to budge. He didn't want, he said, to run for the sake of running. "If the God of Israel wants to preserve us," he said, "He'll preserve us, as He has up until now; and if not, God forbid, then it's a sure sign," he said, "that that's our fate. And if so," he said, "then let it at least be as it's written, 'I shall sleep with my ancestors.'" In short, all he wanted was to be buried like a Jew and remain forever in his own Krushnik. The world's full of evil temptations. But he couldn't have even that satisfaction. Man thinks and God winks, as they say. He forgot to reckon, our rabbi, with those two-legged beasts.

If you remember, the whole business began during the night of the new moon. Ivan and his Cossacks set out to ransack our homes on the pretense of looking for runaway Germans, and in the course of things they did what they always do—what they did, for example, in Kishinev, in Bialystok, in Balta, in Kateri-Neshov, and in other Jewish towns. The only difference was that there they beat people and robbed them, while here they very methodically emptied our pockets, inquiring of each one of us, *"Tschari? tschari?"* ("watches? any watches here?"), not meaning watches in particular: watchchains, rings, earrings, and money-purses would also do. Then when they'd taken it all, everything finished and done with—as the text has it, "emptied out Egypt," carried off all its treasures of wealth—then they proceeded to the people: bound them, beat them, stabbed them, shot them, and hung them. Especially hung them. They hung so many of us there weren't any trees left for hangings. They had to place logs over the rooftops, and there on the logs they continued hanging the Jews of Krushnik, one by one.

Their first victim was our rabbi, the old man, blessed be his memory. The Cossacks broke into his house early, just at daybreak. He'd already put on his prayer shawl and phylacteries and was starting to pray, when they tore in like a flood. "Vodka!" they shouted— meaning they wanted whiskey. Why whiskey at daybreak? Simply out of hunger, if you see what I mean; they were faint and famished, poor men, and so they needed a drop of whiskey. But how would an old rabbi come by whiskey, especially at a time when it was, as they say, strictly forbidden? So he gestured with his hands (not wanting to interrupt his prayers) that he had no vodka to offer them. For that he received a healthy curse, along with a slap for good measure, so that his prayer book fell from his hands. When he bent to pick it up he received another blow to the head from behind. Then the Cossacks lifted him, unconscious, from the floor, wrapped him neatly in his prayer shawl and phylacteries, tied him to a horse (to the horse's tail I mean), and dragged him through town into the marketplace. There they hung him from a tree and set guard over him, with orders that he must hang like that for three days and three nights. No one should dare take him down.

So he hung there, the old rabbi, wrapped in his prayer shawl, beaten and bloodied, in the middle of the marketplace, swaying back and forth in the wind, as though in prayer. Whoever passed by stopped to look, then ran off shuddering to tell his neighbor, and the neighbor told *his* neighbor, and soon people all over town were whispering the news to each other, and then the crowd came running to see. Cows! Cattle! Why were they running? What was so special here? Hadn't they seen a hanged man before? And for that matter, what about me, old fool that I was— why did *I* run to see it? Don't ask how much health it cost me, how many sleepless nights. To this day I see him when I close my eyes—wrapped in his prayer shawl, his face petrified, blue and streaked with blood, swaying back and forth as he stood there saying his prayers. What am I saying? He wasn't standing, he was hanging, if you see what I mean, hanging in prayer!

But let's not talk about it anymore. Silence is best, as they say. Let's talk of happier things. Wasn't there a pogrom in your town? Didn't they hang Jews there? And by the way, what country are *you* running from, Mr. Sholom Aleichem?

Translated by Sacvan Bercovitch

One in a Million

I COULD SWEAR it's him from head to toe. His slightly hooked nose, his warm, dark, smiling eyes, that one bucktooth that juts out when he starts to laugh. He's no youngster now. He must be my age. And I'm past forty.

Should I approach him? He seems very well dressed—a white vest over his belly, a heavy gold chain, a splendid tie, and from what I've heard, he's living the good life, "in the chips" as they say, a real wheeler-dealer.

I am afraid to say hello. Will he think I'm after something? You should know, I've always considered myself a little proud. Not vain, mind you, just proud.

A proud man scorns the world. Well, it's not that he scorns the world but that the world scorns him—especially if he happens to be poor. There's nothing wrong with poverty—it's no sin, so they say. And knock on wood, I'm no millionaire—far from it. Let's understand each other, I belong to that rich class of the well-disguised poor who cloak their

This monologue takes place in Odessa, the major port of Russia on the Black Sea. In the late nineteenth century it was a flourishing city that attracted a large multinational population—not the least being Jews seeking their fortune.

The magic of Odessa entered the Yiddish language in the popular expression, Er lebt vi Got in Odes (literally, he lives like God in Odessa), which translates: he is living the good life. In all probability, Sholom Aleichem had this well-known expression in mind when he wrote this story.   —Translator's Note poverty at home behind a mirror and a grand piano and in public with a showy coat and a new felt hat. But when you really come down to it, they don't even have a crumb to eat or a penny in their pockets.

To be frank, I'm not in the best of straits. Things could be better. I've tried my hand time and again at every kind of hard work and run after enough bad tips—but nothing helps. It's reached such a point I can't stand myself—and neither can others.

Maybe he doesn't give a hoot about me, couldn't care less. The few people who do notice me think, "Watch out, here comes trouble. He wants to wheedle a loan out of me. I won't give him anything." Over my dead body would I ask him for one red cent.

"And how are you?" he asks and looks me straight in the eye.

"How am I?" I say and stare right back.

"How are things going? Pretty well?"

"Not bad."

"Good to hear, thank God," he says and shakes my hand.

"Some people have all the luck," I say to myself and shake his hand. And so we go our separate ways.

But the person whose story I'm telling didn't look at me like that when we met on the boulevard in Odessa. His look was entirely different. I could read straight into his warm, dark, smiling eyes.

And with those smiling eyes he draws me to him and I feel myself at ease. From afar he stretches out his hand to me. He opens his mouth to laugh and his bucktooth protrudes. "Is it?"

"Could it be?"

We tightly grip each other's hand. I must confess that ever since things have not gone well for me, I can't stand rich people. I can't put up with their healthy, happy, fat faces; I can't bear a face that looks content with itself and the world. But this charmer bends over to me somehow so warmly that we embrace each other.

I don't know how to address him. If I am too familiar, am I taking advantage of our past closeness and reminding him of how time flies? But how can I be formal with him? Didn't we pore over the same texts together for so many years in the same schoolroom?

This very thought must have run through his mind too, for as we start talking, we both use language in such a way that during the entire time we rack our brains to avoid being either too intimate or too formal.

He: I keep looking and looking, maybe it's him, maybe not? How goes it?

I: And I kept thinking the whole time, can it really be him? It looks like him. Maybe it's not? Where is he from?

He: From where? I'm already a native. I've lived in Odessa for who knows how long.

I: And I arrived not too long ago . . . to look for a business.

He: A business? Looking for a business? For me it's just the other way around. I have too much business. If only I had as many good employees! It's bad without good help. And what it costs me each year! ["A braggart," I think to myself.] I don't have any luck with them. How many times have I thought to myself: if I had even one reliable man whom I could trust, it would add ten years to my life. What did I say? Ten? Twenty years for sure! I've already tried to keep all kinds of help— cheap help, expensive help, even very high-priced help—they're all the same, there's not a loyal one among them. I once had so many friends. When one of them came to me seeking help, I would shower him with money from head to foot. ["What a liar!" goes through my mind.] And as if for spite, I never meet anyone from the old days. I can really say that this is the first time I've had such a meeting since I settled here. It seems to me we once were really close friends, right?

I: Friends? Anything passes for friendship today! We studied together, we boarded together at a rabbi's, we slept on the same bed together.

He: I can even remember at which rabbi's, at Reb Zorah's on top of the Russian stove throughout the whole winter.

I: And summer in the open air on the ground.

He: Like pigs in the muck, with all the frogs.

I: And Tevye the neighbor standing by his broken window screaming at whoever had thrown stones and scaring the entire household half to death.

He: And at Pironditshke's, who swiped the apples right out of the basket with a spiked pole?

I: And the watermelons? Lifted straight off old Gedaliah's wagon at Succos!

And so on.

It isn't easy to stop talking about the good old days. Our memories flow like water from a tap. But he doesn't get down to brass tacks until we come bit by bit to the present and we tell each other about the good and bad in our lives, the happy and the sad.

Things are going well for one of us, very well. With the other, things are going poorly, really badly. One is rich, a millionaire; the other barely ekes out a living. One spares no expense for his children's upbringing: his oldest daughter is happily married off; the sons are all in the finest schools. The other eats his heart out about his children: his eldest daughter wants to give private lessons and has no students, and his son can't get into the first-rate school. You need "pull" and it costs a lot. One has his own house in Odessa with a garden, all sorts of antiques—in short, a paradise. The other has been wandering a good number of years from one hole to the next. Not too long ago they "took inventory of him" from head to foot, sold his bedding, and threw him out on the street. Steeling himself—"what will be, will be"—he moved to another city! They say it's an answer: "Move away and your luck will change!"

With no one else have I ever opened my heart so fully as now with my friend. And no one else listens with such interest to the bitter end. I feel a load off my chest, a weight off my mind. And I notice how his warm, dark, smiling eyes are moist, and he says to me: "That's enough. Things will be better, I swear it. 'Move away and your luck will change.' I know from my own experience; once things did not turn out well for me either. From now on we will be together again."

"What do you mean," I ask, "by 'together'?"

"What 'by together' means?" he says in a singsong, and his warm, dark eyes are laughing. "'By together' means, when someone has a business and needs help desperately and looks for someone—an honest man, a loyal man, no matter what he costs he's worth twice as much—and with God's help he meets a friend of his whom he hasn't seen for such a long time and learns that unfortunately time hasn't treated his friend well and he's looking for a business, it means simply, they need each other. And what could be better than that today?"

And in order to make this bit of luck seem more real, he draws out his wallet, opens it, and wants to show me a telegram. But my eyes don't fix of the telegram but fall on the wad of bills in his wallet—a nice thick wad of crisp bills in hundreds and five hundreds. And my eyes apparently are wide open, and his eyes meet mine and he guesses why I'm staring and says again in the same singsong: "The business, thank God, can bear it all. And when a new person enters the firm, he needs I'm sure a little extra cash. And there's enough money so why should he not take as much as he needs? What is there to be ashamed of? We all understand what it means to move to a new place with children. I know from experience. I was once in no better shape. I dreamt about greenbacks, too."

And my friend sits down on a bench with me and tells his whole life's story, full of extraordinary events, like tales from the *Thousand and One Nights*. My own life—even with my present troubles—is a bowl of cherries compared to his. I look at him and wonder, "What one man can endure!" And if God could help him after so many troubles, perhaps there's hope for me, too.

And my friend pulls out his wallet again and puts it right under my nose. "Why should one feel embarrassed?" he says to me. "One should take as much as one needs to tide one over."

I ask myself if this isn't a dream and look into the open wallet, and the hundred and five-hundred bills smile at me as do my friend's eyes, and I extend my hand and say: "Two will be enough."

I don't know what I should say: two one hundreds or two five hundreds? And to make it easier for me, he says, "Two thousand, I think, won't go very far."

And he counts out six five-hundred bills and says, "Is three thousand enough on the first go-round?"

"Ah . . ." I couldn't say one word more and fold the wad of bills and stuff them into my breast pocket and feel a strange warmth from them, a soothing feeling.

And so I won't be embarrassed, he adds, "And I should really like to take a look at my old friend's children, may they be well!"

But I don't answer him immediately. My thoughts are elsewhere— there in the breast pocket with a wad of five hundreds which warm and caress me and will not leave me alone. And my thoughts lead to my wife and children. I imagine the happy scene when they suddenly will see so much money and hear of this good luck.

"Well," I say, "we can go straight to my place. I live a few doors away. The children must be home. Shall we go?"

"Why not?" he says, and I can see in his eyes that he knows my thoughts are on the money in my breast pocket because I automatically pat it and sigh with pleasure. And he, that dog, completely understands, and drags the conversation back to those old, foolish, happy days of our childhood and recalls long-forgotten moments as we make our way to my place.

And then I start thinking about my place, my furniture . . . and I am embarrassed for my rich friend and begin to make excuses: "A new apartment . . . recently moved in . . . summertime . . . not yet settled in."

He understands at once what I mean, and before I can go on he says: "Oh, my . . . the usual . . . it's the same thing all over! No better at my place. Come summer and everything's upside down."

And at the same moment I remember the money flat against my chest and it warms and heats and ignites my thoughts. What shall I do first? . . . And quickly I add up in my mind: rent, the butcher bill, the child's tuition, my wife's shoes, my daughter's hat, a coat for myself, some furniture . . . today's debts, yesterday's debts, debts, debts!

Before I know it, the door is opened and one of my children comes toward me looking very sad. My poor children, I'm afraid, know we can't make ends meet. They know what it is to be poor. Not to be able to buy milk or meat at the market. In the morning the rent collector is coming, along with the woman who supplies us with tea, and the wood man, a brazen youth with a short beard who jeers from far off: "For the wood, you could have paid three times over already."

"Where's mother? I ask.

"In the kitchen," the child answers.

"We have no maid now. The maid just went off yesterday," I explain to my rich friend and almost die from shame. And I wonder how my wife will enter, Heaven forbid with greasy hands and God-knows-what clothes.

"It's the same at my place," he says. "They come and go; we have a new maid every week."

I don't know what to do. Shall I let my friend remain seated while I go myself into the kitchen and announce the good news to my wife? That miracles do happen? Or would it be better to remain here with my friend in the parlor?

I say "in the parlor" as if there really were a parlor. A large room, yes, but empty, bare—that is, a few tables, a rug, an old piano, a mirror, plus a lamp (a real ugly one), and a bed smack in the middle of the parlor! And still not made so late in the day! I would give a crisp one-hundred right away just to have someone remove the bed from there. My face turns red.

My friend guesses why I'm acting so strangely and calls out: "A nice apartment—airy, roomy, and not a bad idea to have someone sleep in the parlor. At my place, too, the children sleep in the parlor during the summertime."

"Here comes my only son," and I introduce him to my son who decides, just then, to take off his boots and walk around barefoot. My friend seeing that this little scene bothers me, thinks up a white lie: "In summertime all my children go barefoot, too."

And then my daughter enters, the second oldest. I present her to my old friend. She turns red as a beet, not because she is shy, but because she is so plainly, even poorly dressed. And the proof is in the shoes— everyday shoes but with patches, without heels, bent out of shape and torn.

And just for spite she sits down in such a way that he sees the shoes, and she notices where he's looking, and I notice how they both are staring at her shoes and I'm ready to die. Give me a hole in the ground, I would jump in alive.

"A lovely child," he whispers in my ear, "pretty as a picture."

I want to say something in reply when my eldest daughter, a real beauty, enters. At least she is wearing a decent pair of shoes, but she has put on a jacket made of thin muslin worn out at the elbows. She's not aware that there is a hole at the elbow and she sinks into her chair a little too deeply so that the elbow juts out straight at him. He looks at the elbow, and I look at him. I wink at her. She doesn't understand, becomes red as a beet, gets up and turns her back to go. Don't look, what a mess: her whole jacket is in shreds.

"One's more beautiful than the other," whispers my friend. "With such fine-looking children one must begin saving for the dowry immediately."

"The hell with this guy and his modern stove, his fancy house and courtyard, and all courtyards. They can all go to hell with Odessa itself for all I care."

By now you must have guessed: it's my grumbling wife who enters from the kitchen, bathed in sweat and burning up, the poor thing, without a maid. She must cook the food all by herself—something she has never been used to. The coal stove is smoking, the butcher will no longer give meat on credit, the milkmaid keeps demanding her money and won't leave the kitchen; in the market everything's overpriced; and the children carry on—they want new potatoes for lunch with sweet butter, no less!

I want to stop her, to call her away, first to announce the good news and second to have her change her clothes. But my friend doesn't let me, he holds me back and says: "I'd prefer introducing myself."

And he goes up to her, presents himself, and a dialogue ensues:

He: I knew your husband, madam, way before you.

She: A rare piece of luck!

He: We've been friends from childhood on.

She: Tell me who your friends are and I'll tell you who you are.

He: We studied together, ate together, slept together, and even stole apples from a basket together.

She: That speaks well for both of you.

He: Not only apples alone, but watermelons, too.

She: That's enough. I already know who you are.

My wife pronounces the last few words with so much venom that my friend can't say a word. I wink to her, I give her a high sign with my eyes to stop her sharp needling talk. But she's wound up and answers me: "What are you winking for? I know this type, this friend of yours."

"Madam!" says my friend with the voice of a man who feels himself somewhat insulted. "Madam, from what I see, you don't hold your husband in high esteem. May I remind you that I know him better than you."

"May I remind you," answers my wife in the same words, "that no one asked your opinion. He can stand on his own two feet and doesn't need your help."

I see my friend's face change. His cheeks turn flaming red. The warm, dark, smiling eyes have stopped sparkling and he is sweating as if his life were at stake. What shall I do? I'm finished. I may as well end it all. My surprise has turned sour, ruined. I've forgotten about the money in my breast pocket, I've forgotten about everything. Only one thing remains in my head: How can I take my wife aside? How do I let her know what he has done for us? I plead with my eyes: "Keep quiet! Stop talking!" And just for spite, she speaks up.

"I know all about his good friends and old schoolmates!" she says. "Nothing good will come of it. They're either good-for-nothing bums, or big shots dropping by with a story. Just last week a friend of his showed up from his home town, such a close friend, and from so far away—may he go to hell—and sold my husband such a bill of goods that our heads swirled: he's a real millionaire, a big philanthropist, a soft touch, only one of his kind in the world. And when it came time for my husband to ask for . . . What are you getting all embarrassed for? He's a good friend of yours, isn't he, with whom you once stole apples. And when it came time for my husband to tell him that . . ."

I cannot stand it anymore. I'm losing my temper. I can barely see straight. I must stop this talk at once. And I shout to my wife with a voice that's not mine: "That's eeeeee—nough!!!!!!!"

"What's the matter? Why are you screaming? Wake up!" blurts my wife, frightened to death, and shakes me out of sleep.

I sit up, rub my eyes, and look around. "Where can he be?"

"Who? Whom are you looking for?"

"My blood brother, that friend of mine."

"What blood brother? What friend? You were dreaming. Spit three times to ward off the evil eye! You went to bed late. How many times have I told you that you should stop writing late at night?"

I reach for my pocket and feel for the money. God, it was just there, just as I left it. A wad of crisp five-hundreds! I can still hear the crackle and feel the fresh bills in my hand.

And I remember that tomorrow at ten in the morning the tax collector is coming to draw up a list and auction off my chairs, and the landlord is throwing me out of the apartment, and the butcher wants his money and the milkmaid wants hers, and the woodcutter won't stop either—he comes by all the time and repeats, "Can't pay yet?" . . . And my son has an announcement: he's ready for his exams. Good luck to you, son, you should live to give better news. . . .

I'm bathing in sweat and trembling with chills.

Translated by Seth Wolitz

Once There Were Four

CHARACTERS

Mendele Mocher-Sforim, a fine old man with a gentle voice; referred to as "grandfather"

Bialik, a young poet; contemplative

Ben-Ami, a person prone to excitability

Sholom Aleichem, an old acquaintance, who listens and writes down everything in a notebook

Everyone says mountains are immovable. But I disagree. Mountains move, and how! They run! I discovered this when we four Jewish writers, one of us a poet, took our first walking trip in the famous, eternally snow-covered Alps.

A few miles out of the city—and the mountains seemed almost upon us. Just stretch out a hand and bid them hello. But the closer we came, the farther they moved. Indeed, ran away. We began to walk faster and faster. They outran us.

"Are they teasing us?" I called to the others.

"Who?"

"The mountains."

"I don't understand it," exclaimed my hot-tempered colleague who knew his way in the Alps like a Jew knows his prayer book. "They were never so far before. If you want my advice, we should walk a bit faster."

Urging us on, each time with greater force, he tired even more quickly than the rest of us, grew irritable and angry, and let out his bile in an

254

invective against the "Russian hoodlum with his revolution and his constitution."

"Wait! I want to ask you something," Reb Mendele called out. We all paused for a while. "I want each of you to tell me how you feel at this moment."

It seems my choleric companion was the first to understand the question. He hastened to answer, wiping the sweat from his forehead with the corner of his jacket. "I feel so light I could fly like an eagle, without once looking back."

"As for me," said the young poet, staring at me as he spoke, "I don't feel badly, but I doubt that I could fly."

It was my turn to answer: "I would feel wonderful," I said, "if we could sit down for a while, right here on the grass."

This irritated my excitable colleague who declared that if we continued at this pace, we would spend Sabbath at the foot of the mountain. Turning on me, he asked how I could have undertaken such a hike when I knew that I could hardly walk? Nevertheless, he did fold his umbrella, tuck under his jacket, and throw himself with the rest of us on the fragrant green grass to enjoy a taste of Paradise under God's sky and to beg "grandfather" Mendele for a story. . . .

Have you ever wanted to be someone you're not? I, for example, once wanted *not* to be a Jew—not permanently, God forbid!—but for a short time only, so that I might look with non-Jewish eyes at a group of Jews walking and talking, shouting and arguing and gesticulating. It must be an engrossing sight. An ordinary conversation must look like a quarrel, and a disagreement over a matter of importance—as, for example, the exact time of sunset or the cost of a certain building—like an impending fistfight.

Such were my thoughts as we walked in the Alps. Almost all those we met on the way—Frenchmen, Germans, Englishmen, and others—stopped to gaze in wonder at these odd creatures in strange garments. Perhaps this was because we spoke too loudly and all at once. Speaking all together is an art that only we Jews have mastered. Our assemblies, adjudications, celebrations, and councils are famous the world over. Parliamentary procedure, meaning that every person is required to speak singly, is an innovation for which we have Zionism to thank, and Dr. Herzl in particular. It is surely a fine thing, but not always and not everywhere. How would parliamentary procedure work for four Jewish writers, one of them a poet, climbing together in the famed, eternally snow-covered Alps, and discussing such matters as literature, *Talmud*, history, politics, poetry, and revolution?

The people we meet of other nationalities walk the same mountains, but their progress is dull. They walk in silence or talk so softly one can barely hear a word. Each is aware only of himself and his own stomach. You may consider this a rule: when several people walk together in silence, they are surely engrossed in their stomachs. But Jews are far from such matters. For us the stomach is one of nature's contraptions, an internal pouch and a source of vexation, as our "grandfather" Mendele has so often described it.

In any event, the passersby stared at us in amazement. Some even stopped to listen, waiting for the fight to begin. Dunces! They don't begin to understand that friends as close as we are cannot be found the world over. We may not flatter one another, play cards together, or engage in other such worldly pleasures; but when the Jewish exile occasionally brings us together in one place, our greatest joy is pouring out to one another our bitter hearts. Sometimes, over a nip of brandy, we grow so merry, the tears flow from our eyes. . . .

The sun, strolling across the bright blue Swiss sky, spilled golden sheaves that scattered like stalks of light over the eternal rocks and down the mountainside, falling at last with the serpentine streams into the restless Rhone . . .

We were still at the foot of the mountain which was growing taller, broader, and more beautiful before our eyes. It seemed no longer on the run from us, but to the contrary, it came out to greet us in friendly fashion, though with a touch of hauteur, too. If we four Jewish writers would kindly take the trouble to approach a little higher toward the Throne of God, there we would be exposed to vast marvels, recited to from the Book of Creation, and told of God's mighty powers. From its peak the mountain would show us the foolish little world below where children built tiny houses and called them cities, put tiny carts on wheels and called them trains, played at royalty and politics, at war and at slavery—quite as if they were grown up.

Each of us has a different name for the mountain: "The Sage," "Celebrity," "Reb Begging Your Pardon." Grandfather Mendele, in full flight of fancy, summons forth the greatest of giants, Og King of Bashan, who hoists the mountain on his shoulder and runs with it hundreds of miles in a single breath to hurl it upon the Jews. Suddenly God performs a miracle, and the murderous giant stops short with two enormous teeth growing from his mouth, one up, the other down. Unable to move, neither here nor there, he stands fixed in a singular tragi-comic pose! . . .

"What's its name, this magnificent mountain?"

All eyes turn to our hot-tempered friend, the acknowledged expert on all the mountains, rivers, and streams of the region. Instead of replying, he hesitates, flushes, rubs his forehead, stares up at the mountain's peak, and cries out, as if someone had stamped on his toe: "Tfoo! I've forgotten. Just a second ago I knew it—and now I forget! Can you imagine!"

"Forget?" says Reb Mendele. "If you want to know about forgetting, just ask me. There's no worse punishment on earth than forgetting. To have something fly from your head, like a bird from a cage, just when you need it most! It's an illness, a plague, a tragedy! Why, I could tell you a story—not a fiction either, but a true story—that happened to me in Odessa a few years ago, a story of a hotel . . . "

"I'll tell you a better one, that happened to *me* in Odessa! It's worth hearing!" cried my impulsive colleague.

He was on the point of beginning when he was interrupted by the poet: "My story is even better, though it happened not in Odessa but in Zhitomir!"

"And what about me?" protested the fourth, me myself. "I can tell you a story that took place in three cities at once, and you'll split your sides laughing!"

"Three cities at once? In that case, the honor is yours!" called Grandfather Mendele with a ringing laugh and a wave of his hand as if to say, "You bid for it? The bargain's yours!"

All four of us burst out laughing, and I felt quite the fool. It had been tactless of us to barge in on Grandfather with our stories, and we were now eager to make amends. For some time we pleaded with him to tell us what had happened in Odessa, and Grandfather, if you coax him long enough, always relents. He rolled up his sleeves, as was his habit, and pushed his glasses high up on his high, clever forehead, under the shock of wavy white hair. His small eyes, sharp and piercing, closed somewhat, and his face opened into that radiant, childlike smile that takes fifty years off his age and adds so much charm that you want to sit beside him forever, listening on and on.

Grandfather's Story

This happened, as I told you, some years ago in Odessa—that is, not in Odessa proper, but a couple of train stations away. I was on my way home. It was autumn. The outdoors was cloaked in a mantle of rain. The sky poured tears, the wind howled, the earth mourned for its lost mate, the warm dear sun. From time to time the rain lashed in anger at the sweaty windows of our railway compartment where we sat quite comfortably in the warmth—a companionable group, chatting amiably about the issues of the day.

The passenger opposite me was an educated and well-read man, a Christian as it happened, and a singular friend of the Jews. Now you know that I dislike fawning Jews even more than converts, and I don't fall all over myself with gratitude to every Gentile who has a good word for us either. But for this gentleman I felt a deep affection and an instinctive attraction that goes beyond rational understanding. What can I tell you? I felt so comfortable with him that I would readily have traveled in his company another three days. I was eager to be of some service to him, even in a small way, and happily the opportunity came immediately to hand. Since he was traveling for the first time to *my* city, Odessa, he wanted to know of a good place to stay, a decent hotel. As a longtime resident of the city, could I recommend to him the best hotel in the city?

A hotel? Why, of course!

I grabbed with both hands at this chance to be of help to him, and proceeded to describe in the most glowing colors a well-known hotel, the largest and most beautiful in the city. First, the view: the building was so artfully designed that all its windows faced the sea. Then the spacious, high-ceilinged, bright rooms; the splendid winter garden; the hothouses, reading rooms, the service, the excellent help. There was also the restaurant, the music—in short, I got carried away, as if I were describing Paradise, not a hotel.

With such a dreary outdoors, the prospect of a warm, cheerful oasis in a strange city was ten times more welcome than at any other time. My traveling companion heard me out with grateful shining eyes and a happy expression. I watched him take out his notebook, unclasp a tiny gold pencil, and wait patiently for me to finish so that he could jot down the name of the hotel. So absorbed was I that I failed to notice we were almost in Odessa. Only when people began to rise from their seats and collect their packages did my companion tactfully and with a friendly smile turn to me and ask the name of the hotel.

"Oh, of course! The name? Right away, I'll tell you . . . "

I thought for a moment. My God! What was its name? I knew it a second ago. . . . Damn! It slipped my mind! . . . Uselessly I rubbed my forehead, searched my memory. I simply couldn't remember! You probably think the name was unusual, complicated, hard to remember? Not at all. There is no easier name in the world—in fact, as you'll see, it's impossible to forget! The name was on the tip of my tongue, I had only to pronounce it—but it eluded me. If only the ground could have opened to swallow me!

Seeing my predicament, my companion wanted to effect a rescue, to drag me from the swamp. He applied all his skill and began to recite the names of hotels all over the world: "*Grand Hotel, Belleview, Terminus, Metropole, National, International, Bristol, Paris, Madrid, St. Petersburg, Chicago, San Remo, London, Hamburg, Constantinople . . .* "

No, no, and no again!

Seeing that these were of no use, he turned to national names: "*Hotel France? Montenegro? England? Hotel Russia? Austria-Hungary? Belgium? The Holland? The Brazil? Argentina?*"

Not a hope. We were getting nowhere!

"How about *Hotel Post? Hotel Royale? Hotel Europa? Hotel Louvre? Hotel Imperial?*"

To make it short, I watched him put away his notebook, reattach the tiny gold pencil to his watch fob, courteously bid me good-bye, thank me, and urge me to trouble myself no longer. He would surely, somehow, find his way to that best of hotels.

And as for me, had a grave opened up before me, I would gladly have leapt in. What an embarrassment! What humiliation! I was nothing but a useless old man. There I was each day, repeating my own version of the *Midrash:* better to be wicked all one's life than foolish for a single hour—and to commit such a folly! Who asked you to become such a do-gooder and to recommend an Odessa hotel to a complete stranger? What do you know about hotels anyway, and how can you forget a name that you *know*, that you see very day of your life? . . .

Well, I won't go on. I came home in a state of agitation. I paced the house, rubbing my forehead, in the hope that here, at least, the name would come to me.

"Maybe you know," I asked my wife, "the name of the hotel?"

"Which hotel?"

"She wants *me* to tell *her* which hotel! But I'm asking *you!*"

"Just tell me the name," she says.

Well, go talk to a woman! I would simply have to make my own way to the hotel to see for myself. But when you have just returned from a journey there are eighteen-hundred chores to be taken care of, all kinds of correspondence and business details to get through. So I grow even more nervous and annoyed, and because I am angry with myself and at the world I let it out on the innocent.

Finally night falls. It's hours since we've eaten, time to go to bed, and I'm still struggling with the name of the hotel. Have you ever heard such a story? . . . It was agreed that the next day, at dawn, I would go to the hotel without fail! But I couldn't fall asleep! There I lay, waiting for morning when I could dress and get over to the hotel to look at the sign.

Suddenly I jump out of bed and begin dressing.

"God be with you!" says my wife, frightened almost to death. "Where are you going?"

"I can't stand it any longer," I cry. "I must go and look!"

"Where? At what?"

"Take a lantern, and just come with me!"

I will spare you the description of my wife's plight. You can imagine for yourselves the feelings of a woman whose husband set out on a journey in good health and spirits, and returns home angry, sullen, pacing the house and rubbing his forehead like a madman. Then he suddenly leaps from his bed at night, tells her to light a lamp, and says, "Come on!" And she goes!

What won't a poor wife do for her husband? I say, "Come on!" and she follows. I walk through the mud, and she follows. With God's help we reach the hotel. I raise the lantern and look at the sign. Go ahead, see if you can guess the name! If you had eighteen heads it wouldn't help. The hotel's name is . . . *Odessa!*

The Poet and His Bride

"Well now, tell your story. You said you had a better one."

With these words Mendele addressed himself to our irascible colleague who began to protest that, first of all, he had not said his story was "better"—that had been the poet's claim. And if he had said it, it was not what he had meant to say. To prove his good will, let the poet tell his story first and he would wait his turn.

So it was decided. The poet cleared his throat and spoke as follows:

Each of you, naturally, was once a bridegroom and you had a betrothed. You're all older than I, so perhaps you've already forgotten. But I remember it as though it were yesterday. I was in a state of bliss, the whole world belonged to me! I am engaged to a lovely girl with six hundred rubles for dowry. I have two years free board, and a golden watch in my pocket. Not least, I am in the great city of Zhitomir! It is springtime, the sun is showering diamonds of light, the sky is mirror smooth, the birds sing, and in my heart, a holiday reigns. I want to embrace the world, to kiss everyone! The word *stranger* no longer has meaning. How can anyone be a stranger? If you love someone he is no stranger, and I love everyone: Zimel the tailor who scurries about with his work; Chaim-Hersh the wagoner who reeks of tar; Lazer-Ber the water carrier with his swollen ankles and peeling face; even Ivan the *Goy* who swears whenever he gets drunk that he will kill all the Jews. I could even embrace Ivan and kiss his charming, prickly puss!

If that's how it is with Ivan, you can imagine my feelings for an old friend with whom I grew up and with whom I went to the *yeshiva* at Volozhin. We hungered and grew ragged together. I ran into him the very first day I went walking with my beloved in town! I need hardly explain how eager I was for my betrothed to become acquainted with my friend, and my friend with my betrothed, so that they too might become friends and learn to love one another as I love them, and they me, and all of us the great wide world!

I fell on my friend's neck and kissed him, and drawing my beloved to my side, I introduced them to one another. "This is Miss . . . Miss . . . eh, my fiancée. . . . Her name . . . her name is . . . Oh, yes! And this is . . . this is Mr. . . . Mr. . . . my best and dearest friend. Surely I have told you all about him, my dearest. . . . His name . . . his name is. . . . Well, what is your name? You know what your name is, don't you? Why don't you say something? . . ."

Well you can understand why my friend remained silent. He probably thought that from an excess of happiness I had altogether lost my senses. As for my bride, to this day I don't know what she was thinking. We've been married now, praise God, for several years, but we have never referred to the incident. Neither of us would find it pleasant. There are moments you want to forget, to blot out from memory—but it is impossible. We forget what should be remembered and remember what should be forgotten. That, in a nutshell, is the moral of the story. Now it's someone else's turn.

What Is My Name?

The young poet concluded, and our choleric companion began his account with a curse, as was his wont when speaking of matters he found unpleasant.

When all the uprisings began in our Odessa over the battleship *Potemkin*—with the bombs whizzing over our heads, and the fires and the slaughters—I said, "Let it sink for all I care! I don't want to be here! I'd rather go to the ends of the world, may the devil take them!" And I began preparing for my departure. But it's easy to say *leave!* You think it's just a matter of letting kvass flow from a barrel. You first need a pass! Don't blame me if *kvass* rhymes with *pass* and *mishegass!* . . . Where was I? Oh, yes. You have to work at getting a pass, contact all sorts of people (may their names and memories be erased!), and meet all the petty officials (may the cholera take them this very day!).

"Now that you've exhausted the chapter of curses, perhaps you could stop swearing and get on with your story," Grandfather Mendele suggested.

Am I cursing anyone? To hell with them! It's just a passing comment: may they burn in hell! In short, I started arranging for a passport—and you well know what that means! Get friendly with all the parasites and hand out the money—just like Yom Kippur eve (to distinguish between sacred and profane), when the beggars line up in front of the synagogue.

Every face is an open maw waiting to be filled. Well, I looked into plenty of open maws before I reached the Chief himself.

Having passed through all the circles of hell, I entered his office and found the Chief in the thick of work—scraping with the pen. You know very well that to interrupt an official in the act of scribbling is to put your life on the line. The world may be going under, but you must wait patiently until he finishes. But since I am not so good at standing politely, I decide to cough lightly, sending a herald, as it were, to announce that someone has arrived.

The Chief doesn't pause in his scribbling, so I cough a little louder. This time he raises his head, fixes me with a pair of bloodshot eyes, and hollers in Russian, "What do you want?"

At this reception, of course, I flare up like a match. What is this "What do you want?" Why should he shout at me? And when I get angry, I forget where I am. I see red. I want to break, tear, destroy everything in sight. I remember when I was a child, an orphan, I hated pity more than anything in the world. Once a neighbor made me a wonderful new pair of pants—pants that you see once in a hundred years. She felt sorry for me, you see. She called together the whole neighborhood, showed off every feature of the new pants, and not content with that, called me over to try them on so that everyone could admire their fit. That was the final straw. I ran over, grabbed the pants, and tore into them with my nails and teeth until there was nothing left but shreds and tatters. . . . Where was I? Oh, yes, the Chief has just showered me with his "What do you want?" and I am so angry that I want to make a scene he will never forget. But then I may find myself without a pass. So I control myself this once, approach the table, and hand him my papers. He glances at them and asks, "What is your name?" I remain silent. Seeing that I am silent, he raises his voice several notches and tries again: "What is your name? What are you called?"

My name? As you see me here alive, at that very moment I forgot that in addition to my pen name, I also had my own name. When I say forgot, I mean *forgot*! But completely! All the names of my relatives, friends, and acquaintances parade before me, but one name, my own, has disappeared to where the Holy Sabbath vanishes . . . *Lord of the Universe, tell me: what is my name? What do they call me?* If you'd chopped off my head, I couldn't remember. Meantime, the Chief stares at me as if I were a criminal. Any moment now—I am thinking—he will call me up for a proper sentence, send for two angels of hell to carry me off, and I will be back in exile again. Well, enough! I've had my taste of it, and I don't need any more.

But there is, after all, a great compassionate God above who guides the just, and He inspires me to maintain my composure—*like iron.* These people, if you treat them offhandedly and raise your voice just a little, will melt like putty. And so it was.

The Chief: What is your name?

I: Who? Me?

He: Who else? Me?

I: Exactly as it says in my papers.

He: What does it say in your papers?

I: Can't you read?

He: Who? Me?

I: Who else? Me?

He: (loudly) Wha-a-t! How dare you talk to me like that? Do you know to whom you're speaking?

I: (also loudly) And do you know to whom *you* are speaking?

Hearing me speak in a tone of voice such as he has never in his life heard from a Jew, he looks into the papers and reads my name aloud. And that was all I needed!

What happened subsequently is of little interest. I got out of my predicament safely, and I praise and thank the good Lord every day and every hour for having saved me from exile. May He never have to extricate me from such a dilemma again. . . .

"Amen," we three responded in chorus, and Grandfather Mendele winked to let me know it was now my turn.

A Story of Three Cities

This happened a few years before the "Constitution." I was then making tours to cities and towns on behalf of various organizations throughout Lithuania. Once, around Chanukah time, I received invitations simultaneously from three neighboring cities— Mogilev, Vitebsk, and Smolensk—all three on the same railroad line. The requests came from three separate organizations: the "pure" Zionists, the Labor Zionists, and the Bundists. Naturally these organizations coexisted amicably, like cats and mice. Careful not to speak evil on their friends, the "pure" Zionists let it be known that the *false* Zionists were bringing me to the above-named cities in order to exploit me for their work which bore no relation to Zionism. The Labor Zionists were similarly restrained in their remarks about the "pure" Zionists: they merely regretted the agitation of these Sabbatian heretics, these false Messiahs, for a cause long since dead. . . . The Bundists, however, poured out their wrath on both Zionist groups, and assured me that a tour under the Zionists' auspices would be a guaranteed failure.

In short, I wasn't overjoyed by the prospect before me. What could be done? Finally I conceived of a Jewish plan: unite and divide. I said, "Children, I will come to you on the condition that all three organizations unite for the evenings in all three cities." My proposal was accepted, and there followed a flurry of letters and telegrams regarding the schedule and itinerary.

To which city should I go first? This became the point most difficult to resolve. Each day my route was changed. At first it was decided that I should begin in Mogilev, go from Mogilev to Vitebsk, from Vitebsk to Smolensk, then back to Mogilev—and home. Next it was agreed that I had best start in Smolensk, from Smolensk to Mogilev, from Mogilev to Vitebsk, from Vitebsk back past Mogilev—and home. Then that plan was scratched, and it remained that I should go to Vitebsk, Mogilev, Smolensk, and then back home via Mogilev. Finally they drew up another route "for my convenience": I was to stop first in Smolensk, then proceed to Vitebsk via Mogilev, go from Vitebsk back to Mogilev, and from Mogilev (immediately after the evening's lecture) straight home. The schedule was as follows, and please pay attention: *on the 18th, Smolensk; the 19th, Vitebsk; the 20th, Mogilev.*

On the evening of the 17th I set out, telegraphing ahead to all three cities that I would be there on the specified dates. In the meantime, they prepared all that was necessary—posters, tickets, programs, and so on. While driving to the station, I went over my itinerary again and again, and because of the many changes, naturally enough, I lost track. It seemed to me that I was to be in Vitebsk on the 18th; in Smolensk on the 19th; and in Mogilev on the 20th.

And I acted accordingly. I bought my train ticket and rode calmly to Vitebsk. When I got there, I walked about the depot for half an hour— an hour—two hours—on the chance of spotting one of the Zionists or

Bundists. Has no one come to meet me, to welcome me? They may be Zionists and Bundists, but it still isn't right!

So I hired a carriage and asked the driver to take me to the best hotel. I ordered a room, washed and changed quite serenely, and thought to myself: "If that's the kind of jokers you are, you can take the trouble to search for me in the hotels. Sholom Aleichem is not a needle in a haystack, after all—search long enough and you'll find him."

When I went down to the dining room for lunch, I caught sight of two large posters:

VISITING OUR CITY!!!
SHOLOM ALEICHEM, THE GREATEST JEWISH HUMORIST!
THE 19TH . . .

The 19th? Why the 19th? I call over the waiter, a young Litvak with coarse red hands, a black muzzle, and a white serviette under the arm of his soiled jacket.

"Please tell me, my good man, what's today?"

The waiter blows his nose into the white serviette and says: "Today? Today we have beetroot borscht with cabbage, farfel pudding, and duck, if you like . . . "

"No, that's not what I mean. I mean what day is it today?"

He thinks a while. "What day is it today? Tuesday, the 18th."

"And what is the name of this city?"

"Which city?"

"*This* city. *Your* city. What is it called?"

He stands motionless, stares at me and says: "What do you mean, what's it called? It's called Vitebsk, that's what it's called."

"You're lying!" I retort, "You're dreaming, my friend. The name of your city is Smolensk, not Vitebsk."

"Ha, ha, ha! Ha, ha, ha!"

Apparently the greatest Jewish humorist has impressed the waiter as the greatest fool in the world, for he turns aside and buries his snout in the serviette so that I shouldn't see him choking with laughter. I turn back for another look at the posters. There it is in huge letters:

SHOLOM ALEICHEM IN VITEBSK!

In Vitebsk? All-Merciful God, how can I be in Vitebsk when I'm supposed to be in Smolensk? I don't know what to do with myself. Who needs borscht? Who can think of duck? I must leave for Smolensk. But in order to know my "right place in the liturgy" I decide first to check with my wife. She can telegraph me immediately to tell me where I am to be the first evening. In all matters concerning dates and itineraries, my wife is the expert. And in order to speed things up, I knock out an urgent message: "WHERE AM I TODAY? TELEGRAPH REPLY."

The telegram sent, I feel more relaxed and return to the beetroot borscht, the farfel pudding, and the duck. Then I lie down for a snooze and, as the custom is, fall asleep. In my sleep I am beset by dreams of blonde women and black cats. A bad sign: whenever I dream of blonde women and black cats I can expect the worst. And so it was. Suddenly, as I woke, I realized it was late. If I don't hurry, I'll miss Smolensk. I run to the train, climb aboard, and sitting comfortably in the compartment, I ask the conductor, "When do we arrive in Smolensk?" He pauses, fixes his eyes on the points of his boots, and informs me that we will be in Smolensk at six o'clock the following morning.

"What do you mean, six o'clock tomorrow morning? I must be in Smolensk no later than seven this evening!"

The conductor listens to me patiently and shows me on his watch that from here to Smolensk it takes even the express train no less than twelve hours and some minutes—and since it is already some minutes past four, how can we possibly reach Smolensk today? As it happens he is correct, but what good is that to me? I have lost Smolensk! What am I to do now? Return to Vitebsk? The devil take it! Let me at least figure out where I stand with Mogilev. And no one knows this as well as my wife. At this point I recall that I asked her to wire me in Vitebsk. Now I am enroute to Smolensk. *How will the cat cross the stream?* A learned Jew, as they say, finds a way. So I get busy and write another telegram to my wife and I give it to the conductor at the next station: "TELEGRAPH SMOLENSK. WHEN AM I IN MOGILEV?"

Now, let us take a moment for a bit of language analysis, Tractate Philology, and translate literally two telegrams from the language in which they were written, Russian, into our own Yiddish. In the first I seem to be asking my wife, "Where am I?" (*Srotchi, gdie ya sevodnia?*) In the second, I seem to ask her to telegraph Smolensk while I am still in Mogilev *(Telegraphiroi Smolensk, kogda ya Mogiliovie?)* If you, for example, were to receive two such wires, you could only conclude that the sender has gone mad. And let's not forget that Smolensk is no possum and did not play dead either. At Smolensk they waited for me at the station on the 18th from 1 p.m. till 12 midnight. The audience stormed through the hall and accused the Zionists of having perpetrated a swindle, of having dreamed up a Sholom Aleichem and then run off with the cash. There was nothing for it but to open the money box and refund the tickets. In great dismay, the Zionists and Bundists got together after midnight and sent off a telegram to my home: "WHAT HAPPENED TO SHOLOM ALEICHEM?"

Now let us turn our attention from the prince to the princess. My wife, may she live and be well, when she received these three jolly telegrams, wasted no time and started out immediately to Mogilev. Now this may seem absurd. Why Mogilev? Well, if you'll hear me out, you will see for yourself that she is a sage.

In the first place, she knows me well—we weren't married yesterday. She knows that if I telegraph her from Vitebsk to wire me at Smolensk, I must be in Mogilev. You see, she remembers a previous occasion. I was once in Warsaw on my way home to Kiev for Passover. Suddenly, on the first day of Passover, she gets a wire from me that I am spending the holiday in Holendre, not far from Wapniarke. How did I get to Wapniarke, of all places, which is on the way between Szmerinke and Odessa? Don't ask. I meant no evil, God forbid; my intentions were good. As I was in a terrible hurry to get home, I changed from one express train to another until I found myself on the Odessa line, stranded at the Holendre station. Still, it could have been worse. At least I didn't go as far as Riga! That's what comes of hurrying. No wonder people say, "Haste makes waste." Well, that was in the first place.

In the second place, my wife figured that according to my telegrams the misfortune had occurred not in Vitebsk, nor in Smolensk, but somewhere in between. Accordingly, she could choose no better central point than Mogilev. She was certain that even in the best of circumstances there must have been a collision between two locomotives: the one from Smolensk to Vitebsk with the one from Vitebsk to Smolensk. In such a crash, she assumed, all the cars must have been crushed into splinters—no fewer than two hundred passengers killed, several hundred badly wounded, and among the rest, many deranged, including (it stands to reason) myself.

Generally my wife has a habit, whenever I leave home, of imagining the very worst disasters in the world. Wherever there may be a flood, a collision, a collapsed bridge, a thunderstorm, an earthquake, a conflagration, a sudden epidemic, an ambush of armed guerillas, a snake bite (which occurs once every five hundred years)—she imagines these disasters lurking for me, waiting for me to set out. And when I return home in one piece she can't believe her eyes, staring at me incredulously as though I'd been snatched from the very jaws of death.

This time, too, when she saw me hale and strong, she burst into tears like a child. "Why are you crying, my little fool?" I ask her.

"He wants to know why I'm crying!" she replies. "For him this is another Rovno!"

What has Rovno to do with it, you ask. That's another episode from my travels. If you really want to hear it, I'll tell you what happened in Rovno. A few years ago, I was languishing in Petersburg, trying to get a permit for a Yiddish newspaper, and I decided to go home by way of Vilna. I had told my wife that I was leaving Petersburg on such and such a day; that if I were required to be in Vilna, I would stay there for a day or two, and if not I would come home right from Petersburg. So it was. It turned out that the stopover in Vilna was unnecessary, and knowing how agreeable this news would be to my wife, I sent her a night telegram en route. As sleepy as I was, I translated the words "coming directly" somewhat carelessly; instead of *Yedu priamo*, I wrote *Yedu Rovno*. And since I hadn't seen the children for some time, I added two more words, *Vstretshay dietmi*, meaning "Meet me with the children." Short and sweet. I reach home that evening and rush around the depot like a lunatic. Where is my wife? Where are the children? Not a soul! I ride home—the house is dark as a cemetery. I ring and ring, tear at the bell, pound at the door. At last the cook appears, like a sleepy cat. I grab the swarthy Litvak. "Where is the Mistress? Where are the children?"

"The Mistress?" she says, wiping her nose. "She's not here."

"What do you mean, *see's* not here?" I ask her in Litvakese.

"They all went away."

"What do you mean, went away? Where did they go?"

"How should I know? To Rovno."

"Why on earth to Rovno?"

"You're asking *me*? You told them to join you in Rovno."

"*I* told them to join me in Rovno? *Me?*

"Who then, *me?*" answers the cook, and it seems to me that she is laughing.

You understand? My blood is running out, and she is laughing! I swear to you in all honesty—I'm ashamed to say it, to no one else would I confess this—that never before have I even lifted a finger against another human being! But this sleepy Litvak with her silly laughter so enraged me that I forgot where I was in the world! . . . And how do you think it ended? I had a lawsuit on my hands . . . The word, *Rovno*, cost me plenty, and I had to beg the cook's pardon besides.

In any event, after hearing the good news that my wife and children are in Rovno, I hoist my feet on my shoulders and fly to Rovno. I arrive, but where? What? I can find no one. I make inquiries about a woman with several children. And I am told, "They were here and left." It seems there is nothing left for me to do but to return home. When I get back I find the doctor. What happened? My wife has fallen ill from all her troubles. . . .

"Well, now, let me ask you," I say to my wife after we have both calmed down a little, "why did you fly off with the children to Rovno, and what were you thinking?"

"Don't ask!" she replies. "When I got your telegram telling me to meet you in Rovno with the children, I almost went out of my mind. All kinds of thoughts flew into my head. I thought you had fallen sick somewhere, somewhere around Rovno, with typhus, God forbid, or smallpox."

"What on earth put the idea of smallpox into your head?" I asked, controlling myself.

"That same day I read in the papers that there was smallpox . . . in India."

At this point I can no longer restrain myself and leap up from the chair. "I don't understand! Where is India and where is Petersburg?"

She gazes at me tenderly, like a mother at her child, and says, "Where you're concerned, who knows?"

Now tell me, how much is such a wife worth?

Translated by Etta Blum

Glossary

AGUNA—deserted wife who, according to Jewish law, cannot remarry unless her husband's death is certified

bris—ceremony of circumcision for a male child

Chanukah—Jewish holiday commemorating the rededication of the Temple in Jerusalem by Judah Maccabee in 165 B.C.

cheder—school

Chelm stories—legendary comic stories told about Jews from the town of Chelm

Gemara—a section of the *Talmud*; sometimes refers to the *Talmud* as a whole

Gevalt!—Help!

golem—a human creature without a soul; a Frankenstein

goyisher kop—literally, in Yiddish, a "Gentile head"; used to suggest something less than brilliance of mind

grager—a noisemaker used in celebrating the Jewish holiday of Purim

Haggadah—set form of comments, prayers, and songs recited on the first two nights of the Passover holiday

haroses—paste made of fruit and wine used in the Passover ritual to symbolize the mortar Jews made as slaves in Egypt

Hasidic—refers to Hasidism, a movement of pietistic enthusiasm among East European Jews that flourished in the late eighteenth and early nineteenth centuries and continues to exist even today

havdoleh candle—braided candle used at the ritual that marks the conclusion of the Sabbath

Hershel Ostropolier stories—comic stories about a Jewish scamp named Hershel Ostropolier

Kaddish—mourner's prayer, usually said by the son

khale—Sabbath bread loaf

Kiddish—blessing said over a cup of wine to celebrate the Sabbath or a holiday

kneydlach—dumplings

knishes—pastries usually filled with potatoes, meat, or buckwheat

Kol Nidre—introductory prayer at Yom Kippur

Lag Baomer—spring holiday commemorating spiritual and armed resistance to the Romans

L'chayim!—a toast to life

mazel tov—congratulations

Megillah—scroll; usually refers to the Scroll of Esther, read on Purim

Midrash—a homily or homiletic interpretation

Purim—holiday commemorating the defeat of Haman by Esther

Rambam—Rabbi Moses ben Maimon, Maimonides, 1135-1204, a great rabbinic authority and philosopher

Rashi—most authoritative commentator on the Bible and *Talmud*; lived 1040-1105

reb—mister

rebbe—rabbi, learned man, teacher

rebbetsen—wife of a rabbi

Rosh Hashanah—Jewish New Year

schlemiel—a loser, sometimes used interchangeably with *schlimazel*

schlimazel—a luckless creature of infinite misfortune

seder—ceremonial meal held during the first two nights of Passover

Sephardim—descendants of Spanish and Portuguese Jews

shammes—sexton

Shavuos—Feast of the Pentecost; holiday celebrating the giving of the Torah to Moses

shimenesre—the eighteen blessings said in three daily sets of prayers

Shma Yisroel!—the Jewish creed or cry: "Hear, O Israel!"

shochet—ritual slaughterer

shofar—ram's horn blown on the High Holidays

Sholem aleichem—a greeting: "Peace be unto you"

shprakh—language

shtetl—small town in East Europe inhabited mostly by Jews

shul—synagogue

Simkhas-Torah—holiday after Succos celebrating the completion of a year's reading of the Torah

sliches—penitential prayers recited the week before Rosh Hashanah

Succos—autumn holiday of the harvest, celebrated by meals in the *suke* (or booth), commemorating the desert life of the Jews after the Exodus

tallis—prayer shawl

Talmud—collection of writings constituting traditional Jewish civil and religious law

tefillin—phylacteries

Tisha Bov—the ninth day of the Jewish month of Av; a day of fasting and mourning to commemorate the destruction of the Temple in Jerusalem and other disasters

Torah—Pentateuch, the Five Books of Moses; also a term for Jewish learning in general

treyf—unclean; ritually impure

Vilna Gaon—outstanding Jewish scholar and religious authority, Elijah ben Solomon Zalman (1720-1797), known as the sage of Vilna

yarmulke—skullcap

yeshiva—school of advanced Talmudic and rabbinic studies

Yom Kippur—Day of Atonement

Biographical Notes

SHOLOM ALEICHEM is the pseudonym of Sholom Rabinovitch, born in 1859 in the small Ukrainian town of Pereyeslav. There and in the neighboring *shtetl* (or Jewish town) of Voronkov he spent his youth. He was educated first at a traditional Jewish *cheder* and then at the local government high school; at seventeen he became resident tutor to the daughter of a wealthy Jewish landowner. The predictable romance between tutor and student flourished into a life-long marriage.

Rabinovitch worked briefly as a government rabbi (*rabbiner*), a clerk, and a businessman-speculator, but his writing soon eclipsed all other occupations. After publishing several works in Hebrew, he turned to writing Yiddish fiction in 1883, initiating a prolific and varied literary career. Under the jovial pen name of Sholom Aleichem, the most common term of greeting among Jews, he wrote hundreds of short stories, dramas, novels, feuilletons, and poems. His career coincided with the rapid expansion of the Yiddish press, of which he was one of the major and most popular contributors.

Sholom Aleichem lived with his growing family in Kiev and briefly in Odessa until the pogroms of 1905. Following those disturbances the family left Russia for almost a decade of wandering. In 1906 Sholom Aleichem made his first trip to New York, but was unsuccessful in his attempt to establish himself as a playwright of the flourishing American Yiddish Theatre. He returned to Europe and in 1907 undertook a reading tour through Poland and Russia. He collapsed midway through what had been a triumphant series of personal appearances and spent the following six years recuperating in Southern Italy and Switzerland. In 1914 the family settled in New York, where Sholom Aleichem died on May 13, 1916.

SAUL BELLOW is the distinguished American novelist, author of *Herzog, Humboldt's Gift,* and *Seize the Day,* among other works, and recent winner of the Nobel Prize for Literature.

REUBEN BERCOVITCH has written two novels, *Hasen* and *Odette*, and translated the work of David Bergelson, I. L. Peretz, I. D. Berkowitz, Rachel Weprinsky, and Chaim Grade.

SACVAN BERCOVITCH, professor of English at Columbia University, is the author of *The Puritan Origins of the American Self*, among other works.

ETTA BLUM has published two books of poetry as well as translations of short stories by Eliezer Blum-Alquit, and poems by Jacob Glatstein.

FRANCES AND JULIUS BUTWIN are pioneering translators of Yiddish literature, and Mrs. Butwin is also the coauthor, with her son Joseph, of a critical study of Sholom Aleichem.

GERSHON FREIDLIN has translated works by Ber Mark, Jacob Celemenski, Y. L. Dashevsky, Isaac Raboy, and Raphael Mahler.

HILLEL HALKIN, an American-born writer now living in Israel, is the author of *Letters to an American Jewish Friend*.

NATHAN HALPER was born in New York City, where he attended the Natzionale Radicale Shule and Columbia University; he now lives in Provincetown, Massachusetts.

IRVING HOWE is Distinguished Professor of English at the City University of New York; his most recent books include *World of Our Fathers*, which won the 1977 National Book Award, *Leon Trotsky*, and *Celebrations and Attacks*.

SEYMOUR LEVITAN is currently translating a collection of Rochl Korn's poems and stories.

The late ISAAC ROSENFELD was the author of the novel *Passage from Home*; his essays have been collected as *An Age of Enormity*.

MIRIAM WADDINGTON, professor of English at York University in Toronto, is the author of twelve books of poetry and the editor of *The Collected Poems of A. M. Klein*.

RUTH R. WISSE, Chairman of the Jewish Studies Program at McGill University in Montreal, is the author of *The Schlemiel as Modern Hero, The Shtetl and Other Modern Yiddish Novellas.*

LEONARD WOLF has written, among other books, *The Passion of Israel, A Dream of Dracula, The Annotated Dracula,* and *The Annotated Frankenstein.*

SETH WOLITZ is 1978-1979 fellow at the National Humanities Institute at the University of Chicago and professor of French and Comparative Literature at the University of Texas.

ERADICATING HEART DISEASE

MATTHIAS RATH, M.D.

Published by Health Now
387 Ivy Street
San Francisco, CA 94102 U.S.A.

You can purchase this book at your bookstore,
your health food store or directly from Health Now,
by calling 1-800-624-2442

"An ounce of prevention is worth a pound of cure."

President Bill Clinton in his Health
Care address to the U.S. Congress.

Copyright ©1993 by Matthias Rath, M.D.

All rights reserved. No part of this book may be transmitted in any form or by any means,
electronic or mechnical, including photocopying, recording, or by any information storage
and retrieval system, without written permission of the publisher.

ISBN 0-9638768-0-5

THE NUTRITIONAL DEFICIENCY
THAT DOES NOT MAKE US HUNGRY

Vitamin deficiencies that cause heart attacks, strokes and other cardiovascular diseases do not give us warning signs. Unlike regular hunger, we don't feel stomach pain or any other alarm sign. The first signs that our body cells starve from vitamin deficiency are the outbreak of diseases. These diseases develop primarily in those organs which suffer most from nutritional deficiencies: the heart and the blood vessels.

"New thoughts and new truths go through three stages. First they are ridiculed. Next they are violently opposed. Then, finally they are accepted as being self-evident."

Arthur Schopenhauer

May this book help to make self-evident to all that vitamins are keys to optimum cardiovascular health.

HEART DISEASE - THE EPIDEMIC
OF THE 20TH CENTURY
CAN BE ERADICATED

Cardiovascular disease is the number one killer in the United States and many other countries. Every year, millions of people die from heart attacks and strokes, and millions more are left disabled. Heart disease has become an epidemic disease. Like all epidemics, heart disease is caused by one or only a few factors which have now been identified.

A hundred years ago, Louis Pasteur, Robert Koch, and other brilliant scientists, discovered bacteria as the cause of infectious diseases. This led to the eradication of many infectious diseases and saved millions of lives. Now a medical discovery has been made that can lead to the eradication of heart attacks, strokes, and other forms of cardiovascular diseases.

During recent years an increasing number of studies indicated the benefits of vitamins in relation to cardiovascular disease. Now, finally, a scientific breakthrough was made documenting that vitamin deficiency is in fact the primary cause of heart attacks, strokes, and other cardiovascular diseases. Most importantly, on the basis of these discoveries, we can now prevent cardiovascular diseases by an optimum intake of nutritional supplements. My discoveries which led to this scientific breakthrough are summarized in this book. These discoveries will have a direct impact on your personal health and on the health of millions of people.

I hope that the recommendations of this book will help you personally to achieve and maintain optimum cardiovascular health.

TABLE OF CONTENTS

SECTION C: HOW TO PREVENT CARDIOVASCULAR DISEASE WITH NUTRITIONAL SUPPLEMENTS

SECTION D: HOW TO REVERSE EXISTING CARDIOVASCULAR DISEASE WITH NUTRITIONAL SUPPLEMENTS

SECTION E: HOW TO NEUTRALIZE RISK FACTORS FOR CARDIOVASCULAR DISEASE WITH NUTRITIONAL SUPPLEMENTS

SECTION F: HOW TO EFFECTIVELY TREAT OTHER HEART CONDITIONS WITH NUTRITIONAL SUPPLEMENTS

SECTION G: ERADICATING HEART DISEASE

INTRODUCTION

- How You Can Benefit Immediately From Reading This Book

- The Scope of the Heart Disease Epidemic

HOW YOU CAN BENEFIT
FROM READING THIS BOOK

• **This book is a handbook for optimum cardiovascular health.**

It is an educational book about the number one killer in America.
It contains many illustrations and pictures for better understanding.
It explains how your body functions during health and during disease.
It summarizes the most important heart disease studies and the benefits of vitamins.
It gives my personal recommendations for optimum cardiovascular health.
Most importantly, it shares with you the astonishing health improvements from patients who have already been following the health recommendations of this book.

• **You can improve your health.** Heart attacks and strokes are vitamin deficiency diseases. They are essentially unknown in the animal world, especially in those species that manufacture optimum amounts of their own vitamin C. If you know which vitamins to take and in what amounts, you can prevent heart attacks, strokes, and many other diseases. This book gives first hand answers to your most important questions about heart diseases.

• **You will obtain the latest scientific information on**
How to prevent heart attacks
How to prevent strokes
How to fight angina pectoris, the chest pain from heart disease
How to reduce the clogging of blood vessels after bypass surgery
How to reduce high cholesterol levels
How to alleviate the risk from lipoprotein-a, a newly identified risk factor
    for heart disease - ten times greater than cholesterol
How to prevent blindness and kidney failure in diabetic patients
How to lower high blood pressure
How to fight heart diseases caused by stress, smoking and other factors

The answers to these and other important questions will make this book an invaluable source of information for the rest of your life.

• **You can optimize your health with safe nutritional supplements.** Vitamins, minerals, and other essential nutritional supplements are products of nature. These compounds have effectively maintained health over millions of years. Nutritional supplements can help your body function better without increasing the risk for undesirable side effects.

• **You could increase your life expectancy.** The human body is as young as the walls of its blood vessels. You will learn how to protect your blood vessel system, the largest organ of the human body. Maintaining the stability and flexibility of the blood vessels is an important goal in preventing premature aging of your body. This book describes how you can prevent early aging and achieve a longer and healthier life.

• **You can save money.** Nutritional supplements are not only a very effective way to maintain your health, but also a very economical way. The daily amount of nutritional supplements necessary to prevent heart attacks and strokes costs only a few dimes.

• **You can take better charge of your own health.** This book does not only give you advice for optimum cardiovascular health, it also shares with you the proof: the amazing health improvements of people who have been following the recommendations of this book. This book has been written to encourage you to take better charge of your own health.

• **You can help your loved ones.** This book contains information important to every human being. Share this information with your family, your friends, your neighbors. The medical discoveries reported in this book are also important for their health and their lives. Your loved ones will be grateful to you for passing on this information.

• **You can make all the difference.** The first report that vitamin deficiency is a primary cause of heart attacks and strokes was published more than 50 years ago. Ignoring this report cost the lives of over half a billion people, more than in all wars of mankind together. This unnecessary dying can be stopped, with your help.

Presently, the U.S. Food and Drug Administration is trying to limit the free access of the American people to vitamins, amino acids and other nutritional supplements by making them prescription drugs. By doing so, this federal agency does not serve the interests of millions of Americans who would be deprived of an effective, safe, and affordable way to improve their health.

You can become an advocate for an effective, safe, and affordable health care for yourself and also for the benefit of your loved ones. This book gives you important arguments based on the latest scientific discoveries and clinical studies. Talk about this book within your community, to your local newspaper. Ask them to report about these important discoveries. Contact your political representatives. You can make the difference.

THE PROBLEM:

HEART DISEASE IS A WORLDWIDE EPIDEMIC

- **According to the World Health Organization More Than 12 Million People Die Every Year From Cardiovascular Diseases.**

- **In Most Countries Every Second Death is Caused by Cardiovascular Diseases - Both in Men and Women**

The table on the next page shows you the world-wide scope of the heart disease epidemic. The data were provided by the World Health Organization (WHO) in 1987. Note that some European countries have changed names in the meantime.

In this table the death rates from cardiovascular diseases in men are shown for 32 industrialized nations. For each country the closed rectangles show the death rates from cardiovascular diseases per 100,000 inhabitants. The open rectangles show the death rates from all other causes, in a given country, taken together. In most countries listed cardiovascular diseases are responsible for about every second death.

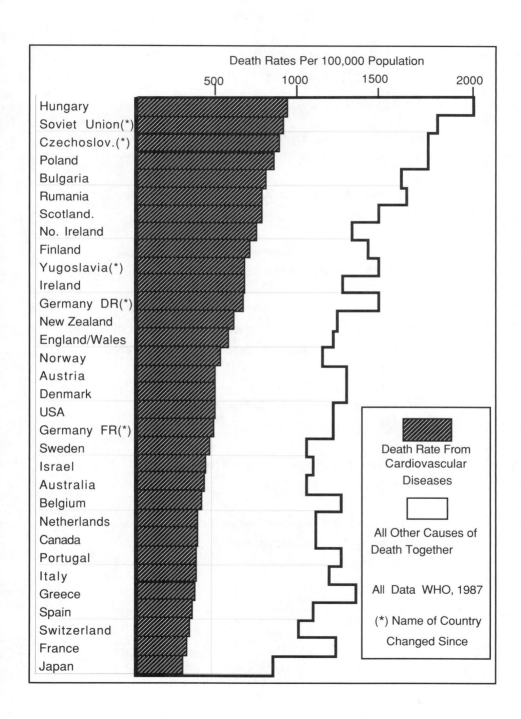

Death Rates Per 100,000 Population

THE PROBLEM:

THE HEART DISEASE EPIDEMIC IN THE UNITED STATES

• Presently, More Than 7 Millions Americans Have Been Diagnosed With Coronary Heart Disease

• Every Year 1.5 Million Americans Will Suffer a Heart Attack.

• 300,000 of These Patients Will Die Suddenly - Before They Can Reach a Hospital or Can Receive Medical Attention.

• Millions of Americans Suffer Presently From Other Forms of Cardiovascular Diseases and Related Diseases:

  • 29 Million Americans Suffer From High Blood Pressure.

  • 8 Million Americans Suffer From Irregular Heartbeat

  • 2.5 Million Americans Suffer From Cerebrovascular Diseases (Atherosclerotic Deposits in the Brain Arteries).

THE PROBLEM:

THE HEALTH CARE COSTS FOR CARDIOVASCULAR DISEASES ARE SKYROCKETING

- 100 Billion Dollars Are Spent in the United States on the Treatment of Cardiovascular Diseases Every Year - $ 200,000 Every Minute.

- The Costs for Coronary Bypass Operations the Most Frequent Surgical Treatment of Heart Disease in the United States Amount to $10 Billion Every Year.

- Survivors of Heart Attacks and Strokes Frequently Become Disabled and Live in Nursing Homes. The Costs for Nursing Homes in the United States Amount to Over $60 Billion Every Year.

Health care costs are skyrocketing in the United States and in many other countries. Exploding health care cost have become the greatest threat to economic recovery. The direct and indirect costs for the treatment of cardiovascular diseases   is the greatest burden among the health care expenses. Everyone interested in economic growth - the government, large and small businesses as well as health maintenance organizations and health insurance companies - must have an immediate interest in promising new ways to control health care costs.

This book presents a fascinating solution to the heart disease epidemic. Many epidemics have occurred throughout history. All these epidemics were caused by one or only a few factors. Infectious diseases, for example, are caused by a bacterium or a virus. Cardiovascular diseases are no exception: they are caused by vitamin deficiencies. That's what this book is all about. Let us now take a closer look at this breathtaking solution to the number one health challenge.

THE SOLUTION:

MOST CARDIOVASCULAR DISEASES ARE VITAMIN DEFICIENCIES

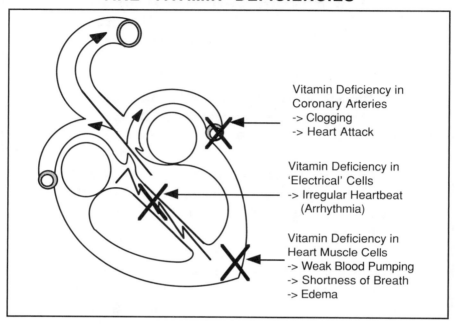

Vitamin Deficiency in Coronary Arteries
-> Clogging
-> Heart Attack

Vitamin Deficiency in 'Electrical' Cells
-> Irregular Heartbeat (Arrhythmia)

Vitamin Deficiency in Heart Muscle Cells
-> Weak Blood Pumping
-> Shortness of Breath
-> Edema

How can vitamin deficiencies cause cardiovascular disease? The heart is the central organ of the cardiovascular system. Its main function is the pumping of blood throughout the human body, 70 times per minute, more than 100,000 times per day. Thus, the heart is the busiest organ of the human body and the organ undergoing the greatest mechanical stress. This mechanical stress is a particular challenge to the millions of cells which make up the heart. These cells need an optimum supply of vitamins and other essential cofactors for their proper functioning. If the heart cells become vitamin deficient they fail and different forms of heart diseases develop.

- Vitamin deficiencies in the blood vessels of the heart (coronary arteries) lead to the clogging of these arteries and to heart attack.
- Vitamin deficiencies in the electrical cells of the heart lead to irregular heartbeat (arrhythmia).
- Vitamin deficiencies in the heart muscle cells lead to impaired blood pumping, to shortness of breath and to edema.

Optimum intake of vitamins helps prevent cardiovascular diseases.

THE SOLUTION:

A DAILY NUTRITIONAL REGIMEN FOR OPTIMUM CARDIOVASCULAR HEALTH

Below are my key recommendations for cardiovascular health: a daily nutritional supplement plan based on the latest scientific discoveries in cardiovascular and nutritional medicine.
• These recommendations contain all the ingredients you will read about in this book.
• These recommendations are being followed by several thousand people.
• Health improvements of people following these recommendations are documented in this book.
• These recommendations are made for everybody who wants to maintain optimum health of the heart and blood vessels.
• These recommendations are made particularly for those among my readers with existing heart disease.

<u>My daily cardiovascular health recommendations
are based on the following nutrients:</u>

Vitamin C	(Blood Vessel Stability, Deposit Removal, Cell Fuel, Antioxidant)
Vitamin E	(Deposit Removal, Antioxidant)
Beta Carotene	(Antioxidant)
L-Proline	(Blood Vessel Teflon, Atherosclerotic Deposit Removal)
L-Lysine	(Blood Vessel Teflon, Atherosclerotic Deposit Removal, Cell Fuel)
L-Carnitine	(Cell Fuel)
Coenzyme Q10	(Cell Fuel)
Vitamin B-1	(Cell Fuel)
Vitamin B-2	(Cell Fuel)
Vitamin B-3 (Niacin)	(Cholesterol-Lowering, Cell Fuel)
Vitamin B-3 (Niacinamide)	(Cell Fuel)
Vitamin B-5 (Pantothenate)	(Cell Fuel)
Vitamin B-6	(Cell Fuel)
Vitamin B-12	(Blood Cell Factor, Cell Fuel)
Folic Acid	(Blood Cell Factor, Cell Fuel)
Vitamin D	(Bones)
Biotin	(Cell Fuel)

Calcium, Magnesium, Zinc, Manganese, Copper, Selenium, Chromium, Molybdenum (Minerals And Trace Elements Are Required For Many Cell Functions).

At the end of this book you will find detailed information about these recommendations.

STRIKING EVIDENCE

The following testimonials are from patients who have followed my recommendations for cardiovascular health. Their health improvements are striking evidence for the value of vitamins and essential nutrients in the treatment of heart disease.

G.P. is a patient with a severe heart muscle weakness. G.P. is an entrepreneur in his fifties. Three years ago his life was changed by a sudden occurrence of cardiac failure, a weakness of the heart muscle leading to a decreased pumping function and to an enlargement of the heart chambers. The patient could no longer fully meet his professional requirements and had to give up his sport activities. On some days he felt so weak that he couldn't climb stairs and he had to hold his drinking glass with both hands. Because of the continued weak pumping function of the heart and the unfavorable prognosis of this disease, his cardiologist recommended a heart transplant operation: "I recommend you get a new heart."

At this point the patient started to follow my cardiovascular health recommendations. His physical strength improved gradually. Soon he could again fulfill his professional obligations on a regular basis and was able to undertake daily bicycle rides. After two months his cardiologist noted a decrease in size of the previously enlarged heart in the echocardiography examination, another sign of a recovering heart muscle. One month later, the patient was able to undertake a business trip abroad by plane, and he could attend to his business affairs without any physical limitations.

H.K. is a 76 year old patient with coronary heart disease. For several months he had been suffering from shortness of breath and chest pain (angina pectoris) which occurred during regular walking. He was hospitalized in January 1993, after suffering a life-threatening angina pectoris attack. During the hospital stay, he was taken to the intensive care unit because of cardiac failure and a severely irregular heart beat. The symptoms continued throughout the ten-week hospital stay. When he was dismissed from the hospital, the symptoms had only slightly improved despite a combination of multiple cardiac drugs. Chest pain, shortness of breath and irregular heartbeat continued to occur after only a few steps when climbing stairs. The physician who had treated H.K. during his hospital stay gave him a very unfavorable prognosis with respect to life expectancy.

The first week after leaving the hospital the patient started to follow my cardiovascular health recommendations. His general as well as his physical strength improved. Two and a half weeks later, he could walk again for up to one hour, even uphill, without shortness of breath. The patient was again able to undertake his daily activities without any help from outside. His physician wrote: "Overall the patient became more mobile, more secure, less dependent and thereby more confident about his further life. Control examinations are now planned to document the obvious clinical improvements of the patient."

B.M. is a 64 year old patient with irregular heartbeat. She has experienced tachycardia (rapid heartbeats) as well as irregular heartbeat for two months. The drugs prescribed by her doctor did not bring relief. Then she started to follow my cardiovascular health recommendations. In her letter to me she wrote "What a smart decision that was! Within a few days the tachycardia stopped and I've not experienced any loud or irregular heartbeats. It's like a miracle. Because of your research I'm able to continue working." Interestingly, the patient had already been taking some of the recommended nutrients. "It must be the combination of nutrients in your recommendation," she wrote.

H.W. is a 64 year old patient who has been suffering for many years from heart muscle weakness, arrhythmia, and shortness of breath. H.W. lives in a senior citizens home. He had difficulties climbing stairs and had to pause after about 200 yards when walking because of shortness of breath. Only two weeks after starting to follow my recommendations for cardiovascular health, he wrote: "During the past two weeks significant changes have occurred. I no longer have difficulties climbing stairs. I can walk without pausing for one mile and more, even uphill. Overall, I feel more energy and courage to live." Moreover, because of the significant improvements in the patients' health, his physician showed interest in these cardiovascular health recommendations.

J.S. wrote: "Dear Dr. Rath: How delightful, after following your recommendations for just 2 months one notices the absence of irregular heartbeats, and the freedom to breathe freely. Confidence is restored as one has increased vigor and endurance. In a word, one spends less time thinking about their heart and more time enjoying life. Your cardiovascular health recommendations have become the answer for resolving coronary problems. I am happy to have this opportunity of expressing my gratitude for your advanced medical research and for your cardiovascular recommendations."

<u>Remarkable Facts About These Patients</u>

• All patients had been taking regular drugs. Not these conventional drugs but nutritional supplements brought ultimate relief to these patients. This means that vitamin deficiencies are not only frequently related to heart diseases but are their primary cause.

• If this nutritional formula can help severely ill patients - imagine what it can do for your cardiovascular health.

THE KEYS TO

CARDIOVASCULAR HEALTH

THE KEYS TO CARDIOVASCULAR HEALTH

The key mechanisms which keep our cardiovascular system healthy have striking parallels to the technical world we live in. The symbols used in the following figure connect these two worlds - the technical world outside and the biological world within our body. This figure can help you memorize the keys to optimum cardiovascular health and will help you to better understand your own body. The keys to cardiovascular health are:

Stability

Stability of the human body and its organs is the most important key. Without stability we could not walk upright and our body would fall apart. The stability of our body is guaranteed by an optimum daily intake of vitamin C. Vitamin C increases the production of collagen molecules which strengthen the blood vessels and act like iron reinforcement rods in a skyscraper building. A reinforced blood vessel wall is the basic protection against atherosclerotic deposits and cardiovascular disease.

Deposit Removal

The atherosclerotic deposits in the wall of our blood vessels are like a plaster cast. They are only necessary because the vessel wall has become weakened by vitamin deficiency and threatens to break apart. With continued low vitamin intake over many years these atherosclerotic deposits become the body's blood vessel repair mechanism. Optimum daily intake of vitamin C, vitamin E, as well as the natural amino acids proline and lysine can help reduce these deposits and thereby reverse existing cardiovascular disease. Deposit removal from our arteries is like waste removal in our daily life.

Cell Fuel

The heart and the blood vessels are composed of millions of cells whose proper function determines cardiovascular health. Every single one of these cells works like a factory. Vitamin C, the B-vitamins, carnitine, coenzyme Q-10, and certain minerals and trace elements are critical fuel for the body's cell factories and are therefore a key to optimum cardiovascular health.

Antioxidant Protection

Cigarette smoke, and the smog polluted air in our cities contain dangerous small particles called free radicals. Free radicals damage our body and particularly our blood vessel system. Vitamin C, vitamin E, and beta carotene are powerful natural antioxidants which can neutralize free radicals before they can cause damage and cardiovascular disease. Antioxidant protection of our body is nothing else than a biological anti-rust protection.

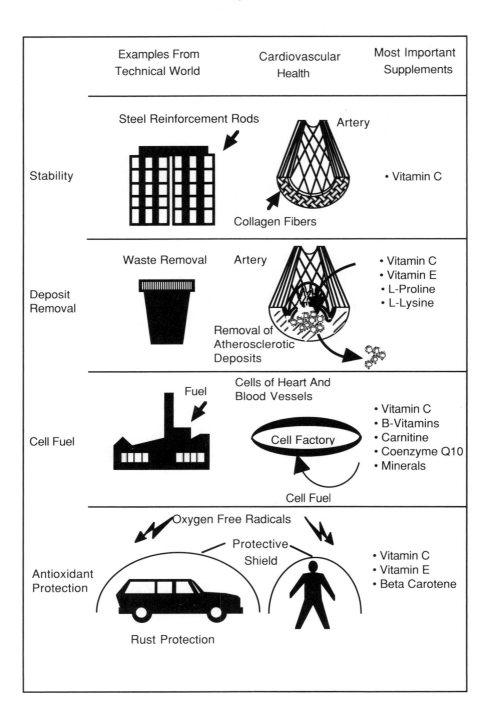

	Examples From Technical World	Cardiovascular Health	Most Important Supplements
Stability	Steel Reinforcement Rods	Artery / Collagen Fibers	• Vitamin C
Deposit Removal	Waste Removal	Artery / Removal of Atherosclerotic Deposits	• Vitamin C • Vitamin E • L-Proline • L-Lysine
Cell Fuel	Fuel	Cells of Heart And Blood Vessels / Cell Factory / Cell Fuel	• Vitamin C • B-Vitamins • Carnitine • Coenzyme Q10 • Minerals
Antioxidant Protection	Oxygen Free Radicals / Rust Protection	Protective Shield	• Vitamin C • Vitamin E • Beta Carotene

WHY ANIMALS DON'T GET HEART ATTACKS

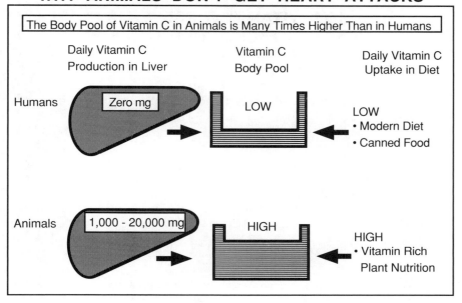

The Body Pool of Vitamin C in Animals is Many Times Higher Than in Humans

While millions of humans die every year from heart attacks and strokes, these diseases are essentially unknown in the animal world. Understanding why animals don't get heart attacks must inevitably lead us to eradicate this disease in humans and thus save millions of lives.

Animals do not get heart attacks because they are able to manufacture high amounts of vitamin C in their own bodies. The average amount they produce every day ranges between 1 and 20 grams (1,000 milligrams - 20,000 milligrams) compared to human body weight. In addition, most animals further increase their body pool of vitamin C by vitamin rich plant nutrition. In contrast, we human beings cannot produce our own vitamin C. Our ancestors lost this ability millions of years ago and ever since we have been dependent on getting enough vitamin C in our diet. To make things worse, our modern diet does not contain the amounts of vitamin C needed for optimum health. Most of the vitamins are destroyed in canned food as well as in cooked food. As a result, the vitamin C pool in the body of most animals is often ten times, perhaps a hundred times, higher than in our human bodies. Consequently, their bodies are reinforced many times more by collagen, and their blood vessels are much more stable than ours.

**Animals don't get heart attacks and strokes
because their bodies manufacture enough vitamin C.**

HOW VITAMIN C PREVENTS HEART ATTACKS AND STROKES

The following figure illustrates an important discovery: cardiovascular diseases are a form of early scurvy.

Column A: Optimum intake of vitamin C is the single most important measure to prevent heart attacks and strokes. Vitamin C has many functions in the body. Among the most important is the production of collagen. Optimum intake of vitamin C produces many collagen molecules which guarantee a strong and elastic blood vessel wall. A blood vessel wall strengthened by vitamin C does not allow atherosclerotic deposits to develop.

Column C: The opposite of a vitamin C- stabilized blood vessel wall is the vessel wall during scurvy. Scurvy, the sailor's disease of earlier centuries, is a deadly disease caused by a complete lack of vitamin C in the diet. In this condition very little collagen is produced in the body and the blood vessels virtually break apart. As a consequence, the blood leaks through the vessel wall just like water leaks through a brittle garden hose. Eventually scurvy leads to massive blood loss through vitamin C-depleted and leaky blood vessel walls. During the ship voyages in earlier centuries thousands of sailors died from scurvy and scorbutic blood loss within a few months.

Column B: Cardiovascular diseases lie exactly between these two conditions. Our average diet contains enough vitamin C to prevent open scurvy but not enough to guarantee a stable blood vessel wall. As a consequence, over many years, fat globules and other risk factors from the blood enter the blood vessel wall and lead to the development of atherosclerotic deposits. Local growth of cells inside the vessel wall further increases these deposits. Deposits in the arteries of the heart lead to heart attack; deposits in the arteries of the brain lead to stroke.

Optimum daily intake of vitamin C in our diet stabilizes the walls of the blood vessels and helps prevent heart attacks and strokes.

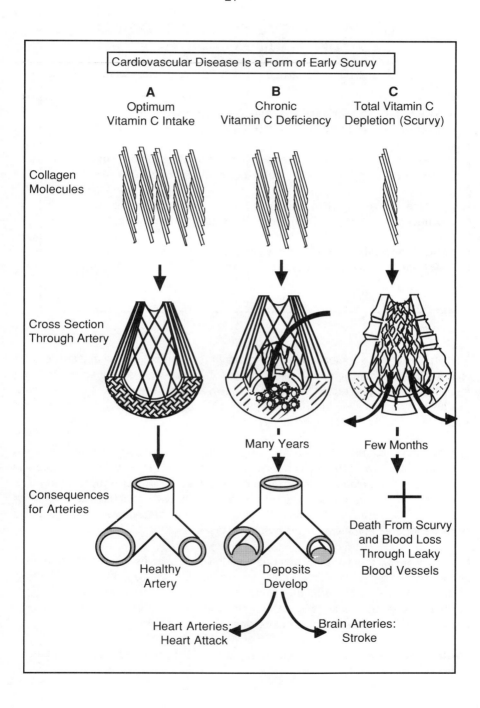

Cardiovascular Disease Is a Form of Early Scurvy

A
Optimum
Vitamin C Intake

B
Chronic
Vitamin C Deficiency

C
Total Vitamin C
Depletion (Scurvy)

Collagen
Molecules

Cross Section
Through Artery

Many Years

Few Months

Consequences
for Arteries

Healthy
Artery

Deposits
Develop

Death From Scurvy
and Blood Loss
Through Leaky
Blood Vessels

Heart Arteries:
Heart Attack

Brain Arteries:
Stroke

VITAMINS PREVENT HEART DISEASE
- THE CLINICAL EVIDENCE -

- **Vitamin C Cuts Heart Disease Rate Almost in Half (Documented in 11,000 Americans Over 10 Years)**

- **Vitamin E Cuts Heart Disease Rate by More Than One Third (Documented in 36,000 Americans Over 6 Years)**

- **Beta Carotene (Provitamin A) Cuts Heart Disease Rate Almost in Half (Documented in 36,000 Americans)**

- **No Prescription Drug Has Ever Been Shown to Help Prevent Heart Disease Similar to These Vitamins**

Vitamins belong to the most powerful agents in the fight against heart disease. This fact has been established by studies on thousands of people over many years. The results of the largest recent studies are shown above. These results are so clear that anybody questioning the value of vitamins in the prevention of heart disease can safely be considered as uninformed.

The best documented vitamins for the prevention of cardiovascular diseases are vitamin C, vitamin E, and beta carotene. These vitamins are natural antioxidants and they prevent the biological rusting of our blood vessels. No prescription drug was ever shown to cut the rate for heart diseases as effectively as these vitamins. Thus optimum dietary intake of vitamin C, vitamin E, and beta carotene is the basic measure for the prevention of cardiovascular diseases.

Now, a scientific breakthrough has been made which enables us not only to prevent the development of cardiovascular diseases more effectively but also to help remove existing deposits in our arteries - without surgery. This breakthrough was made possible by recent discoveries about the mechanisms of how atherosclerotic deposits develop in the wall of our blood vessels.

Nutritional supplements can help prevent cardiovascular diseases.

A NEW RISK FOR YOUR HEART
10 TIMES GREATER THAN CHOLESTEROL

Lipoprotein(a) is by far the greatest risk factor known today for
- **Heart attacks**
- **Strokes**
- **Clogging of bypass vessels after coronary bypass surgery**
- **Clogging after angioplasty**

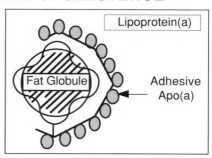

Until now we have been told that cholesterol or LDL (low density lipoprotein or "bad cholesterol") are the main risk factors for our blood vessels. Recent scientific discoveries have antiquated this theory. A new risk factor for your heart has been identified which is a 10 times greater risk for your heart than "bad cholesterol". The name of this "very bad cholesterol" is lipoprotein(a).

What is lipoprotein(a)? Cholesterol and other fat molecules are transported in our blood in the form of small fat globules called lipoproteins. The most well-known among them is low density lipoprotein, LDL. Lipoprotein(a) is an LDL fat globule with a biological adhesive tape wrapped around. This adhesive is called apoprotein(a) or apo(a). The adhesive apo(a) makes the lipoprotein fat globule stick inside the blood vessels. Many of these sticky fat globules then lead to fatty deposits and to clogging of arteries. The main problem is not the fat globule but the adhesive tape: less adhesive - less risk for heart disease.

What is the normal function of lipoprotein(a)? Lipoprotein(a) is the body's top repair molecule. Whenever our blood vessels are weakened by vitamin C deficiency, the vessel walls develop small lesions. In this situation, lipoprotein(a) functions as a first aid ambulance; it enters the vessel wall and tries to repair the damage. However, with low vitamin C in the diet over many years, this repair goes on and on; many fatty lipoprotein(a) molecules are deposited in the blood vessel wall, and eventually atherosclerotic deposits develop.

We have gained a new understanding of cardiovascular disease. Heart attacks and strokes are caused by an overcompensating or overshooting repair mechanisms for blood vessel walls weakened by a deficiency in vitamins, particularly in vitamin C. Atherosclerotic deposits are the bodies plaster cast to stabilize weakened blood vessels. Lipoprotein(a) is the most effective repair molecule and - with ongoing repair - becomes the greatest risk factor for heart attacks and strokes. If lipoprotein(a) is so important, why haven't you heard about it?

**Cardiovascular disease is an overshooting repair mechanism
for blood vessels weakened by vitamin deficiency.**

WHY YOU HAVE HEARD ABOUT CHOLESTEROL - BUT NOT ABOUT LIPOPROTEIN(a)

Why Cholesterol Is Known	Why Lipoprotein(a) Is Unknown
<u>Reason #1:</u>	<u>Reason #1:</u>
Cholesterol was found long ago	Lipoprotein(a) is a newly identified risk factor
<u>Reason # 2:</u>	<u>Reason # 2:</u>
Cholesterol - lowering prescription drugs are available ↓	No prescription drugs are available which lower the risk from lipoprotein(a) ↓
Many clinical studies are available ↓	Clinical studies are rare ↓
The results of these studies are published in medical journals, newspapers, and other media ↓	No studies are published in medical journals, newspapers and other media ↓
Everybody knows about cholesterol	Hardly anybody knows about lipoprotein(a)

Three More Reasons Why This Book Is Needed

- To inform you about lipoprotein(a) - the risk factor for your heart you had not heard about despite the fact that it is ten times more dangerous than cholesterol.

- To inform you about the value of vitamin C, vitamin B3, lysine and proline - effective, safe, and affordable nutrients which lower the risk from lipoprotein(a) and which can reverse existing cardiovascular disease.

- You will get little education from elsewhere as long as no patentable prescription drugs are available. Moreover, it may take ten years or more until such drugs could become available.

A SCIENTIFIC BREAKTHROUGH - THE REVERSAL OF EXISTING CARDIOVASCULAR DISEASES WITHOUT SURGERY

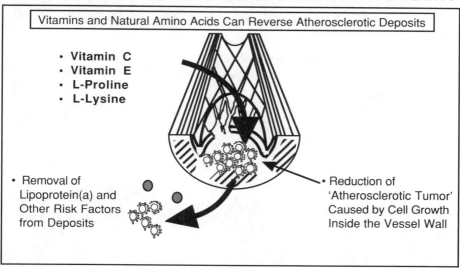

Vitamins and Natural Amino Acids Can Reverse Atherosclerotic Deposits

- **Vitamin C**
- **Vitamin E**
- **L-Proline**
- **L-Lysine**

• Removal of Lipoprotein(a) and Other Risk Factors from Deposits

• Reduction of 'Atherosclerotic Tumor' Caused by Cell Growth Inside the Vessel Wall

An old dream of mankind has come true: the non-surgical reversal of existing cardiovascular disease. The nutritional supplements vitamin C, and the natural amino acids L-proline and L-lysine are the keys to reverse existing deposits and thereby reverse heart disease. What are the secrets behind this breakthrough?

• *Blood vessel stability.* Vitamin C restores stability and elasticity of a weakened blood vessel wall. This stability is the basis for restoring blood vessel health.
• *A teflon layer in the vessel wall.* High intake of the natural amino acids lysine and proline provide a teflon layer around lipoprotein(a) and in the blood vessels. This teflon layer helps release lipoprotein(a) and other fat globules from their deposits in the blood vessel walls.
• *Decrease of the 'atherosclerotic tumor'.* Growth of cells in the blood vessel walls is part of the overshooting repair mechanism causing a small 'atherosclerotic tumor' inside the vessel wall. Vitamin E, and potentially vitamin C, lysine and proline can decrease this 'tumor' and thereby further reverse existing cardiovascular disease.

Until now coronary bypass surgery and angioplasty of the coronary arteries have been the standard treatments to reverse existing heart disease. On the basis of the above discoveries, safe and affordable nutritional supplements can become the method of choice to reverse existing heart disease without surgery.

Nutritional supplements can help reverse existing heart disease - without surgery.

WHEN TO START PROTECTING
YOUR BLOOD VESSELS AND YOUR HEART

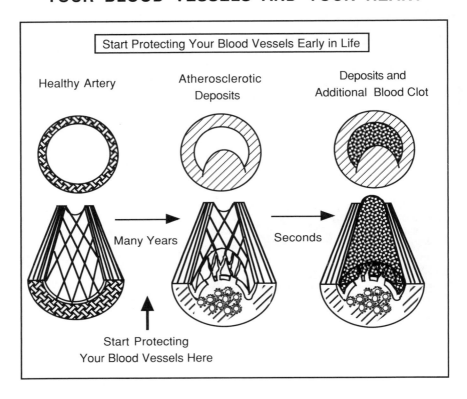

At birth the walls of the arteries are clean and show no deposits. The changes in a blood vessel leading to a heart attack and stroke occur in two stages. The first stage, the development of atherosclerotic deposits, continues over many years. The second stage, the formation of a blood clot occurs within a few seconds. Blood clots frequently form around atherosclerotic deposits leading to a total interruption of the blood flow and thereby to heart attacks and strokes. This happens so fast that many patients die immediately without being able to reach a hospital.

The time to start protecting your blood vessels and your heart is during the first stage. Since atherosclerotic deposits have been found in the arteries at age twenty and younger, preventing the build-up of deposits early in life is the safest way to prevent a heart attack .

The right time to start protecting your heart is now!

HOW YOU CAN IMPROVE THE PERFORMANCE OF YOUR HEART

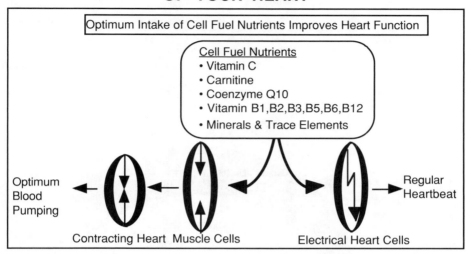

Protecting the blood vessels of the heart guarantees an optimum supply of oxygen to heart muscle cells. Optimum performance of the heart, however, also requires an optimum intake of those essential nutrients which are critically needed as fuel for these heart cells.

The heart is made up of millions of single cells which cooperate like the members of a music orchestra. Their common aim is to coordinate the regular pumping of the blood through the human body. Most of the heart cells are muscle cells which contract about 70 times per minute, each time pumping about the volume of a tea cup of blood into the circulation. Vitamin C, the B-vitamins, carnitine, coenzyme Q-10, as well as certain minerals and trace elements are critically needed as fuel for every single cell. A deficiency of these fuel nutrients in the contracting muscle cells leads to a weak pumping function of the heart. As a result only half a cup of blood may be ejected into the circulatory system with every heart beat. This typically leads to weakness of the body, shortness of breath, the accumulation of body water in the legs and other parts of the body (edema).

Another type of heart cells, electrical cells, are responsible for igniting the heartbeat. These electrical cells work automatically, without our telling them what to do. A deficiency of fuel nutrients in the heart's electrical cells can lead to many forms of irregular heartbeat (arrhythmias). Resupplementing important fuel nutrients for all heart cells can help improve many different diseased conditions of the heart.

Optimum daily intake of cell fuel nutrients optimizes the performance of your heart.

HOW YOU CAN PROTECT YOUR BLOOD VESSELS AND YOUR BODY FROM FREE RADICAL DAMAGE

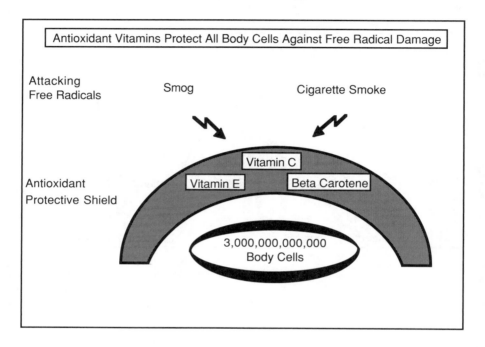

Free radicals are present in the polluted air in large cities where we live and work. In addition, cigarette smoke generates huge amounts of free radicals. Free radicals are aggressive molecules which damage our body. This damage is called oxidation and is nothing else than biological rusting. Oxidation damages our bodies in the same way rust damages our cars. This biological rusting is particularly harmful for the heart, the blood vessels and for the fat globules circulating in the blood. Virtually no molecule in the body is safe from attack by free radicals - unless we are protected by antioxidants.

Vitamin C, vitamin E and beta carotene are the most important natural antioxidants known. Antioxidants are able to scavenge and neutralize free radicals. Regular and optimum daily intake of these antioxidants forms a shield that protects your cardiovascular system and your whole body from damage. Moreover, antioxidants can protect your body from early aging, thereby adding valuable years to your life.

Optimum daily intake of natural antioxidants is the best protection against damage from free radicals.

<u>NOTES</u>

THE NATURE OF
CARDIOVASCULAR DISEASE

- How the Heart Works

- How the Blood Vessel System Functions

- How Cardiovascular Diseases Develop

- Why Vitamin Deficiencies Are the Primary
  Cause of Cardiovascular Diseases

HOW THE BLOOD CIRCULATION WORKS

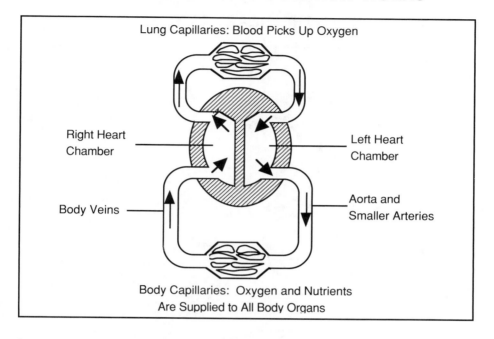

The cardiovascular system is composed of the heart and the blood vessels. The heart is the central pumping device of the blood vessel system. Its role is to pump blood through the blood vessel pipeline, thereby delivering oxygen and nutrient supplies to all parts of the body.

The blood vessel system is the largest organ of the human body.
- **It is 60,000 miles long**
- **It has a surface area of more than half an acre**

There are three different forms of blood vessels: arteries, veins, and capillaries.
- *Arteries* transport blood enriched in oxygen and nutrients from the heart to the head, the internal organs, the limbs, and all other parts of the body.
- *Veins* transport blood from the different parts of the body back to the heart and to the lungs where it is re-loaded with oxygen.
- *Capillaries* are the tiny blood vessels between the arteries and the veins. They are only one-tenth as thick as a human hair. Oxygen and nutrients filter through the thin walls of the capillaries to the surrounding body tissue and into millions of body cells. In turn, cellular waste filters back from the tissue into the capillaries to be removed by the blood stream.

The cardiovascular system is the pipeline delivering nutrients and oxygen to all parts of the body.

HOW THE HEART IS BUILT

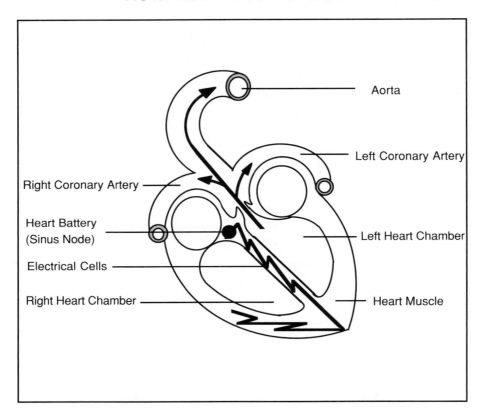

The heart is built of four chambers, the two most important of which are the right and the left heart chamber. The left heart chamber is responsible for pumping the blood into the aorta, the body's main artery.

The heart muscle is composed of millions of muscle cells. The task of most of these muscle cells is to contract the heart muscle and thereby pump blood into the circulatory system. The heart also contains cells with the fascinating ability to generate electricity. The 'battery' of the heart (the sinus node) generates the electricity needed for the heartbeat. Special electrical cells transport this biological electricity to all heart muscle cells. Within a split second this electricity arrives at millions of heart muscle cells igniting their contraction and thereby causing the heart to pump.

HOW THE HEART WORKS

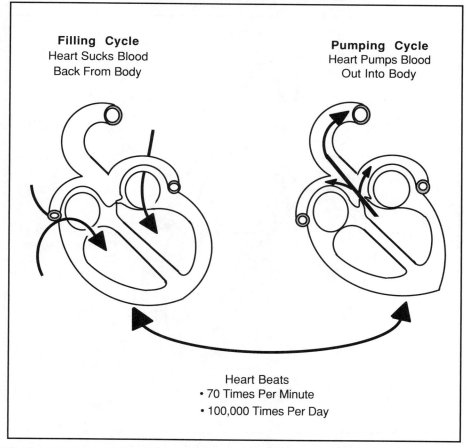

Filling Cycle
Heart Sucks Blood
Back From Body

Pumping Cycle
Heart Pumps Blood
Out Into Body

Heart Beats
• 70 Times Per Minute
• 100,000 Times Per Day

The heart is the pumping station for the blood in our body. As do mechanical pumps, the heart works in two cycles, a filling cycle and a pumping cycle. During the filling cycle the heart sucks blood from the blood circulation and fills its chambers. During the pumping cycle the heart muscle contracts and pumps the blood into the circulation.

The left heart chamber ejects blood into the aorta, the main artery of the human body. With every heart beat the heart ejects about one teacup of blood into the aorta. In this way 2,500 gallons of blood are pumped by the heart during one day.

The blood wave in the arteries caused by the pumping heart is the pulse. By using our finger tips we can feel this pulse wave in the arteries of the neck, the wrist, and in other arteries of the body. By measuring our pulse we are able to determine how fast our heart beats.

HOW THE HEART IS NOURISHED

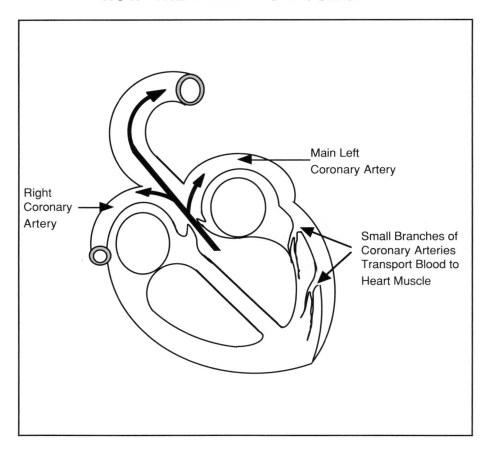

Since the heart is the pumping station for the blood, one could assume the heart muscle gets its oxygen and nutrition from the blood inside the pump, but this is not the case. The main blood supply for oxygen and nutrients to millions of heart muscle cells comes from outside - through the coronary arteries. The coronary arteries received their name from the Latin word for crown (corona). In fact, the coronary arteries surround the heart like a crown and ride directly on the heart muscle. From the aorta one coronary artery branches off to the right side of the heart and one coronary artery branches off to the left side of the heart and divides into two larger branches. From these large coronary arteries smaller blood vessels branch off delivering oxygen and nutrients to millions of heart muscle cells. Optimum blood flow through the coronary arteries is essential for the proper functioning of the heart. Interruption of the blood flow through the coronary arteries leads to heart attacks.

WHY THE CORONARY ARTERIES ARE THE MOST STRESSED ARTERIES OF THE HUMAN BODY

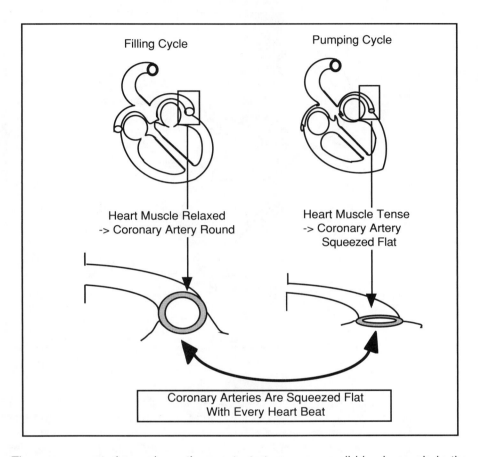

The coronary arteries undergo the greatest stress among all blood vessels in the human body. Because these blood vessels are tightened to the surface of the heart, they are forced to follow its every movement. Every heartbeat involves a contraction of the heart muscle. This rhythmic spasm of the heart squeezes flat the coronary artery running atop the heart muscle. Since the heart beats about 100,000 times per day the coronary arteries on top of the heart are squeezed flat 100,000 times every day. It is easy to understand that this squeezing mechanism exerts great mechanical stress on the wall of the coronary arteries. Just think of stepping on a garden hose and squeezing it flat 100,000 times a day. The continuous mechanical squeezing of the coronary arteries causes small lesions of the blood vessel wall. In a blood vessel wall weakened by vitamin C deficiency these lesions occur frequently and cause the development of atherosclerotic deposits and heart attacks.

HOW A HEART ATTACK OCCURS

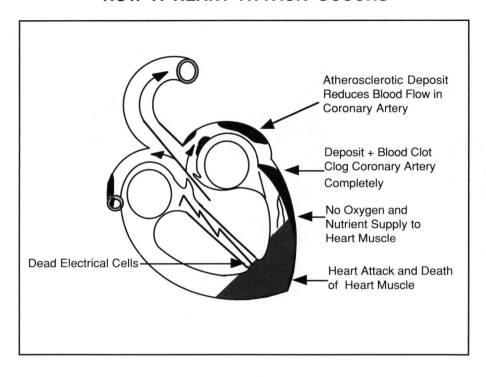

Atherosclerotic Deposit
Reduces Blood Flow in
Coronary Artery

Deposit + Blood Clot
Clog Coronary Artery
Completely

No Oxygen and
Nutrient Supply to
Heart Muscle

Dead Electrical Cells

Heart Attack and Death
of Heart Muscle

This year more than one and a half million Americans will suffer a heart attack. Heart attacks are caused by interruption of the blood flow through the coronary arteries. The development of atherosclerotic deposits leads to narrowing of the blood vessel and to a decreased blood flow through the arteries. At this stage patients frequently experience the alarm sign of heart disease - chest pain or angina pectoris. In most cases a blood clot has formed in the neighborhood of an atherosclerotic deposit. This event leads to clogging of the coronary artery and to a complete interruption of the blood flow. As a result, millions of heart muscle cells suffocate from lack of oxygen and nutrients, and many of these cells die. In general, heart attacks lead to the irreversible damage and death of a portion of the heart muscle. The effect of a dead heart muscle portion for the functioning of the heart is comparable to the failure of one cylinder in a motor: the performance is permanently impaired.

HOW A STROKE OCCURS

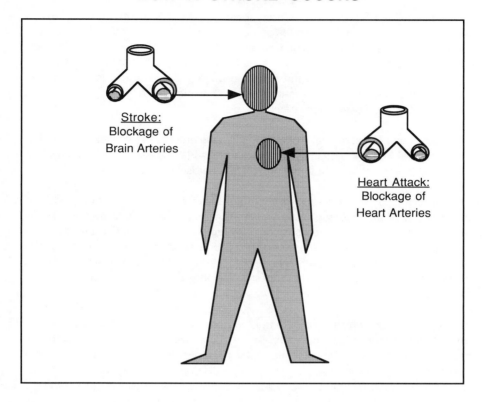

Stroke:
Blockage of
Brain Arteries

Heart Attack:
Blockage of
Heart Arteries

While heart attacks are caused by clogging of the heart arteries, strokes are caused by clogging of the brain arteries. Atherosclerotic deposits frequently develop in the arteries of the neck (carotid arteries) and the brain (cerebral arteries). If the blood flow to the brain is interrupted a stroke occurs and millions of brain cells suffocate and eventually die. Since brain cells coordinate the movement of every part of our body, their death frequently leads to paralysis - the typical sign of a stroke.

Why is a stroke a frequent form of cardiovascular disease? The arteries of the brain are located close to the pumping station, the heart. As in the technical world, the pressure in a pipeline is greatest immediately adjacent to a pumping station. The arteries of the heart and the brain have a a relatively high blood pressure compared to other blood vessels of the body. This pressure stresses the walls of the blood vessels, particularly if additional blood flow turbulences exist in branching areas of the arteries. If this pressure stress meets an arterial wall weakened by vitamin deficiency, deposits develop and eventually strokes occur. Now we can also explain why patients with high blood pressure carry a particular risk for strokes.

HOW ATHEROSCLEROTIC DEPOSITS DEVELOP

Atherosclerotic deposits develop as a response to small lesions in the blood vessel wall. We already know that these lesions are caused by mechanical stress on the arteries in combination with a blood vessel wall weakened by vitamin deficiency. These small lesions occur in the barrier cells (endothelium) between the blood stream and the blood vessel walls. On the following page you will take a look inside an atherosclerotic deposit of a human artery. This picture is magnified under a microscope. Several observations can be made:

• The black area represents fat globules which have entered the vessel wall from the blood stream. Inside the blood vessel wall thousands of these fat globules are laid down and thereby contribute to the growth of atherosclerotic deposits.

• This picture also shows a second important factor contributing to the buildup of deposits - a small 'atherosclerotic tumor'. This local 'tumor' is formed inside the blood vessel wall by muscle cells which grow rapidly during cardiovascular diseases and thereby further narrow the blood flow in the arteries. The deposition of risk factors and a local tumor build up an 'atherosclerotic plaster cast' inside the vessel walls. The function of this cast is to stabilize these walls weakened by vitamin deficiency.

• A third mechanism which contributes to the development of deposits is caused by an impaired waste collection system in the vessel wall. The waste collectors are certain white blood cells which normally circulate in our blood. These waste collection cells enter the vessel wall and pick up deposited fat globules and other waste products from the vessel wall. If these waste collector cells overload themselves they become unable to move back into the blood stream and they get stuck inside the blood vessel wall. In this situation the waste collectors themselves become part of the problem: they contribute to the further build up of atherosclerotic deposits.

Of particular significance for the development of atherosclerotic deposits is the fat globule lipoprotein(a) a newly identified risk factor for cardiovascular disease. Together with my colleagues at Hamburg University, I reported the most comprehensive studies on lipoprotein(a) in human arteries yet. Several thousand data samples were collected from patients undergoing bypass surgery as well as from human arteries at autopsy. We discovered that lipoprotein(a) is the primary risk factor for the development of atherosclerotic deposits in human arteries. Let us now have a closer look at some of these mechanisms.

For More Information: Lipoprotein(a) And Atherosclerosis: Rath M 1989; Niendorf A 1990; Beisiegel U 1990; Rath M 1991a; Lawn RM 1992. Previous Atherosclerosis Concepts: Brown MS 1984, Steinberg D.1989; Ross R 1993.

39

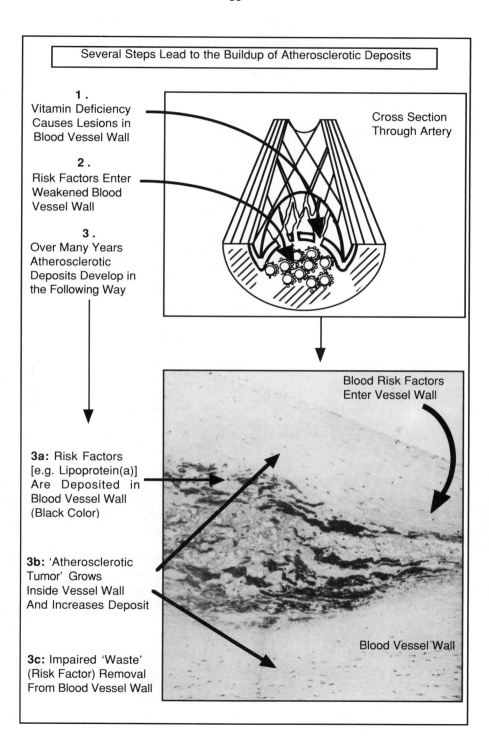

Several Steps Lead to the Buildup of Atherosclerotic Deposits

1. Vitamin Deficiency Causes Lesions in Blood Vessel Wall

2. Risk Factors Enter Weakened Blood Vessel Wall

3. Over Many Years Atherosclerotic Deposits Develop in the Following Way

Cross Section Through Artery

3a: Risk Factors [e.g. Lipoprotein(a)] Are Deposited in Blood Vessel Wall (Black Color)

3b: 'Atherosclerotic Tumor' Grows Inside Vessel Wall And Increases Deposit

3c: Impaired 'Waste' (Risk Factor) Removal From Blood Vessel Wall

Blood Risk Factors Enter Vessel Wall

Blood Vessel Wall

HOW LIPOPROTEIN(a) FORMS DEPOSITS IN THE BLOOD VESSEL WALL

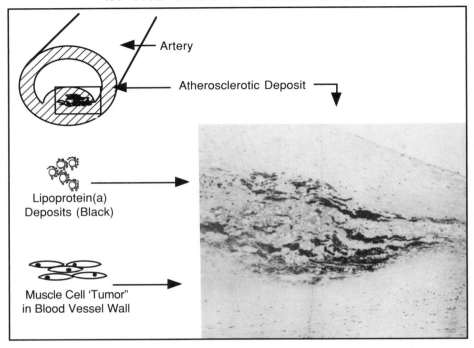

There are different ways by which the lipoprotein(a) particle contributes to the growth of atherosclerotic deposits:

- *By its own size.* Among all the particles swimming in our blood, lipoprotein(a) is one of the largest. For example, one lipoprotein(a) particle is 10,000 times bigger than hormone molecules and most other proteins in our body. Many lipoprotein(a) particles together can easily form a bulge within an atherosclerotic deposit.

- *By capturing other fat globules.* Once deposited inside the blood vessel wall, the sticky lipoprotein(a) molecule captures other fat globules from the blood, such as LDL (low-density lipoproteins), and makes them glue inside the blood vessel wall as well.

- *By stimulating the growth of cells inside the blood vessel wall.* Lipoprotein(a) also stimulates the growth of muscle cells inside the blood vessel wall. In this way lipoprotein(a) stimulates the atherosclerotic tumor to grow thereby further decreasing blood flow in the arteries of the heart or of other organs.

Further Information: Binding of Lipoproteins: Rath M 1991a , Trieu VN 1991. Cell growth: Grainger DJ 1993.

IMPAIRED WASTE COLLECTION FROM THE BLOOD VESSEL WALL FURTHER INCREASES DEPOSITS

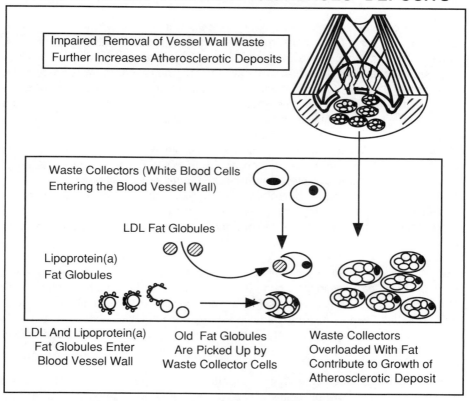

Impaired Removal of Vessel Wall Waste
Further Increases Atherosclerotic Deposits

Waste Collectors (White Blood Cells Entering the Blood Vessel Wall)

LDL Fat Globules

Lipoprotein(a) Fat Globules

LDL And Lipoprotein(a) Fat Globules Enter Blood Vessel Wall

Old Fat Globules Are Picked Up by Waste Collector Cells

Waste Collectors Overloaded With Fat Contribute to Growth of Atherosclerotic Deposit

Fat globules (lipoproteins) which have been stuck inside the vessel wall for some time gradually age. This aging process is greatly accelerated by free radicals and the biological rusting process you have already learned about. These aged or rusted fat globules are eaten up by the waste collector cells which had entered the vessel wall from the blood stream. Of course, these waste collectors become primarily overloaded in those areas of the vessel wall where atherosclerotic deposits develop. Under the microscope these fat-loaded waste collector cells look foamy, so they have also been named foam cells. Many foam cells inside the blood vessel wall further accelerate the development of atherosclerotic deposits. Aged or biologically rusted lipoprotein(a) fat globules, LDL (low-density lipoprotein), and VLDL (very low-density lipoproteins) can all cause foam cell formation.

Let us now have a closer look at lipoprotein(a) and how this newly identified risk factor relates to already known heart risk factors such as cholesterol.

Further Information: Oxidation of LDL: Steinberg D 1989. Vitamin C as Antioxidant: Frei B 1989.

WHAT IS LIPOPROTEIN (a)

For half a century it was thought that cholesterol entering the vessel wall from the blood was the main factor leading to the buildup of deposits. More recently, LDL cholesterol was proposed to be the villain for the development of atherosclerotic deposits. Today we know that these factors play only a secondary role. Atherosclerotic deposits are essentially the result of the newly identified risk factor lipoprotein(a). This figure explains what cholesterol, low density lipoprotein (LDL) and lipoprotein(a) have in common and what sets them apart.

Cholesterol. Cholesterol is a very important molecule for the growth of every cell in our bodies. Cholesterol molecules do not swim in the blood like fat in the soup. Thousands of cholesterol molecules are packed together with other fat molecules in tiny round globules called lipoproteins. Millions of these fat transporting vehicles circulate in our body at any time. The best-known among these are high density lipoproteins (HDL, or "good cholesterol") and low density lipoprotein (LDL, or "bad cholesterol").

LDL Cholesterol. Most of the cholesterol molecules in the blood are transported in millions of LDL particles in the blood. By carrying cholesterol and other fat molecules to our body cells, LDL is a very useful transport vehicle to supply nutrients to these cells. LDL has been named the "bad cholesterol" during the years when researchers missed the real villain - the "very bad cholesterol" - which causes blood vessel deposits: lipoprotein(a).

Lipoprotein(a). Lipoprotein(a) is an LDL particle with an additional adhesive protein wrapped around it. This biological adhesive tape is named apoprotein(a), or apo(a). The letter (a) could in fact stand for 'adhesive'. The adhesive apo(a) makes the lipoprotein(a) fat globule one of the stickiest particles in our body. In brief:

• The adhesive apo(a) is responsible for millions of lipoprotein(a) fat globules sticking inside the walls of the blood vessels and forming atherosclerotic deposits.
• LDL has no adhesive tape and therefore is much less of a risk factor for cardiovascular disease.
• The adhesive tape is the real risk - not cholesterol or the fat globule.
• Less adhesive means less risk for heart disease.

This figure can also explain why most cardiovascular researchers have missed this important risk factor for 30 years. Lipoprotein(a) and LDL look alike, and one has to specifically look for the adhesive apo(a) to find out the scientific truth. This was achieved by our studies at Hamburg University .

Further Information: Lipoprotein(a) general aspects: Berg K 1963; Utermann G 1989; Scanu A 1991; Adhesive properties: Rath M 1991b and 1992f.

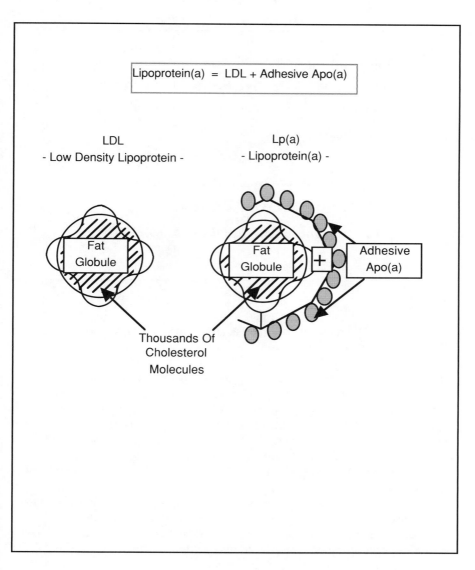

LIPOPROTEIN(a) IS THE GREATEST RISK FACTOR FOR CARDIOVASCULAR DISEASE KNOWN TODAY

- Lipoprotein(a) Is a Heart Risk Factor 10 Times Greater Than LDL, the "Bad Cholesterol'
- Lipoprotein(a) Is by Far the Greatest Risk Factor
  - For Heart Attacks
  - For Strokes
  - For Clogging of Bypass Blood Vessels After Coronary Bypass Surgery
  - For Clogging of Arteries After Angioplasty

Today lipoprotein(a) has been confirmed as the leading risk factor for many forms of cardiovascular diseases:

- Lipoprotein(a) is a ten times greater risk factor for heart disease than LDL cholesterol. This fact was revealed during a recent reevaluation of the Framingham Heart Study, the largest cardiovascular risk factor study ever conducted.
- Lipoprotein(a) is the greatest risk factor known today for heart attacks. This fact was established in studies of survivors with myocardial infarction, and by angiography studies in patients with coronary heart disease.
- Lipoprotein(a) is the greatest risk factor known today for atherosclerosis of the brain arteries and for strokes.
- Lipoprotein(a) is the greatest risk factor known today for the clogging of bypass blood vessels after a patient has undergone coronary bypass surgery.
- Lipoprotein(a) is the greatest risk factor known today for the restenosis (formation of new deposits or blood clots) of coronary arteries after coronary angioplasty (balloon catheterization or similar procedures which mechanically remove atherosclerotic deposits).

Further Information: Lipoprotein(a) And Coronary Heart Disease: Kostner G 1983; Dahlen GH 1986; Rhoads GG 1986; Genest J 1991. Stroke: Zenker G 1986; Murai AS 1986. Coronary Bypass: Hoff HF 1988. Angioplasty: Hearn JA 1992.

YOU SHOULD KNOW YOUR
LIPOPROTEIN(a) BLOOD LEVELS

---

0 - 20 mg/dl   **Low Risk for Heart Disease**

20 - 40 mg/dl   **Medium Risk for Heart Disease**

> 40 mg/dl   **High Risk for Heart Disease**

Lipoprotein(a) blood levels vary greatly between one individual and another. What do we know about the factors influencing the lipoprotein(a) levels in the blood:

• Lipoprotein(a) levels are largely determined by inheritance.

• Special diet does not influence lipoprotein(a) blood levels.

• None of the presently available lipid-lowering prescription drugs lowers lipoprotein(a)blood levels.

• Vitamin C and vitamin B3 can lower blood levels of lipoprotein(a) (see Section E). Together with the natural amino acids lysine and proline (see Section D) the risk from lipoprotein (a) can be significantly lowered by nutritional supplements.

Everybody should know their lipoprotein(a) blood level. The above figures give you a basic guideline to properly read the results of your lipoprotein(a) blood test and to find your personal risk. People whose lipoprotein(a) concentrations are greater than 30 mg/dl (milligrams per hundred milliliter) have a two-fold increased risk of developing cardiovascular disease. On the following page you will find a more detailed interpretation of the risk from lipoprotein(a) testing in combination with LDL testing.

Further Information: Inherited Lipoprotein(a) Levels: Utermann G 1989; Koschinsky M 1990. Risk Factor Analysis: Armstrong VOW 1986. Vitamin Therapy: Carlson LA 1989; Rath M 1991a, 1992c and 1992e.

LIPOPROTEIN(a), AND LDL-CHOLESTEROL - HOW TO INTERPRET YOUR PERSONAL RISK

Most of us know our LDL-cholesterol levels but hardly anybody knows their lipoprotein(a) blood levels. This page will help you to interpret your blood measurements of LDL- cholesterol in combination with lipoprotein(a) and to better determine your risk for cardiovascular disease:

• *Low levels of lipoprotein(a) (below 30 mg/dl) and high levels of LDL cholesterol (above 150 mg/dl).* High levels of LDL cholesterol alone are only a moderate risk factor. The explanation is simple. The LDL particles lack the adhesive apo(a) and are therefore much less likely to stick inside the blood vessel wall and much less likely to contribute to the development of atherosclerotic deposits.

• *High levels of lipoprotein(a) (above 30 mg/dl) and low levels of LDL cholesterol (below 150 mg dl).* High levels of lipoprotein(a) in the blood, even when LDL cholesterol levels are low, increase your risk of developing cardiovascular disease about twofold. You already know the reason: via the adhesive apo(a), the lipoprotein(a) particles stick inside the blood vessel wall and millions of them eventually lead to the buildup of atherosclerotic deposits.

• *High levels of lipoprotein(a) levels and, in addition, LDL cholesterol levels high.* Patients with this combination of risk factors are two to five times more likely to suffer a heart attack or stroke than a person with normal levels of these risk factors. Why is that? On the one hand, lipoprotein(a) particles stick inside the blood vessel wall. On the other hand, the adhesive apo(a) can also capture additional lipoproteins and retain them inside the blood vessel walls. LDL fat globules are the most important among these lipoproteins gluing to lipoprotein(a) particles. The additional retention of many LDL and VLDL fat globules in the vessel wall by many lipoprotein(a) particles already deposited there further speeds up the development of atherosclerotic deposits. This is why the risk for heart diseases increases manifold in persons with high lipoprotein(a) blood levels as well as high LDL blood levels.

Further Information: Serum Lp(a) Concentrations: Armstrong VW 1986; Seed BH 1990; Rath M 1992e. LDL - Cholesterol Concentrations: See Also Recommendations From the American Heart Association.

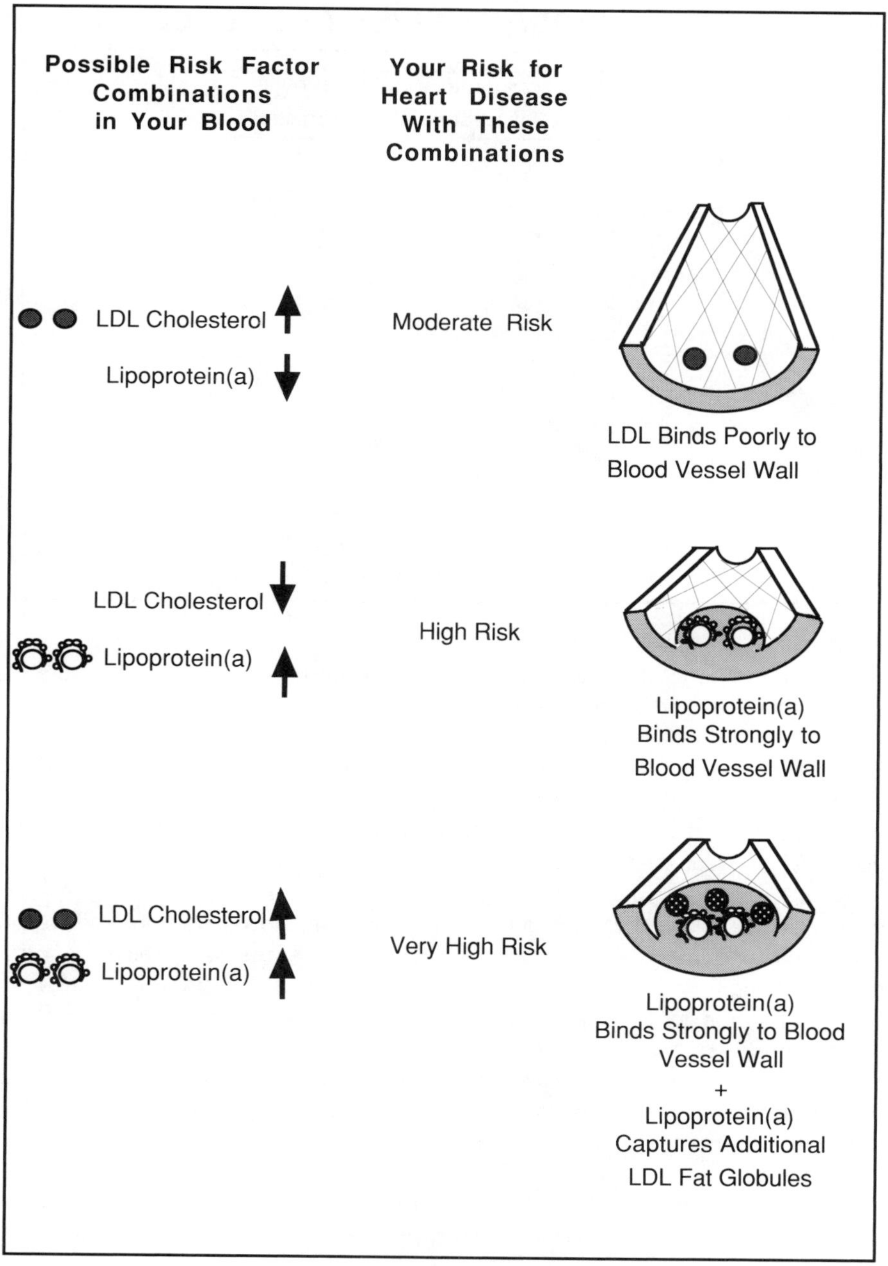
Possible Risk Factor Combinations in Your Blood
Your Risk for Heart Disease With These Combinations
LDL Cholesterol
Lipoprotein(a)
Moderate Risk
LDL Binds Poorly to Blood Vessel Wall
LDL Cholesterol
Lipoprotein(a)
High Risk
Lipoprotein(a) Binds Strongly to Blood Vessel Wall
LDL Cholesterol
Lipoprotein(a)
Very High Risk
Lipoprotein(a) Binds Strongly to Blood Vessel Wall
+
Lipoprotein(a) Captures Additional LDL Fat Globules

RISK FOR LIPOPROTEIN(a) DEPOSITS INCREASES WITH HIGH LIPOPROTEIN(a) BLOOD LEVELS

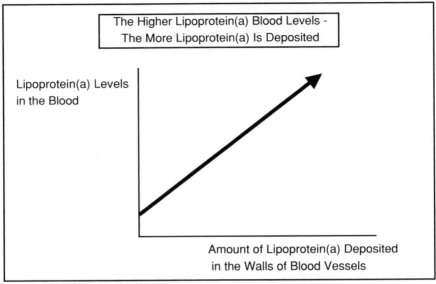

How important it is to know your lipoprotein(a) blood levels can be seen from the figures on this page and on the following page:

- First, the more lipoprotein(a) you carry in your blood, the greater is your risk that this lipoprotein(a) is actually deposited in your blood vessels.
- Second, the size of atherosclerotic deposit increases with the amount of lipoprotein(a) deposited.

The above figure shows that the higher the lipoprotein(a) blood levels are, the greater the risk that lipoprotein(a) is deposited inside the vessel wall. This is another important finding from our studies in human arteries. Similar results were obtained by colleagues from Baylor College of Medicine in Houston, Texas. They investigated the atherosclerotic deposits in the venous blood vessels used for coronary bypass surgery. The researchers in Texas came to the same conclusion: the higher the lipoprotein(a) blood level in the patient, the more lipoprotein(a) was deposited in the bypass blood vessels.

Another important question was whether there is a relation between the size of the blood vessel deposit and the amount of lipoprotein(a) deposited therein.

Further Information: Rath M 1989; Cushing GL 1989.

EXTENT OF ATHEROSCLEROTIC LESION INCREASES WITH AMOUNT OF LIPOPROTEIN (a) DEPOSITED

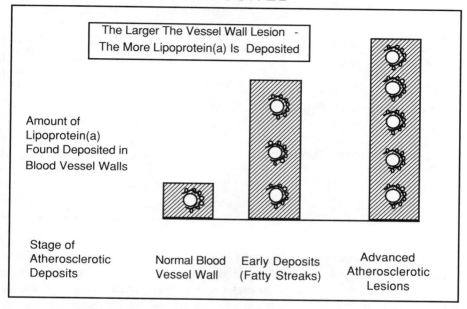

The Larger The Vessel Wall Lesion - The More Lipoprotein(a) Is Deposited

Amount of Lipoprotein(a) Found Deposited in Blood Vessel Walls

Stage of Atherosclerotic Deposits

Normal Blood Vessel Wall

Early Deposits (Fatty Streaks)

Advanced Atherosclerotic Lesions

The larger the size of atherosclerotic deposits in the vessel walls, the more lipoprotein(a) is found to be stuck inside these deposits. Analysis of several hundred deposits from human arteries showed the following results:

- Normal blood vessel walls generally contain some lipoprotein(a).
- Early deposits (fatty streaks) already have a much higher amount of lipoprotein(a) accumulated.
- Advanced deposits, the atherosclerotic plaques about to clog the artery and to cause heart attacks and strokes, contain the highest amount of lipoprotein(a).

The conclusion from these studies is that by lowering your lipoprotein(a) blood levels you can reduce the deposition of lipoprotein(a) in the blood vessel wall and thereby decrease your risk for heart attacks and strokes. Two vitamins, vitamin C and vitamin B3, are the only factors known to reduce effectively the blood levels of lipoprotein(a). These and further therapeutic recommendations will be extensively discussed in the Section D and Section E of this book.

On the following pages I would like to share with you how these discoveries lead to an entirely new understanding about the nature of cardiovascular diseases.

Further Information: Lipoprotein(a) in Human Blood Vessels: Niendorf A 1990; Beisiegel U 1990; Rath M 1989.

THE LIPOPROTEIN(a) - VITAMIN C CONNECTION

	Humans	Animals
Vitamin C High	NO	YES
Lipoprotein(a) High	YES	NO
Cardiovascular Diseases Frequent	YES	NO

Perhaps the most important fact about lipoprotein(a) is that this risk factor is primarily found in human beings while other living beings have little or no lipoprotein(a) at all. In 1987, while researching the role of lipoprotein(a) in cardiovascular disease, I made an amazing discovery: the lipoprotein(a) - vitamin C connection. I noticed that animals producing vitamin C in their own bodies have little or no lipoprotein(a). In contrast, we human beings, unable to manufacture our own vitamin C, apparently make ample use of lipoprotein(a). Moreover, we thereby evidently increase the risk for cardiovascular diseases.

The lipoprotein(a) - vitamin C connection says:
• high vitamin C levels - little or no need for lipoprotein(a) molecules
• low vitamin C levels - great need for lipoprotein(a) molecules.

Immediately following the discovery of the lipoprotein(a) - vitamin C connection, I conducted the first clinical test to prove this discovery: In 1987, the first person with high lipoprotein(a) blood levels was given vitamin C with the specific aim to lower this risk factor. The encouraging results were later confirmed in a pilot clinical study (see Section F).

What is the secret behind the lipoprotein(a) - vitamin C connection?

Further Information: Rath M 1990.

VITAMIN C DEFICIENCY IS THE PRIMARY CAUSE OF CARDIOVASCULAR DISEASE

- BLOOD VESSEL STABILITY IS THE KEY -

The lipoprotein(a) - vitamin C connection leads us directly to the nature of cardiovascular disease:

• The underlying cause of cardiovascular disease is a low intake of vitamins, particularly of vitamin C.
• Vitamin C deficiency leads to lesions and instability in the blood vessel walls, and the cell barrier between the blood stream and the blood vessel wall becomes leaky.
• Lipoprotein(a) molecules, the body's first aid molecule for blood vessel repair, enter the blood vessel wall.
• Lipoprotein(a) is an ideal repair molecule because the adhesive tape apo(a) makes up for the lack of collagen molecules in the blood vessel wall. In this way the adhesive apo(a) renders stability to the weakened blood vessel wall.
• With low intake of vitamin C over many years this repair mechanism overshoots and atherosclerotic deposits develop.

Thus, atherosclerotic deposits are an overcompensating or overshooting repair process of the vessel wall which is chronically weakened by vitamin deficiency.

Neither cholesterol, nor fat globules, nor any other blood risk factor is the primary cause of cardiovascular disease. The primary cause of cardiovascular disease is the instability of the blood vessel wall. Vessel wall stability is the key behind the lipoprotein(a)- vitamin C connection. Evidently, blood vessel stability can be achieved in two ways:

Alternative #1: An optimum intake of vitamin C resulting in optimum collagen production and in blood vessel reinforcement.

Alternative #2: By the deposition of lipoprotein(a) and of other risk factors resulting in the formation of atherosclerotic deposits. Atherosclerotic deposits are the blood vessels plaster cast which stabilize the vessel walls weakened by vitamin deficiency.

In summary, the primary cause of cardiovascular disease is a blood vessel wall which is weakened by an insufficient intake of vitamin C. On the following pages I will share with you the already available evidence for this new understanding of this disease.

Further Information: Rath M 1991a.

Two Alternatives to Stabilize Your Blood Vessels

Alternative # 1   Alternative # 2

Molecules
Responsible
for Stability

Collagen Molecules   Repair Molecules
                                      e.g. Lipoprotein(a)

A Look Inside
Our Arteries

Healthy Artery Wall: Weakened Artery Wall:
Reinforced by Sufficient   Stability Provided by
Collagen Molecules   Atherosclerotic Plaster Cast

You Have   Optimum Vitamin C   Insufficient Vitamin C
the Choice by   Intake in Your Diet   Intake in Your Diet

Which Alternative Do You Prefer?

VITAMIN C DEFICIENCY IS THE PRIMARY CAUSE OF CARDIOVASCULAR DISEASE

- EARLY CLINICAL EVIDENCE -

1941: The Canadian cardiologist J.C. Paterson reports that more than 80% of his heart disease patients have vitamin C deficiency as a significant risk factor.

1948: The American doctors R.W. Trimmer and C.J. Lundy report that 70% of their patients with coronary artery disease have very low vitamin C blood levels.

Already half a century ago first clinical reports showed that patients with cardiovascular diseases have much lower vitamin C blood levels than healthy persons. This study was published in 1941 by the Canadian cardiologist J.C. Paterson. He found that more than 80% - or four out of five - of his patients with heart disease suffered from vitamin C deficiency.

In 1948, the American doctors R.W. Trimmer and C.J. Lundy found similar results in their coronary heart disease patients. In the medical journal *American Practitioner* they reported the measurements of vitamin C blood levels in 556 patients with various diseases. Two out of three patients with coronary heart disease were found to have very low vitamin C blood levels. Moreover, among all diseases investigated vitamin deficiencies were widest spread among heart disease patients.

Thus, a low vitamin C intake and low vitamin C blood levels were found to be leading risk factor for cardiovascular diseases long ago.

Measurements of vitamin C concentration in the blood vessel wall showed similar results.

Further Information: Paterson JC 1941; Trimmer RW 1948; Knox EG 1973.

VITAMIN C DEFICIENCY IS THE PRIMARY CAUSE OF CARDIOVASCULAR DISEASE
- FURTHER EVIDENCE -

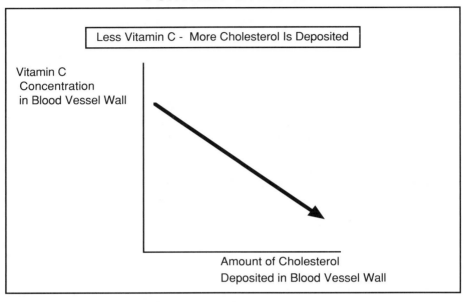

A low concentration of vitamin C in the blood vessel wall leads to fatty deposits inside the wall. In 1979 Dr. A. Hanck and his colleagues from the University of Basel, Switzerland published an important study. They measured the concentrations of vitamin C in human blood vessels, and at the same time they determined the amount of cholesterol deposited. The figure above shows their findings.

- The lower the vitamin C content of the vessel wall, the more cholesterol was deposited.
- A blood vessel wall rich in vitamin C was evidently protected against fatty deposits.

Dr. Hanck and his colleagues confined their study to measuring the deposition of cholesterol in the vessel wall; they did not include lipoprotein(a) in their analysis at that time.

On the previous pages we have learned how vitamin deficiencies lead to cardiovascular disease. Moreover, we have seen that patients with heart disease frequently have low vitamin C concentrations in their bodies. On the following page I will share with you the proof for this new understanding of cardiovascular disease.

Further Information: Hanck A 1979.

VITAMIN C DEFICIENCY IS THE PRIMARY CAUSE OF CARDIOVASCULAR DISEASE
- THE PROOF -

Vitamin C deficiency is the primary cause of cardiovascular disease. This revolutionary new insight into the number one killer diseases has, of course, to be proven. The key question is: can it be shown that a low intake of vitamin C in the diet actually causes atherosclerotic deposits to develop? For ethical reasons, this question can, of course, not be answered by a study using human beings. It is therefore necessary to answer this important question with a suitable animal model.

This animal model is available. Guinea pigs, like human beings, cannot produce their own vitamin C and they are therefore also dependent on sufficient intake of vitamin C in the diet. What happens to blood vessels of guinea pigs if they receive a diet low in vitamin C? To answer this question the following study was carried out: A group of guinea pigs received 60 mg of vitamin C in their diet (compared to the human body weight). This amount was chosen because the 'official' Recommended Daily Allowance (RDA) for vitamin C is 60 mg. A second group of guinea pigs received about 5,000 mg vitamin C per day (compared to the human body weight). After five weeks the arteries of both groups of animals were analyzed. The dramatic findings are shown on the next page:

- *Picture A*: Animals on a diet rich in vitamin C showed no atherosclerotic deposits. Optimum collagen reinforcement evidently protected their blood vessels effectively. Picture A shows the main artery of a guinea pig with optimum vitamin C in the diet. Note that no fatty deposits (white areas) are visible.
- *Picture B*: In contrast, animals on a diet low in vitamin C rapidly developed atherosclerotic deposits in their arteries. Picture B shows the main artery of a guinea pig with insufficient vitamin C in the diet. The white areas represent the atherosclerotic deposits (arrows) in the blood vessel wall.

It is important to understand that both groups of animals received exactly the same amounts of cholesterol and other fats in their diet. Vitamin C was the only factor varying between the two groups. This experiment thus proves that one factor - too little vitamin C in the diet - causes atherosclerotic deposits to develop. As mentioned above, the guinea pig and the human body share exactly the same problem - both are dependent on optimum intake of vitamin C in the diet. Because of this fact we can directly translate the results of this experiment to our human bodies. Thus, with this experiment we were able to scientifically prove that vitamin C deficiency is the primary and direct cause of heart attacks and strokes.

A note by the author: Animal experiments should be kept at an absolute minimum. These experiments should be limited to gaining information which can help to save human lives. The experiment described above and the figure shown will likely stay with my readers throughout their lives, and hopefully will help to prolong them.

Further Information: Willis GC 1952; Gore I 1965; Ginter E 1978; Rath M 1990b.

56

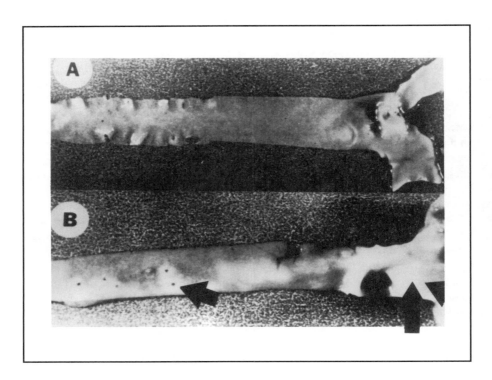

VITAMIN C DEFICIENCY IS THE PRIMARY CAUSE OF CARDIOVASCULAR DISEASE
- THE PROOF -

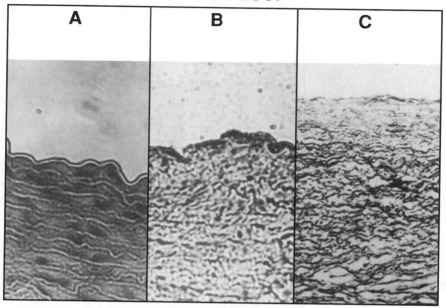

Let us now have a closer look inside vessel walls with sufficient and insufficient vitamin C content. The above pictures A and B show a cut through the blood vessel wall of guinea pigs magnified under a microscope. For comparison, picture C gives you a look inside a human blood vessel. We can make the following observations:

• *Picture A* shows the blood vessel wall from a guinea pig on a *high* vitamin C diet: Two features are important to note. First, the barrier (fine white line) between the blood stream and blood vessel wall is intact. Thus, few risk factors can enter the blood vessel wall from the blood stream. Second, the blood vessel wall itself shows a regular structure of collagen molecules inside the blood vessel wall. This regular structure guarantees optimum stability and elasticity of these blood vessel walls.

• *Picture B* shows the blood vessel wall from a guinea pig on a *low* vitamin C diet: Again two features are noteworthy: First, the barrier between the blood stream and blood vessel wall is disrupted and broken. It is evident that this blood vessel wall is open for many risk factors entering from the blood stream. Second, the vitamin C deficient blood vessel wall shows a very disorganized collagen pattern. These collagen molecules are unable to provide stability and elasticity to the wall. These weak vessel walls develop atherosclerotic deposits as a 'cast' to improve stability.

• *Figure C* shows a similar slice through an atherosclerotic human artery. Again, disrupted collagen molecules are the basis for the development of atherosclerotic deposits. Please compare picture C with pictures A and B.

Our new understanding of cardiovascular disease is summarized on the next page.

The Principles of Cardiovascular Disease

• The primary cause of cardiovascular disease is vitamin C deficiency leading to weakness of the blood vessel walls.

• Cardiovascular disease begins with the deposition of repair molecules inside the blood vessel wall.

• If vitamin deficiency continues over many years these repair molecules become risk factors, the vessel wall repair mechanism overshoots, and cardiovascular disease develops.

• Lipoprotein(a) is the most effective vessel wall repair molecule and therefore - over time - becomes the greatest risk factor for cardiovascular disease.

HEART ATTACKS, STROKES, AND PERIPHERAL VASCULAR DISEASES

Why Some Forms of Cardiovascular Diseases Are More Frequent Than Others			
	Heart Attacks (7 Million)	Strokes (3 Million)	Peripheral Vascular Disease (1 Million)
Weak Blood Vessel Wall (Vitamin C Deficiency)	# 1	# 1	# 1
Higher Blood Pressure in Arteries Close to Heart	# 2	# 2	No
Mechanical Stress on Blood Vessel Wall	# 3	No	No
High Levels of Blood Risk Factors	Optional	Optional	# 2

We can now explain why heart attacks are more frequent than strokes and strokes more frequent than the clogging of arteries in the bodie's periphery:
• Seven million Americans are diagnosed with diseases of the heart arteries.
• Three million Americans are diagnosed with diseases of the brain arteries.
• An estimated one million Americans are diagnosed with cardiovascular. diseases in other organs and the extremities of the body (periphery).

The answer for this phenomenon is summarized in the above figure:
• The underlying cause of all forms of cardiovascular diseases is a weakness of the blood vessels as a result of vitamin deficiencies (#1).
• The more *additional local* factors challenge this instable blood vessel wall the more often the vascular system fails at this specific location.
• One additional local challenge is the higher blood pressure in the arteries of the heart and the brain explaining heart attacks and strokes (#2).
• The greatest local challenge is the mechanical stress for the coronary arteries explaining heart attack as the leading cardiovascular disease (#3).
• High levels of blood risk factors alone cannot explain the local failure of the cardiovascular system in form of heart attacks or strokes. But if these risk factors are present *in addition* , heart attacks and strokes occur earlier.
• In contrast, peripheral vascular diseases are caused by a direct damage of certain blood risk factors to the wall of the entire blood vessel pipeline. Vascular diseases in smokers and diabetics are examples (Section E).

THE PIPELINE PHENOMENON

This new understanding suddenly enables us to explain an unsolved puzzle in our bodies: the pipeline phenomenon. The human blood vessel system is a pipeline. If this pipeline were cut open, laid out, and measured it would be huge. Each small square in the adjacent figure represents two square yards (about two square meters). The blood vessel surface area of one person amounts to half the size of a football field. The black square in the middle represents the surface area of those arteries which fail a million times over: the coronary arteries where heart attacks occur. As you can see this area of the coronary arteries is only a small fraction when compared to the whole pipeline. Why is there only one black square and why are not all the squares black?

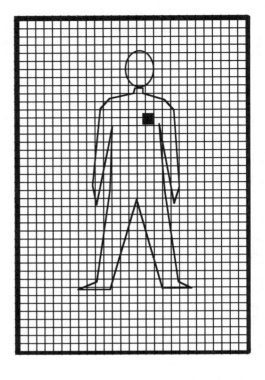

All presently available theories for cardiovascular diseases assume that high concentrations of a risk factor in the blood are the primary villains. The cholesterol theory, for example, assumes that high cholesterol levels damage the blood vessel wall and thereby lead to the development of atherosclerotic deposits. It is, however, evident that in this case the damage to the blood vessel wall would occur in all blood vessels throughout the body. Just as bad water quality damages a water pipeline everywhere, cholesterol would lead to the clogging of arteries, veins, and capillaries throughout our body. If this theory was valid, we would suffer from infarctions of our fingers, nose, elbows - essentially every part of our body. In our picture above, all squares would turn black. This is obviously not the case.

Thus not bad water quality is the primary problem but the instability of the wall of the water pipeline. The very local failure of our cardiovascular system in the arteries of the heart is the result of the instability of the blood vessel wall in combination with great mechanical stress in these coronary arteries. The logic behind the figure above does not take a medical degree - it is a simple physical problem. A plumber finds similar technical problems in his daily work.

The logical answer to the pipeline phenomenon directly leads us to new ways in the prevention and treatment of cardiovascular disease.

VITAMIN C AND OTHER ESSENTIAL NUTRIENTS CAN PREVENT AND REVERSE CARDIOVASCULAR DISEASES

In this section we have seen that the primary cause of cardiovascular disease is the instability of the blood vessel walls caused by a deficiency in vitamins, primarily in vitamin C.

The following sections of the book will show you that dietary vitamin supplementation is a powerful way to protect your blood vessels and your heart and to treat virtually any cardiovascular disease you may have.

- *Aim Number One (Section C):* Maintaining and restoring the stability
  of your blood vessel walls and preventing free radical damage -
  Needed: • Vitamin C
             • Vitamin E
             • Beta Carotene
             • Other essential nutrients

- *Aim Number Two(Section D):* Reversing cardiovascular disease by
  decreasing atherosclerotic deposits in your blood vessel walls -
  Needed: • Vitamin C
             • Vitamin E
             • L-Proline
             • L-Lysine
             • Other essential nutrients

- *Aim Number Three (Section E):* Lowering the levels of lipoprotein(a)
  and of other risk factors for cardiovascular diseases in your blood -
  Needed: • Vitamin C
             • Vitamin B3 (Niacin)
             • Other B vitamins
             • Other essential nutrients

NOTES

HOW TO PREVENT CARDIOVASCULAR DISEASES WITH NUTRITIONAL SUPPLEMENTS

This Section Will Summarize the Evidence That Vitamin C, Vitamin E, and Beta Carotene Can Prevent Cardiovascular Diseases

64

"Vitamin C linked to heart benefits" was a headline in the *New York Times* on May 8, 1992. The newspaper article referred to one of the largest studies on vitamin C carried out thus far. Dr. James Enstrom from the School of Public Health at the University of California Los Angeles (UCLA) and his colleagues studied more than 11,000 Americans for an average of 10 years. Their findings are summarized on the next two pages.

VITAMIN C CUTS HEART DISEASE RATE IN HALF

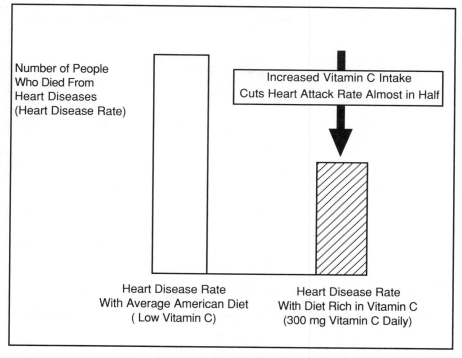

In their study Dr. Enstrom and his colleagues compared the number of deaths from heart disease (heart diseases rate) between Americans following an average diet (low vitamin C intake) and those taking additional vitamin C (on average 300 mg vitamin C per day). In this large-scale study the researchers followed more than 11,000 people for an average of ten years. They found that among those people supplementing their diet with vitamin C much less people died from cardiovascular diseases:

- In men, 300 mg of vitamin C in the diet from food or supplements cut the rate of heart disease in half.
- In women, 300 mg of vitamin C per day in the diet decreased the rate of heart disease by one-third.

Thus, the daily intake of the moderate amount of 300 mg vitamin C saved every second man and one out of three women from suffering a heart attack or stroke.

**No study with any other drug has ever shown
a similar cut of heart diseases.**

Further Information: Enstrom JE 1992.

VITAMIN C ADDS YEARS TO YOUR LIFE

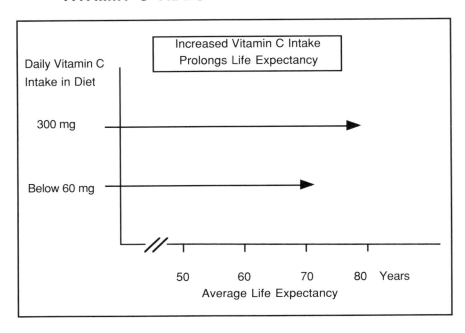

Daily Vitamin C Intake in Diet

Increased Vitamin C Intake Prolongs Life Expectancy

300 mg

Below 60 mg

50   60   70   80   Years
Average Life Expectancy

In the same study the researchers also investigated the question whether vitamin C intake affects life expectancy. Their striking finding was that those Americans with a higher dietary intake of vitamin C lived much longer than those with a low intake of this vitamin:

• Men having a daily vitamin C intake of 150 mg lived two years longer compared to the average American life span.
• Men having a daily vitamin C intake of 300 mg lived six years longer compared to the average American life span.
• In women a similar trend was observed.

Imagine! If 300 mg of vitamin C prolong your life for several years, what can you expect from taking 1,000 mg (1 gram) and more? We can now better understand why animals producing between 1,000 and 20,000 mg of vitamin C every day in their bodies don't get heart attacks and strokes. Moreover, we can now also understand that the eradication of heart disease among humans is a realistic goal.

USA: MORE VITAMIN C - LESS HEART DISEASE

The More Vitamin C Was Consumed -
The Fewer People Died From Heart Disease

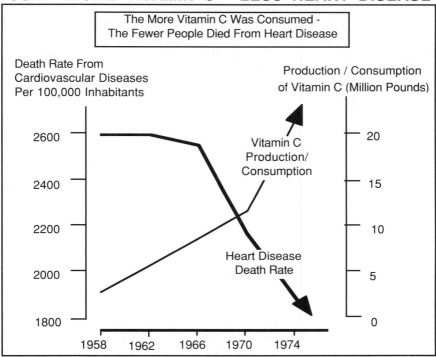

Death Rate From
Cardiovascular Diseases
Per 100,000 Inhabitants

Production / Consumption
of Vitamin C (Million Pounds)

Vitamin C
Production/
Consumption

Heart Disease
Death Rate

2600	20
2400	15
2200	10
2000	5
1800	0

1958   1962   1966   1970   1974

The findings reported on the previous pages are further confirmed by a look at the heart disease statistics in the United States over the past 35 years
• Vitamin C consumption in the United States increased several fold.
• The heart disease rate in the U.S. dropped by one-third.
• The U.S. became the country with the highest per capita consumption
  of vitamin C in the world and, concurrently, had the greatest decrease in
  heart disease rates.
Other public health programs, such as the anti-smoking program and the dietary recommendations of the American Heart Association may have also contributed to this success. The fact remains, however, that a similar decrease in heart disease is not found in any other country despite dietary and other public health programs.

**The United States of America has become a model nation
for reducing heart disease by broad use of vitamin supplements.
A similar reduction of heart diseases is now
also possible in other countries.**

Further information: Vitamin C and Heart Disease Decline: Ginter E 1979.
Heart Disease Statistics in US: Statistical Bulletin 1989; Heart Facts 1987.

THE LARGEST HEALTH STUDY
EVER CONDUCTED
DOCUMENTS HEART BENEFITS OF VITAMIN C

Nature itself carried out the largest study in the history of our planet.
Below you will find the study protocol of this amazing study:

Study Protocol of the World's Largest Health Study:

Substance Tested: Vitamin C

Aim of The Study : To study the effect of vitamin C on
heart disease prevention

Study Groups: Two groups were included:

• Group A: Living beings able to manufacture
vitamin C in their bodies. This group included most
animals on earth.

• Group B: Living beings unable to manufacture vitamin
C and frequently having a low dietary intake of this
vitamin. This group included all human beings.

Study Size: • Group A: Several trillion study participants.

• Group B: Several billion study participants.

Study Duration: Several thousands of human generations.

Study Results: • Group A: Cardiovascular diseases are essentially
unknown in this study group.

• Group B: Every second study participant of this group
died from heart attacks and strokes.

The fact remains, however, that in none of the domestic species, with the rarest of exceptions, do animals develop arteriosclerotic diseases of clinical significance. It appears that most of the pertinent pathological mechanisms operate in animals and that arteriosclerotic disease in them is not impossible; it just does not occur. If the reason for this could be found, it might cast some very useful light on the human disease.

Veterinary Pathology
Smith and Jones, 1958

In 1958 two veterinary doctors published a textbook of veterinary medicine. Throughout their professional life these doctors had treated many animals and had ample opportunity to study the blood vessel system of many kinds of animals. With amazement they discovered that - in whatever animal species they looked - they hardly ever found that cardiovascular disease had developed.

They felt that this observation was so remarkable that they reported it in their textbook on veterinary medicine. The essence of their statement above is that cardiovascular disease "just does not occur" in animals. "If the reason for this could be found, it may cast some very useful light on the human disease."

Unfortunately, the veterinary doctors did not have an explanation for their remarkable observation at that time. Today this observation can be explained: Animals don't have heart disease because they manufacture high amounts of vitamin C in their body which helps to stabilizes their blood vessels. This book may eventually help to cast light on heart disease in human beings.

PROTECTING YOUR BLOOD VESSEL WALL AGAINST FREE RADICAL DAMAGE

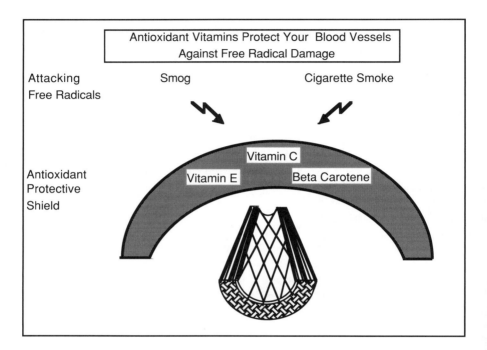

Because of its many protective functions vitamin C is the single most important vitamin for the prevention of cardiovascular diseases. Other vitamins, particularly vitamin E and beta carotene, play also an important preventive role.

In earlier sections of this book I introduced you to free radicals, biochemically aggressive molecules which are contained in high concentrations in the smog-polluted air of our cities and in cigarette smoke. We have also discussed the damage these free radicals do to the walls of our blood vessels and other parts of our bodies. We have also seen that fat globules staying inside our blood vessel walls can be attacked by these free radicals leading to an increased uptake of these fat globules by waste-collecting cells. These fat-loaded waste collecting cells also contribute to the development of atherosclerotic deposits.

Most importantly, this whole mechanism can be prevented by an optimum intake of vitamin C, vitamin E, and beta carotene. These antioxidant vitamins can neutralize free radicals and thereby protect the blood vessel system. The following pages will show that supplementing your diet with antioxidant vitamins is a powerful way to prevent heart attacks and strokes.

ANTIOXIDANT VITAMINS REDUCE THE RISK FOR CARDIOVASCULAR DISEASES

- **Vitamin C Cuts Heart Disease Rate Almost in Half (Documented In 11,000 Americans Over 10 Years)**

- **Vitamin E Cuts Heart Disease Rate by More Than One Third   (Documented in 36,000 Americans Over 6 Years)**

- **Beta Carotene (Provitamin A) Cuts Heart Disease Rate by 30%   (Documented in 36,000 Americans Over 6 Years)**

- **No Prescription Drug Has Been Shown to Be as Effective as These Vitamins in Preventing Heart Disease**

In recent years a number of large scale clinical and epidemiological studies have been carried out with vitamin C, vitamin E, and beta carotene. All these studies documented a preventive effect of these antioxidant vitamins on cardiovascular diseases. The results of these studies can be summarized in the following way: At the present time there is no medical treatment known to prevent cardiovascular diseases more effectively than vitamin C, vitamin E and beta carotene.

Interestingly, the results of one study suggest that the daily amounts of vitamin C needed for cardiovascular protection are more than 300 mg per day. This amount is five times higher than the 'official' recommendation of 60 mg per day.

The following facts show why vitamin C is needed in high amounts:
- Vitamin C is the most powerful among all natural antioxidants and no free radical damage occurs as long as vitamin C is present.
- Vitamin C is the first among these antioxidant vitamins to be destroyed in the battle against the attacking free radicals.
- Antioxidant vitamins can partially make up for each other. An important function of vitamin E and beta carotene is that they back up vitamin C in the antioxidative defense. Optimum amounts of vitamin E and beta carotene in the diet can save vitamin C molecules in the body from becoming depleted.

Further Information: Vitamin E Clinical Studies: Riemersma RA 1991; Rimm EB 1991. Beta Carotene: Rimm EB 1991; Gerster H 1991 (Review). Vitamin C The Strongest Antioxidant: Frei B 1989; Niki E 1987.

EUROPE: MORE VITAMINS -
LESS HEART DISEASE

Further evidence for the benefit of high intake of dietary vitamins in the prevention of heart diseases comes from studies in Europe. The study shown above included several thousand people from six European countries ranging from the northern to the southern parts of Europe. The rate of cardiovascular disease in these countries was compared to the blood levels of vitamins C, E, and cholesterol found in these populations. The following remarkable findings were made:

• The rates of cardiovascular disease are highest in northern European countries and lowest in southern European countries close to the Mediterranean Sea.
• Vitamin C and vitamin E blood levels are highest in southern European countries where the diet contains more fruits and vitamin rich nutrition. In contrast, people living in northern European countries have on average much lower vitamin C and vitamin E blood levels.
• Heart disease rate is highest in those countries where people had, on average, a lower vitamin intake and therefore a lower vitamin blood level.
• The rates for heart disease are lowest in those countries where people have, on average, a high vitamin intake and therefore high vitamin blood levels.
• Lower levels of vitamins are a greater risk for cardiovascular diseases than high levels of cholesterol.

These findings should also end speculation about the causes for low heart disease rates in countries such as France and Greece. It has been speculated that the lower rate of heart disease in France is due to high red wine consumption, whereas in Greece olive oil consumption was held responsible. The answer for the low rate of heart disease in these two countries is much simpler: the inhabitants of these two southern European countries enjoy a diet high in fruits and vitamin-rich nutrition.

The alarming studies above included only populations from western European countries. Even more alarming is the situation in eastern European countries. The statistics of the World Health Organization at the beginning of this book show that heart disease rates in some middle and eastern European countries were even higher than in northern Europe. Dr. Emil Ginter from the University of Bratislava explained this fact as the result of an average diet low in fruits, high in fats, and also of a high degree of air pollution abundantly containing free radicals.

**Countries with a high rate of cardiovascular diseases
can lower this rate by promoting a higher intake of vitamins
among their population.**

Further Information: Western Europe: Gey KF 1987 and 1991. Eastern Europe: Ginter E 1991.

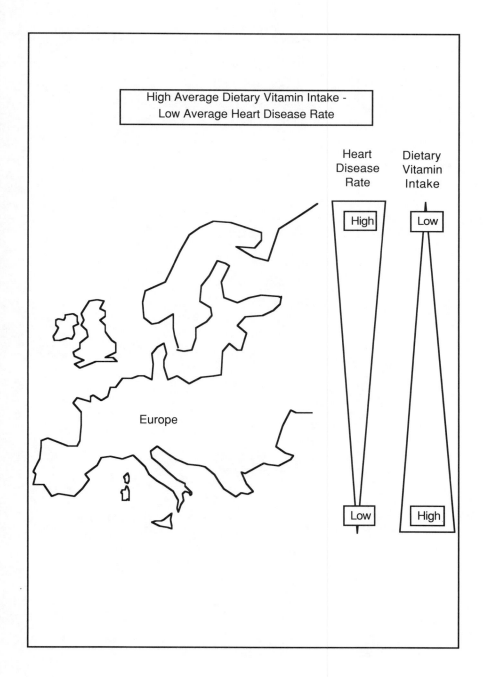

<u>NOTES</u>

SECTION   D

HOW TO REVERSE EXISTING CARDIOVASCULAR DISEASE WITH NUTRITIONAL SUPPLEMENTS

- Reduce Existing Atherosclerotic Deposits

- Improve the Blood Supply to a Suffocating Heart

- Reduce Angina Pectoris Pain

DIETARY VITAMIN C SUPPLEMENTATION REVERSES ATHEROSCLEROTIC DEPOSITS

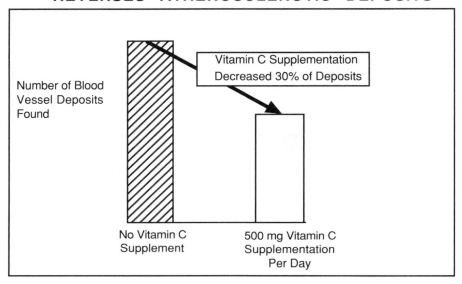

After all what you already know about vitamin C it should come as no surprise that this vitamin was also shown to reverse existing atherosclerotic deposits. In 1954 the Canadian cardiologist C. G. Willis published a landmark clinical study in which he had analyzed the size of the deposits in the leg arteries of his patients by angiography. This method uses a radioactive dye injected into the blood vessel system of the patients to measure the size of the deposits in the blood vessel walls. Today, angiography has become the standard method for evaluating coronary artery disease and other forms of cardiovascular disease.

After having measured the initial size of the deposits, Dr. Willis gave ten of his patients a daily vitamin C supplementation of 500 mg. After a period of two to six months, the patients returned to his clinic and received a control angiography. The size of the atherosclerotic deposits could then be compared with their size before vitamin C supplements were taken. In those patients taking 500 mg per day, 30% of the atherosclerotic deposits were found to be decreased. In a control group of patients who did not receive any vitamin C supplementation, none of the deposits had decreased. This is the first clinical report that vitamins can reverse existing cardiovascular disease. Unfortunately, this important study was not followed up until today.

What are the signals for a patient who has developed coronary heart disease?

Further Information: Willis GC 1954.

DEPOSITS IN CORONARY ARTERIES LEAD TO A SUFFOCATING HEART MUSCLE AND TO ANGINA PECTORIS

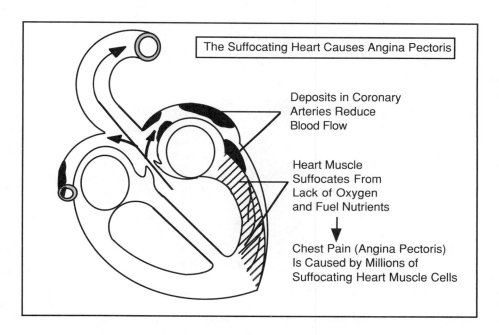

The Suffocating Heart Causes Angina Pectoris

Deposits in Coronary Arteries Reduce Blood Flow

Heart Muscle Suffocates From Lack of Oxygen and Fuel Nutrients

Chest Pain (Angina Pectoris) Is Caused by Millions of Suffocating Heart Muscle Cells

The typical alarm signal for a patient who has developed coronary heart disease is angina pectoris. Angina pectoris is a sharp pain typically occurring in the middle of the chest and spreading into the left arm. Since there are many 'untypical' forms of angina pectoris it is always best to consult your doctor about any form of chest pain.

What causes angina pectoris? Angina pectoris is caused by heart muscle cells suffocating from lack of oxygen and nutrition. Growing atherosclerotic deposits in the coronary arteries gradually decrease the blood flow to the heart muscle cells. When the blood flow in a coronary artery is reduced to about 25% of normal, the heart cells receiving their blood supplies from this artery begin to suffocate from lack of oxygen and nutrition. The pain from millions of suffocating heart cells is projected to the chest. This is what you experience as angina pectoris.

Typically, angina pectoris occurs with increased physical activity such as climbing stairs, and exercising. In this condition the heart muscle cells have to work at maximum effort, and they need a maximum supply of oxygen and nutrients. In patients with coronary artery disease, the reduced blood flow cannot meet the increased demand of the heart muscle cells and angina pectoris occurs.

REVERSING HEART DISEASE
AND DECREASING ANGINA PECTORIS

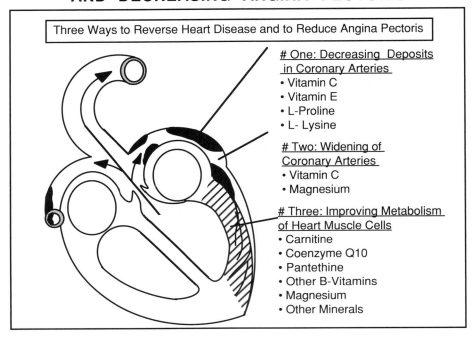

Three Ways to Reverse Heart Disease and to Reduce Angina Pectoris

One: Decreasing Deposits in Coronary Arteries
• Vitamin C
• Vitamin E
• L-Proline
• L- Lysine

Two: Widening of Coronary Arteries
• Vitamin C
• Magnesium

Three: Improving Metabolism of Heart Muscle Cells
• Carnitine
• Coenzyme Q10
• Pantethine
• Other B-Vitamins
• Magnesium
• Other Minerals

Angina pectoris is the typical signal for existing heart disease. Reversing heart disease therefore leads to a decrease or to a complete cessation of angina pectoris pain. In the past coronary bypass surgery or angioplasty (e.g. balloon catheterization) of the coronary arteries were the only ways to achieve this aim. Now a non-surgical way is available: The reversal of existing heart disease with selected nutritional supplements. These essential nutrients can help to improve the blood supply to the heart muscle cells by:

• *Number one*: Improving the coronary blood flow by reversing the deposits in the arteries. The most important nutritional supplements contributing to this goal are vitamin C, vitamin E, L-proline, L-lysine, and antioxidant vitamins.

• *Number two*: Increasing the blood flow in the coronary arteries by widening the coronary arteries. The key essential nutrients for this are vitamin C and magnesium.

• *Number three*: Improving the level of fuel nutrients for suffocating heart muscle cells. This aim can be achieved by supplementing your diet with the following essential nutrients: carnitine, coenzyme Q10, pantethine and other B vitamins, magnesium, as well as other minerals and trace elements.

By following these recommendations, angina pectoris will decrease in most cases within weeks. The following page lists the essential nutrients which can help you reverse existing heart diseases in your body.

NUTRITIONAL RECOMMENDATIONS TO REVERSE HEART DISEASE

Below are my recommendations to help you to reverse existing heart diseases and to achieve optimum cardiovascular health.

These recommendations are based on recent scientific discoveries and the most important effects of the ingredients are given in parentheses. These recommendations are already being followed by several thousands people in the United States and in other countries.

On the following pages I shall share with you the letters from some of the patients following my recommendations.

Vitamin C (Restoring Blood Vessel Stability, Deposit Removal, Antioxidant,Others)
Vitamin E (Antioxidant, Deposit Removal)
Beta Carotene (Antioxidant)
L-Proline (Blood Vessel Teflon, Atherosclerotic Deposit Removal)
L-Lysine (Blood Vessel Teflon, Atherosclerotic Deposit Removal, Cell Fuel)
L-Carnitine (Cholesterol Decrease, Triglyceride Decrease, Cell Fuel)
Coenzyme Q10 (Cell Fuel)
Vitamin B-1 (Cell Fuel)
Vitamin B-2 (Cell Fuel)
Vitamin B-3 (Niacin) (Cholesterol Decrease, Triglyceride Decrease, Cell Fuel)
Vitamin B-3 (Niacinamide) (Cell Fuel)
Vitamin B-6 (Cell Fuel)
Vitamin B-12 (Blood Cell Factor, Cell Fuel)
Folic Acid (Blood Cell Factor, Cell Fuel)
Vitamin D (Cell Fuel)
Biotin (Cell Fuel)
Pantothenate (Cholesterol Decrease, Triglyceride Decrease, Cell Fuel)
Calcium, Magnesium, Zinc, Manganese, Copper, Selenium, Chromium, Molybdenum (Minerals And Trace Elements Are Required For Many Cell Functions).

You will find detailed information about these recommendations
at the end of this book.

REVERSING HEART DISEASE AND ALLEVIATING SUFFOCATING HEART WITHIN WEEKS
- THE PROOF -

TESTIMONIALS FROM PATIENTS WITH ANGINA PECTORIS WHO ARE FOLLOWING MY CARDIOVASCULAR HEALTH RECOMMENDATIONS

Dear Dr. Rath:

In May, 1992 some extraordinary physical exertion on my part (heavy lifting) brought on pain that was especially noticeable in my left arm and left shoulder. I thought that I had badly strained these muscles in my upper body. There was so much discomfort that I was not able to sleep until the morning hours. By the next morning the pain had progressed to the middle of my chest and I then recognized the pain as angina.

Immediately, I started a series of treatments. During the treatments and after, I started a walking program. Although my walking did not cause any severe angina pain, there was still a tightness in my chest and a necessity to slow down my pace because of a shortness of breath.

It wasn't until I started following your cardiovascular health recommendations that I experienced a difference. Remarkably, within a month the discomfort from walking had entirely disappeared.

Presently, I am walking 2.5 miles at least 3 days per week at a very fast clip with no discomfort whatsoever. I am cognizant that the buildup within my blood vessel walls occurred over a long time period, so I am prepared to continue following your recommendations on a continuous basis. It's a small price to pay for arteries that are free of atherosclerotic deposits.

Thanks for your cardiovascular recommendations! I feel that you have made a tremendous scientific breakthrough in the treatment of heart disease.

I look forward to your upcoming book.

M.L., USA

Dear Dr. Rath:
I had been having chest pain (angina pectoris) for several years on the average of about every three weeks. Since I started follow your cardiovascular health recommendations over 90 days ago, I have only had chest pain one time, which was about three weeks after receiving my first bottle.
I am following your cardiovascular health recommendations because I feel that proper nutrition can prevent eighty percent of our health problems.

E.T., USA

From a patient's letter to his doctor:
I can't wait to see you in six weeks. Since following Dr. Rath's cardiovascular health recommendations I have had no angina. This past May I walked and climbed the rugged ocean trails of the rain forest without so much as a twinge. And recently, I have walked the last 2-18 holes of golf - something unheard of since my heart attack.
In closing, I and my family are very pleased and would like to thank you.

J.T., Canada

Dear Dr. Rath:
I am happy to write to you telling you of the benefits that I have received since starting to follow your recommendations for cardiovascular health. It has been approximately one month since I began and I have been able to notice a remarkable improvement in my energy and vitality. Several of my neighbors have commented that I look better than I have for years.
It was a little over three years ago that I suffered a brain-stem stroke which has left me with a little disability in my walking and some weakness. However, since that time I have had surgery for a narrowing of the arteries (endarterectomy). Recovery from that surgery was uneventful. Then in 1992 I developed a blood disorder with low platelets (down to 3,000). Treatment has been extensive including chemotherapy, blood infusions, and even a splenectomy. A complication to all of this was blood clots in both legs. It appears that all is beginning to turn around and a lab report just today showed that my platelets have gone up to 38,000. I believe that your recommendations are having a marked effect on my getting better.

G.S., USA

82

Dear Dr. Rath:
I have asthma, controlled high blood pressure and angina. After following your recommendations for cardiovascular health I feel wonderful - I feel like I have more energy and can do my work easier - no chest pain, coughing or leg pains - my whole body feels light, as if I lost weight. It is a very good feeling.
Thank you for helping us in our older years.
Sincerely,

B. , Canada

Dear Dr. Rath:
I am 60 years old, my weight and general health are normal.
In January of this year I began experiencing chest pains when exercising. In April, my doctor told me, on the basis of an ECG, that I had suffered a heart attack. He continued prescribing a beta blocker which I had been taking for high blood pressure for many years.
In May I started following your recommendations for cardiovascular health and also went on a very strict vegetarian, no fat diet. My chest pain during exercise began to lessen after just two weeks of this regimen. I have now been on my diet and followed your recommendations for 2 months, and I now have no chest pain or breathlessness at all, even cycling or walking energetically for several hours at a time. I also feel better than I have felt for years, with lots of energy and high spirits. My confidence level in my heart condition is so good that I no longer carry nitro pills with me when setting out on a bicycle ride or a walk. I feel young and bright, and I look great. (People I run into say how good I look).
Since the only changes in my lifestyle have been your cardiovascular recommendations and diet, I have to say that one or both of these factors have caused this dramatic change in my health. For what it is worth, I tend to think that the combination of both these factors together is what has caused my health to improve.
Yours truly,

K.P., Canada

Further testimonials are documented throughout this book.

HOW NUTRITIONAL SUPPLEMENTS REVERSE EXISTING ATHEROSCLEROTIC DEPOSITS

There is no better proof for a new therapy than the personal testimony of those following this therapy. On the previous pages I shared with you how much everybody - even patients with severe heart conditions - can benefit from following the recommendations of this book. However, I still owe you a more detailed explanation how this is possible. How can nutritional supplements achieve these remarkable health improvements? You already know that several factors contribute to an improved blood supply to the suffocating heart and to the reversal of heart disease: A decrease of atherosclerotic deposits in the coronary arteries, a relaxation of the coronary artery, and an improved metabolism of the heart muscle cells.

Of particular importance is the reversal of existing atherosclerotic deposits in the wall of the coronary arteries. A decrease of the deposit size results in an improved blood supply to the heart muscle - a result which was previously only achieved by surgical procedures. Because of the importance for patients and doctors I will focus here on the role of nutritional supplements in the reversal of atherosclerotic deposits.

There are several ways by which nutritional supplements can reverse atherosclerotic deposits.

• By increasing the blood levels of HDL (high-density lipoprotein) particles. These transport particles are also called "good cholesterol" because they are able to pick up fat from the deposits in the blood vessel wall and thereby decrease the fat content of the vessel wall. Vitamin C, but also vitamin E, are powerful agents increasing HDL blood levels, particularly in those patients with low levels of this useful particle. Thus, vitamin C and vitamin E help reverse existing heart diseases by improving the waste removal from the vessel wall.

• A new therapeutic approach is the use of L-lysine and L-proline. These natural amino acids provide a teflon layer which detaches lipoprotein(a) and other risk factors from their deposits inside the blood vessel wall. By releasing thousands of lipoprotein(a) particles from the blood vessel wall lysine and proline help reverse existing cardiovascular disease.

• Vitamin E has already been shown to inhibit the muscle cells in the vessel wall responsible for 'atherosclerotic tumor' growth. Vitamin C and the natural amino acids L-proline and L-lysine promise to be also effective agents to stop and reverse atherosclerotic tumors, thereby improving blood flow in the arteries.

On the following pages we will take a closer look at these different mechanisms.

VITAMINS REVERSE ATHEROSCLEROTIC DEPOSITS BY INCREASING HDL LEVELS

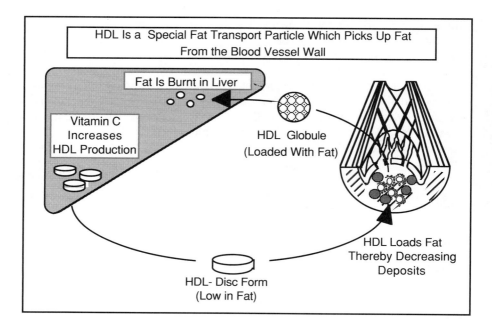

HDL Is a Special Fat Transport Particle Which Picks Up Fat From the Blood Vessel Wall

Fat Is Burnt in Liver

Vitamin C Increases HDL Production

HDL Globule (Loaded With Fat)

HDL Loads Fat Thereby Decreasing Deposits

HDL- Disc Form (Low in Fat)

Vitamin C increases the production of high density lipoprotein particles (HDL, "good cholesterol") in the liver. As a result the blood levels of HDL rise with vitamin C supplementation. HDL is a unique fat transport vehicle. Produced by the liver, the HDL particles circulate in the blood. Eventually, they enter the blood vessel walls, suck up fat molecules deposited there, and transport them back to the liver where the fat is burnt. The greater the number of HDL particles produced, the more HDL which can remove deposited fat from the blood vessel wall, and the greater the chance to reverse atherosclerotic deposits.

Like vitamin C, vitamin E is also known to increase HDL blood levels. Thus, dietary supplementation of vitamin C and vitamin E helps to reverse heart disease by increasing HDL levels. On the following pages I will introduce you to new therapeutic approaches which further accelerate the reversal of atherosclerotic deposits.

Further Information: Metabolic Transport of HDL: Breslow JL. Vitamin C And HDL: Bates JL 1977; Jacques PF 1987. HDL And Vitamin E: Hermann WJ 1979.

A TEFLON-LIKE PROTECTION LAYER
FOR YOUR BLOOD VESSEL WALLS

The risk for cardiovascular disease from lipoprotein(a) can be further reduced by preventing the deposition of lipoprotein(a), via the adhesive apo(a), inside the blood vessel wall. As we already know, the binding of lipoprotein(a) particles inside the blood vessel wall leads to development of atherosclerotic deposits. Less adhesiveness must therefore lead to less deposition of lipoproteins(a) particles. Two natural anti-adhesives have been identified:

* The amino acid L- lysine
* The amino acid L- proline

These amino acids act like a teflon layer around the lipoprotein(a) particle and inside the blood vessel wall. Natural anti-adhesives are an important new way to reduce the risk for cardiovascular disease. Dietary supplementation of lysine and L-proline has the following therapeutic effects in your body:

• Preventing further deposition of lipoprotein(a) fat globules inside your blood vessel walls.
• Releasing already deposited lipoprotein(a) from your blood vessel walls.
• Releasing also other fat globules (e.g. LDL) which had been captured inside the vessel wall via the adhesive apo(a).

For preventive purposes I recommend a dosage of 500 mg of lysine and 500 mg of proline per day. For therapeutic purposes this dosage can be increased up to several grams per day. This dosage range is safe from any side effects.

What else should you know about these two amino acids?
L-lysine: Lysine is an essential amino acid, which means that our bodies cannot manufacture lysine. We are therefore entirely dependent on an optimum intake of this amino acid in the diet. Meat is an important source for lysine. While no 'official recommendations have been established for this amino acid, we now understand that we frequently do not get enough of this amino acid in the diet. This is particularly true for patients at risk for cardiovascular diseases.

L-Proline: Proline is a non-essential amino acid which means that our body can manufacture a certain amount of it. However, under certain conditions the amount of proline manufactured in the body may not be enough to meet the requirement. This is particularly true for patients at risk for cardiovascular diseases. It should be noted that proline is several fold more effective in neutralizing the adhesive risk from lipoprotein(a) than natural lysine.

Further Information: Therapeutic Recommendation of Lysine: Rath M 1991a. Lp(a) And Proline Trieu VN 1991. Therapeutic Recommendation of Proline: Rath M 1992e. Proline Metabolism: Phang JM.

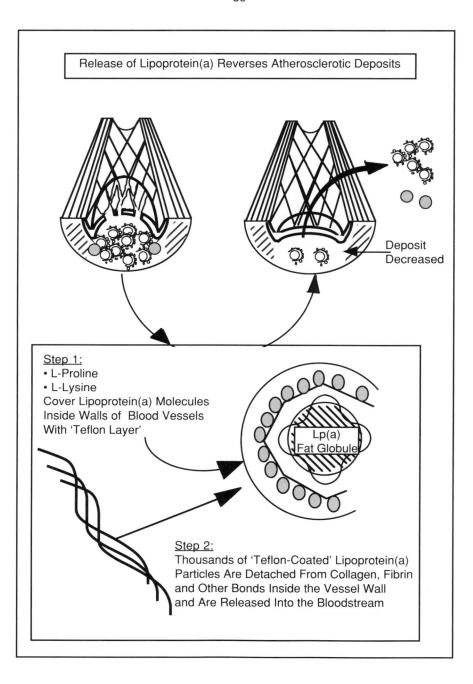

Release of Lipoprotein(a) Reverses Atherosclerotic Deposits

Deposit
Decreased

Step 1:
• L-Proline
• L-Lysine
Cover Lipoprotein(a) Molecules
Inside Walls of Blood Vessels
With 'Teflon Layer'

Lp(a)
Fat Globule

Step 2:
Thousands of 'Teflon-Coated' Lipoprotein(a)
Particles Are Detached From Collagen, Fibrin
and Other Bonds Inside the Vessel Wall
and Are Released Into the Bloodstream

A MEDICAL BREAKTHROUGH
FROM THE LABORATORY BENCH

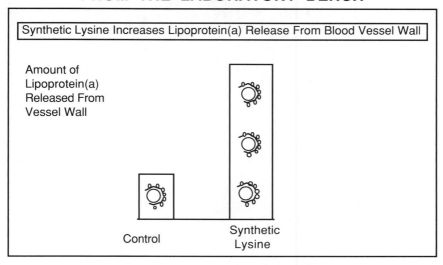

Synthetic Lysine Increases Lipoprotein(a) Release From Blood Vessel Wall

Amount of Lipoprotein(a) Released From Vessel Wall

Control

Synthetic Lysine

How was the therapeutic value of lysine discovered? As with most discoveries in medicine it started at the laboratory bench. While working on the lipoprotein(a) research project at Hamburg University I used lysine to isolate lipoprotein(a) from the blood. The finding that lipoprotein(a) was deposited inside the blood vessel wall as an entire particle bound via the adhesive apo(a) suggested the therapeutic use of lysine as a possible anti-adhesive. The natural amino acid had the advantage of having no side effects and being immediately available as a nutritional supplement.

The above figure shows a subsequent experiment in which synthetic lysine was tested for its ability to release lipoprotein(a). These experiments confirmed that synthetic lysine was in fact able to release lipoprotein(a) from atherosclerotic deposits. Later I proposed the therapeutic use of lysine in the treatment of cardiovascular diseases.

In the same year Dr. Trieu and his colleagues published their experiments showing that the amino acid proline was another substance which can reduce the stickiness of lipoprotein(a) and the therapeutic benefits of the combined use of lysine and proline became evident.

The cardiovascular recommendations of this book are based on these recent scientific discoveries in cardiovascular and nutritional medicine. The remarkable health improvements achieved with these recommendations are no coincidence. They are based on an improved understanding of cardiovascular diseases and on the new therapeutic approaches resulting therefrom.

THE COMING SCIENTIFIC BREAKTHROUGH : VITAMIN E, VITAMIN C, LYSINE AND PROLINE, COULD REVERSE "ATHEROSCLEROTIC TUMORS"

This and the following page will give you a glimpse into current scientific research documenting the benefits of nutritional supplements in reversing cardiovascular diseases.

We have seen earlier that an important part of the atherosclerotic deposit is contributed by an 'atherosclerotic tumor' growing around the deposits inside the vessel wall. We also know that this local 'tumor ' is caused by muscle cells inside the vessel wall which multiply uncontrolled in the neighborhood of deposits. Halting or reversing this vessel wall 'tumor' will help reverse cardiovascular diseases and improve blood flow in the arteries. Towards this end, any substance which inhibits the growth of the muscle cells in the vessel wall is of great therapeutic value. It should come as no surprise that vitamins and other essential nutrients are prime candidates to accomplish this therapeutic goal.

Vitamin E (alpha-tocopherol) has already been shown experimentally to inhibit muscle cell growth by 50%. This powerful effect can be achieved in dosages which are comparable to the blood levels of vitamin E in a person taking dietary supplements of this vitamin. It is likely that vitamin C will be found to have a similar effect.

Moreover, the amino acids lysine and proline could further decrease the size of the atherosclerotic tumor. Recently, Dr. Grainger and his colleagues at Stanford University published a report that lipoprotein(a) actively promotes the growth of these muscle cells thereby accelerating the growth of 'atherosclerotic tumors'. The pathway described by these researchers can be inhibited by lysine and proline. Thus at least four nutritional supplements are likely to inhibit and reverse the 'atherosclerotic tumors' in the vessel wall and thereby reverse existing cardiovascular diseases.

I am aware that these pages are of rather technical nature. On the other hand I wanted to share with you the fascination of medical science - the steps from an idea in the laboratory, to its verification by experiments and, finally, to its successful clinical introduction to improve the health of millions of people. What is most fascinating about research with nutritional supplements is that they are safe and affordable. In other words, you can immediately start to take advantage of the medical discoveries I am sharing with you on these pages.

Further Information: Vitamin E and Muscle Cells: Boscoboinik D 1991.
Lipoprotein(a) and Muscle Cells: Grainger DJ 1993.

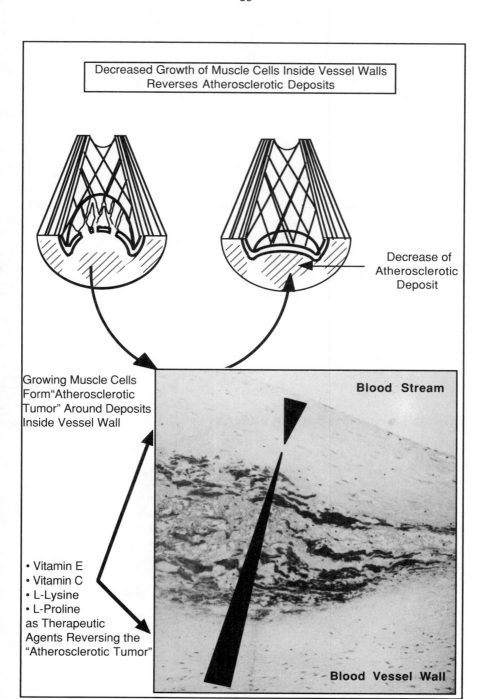

Decreased Growth of Muscle Cells Inside Vessel Walls
Reverses Atherosclerotic Deposits

Decrease of
Atherosclerotic
Deposit

Growing Muscle Cells
Form "Atherosclerotic
Tumor" Around Deposits
Inside Vessel Wall

- Vitamin E
- Vitamin C
- L-Lysine
- L-Proline
as Therapeutic
Agents Reversing the
"Atherosclerotic Tumor"

Blood Stream

Blood Vessel Wall

REVERSING CARDIOVASCULAR DISEASES WITH NUTRITIONAL SUPPLEMENTS

Reversing existing atherosclerotic deposits without surgery has been one of the greatest challenges in medicine. In this section I have summarized for you the evidence that nutritional supplements can reverse atherosclerotic deposits, can effectively improve the blood supply to the suffocating heart and can free the patient from angina pectoris.

I have shared with you my recommendations for achieving this goal by utilizing a comprehensive, scientifically based, program of essential nutrients. Most importantly, I have shared with you the already available proof: Testimonials from grateful patients who are following my nutritional recommendations.

All these patients were on regular medication for treatment of their heart conditions. However, they found ultimate relief only when their bodies and their cardiovascular systems were resupplemented with vitamins and other essential nutrients. Their health improvements can be summarized as follows:

• Free of angina pectoris within only weeks
• Free of shortness of breath
• Free of irregular heartbeats
• More physical and mental energy

I am not aware of any other drug or any other treatment which is able to accomplish such remarkable health improvements within such a short time.

Moreover, an additional report is available on the lysine and vitamin C component of my recommendations. Based on my early discoveries, my former colleague Linus Pauling reported the decrease of angina pectoris after five months in a patient taking high amounts of lysine and vitamin C. While this result is encouraging it also shows the limitations of a therapeutic approach based on two components: Much higher amounts of supplements and a longer time are needed to help the patient.

In summary, the recommendations of this book are the most effective treatment presently available to prevent and treat cardiovascular diseases. Since this treatment is based exclusively on natural ingredients everyone can start immediately to take advantage of this medical breakthrough.

Further Information : Pauling L 1991.

HEART ATTACKS AND STROKES
CAN BE ERADICATED

We are now able to summarize our present knowledge of the causes, the prevention, and the treatment of coronary heart disease and other forms of cardiovascular diseases as follows:

• Heart attacks, strokes and other cardiovascular diseases are primarily caused by vitamin deficiencies.

• Optimum supplementation with vitamins and other essential nutrients is the basic therapeutic measure for prevention and successful treatment of cardiovascular diseases.

• I encourage my colleagues in clinical medicine to help spread this information as soon as possible for the benefit of your own patients and millions of others.

A special note is in order for patients with coronary heart disease or other forms of cardiovascular diseases:

• You should start immediately to supplement your diet with vitamins and other essential nutrients.

• While following the recommendations of this book, do not discontinue your regular medication without consulting your doctor.

• Share your health improvements with your doctor. Together you can make the best decisions to reduce your regular medication.

"CALL FOR EXCELLENCE IN HEALTH CARE"

AN OPEN INVITATION TO THE
PHARMACEUTICAL COMPANIES
OF THE WORLD
BY THE AUTHOR OF THIS BOOK

More than ten million Americans suffer presently from different forms of cardiovascular disease. They need the best treatment science and medicine can offer. Many millions more need medical advice and help to prevent these diseases. And they need it now.

Pharmaceutical companies are an important part of the health care system and they share an overall responsibility to provide the best health care possible. Over the years many prescription drugs became available which were able to help many patients. This book reports about a new therapeutic approach based on nutritional supplements. This therapeutic approach is effective, safe and it is affordable to all Americans. Moreover, the nutritional recommendations of this book are helping heart disease patients to improve their health beyond any treatment with conventional drugs. Thus, the recommendations of this book are likely to improve the cardiovascular health of millions of Americans beyond the present health standard.

I call upon you, the pharmaceutical companies offering drugs for the treatment of cardiovascular diseases, to compare your products in clinical studies with the recommendations of this book. Our common responsibility towards millions of lives urges us to document the treatment for cardiovascular disease which is

- the most effective in preventing heart attacks and strokes
- the most effective in reducing atherosclerotic deposits
- the most effective in reducing angina pectoris pain
- without side-effects
- affordable to everybody

The results of these studies can have far-reaching implications for the health care system of the United States as well as of many other countries.

NOTES

SECTION E

HOW TO NEUTRALIZE
RISK FACTORS FOR
CARDIOVASCULAR DISEASE
WITH
NUTRITIONAL SUPPLEMENTS

Neutralize Inherited Risk Factors Such as
- **High Lipoprotein(a) Levels**
- **High Cholesterol Levels**
- **High Triglyceride Levels**
- **Low HDL Levels**
- **High Blood Sugar In Diabetic Patients**
- **High Blood Pressure**

Neutralize the Cardiovascular Risk
From External Risk Factors Such as
- **Smoking**
- **Stress**
- **Birth Control Pill**
- **Dialysis Procedures**

RISK FACTORS FOR HEART DISEASE ARE REPAIR FACTORS FOR VITAMIN DEFICIENT BLOOD VESSEL WALLS

Earlier in this book we redefined cardiovascular disease as an overshooting repair for a blood vessel wall deficient in vitamins, particularly in vitamin C. This new understanding also gives a new meaning to blood risk factors: Risk factors for cardiovascular disease are repair factors for blood vessel walls weakened by vitamin deficiency.

- The more effective a blood factor is in repairing the blood vessel wall, the more likely it accumulates in the blood vessel wall and leads to cardiovascular disease.

- These repair factors include cholesterol, triglycerides, lipoprotein(a), low density lipoproteins (LDL), very low density lipoproteins (VLDL), as well as clotting factors and dozens of lesser risk factors. Lipoprotein(a) is the greatest risk factor by far because it is the most effective repair molecule and easily accumulates inside the vessel wall.

The figure on the following page summarizes the fascinating blood vessel repair program in our body involving different organs:

- *1. Vessel Wall:* Low dietary intake of vitamins, particularly a deficiency in vitamin C, leads to lesions in the blood vessel wall. A local repair mechanism is initiated.

- *2. Liver:* At the same time the liver starts to produce a higher amount of repair factors which lead to increased levels of these repair factors in the blood. The function of these repair factors is to mend the blood vessel wall destabilized by vitamin deficiency. With an ongoing repair these repair factors become risk factors and build up atherosclerotic deposits.

As you already know, high intake of vitamin C keeps the blood vessel wall healthy and stable and no repair is needed. Consequently, the liver does not have to produce high amounts of repair or risk factors. On the basis of this new understanding it comes as no surprise that vitamin C, but also certain other vitamins, decrease the blood levels of most risk factors for cardiovascular disease known today. In this section we will discuss in greater detail which nutrients are particularly effective in lowering high blood levels of these risk factors.

Further Information: Rath M 1991a.

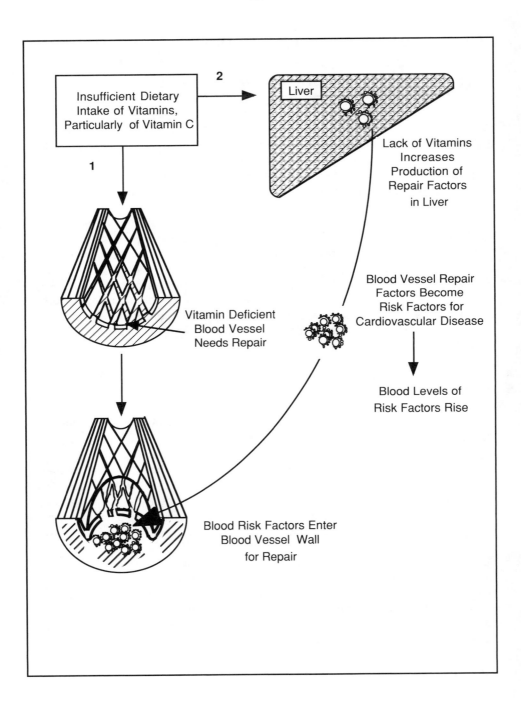

VITAMIN C LOWERS LIPOPROTEIN(a)
BLOOD LEVELS

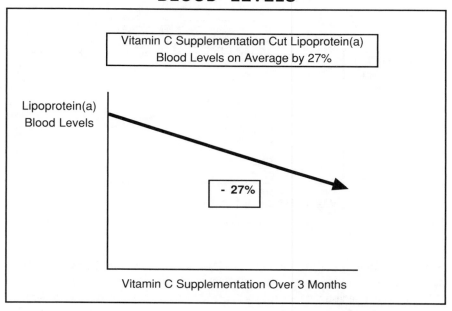

Vitamin C Supplementation Cut Lipoprotein(a)
Blood Levels on Average by 27%

Lipoprotein(a)
Blood Levels

- 27%

Vitamin C Supplementation Over 3 Months

At present no prescription drug is known to lower lipoprotein(a) blood levels or reduce the risk for cardiovascular disease from this tremendous risk factor.   In contrast, two vitamins are known to decrease lipoprotein(a) blood levels. Vitamin C and vitamin B3 (nicotinic acid) can decrease the production of lipoprotein(a) in the liver and thereby reduce the concentrations of these risk factors in the blood.

A clinical pilot study I initiated was able to show that vitamin C can lower lipoprotein(a) plasma blood levels. Eleven patients with cardiovascular disease and very high levels of lipoprotein(a) took 9 grams (9000 milligrams) of vitamin C per day for 14 weeks. Their lipoprotein(a) blood levels dropped on average by 27%.

In order to reduce the lipoprotein(a) blood concentration, it may   actually be necessary to take relatively high amounts of vitamin C (several grams per day). Smaller amounts of vitamin C (less than 1 gram per day) may not be sufficient to lower lipoprotein(a) levels. Following this pilot clinical study, physicians have reported to me the successful lowering of lipoprotein(a) with vitamin C.

Another vitamin known to lower lipoprotein(a) blood levels is vitamin B3.

Further Information: Rath M 1992c.

VITAMIN B3 (NICOTINIC ACID) LOWERS LIPOPROTEIN(a) BLOOD LEVELS

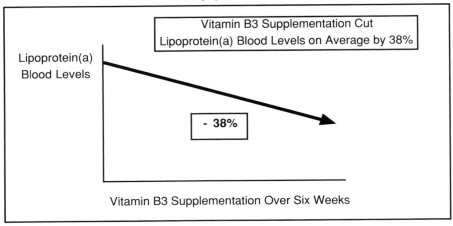

In a clinical study from the King Gustav Research Institute in Stockholm, Sweden, vitamin B3 (nicotinic acid) was shown to lower lipoprotein(a) blood levels. Four grams of nicotinic acid decreased lipoprotein(a) blood levels by 38% over a period of one and one-half months. The higher the lipoprotein(a) blood level was at the beginning of the treatment, the greater was the effect of nicotinic acid in lowering the blood level of this risk factor.

In order for vitamin B3 to be effective, it must be taken in the form of nicotinic acid (niacin); niacinamide was not shown to be effective. When starting to take nicotinic acid in higher amounts, some patients react with a slight skin rash. This rash is nothing unusual and reflects the adaptation of the body to this vitamin when taken in higher dosages. This skin rash is easily avoided by starting with lower amounts of nicotinic acid and slowly increasing the daily intake. In the above study, the regimen was as follows: first day - 250 mg of nicotinic acid at lunch, 500mg at dinner, and 500 mg in the evening. The dosage was increased gradually until after the third day, the full dose of 4 grams per day was taken in the form of four 1-gram dosages per day. In this way, the skin rash was avoided.

Thus, while no available prescription drug is able to lower the cardiovascular risk from lipoprotein(a), two vitamins, vitamin C and vitamin B3 are the first choice in reducing the blood levels from this risk factor.

Further Information: Carlson LA 1989; Guraker A 1985.

VITAMIN C DECREASES HIGH BLOOD LEVELS OF CHOLESTEROL AND TRIGLYCERIDES

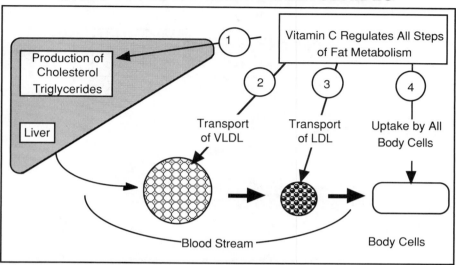

High blood levels of triglycerides are an increased risk for cardiovascular disease. High levels of cholesterol, especially together with high levels of lipoprotein(a), also increase the risk for cardiovascular disease. Reducing high blood concentrations of cholesterol and triglycerides are therefore important therapeutic aims. In some cases diet can be helpful to achieve this aim. In most cases, however, patients with high blood levels of cholesterol and triglycerides suffer from an inherited disorders. The key, to neutralize the risk from triglycerides and cholesterol is to control the inherited disorder. How can this be accomplished? The above figure shows as an example how vitamin C regulates all steps of cholesterol and triglyceride metabolism.

Cholesterol and triglyceride molecules are produced in the liver and transported to the body cells in the form of lipoproteins, the fat globules in the blood that we have already learned about.
• Transport problems with very low density (VLDL) lipoproteins lead frequently to high triglyceride levels in the blood.
• Transport problems with LDL lipoproteins lead frequently to high cholesterol levels.
• Vitamin C can lower cholesterol and triglyceride blood levels by lowering the production rate in the liver (1), by optimizing their transport in the blood stream (2 and 3), and by enhancing their uptake by millions of body cells (4). Thus vitamin C regulates virtually all steps of these fat molecules known today.

The following pages show clinical studies in which this normalizing effect was documented for vitamin C as well as for other vitamins.

Further Information: Cholesterol Regulation: Harwood HJ 1986; Aulinskas TH 1983; Ginter E 1974. Triglyceride Regulation: Sokoloff B 1966. Review: Hemilä H 1992.

VITAMIN C LOWERS HIGH CHOLESTEROL BLOOD LEVELS

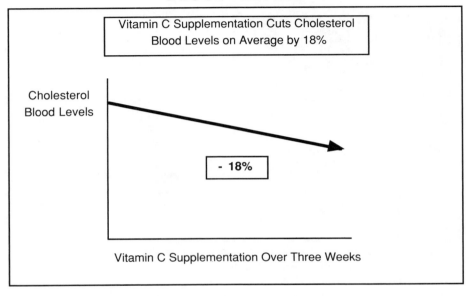

A multitude of clinical studies are available documenting the effect of vitamin C to lower high blood levels of cholesterol. In a recent comprehensive review Dr. Hemilä from the University of Helsinki analyzed almost 200 clinical studies on the role of vitamin C and cholesterol. In summary, he found that the higher the cholesterol level in the blood, the greater the effect of vitamin C supplementation in decreasing elevated blood levels of this risk factor.

In the above study carried out by Dr. E. Ginter from the University of Bratislava, vitamin C was shown to lower high blood cholesterol levels. One gram of vitamin C given for a period of three weeks lowered the blood levels of cholesterol, on average, by 18%.

In some patients higher dosages of vitamin C may be necessary to decrease blood cholesterol levels.

Further Information: Ginter E 1978. Review: Hemilä H 1992.

VITAMIN C LOWERS TRIGLYCERIDE LEVELS

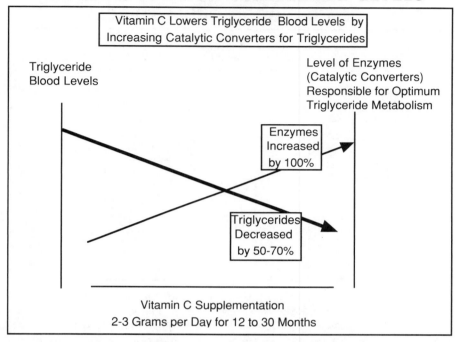

A series of available clinical studies show that vitamin C supplementation lowers elevated blood levels of triglycerides. One of the most interesting studies was reported by Dr. Sokoloff and his colleagues from the Southern Institute in Lakeland, Florida. Sponsored by the National Heart Institute and the American Heart Association the researchers investigated the effects of high dosages of vitamin C on triglyceride levels and on other blood factors.

2-3 grams of vitamin C per day given over several months lowered the blood levels of triglycerides on average by 50-70%. Interestingly, this remarkable reduction was only observed in patients with initially high levels of triglycerides. This fact shows that vitamins have primarily a regulatory effect: they lower blood factors only when necessary.

Of particular importance was that the researchers also investigated the mechanism *how* vitamin C lowers triglyceride blood levels. They found that vitamin C increases the production of the catalytic converters (enzymes) responsible for optimum triglyceride metabolism. Vitamin C supplementation increased the amount of these enzymes on average by 100%. Other clinical studies with vitamin C, vitamin E, carnitine and pantethine confirmed the regulative effect of vitamins on triglycerides: High levels of triglycerides are lowered, normal levels are not affected.

Further Information: Vitamin C: Sokoloff B 1966; Koh ET 1984; Review: Hemilä H 1992. Vitamin E: Hermann WJ 1979. Carnitine: Opie LH 1979.

VITAMIN C INCREASES LOW BLOOD LEVELS OF HDL (GOOD CHOLESTEROL)

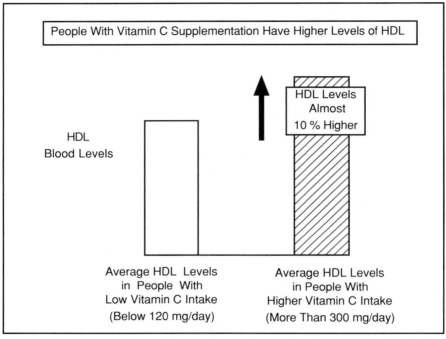

People With Vitamin C Supplementation Have Higher Levels of HDL

HDL Levels Almost 10 % Higher

HDL Blood Levels

Average HDL Levels in People With Low Vitamin C Intake (Below 120 mg/day)

Average HDL Levels in People With Higher Vitamin C Intake (More Than 300 mg/day)

Vitamin C does not only lower the amounts of risk factors such as cholesterol, triglycerides, lipoprotein(a) and others; it also increases the production of "good cholesterol" or HDL (high density lipoproteins). We have already learned that HDL particles pick up fat from the deposits in the arteries and bring it back to the liver. Thus, higher levels of HDL reduce the risk for cardiovascular diseases.

A series of clinical studies show that vitamin C increases the concentrations of HDL in our blood. In the clinical study shown above, Dr. Jacques and his colleagues from Tufts University, in Boston, reported that people taking 300 mg of vitamin C per day had, on average, a 9% higher blood level of HDL than people taking less than 120 mg of vitamin C per day. It is conceivable that vitamin C taken in daily amounts of 1000 mg and above leads to even higher blood levels of this beneficial transport vehicle, particularly in patients with initially very low levels of HDL.

Other vitamins which haven been shown to raise HDL levels include vitamin E and certain B vitamins.

Further Information: Vitamin C: Jacques PF 1987; Bates CJ 1977. Vitamin E: Hermann WJ 1979. Vitamin B5: Avogaro P 1983; Cherchi A 1983.

OTHER VITAMINS AND ESSENTIAL NUTRIENTS NORMALIZING BLOOD FAT LEVELS

**In Addition to Vitamin C,
Other Nutritional Supplements Are Also Important
for Normalizing Blood Risk Factors:**

- **Vitamin B3 (Nicotinic Acid, Niacin)**
- **Vitamin B5 (Pantethine)**
- **Vitamin E**
- **Carnitine**

Besides vitamin C, other vitamins and essential nutrients also help to normalize impaired levels of blood fats. Clinical studies have shown that vitamin B3 (nicotinic acid), vitamin B5 (pantothenic acid or the biologically active form pantethine), vitamin E as well as L-carnitine are effective in normalizing blood fat levels.

It is important to understand that these nutritional supplements do not just *lower* blood concentration of certain factors. Instead, they *normalize* these blood factors towards a normal range.
- They decrease high blood levels of risk fats (cholesterol, triglycerides) and fat transport particles (lipoprotein(a), LDL cholesterol, VLDL (very low-density lipoprotein) -cholesterol.
- They increase the blood levels of beneficial particles (e.g. HDL).
- The further off the normal range the blood fats are in a person, the greater the normalizing effect of these essential nutrients.

The comprehensive normalizing effects of these nutrients on the risk factor profile in our blood is amazing. It reflects the need of our body to regulate factors that are out of range back towards a normal range. In order to do so, our body evidently needs the right fuel from outside. Vitamins and other essential nutrients are nature's choice as fuel and therefore the most effective and safest way to achieve this goal.

Disorders of fat molecules are not the only risk factors neutralized by vitamin supplements. On the next pages you will see how vitamin C and other essential nutrients help to decrease the risk for cardiovascular disease in diabetic patients with disorders of their sugar metabolism.

Further Information: Lipid-Lowering Effect of Niacin: Altschul R 1955. Vitamin E: Hermann WJ 1979. Carnitine: Opie LH 1979. Pantethine: Avogaro P 1983; Cherchi A 1983; Gaddi A 1984; Miccoli R 1984.

CARDIOVASCULAR DISEASE IN DIABETES CAN OCCUR ANYWHERE

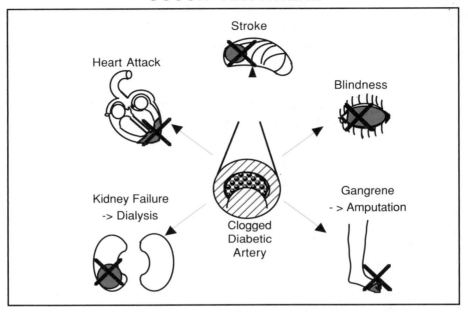

In the United States six million people suffer from diabetes, a disease characterized by too high levels of sugar in the blood. If untreated, these high levels of sugar lead to an impairment of the blood vessel walls and cardiovascular disease develops. Even if treated with insulin or other drugs, the risk for cardiovascular disease in these patients is high. The form of cardiovascular disease occurring in diabetic patients is particularly malicious. Circulatory problems and clogging of arteries can occur in virtually every part of the blood vessel system. Any of the following events can strike a diabetic patient at any time:

- Blindness from clogging of the arteries of the eye
- Kidney failure from a clogging of the arteries of the kidneys, requiring dialysis
- Infarctions in the foot arteries eventually requiring amputation
- Heart attacks from clogging of the coronary arteries
- Strokes from clogging of the brain arteries

Some progress has been made in recent years to retard the development of cardiovascular diseases in diabetic patients. However, no breakthrough has been made towards its prevention. On the following pages we will see that a major therapeutic breakthrough for diabetic patients is the optimum intake of vitamin C.

HOW CARDIOVASCULAR DISEASE DEVELOPS IN DIABETIC PATIENTS

The unique feature of cardiovascular disease in diabetic patients is that the walls of the blood vessel are damaged throughout the pipeline system. Since diabetic patients have elevated blood levels of sugar, the sugar molecules must be involved in causing this particular form of cardiovascular disease. How does this happen? The figure on the following page gives the explanation. The key for this figure is to understand the similarity between the sugar molecules and the vitamin C molecules. These two molecules look almost alike, and our body is frequently unable to keep them apart.

Figure A shows the situation in a healthy person. We already know that the bloodstream is separated from the blood vessel wall by a thin layer of barrier cells called endothelial cells. The walls of these endothelial cells contain small biological pumps which are specialized to pump sugar molecules *and* vitamin C molecules from the bloodstream into these cells. In a healthy person this pump transports an optimum amount of sugar molecules and of vitamin C molecules into the blood vessel wall, enabling a normal function of the vessel wall and preventing cardiovascular disease.

Figure B shows the situation in the blood and in the vessel wall of a diabetic patient. High levels of sugar are circulating in the blood. The pumps located in millions of barrier cells in the blood vessel wall are mixed up. These pumps cannot distinguish between glucose molecules and vitamin C molecules because these two molecules look so much alike. As a result of this fateful mixup the pumps in the cell walls transport into the vessel wall primarily sugar molecules abundantly available in the blood of diabetic patients. Two major problems result:
- Too many sugar molecules enter the cells of the blood vessel wall and impair its normal function.
- Too little vitamin C is transported into the blood vessel wall. The cell pumps are overloaded with sugar molecules and few vitamin C molecules are pumped inside the blood vessel wall which becomes depleted of vitamin C.

Thus, in diabetic patients an overload of sugar and a depletion of vitamin C lead to the thickening of the vessel walls throughout the blood vessel pipeline and eventually to cardiovascular disease.

Figure C shows the logical way to prevent cardiovascular disease in diabetic patients. A high dietary intake of vitamin C corrects the imbalance between glucose and vitamin C in the blood. Because of the high concentration of vitamin C in the blood, the blood can pump more vitamin C molecules into the blood vessel wall. An optimum amount of vitamin C molecules in the blood vessel wall is the basic prevention and treatment for cardiovascular diseases in diabetic patients.

Further Information: Mann GV 1975, Kapeghian JC 1984.

106

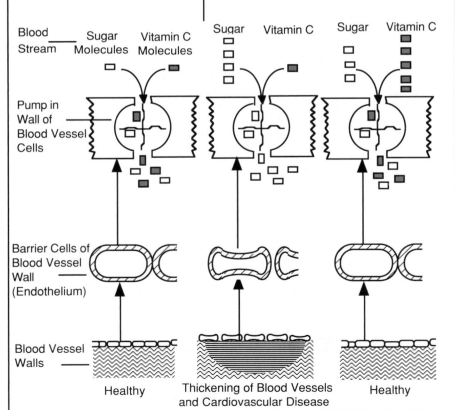

VITAMIN C LOWERS BLOOD SUGAR LEVELS, INSULIN REQUIREMENT, AND SUGAR EXCRETION IN THE URINE

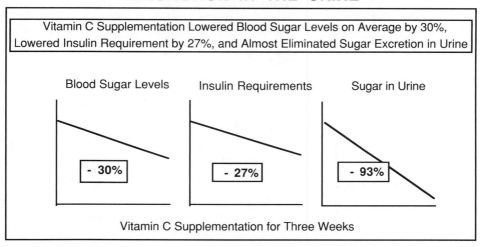

Vitamin C Supplementation Lowered Blood Sugar Levels on Average by 30%, Lowered Insulin Requirement by 27%, and Almost Eliminated Sugar Excretion in Urine

Blood Sugar Levels   Insulin Requirements   Sugar in Urine

- 30%   - 27%   - 93%

Vitamin C Supplementation for Three Weeks

Vitamin C can also help diabetic patients in other important ways. In 1937 Dr. Pfleger and his colleagues from the University of Vienna, Austria, published a clinical study showing the striking benefits for improving the health of diabetic patients. The doctors followed patients taking about half a gram of vitamin C (300 mg to 500mg) every day. Within two to three weeks the following remarkable results were achieved with this moderate amount of vitamin C supplementation:

• The sugar (glucose) levels in the blood decreased on average more than 30%.
• The insulin requirement for the patients could be significantly reduced; on average, one of four insulin units could be spared.
• The excretion of sugar in the urine decreased more than 90% and could almost be completely prevented.

It is amazing that a study as important as this could be neglected for more than 55 years. Just imagine how many patients could have received help if this clinical study had been followed up and if the results of these studies had been documented in medical textbooks. Without any doubt, vitamin C could have long been the basic treatment to prevent and to effectively control diabetic disease.

In the clinical study shown above, a relatively moderate amount of vitamin C was given. Let us see how diabetic patients benefit by further increasing the amount of daily vitamin C intake.

Further Information: Pfleger R 1937; Stepp W 1935; Sherry S 1947.

THE HIGHER THE VITAMIN C IN THE DIET - THE LOWER THE REQUIREMENT FOR INSULIN

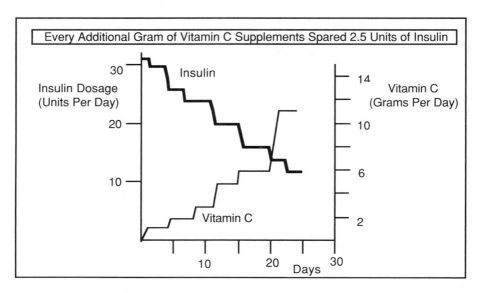

Diabetic patients may be able to significantly reduce their insulin requirement by taking larger amounts of vitamin C. This encouraging result was contained in a case report from a patient published by researchers from Stanford University in California. The patient was 20 years old and had been injecting himself with 32 units of insulin every morning for four years. The effect of vitamin C on lowering blood sugar levels was studied in the following form: increasing amounts of vitamin C were taken in the diet every hour from 7 a.m. to 1 a.m. The patient increased his amount of vitamin C gradually until he reached 11 grams per day on the 23rd day. By that time his insulin requirement had dropped from 32 units to 5 units per day. In summary:

• The greater the vitamin C intake, the lower the insulin requirement.
• For every additional gram of dietary vitamin C supplementation, 2.5 units of insulin could be spared.

This important publication on the value of vitamin C for diabetic patients was published in 1973. Because of the importance of their findings the authors underlined the immediate need for well controlled large scale studies. Until now, 20 years later, none of these large scale studies has been carried out. This is even more regrettable, since the simple measure of a daily vitamin C regimen may be able to entirely eradicate cardiovascular complications in diabetic patients and enable them to lead their lives without fear of blindness, strokes, kidney failures, or amputation of their limbs.

Further Information: Dice JF 1973.

TESTIMONIAL FROM A DIABETIC PATIENT FOLLOWING MY NUTRITIONAL RECOMMENDATIONS FOR OPTIMUM CARDIOVASCULAR HEALTH

Dear Dr. Rath:

I started following your nutritional recommendations three months ago. I'm 29 years old and was recently diagnosed with Type II Diabetes. Since following your recommendations on a regular basis, I have found my blood glucose level to remain around 100, even when under stress which previously raised my blood glucose level.

Your recommendations and 1-2 extra grams of vitamin C have relieved the primary negative symptoms that I have experienced such as weakness from low blood sugar levels, pain in the right side from high blood sugar, and painful urination from the higher blood sugar levels.

I have found only positive results from following your recommendations.

Sincerely,

A.M., USA

DIABETIC DISEASES CAN BE ERADICATED

Our present knowledge of the causes, the prevention, and the treatment of diabetes mellitus can be summarized as follows:

- Diabetes is an inherited disorder which is activated by vitamin deficiency.

- Optimum supplementation with vitamin C and of other essential nutrients is the basic therapeutic measure for the prevention and treatment of diabetes and related cardiovascular complications.

- I encourage my colleagues in clinical medicine to help spread this information as soon as possible for the benefit of their own patients and millions of other patients suffering from this disease.

A special note for patients with diabetes is in order:

- You should start immediately to supplement your diet with vitamin C and with other important vitamins.

- By doing so you may need less of your current medication. Continuing your regular medication (e.g. insulin) while taking higher amounts of vitamins may lower your sugar level too much.

- Thus, while starting a vitamin regimen you should have your blood sugar checked more frequently. Once you have started to take vitamin supplements you should continue to do so on a regular basis.

- Share your health improvements with your doctor. Together you can make the best decisions to reduce your previous medication.

- Vitamins have a normalizing effect on blood sugar levels. Thus, they do not affect the blood sugar levels of healthy persons.

DIFFERENT WAYS IN WHICH VITAMIN C REDUCES THE RISK FOR CARDIOVASCULAR DISEASE

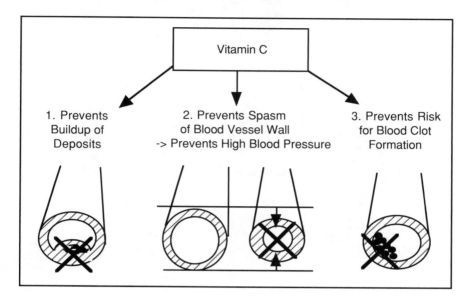

Vitamin C reduces the risk for cardiovascular disease in many different ways:

- by preventing the buildup of deposits
- by relaxing the blood vessel wall and lowering the blood pressure
- by decreasing the risk of blood clotting and keeping the blood at optimum viscosity

These broad cardiovascular benefits of vitamin C are no coincidence. The explanation is found in the molecules of inheritance (genes) in our bodies (for details see Section G of this book).

In the previous chapters we have described the role of vitamin C and other essential nutrients in preventing the buildup of atherosclerotic deposits and other forms of thickening of the blood vessel wall. The next pages describe the role of vitamin C in helping to relax the blood vessel wall, thereby lowering the blood pressure.

Further Information: Review: Clemetson CAB 1989; Rath M 1991a and 1992a.
Anti-Clotting Effect: Spittle CR 1973; Bordia AK 1979 and 1985; Salonen JT 1991.

HOW VITAMIN C LOWERS HIGH BLOOD PRESSURE

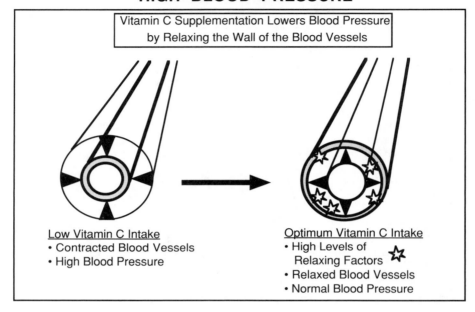

Vitamin C Supplementation Lowers Blood Pressure by Relaxing the Wall of the Blood Vessels

Low Vitamin C Intake
• Contracted Blood Vessels
• High Blood Pressure

Optimum Vitamin C Intake
• High Levels of Relaxing Factors
• Relaxed Blood Vessels
• Normal Blood Pressure

High blood pressure is generally the result of a blood vessel wall suffocating from a deficiency in vitamin C and other essential nutrients.

Vitamin C deficiency increases the blood pressure by
•   leading to a long term buildup of atherosclerotic deposits
•   causing spasms of the blood vessel wall.

Vitamin C supplementation lowers high blood pressure by
•   preventing and reversing atherosclerotic deposits
•   by relaxing the blood vessel wall.

The blood vessel relaxing effect of vitamin C is shown on this page. Vitamin C increases the concentration of small relaxing factors (nitric oxide, prostacyclin) in the blood vessel wall. As a result, the blood vessel wall relaxes, the diameter of the blood vessel increases and the blood pressure is lowered. This relaxing effect can occur rather quickly and an initial blood pressure lowering effect of vitamin C may be seen within a few days.

Further Information: Vitamin C and Prostacyclin: Beetens J 1986. Nitric Oxide: Rath M 1991 a.

VITAMIN C LOWERS BLOOD PRESSURE

Vitamin C Supplementation Decreased High Blood Pressure

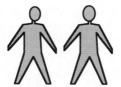

One Gram Vitamin C Per Day
Lowered High Blood Pressure
in Two Out of Three Patients

A number of studies are available showing that low dietary intake of vitamin C increases the risk for high blood pressure. The most comprehensive of these investigations was carried out by Dr. McCarron and his colleagues from the Oregon Health Science University in Portland. The researchers analyzed the blood pressure of 10,372 persons of all ages in relation to their dietary habits. They found that the single most important factor associated with high blood pressure was a low dietary intake of vitamin C and vice versa. Vitamin A deficiency was also found to increase the risk for high blood pressure while the amount of cholesterol in the diet had no effect.

In the study shown above Dr. Koh from the Alcorn State University reported that a dietary supplementation of one gram of vitamin C was able to lower the blood pressure in his patients. He had investigated 23 women with slightly elevated blood pressure between 140-160 mm Hg (systolic value) and 90-100 mm Hg (diastolic value). Remarkably, 64% of the women were able to lower their diastolic pressure, the more important value for decreasing the risk for heart disease. Vitamin C supplementation lowered the systolic as well as the diastolic pressure on average by more than 5%.

Another important nutrient which is able to lower high blood pressure is magnesium, which functions as Nature's calcium blocker. Patients with high blood pressure among my readers should immediately supplement their diet with vitamin C, magnesium and other essential nutrients recommended in this book.

Further Information: Vitamin C: McCarron DA 1984; Salonen JT 1987; Koh ET 1984. Magnesium: Turlapaty PDMV 1980; Iseri LT 1984.

VITAMIN C DECREASES THE CARDIOVASCULAR RISK FROM EXTERNAL RISK FACTORS

Until now we have discussed the beneficial role of vitamin C and other essential nutrients for decreasing mostly inherited *or internal risk factors* for cardiovascular disease. Vitamins, in particular vitamin C, also neutralize most *external risk factors*.

Smoking
Smoking cigarettes dramatically increases the risk for cardiovascular disease. Cigarette smoke contains an abundant amount of free radicals. We already know that these aggressive molecules have a toxic effect on the blood vessel wall. Moreover, these free radicals destroy vitamin C and other antioxidant vitamins. Thus chronic smokers deplete their body pool of antioxidant vitamins much faster than a normal person. By ceasing to smoke and by resupplemention vitamin C, vitamin E, and beta carotene smokers can greatly reduce the risk for cardiovascular disease.

Stress
Chronic stress increases the risk for cardiovascular disease. How does this happen? Physical or emotional stress increases the production of adrenalin molecules in the body. For every molecule of adrenalin produced, one molecule of vitamin C is destroyed. Thus, long term stress destroys many molecules of vitamin C and, if not resupplemented, depletes the body pool of vitamin C. It is not stress itself that causes cardiovascular disease, but the chronic vitamin C depletion in the body and the blood vessels which occurs during chronic stress.

Unhealthy Diet
High fat dietary habits can increase the risk for cardiovascular disease. Once taken up by meals, cholesterol, triglycerides and other fat molecules need to be processed through our body. For every molecule of cholesterol processed, at least one molecule of vitamin C is destroyed - used up as fuel in metabolic converter (enzymatic) reactions. Similarly, high levels of triglycerides and other fats lead to an accelerated depletion of the body's vitamin C pool. Thus, it is not the diet itself that increases the risk for cardiovascular disease, but the systematic depletion of vitamin C and other fuel vitamins in the body.

Further Information: Smoking: Smith JL 1987. Adrenalin: Levine M 1986. Cholesterol: Ginter E 1974. Triglycerides: Sokoloff B 1966.

Birth Control Pill
Women taking birth control pills over years greatly increase their risk for cardiovascular diseases. How can this be explained? Several studies have shown that certain hormones and hormonal birth control pills significantly reduces the body's vitamin C pool. Not the birth control pill itself but the depletion of the vitamin body pool increases risk for cardiovascular disease in these women. If you are presently taking hormonal birth control pills or if you have been taking them in the past you should immediately start to resupplement your vitamin body pool. By doing so you greatly decrease the risk to develop cardiovascular disease.

Diuretic Drugs
Taking diuretic drugs can increase your risk for cardiovascular disease. What is the explanation? Diuretic drugs help the body to get rid of accumulated water. With the increased excretion of water through the kidneys into the urine not only water but also water-soluble vitamins and other essential nutrients disappear. If not resupplemented, a chronic vitamin deficiency develops. Thus, patients taking diuretic drugs should always be sure to have a sufficient resupplemention of vitamins and other essential nutrients in their diet (see also chapter ' heart failure' , Section F).

Certain Other Drugs
Besides hormones and diuretic drugs, other medication can also lead to a decreased body pool of vitamin C and other essential nutrients. This effect can be explained in part as follows. After taking a chemical drug, the liver has to detoxify these substances. This form of 'chemical waste' removal involves metabolic converters (enzymes) and other biochemical processes which use up vitamin C and other essential nutrients at a high rate. One of these drugs is interferon. Unfortunately, no systematic screening has been carried out on the vitamin depleting effect of chemical drugs. It is therefore safe to take additional vitamin supplements whenever you have to take chemical drugs.

Further Information: Birth Control Pill: Briggs M 1972; Rivers JM 1975. Detoxification: Review in: Halliwell B 1985; Burns JJ 1987.

Blood Dialysis

Patients with kidney failure must have their blood detoxified regularly. In order to do so their blood is filtered through fine membranes which help to get rid of the small toxic molecules that have accumulated in the blood. Unfortunately, not only the small toxic molecules disappear in this process, but the small beneficial molecules such as vitamins and other essential nutrients are also lost. This explains why patients undergoing chronic dialysis frequently develop cardiovascular diseases in addition to their kidney failure. Regular vitamin supplementation should decrease this risk and prevent the development of cardiovascular disease in dialysis patients.

In summary, the most effective way to decrease your cardiovascular risk from external risk factors is to make sure that your body gets an optimum amount of vitamin C and other essential nutrients.

The figure on the following page summarizes how vitamin C supplementation neutralizes the risk from the different external risk factors discussed on these pages. Smoking, stress, a high fat diet, birth control pills, certain other drugs and clinical procedures deplete your vitamin body pool. Many vitamins are depleted by these risk factors; however, the depletion of vitamin C is the most frequent and the most important among them. If the vitamin C body pool is depleted by one or more of these risk factors, the risk for cardiovascular disease increases. Resupplementing your vitamin body pool by an optimum dietary intake of nutritional supplements neutralizes these risk factors and helps you to prevent cardiovascular disease.

Further Information: Vitamin Depletion From Dialysis: Blumberg A 1983.

VITAMINS NEUTRALIZE EXTERNAL RISK FACTORS FOR CARDIOVASCULAR DISEASE

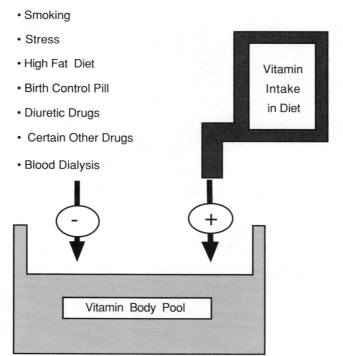

External Risk Factors
Decreasing Vitamin
Body Pool

- Smoking
- Stress
- High Fat Diet
- Birth Control Pill
- Diuretic Drugs
- Certain Other Drugs
- Blood Dialysis

Vitamin
Intake
in Diet

−

+

Vitamin Body Pool

<u>NOTES</u>

SECTION   F

HOW TO SUCCESSFULLY TREAT OTHER HEART CONDITIONS WITH NUTRITIONAL SUPPLEMENTS

- Improve Quality of Life After a Heart Attack

- Reduce Risk for Clogging After Angioplasty

- Protect Bypass Vessels After Coronary Bypass Surgery

- Decrease Restenosis After Coronary Angioplasty

- Successfully Treat Heart Failure

- Successfully Treat Irregular Heartbeat (Arrhythmia)

WHAT ARE THE CONSEQUENCES OF A HEART ATTACK

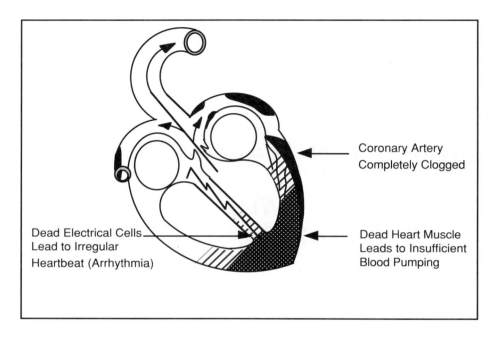

Coronary Artery Completely Clogged

Dead Electrical Cells Lead to Irregular Heartbeat (Arrhythmia)

Dead Heart Muscle Leads to Insufficient Blood Pumping

In previous sections we have seen how atherosclerotic deposits in coronary arteries reduce the blood flow in these arteries, thereby causing the heart muscle to suffocate. A heart attack is caused by complete clogging of a coronary artery and by the total cut-off of millions of heart muscle cells from oxygen and nutrition. Two severe consequences result from a heart attack.

- If the heart muscle cells are cut off from the blood circulation for several hours they die off. As a result, a certain portion of the heart muscle becomes defunct. A heart muscle of which 25% is destroyed by a heart attack is like a four cylinder motor running on three cylinders.
- In a similar way, the electrical cells of the heart can be affected by a heart attack, resulting in their death or severe irritation and leading to irregular heart beat (arrhythmia). Severe electrical irritation (fibrillation of the heart chamber) and other grave forms of arrhythmia are the most frequent causes of death after a heart attack.

The larger the size of the dead heart muscle, the greater the impairment of blood pumping, the greater the risk for arrhythmias and the less likelihood of surviving a heart attack.

HOW TO IMPROVE THE QUALITY OF LIFE AFTER A HEART ATTACK

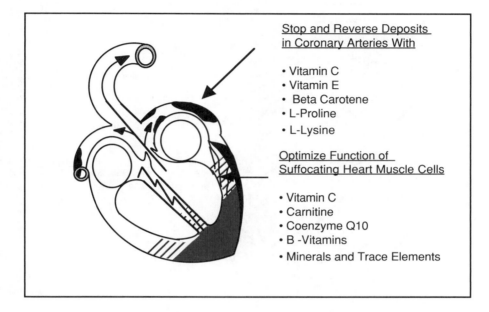

Stop and Reverse Deposits
in Coronary Arteries With

• Vitamin C
• Vitamin E
• Beta Carotene
• L-Proline
• L-Lysine

Optimize Function of
Suffocating Heart Muscle Cells

• Vitamin C
• Carnitine
• Coenzyme Q10
• B -Vitamins
• Minerals and Trace Elements

Anybody suffering a heart attack should immediately contact a hospital and get emergency care. The sooner you obtain the proper medical attention, the greater the chances of limiting lasting damage to your heart muscle cells. Every minute counts. If a heart attack has occurred some time ago, you should continue to consult regularly with your physician. In addition, this page will give you valuable information about how to improve the quality of your life after a heart attack.

It is important to understand that once a heart attack has led to the death of heart muscle cells, these cells seldom regenerate. Therefore, the primary aims after a heart attack are the following:

• Halting the further growth of atherosclerotic deposits in the coronary arteries and thereby preventing the reoccurrence of a heart attack. The essential nutrients for achieving this aim are vitamin C, other antioxidant vitamins, as well as the amino acids lysine and proline.
• Optimizing the function of those heart muscle cells which are still alive. The essential nutrients for achieving this aim are carnitine, coenzyme Q10, panthetine, other B vitamins, magnesium, as well as other minerals and trace elements.

WHAT IS A CORONARY ARTERY BYPASS

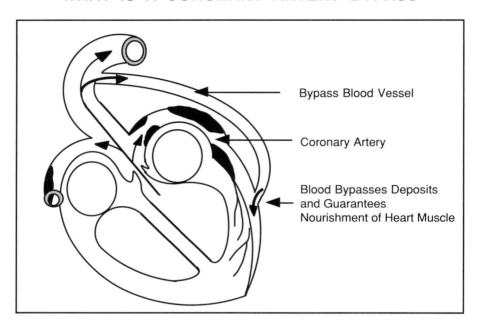

Bypass Blood Vessel

Coronary Artery

Blood Bypasses Deposits and Guarantees Nourishment of Heart Muscle

A coronary bypass operation becomes necessary if one or more coronary arteries have developed severe atherosclerotic deposits which threaten to clog the arteries and to cause a heart attack. In order to avoid a heart attack, a blood bypass is constructed surgically which guarantees the blood flow to all parts of the heart muscle.

During bypass surgery usually a vein is taken from the leg and reimplanted as a bypass blood vessel. Generally, one end of this bypass is attached to the aorta and the other end to the coronary artery further down on the outside of the heart muscle. In this way, the atherosclerotic deposits in the coronary artery are bypassed and the blood flow through the bypass blood vessel guarantees optimum blood supply for the proper function of the heart muscle.

WHAT ARE THE MAIN PROBLEMS
AFTER CORONARY BYPASS SURGERY

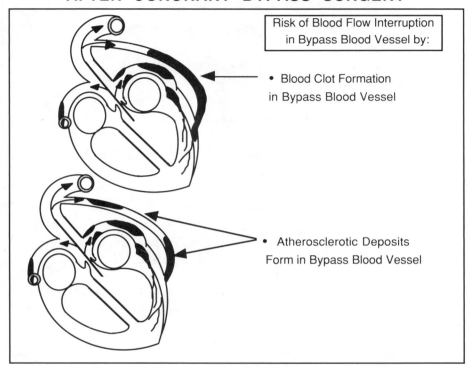

Risk of Blood Flow Interruption
in Bypass Blood Vessel by:

• Blood Clot Formation
in Bypass Blood Vessel

• Atherosclerotic Deposits
Form in Bypass Blood Vessel

The overall success of a coronary bypass operation is threatened by two main problems: blood clots and atherosclerotic deposits in the bypass blood vessels.

• *Problem number one*: a blood clot forms in the bypass blood vessels, cutting off the blood flow through them. This complication occurs shortly after the operation, generally within hours or a few days. If untreated, this blood clot will completely cut off the blood flow through the bypass blood vessel and thereby make the previous operation ineffective.

• *Problem number two*: atherosclerotic deposits develop inside the wall of the bypass blood vessel. The development of atherosclerotic deposits in bypass blood vessels is a long term process. Generally, it takes several months or several years for these deposits to develop. Similar to the atherosclerotic deposits in the regular coronary arteries, the deposits in the bypass blood vessel can lead to a decreased blood flow and eventually to clogging.

The consequences in each case are the same: an interruption of the blood flow through the bypass blood vessels and an increased risk for a heart attack. Keeping the bypass blood vessels patent avoids further bypass operations and heart attacks. The following page summarizes the most important nutritional supplements which help you to achieve this aim.

HOW TO IMPROVE QUALITY OF LIFE
AFTER CORONARY BYPASS SURGERY

Protect Your Bypass Blood Vessels With the Help of

- **Vitamins Preventing Blood Clot Formation**
  - **Vitamin C**
  - **Vitamin E**
  - **Beta Carotene**

- **Vitamins and Natural Amino Acids Preventing Development of Atherosclerotic Deposits**
  - **Vitamin C**
  - **Other Antioxidant Vitamins**
  - **Lysine**
  - **Proline**

There are several ways in which nutritional supplements help to maintain healthy bypass blood vessels and thereby improve the quality of life after bypass surgery:

- *Preventing blood clot formation in bypass vessels*: vitamin C, vitamin E and beta carotene have all been shown to have important properties which help to prevent formation of blood clots. In addition, vitamin C has also been shown to help dissolve blood clots once they have been formed. These important properties of vitamin C , vitamin E, and beta carotene should be utilized routinely in minimizing the complications of blood clot formation after coronary bypass and other surgeries.
- *Preventing atherosclerotic deposits in bypass blood vessels*: atherosclerotic deposits in venous bypass vessels closely resemble the deposits in normal arteries. Lipoprotein(a) again, plays a critical role in the development of these bypass deposits. Thus, the vitamins and other essential nutrients recommended for the treatment of atherosclerotic deposits are also beneficial for preventing development of the deposits in bypass blood vessels. The most important among them are vitamin C, vitamin E, beta carotene, L-lysine and L-proline.

A note for those among my readers who are taking blood-thinning medication: The vitamins mentioned above have a natural effect of keeping your blood in optimum flow condition (viscosity). They may, therefore, enhance the effect of your blood thinning medication. Ask your doctor about additional controls and take your vitamins as regularly as you take other medication.

Further Information: Anti-clotting effect: Bordia AK 1979 and 1985; Beetens J 1986; Kojima S 1986; Salonen JT 1991.

WHAT IS CORONARY ANGIOPLASTY

Coronary bypass surgery installs a new blood vessel pipeline for optimum blood supply to the heart muscle. In contrast, coronary angioplasty is the 'rotor rooter' approach to remove atherosclerotic deposits mechanically by means of a balloon or, more recently, by scraping methods. For this purpose a catheter is inserted into the leg artery and moved forward through the aorta until the catheter tip reaches the coronary artery close to the deposits. At this point normally a balloon at the tip of the catheter is inflated with high pressure which squeezes the atherosclerotic deposits flat to the wall of the coronary arteries. In many cases the blood flow through the coronary artery can be improved by this procedure.

However, complications occur in one out of three patients . The nature of these complications is directly related to the fact that angioplasty necessarily causes mechanical damage to the inside of the blood vessel wall. The most frequent complications are blood clot formation and rapid grow of new deposits at the same location as before (restenosis).

What factors influence the rate of restenosis after angioplasty? We already know that lipoprotein(a) is nature's top repair molecule and it is therefore no surprise that high lipoprotein(a) levels are a leading cause for restenosis. Dr. Hearn and his colleagues from Emory University in Atlanta found that angioplasty patients with lipoprotein(a) blood levels above 19 mg/dl had a fivefold greater risk for restenosis than those patients below this margin. For patients with lipoprotein(a) levels above 40 mg/dl the restenosis risk after angioplasty was more than ten fold higher.

Thus, for patients who have to undergo angioplasty, the overall success rate can be greatly reduced by neutralizing the risk from lipoprotein(a) and by following the recommendations of this book.

Further Information: Hearn JA 1992.

Angioplasty Is a Mechanical Procedure to Improve Blood Flow to Suffocating Heart Muscle

Figure A:

Balloon Catheter Is Inserted in Leg Artery

Deflated Catheter Tip Reaches Coronary Artery

Deposits in Coronary Arteries Reduce Blood Flow

Figure B:

Inflated Balloon Catheter Squeezes Deposits in Coronary Arteries Flat - Vessel Wall is Injured During This Procedure

Success Rate of This Procedure:
- 70% of Patients Get Improved Blood Flow to Heart Muscle
- 30% Have Complications - Requiring Repetition of Procedure or Coronary Bypass Operation

HOW TO IMPROVE THE SUCCESS RATE AFTER ANGIOPLASTY

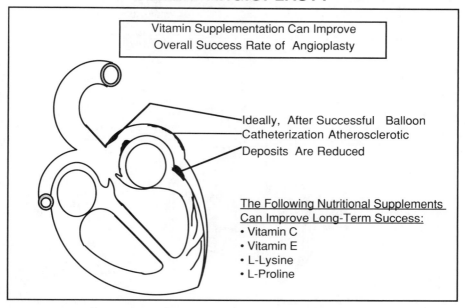

Vitamin Supplementation Can Improve
Overall Success Rate of Angioplasty

Ideally, After Successful Balloon
Catheterization Atherosclerotic
Deposits Are Reduced

The Following Nutritional Supplements
Can Improve Long-Term Success:
• Vitamin C
• Vitamin E
• L-Lysine
• L-Proline

The essential nutrients needed to minimize restenosis after angioplasty are much the same as the recommendations for blood vessel protection in general. During and after angioplasty the achieve the following therapeutic effects:
• Vitamin C accelerates healing of the blood vessel lesion by collagen formation
• Vitamin E gives important antioxidant protection
• Vitamin C, vitamin E, and beta carotene decrease the risk for blood clot formation
• Lysine and proline help to neutralize the risk from lipoprotein(a)

Vitamin E has already been shown to prevent restenosis after angioplasty. 115 patients undergoing coronary angioplasty were studied. Half of these patients received 1,200 International Units of vitamin E per day; the other half received an inactive placebo. After four months the rate of restenosis of the coronary arteries was compared between the two groups. The patients receiving vitamin E had a much less restenosis than those patients without vitamin E.

Any patient among my readers who is about to undergo angioplasty should immediately start to take nutritional supplements. By protecting your blood vessels before, during, and after angioplasty with nutritional supplements you can maximize the overall success of this procedure. In the remaining part of this section I will describe how patients with other heart conditions can benefit from taking nutritional supplements.

Further Information: DeMaio SJ 1992.

WHAT CAUSES HEART FAILURE

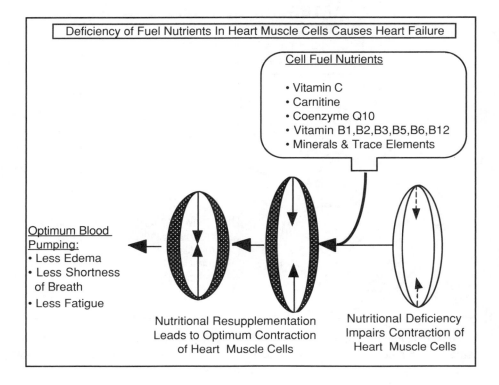

Deficiency of Fuel Nutrients In Heart Muscle Cells Causes Heart Failure

Cell Fuel Nutrients

• Vitamin C
• Carnitine
• Coenzyme Q10
• Vitamin B1,B2,B3,B5,B6,B12
• Minerals & Trace Elements

Optimum Blood Pumping:
• Less Edema
• Less Shortness of Breath
• Less Fatigue

Nutritional Resupplementation Leads to Optimum Contraction of Heart Muscle Cells

Nutritional Deficiency Impairs Contraction of Heart Muscle Cells

Heart failure is a disease caused by weakness of the heart muscle which impairs the pumping of blood into the circulation. Heart failure frequently develops after a heart attack or in patients with high blood pressure. Heart failure can also occur spontaneously without any previous heart condition. The common underlying cause of heart failure is the same: an exertion of the heart muscle and a depletion of heart muscle cells in vitamins and other cell fuel nutrients.

In patients with heart failure millions of heart muscle cells suffocate from a lack of essential nutritional fuel. This cell fuel is needed for thousands of biochemical reactions in each cell. A heart without cell fuel is like a motor without oil - it does not work properly. Heart muscles lacking essential fuel nutrients are not able to contract properly . As a consequence, the heart muscle does not pump enough blood into the body's circulation.

HEART FAILURE CAUSES
IMPAIRED BLOOD PUMPING

The figure on the following page summarizes the consequences of a vitamin deficient heart muscle for the body of the patient.

• Figure A: Instead of one cup which leaves the heart normally with every heart beat, half a cup of blood or even less will be ejected into the circulation. This amount of blood is too little to supply the various organs of the body with oxygen and nutrients. As a consequence, shortness of breath, water retention (edema) and general weakness occur.

• Figure B: In contrast, an optimum dietary intake of essential fuel nutrients for the heart muscle cells optimizes the contraction of every cell. As a result, the whole heart muscle regains its strength and pumps sufficient blood into the circulation. The different organs of the body receive adequate oxygen and nutrients and the patient can enjoy a life without major restraints.

Unfortunately, the fact that heart failure is frequently caused by vitamin deficiencies is hardly known. In today's medical text books the causes of heart failure are described as largely unknown. The fatal consequences of this insufficient understanding for millions of heart failure patients are shown on the following pages.

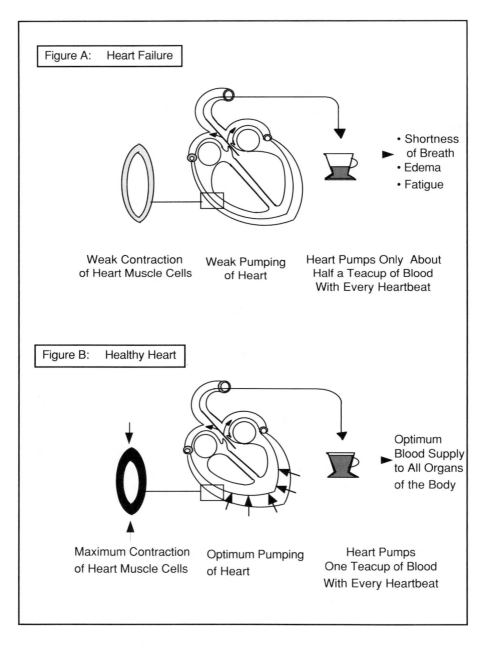

Figure A: Heart Failure

• Shortness of Breath
• Edema
• Fatigue

Weak Contraction of Heart Muscle Cells

Weak Pumping of Heart

Heart Pumps Only About Half a Teacup of Blood With Every Heartbeat

Figure B: Healthy Heart

Optimum Blood Supply to All Organs of the Body

Maximum Contraction of Heart Muscle Cells

Optimum Pumping of Heart

Heart Pumps One Teacup of Blood With Every Heartbeat

THE HEART FAILURE EPIDEMIC

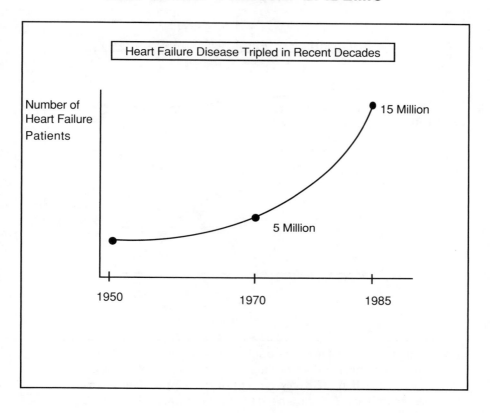

In recent years heart failure has spread like an epidemic. In the western industrialized countries, about 15 million people suffer from heart failure today. During recent decades the number of heart failure patients who had to be hospitalized because of this disease increased threefold.

Equally alarming is the short life expectancy of patients once they are diagnosed with heart failure.

Further Information: Packer M 1987.

HEART FAILURE PATIENTS
HAVE A SHORT LIFE EXPECTANCY

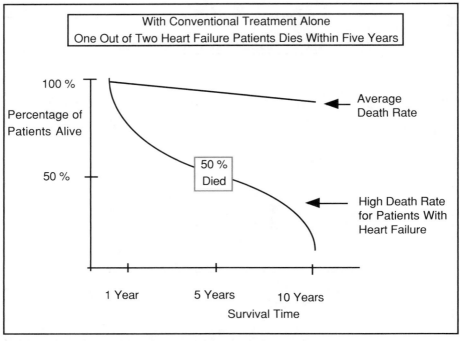

Patients with heart failure have a very unfavorable prognosis:
- One out of two patients dies within the first five years after the heart failure is diagnosed. After ten years only one or two patients out of ten are still alive.
- For many heart failure patients a heart transplant operation remains the only hope.

Both, the epidemic proportion of heart failure (previous page) and the bad prognosis of this disease (this page) are no coincidence. They are the direct result of the fact that vitamin deficiencies are not yet known and understood as the underlying cause of this disease. Consequently, no effective treatment has been available.

Those among my readers who are candidates for a heart transplant operation may be interested to read the testimonial of a former heart transplant candidate (G.P.) who started to follow my cardiovascular recommendations. By refilling his suffocating heart cells with vitamins and other essential nutrients his heart performance greatly improved. He was able to cancel the scheduled heart transplant operation and he is now leading a normal life.

On the next page we will see that the conventional medical treatment of heart failure leads to a vicious cycle which is responsible for the bad prognosis of this disease.

Further Information: Mc Kee PA 1971.

THE FATAL CONSEQUENCES OF INCOMPLETE TREATMENT OF HEART FAILURE

Heart failure leads to water accumulation (edema) in the legs, lungs, and other parts of the body. To remove accumulated water from the body heart failure patients have to take diuretic drugs. At this point of the treatment the patient enters a vicious cycle which is explained in the adjacent figure. The understanding of this vicious cycle is a clue to the successful treatment of heart failure disease in the future.

Nutritional deficiencies of the heart muscle cells lead to a weak pumping of the heart. The low blood output into the arteries results in low blood pressure, which has direct consequences for the proper function of the kidneys. The primary role of the kidneys is to filter body water into urine. With low blood pressure, less water is filtered out and, instead of leaving the body via urine, it accumulates in the legs and other parts of the body. As a result, edema occur in the feet and legs as well as in the lungs, where it leads to shortness of breath and eventually, to lung edema.

In order to eliminate the abundant body water and to provide relief to the patient diuretic medication is given. On one side, this medication increases the filter function of the kidneys and flushes out the body water into the urine. Unfortunately, diuretic drugs also flush out the small vitamins and other essential nutrients into the urine. The body's loss of essential nutrients further aggravates the lack of fuel nutrients for the heart muscle cells, hereby further aggravating the heart failure. A vicious cycle begins.

A weakened heart leads to even more water accumulation in the body. Higher dosages of diuretic medication is required, further depleting the body of essential nutrients and further weakening the heart. We suddenly understand why heart failure has such a poor prognosis and why there is no other alternative for many patients than to receive a new heart - or to die before a suitable donor heart can be found.

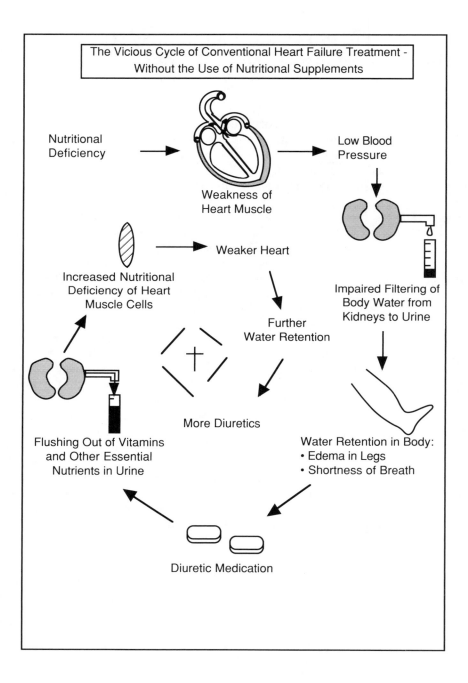

The Vicious Cycle of Conventional Heart Failure Treatment -
Without the Use of Nutritional Supplements

Nutritional Deficiency

Weakness of Heart Muscle

Low Blood Pressure

Weaker Heart

Increased Nutritional Deficiency of Heart Muscle Cells

Impaired Filtering of Body Water from Kidneys to Urine

Further Water Retention

More Diuretics

Flushing Out of Vitamins and Other Essential Nutrients in Urine

Water Retention in Body:
• Edema in Legs
• Shortness of Breath

Diuretic Medication

HOW VITAMINS CAN INTERRUPT
THE VICIOUS CYCLE OF HEART FAILURE

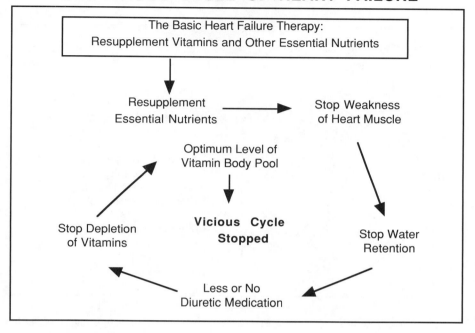

With this page I am addressing my colleagues in clinical medicine:
In the attempt to help our patients we have learned to prescribe diuretic medication. While improving the immediate problems for the patient, the water accumulation in the body, diuretic medication depletes the patient's body of water soluble vitamins and thereby starts a vicious cycle. While diuretic medication may still be needed in severe cases, no one should prescribe diuretic drugs any longer without alerting the patients to resupplement their bodies with vitamins and essential nutrients.

Patients and doctors should be equally interested in interrupting the vicious cycle of heart failure with an optimum supplementation of vitamins and other essential nutrients in the diet. Most important among these essential nutrients are:

• Vitamin C
• Carnitine
• Coenzyme Q10
• B vitamins
• Minerals and trace elements

The following pages will highlight some of the clinical evidence for the importance of essential vitamins and nutrients in the treatment of heart failure.

CARDIOMYOPATHIES ARE PRIMARILY CAUSED BY VITAMIN DEFICIENCY

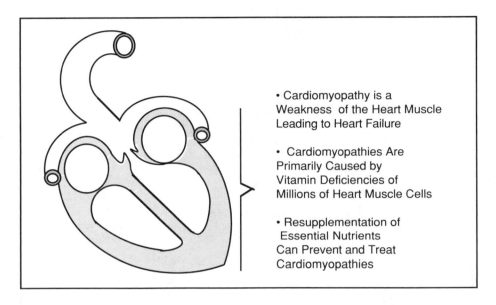

• Cardiomyopathy is a Weakness of the Heart Muscle Leading to Heart Failure

• Cardiomyopathies Are Primarily Caused by Vitamin Deficiencies of Millions of Heart Muscle Cells

• Resupplementation of Essential Nutrients Can Prevent and Treat Cardiomyopathies

The best documented form of heart failure in which vitamins and other essential nutrients were proven to be most effective are cardiomyopathies. What are cardiomyopathies? The Latin word cardiomyopathy means 'disease of the heart muscle'. The unique feature of this form of heart failure is that it occurs frequently without any other heart condition being present. This fact makes cardiomyopathy an ideal disease to identify the underlying problem of heart failure in general and to document an effective treatment for this disease.

According to the current medical textbooks the causes for cardiomyopathy are still largely unknown. However, during recent years scientific evidence showed that cardiomyopathy is primarily a vitamin deficiency disease. Dr. Karl Folkers and his colleagues from the University of Austin, Texas, are pioneers of cardiomyopathy research and nutrition. They have shown that coenzyme Q10 (ubiquinon), an important cell fuel nutrient, greatly improved the health of cardiomyopathy patients. Dr. Folkers recently reviewed the available clinical studies of coenzyme Q10. This review included 25 Japanese clinical reports from 110 physicians in 41 medical institutions. The summary of ten years of clinical research showed that an average of 70% of the patients with cardiomyopathy and heart failure benefited from a dietary supplementation of coenzyme Q10.

Further Information: Folkers K 1985; Mortensen SA 1990.

COENZYME Q10 BENEFITS PATIENTS WITH HEART FAILURE

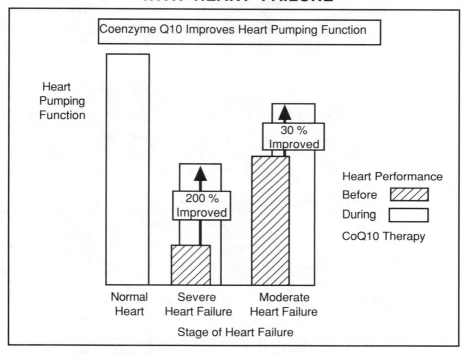

Coenzyme Q10 Improves Heart Pumping Function

Heart Pumping Function

30 % Improved

200 % Improved

Heart Performance

Before

During

CoQ10 Therapy

Normal Heart   Severe Heart Failure   Moderate Heart Failure

Stage of Heart Failure

Coenzyme Q10 (ubiquinon), is a critical fuel for the functioning of the miniature power plants or bioenergy centers in each cell of our body. It is essential for the proper 'breathing' of our cells. Coenzyme Q10 was found to be much lower in the blood and in the heart muscle of patients with heart disease compared to healthy persons.

The figure above summarizes the results from a study by Dr. Langsjoen, Dr. Folkers and their colleagues. They gave 100 mg of coenzyme Q10 per day to 88 patients with heart failure. In this study more than 75% of these patients showed a significant improvement in the pumping function of their heart as well as their overall well being.

The following improvements were observed after few weeks of taking coenzyme Q10:
• Patients with very severe forms of heart failure benefited the most from coenzyme Q10 supplementation. The pumping function of these patients increased more than 200% while taking coenzyme Q10.
• In general, the more severe the heart failure condition in a patient, the greater was the benefit from taking coenzyme Q10.
• Coenzyme Q10 had no side effects.

Further Information: Langesjoen PH 1988; Mortensen SA 1990.

COENZYME Q10 PROLONGS THE LIFE OF PATIENTS WITH HEART FAILURE

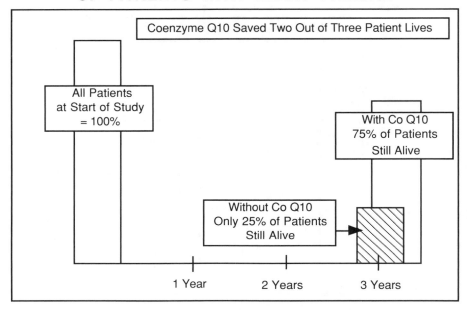

More recently the same group of doctors published the long-term results of their studies with coenzyme Q10 in heart failure patients. By now they had followed 137 patients with heart failure over a period of three years. The reported health benefits from coenzyme Q10 are very encouraging:

- After three years, *three out of four* heart failure patients taking coenzyme Q10 were still alive.

- In contrast, when heart failure patients received only conventional drugs only *one out of four* patients was still alive after three years.

Thus, the life of every second patient with heart failure could be saved by the simple measure of supplementing the diet with coenzyme Q10. Moreover, the dramatic improvement of the survival rate and the quality of life of the patients shows that a lack of coenzyme Q10 in the heart muscle cells is an important cause for heart failure. These scientists conclude that coenzyme Q10 constitutes the first therapy that significantly improves the survival rate of patients with heart failure.

Further Information: Langsjoen PH 1990.

LESS CARNITINE IN THE HEART MUSCLE CELLS-MORE SEVERE HEART FAILURE

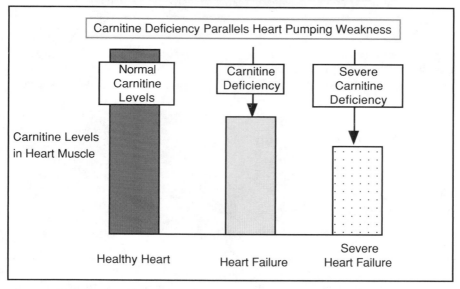

Another important nutrient which is frequently deficient in heart failure patients is carnitine, a natural amino acid. Its main role is to improve the energy level of the cell by transporting energy molecules (fatty acids) to the power plants of each cell. Carnitine also removes useless fuel from the power plants inside each cell (waste removal) and thereby helps to improve their function.

Low levels of carnitine lead to an impaired function of the cellular power plants and consequently to a low energy level in the heart muscle. An important study was carried out by my colleagues at the German Heart Center in Berlin. They measured carnitine in small pieces of heart muscle routinely taken from heart failure patients for diagnostic purposes. The following significant findings were made in this study:

• The highest levels of carnitine were found in the heart muscle cells of healthy hearts.
• The weaker the heart function of the patient, the lower the amount of carnitine measured in the heart muscle cells.

Thus, carnitine deficiency was found to be closely related to the degree of severity of heart failure.

Further Information: Regitz V 1990.

CARNITINE BENEFITS HEART FAILURE PATIENTS

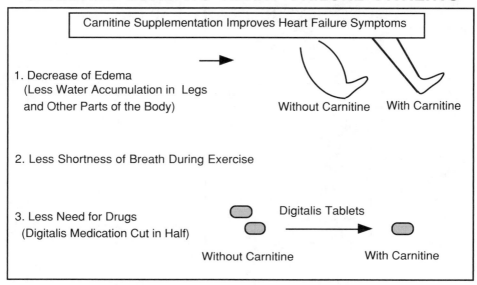

Carnitine Supplementation Improves Heart Failure Symptoms

1. Decrease of Edema
   (Less Water Accumulation in Legs
   and Other Parts of the Body)

Without Carnitine   With Carnitine

2. Less Shortness of Breath During Exercise

3. Less Need for Drugs
   (Digitalis Medication Cut in Half)

Digitalis Tablets

Without Carnitine   With Carnitine

Since carnitine deficiency is obviously an important factor for the development of heart failure, it is no surprise that dietary carnitine supplementation greatly benefits patients with heart failure.

Dr. Ghidini and his colleagues from Verona, Italy, conducted a study with 38 patients, all of whom were suffering from heart failure. The physicians gave two grams of L-carnitine to half of the patients for 40 to 45 days and compared the performance of their heart to the other half of the patient group, who did not receive carnitine. All patients continued their conventional therapy, including digitalis medication. The patients receiving additional carnitine showed remarkable improvement of their heart function. Patients receiving carnitine had:

• Less water accumulation in their bodies (less edema)
• An increased natural water excretion from their bodies
• Less shortness of breath
• A normalized heart beat rate.
• Taking carnitine was safe and no side effects were observed.

As a consequence of these remarkable improvements, the patients could cut their conventional drugs (digitalis) in half. The physicians noted that L-carnitine treatment also reduced the blood levels of cholesterol and triglycerides in the patients' blood.

Further Information: Ghidini O 1988.

TESTIMONIALS FROM PATIENTS WITH HEART FAILURE WHO ARE FOLLOWING MY CARDIOVASCULAR HEALTH RECOMMENDATIONS

Dear Dr. Rath:

I am happy to report that your cardiovascular health recommendations have improved my life! Now I can climb the stairs readily and without shortness of breath. I can also resume hiking for 3-4 miles a day without feeling tired and exhausted. I do have an energetic outlook towards life, and I am sure it's due to your recommendations.

Thank you very much for all the research you have done and are continuing to do for people with circulatory problems.

Yours truly,

A.G., USA

Dear Dr. Rath:

I am 64 years old and for four years have been suffering from heart failure, arrhythmia, and shortness of breath. I had difficulty in climbing stairs, and while walking I had to pause frequently. I have been following your cardiovascular health recommendations for the past two weeks and I notice remarkable changes: I can climb stairs without any problems. I can now walk one mile or more, even uphill. Before, I had to pause after about 200 yards. I have more energy for living.

Because of my health improvements my physician showed interest in your recommendations for cardiovascular health.

G.W., Germany

Dear Dr. Rath:

I would like to inform you about two patients to whom I have applied your cardiovascular health recommendations during the past few weeks. H. K. is a patient with coronary heart disease. A few months ago he began to have increasing shortness of breath and frequent angina pectoris attacks. After a severe angina pectoris attack, the patient had to be admitted to the hospital in a life-threatening condition. During the fifth week of his hospital stay, his condition became even worse. With *heart failure* and severe arrhythmia the patient had to be transferred to the intensive care unit for several days. During the entire duration of his hospital stay the patient received several drugs to treat the angina pectoris symptoms. After two and a half months the patient was discharged from the hospital. Angina pectoris attacks continued to occur with minimum exertion, and particularly in the morning hours. When discharging the patient the clinician gave a very unfavorable prognosis with respect to the life expectancy of the patient. His medication consisted of nitrates, calcium antagonists, digitalis, and a diuretic drug.

A few days after leaving the hospital the patient started to follow your cardiovascular health recommendations in addition to his other medications. By doing so, a gradual improvement occurred in the patient's cardiovascular health as well as in his general condition. In the meantime, the patient can walk up to one hour, even uphill, without significant shortness of breath. The patient is following his regular daily activities without any restraints or help from outside. In general, the patient became more mobile, more secure, less dependent, and because of that, more confident with respect to his future life expectancy. Further tests are planned to document the remarkable clinical improvement of the patient.

The second case history is the report of a woman who developed symptoms of cardiac failure in connection with a severe viral infection. The heartbeat was irregular. By following your cardiovascular recommendations a rapid improvement in the patient's health began. After two months the cardiovascular functions had stabilized, and the heartbeat was regular. Moreover, the patient became more active again and she is now able to carry out her daily activities in house and garden without difficulty. Your cardiovascular health recommendations will be continued.

I wish you further success with the cardiovascular recommendations you developed.

J.K., M.D., Germany

HEART FAILURE CAN BE ERADICATED

Our present knowledge of the causes as well as the prevention and the treatment of heart failure can be summarized as follows:

- Heart failure is primarily caused by vitamin deficiencies. In many cases vitamin deficiency is the direct cause of heart failure. In other cases, e.g. after a heart attack, vitamin deficiencies further impair heart muscle function and aggravate heart failure.

- Optimum supplementation with vitamins and other essential nutrients is the basic measure for prevention and treatment of heart failure.

- Any treatment of heart failure with diuretic drugs greatly increases the need for vitamin supplementation for the patient.

- I encourage my colleagues in clinical medicine to help spread this information as soon as possible for the benefit of your own patients and thousands of other patients.

A special note is in order for heart failure patients among my readers:

- You should start immediately to supplement your diet with vitamins and other essential nutrients.

- While following the recommendations of this book, do not discontinue your regular medication without consulting your doctor.

- Share your health improvements with your doctor. Together you can make the best decisions to reduce your regular medication.

We now turn to another frequent heart diseases which is essentially preventable.

WHAT CAUSES IRREGULAR HEARTBEAT

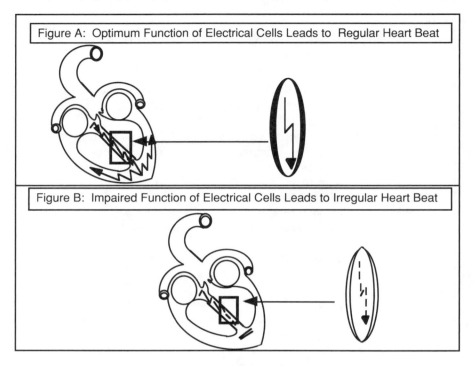

Figure A: Optimum Function of Electrical Cells Leads to Regular Heart Beat

Figure B: Impaired Function of Electrical Cells Leads to Irregular Heart Beat

Currently eight million Americans suffer from irregular heartbeat (arrhythmia). Arrhythmia is primarily caused by vitamin deficiencies of the electrical heart cells and can be prevented by optimum intake of essential nutrients.

The electrical impulse responsible for the heartbeat is generated in the battery cells of the heart (sinus node). This impulse of biological electricity is transported through a "wire" of cells in the middle of the heart which are specialized for transporting electricity. Eventually this electrical impulse reaches millions of heart muscle cells and stimulates them to contract for the heart beat. The proper generation and transport of biological electricity in the heart is responsible for a coordinated contraction of the heart muscle and for a regular heartbeat.

The generation and transport of the electricity needed for regular heartbeat depends on optimum supply of the electrical cells with vitamins and other essential nutrients. If these electrical cells do not receive an optimum amount of these fuel nutrients, either the generation of the electrical impulse or the transport of the electricity can be disturbed or interrupted. Thus, the lack of fuel nutrients in the electrical cells of the heart causes irregular heart beat and arrhythmia.

THE BASIC TREATMENT OF IRREGULAR HEARTBEAT

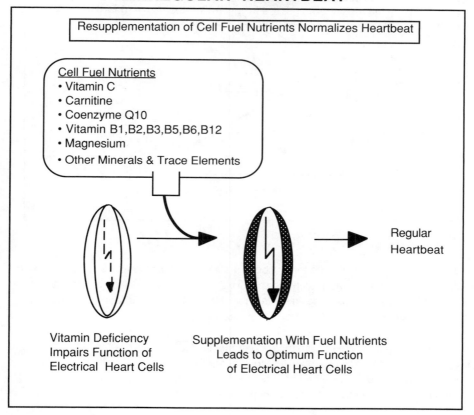

Resupplementation of Cell Fuel Nutrients Normalizes Heartbeat

Cell Fuel Nutrients
• Vitamin C
• Carnitine
• Coenzyme Q10
• Vitamin B1,B2,B3,B5,B6,B12
• Magnesium
• Other Minerals & Trace Elements

Regular Heartbeat

Vitamin Deficiency Impairs Function of Electrical Heart Cells

Supplementation With Fuel Nutrients Leads to Optimum Function of Electrical Heart Cells

Vitamin deficiency and a lack of fuel nutrients in the electrical cells of the heart are primary causes of irregular heart beat. Resupplementation of vitamins and other essential fuel nutrients in the diet is the basic therapeutic measure to prevent and to treat arrhythmias.

As for the other muscle cells in the heart, the following fuel nutrients are particularly important: vitamin C, carnitine, coenzyme Q10, other B vitamins, magnesium, as well as other minerals and trace elements.

Some of the essential nutrients with antiarrhythmic properties will be discussed in more detail on the following pages.

MAGNESIUM REDUCES IRREGULAR HEARTBEAT

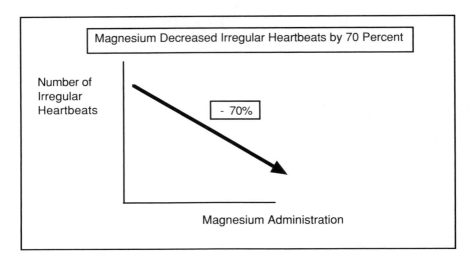

Magnesium is one of the essential body salts and of particular importance is its balance with calcium. Magnesium is nature's physiologic calcium blocker and is a powerful agent in normalizing irregular heartbeat. Moreover, magnesium has been shown to improve different forms of arrhythmias:

• Rapid beating of the heart chambers (ventricular tachycardia)
• Fibrillation of the heart chamber (ventricular fibrillation)
• Irregular heartbeat originated in the smaller chambers of the heart
  situated above the main chambers (supraventricular arrhythmia)

In the clinical study shown above, Dr. Iseri and his colleagues from the University of California showed that magnesium is able to lower the number of irregular heartbeats by more than 70%. Moreover, magnesium helped to normalize rapid heartbeats. In the studies mentioned above, magnesium was given to patients with severe forms of arrhythmia.

In summary, magnesium - nature's calcium antagonist- can reduce most forms of irregular heartbeats and arrhythmia.

Further Information: Iseri LT 1984 and 1986; Turlapaty PDMV 1980.

CARNITINE REDUCES IRREGULAR HEARTBEAT

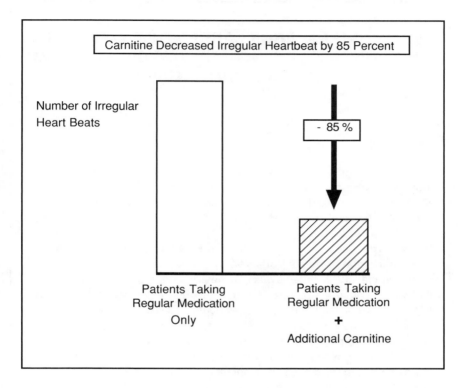

Carnitine Decreased Irregular Heartbeat by 85 Percent

Number of Irregular Heart Beats

- 85 %

Patients Taking
Regular Medication
Only

Patients Taking
Regular Medication
+
Additional Carnitine

The amino acid L-carnitine also reduces irregular heartbeat. In a clinical study reported by Dr. P. Rizzon and his colleagues from the University of Bari, Italy, the effect of carnitine on reducing arrhythmias was studied in patients who had just suffered a myocardial infarction. Arrhythmias are a frequent cause of death after a heart attack has occurred. Thus, the reduction of arrhythmias by use of carnitine can greatly increase the chance of a patient to survive a heart attack.

In the study shown in the figure above, 28 patients received L-carnitine for several days during their hospital stay. During that time the heart beat was recorded and the numbers of irregular heartbeats were counted. Patients receiving carnitine had up to 85% less irregular heartbeats than those heart attack patients who did not receive L-carnitine. These remarkable results with carnitine were achieved in acute therapy. In the same way, carnitine given as dietary supplement helps prevent and reduce irregular heartbeat.

Further Information: Rizzon P 1989.

TESTIMONIALS FROM ARRHYTHMIA PATIENTS WHO ARE FOLLOWING MY CARDIOVASCULAR HEALTH RECOMMENDATIONS

Dear Dr. Rath:

Two months ago, I was experiencing loud heartbeats, tachycardia and irregular beating of the heart. I saw my doctor who promptly put me on antiarrhythmic medication. I can honestly say this medication did me absolutely no good.

Because I've tried to investigate alternative treatments for my ailments (I've had diabetes for 38 years) I began to follow your recommendations for cardiovascular health. What a smart decision that was! Within a few days, the tachycardia stopped and I've not experienced any loud or irregular heartbeats. It's like a miracle. It must be the combination of nutrients you suggest because I had been taking Coenzyme Q10 separately from my regular vitamins. I tell everyone I know about the benefits of your cardiovascular recommendations and mention it during the diabetic seminars that I am conducting. At the last seminar I handed out copies of your letter, with a list of the ingredients in your recommendations. I hope you won't mind.

Thank you for sending me a copy of the letter you sent to Pres. Clinton, V.P. Gore, and Hillary Clinton.

Because of your research, I'm able to continue working.

B.M., USA

149

Dear Dr. Rath,

How delightful, after following your cardiovascular health recommendations for just 2 months, one notices the absence of irregular heartbeats, and the freedom to breathe freely. Confidence is restored as one has increased vigor and endurance. In a word, one spends less time thinking about their heart and more time enjoying life.
All this by simply following your cardiovascular health recommendations, which have become the answer for resolving coronary problems.

I am happy to have this opportunity of expressing my gratitude for your advanced medical research and for your cardiovascular health recommendations .

J.S., USA

Dear Dr. Rath:

Before following your cardiovascular health recommendations, I used to wake up with a pumping feeling in my chest, no pain, just discomfort. Upon changing position, it would stop. I no longer have that problem. I even forget I have a heart. I feel better now than ever in my life!

J.A., USA

ARRHYTHMIAS CAN BE ERADICATED

Our present knowledge of the causes, the prevention, and the treatment of arrhythmias can be summarized as follows:

- Arrhythmias are primarily caused by vitamin deficiencies of the electrical heart cells. In many cases vitamin deficiency is the direct cause of irregular heartbeat. In other cases, e.g. after a heart attack, vitamin deficiencies can contribute to life threatening arrhythmias.

- Optimum supplementation with vitamins and other essential nutrients is the basic therapeutic measure for prevention and treatment of arrhythmias.

- I encourage my colleagues in clinical medicine to help spread this information as soon as possible for the benefit of your own patients and millions of others.

A special note is in order for patients with irregular heartbeat among my readers:

- You should start immediately to supplement your diet with vitamins and other essential nutrients.

- While following the recommendations of this book, do not discontinue your regular medication without consulting your doctor.

- Share your health improvements with your doctor. Together you can make the best decisions to reduce your regular medication.

HOW YOU CAN LIVE LONGER AND STAY HEALTHY

> ## "Your Body Is as Old as
> ## Your Cardiovascular System."

Aging is a slow form of cardiovascular disease. The speed at which your body ages is directly dependent on the health of your cardiovascular system. All organs of your body are connected by a 60,000 miles long blood vessel pipeline.

• If your body is unprotected, the aging process leads to a gradual thickening of your blood vessel walls. This wall thickening eventually leads to malnutrition of millions of body cells in every organ and every other part of your body.

• Vitamins and other essential nutrients protect your blood vessels. Optimizing the health of your blood vessel system is the most effective way to prevent your body from early aging, to live longer, and to enjoy a healthy life.

Further Information: Biosca DG 1982; Pauling L 1986

OTHER RECOMMENDATIONS TO
MAINTAIN OPTIMUM CARDIOVASCULAR HEALTH

What Else You Can Do to Protect Your Cardiovascular System:

- **Exercise Regularly**
- **Eat a Prudent Diet**
  - **Rich in Fruits, Vegetables, and Fiber**
  - **Low in Fat and Sugar**
- **Stop Smoking**
- **Find Time to Relax**

In addition to nutritional supplements, the body also greatly benefits from a healthy lifestyle in general. Important for the health of the cardiovascular system are regular exercise, a diet rich in fruits, vegetables, and fiber and low in sugar and fats. By all means you should stop smoking in order to prevent toxic substances from cigarette smoke to damage your blood vessels and other parts of your cardiovascular system.

Those among my readers who are interested in learning more about a healthy cardiovascular lifestyle will find additional advice in books written on this subject by Dr. Dean Ornish, Dr. Julian Whitaker and other colleagues.

<u>NOTES</u>

HOW OUR ANCESTORS LOST THE ABILITY TO MANUFACTURE VITAMIN C

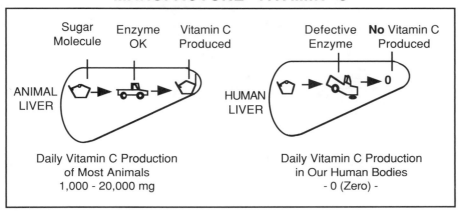

Throughout this book we have seen that vitamins, particularly vitamin C, play a critical role in maintaining and restoring cardiovascular health. Vitamin C is so important that animals manufacturing a sufficient amount of this vitamin in their bodies generally don't suffer heart attacks; humans, unable to manufacture their own vitamin C, die by the millions from cardiovascular diseases. How did the human race lose the ability to manufacture vitamin C? What were the consequences for our ancestors? What are the consequences for our own health today?

Most living species produce a sufficient amount of vitamin C in their own bodies. They do so by converting sugar molecules into vitamin C. In this way they manufacture between 1,000 mg and 20,000 mg (1 to 20 grams) per day compared to the human body weight. Converting sugar into vitamin C requires enzymes. Enzymes are biological catalysts or converters, symbolized in the figure above as a car. Several of these cars (enzymes) are necessary for converting a sugar molecule into a vitamin C molecule. If one of these cars breaks down, this pathway is cut and no vitamin C molecules can be produced.

Thousands of generations ago our ancestors lost the ability to convert sugar molecules into vitamin C in their livers. This was the result of an "accident" in the genes (molecules of inheritance) illustrated in the figure above as a car breakdown. As a result of this genetic accident all descendants, including all human beings living today, are dependent on sufficient dietary intake of vitamin C. For many thousands of generations this genetic mishap did not bother our ancestors greatly since they found plenty of vitamins in their diet consisting mainly of fruits, vegetables, and other vitamin rich plant nutrition. A sufficient vitamin supply in the diet of our ancestors guaranteed the stability of their bodies, and in particular, of their blood vessels. This changed dramatically with the dawn of the Ice Ages.

Further Information: Burns JJ 1957; Nishikimi M 1991.

DURING THE ICE AGES SCURVY BECAME THE GREATEST THREAT TO THE SURVIVAL OF OUR ANCESTORS

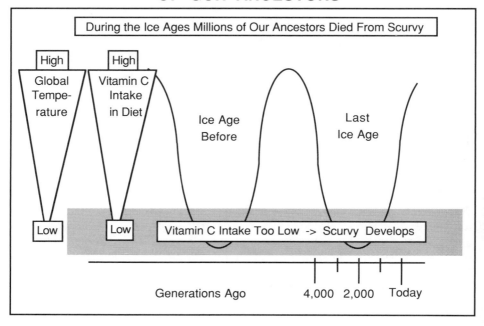

During the Ice Ages Millions of Our Ancestors Died From Scurvy

Several thousands of generations ago the global temperature dropped and the Ice Ages started. We know today that several Ice Ages have occurred on our planet. Each Ice Age lasted over several thousands of generations for our ancestors. The last Ice Age occurred between 4,000 and 500 human generations ago. During the peak of this Ice Age half of Europe and North America were covered with ice. Yet we know from skeletons found that our ancestors were living under these harsh climatic conditions. Their malnourished bones show the greatest problem for our ancestors: they were fighting a daily battle for food, and their vitamin intake was close to zero.

During the Ice Ages malnutrition and lack of vitamins in their diet became a constant threat to the survival of our ancestors. Among all deficiencies a lack of vitamin C was the greatest problem. While other living beings produced their own vitamin C in their bodies, our ancestors had lost this ability. In addition, they now found little vitamin C in their diet. The inevitable consequence for many of them was scurvy, a deadly disease. During the thousands of generations that the Ice Ages lasted, millions of our ancestors died from lack of dietary vitamin C and from scurvy. Thus for thousands of human generations, the vitamin C deficiency disease, scurvy, was the greatest threat to the survival of the human race.

Further Information: Rath M 1992a and 1992d.

SCORBUTIC BLOOD LOSS WAS THE MAIN CAUSE OF DEATH DURING THE ICE AGES

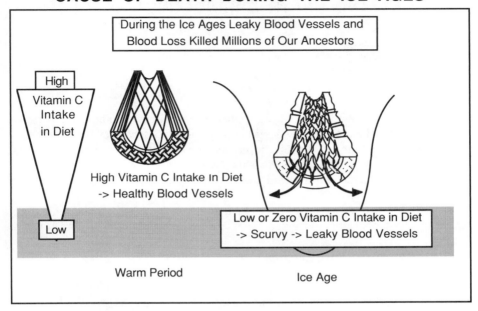

During the Ice Ages Leaky Blood Vessels and Blood Loss Killed Millions of Our Ancestors

High
Vitamin C Intake in Diet

High Vitamin C Intake In Diet -> Healthy Blood Vessels

Low

Low or Zero Vitamin C Intake in Diet -> Scurvy -> Leaky Blood Vessels

Warm Period

Ice Age

Scurvy is a deadly disease. Death is primarily caused by massive blood loss through a leaky blood vessel wall. During the Ice Ages scurvy and leaky blood vessels killed millions of our ancestors.

The total lack of vitamin C in the diet leads to a minimum production of collagen, the body's cement molecules. The first organs to fail are the blood vessel walls. During scurvy, these walls become destabilized: blood leaves the blood stream and leaks out. We know that bleeding of the gums was an early sign of scurvy during the long ship voyages of earlier centuries. The sailors on these journeys eventually died from massive bleeding inside and outside their bodies. They died after only a few months due to a lack of vitamin C in their diet.

During the Ice Ages vitamin C in the diet of our ancestors was scarce not only for a few months - but for many thousands of years. Over thousands of generations the scurvy epidemic raged among our ancestors. Millions of our ancestors died from massive blood loss through leaky blood vessels. If the human race were to survive, the bodies of our ancestors had to come up with ways to protect the blood vessels from becoming leaky. We know today that they did come up with solutions.

Further Information: Rath M 1992a and 1992d.

REPAIR MOLECULES BECAME MATTERS OF LIFE AND DEATH DURING THE ICE AGES

Protection of the blood vessel wall during vitamin C deficiency was a matter of life and death for our ancestors living during the Ice Ages. What did they come up with? How were they able to protect their blood vessels?

The keys for the blood vessel protection were repair molecules. These repair molecules entered the blood vessel wall during vitamin C deficiency with the aim of repairing and stabilizing it. Favorite repair molecules were lipoprotein(a), other fat transporting particles, other adhesive molecules able to mend the leaky blood vessels, clotting factors which could coagulate the blood before it leaked out, and many other repair factors. During the Ice Ages these repair factors had a great advantage, in fact so great that they became life saving. Only those among our ancestors who had inherited these repair molecules could survive the threat of scurvy.

These repair factors had to meet two requirements:
• to rise and to become effective whenever the body level of vitamin C drops
• to stabilize and repair the blood vessel during vitamin C deficiency

The advantage of these repair molecules during the Ice Ages is shown in the following figure. Let's imagine an Ice Age family living during the height of the last Ice Age, about 50,000 years ago. Our Ice Age family has four children, three of whom have not inherited any repair molecules. Without repair molecules their blood vessels are unprotected from scurvy. Immediately after these babies are born their blood vessels become leaky since lack of vitamin C is a lasting threat during the Ice Ages. All three children die as babies or during childhood from scurvy and from massive blood loss through their leaky blood vessels.

Luckily, one child in our family has inherited the lipoprotein(a) repair molecule (or another type of repair molecules or repair mechanism). With low vitamin C intake the lipoprotein(a) molecule enters the blood vessel wall and prevents it from leaking. This child is fortunate enough to survive childhood and to become an adult. Most importantly this child now can have children on its own and can pass on the information for this repair molecule to its children, grandchildren, and further generations via the genes (molecules of inheritance).

During the Ice Ages only those among our ancestors who carried these repair molecules in their genes stayed alive to pass these repair genes on to the next generation. This repair information was then passed on in their genes from one generation to the next, from the Ice Ages to our bodies today.

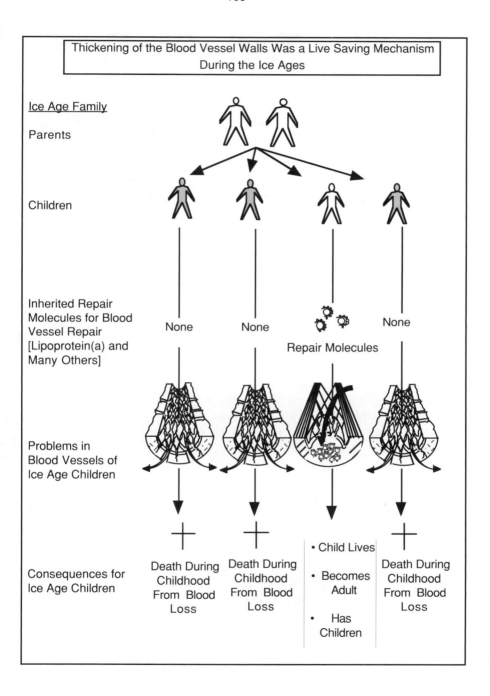

TODAY'S CARDIOVASCULAR DISEASES ORIGINATED DURING THE ICE AGES

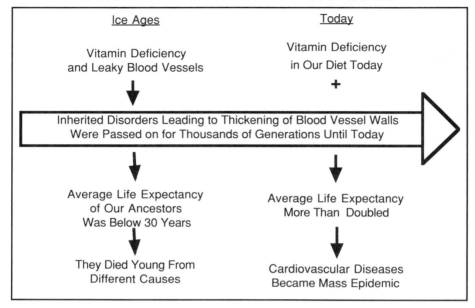

Ice Ages

Vitamin Deficiency
and Leaky Blood Vessels

Today

Vitamin Deficiency
in Our Diet Today

+

Inherited Disorders Leading to Thickening of Blood Vessel Walls
Were Passed on for Thousands of Generations Until Today

Average Life Expectancy
of Our Ancestors
Was Below 30 Years

Average Life Expectancy
More Than Doubled

They Died Young From
Different Causes

Cardiovascular Diseases
Became Mass Epidemic

Inherited disorders leading to the thickening of the blood vessel wall or protecting in another way against death from scurvy were greatly favored during the Ice Ages. Moreover, the genetic information for these diseases was passed on over thousands of generations until today. Thus, our bodies today contain genetic information greatly influenced and shaped during the extreme nutritional conditions of the Ice Ages. On the basis of this new understanding we can suddenly explain

- Why most inherited disorders known today lead to cardiovascular diseases
- Why most people living today carry some form of inherited disorder predisposing them for cardiovascular diseases
- Why today every second death is caused by heart attacks, strokes, or other forms of cardiovascular disease

We can now also explain the close connection of cardiovascular disease to vitamin deficiencies. Throughout this book you may have wondered about the broad effectiveness of vitamins, particularly of vitamin C, in the prevention of heart diseases. The Ice Age-vitamin deficiency-cardiovascular disease connection is the reason why

- all disease mechanisms leading to heart attacks and many other forms of cardiovascular diseases can be prevented by supplementation of vitamin C and other essential nutrients
- all blood risk factors known today in clinical cardiology can be neutralized by vitamin C and other essential nutrients.

DEFUSING INHERITED TIME BOMBS IN OUR BODIES

The Ice Ages greatly influenced the genetic information we received from our parents, grandparents, and earlier generations in our blood lines. As a result, most of us carry genetic information in our bodies predisposing us to develop some form of cardiovascular disease as we grow older. Since we don't know when this disease will strike we carry a genetic time bomb in our body. These time bombs can be high lipoprotein(a) levels, high triglyceride levels, diabetes, and many other inherited disorders which predispose us to develop cardiovascular diseases. I will use the picture of an inherited biological time bomb ticking in our bodies to illustrate the importance of this discovery for your personal health.

When this time bomb explodes it leads to a heart attack in one person, to strokes in another person, and to diabetic cardiovascular disease in yet another person. Since we are unable to change our molecules of inheritance we cannot get rid of the time bomb itself. But we can do something else - we can defuse this bomb and prevent its activation. How do we do this?

The discovery of the Ice Age-cardiovascular disease connection reveals the answer: Inherited time bombs leading to cardiovascular disease are all activated in the same way - by a low dietary intake of vitamins, particularly of vitamin C. The thickening of our blood vessel walls today is triggered in the same way as it was triggered in the bodies of our ancestors during the Ice Ages: by vitamin deficiency. Consequently, optimum vitamin supplementation in our diet will defuse and deactivate the inherited time bombs in our bodies thereby preventing its explosion in form of heart attacks or strokes.

The following figure summarizes this important mechanism which directly affects the health of millions of people.

Figure A:

- Most of us carry inherited time bombs in our bodies predisposing us to cardiovascular disease later in life if we do not protect ourselves.
- If the bomb explodes a heart attack, stroke, or any other form of cardiovascular diseases strikes.
- The common trigger mechanism for the activation of the inherited bomb is an insufficient dietary vitamin intake and a low vitamin body pool.
- Optimum vitamin supplementation and an optimum level of the vitamin body pool keeps the inherited time bomb inactive and keeps the person healthy.

Figure B:

- Everybody carries a different type and different size of inherited time bomb in the body.
- The more aggressive the inherited disorders, the bigger the time bomb.
- The bigger the time bomb, the earlier it normally explodes leading to heart attacks and strokes early in life (in the thirties, forties, or fifties).
- The bigger the bomb, the higher the required level of the vitamin body pool to defuse and deactivate the inherited time bomb.
- Since most of us don't know what size of inherited time bomb we carry it is safe to take vitamin supplements on a regular basis.

Figure B also gives you an example for this discovery:

Patient 1 carries the genetic time bomb 'diabetes' which -if unprotected- will lead to diabetic cardiovascular diseases later in this patient's life. The vitamin body pool drawn in this figure is sufficient to keep the time bomb defused at the present time.

Patient 2 carries the genetic time bomb 'high lipoprotein(a) level' which will lead to a heart attack or stroke. The vitamin body pool drawn in this figure is not sufficient to keep this time bomb inactive and therefore atherosclerotic deposits are already building up in the arteries of this patient.

Patient 3 has both inherited disorders 'diabetes' and 'high lipoprotein(a)' and therefore carries a huge inherited time bomb in the body. The vitamin body pool drawn in this figure is by far not enough to keep this huge time bomb defused; in fact the fuse has already burnt down and the bomb is just about to explode in form of a heart attack or stroke.

Thus, the higher the inherited risk, the more vitamins are needed to prevent the outbreak of cardiovascular diseases.

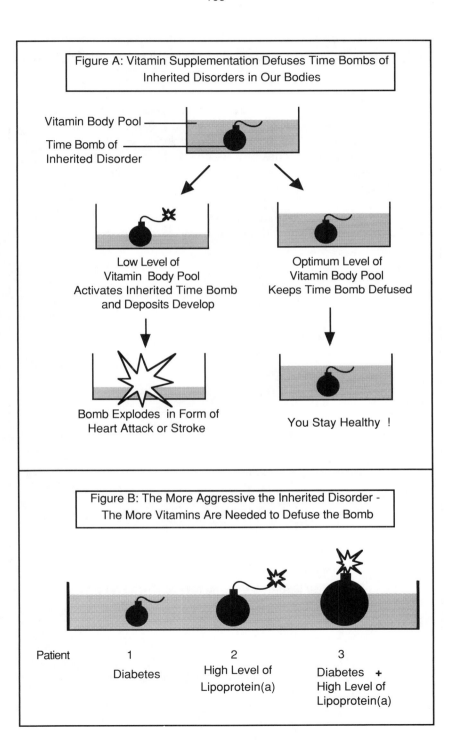

Figure A: Vitamin Supplementation Defuses Time Bombs of Inherited Disorders in Our Bodies

Vitamin Body Pool

Time Bomb of Inherited Disorder

Low Level of
Vitamin Body Pool
Activates Inherited Time Bomb
and Deposits Develop

Optimum Level of
Vitamin Body Pool
Keeps Time Bomb Defused

Bomb Explodes in Form of
Heart Attack or Stroke

You Stay Healthy !

Figure B: The More Aggressive the Inherited Disorder -
The More Vitamins Are Needed to Defuse the Bomb

Patient   1   2   3
             Diabetes   High Level of   Diabetes +
                            Lipoprotein(a)   High Level of
                                                 Lipoprotein(a)

THESE DISCOVERIES MAY LEAD TO
THE ERADICATION OF MANY OTHER DISEASES

The Ice Age-vitamin deficiency-cardiovascular disease connection says: "Inherited diseases leading to thickening of blood vessel walls or protecting the vessel wall in another way during vitamin deficiency originated during the Ice Ages or were greatly favored during that time. These diseases can be prevented and treated by optimum intake of vitamins, particularly vitamin C."

On the basis of this discovery the following diseases may now be eradicated as well since they involve - in many different ways - thickening of the blood vessel walls :

- Diabetes
- Homocystinuria
- Morbus Cushing
- Addison's Disease
- Alzheimer's Disease
- Amyloidosis
- Neurofibromatosis
- Cystic Fibrosis
- Multiple Sclerosis
- Muscular Dystrophy
- Parkinson's Disease
- Rheumatoid Arthritis
- Lupus Erythematodes
- Scleroderma
- Connective Tissue Disorders
- Metabolic Storage Diseases
- Inherited Disorders Leading to High Blood Pressure
- Inherited Disorders Leading to Increased Blood Clotting

Further Information: Genetic Disorders Associated With Cardiovascular Diseases (Reviews): Perloff JK 1992; Pyeritz RE 1992; Stollermann GH 1992; Williams GH 1992. Vitamin Deficiency And - Homocystinuria: McCully KS 1971. - Addison's Disease: Wilkinson JF 1936. - Diabetes: Pfleger R 1937; Mann GV 1975.

Diseases involving the thickening of arteries can be divided into two main groups. The first group includes those diseases leading to open cardiovascular problems such as heart attacks and strokes, which have been the main focus of this book.

These pages are devoted to the second group of diseases. This group of diseases leads to a thickening or hardening of many body tissues but at the same time also leads to a thickening of the patient's blood vessel walls. This fact suggests that these disorders also originated during to the Ice Ages, when they protected our ancestors from scorbutic blood loss and from death. These diseases were less efficient than typical cardiovascular disorders in protecting the blood vessels; however, they were better than no protection at all.

We now understand that not only lipoprotein(a) and other fat globules stabilized the blood vessel wall during vitamin deficiency and pre-scurvy, but also complex sugar molecules, amyloids and other large proteins, connective tissue molecules, even immune complexes deposited in the blood vessel wall were of advantage. There were few molecules in the bodies of our ancestors which nature did not try out as a protective mechanism to avoid the alternative: death from scurvy and from scorbutic blood loss.

These discoveries are not only of scientific value. They are of great importance for thousands of patients suffering from any of the diseases listed on the previous page. The Ice Age - vitamin deficiency - vascular wall connection says that these diseases can be prevented and treated by optimum intake of vitamins and other essential nutrients. This fact is even more significant since for most of the dreaded diseases above no other effective treatment is available today.

With the authority of the scientist who made these discoveries I am urging my readers:

• *Patients* with any of the diseases listed above should immediately supplement their diet with vitamin C and other essential nutrients discussed in this book.

• *Doctors* who treat patients with disorders listed above should inform their patients about this therapeutic possibility since for most of these diseases no other effective treatment is available.

• *Researchers* active in developing treatments for these diseases should immediately include vitamin C and other essential nutrients in their research efforts.

YOUR CARDIOVASCULAR HEALTH DEPENDS ON AN OPTIMUM VITAMIN POOL IN YOUR BODY

How are the different risk factors for cardiovascular disease connected? Is smoking more important than an inherited disorder for diabetes? The following figure summarizes the answer.

Three factors determine whether and when you suffer a heart attack and stroke:

- *Internal Risk Factors:* The size of the time bomb of inherited disorders in your body which we discussed in this section of the book.

- *External Risk Factors:* The rate at which external risk factors drain your body pool in vitamins, particularly in vitamin C, a mechanism we discussed in an earlier section of this book. Smoking, stress, being overweight and other forms of an unhealthy lifestyle deplete your body of vitamins. The more of these risk factors you accumulate, the faster your vitamins body pool drops.

- *Your Vitamin Body Pool:* Ultimately, your health is determined by the level of your vitamin body pool. By supplementing your diet with vitamins and with other essential nutrients you can neutralize an increased cardiovascular risk caused by any internal or external risk factors.

The adjacent figure shows the two faucets by which you can regulate your personal vitamin body pool.

- *Faucet number one:* Optimum vitamin intake. This is the most important regulation of your vitamin body pool. An optimum intake of vitamins and other essential nutrients is the safest way to achieve an optimum level of your vitamin body pool and thereby optimum cardiovascular health.

- *Faucet number two:* Decreasing external risk factors. Since we cannot influence our inherited risk factors we should always try to minimize our external risk factors. Above all, stop smoking.

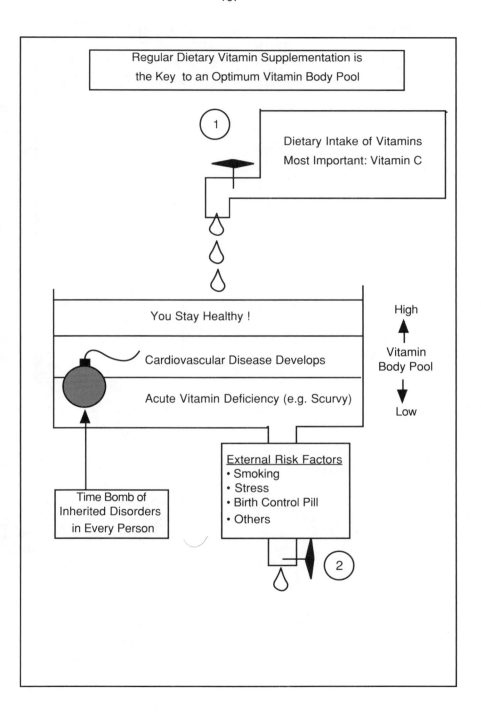

THE ERADICATION OF HEART DISEASE IS IN SIGHT

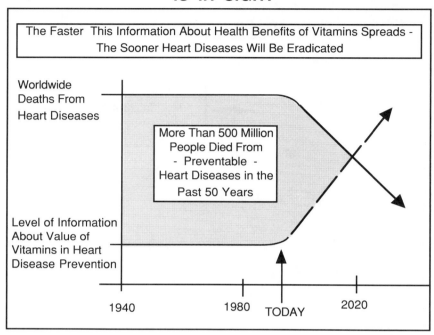

How fast cardiovascular diseases can be eradicated depends on how fast information about the value of vitamins in the prevention of these diseases is spread.

In 1941 the Canadian Cardiologist Dr. Paterson reported that four out of five heart diseases patients had low vitamin C blood levels as as leading risk factor. Thus more than 50 years ago the first alarm bells were rang. How many lives could have been saved if this report would have entered the textbooks of medicine? According to the World Health Organization more than 12 million people die every year from heart attacks and strokes. Thus, during the past half century about half a billion people died prematurely from cardiovascular diseases - more than in all wars of mankind taken together. Thus, ignoring these early studies on the value of vitamins in heart diseases prevention had a terrible death toll.

Most regrettably, the death of most of these people could have been prevented. In many countries of the world there is hardly any family which has not suffered the loss of a father, a sister, an uncle who died from a heart attack or stroke. The scope of this drama is worldwide and we have to ask: Why are people still dying from preventable diseases?

WHY PEOPLE CONTINUE TO DIE FROM PREVENTABLE DISEASES

I am frequently asked
"Why did nobody tell us this important information before?"
This page will give you an answer:

Vitamins are not patentable.

Vitamin sales give small profits.

Little interest exists from pharmaceutical companies.

Vitamin research receives scarce financial support.

Little money is made available for clinical studies with vitamins.

Few reports about value of vitamins are published in medical journals .

Health benefits of vitamins are hardly ever mentioned in medical textbooks.

Few universities teach nutritional medicine.

Few medical students learn about nutritional medicine.

Few doctors know and practice nutritional medicine.

Millions of people continue to die from heart disease
and from other preventable diseases.

HOW WE CAN STOP
THIS UNNECESSARY DEATH TOLL
AND HELP CREATE
A BETTER AND HEALTHIER TOMORROW

The key to turning this dreadful development around is information. The message of this book should reach every country and every family as soon as possible. You can help. Talk to your family, to your friends, and your colleagues about this book. You can also send a copy of this book to your local newspaper, radio or TV station for review. Other steps which should be taken immediately include:

- *Doctors, health care professionals, students, and educational institutions* in the health care field share an ethical responsibility to introduce nutritional research and nutritional medicine into their teaching programs. No future doctor should leave medical school without a profound knowledge in nutritional medicine.

- *Scientists and researchers* have an urgent responsibility. More research and more clinical studies are needed to document the health values of essential nutrients. New nutritional compositions should be developed based on scientific research and clinical tests. Universities and other public institutions should develop a focus in this important area of medicine.

- *Scientific and medical journals as well as the media in general* share a responsibility in disseminating the scientific progress made in this important area of medicine. They should regularly report the research and clinical studies in nutritional medicine.

On the next page you will find some personal recommendations for you.

MY PERSONAL RECOMMENDATIONS FOR YOU

- Use this book as your personal advisor to improve your cardiovascular health and to add valuable years to your life.

- Follow the recommendations of this book and optimize your cardiovascular health with nutritional supplements. Enjoy leading a healthy life style.

- If you have a heart condition inform your doctor about the health improvements you achieve by following the recommendations of this book. Do not stop taking your regular medication without consulting your doctor.

- Talk to your family, friends, and colleagues about how you feel while following the recommendations of this book.

- Enjoy taking control of your own health and look forward to a life without cardiovascular ailments and to all those years you will add.

_____

_____

The health improvements grateful patients shared with you throughout this book may help you personally. In return, I encourage you to also share the health improvements you may experience while following the recommendations of this book. While staying anonymous, your health message can be of great importance to thousands of other people. You can send your letter directly to me at the address you find at the end of this book.

"CALL FOR EXCELLENCE IN HEALTH CARE"

AN INVITATION TO
MY COLLEAGUES IN MEDICINE AND
IN OTHER HEALTH CARE PROFESSIONS

This book provides the scientific rationale as well as clinical evidence for a great advancement in medicine. Before long, nutritional medicine will reach all health care areas and millions of people will benefit from it. But this advancement does not come by itself - it needs your support.

• I invite my colleagues in medicine and in other health care professions to further improve the health of your patients by making use of the nutritional recommendations of this book. I invite you to document the health improvements of your patients and, if possible, conduct clinical tests and studies to further document the health benefits of essential nutrients.

• I invite the health maintenance organizations and health insurance companies to take advantage of this medical breakthrough. The testimonials from patients documented in this book are just the tip of the iceberg. Imagine the efficiency improvement for our health care system if these recommendations are followed by your members or policy holders.

• I invite the medical students and all future health professionals to help promote this fascinating area of nutritional medicine during your lifetime. Take this book to your medical school and help to make nutritional medicine part of the ongoing education.

I founded Health Now to promote research, clinical studies as well as education in nutritional medicine. We are open for any form of collaboration in this area and we will help you in any way we can. If you are interested - don't hesitate to contact us.

Based on the scientific discoveries reported in this book a series of political measures are also immediately needed. On the following pages I would like to share with you my open correspondence with the White House in Washington.

SAVE LIVES AND REDUCE THE HIGH COSTS OF HEART DISEASE

Open Letter to President Bill Clinton, Vice-President Al Gore, and Health Care Task Force Chair Hillary Clinton

Dear President Clinton,
Dear Vice-President Gore,
Dear Hillary Clinton:

This letter is to inform you about recent scientific discoveries that open the way to significantly reduce the risk for heart attack and stroke for millions of people. At the same time these discoveries will lead to a necessary change and a significant improvement of America's health care and to a great reduction of health care costs.

The facts on heart disease are alarming:
• Ever year more than 1 million Americans die from heart disease - two Americans every minute.
• Every year more than 100 billion US dollars in health care costs are spent for heart disease alone - 200,000 US dollars every minute.

Over the years scientific knowledge has accumulated about the value of vitamins and other essential nutrients in the prevention of heart disease. In my former capacity as Director of Cardiovascular Research at the Linus Pauling Institute of Science and Medicine in Palo Alto I had the opportunity to review much of this evidence. In addition, I have contributed to this knowledge a series of discoveries which provide us with a new understanding of heart disease and with effective treatments for it.

• Heart disease is a vitamin deficiency disease. Heart attacks and strokes are essentially unknown in all animals producing sufficient vitamin C in their bodies. Among humans, unable to produce their own vitamin C and frequently having a low dietary intake of vitamins, this disease became a leading cause of death. Virtually every form of heart disease known today can be induced by vitamin C deficiency.

• Vitamin C stabilizes the wall of the blood vessels and is needed for the production of collagen, the reinforcement for the blood vessel wall and other parts of the human body. A reinforced blood vessel wall does not allow atherosclerotic deposits to develop. Thus heart attacks and strokes can largely be prevented by an optimum intake of vitamin C.

• The most important risk factor for heart disease known today is *lipoprotein-a* which directly or indirectly causes over 50% of all heart attacks and strokes. Neither diet nor any of the presently available cholesterol-lowering prescription drugs is known to affect this newly identified risk factor. In contrast, vitamin C and vitamin B3 as well as the natural amino acids lysine and proline can be therapeutically effective. Moreover, these nutritional supplements have the potential to reduce existing atherosclerotic deposits and thereby to reverse existing heart disease in a non-surgical way.

A century ago scientific discoveries were made which lead to the control of infectious diseases. The scientific knowledge available today on the important role of vitamins and other essential nutrients in the fight against heart disease will lead to the control of this disease during the next decades. As the physician and scientist who made the discoveries which lead to the recent scientific break-through I feel it is incumbent upon me to inform you about this development in order to enable your administration to make appropriate decisions towards a significant improvement of human health. These discoveries are summarized in my recent paper "Reducing the Risk for Cardiovascular Disease with Nutritional Supplements" and in my forthcoming book entitled "The Abolition of Heart Disease".

It is no coincidence that the U.S., the nation with the highest per capita vitamin consumption, has already achieved the greatest decrease in the rate for heart disease among all industrialized nations. In a recent epidemiological study from the University of California at Los Angeles involving more than 11,000 Americans a modest dietary Vitamin C supplementation cut the heart attack rate in half and increased life expectancy for up to six years. No other drug or compound has ever been shown to have a similar effect.

Half a century ago clinical studies had documented that low vitamin C levels in the blood were a leading risk factor for heart disease. Unfortunately these reports were ignored, and in the 50 years since, more than half a billion people died - unnecessarily - from heart attacks and strokes. The death toll from these preventable diseases is greater than from all wars of mankind combined. There is no rational explanation why this important information has been ignored. There may, however, be an economic reason. Vitamins and other essential nutrients are not patentable and have had few advocates promoting this knowledge essential for millions of patients. What is particularly alarming is that today the Food and Drug Administration intends to make vitamins and essential nutrients prescriptive drugs and thereby to limit their free and affordable access.

There is no scientific, ethical, or economic reason to neglect this important information any longer. The health of millions of Americans can and must immediately be improved by optimum use of nutritional supplements in the prevention and therapy for heart disease and many other diseases. A change of the Nation's health care towards an effective therapy at low cost will also have immediate implications for the economy. Effective, safe, and affordable health care on the basis of nutritional supplements is a realistic and logical way - I believe the only way - to implement your most important campaign promises:

- Provide health care to all Americans at affordable costs
- Reduce health care spending
- Decrease the budget deficit
- Increase the competitiveness of Americas businesses by decreasing their health care expense burden

In the name of millions of present and future patients I urge you and your administration to immediately initiate a scientific and clinical program through the National Institutes of Health and by other measures you consider appropriate to irreversibly establish the benefits of nutritional supplements for human health. Your support for this new era of medicine will require courageous stands against some pharmaceutical companies but the immediate benefits for the health of the people, for thousands of small and large businesses, and for the overall economy of this country will reward this courage manifold.

You and your administration now have a historic opportunity to lead an international medical and scientific effort to greatly reduce death and disability from heart disease. 50 years ago the Manhattan Project, a joint effort by the world's leading scientists initiated by President Roosevelt, ended the Second World War by creating the atomic bomb. Now is the time to initiate a scientific effort to win another war - the war against heart attacks, strokes and other diseases. The goal is clearly defined: a significant reduction of heart disease as a cause for human mortality in this generation and in future generations of mankind.

Towards this goal I have recently founded a company committed to the promotion of nutritional medicine by focussing on research and clinical studies as well as educational services. We will pursue the goals outlined above through collaboration with physicians, scientists, health organizations and we are open to any form of collaboration with your administration.

Very truly yours,

Matthias Rath, M.D.

For more information please contact
Health Now, 387 Ivy Street, San Francisco, California 94102

A FIRST RESPONSE FROM THE WHITE HOUSE

THE WHITE HOUSE

Dear Friend:

Thank you for writing and sharing your views on health care reform. President Clinton is committed to reforming our nation's health care system—controlling runaway costs and providing security to every American family.

It won't be easy and it won't happen overnight, but with your help, we will bring costs under control while maintaining quality medical care and preserving the choice so important to us all.

Thank you again for your views and for your support.

Hillary Rodham Clinton

This response from the White House and from Mrs. Hillary Rodham Clinton is an important document. With her signature Mrs. Clinton acknowledges that the White House was informed about the possibility that heart diseases, the leading diseases in America, can be eradicated.

On the next page I will share with you my open response letter to Mrs. Rodham Clinton.

176

Contributing to the eradication of heart diseases by optimum use of nutritional supplements.

ERADICATE HEART DISEASE AND SAVE BILLIONS IN HEALTH CARE COSTS - NOW!

An Open Response by Dr. Matthias Rath
to a Letter From Hillary Clinton And The White House

Dear Mrs. Rodham Clinton:

Thank you for your response to my Open Letter 'Save Lives and Reduce The High Costs of Heart Disease' in which I informed you about the discovery that heart attacks and strokes are caused by vitamin deficiencies and can be eradicated.

Your response is an encouragement for all of us promoting nutritional and preventive medicine. On the other hand, I take the fact that your response was sent during the final deliberations of the health-care reform task force as a signal. Your administration needs help to provide effective health care available and affordable for every American family. Nutritional medicine as an essential part of general medicine is the only way to achieve this goal.

In the meantime I have discovered that not only heart attacks and strokes but also other forms of heart disease, such as cardiac failure and arrhythmia, are frequently caused by a lack of vitamins as the essential fuel of heart muscle cells. On the basis of these discoveries I have developed a nutritional supplement formula with the aim to maintain and to restore optimum cardiovascular health. With this letter you will find testimonials from heart disease patients taking this formula. They relate that even severe symptoms of heart disease such as angina pectoris, shortness of breath, as well as arrhythmias disappeared within weeks, enabling the patients to lead a normal life again.

These heart disease symptoms had persisted despite conventional cardiac drug therapy. The fact that not conventional drugs but nutritional supplements brought ultimate relief to these patients indicates that vitamin deficiencies are not only related to heart diseases but are frequently their primary cause. This letter is an open and public advocacy for one of the greatest breakthroughs in medicine in this century.

I have now outlined to the White House and to the American public the historic opportunity to eradicate heart disease. Moreover, I have provided first clinical evidence that these discoveries can immediately be applied to save millions of human lives and billions of health care dollars. The scientific basis for this new era of medicine is established - what is needed now is the political will and support to implement it.

I would welcome the opportunity to meet with you and your advisors to further evaluate the scientific evidence already available. Moreover, I am proposing the initiation of a federal scientific task force to promote research and clinical studies in nutritional medicine. The immediate goal for this task force is clearly defined: eradication of heart disease as a cause of human mortality.

I am looking forward to hearing from you again.

Sincerely,

Matthias Rath

Health Now, 387 Ivy Street, San Francisco, CA 94102

ADVOCACY FOR A NEW ERA IN MEDICINE - A PERSONAL CHRONOLOGY

1940 - 1980 Early research and clinical studies in nutritional medicine are largely ignored. Proponents of vitamins are frequently considered "quacks."

1980's More research and clinical studies are published about the health value of vitamins and nutritional supplements. The value of vitamins A, C and E as natural antioxidants becomes known.

1987 Discovery of the connection between cardiovascular disease, lipoprotein(a) and vitamin C. For the first time vitamin C is given to a person with high lipoprotein(a) levels in order to lower this risk factor.

1989 September: Together with my colleagues from Hamburg University, publication of our findings about the critical role of lipoprotein(a) in human atherosclerosis.

1990 August: Publication of the connection between lipoprotein(a), vitamin C and cardiovascular disease.

1991 April: Submission to the Proceedings of the National Academy of Science of the paper "Solution to the Puzzle of Human Cardiovascular Disease: Its Primary Cause is Vitamin C Deficiency Leading to the Deposition of Lipoprotein(a) and Fibrin/Fibrinogen in the Vascular Wall".

1991 June: After having originally accepted publication of this paper, the editor of the Proceedings denies publication.

1991 November: Publication of the paper "Solution" in the Journal of Orthomolecular Medicine, with a foreword quoted from a letter written by Galileo Galilei in the 17th century who discovered that the earth circles the sun and not the sun the earth: "My dear Kepler, what do you say of the leading philosophers here to whom I have offered a thousand times of my own accord to show my studies, but who, with the lazy obstinacy of a serpent who has eaten his fill, have never consented to look at the planets, or moon, or telescope? Verily, just as serpents close their ears, so do men close their eyes to the light of truth."

I also added to the foreword that this paper had originally been accepted by the Proceedings of the National Academy of Sciences. "Under questionable circumstances this decision was later revoked by the editor. We are aware that this pullback was not the decision of an individual. It happened in the interests of those who are personally or economically dependent on the present dogma of human cardiovascular disease. We are confident that the scientific historians will make the proper judgment on this interesting development. We are indebted to the Journal of Orthomolecular Medicine for the publication of this article without delay and we know that this decision will not be to the disadvantage of this journal. Above all, we are convinced that the uncompromised publication of this article lies in the interest of millions of patients, and perhaps every human being."

November 1991: Copies of the "Solution" paper were distributed at the American Heart Association meeting in Anaheim, California. From there this important publication reached doctors and scientists in many countries.

January 1992: Press conference by the American Heart Association. Then president Dr. Virgil Brown essentially acknowledged the potential health value of megadoses of vitamins in the prevention of cardiovascular disease.

February 1992: Scientific conference on the health benefits of vitamins sponsored by the New York Academy of Science in Arlington, Virginia, under the title "Beyond Deficiency." The author's latest publication "A Unified Theory Of Human Cardiovascular Disease Leading to The Abolition of This Diseases As A Cause For Human Mortality" is distributed to the participants of this conference as well as to media representatives at the conference.

April 1992:The publication "A Unified Theory Of Human Cardiovascular Disease Leading to The Abolition of This Diseases As A Cause For Human Mortality" is sent out to the press.

April 1992: *Time Magazine* appears with a title page "The Real Power Of Vitamins - New research shows they may help fight Cancer, Heart Disease, and the ravages of Aging." This issue of *Time* becomes the best selling issue ever. *Newsweek, US News And World Report, Readers Digest*, and many others follow.

May 1992: Dr. James Enstrom and his colleagues from the University of California in Los Angeles publish their findings from 11,000 Americans that vitamin C significantly cuts heart disease rates and prolongs life. This study makes front page news.

September 1992: Health Now is founded, a company promoting nutritional medicine through research, clinical studies as well as educational services.

February 1993: Open Letter To President Clinton, Vice President Gore, and Hillary Rodham Clinton informing The White House about the discovery that heart diseases are vitamin deficiencies and can now be eradicated.

May 1993 : A first response from The White House acknowledging having received information about the historic opportunity to eradicate cardiovascular diseases.

SOME DISCOVERIES
MADE BY THE AUTHOR

Major Scientific Discoveries

• Discovery of the Ice Age - cardiovascular disease connection. This discovery explains that today's cardiovascular diseases and many related diseases originated during the Ice Ages.

• Discovery that cardiovascular diseases can largely be eradicated in this generation and in future generations of mankind. This discovery is based on the Ice Age - vitamin deficiency - cardiovascular disease connection and on the discovery that heart diseases are primarily vitamin deficiencies.

• Discovery of the lipoprotein(a) - vitamin C connection. Lipoprotein(a) is primarily found in humans and other living beings unable to synthesize vitamin C. Vice versa, animals synthesizing vitamin C have less or no lipoprotein(a).

• L-lysine and related compounds can release lipoprotein(a) from atherosclerotic deposits and thereby reverse cardiovascular disease.

• Discovery of the 'protein code', the communication code of protein molecules in our body. This discovery deciphers the language by which our body molecules 'talk' to each other during health and disease. After the discovery of the genetic code more than thirty years ago the 'protein code' has remained the missing link of biological communication. This most recent discovery was published in early 1993.

Discoveries Which Can Immediately Improve Your Personal Health

The following diseases may now be completely eradicated:

• Heart attacks

• Strokes

• Peripheral forms of cardiovascular diseases;

• Heart failure

• Arrhythmias

• Inherited disorders causing high blood pressure

• Inherited disorders causing increased blood clotting

• Diabetes, Morbus Cushing, Addison's disease, and other hormonal disorders leading to cardiovascular diseases

• Alzheimer's disease, neurofibromatosis, muscular dystrophy, Parkinson's disease, multiple sclerosis and other disorders of the nervous system which also involve the cardiovascular system

• Rheumatoid arthritis, polyarteritis, lupus erythematodes, scleroderma and other immunological disorders which also involve the cardiovascular system

• Inherited disorder causing tissue storage diseases

• Inherited disorders of the connective tissue

Some of these diseases had been connected to nutritional deficiencies earlier; for most of them this book is the first report. Moreover, the opportunity to eradicate any of the above diseases is reported here for the first time. The discovery of the Ice Age - vitamin deficiency - cardiovascular disease connection was necessary for this medical breakthrough.

We can now eradicate heart disease and several dozen of related diseases by optimum use of nutritional supplements.

Doctors, scientists, health care providers, politicians, all of us now share a historic opportunity to achieve this goal as soon as possible - for the benefit of this generation and of future generations of mankind.

REFERENCES

For editorial reasons only the first author and the year is given in the text references.

Acheson RM and Williams DRR. (1983) Does consumption of fruit and vegetables protect against stroke ? Lancet 1: 1191-1193.

Armstrong VW, Cremer P, Eberle E, et al. (1986) The association between serum Lp(a) concentrations and angiographically assessed coronary atherosclerosis. Dependence on serum LDL levels. Atherosclerosis 62: 249-257.

Altschul R, Hoffer A and Stephen JD. (1955) Influence of nicotinic acid on serum cholesterol in man. Archives of Biochemistry and Biophysics 54: 558-559.

Aulinskas TH, Van Westhuyzen DR and Coetzee GA. (1983) Atherosclerosis 47: 159-171.

Avogaro P, Bon G B and Fusello M. (1983) Effect of pantethine on lipids, lipoproteins and apolipoproteins in man. Current Therapeutic Research 33: 488-493.

Bates CJ, Mandal AR, Cole TJ. (1977) HDL cholesterol and vitamin-C status. The Lancet II: 611.

Beetens J, Coene M-C, Verheyen A, Zonnekyn L & Hermann AG (1986) Prostaglandins.

Beisiegel U, Niendorf A, Wolf K, Reblin T and Rath M. (1990) Lipoprotein(a) in the arterial wall. European Heart Journal 11 (Supplement E): 174-183.

Berg K. (1963) A new serum type system in man - the Lp system. Acta Pathologica Scandinavia 59: 369-382.

Biosca DG, Mizushima S, Sawamura M, Nara Y, and Yamori Y. The effect of nutritional prevention of cardiovascular diseases on longevity. Nutritional Review 50: 407-412.

Blumberg A, Hanck A and Sandner G. (1983) Vitamin nutrition in patients on continuous ambulatory peritoneal dialysis (CAPD). Clinical Nephrology 20: 244-250.

Bordia AK. (1979) The effects of vitamin C on blood lipids, fibrinolytic activity and platelet adhesiveness in patients with coronary artery disease. Atherosclerosis 35; 181-187.

Bordia A and Verma SD. (1985) Clinical Cardiology 8: 552-554.

Boscoboinik D, Szewczyk A, Hensey C and Azzi A. (1991) Inhibition of cell proliferation by alpha -tocopherol. Journal of Biological Chemistry 266: 6188-6194.

Breslow JL. (1989) Familial disorders of high density lipoprotein metabolism. In: Scriver CR, Beaudet AL, Sly WS, Valle D (editors). The Metabolic Basis of Inherited Disease. p. 1251-1266. McGraw-Hill, New York, St. Louis, San Francisco

Briggs M and Briggs M. (1972) Vitamin C requirements and oral contraceptives. Nature 238: 277.

Brown MS and Goldstein JL. (1984) How LDL receptors influence cholesterol and atherosclerosis. Scientific American 251: 58-66.

Burns JJ. (1957) Missing step in man, monkey and guinea pig required for the biosynthesis of L-ascorbic acid. Nature 180: 553.

Burns JJ, Rivers JM, Machlin LJ, editors. (1987) Third Conference on Vitamin C. Annals of the New York Academy of Sciences 498.

Carlson LA, Hamsten A and Asplund A. (1989). Pronounced lowering of serum levels of lipoprotein Lp(a) in hyperlipidemic subjects treated with nicotinic acid. Journal of Internal Medicine (England) 226: 271-276.

Cherchi A, Lai C, Angelino F, Trucco G, Caponnetto S, Mereto PE, Rosolen G, Manzoli U, Schiavoni G, Reale A, Romeo F, Rizzon P, Sorgente I, Strano A, Novo S, and Immordino R. (1985) International Journal of Clinical Pharmacology, Therapy and Toxicology: 569-572.

Clemetson CAB. (1989) Vitamin C, Volume I-III. CRC Press Inc., Florida.

Cushing GL, Gaubatz JW, Nave ML, Burdick BJ, Bocan TMA, Guyton JR, Weilbaecher D, DeBakey ME, Lawrie GM and Morrisett JD. (1989) Quantitation and localization of lipoprotein(a) and B in coronary artery bypass vein grafts resected at re-operation. Arteriosclerosis 9: 593-603.

Dahlen GH, Guyton JR, Attar M, Farmer JA, Kautz JA and Gotto AM, Jr. (1986) Association of levels of lipoprotein LP(a), plasma lipids, and other lipoproteins with coronary artery disease documented by angiography. Circulation 74: 758-765.

DeMaio SJ, King SB, Lembo NJ, Roubin GS, Hearn JA, Bhagavan HN and Sgoutas DS. (1992) Vitamin E supplementation, plasma lipids and incidence of restenosis after percutaneous transluminal coronary angioplasty (PTCA). Journal of the American College of Nutrition 11: 68-73.

Dice JF and Daniel CW. (1973) The hypoglycemic effect of ascorbic acid in a juvenile-onset diabetic. International Research Communications System: 1: 41.

Enstrom JE, Kanim LE and Klein MA. (1992) Vitamin C intake and mortality among a sample of the United States population. Epidemiology 3: 194-202.

Ferrari R, Cucchini, and Visioli O. (1984) The metabolical effects of L-carnitine in angina pectoris. International Journal of Cardiology 5: 213-216.

Folkers K and Yamamura Y (editors). (1976,1979,1981,1984,1986) Biomedical and clinical aspects of coenzyme Q. Volume 1-5. Elsevier Science Publishers, New York.

Folkers K, Watanabe T, Kaji M. (1977) Critique of coenzyme Q10 in biochemical and biomedical research and of ten years of clinical research on cardiovascular disease. Journal of Molecular Medicine 2: 431-460.

Folkers K, Vadhanavikit S and Mortensen SA. (1985) Biochemical rationale and myocardial tissue data on the effective therapy of cardiomyopathy with coenzyme Q10. Proceedings of the National Academy of Sciences USA 82: 901-904.

Frei B, England L and Ames BN. (1989) Ascorbate is an outstanding antioxidant in human blood plasma. Proceedings of the National Academy of Sciences USA 86: 6377-6381.

Gaby SK, Bendich A, Singh VN and Machlin LJ (editors). (1991) Vitamin Intake and Health, Marcel Dekker Inc. N.Y.

Gaddi A, Descovich GC, Noseda G, Fragiacomo C, Colombo L, Craveri A, Montanari G, and Sirtori CR. (1984) Controlled evaluation of pantethine, a natural hypolipidemic compound, in patients with different forms of hyperlipoproteinemia. Atherosclerosis 5: 73-83.

Galeone F, Scalabrino A, Giuntoli F, Birindelli A, Panigada G, Rossi, and Saba P. (1983) The lipid-lowering effect of pantethine in hyperlipidemic patients: a clinical investigation. Current Therapeutic Research 34: 383-390.

Genest J Jr., Jenner JL, McNamara JR, Ordovas JM, Silberman SR, Wilson PWF and Schaefer EJ. (1991) Prevalence of lipoprotein(a) Lp(a) excess in coronary artery disease. American Journal of Cardiology 67: 1039-1045.

Gey KF, Stähelin HB, Puska P and Evans A. (1987) Relationship of plasma level of vitamin C to mortality from ischemic heart disease.110-123. In: Burns JJ, Rivers JM, Machlin LJ (editors): Third Conference on Vitamin C. Annals of the New York Academy of Sciences 498.

Gey KF, Puska P, Jordan P and Moser UK. (1991) Inverse correlation between plasma vitamin E and mortality from ischemic heart disease in cross-cultural epidemiology. American Journal of Clinical Nutrition 53: 326, Supplement.

Ghidini O, Azzurro M, Vita A, and Sartori G. (1988) Evaluation of the therapeutic efficacy of L-carnitine in congestive heart failure. International Journal of Clinical Pharmacology, Therapy and Toxicology 26: 217-220.

Ginter E. (1973) Cholesterol: Vitamin C controls its transformation into bile acids. Science 179: 702.

Ginter E (1976) Vitamin C and plasma lipids. New England Journal of Medicine 294: 559-560.

Ginter E. (1978) Marginal vitamin C deficiency, lipid metabolism, and atherosclerosis. Lipid Research 16: 216-220.

Ginter E. (1979) Decline of coronary mortality in United States and vitamin C. Journal of Clinical Nutrition 32: 511.

Ginter E (1991) Vitamin C deficiency cholesterol metabolism and atherosclerosis. Journal of Orthomolecular Medicine 6: 166-173.

Gore I, Fujinami T, and Shirahama T. (1965) Endothelial changes produced by ascorbic acid deficiency in guinea pigs. Archives of Pathology 80: 371-376.

Grainger DJ, Kirschenlohr HL, Metcalfe JC, Weissberg PL, Wade DP and Lawn RM. (1993) Proliferation of human smooth muscle cells promoted by lipoprotein(a). Science 260: 1655-1658.

Guraker A, Hoeg JM, Kostner G, Papadopoulos NM and Brewer HB Jr. (1985) Levels of lipoprotein Lp(a) decline with neomycin and niacin treatment. Atherosclerosis 57: 293-301.

Halliwell B and Gutteridge JMC (editors). (1985) Free radicals in biology and medicine. Oxford University Press, London, New York, Toronto.

Hanck A and Weiser H. (1979) The influence of vitamin C on lipid metabolism in man and animals. International Journal for Vitamin and Nutrition Research 19: 83-93.

Harwood HJ Jr, Greene YJ and Stacpoole PW (1986) Inhibition of human leucocyte 3-hydroxy-3-methylglutaryl coenzyme A reductase activity by ascorbic acid. An effect mediated by the free radical monodehydroascorbate. Journal of Biological Chemistry 261: 7127-7135.

Hayashi K. (1980) Scanning electron microscopic observations on the aortic endothelium in hypovitamin C guinea pigs with or without cholesterol administration. Nagoya Medical Journal 25: 155-168.

Hearn JA, Donohue BC, Ba'albaki H, Douglas JS, King SBIII, Lembo NJ, Roubin JS and Sgoutas DS. (1992) Usefulness of serum lipoprotein(a) as a predictor of restenosis after percutaneous transluminal coronary angioplasty. The American Journal of Cardiology 68: 736-739.

Heart Facts, American Heart Association, 1987.

Hermann WJ JR, Ward K and Faucett J. (1979) The effect of tocopherol on higdensity lipoprotein cholesterol. American Journal of Clinical Pathology 72: 848-852.

Hemilä H. (1992) Vitamin C and plasma cholesterol. In: Critical Reviews in Food Science and Nutrition 32 (1): 33-57, CRC Press Inc., Florida.

Hoff HF, Beck GJ, Skibinski CI, Jürgens G, O'Neil J, Kramer J and Lytle B. (1988) Serum Lp(a) level as a predictor of vein graft stenosis after coronary artery bypass surgery in patients. Circulation 77: 1238-1244.

Hulley SB, Rosenman RH, Bawol RD and Brand RJ. (1980) The association between triglyceride and coronary heart disease. New England Journal of Medicine 302: 1383-1389.

Ide T. (1922) Gefässveränderungen bei der Möller-Barlowschen Krankheit. Zeitschrift für Kinderheilkunde. 165-177.

Iseri LT. (1986) Magnesium and cardiac arrhythmias. Magnesium 5: 111-126.

Iseri LT and French JH. (1984) Magnesium: nature's physiologic calcium blocker. American Heart Journal 108: 188-193.

Jacques PF, Hartz SC, McGandy RB, Jacob RA and Russell RM. (1987) Ascorbic acid, HDL, and total plasma cholesterol in the elderly. Journal of the American College of Nutrition 6: 169-174.

Kamikawa T, Kobayashi A, Emaciate T, Hayashi H, and Yamazaki N. (1985) Effects of coenzyme Q10 on exercise tolerance in chronic stable angina pectoris. American Journal of Cardiology 56: 247-251.

Kapeghian JC and Verlangieri J. (1984) The effects of glucose on ascorbic acid uptake in heart endothelial cells: possible pathogenesis of diabetic angiopathies. Life Sciences 34: 577-584.

Knox EG. (1973): Ischemic heart disease mortality and dietary intake of calcium. The Lancet 1: 1465.

Koh ET (1984) Effect of Vitamin C on blood parameters of hypertensive subjects. Oklahoma State Medical Association Journal 77: 177-182.

Kojima S, Soga W, Hagiwara H, Shimonaka M, Saito Y, and Inada Y. (1986) Visible fibrinolysis by endothelial cells: effect of vitamins and sterols. Bioscience Reports 6: 1029-1033.

Kostner GM, Avogaro P, Cazzolato G, Marth E, Bittolo-Bon G and Qunici GB. (1981) Lipoprotein Lp(a) and the risk for myocardial infarction. Atherosclerosis 38: 51-61.

Langsjoen PH, Folkers K, Lyson K, Muratsu K, Lyson T, and Langsjoen P. (1988) Effective and safe therapy with coenzyme Q10 for cardiomyopathy.

Klinische Wochenschrift 66: 583-590.

Langsjoen PH, Folkers K, Lyson K, Muratsu K, Lyson T, and Langsjoen P. (1990) Pronounced increase of survival of patients with cardiomyopathy when treated with coenzyme Q10 and conventional therapy. International Journal of Tissue Reactions XIII (3) 163-168.

Lawn RM. (1992) Lipoprotein(a) in heart disease. Scientific American. June: 54-60.

Leaf A and Hallaq HA. (1992) The role of nutrition in the functioning of the cardiovascular system. Nutrition Review 50: 402-408.

Levine M. (1986) New concepts in the biology and biochemistry of ascorbic acid New England Journal of Medicine 314: 892-902.

Mann GV and Newton P. (1975) The membrane transport of ascorbic acid. Second Conference on Vitamin C. 243-252. Annals of the New York Academy of Sciences.

McBride PE and Davis JE. (1992) Cholesterol and cost-effectiveness implications for practice, policy, and research. Circulation 85: 1939-1941.

McCarron DA, Morris CD, Henry HJ and Stanton JL. (1984) Blood pressure and nutrient intake in the United States. Science 224: 1392-1398.

McCully KS. (1971) Homocysteine metabolism in scurvy, growth and arterio-sclerosis. Nature 231: 391-392.

McKee PA, Castelli WP, McNamara PM and Kannel WB. (1971) The natural history of congestive heart failure: the Framingham study. New England Journal of Medicine 285: 1441-1445.

McLean JW, Thomlinson JE, Kuang WJ, Eaton DL, Chen EY, Fless GM, Scanu AM and Lawn RM. (1987) c-DNA sequence of human apolipoprotein(a) is homologous to plasminogen. Nature 300: 132-137.

Miccoli R, Marchetti P, Sampietro T, Benzi L, Tognarelli M and Navalesi R. (1984) Effects of pantethine on lipids and apolipoproteins in hypercholesterolemic diabetic and nondiabetic patients. Current Therapeutic Research 36: 545-549.

Mortensen SA, Vadhanavikit S, Muratsu K and Folkers K. (1990) Coenzyme Q10: clinical benefits with biochemical correlates suggesting a scientific breakthrough in the management of chronic heart failure. International Journal of Tissue Research XII (3): 155-162.

Murad S, Grove D, Lindberg KA, Reynolds G, Sivarajah A, and Pinnell S. (1981) Regulation of collagen synthesis by ascorbic acid. Proceedings of the National Academy of Sciences USA 78: 2879-2882.

Murai AS, Miiyahara T, Fukimoto N, Matsuda M & Kamayama M (1986) Lp(a) Lipoprotein as a risk factor for coronary heart disease and cerebral infarction. Atherosclerosis 59: 199-204.

Myllyla R, Majamaa K, Gunzler V, Hanuska-Abel HM and Kivirikko KI. (1984) Ascorbate is consumed stoichiometrically in the uncoupled reactions catalyzed by prolyl-4-hydroxylase and lysyl hydroxylase. Journal of Biological Chemistry 259: 5403-5405.

Niendorf A, Rath M, Wolf K, Peters S, Arps H, Beisiegel U and Dietel M. (1990) Morphological detection and quantification of lipoprotein(a) deposition in atheromatous lesions of human aorta and coronary arteries. Virchow's Archives of Pathological Anatomy 417: 105-111.

Niki E. (1987) Interaction of ascorbate and alpha-tocopherol. In Burns JJ, Rivers JM, Machlin LJ, editors: Third Conference on Vitamin C. Annals of the New York Academy of Sciences 498: 186-198.

Nishikimi M and Yagi K. (1991) Molecular basis for the deficiency in humans of gulonolactone oxidase, a key enzyme for ascorbic acid biosynthesis. Journal of Clinical Nutrition 54: 1203S-1208S.

Opie LH. (1979) Review: Role of carnitine in fatty acid metabolism of normal and ischemic myocardium. American Heart Journal 97: 375-388.

Packer M. (1987) Prolonging life in patients with congestive heart failure: the next frontier. Circulation 75 Supp IV: 1-3.

Paterson JC (1941): Canadian Medical Association Journal 44: 114-120.

Pauling L (1986): How to Live Longer and Feel Better. WH Freeman and Company, New York.

Pauling L. (1991) Case report: Lysine/ascorbate-related amelioration of angina pectoris. Journal of Orthomolecular Medicine 6: 144-146.

Perloff JK (1992) Neurological disorders and heart disease. p.1810-1826. In: Braunwald E (editor): Heart Disease - A Textbook of Cardiovascular Medicine. WB Saunders Company, Philadelphia.

Pfleger R and Scholl F. (1937) Diabetes und vitamin C. Wiener Archiv für Innere Medizin 31: 219-230.

Phang JM and Scriver CR. (1989) Disorders of proline and hydroxyproline metabolism. p. 577-597 In: The Metabolic Basis of Inherited Diseases. McGraw Hill, New York, St. Louis, San Francisco.

Pyeritz RE. (1992) Genetics and cardiovascular disease. p.1622-1655. In: Braunwald E (editor): Heart Disease - A Textbook of Cardiovascular Medicine. WB Saunders Company, Philadelphia.

Ramirez J and Flowers NC. (1980) Leukocyte ascorbic acid and its relationship to coronary artery disease in man. American Journal of Clinical Nutrition 33: 2079-2087.

Rath M, Niendorf A, Reblin T, Dietel M, Krebber H-J, and Beisiegel U. (1989) Detection and quantification of lipoprotein(a) in the arterial wall of 107 coronary bypass patients. Arteriosclerosis 9: 579-592.

Rath M and Pauling L. (1990a) Hypothesis: Lipoprotein(a) is a surrogate for ascorbate. Proceedings of the National Academy of Sciences USA 87: 6204-6207.

Rath M and Pauling L (1990b) Immunological evidence for the accumulation of lipoprotein(a) in the atherosclerotic lesion of the hypoascorbemic guinea pig. Proceedings of the National Academy of Sciences USA 87: 9388-9390.

Rath M and Pauling L. (1991a) Solution to the puzzle of human cardiovascular disease: Its primary cause is ascorbate deficiency, leading to the deposition of lipoprotein(a) and fibrinogen/fibrin in the vascular wall. Journal of Orthomolecular Medicine 6: 125-134.

Rath M and Pauling L. (1991b) Apoprotein(a) is an adhesive protein. Journal of Orthomolecular Medicine 6: 139-143.

Rath, M., Pauling, L. (1992a) A unified theory of human cardiovascular disease leading the way to the abolition of this disease as a cause for human mortality. Journal of Orthomolecular Medicine 7: 5-15.

Rath M and Pauling L. (1992b) Plasmin-induced proteolysis and the role of apoprotein(a), lysine, and synthetic lysine analogs. Journal of Orthomolecular Medicine 7: 17-23.

Rath M. (1992c) Lipoprotein-a reduction by ascorbate. Journal of Orthomolecular Medicine 7: 81-82.

Rath M. (1992d) Solution to the puzzle of human evolution. Journal of Orthomolecular Medicine 7: 73-80.

Rath M. (1992e) Reducing the risk for cardiovascular disease with nutritional supplements. Journal of Orthomolecular Medicine 7: 153-162.

Rath M. (1992f) Cationic-anionic and anionic-cationic oligopeptides in apoprotein-a and other proteins as modulators of protein action and of biological communication. Journal of Applied Nutrition 44: 62-69.

Rath M. (1993) Discovery of new elements of biological communication leading the way to the abolition of infectious diseases, cancer, and other diseases as causes of human mortality. Journal of Orthomolecular Medicine 8: 11-20.

Regitz V, Shug AL, and Fleck E. (1990) Defective myocardial carnitine metabolism in congestive heart failure secondary to dilated cardiomyopathy and to coronary, hypertensive and valvular heart diseases. American Journal of Cardiology 65: 755-760.

Rhoads GG, Dahlen G, Berg K, Morton NE and Dannenberg AL. (1986) Lp(a) Lipoprotein as a risk factor for myocardial infarction. Journal of the American Medical Association 256: 2540-2544.

Riemersma RA, Wood DA, Macintyre CCA, Elton RA, Gey KF and Oliver MF. (1991) Risk of angina pectoris and plasma concentrations of vitamins A, C, and E and carotene. The Lancet 337: 1-5.

Rimm EB, Stampfer MJ, Ascherio AA, Giovannucci E, Colditz GA, and Willett WC. (1993) Vitamin E consumption and the risk of coronary heart disease in men. New England Journal of Medicine 328: 1450-1449.

Rivers JM. (1975) Oral contraceptives and ascorbic acid. American Journal of Clinical Nutrition 28: 550-554.

Rizzon P, Biasco G, Di Biase M, Boscia F, Rizzo U, Minafra F, Bortone A, Silprandi N, Procopio A, Bagiella E and Corsi M. (1989) High doses of L-carnitine in acute myocardial infarction: metabolic and antiarrhythmic effects. European Heart Journal 10: 502-508.

Rose WC, Johnson JE and Haines W. (1950) The amino acid requirement of man. Journal of Biological Chemistry 182: 541-556.

Ross R. (1993) The pathogenesis of atherosclerosis: a perspective for the 1990s. Nature 362: 801-846.

Salonen JT, Salonen R, Ihanainen M, Parviainen M, Seppänen R, Seppänen K and Rauramaa R. (1987) Vitamin C deficiency and low linolenate intake associated with elevated blood pressure: The Kuopio Ischemic Heart Disease Risk Factor Study. Journal of Hypertension 5 (Supplement 5): S521-S524.

Salonen JT, Salonen R, Seppänen K, Rinta-Kiika S, Kuukka M, Korpela H, Alfthan G, Kantola M, and Schalch W. (1991) Effects of antioxidant supplementation on platelet function: a randomized pair-matched, placebo-controlled, double-blind trial in men with low antioxidant status. American Journal of Clinical Nutrition 53: 1222-1229.

Sauberlich HE and Machlin LJ (editors). (1992) Beyond deficiency: new views on the function and health effects of vitamins. Annals of the New York Academy of Sciences 669.

Scanu M, Lawn RM and Berg K. (1991) Lipoprotein(a) and atherosclerosis. Annals of Internal Medicine 115: 209-218.

Seed BM, Hoppichler F, Reaveley D, McCarthy S, Thompson GR, Boerwinkle E, and Utermann G. (1990) Relation of serum lipoprotein(a) concentration and apolipoprotein(a) phenotype to coronary heart disease in patients with familial hypercholesterolemia. New England Journal of Medicine 322: 1494-1499.

Sherry S and Ralli EP. (1947) Further studies of the effects of insulin on the metabolism of vitamin C. Journal of Clinical Investigation 27: 217.

Simon JA . (1992) Vitamin C and cardiovascular disease: a review. Journal of the American College of Nutrition 11: 107-125.

Smith JL. and Hodges RE (1987) Serum levels of vitamin C in relation to dietary and supplemental intake of vitamin C in smokers and nonsmokers. In: Burns JJ, Rivers JM, Machlin LJ (editors): Third Conference on Vitamin C. Annals of the New York Academy of Sciences 498.

Smith HA and Jones TC (editors). (1958) Veterinary Pathology. 3rd Edition. Lea and Febiger, Philadelphia.

Sokoloff B, Hori M, Saelhof CC, Wrzolek T, Imai T. (1966) Aging, atherosclerosis and ascorbic acid metabolism. Journal of the American Gerontology Society 14: 1239-1260.

Spittle CR. (1973) Vitamin C and deep-vein thrombosis. The Lancet 7822, 2: 199-201.

Statistical Bulletin (1989,I-III) Continued Progress Against Cardiovascular Diseases. United States National Center of Health Statistics.

Steinberg D, Parthasarathy S, Carew TE, and Witztum JL. (1989) Beyond cholesterol. Modifications of low-density lipoprotein that increase its atherogenicity. New England Journal of Medicine 320: 915-924.

Stepp W, Schroeder H. and Altenburger E. (1935) Vitamin C und Blutzucker. Klinische Wochenschrift 14 [26]: 933-934.

Stollerman GH (1992) Rheumatic fever and other rheumatic diseases of the heart. p.1721-1741. In: Braunwald E (editor): Heart Disease - A Textbook of Cardiovascular Medicine. WB Saunders Company, Philadelphia.

Thomsen JH, Shug AL, Yap VU et al. (1979) Improved pacing tolerance of the ischemic human myocardium after administration of carnitine. American Journal of Cardiology 43: 300-306.

Trieu VN, Zioncheck TF, Lawn RM, and McConathy WJ (1991) Interaction of apolipoprotein(a) with apolipoprotein B-containing lipoproteins. Journal of Biology and Chemistry 226: 5480-5485.

Trimmer RW, Lundy CJ. (1948) A nutrition survey in heart disease. American Practitioner II. No. 7:448-450.

Turlapaty PDMV and Altura BM. (1980) Magnesium deficiency produces spasms of coronary arteries: relationship to etiology of sudden death ischemic heart disease. Science 208: 198-200.

U.S. Dept. of Health & Human Serv. Public Health Service, Centers for Disease Control (1989) Vital and Health Statistics. Current estimates for the national health interview survey, 1988. National Center for Health Statistics.

Utermann G. (1989) The mysteries of lipoprotein(a). Science 246: 904-910.

Wilkinson JF, Manch MD, Ashford CA. (1936) Vitamin C deficiency in Addison's disease. The Lancet X/24: 967-970.

Willis GC. (1953) An experimental study of the intimal ground substance in atherosclerosis. Canadian Medical Association Journal 71: 17-22.

Willis GC, Light AW, Gow WS. (1954) Serial arteriography in atherosclerosis. Canadian Medical Association Journal 71: 562-568.

Williams GH and Braunwald E (1992) Endocrine and nutritional disorders and heart disease. p.1827-1855. In: Braunwald E (editor): Heart Disease - A Textbook of Cardiovascular Medicine. WB Saunders Company, Philadelphia.

Zenker G, Koeltringer P, Bone G, Kiederkorn K, Pfeiffer K and Jürgens G. (1986) Lipoprotein(a) as a Strong Indicator for Cardiovascular Disease. Stroke 17: 942-945.

INDEX

<u>NOTES</u>

NOTES

ABOUT THE AUTHOR

Dr. Rath is a leading expert in cardiovascular disease and nutrition. He has held research and clinical positions at the University of Hamburg, Germany, and the German Heart Center in Berlin. Subsequently, he became Director of Cardiovascular Research at the Linus Pauling Institute of Science and Medicine in Palo Alto, California. In 1992 Dr. Rath founded Health Now, a company promoting nutritional medicine through scientific research as well as through educational services. Over the years Dr. Rath's work has appeared in scientific journals of the American Heart Association, the National Academy of Sciences as well as in other scientific journals. Some of his scientific discoveries are listed on page 179 and 180 of this book.

ACKNOWLEDGEMENTS

The author would like to thank all those who have made this book possible with their encouragement, their criticism, and their help. Special thanks go to Jeffrey Kamradt and Bernard Murphy (SCORE) for their help with the publication of this book. Pictures are used from publications in Virchow's Archives of Pathology (pages 39,40,89) and from the Proceedings of the National Academy of Sciences (page 56).

A DAILY PROGRAM OF ESSENTIAL NUTRIENTS FOR OPTIMUM CARDIOVASCULAR HEALTH

VITAMINS

Vitamin C	900	- 3,000 mg
Vitamin E (d-Alpha Tocopherol)	200	- 600 I.U.
Vitamin A (Beta-Carotene)	2,500	- 8,000 I.U.
Vitamin B-1 (Thiamine)	10	- 40 mg
Vitamin B-2 (Riboflavin)	10	- 40 mg
Vitamin B-3	65	- 200 mg
Vitamin B-5 (Pantothenate)	60	- 200 mg
Vitamin B-6 (Pyridoxine)	15	- 50 mg
Vitamin B-12 (Cyanocobalamin)	30	- 100 mcg
Vitamin D	200	- 600 I.U.
Folic Acid	130	- 400 mg
Biotin	100	- 300 mcg

MINERALS

Calcium	50	- 150 mg
Magnesium	60	- 200 mg
Potassium	30	- 90 mg
Phosphate	20	- 60 mg
Zinc	10	- 30 mg
Manganese	2	- 6 mg
Copper	500	- 2,000 mcg
Selenium	30	- 100 mcg
Chromium	15	- 50 mcg
Molybdenum	6	- 20 mcg

OTHER IMPORTANT NUTRIENTS

L-Proline	150	- 500 mg
L-Lysine	150	- 500 mg
L-Carnitine	50	- 150 mg
L-Arginine	50	- 150 mg
L-Cysteine	50	- 150 mg
Inositol	50	- 150 mg
Coenzyme Q-10	10	- 30 mg
Pycnogenol	10	- 30 mg

The first values are my minimum daily recommendations for a healthy person. People and patients with additional needs can adjust accordingly.

HOW YOU CAN GET MORE INFORMATION

- If you have difficulties finding the nutrients
  recommended in this book elsewhere
  HEALTH NOW can refer you to sources.

- If you or your doctor have difficulties identifying
  a laboratory that does the lipoprotein(a) testing
  HEALTH NOW can refer you to diagnostic
  laboratories performing this test.

- You can also order additional copies of this book
  directly through HEALTH NOW.

- Dr. Rath founded HEALTH NOW to promote
  nutritional medicine through scientific research
  and through educational services.

- Parts of the revenues from the sales of this book are
  designated for further clinical studies with
  nutritional supplements in the fight against heart
  disease, strokes, diabetes and other diseases.

HEALTH NOW, 387 Ivy Street, San Francisco,
California 94102, USA
Tel: 1-800-624-2442 or 916-939-1007 (from overseas).

BOOKS AVAILABLE FROM HEALTH NOW

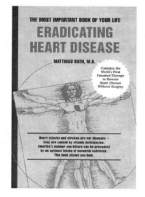

"America's Most Successful Cardiovascular Health Program' is currently followed by over 20,000 Americans.

This book documents the success of this program in form of testimonial letters from patients with coronary heart disease, high blood pressure, irregular heartbeat, heart failure, diabetes and other cardiovascular conditions.

161 pages $12.95

"Why Animals Don't Get Heart Attacks- But Humans Do" is a brief introduction to the breakthrough in cardio-vascular disease and nutrition led by Dr. Rath.

In this short handbook the reader finds the answer to the most striking medical puzzle of our time: "Why does every second man and women die from a disease that is essentially unknown in the animal world?"

2nd edition, 63 pages $8.95

"Eradicating Heart Disease" is a detailed documentation about this medical breakthrough.

In several chapters patients with different cardiovascular conditions find specific answers to the question which essential nutrients can help to optimize their cardiovascular health.

197 pages $ 14.95